S0-BDO-023

Caesar Ascending - Invasion of Parthia

By R.W. Peake

Caesar Ascending-Invasion of Parthia

Also by R.W Peake

Marching with Caesar®- Birth of the 10th

Marching with Caesar-Conquest of Gaul

Marching with Caesar-Civil War

Marching with Caesar-Antony and Cleopatra, Parts I & II

Marching With Caesar-Rise of Augustus

Marching With Caesar-Last Campaign

Marching With Caesar-Rebellion

Marching With Caesar-A New Era

Marching With Caesar-Pax Romana

Marching With Caesar - Fraternitas

Caesar Triumphant

R.W. Peake

Critical praise for the Marching with Caesar series:

Marching With Caesar-Antony and Cleopatra: Part I-Antony

"Peake has become a master of depicting Roman military life and action, and in this latest novel he proves adept at evoking the subtleties of his characters, often with an understated humour and surprising pathos. Very highly recommended."

Marching With Caesar-Civil War

"Fans of the author will be delighted that Peake's writing has gone from strength to strength in this, the second volume...Peake manages to portray Pullus and all his fellow soldiers with a marvelous feeling of reality quite apart from the star historical name... There's history here, and character, and action enough for three novels, and all of it can be enjoyed even if readers haven't seen the first volume yet. Very highly recommended."
~The Historical Novel Society

"The hinge of history pivoted on the career of Julius Caesar, as Rome's Republic became an Empire, but the muscle to swing that gateway came from soldiers like Titus Pullus. What an amazing story from a student now become the master of historical fiction at its best."
~Professor Frank Holt, University of Houston

3

Caesar Ascending - Invasion of Parthia by R.W. Peake

Copyright © 2015 by R.W. Peake

All rights reserved. This book or any portion thereof may not be reproduced or used in any manner whatsoever without the express written permission of the publisher except for the use of brief quotations in a book review.
Cover Art by Marina Shipova
Cover Artwork Copyright © 2015 R. W. Peake
Maps created through Google Maps © 2015
Captions and Map Overlays added by the Author
All Rights Reserved

Foreword

One of the most pleasant aspects of this "job" is the interaction with the readers of both the *Marching With Caesar*® series, and the standalone, alternate history *Caesar Triumphant*, of which this book is the "prequel".

And, while *Caesar Triumphant* isn't my bestselling book by any means, it probably has generated more comment and controversy than the others combined. Now, I knew going into CT that my story of Caesar and his army invading the Isle of Wa, or as we know it today, Japan, was an either/or kind of book; readers would either love it or they would hate it.

Honestly, I was expecting a lot more of the latter than I have actually gotten, in the form of bad reviews and/or angry mail. But in the slightly more than two years since I released CT, far and away the most common comment and suggestion I've received is the direct reason why this book is in your hands.

"I'd love to read about Caesar's invasion of Parthia, and what happens *before* he gets to Japan."

This is basically a compilation and summary of that sentiment expressed, several times a month, ever since CT came out. And far be it from me to ignore the wishes of my readers!

In some ways, this book was more difficult to write than CT, simply because there is a quasi-historical basis for this part of the story. It is a recognized historical fact that Caesar was planning for a campaign against the Parthians, with the intent of not only avenging the ignominious defeat and death of his friend and fellow Triumvirate Marcus Licinius Crassus, but to retrieve the seven standards lost in Crassus' ill-fated, and frankly, poorly led campaign.

Because of this, I tried to do as much research as I could, particularly about the forces of the Parthian Empire that would have been arrayed against Caesar and his Legions. And, as I quickly learned, there is a paucity of what I would call in-depth and credible information about the Parthians of Caesar's day (I will discuss this more fully in the Historical Notes.).

But, while this was in some ways a more difficult book to write from that aspect, one thing I enjoyed a great deal, and I hope you

5

readers will also, was in bringing the first Titus Pullus, Sextus Scribonius, Quintus Balbus, Diocles, and Gaius Porcinus back to "life." It will probably not surprise anyone to learn that I consider them, Titus and Scribonius in particular, old, familiar friends and comrades with whom I've shared many adventures. However, even this reunion wasn't without its difficulties, but that had more to do with where this fits with CT and accounting for the myriad details that were mentioned by the characters in that story that happened previously. As I learned, while my memory is very good, keeping track of every single event and detail in the dual worlds of MWC and CT proved to be a real challenge.

I bring this up as a preemptive way of apologizing if, in fact, there is something I missed, where one of you readers go, "Wait, I thought that happened to Balbus and not Scribonius", or "That didn't happen until Titus was Camp Prefect, after Caesar was assassinated"...which, of course, doesn't happen in this version.

On that note, those who have read *Caesar Triumphant* will probably notice that the Prologue in this book is the same. I decided to put this in because, once this series is finished, which in this case means everything that leads up to Caesar's invasion of Japan, starting with what you are about to read, this is the most appropriate place to put the Prologue.

Thanks as always to Beth Lynne of BZHercules, my editor, and Marina Shipova, who produced this cover, and with that, I hope you enjoy *Caesar Ascending*.

Prologue

Even for a man with the prodigious energy of Gaius Julius Caesar, this day promised to be one of the busiest in a career filled with sleepless nights and long days. It didn't help that he was roused even earlier than he had planned because of the restless thrashing about of Calpurnia. By his estimate, he had barely been asleep a full watch when he was awakened, although he wasn't sure whether it was from the movement of their bed as she waved her arms or the tortured moans that escaped her lips. Rousing himself, he looked over at her with concern and was forced to dodge one of her arms as they flailed wildly about in a clear attempt to ward off whatever demons were assaulting her in the recesses of her subconscious. If this had been the first time, Caesar would have been extremely alarmed, but it had become an unfortunately regular occurrence, and what made it more disturbing—at least for his wife—was that this dream was always the same. He knew from bitter experience that waking her when she was like this was the worst thing he could do, so, heaving a sigh, he decided that since the chances of more sleep were practically non-existent, he might as well get started on what was going to be a challenging day. So much to do, he thought, here on these Ides of March, the day before he was to leave to meet his army for the Parthian campaign. Perhaps Calpurnia had done him a favor, although there was a part of him that was honest with himself: leaving before Calpurnia was awake would allow him to avoid a scene that had become quite tiresome, as his wife had essentially begged him to retire from public life. And all because of some silly dreams! No! He was Caesar, and Caesar wasn't subject to such superstitious nonsense. Still, if it had been just Calpurnia's dreams, it would have been relatively easy to dismiss, even if it caused his wife distress. He couldn't say he loved her, exactly, but he did hold her in very high regard, and he did have affection for her. But it wasn't just Calpurnia's dreams Caesar was forced to acknowledge, however grudgingly, and only to himself. No, there were many other signs, rumors, and whispers of plots by the jealous mediocrities who were, unfortunately, members of his own class, at least by birth. Still, Caesar refused to show that he feared any man, or any group of men; to do so would be unthinkable, especially for a man who had walked into the

7

maelstrom of missiles at Munda and emerged completely unscathed. Nevertheless, the knowledge that there were plots was there, even if he forced it into the recesses of his mind.

Before he could leave his villa—the official residence of the Pontifex Maximus that he had occupied for many years by this point—like all members of his class, it was customary for Caesar to meet with some of his clients, who always gathered at the crack of dawn to press their petitions with their patron. It might have been customary, but no Roman of his time—or of the past, for that matter—had as many clients as Gaius Julius Caesar. That meant that the vestibule of his residence was always jammed full of men, most of them waving scrolls that contained the details of their particular woes or requests, all of them shouting his name. It was always chaotic, but it was even more than usually so on this day, as every man there knew that the Dictator for Life was leaving for the wastes of Parthia. Consequently, there was a din that Caesar was sure would rouse his wife, so while it made him angry to do so, he made the decision to conduct his daily audience as he walked to what was going to be the most important part of his day and probably one of the more crucial days of his time as Dictator. The fact that the Senate wasn't meeting in the Curia—it had burned down and had yet to be rebuilt—forced the body of men who ostensibly ruled Rome to meet in the only building large enough to hold their newly inflated numbers, Pompey's Theater—and the delicious irony of that location wasn't lost on Caesar. In all honesty, he had what men like Cicero would call a perverse streak that colored his sense of humor, and perhaps it was perverse to exercise his role as First Man in Rome at the very feet of the Roman he had defeated for that title. But Caesar was also practical, and there simply was no better place to hold a meeting that would undoubtedly be attended by every Senator currently in Rome.

With his lictors clearing the way, shoving the mass of men who were still arriving to present their cases to the Dictator, Caesar walked slowly from his residence in the heart of the Roman Forum, surrounded by his petitioners. His pace was leisurely, but this was not his norm; the combination of the early start and the sheer number of men with requests to be heard meant that he couldn't move with his usual speed. Using his lictors, Caesar would signal to them to allow one man at a time to approach him and walk at his side, where he would have a very short time to make his case. Although almost all of the supplicants had come bearing scrolls containing the particulars of their grievances or pleas, Caesar rarely looked at any of them, preferring instead to listen briefly, then ask one or two questions that always demonstrated that he had, indeed, been paying attention. Some of the cases were straightforward, so Caesar was able to adjudicate them with a quick aside to one of the half-dozen secretaries trailing in his wake—each of them responsible for a particular area of their master's concerns—whereupon the scribe would hastily jot down the notes Caesar dictated. Other matters, however, did require more of his attention, so with these, Caesar slowed even further, giving him time to ask more questions and, in one or two cases, actually deigning to look very quickly at the proffered scroll, ignoring the hopeful look on the petitioner's face as he took this to be a positive sign of his patron's interest. It was in this manner that what was a crowd totaling some two hundred — exclusively male—Romans made their way along the Via Sacra, the main thoroughfare that passed through the Forum, heading in a roughly northerly direction towards the base of the Capitoline Hill, the most sacred of the seven hills of Rome.

Just before Caesar and his entourage reached the foot of the Capitoline, the crowd—growing in number, as the ranks of the petitioners swelled with the early risers of the city, drawn to the sight of the most powerful man in Rome—now numbered several hundred. It was always this way with Caesar. As reviled as he was by some members of his own class, he was adored and revered by that teeming mass of people that their betters sneeringly referred to as the Head Count, when they weren't just calling them "the mob." Many among the crowd called out his name, which only added to the commotion and din, all of them hoping that he would at least look in their direction, or better yet, acknowledge their hail with a wave, giving them something to tell their children and grandchildren about; the day that the greatest man in Rome actually acknowledged their existence. And Caesar, knowing as he did that the source of his power rested on the twin pillars of these nameless, faceless people and the Legions, whose ranks were filled by men of the same class, took more of his time in acknowledging these shouts and waves than he did with his petitioners, even stopping from time to time to share a quick word with a butcher or a tanner. And some of them, much to their astonishment and delight, he actually knew by name! The fact that his recall of them was just another way for Caesar to demonstrate his most formidable and useful gift, the astonishing memory that never forgot a fact, face, or name, didn't matter to them at all. That he remembered them was all they cared about. Yet, even as Caesar did this, there was a part of him that was untouched by this tumult, and was devoting only a portion of that gifted intellect to the activity around him. It was always this way, he thought, when they reached this part of the Forum, because to the right, at the corner of the Vicus Iugarius and Via Sacra, was the partially completed Basilica he had commissioned to honor his daughter Julia, now dead for almost a decade.

Even now, after so much time, he felt a familiar tightness in his chest at the loss of his firstborn child, because as fond as he might have been of Caesarion, his child by Cleopatra, Julia was not only pure Roman, she had also been a beautiful, captivating child that had grown into a woman with even more wonderful qualities about her. While her marriage to Pompey Magnus had been arranged for strictly political considerations—as all marriages of the upper classes were—Caesar had been both relieved and happy to see that she had been genuinely happy in her marriage. Although Caesar would never say it, he had personally never really understood how his beautiful daughter had been able to look at Pompey—who had long since passed into the land of the middle-aged man, with the receding hair, jowls, and thickening waist, something that Caesar himself hadn't suffered from—and seen something to love in him. It was just another example of how silly women could be about such things, he mused.

Shaking himself from his thoughts, inwardly at least, he stopped at the corner of the two streets. However, this was prearranged, and was his signal to his lictors that his audience was now over. This was always the most irritating part of his day, because some men refused to take the hint and disperse on their own, forcing the lictors to muscle them away from their charge. It was one of the times when Caesar was acutely aware of appearances, understanding that his enemies pointed to this simple exercise of extricating himself as an example of haughtiness and as a sign that he believed himself to be above the rest of them. The fact that, to one degree or another, every one of Caesar's rivals did essentially the same thing—albeit with a much smaller crowd and in the privacy of their own villas—was something his enemies universally ignored. Dispersing the crowd took some doing, more than normally, and although Caesar understood why this was the case, it was still trying his patience. He needed at least a few moments of solitude as he made his way around the base of the Capitoline to the

Campus Martius where Pompey's Theater was located so that he could marshal his thoughts.

Once the way was cleared, Caesar resumed walking, but as much as he had on his mind, when he spotted a lone figure squatting in his accustomed spot—where there was a small street off the Vicus Iugarius that led to the Velabrum—he couldn't resist the urge to have a little fun. Somewhat unusually, Caesar didn't know the man's name, but that was because, as far as he knew, nobody knew it. He was just referred to as The Seer because of the way he made his living: soliciting passersby with offers to tell their future. For some time now, The Seer had called out to Caesar, every single time he saw him, the same prediction he had first made several months earlier. And since today was the day about which Caesar had been warned by The Seer, and since the day had dawned bright and clear, Caesar decided it was time to take The Seer down a notch.

"Good morning, Seer," Caesar called out genially, raising his voice so that not just his entourage, but also anyone within earshot could hear, knowing that what he was about to say would be known through every precinct of Rome by sunset. "You said that the Ides of March would see my doom, but here I am! The Ides have come, and," he made a point to peer down at himself, affecting surprise before he returned his gaze back to the squatting man, giving him a grin, "I'm all in one piece!"

As he expected, this brought a hearty round of laughter, not just from his lictors and scribes, but from the dozens of men nearby. For his part, The Seer didn't seem to be in the least bit embarrassed, and, in fact, smiled back at Caesar, although he said nothing, at least at first. Caesar had already turned away and was resuming his walk when The Seer called out, "Yes, Caesar. You're right; the Ides have come. But they're not finished yet."

Although he heard The Seer's response, Caesar didn't turn back around, not wanting to prolong the exchange. And yet, despite continuing on his way, something was...wrong. Shaking his head, Caesar chided himself for allowing the superstition of a beggar in the Forum to burrow its way into his own brain, so to show that he had dismissed the thought, he lengthened his stride.

Then, without knowing how, Caesar found himself coming to a stop. Turning around, he could still view The Seer watching him calmly, his face expressionless. And Caesar would wonder for the rest of his days how it happened, but he began walking again. This time, however, it was back towards the Forum, away from Pompey's Theater, and away from his death.

Chapter One

"We're going to do what??"

Gaius Octavius immediately winced at his own outburst, although his superior didn't seem to be upset at all; the fact that the man was also his uncle, great-uncle on his mother's side, meant that Caesar was more indulgent with his subordinate than he might have normally been. And it did not hurt that Gaius Julius Caesar loved to surprise people, no matter who they were.

"Why, nephew," Caesar teased his young Master of the Horse, "it's not like you not to listen! You didn't hear me the first time?"

"I heard you," Octavius replied waspishly. "It's just I find it hard to believe."

"It is hard to believe," Caesar agreed, "which is why we're doing it."

That, Octavius understood, was certainly the truth, but he was nevertheless plagued with doubts, and a part of him wondered how much the close call his uncle had experienced just two days before was playing a role in Caesar's decision. Given the absolute frenzy of the previous two days, he had to believe that it did.

Deciding a change of tactics was in order, Octavius chose instead to focus on the practical challenges that came with Caesar's plan, and not waste any more time bemoaning the almost breathtaking level of what his detractors would describe as just another example of Caesar's monstrous hubris.

"I understand the advantage of surprise this will certainly give us," he began carefully. "But what about the specifics of how you plan on doing it?"

If Caesar was vexed at his nephew's refusal to accept his decision, he didn't show it, instead leaning back on his desk, crossing his arms and asking calmly, "What specifics are you referring to, Gaius?"

"By taking the most direct route to Syria," he began, "we'll have the stretch between Crete and Cyprus where there's absolutely nowhere to land in case of a storm. That's three hundred miles of open water, and in the middle of Our Sea, where there's no protection from the elements."

"Actually," Caesar interjected mildly, "you're incorrect."

Puzzled, Octavius argued, "Uncle, I've looked at the map! Believe me, there's nothing out there between those two!"

This prompted a smile from Caesar, amused that his normally astute nephew had mistaken his objection. "Oh, you're right about that," he granted.

"So what am I incorrect about, then?"

Octavius felt his cheeks start to burn, recognizing that Caesar was toying with him, but completely flummoxed as to the cause.

"You said the distance is three hundred miles," Caesar replied calmly, "but in truth, it's a bit more than five hundred. Because we're not stopping at Cyprus."

This caused Octavius' mouth to drop in astonishment, yet at the same time, he experienced an initial rush of excitement, as his first reaction was that, at last, he had caught Caesar out. Fortunately for him, this sensation didn't last long, as his more pragmatic and detached side pointed out how impossible it was to catch Caesar by surprise about anything. Except, the thought came unbidden to him, creating such a rush of unease that he felt his stomach twist, for the other day. Caesar clearly hadn't expected that Brutus, Cassius, and that bunch of jackals would be waiting at Pompey's Theater with their *pugiones* secreted away in the folds of their *togae* intent on murdering the Dictator for Life. Not surprisingly, Octavius didn't think it wise to point this outright then; the gods knew there had been enough rancor and acrimony over the last two days, and he understood that it worked in his own interests to let Marcus Antonius carry that particular flail.

Consequently, Octavius forced himself to remain as dispassionate as he could, acknowledging his uncle's correction with a nod, saying instead, "You're right, of course. But," he felt compelled to point out, "doesn't that make it even more difficult?"

"Oh, I didn't say it wouldn't be a challenge," Caesar agreed, "nor that it wouldn't entail a fair amount of risk. But I've talked with Volusenus at length about this, and his calculations agree with mine. We'd cut a month off the time it normally takes to transport an army using the old route, following the coast. And," he pointed out, "ultimately, there's really only that one stretch to worry about. Besides," he finished with a shrug, "this route's been used before, and it's made more than one man rich. It's a difference of more than 700 miles, Gaius."

This, Octavius knew, was something he couldn't argue. Every season, there were a few intrepid ship masters who risked their lives

14

to take this most direct route between the East and Rome, but while he certainly could not swear this was the case, Octavius distinctly recalled hearing that the failure rate for these men was such that it was essentially a flip of the coin as to whether they arrived as rich men or died impoverished, taking their crews with them.

"What would you consider an acceptable loss?" he asked Caesar.

This question seemed to surprise Caesar, although he answered readily enough. "If we lose one ship in ten, that would be a serious but not catastrophic loss."

Octavius' first instinct was to argue the point because, on the face of it, to lose this number of ships would essentially mean each Legion would be marching with nine instead of ten Cohorts, which in Caesarian Legions meant a loss of six hundred men per Legion. But as he considered it for a moment, he was forced to recognize that the reality was quite different: of the two-thousand-ship fleet, a large number of those ships carried nothing but cargo in the form of supplies, or perhaps the horses for the Gallic cavalry that would be shipping with the Legions. As Caesar's titular second in command, despite his youth, Octavius was well aware that, as much as was being transported, the Dictator had been stockpiling massive quantities of supplies in Syria, which would be distributed and packed for the campaign once the army had made the crossing. And just that process, Octavius knew, would take almost a month by itself. When the campaign was originally conceived, the plan had been to actually not embark on the invasion of Parthia until the next season, after the army had integrated with the auxiliaries and extra cavalry, mostly from Galatia, that were already there and waiting. Suddenly, it hit Octavius with the power of a thunderbolt, and he stared at his uncle who, still sitting on the edge of the desk, was regarding him with that same smile.

"So if you cut a month off the voyage," Octavius began, "then does that mean...?"

"That I'm not prepared to wait until next year to actually cross into Parthia?" Caesar responded. He paused for a moment, the icy blue eyes practically sparkling as the corners turned down in what Octavius had long since learned was Caesar's amused expression, then finished, "Why, yes, Gaius. That's exactly what it means. We're going to be invading Parthia this year, not next."

"You know," Sextus Scribonius, the Secundus Pilus Prior of the 10th Legion, known throughout the Republic as the 10th Equestris, spoke in a thoughtful manner that alerted his superior and best friend, Titus Pullus, that Scribonius had actually put a great deal of time into what he was about to pose, "I wouldn't be a bit surprised if Caesar doesn't wait until next year to take us into Parthia."

His dinner companion, who along with being Scribonius' closest friend, was also the Primus Pilus of the 10th, and in his own, albeit smaller way, was almost as famous as Caesar, stared at Scribonius incredulously from his spot across the table.

"*Gerrae!*" Pullus exclaimed. "You're mad! By the time we get organized and ready, it'd be Sextilis, at the earliest!" Stabbing a huge, blunt finger at his friend, Pullus finished, "This is one time I think you've overthought this, Sextus!"

Completely unfazed, and in fact long accustomed to his friend's bluster, Scribonius didn't immediately reply, only partially because he was still munching the piece of bread he had stuffed into his mouth. Mostly it was because he knew how much it infuriated Titus Pullus when his excited agitation was met by a corresponding calm. Of all the men in the 10th Equestris, it could safely be said that the number of them who weren't intimidated, and frankly, scared of their Primus Pilus, could be counted on one hand, with three fingers left over, and Scribonius was one of them. The other, Quintus Balbus, was also at the table, watching the exchange with a quiet amusement, although it would have been impossible for anyone who did not know Balbus well to tell this was the case. As both Pullus and Scribonius loved to remind Balbus, his was a face only his mother could love, and since she was long dead, she didn't count. Even before suffering the horrific wound that resulted in the loss of an ear, and the entire side of his face being covered in a knotted mass of scar tissue, Balbus had never been considered handsome. Luckily for him, success in the Legions wasn't predicated on a man's looks, but on how well he could kill another man, and in this, Balbus had been gifted by the gods. Balbus was the Primus Pilus Posterior, the commander of the Second Century of the First Cohort, which meant he was technically the second in command. The very thought made Balbus shudder in horror, although it wasn't only because of the burden that came from commanding one of Caesar's most veteran Legions; the only way Balbus would become Primus Pilus was if Titus Pullus died. And this was such an unfathomable thought that Quintus Balbus actually took a great deal of comfort in it, secure in his belief that there wasn't a man anywhere

16

in the world, even the unknown part of it, who could slay Titus Pullus. Watching his two best friends bickering was an oddly comforting scene, but while he wouldn't have offered his own opinion, unless Pullus asked it of course, silently, he thought Scribonius was right.

Oblivious to Balbus' musings, Scribonius countered with, "I'm guessing that if Diocles told me, he already told you that Caesar's decided to change the route across Our Sea?"

Pullus' face, lined with the signs of weather and bearing a wide scar that followed the contour of his cheekbone, showed his sudden uncertainty.

"Yes, of course he did," Pullus replied, but he was still unwilling to cede the point. "But while it's true that we're cutting a significant chunk of time off the voyage, we still have to get organized when we get to Antiochus. That's going to take a month, easily."

"Unless Caesar has already sent someone he trusts ahead to ensure everything's ready, in a Liburnian." Now Scribonius grinned, despite having a mouthful of bread, happy to play the last stone in this particular game between him and Pullus.

"Where by Pluto's balls did you hear that?" Pullus demanded, yet such was his faith in Scribonius, it never occurred to him that his longtime friend might be playing a trick. Before Scribonius could answer, Pullus turned in his chair, and now it was his slave Diocles who had to endure the stabbing finger as Pullus asked accusingly, "And why did you tell him about this before you told me?"

"I didn't!" Diocles insisted, shooting an irritated glance at Scribonius in a manner that if another Roman witnessed it who was unaware of the particulars of the relationships among this quartet, the Roman would more than likely admonish Pullus to whip this impertinent slave. "This is the first I'm hearing about it too!"

This mollified Pullus, who resumed glaring at Scribonius, who was looking just a bit too smugly satisfied for the Primus Pilus.

"I wonder if you'd still be sitting there with that *cac*-eating smile if I dumped you on your ass," he grumbled, but again, Scribonius wasn't fazed in the slightest.

"I absolutely would." He laughed. "Just seeing your expression would be worth it!"

Pullus, as Scribonius had known, did no such thing, instead returning to his bowl of stew, mumbling something about some men who knew too much. However, also as Scribonius expected, before another mouthful had been consumed, the giant Roman was chuckling, and quickly, the rest of the company joined in.

The venture that so consumed the interest of not just Gaius Octavius in his role as Master of the Horse, or Titus Pullus as Primus Pilus of a Legion, but every man throughout the ranks was simple in its ambition, yet breathtaking in its scope and execution. For more than a decade now, the defeat of Caesar's former political partner and personal friend, Marcus Licinius Crassus, had hung over all Romans, but particularly so with the men who marched under the standard of a Legion of Rome. Consequently, when Caesar had announced his plans to avenge Crassus and recover the seven lost Legion eagles, he had received much approbation from all of Roman society—civilian and military. The Legion eagle was the symbol of Rome's military might and for which every Legionary worth his salt was willing to fight, kill, and, if necessary, die for in order to keep it with its Legion. As far as the standards themselves, they were relatively simple: a carved, wooden eagle affixed to the top of a sturdy ten-foot pole, and the eagle was gilt in silver, but it was what it represented to every man in the ranks and to Roman civilians that made the eagles so special. Now, Gaius Julius Caesar, Dictator for Life and the most powerful man in Rome, was about to embark, leading an army of hardened veterans on his quest to retrieve them, yet the events that had occurred, or almost had happened on the Ides just two days before, had required him to alter his original plan. Rather than taking ship for a voyage of short duration across to Illyria, whereupon Caesar originally planned to subdue the recalcitrant barbarians of Dacia, then march overland through Moesia and cross the narrow strait over to Asia Minor in a whirlwind of almost non-stop activity, the Dictator had made the decision to forego this part of the campaign. The fact that such drastic changes were made in such a short span of time was surprising only to those who didn't know Caesar, yet even for his own prodigious talents, the previous days had been taxing. Only a relatively few men close to Caesar knew how badly shaken he'd been by the failed attempt to assassinate him at Pompey's Theater, but while Caesar wasn't normally one for introspection and examining the ramifications of his actions in anything other than a straightforward, action/reaction sense, that this event gave him pause was understandable. One of Caesar's many qualities was his ability to be brutally honest with himself about his motives, even if he might not publicly announce those motives to others, or even lie outright about them. Therefore, he wasn't particularly surprised that a group of Roman patricians or high-ranking plebeians had conspired to kill him; the identity of some of them, however, had rocked him to his very core. More than the sense of betrayal, though, there was a practical aspect to the whole sordid affair that, more than anything, was responsible for his sudden alteration of a campaign that had been in the planning for more than a year. Ultimately, he had intended to endow men in whom he'd trusted during his Gallic campaign with enormous responsibilities, and knowing that some of these very men had been in on the plot to kill him had made their continuing participation...problematic. Even as this thought passed through Caesar's mind, he experienced a sense of rueful amusement at the simplistic characterization, because while it was certainly a problem, the scope of it was almost beyond comprehension. Specifically, Decimus Brutus and Gaius Trebonius, both of whom had proven to be such able lieutenants, displaying an ability to act on their own initiative while following the guiding principles as set out by Caesar, couldn't be trusted any longer. In fact, they, and the other conspirators who hadn't managed to flee when Caesar sent his German bodyguards to Pompey's Theater to seize them, were now in the Tullianum, the cramped, dank, and dark cell that was little more than a pit in the ground, waiting for Caesar's decision about what to do with them. He wasn't surprised that the segment of those who styled themselves The Boni were expressing their outrage over what they were trying to claim was an unlawful seizure of members of the Senate, although once the residences of the conspirators had been thoroughly searched and a variety of documents had been discovered that provided enough detail whereby even a man like Cicero couldn't argue that there had in fact been a plot in the first place, not to mention that when each conspirator's person was searched, every one of them was carrying a weapon. Oh, Caesar mused wryly, it wasn't for a lack of trying on the aging orator's part, and while the Dictator didn't think much of Cicero when it came to martial matters, neither could he deny the fact that Cicero's appearance at Caesar's villa took courage. Although Caesar also understood that Cicero was acting as an emissary of sorts as well, and he didn't fault the man for doing so, the fact that no less than three conspirators had been in possession of correspondence that definitively indicated Cicero was, while not in on the plot, at least generally aware that such a thing was afoot played a role in the orator's appearance.

Still, as shocked as he had been when the search of Brutus and Trebonius by his bodyguards revealed that, like the others gathered there, they were secretly carrying their own *pugiones*, which was specifically forbidden at Senate meetings, he had been rocked to his core at learning that Marcus Junius Brutus was involved as well. Despite the gossip, or perhaps because of it, that Brutus was actually Caesar's son, the result of his long-standing affair with Brutus' mother Servilia, Caesar knew Brutus wasn't his blood, but he still regarded the younger man with a regard that came close to that of father and son. Now, however, Brutus was involved in this plot that, if Caesar hadn't actually listened to the man he only knew as The Seer, who was perched at his usual spot at the edge of the Forum, directly along the path Caesar was taking from his villa to Pompey's Theater, it would have undoubtedly succeeded. This knowledge also shook Caesar, but when he tried to reward The Seer, the man was nowhere to be found. Caesar had actually, very briefly, toyed with the idea of extending the policy of clemency he had practiced during his war with Pompey, and after his death, Pompey's sons, but quickly discarded it. No, there was a point where forgiveness would not only be viewed as weakness by others of not just Caesar's class but by all class of Roman citizen, and Brutus and the others had crossed their own particular Rubicon in advancing this plot. Nevertheless, Caesar was loath to order the execution of every last one of them without benefit of trial, as was his right as Dictator, yet neither could he leave Rome with this nest of vipers at his back, working in his absence to undo all that he had accomplished. While he trusted Marcus Antonius personally and didn't doubt his loyalty, Caesar wasn't as certain about the man's devotion to duty, nor his steadfastness in supporting Caesar's programs. Marcus Antonius, as Caesar knew all too well, was nothing if not impulsive, but he was also implacable and ruthless when it came to those Caesar deemed as enemies. Perhaps, Caesar reflected, the idea of what Antonius would do, backed by the power that came with the Dictatorship, would be enough to keep some of these men in check. Oh, he would undoubtedly execute at least some of the conspirators; Casca and his no-account brother, although the latter would require a message being sent to where he was living in exile out in the vast wastelands of Scythia; Cimber and, Caesar thought with grim amusement, that Tribune of the Plebs Aquila would be executed, not in private as was customary, but by public beheading. However, Caesar wouldn't be present; he was about to depart for Brundisium where his army awaited, and he would give Antonius instructions to wait to execute those whose lives were forfeit until he received a message that Caesar had in fact departed Italia and arrived safely at

Antiochus. That way, this act of vengeance wouldn't appear to be personally motivated; Caesar wanted to avoid the taint of what The Boni had been accusing him of, acting like a king. This was business of the state, and as such, the duly appointed representative of the Dictator was merely acting in his capacity as such. Of course, Caesar recognized, this meant a change within his own organization, and as usual, he wasted no time in sending a messenger, summoning the two men who this would impact.

Gaius Octavius didn't take the news of his demotion well, although to those who didn't know him, it would have been impossible for them to tell. But Caesar did know him, so he recognized the signs of his young nephew's repressed rage in the way his ears, unfortunately his most prominent feature because of the way they stuck out at almost a right angle from his head, had turned bright pink. In every other sense, however, the youngster's demeanor betrayed none of his inner thoughts, a trait that Caesar thought boded well for this youngster in whom so many hopes for his future resided. In contrast, Marcus Antonius made no effort to hide his feelings, his handsome features wreathed in a smile as he actually rubbed his hands together in obvious relish at the thought of what it would mean to wield such power.

"May I ask why, uncle?" Octavius asked politely, but it was his use of the familial title in front of others that gave Caesar another hint of the state of his nephew's mind because he was normally careful to refer to Caesar by either his name or title when in the company of other men.

Although, Caesar reflected, it was true that Antonius was family as well, albeit more distantly related.

"You may," Caesar allowed, then went on to explain, "and it has nothing to do with your abilities, young Gaius." While Octavius' features flushed even darker, Caesar's emphasis of the boy's youth was calculated, and was in its own way, a warning to Octavius. Going on, Caesar said, "It has to do with my decision concerning the conspirators."

"You're going to execute them!" Antonius practically crowed, and now made no attempt to hide his glee at the idea. "And you need someone like me to do it for you! Not the boy here." He jerked a careless thumb over at Octavius.

Unsurprisingly, this served to enrage Octavius further, yet he still managed to keep his mouth shut, although this was not what Caesar noticed. Instead, it was the look he exchanged with his young nephew that informed the Dictator that, unlike Antonius, Octavius understood there was more to this decision than Antonius believed.

"*Some* of the conspirators are going to be executed," Caesar agreed. "But not all of them. And I need my Master of the Horse to fulfill the sentence. Here in Rome."

For the first time, Octavius' expression changed as the ghost of a smile played on his lips. Meanwhile, Antonius looked nothing more than confused.

"Wait." The burly older man held up a hand. "What do you mean, 'some' of them? Surely you're not going to spare any of these vermin! They deserve to die, Caesar!"

"I meant just what I said," Caesar replied calmly, unwittingly behaving in much the same way as Scribonius did to Pullus, except that it was Antonius fulfilling the latter's role. "Some of them will die, but I'm going to spare some of them as well."

"You can't do that!" Antonius blurted out, and because of his position behind the older man, Octavius made no effort to hide a grin that was tinged with malice.

Caesar's response, at first, was not to reply, verbally at least, but he had perfected the ability to use his eyes, a vivid blue, to express himself in ways that words could not, and Antonius was now subjected to a stare that was more terrifying than anything Caesar could have uttered.

"I assure you, Antonius," Caesar finally spoke, his voice calm, but one didn't have to know the man to hear the menace in his tone, "I can do exactly that." Turning away from the pair, he picked up a tablet from his desk, then proffered it to his new Master of the Horse. "These are the men you'll have executed." He paused for an instant, then added, "In the Forum. On the Rostra."

For a brief moment, Octavius and Antonius were allied in their thoughts, and both of them visibly reacted, one with a gasp, another with a sharply indrawn breath. Hearing each other respond in a similar manner caused the pair to exchange a glance, although for once willing to defer to an older man, Octavius gave a slight nod to Antonius in a silent encouragement.

"Caesar," Antonius, the memory of the stark terror from just a moment before still strong, made sure to modulate his tone, "that's

22

never been done before. I mean," he added unnecessarily, "executing men of our rank in such a public setting."

"These are new times, Antonius." Caesar's reply came so quickly that it told Octavius that his uncle had given this much thought. "And what these…men," despite his internal admonition to remain impassive, Caesar's lip curled in contempt, "did, or *tried* to do is unprecedented. No," he shook his head adamantly, "their despicable treachery deserves to be punished so that all of the citizens of Rome can see. Much of my support comes from the people, and I've heard them howling for blood."

That, both men knew, was no exaggeration. Indeed, there were crowds hanging about the Tullianum during the daylight hours, constantly agitating for the men guarding the prisoners to step aside and let the crowd dispense their own brand of justice on those men they considered traitors to Rome. It was why Caesar had only his Germans serving as guards, knowing they wouldn't be swayed by either the appeals of the mob or the violence they threatened. Conversely, the average Roman citizen had been raised on stories of German bloodthirstiness and barbarity, meaning they weren't ready to tempt men who wouldn't hesitate at separating heads from bodies.

But it was Octavius who raised the more practical problem, asking, "But how will they react when they see only some of them being executed?" He paused for a moment, then plunged ahead, knowing as he did he was treading in dangerous territory just mentioning the name. "Especially Brutus?"

As Octavius feared, Caesar visibly stiffened at the mention of the man's name, but his tone remained neutral as he nodded. "That," he admitted, "is a risk. And it's not a small one. But," he closed his eyes and, for the first time since the whole sorry business had begun, both Octavius and Antonius caught a glimpse of the turmoil this man was feeling, "I owe it to Servilia to spare her son. And," he opened his eyes, pinning each of them in turn with a stare that was challenging them to dispute him, "I know he was practically dragged into it by Cassius." Despite their personal feelings on the matter of Brutus, neither man thought it wise to argue, and Caesar continued, "But that doesn't mean he won't be punished. Just not as severely as the Casca brothers, Cimber, Cinna, Aquila, and the rest of them."

Only then did Antonius actually read the names on the tablet Caesar had handed to him, and in a move that told Caesar the depth of his ambivalence, the older man turned and, without a word, handed the tablet to Octavius. The younger man glanced down at it, his eyebrows suddenly plunging down as he looked at Caesar with an expression that betrayed his consternation.

"Caesar," he still managed to retain control of his emotions, "while I understand about Brutus, how is it possible that Cassius' name isn't on this list to be executed? You said it yourself; he was the prime mover of the conspiracy, at least from what we've determined so far."

If anything, Caesar actually dreaded this part of the conversation with the pair more than the subject of Brutus, because he honestly didn't have a good answer.

"I understand your question," Caesar replied carefully, "and of all the names there, this is the one I've struggled with the most. But I've decided that he's still going with me on this campaign."

"What?" Antonius couldn't contain himself any longer. "You're going to take a man who plotted to kill you on campaign? How will you ever be able to take a restful breath?"

"I do have five hundred Germans guarding me day and night," Caesar began, but Octavius surprised himself when he felt compelled to point out, "Who wouldn't have been any help if you'd walked into Pompey's Theater."

For an instant, the young man was sure he'd committed a huge blunder, because Caesar's face darkened and his lips thinned down into a bloodless line as he struggled to keep his composure, yet the Dictator's tone was calm as he acknowledged, "That's certainly true, Gaius. But it will only be Cassius, and he'll never be with me alone. And," he finished grimly, "if he even twitches in a way that I don't like, Gundomir will separate his traitorous head from his shoulders the instant I lift a finger."

While it was certainly true that Caesar would be on his guard, to Octavius it sounded like it would be an exhausting, enormously tense situation, but he had seen enough of Caesar's temper and held his counsel. Somewhat to his surprise, Antonius seemed to be of a like mind, because while he clearly disapproved, he likewise said no more about it. Seeing the pair were finished, Caesar then turned to the practical aspects of this new assignment of duties. By the time he was through, the sun had set, and Caesar was still intent on departing for Brundisium the next day.

Throughout the Republic, Gaius Julius Caesar, Dictator for Life, was renowned as much for his luck as his skill on the battlefield. This decision of his only added to the luster of what had already become legendary. Not only did the massive fleet make better time than expected, thanks to a steady wind that remained consistent from a northerly direction, the only foul weather occurred on the third day, when the fleet was still hugging the coast of Greece. And on the vast stretch that Octavius was rightly concerned about, while they did lose ships, the number wasn't the one in ten Caesar would have settled for, but ten total. Not just the voyage seemed to be blessed with even more than a usual dose of Caesar's Luck, although while the men in the ranks attributed the next event to that luck, the senior officers like Titus Pullus, the other Primi Pili, and by extension, their Pili Priores knew that it was based in Caesar's decision to send two of his ablest men when it came to organizational logistics ahead to Antioch. Once there, the two men, dividing the tasks between them and aided by virtue of their Legate rank, worked tirelessly to prepare the massive amount of supplies already cached there. Thanks to the overall organizational ability that seemed inborn in Romans, the pair quickly inventoried what was on hand. In itself this would have been a help, but they took matters further by subdividing the supplies into the amounts that would be carried by each Legion. While Antioch was a large city, its commercial center wasn't generally where local merchants stored the bulk of their goods, whatever they may have been; instead, the two Legates sent members of their staff, scouring the city for the location of all buildings capable of storing the massive quantity of consumables, leather goods, iron, and other essentials that was crucial to the success of a Legion. In their conception, the Legions of Rome were largely self-sufficient entities, at least when it came to the materials needed to repair gear, or replace items if needed, but despite initially despairing that such a decentralized system of supply would complicate matters further, after some thought, it was Volusenus who realized there was a hidden benefit. What that was became apparent when, as the fleet carrying Caesar and his army arrived and began the monstrously complicated unloading process, instead of sending the Legions directly into the camp that had been prepared for them by the Legions that had already been in Syria, each one was instead marched to a certain area of the city. Waiting there for them were the supplies

25

allocated for their Legion, most of which had already been broken down into the smaller containers and sacks that would be transported on the Legion mules. Those mules had been the responsibility of Aulus Ventidius Bassus, both when he was still in Italia, and once in Syria, because Caesar had deemed that waiting the extra time it would have taken for the final contingent of mules, raised by breeders in Transalpine Gaul, wasn't acceptable. Instead, the man known as Ventidius, or more commonly by the men of the ranks as The Muleteer, owing to his humble beginning in Caesar's service as a breeder who supplied the Dictator, had scoured Syria to make up the shortfall of one thousand mules that were, presumably, recently arrived at their final destination of Brundisium, only to find the army and the fleet carrying it long departed. As the men discovered when they arrived, unlike what they expected, the supplies waiting for them weren't in one central location, which was inevitably a scene of chaos as the hapless Quaestor, the quartermaster of the army, and his staff of Tribunes, tried to ensure that one Legion didn't filch more for themselves from the warehouses than they had been allocated. Which, inevitably, caused disagreements between men of different Legions that could quickly escalate into something ugly, as their affinity for each other and their bond was temporarily set aside in their desire to help their Legion by stealing an extra sack of grain, or more often, more amphorae of the wine allotment. This time in Antioch, the only squabbling was within a Legion, after each of them marched to a different section of the city where the warehouses that had been seized by Volusenus were waiting. In essence, what would have taken more than a week, at a minimum, before everything was sorted out and each Primus Pilus was satisfied with their allotment, took two days. The only slight hitch was in the integration of the Syrian mules, but while Volusenus may have been a shade better at organizational matters than the Muleteer, it wasn't by much. Subsequently, much, much more quickly than anyone had expected, Caesar's army was ready to march out of Antioch, heading to their staging area at Zeugma, which Caesar had selected as the spot from which his great campaign would begin.

The best illustration of how stunning a feat had been pulled off could be summed up in a conversation between Sextus Scribonius and Titus Pullus. This took place at the evening meal, in the camp outside Antiochus, the night before Caesar had announced they would depart the city.

"I told you so," Scribonius began with a grin, lifting his wine cup in a mock salute towards his Primus Pilus.

Scribonius didn't have to preface his remark for Pullus, or Balbus or Diocles either, for that matter, to know to what he was referring.

And the huge Primus Pilus took defeat with his usual grace, prompting him to retort in a surly tone, "Go ahead; rub it in." He paused long enough to take a swallow from his cup, but there was a slight curling of his lip when he took a huge breath, and said, "I was wrong."

As Pullus expected, this caused Scribonius to leap up from the table, whooping with delight, whereupon he turned to receive the congratulations and overly effusive praise of Diocles and Balbus, whose scarred face was split into what anyone else would think was a grimace, but the others knew was his version of a smile.

"Friends," Scribonius intoned with a solemnity that was completely false, "I'm happy you're here to witness the defeat of the mighty Titus Pullus, hero of the Equestrians!"

Suddenly, Diocles disappeared from the main room of the Primus Pilus' quarters, only for an instant, returning with what appeared to be a crown, but one where the top was crenellated, looking like a fortified wall, which was exactly what it was supposed to represent. It was a *corona murales*, one of two that had been won by Titus Pullus over the course of a career that was almost unparalleled by any other man in the Roman Legions. The instant Scribonius and Balbus saw the object in his hand, the pair began roaring with laughter, while Pullus visibly fumed, glaring at his diminutive Greek.

"Master Sextus," Diocles announced, holding the crown up in front of him, "such an auspicious occasion such as this one must be marked with an award appropriate to the event! I can't get my hands on something that's truly worthy of the moment, but this trinket will have to suffice."

As Diocles ceremoniously held the crown as far above his head as his arms would stretch, Scribonius was forced to bend at the waist to allow the Greek to set the crown atop his head, which the Greek purposely set at an angle that could only be described as jaunty.

Scribonius immediately struck a pose in the style of those that graced the public spaces of any town or city owned or dominated by Rome, asking rhetorically, "Do you think this is an appropriate posture? I want my statue to represent the right balance of *gravitas* and humility."

Under normal circumstances, Titus Pullus neither appreciated nor tolerated being the butt of a joke, but even he could contain himself no longer, joining in with these men who had been his longest and best friends.

"Well," he finally managed, "it *is* such a momentous event. It's the first time you've beaten me at anything, after all." He grinned at Scribonius, adding as he did, "But it might be time to remind you just how much better I am than you. Are you up to a sparring session, say, tomorrow?"

"No." Scribonius laughed. "I still have bruises from the last time. But," despite recognizing that Titus Pullus was a master with the *gladius*, and was indeed famous not just in the 10th but the entire army, the Secundus Pilus Prior had a fair amount of pride, which caused him to point out, "have you forgotten that I *have* taken you before?"

"That was four years ago, and I had a cold!" Pullus protested, prompting mock jeers from the others.

After a pause, the Primus Pilus returned the subject to the matter that had prompted this moment of levity.

"What's the status of the new mules?"

While this was a pertinent question, Pullus had directed it not to his fellow Centurions, but to Diocles, who, in addition to being Pullus' body servant, served as the chief clerk for the Legion. Such was the Greek's ability at remembering the vast amount of information that was involved in running a Legion of Rome that he didn't need to consult a tablet or scroll.

"For the most part, the Centurions report that their complement is at least trained enough to accept their load," he began, except that was where the good news ended. "But that's about as far as it goes." Now he did consult not just one, but a small stack of tablets, which represented the reports of each Cohort. "The Ninth Cohort in particular isn't very happy. Pilus Prior Glaxus insists that he got more of the new mules than any other Cohort."

This elicited a part sigh, part curse from Pullus, who asked Diocles, "Did you assure him that we divided the new mules evenly across all ten Cohorts? Including," he pointed out, "my own?"

"Yes, Master," Diocles assured him, using the title that the Greek, not the Roman, insisted on using in the presence of others, even these two closest friends. "I did, but I don't think he believes me."

This slur against Diocles served to turn Pullus' irritation to anger, which he expressed by slamming his flat hand on the top of the table.

"Well, he and I are going to have a talk about that," he said tightly, causing Scribonius and Balbus to exchange a wryly amused glance; despite their friendship with Pullus, each of them had been subjected to these "talks" at the hands of their Primus Pilus, and neither of them envied the Nones Pilus Prior.

Who, both of them thought simultaneously, should have known better, since Marcus Glaxus had not too long before been Pullus' Optio.

With the rest of the business concluded, both Scribonius and Balbus excused themselves, even though it was still relatively early, but as Scribonius put it, "We've got a big day tomorrow, and I need to make sure my boys have everything ready."

Balbus gave the same reason and, quickly, the quarters were empty except for Diocles and Titus Pullus. Still seated at the table, Pullus stared reflectively down into his cup, welcoming the feeling of nerves as an old friend that always came on the embarkation of a campaign.

Then, he glanced up and told Diocles, "Go get Gaius. I want to talk to him before we march tomorrow."

Although there were literally hundreds of men in the 10th whose *praenomen* was Gaius, and thousands more scattered throughout the army, Diocles didn't need anything more than that name, knowing exactly to whom Pullus was referring. Answering only with a nod, the Greek disappeared, leaving the Primus Pilus to his thoughts.

The recipient of the summons, however, was not in as composed a state of mind. A Primus Pilus summoning a lowly Gregarius by itself was enough to cause a certain level of anxiety; that Gaius Porcinus was the nephew of Titus Pullus actually didn't help matters. Compounding it all was that Porcinus was a new addition to the First Century, Second Cohort of the 10th, and this was his first campaign. This fact accounted for Porcinus' presence in not only one of the senior Cohorts, but in the First Century, because Titus Pullus, using the prerogative that came with his rank, had decided that there was only one man he trusted to not only train Porcinus to a standard that met the level expected of a legendary Legion like the 10th, but who would keep an eye on him with a fidelity second only to that of Pullus himself. Consequently, Porcinus' Centurion was Sextus Scribonius, who had known beforehand that one of his men would be summoned into the presence of the Primus Pilus. None of this mattered to

Porcinus at the moment, of course; he was dimly aware that his placement in the First of the Second, as it was called, was no accident, but ever since his uncle, his mother's younger and only brother had appeared at his family farm in Baetica a bit more than a decade before, when Caesar's Gallic campaign was still ongoing, young Gaius Porcinus had sworn to himself that he would follow in the *caligae* of his giant uncle, who even then was on his way to becoming a legend in the Legions. After his uncle had returned to the army, Porcinus had begun his own training regimen, yet as he was growing up, he had attributed most of Titus Pullus' success to the fact that, by some accident or a gift from the gods, Pullus was much, much larger than the average Roman. More than a foot taller, but beyond that, he had been blessed with a frame that seemed made to put on muscle, and thanks to Titus Pullus' hardscrabble upbringing, one in which his father Lucius was a drunken sot who hated his only son, blaming him for the death of his wife when Titus was born, the young Pullus had ample opportunity to build muscle. But what Porcinus was just beginning to discover on his own was that, while this gave his uncle an undeniable advantage, there was more to the success of Titus Pullus than mere physical strength. In its simplest terms, Titus Pullus had been born with an ambition that would have done even Caesar justice, and he had devoted himself fully and wholly to the profession of arms. This dedication was based in a straightforward but powerful driving force; Titus Pullus was determined to elevate his family from the lowest rung on the social ladder of Roman citizen, sneeringly called the Head Count by those Romans of the higher classes, up into the order of Equestrians. In order to do so, he had to accumulate a personal fortune totaling over four hundred thousand *sesterces*, a sum so fantastic that Porcinus could barely fathom it as a concept, let alone an actual number. And Titus Pullus had determined that his best, really his only, path led through the army; it was just his good fortune that he had answered the call of a *dilectus* held by the then-Praetor of Hispania, a man who was now Dictator for Life. Over the years, Caesar had recognized in this large, bumptious, and somewhat insecure boy the makings of a fine Legionary, and more importantly, a great Centurion. Pullus had rewarded his general's faith with an unswerving loyalty, one that had cost Pullus his longest and closest friendship in Vibius Domitius, back when the 10th had mutinied after the battle on the dusty plains of Pharsalus. In that moment, Pullus, who had been Secundus Pilus Prior at the time, came dangerously close to striking down his own Optio, Domitius, when the latter had tried to convince Pullus to join the mutiny. The dramatic moment of their confrontation had been witnessed by Caesar, who had gone on to reward Pullus, but just like Scribonius and Balbus, Porcinus knew it was a day his uncle had no interest in reliving, nor hearing about from others. Now Porcinus was standing outside the Legion office, while Diocles entered first to announce he had been successful in retrieving Pullus' nephew, whereupon he was immediately waved in to the private quarters of the Primus Pilus. Diocles left them alone, knowing that his master wanted privacy for this discussion; besides, he still had much to do.

"So," Pullus began immediately, waving his nephew to a seat at the table as he spoke, "are you ready?"

"Well," Porcinus replied cautiously, "I'm all packed, and I put the things I'm not taking into my strongbox."

Pullus waved a dismissive hand, interrupting, "That's not what I'm talking about. Are you *ready*?"

Truthfully, Porcinus was certain he knew what his uncle meant before he opened his mouth, but he decided buying time before answering was the wisest course.

Finally, he answered, speaking slowly, "I suppose I am. At least," he gave a slight shrug, "as ready as I can be without knowing what to expect."

This, in truth, was exactly the answer for which Pullus was looking; over his long career, he had heard far too many men boast about their eagerness to go into battle for the first time, and invariably, those were the men whose nerve failed them and brought shame to themselves, and most importantly to a man like Pullus, the Legion. Hearing his nephew give this realistic assessment of his state of mind actually served to settle Pullus' own misgivings, which he tried to disguise with little success from those who knew him best.

"Scribonius says you're still dropping your shield too much," Pullus said sternly. Then, leaning forward, he stabbed his finger at his nephew. "I thought we'd worked enough to break that bad habit! Do you need another bout or two with me to remember what I taught you?"

"No," Porcinus replied instantly, unconsciously echoing his Pilus Prior's reaction from a short while before, which prompted a small smile to play across Pullus' lips. "I don't need another beating, uncle! I'll remember!"

31

"See that you do," Pullus growled before turning to the subject that, if Porcinus had known, he would have been astonished to learn that his famous uncle felt the kind of fear about someone else that Porcinus felt towards his uncle, especially considering who that person was. "Did you write your mother?"

Porcinus' crestfallen expression elicited a groan from his uncle, and Pullus muttered, "Pluto's cock, your mother will flay me alive!"

As Pullus glared at his nephew, Porcinus could only offer a shrug and half-hearted protest. "I meant to, but I've been so busy that..."

"Don't tell me how busy you've been," Pullus snapped. "I know exactly how busy a man is when he's about to go on campaign. That's no excuse! I swore to your mother that the next letter that came from the 10th wouldn't be from me, but from her son! That's who she wants to hear from!"

"Yes, sir," Porcinus replied meekly, yet if he thought this was the extent of his uncle's ire, he quickly learned differently when Pullus summoned Diocles.

"I know you've got a lot to do, but so do I," Pullus said, then pointed at his hapless nephew, instructing the Greek, "and I want you to take this boy out to your office, give him a wax tablet, then stand over him and make sure he writes his mother! I want it done tonight so I can leave it with the outgoing mail tomorrow when we leave!"

"But that'll take me at least a third of a watch," Porcinus protested, but Pullus was unmoved.

"I guess it's a good thing you're finished doing everything else then." Standing up, Pullus reached for his *vitus*, the twisted vine stick that announced his authority to all whenever he was not in full uniform, although of all the Centurions in the army, he needed it the least. "I have to go to the *praetorium* for the final briefing with Caesar. I expect you to be done when I get back. Or," he added with a glimmer of a smile that wasn't meant to put Porcinus at ease, "still working on it."

With that, he left his quarters, leaving Diocles and Porcinus behind. Neither of them spoke, at least not until they heard the outer door slam, signaling that Pullus had left the building. Then Diocles turned to the younger man, who looked thoroughly miserable, favoring Porcinus with a smile of his own. Even if he had loathed the boy, he would have suggested what he was about to, for the simple reason he wanted to save his own time, but the truth was that Diocles had become extremely fond of the young Legionary, simply because he was inherently likable, a trait that had served the boy well. Earnest

32

in his desire to make Pullus proud, but willing to not only do the work, he also refused to use his status as Pullus' nephew to his advantage. Consequently, he had been accepted into the ranks of the First of the Second more rapidly than just about any Gregarius Diocles had ever seen. While he resembled Pullus in a couple of ways—he was almost as tall as Pullus, but he had a much, much leaner build, although he had a deceptive strength, and there was a similarity in their facial features—more than anything, they shared a willingness to do the work necessary to become the best Legionaries they could be.

Therefore, Diocles didn't mind suggesting, "How about this, Gaius? How about you dictate what you want to say to your mother, and I write it down. That way, we'll both get out of here faster."

Porcinus didn't reply verbally, but he didn't need to; the expression of relief was more than enough.

An army on the march is an impressive sight, no matter to which nation or people it belonged. But an army of Rome, one led and organized by the most famous general in Roman history, presented a spectacle of such magnitude that, as Pullus and Scribonius agreed that night after their exit from Antioch, rivaled any of the four triumphs in which they had marched for Caesar. Certainly the crowds weren't as large, but this was because Rome was larger than Antioch, although both agreed it was extremely likely that every single citizen of the city was out lining the streets of the route the army took out of Antioch. And while it was also true there weren't small children strewing flower petals in their path, the crowd was still wildly enthusiastic. Which, as Scribonius pointed out, was probably due to the idea the men of the Legions were vacating the area, meaning that husbands and fathers could breathe easier. Whatever the cause, it still left an impression, not just on the hoary veterans, but especially with men like Gaius Porcinus, who despite his internal admonition that this sendoff was ultimately meaningless, felt his chest swell with pride as he took in the sights and sounds. If he had known the citizens of Antioch who he marched past as a man of the 10th Legion, which Caesar had given the signal honor of being the vanguard, would be standing there for more than a full watch, only then would he have had an idea of how massive an enterprise this was. This army consisted of eleven Legions, five thousand cavalry, and ten thousand auxiliaries, along with the attendant baggage train that was required to support an endeavor of this size and, in fact, it wouldn't be until several days later, when the

10th was given what the men called "the dirty end of the sponge" marching as the rearguard of the army, before Porcinus experienced a taste of what this really meant.

This first day, however, was one of pomp, panoply, and served as a graphic example of the immense power of Rome. Which, as every veteran in the ranks understood, would be needed to accomplish the goal Caesar had set for them. What only a relatively small number of men knew—the senior officers, the Primi Pili and, of course, many of the clerks in the *praetorium*—was that as massive an army as this already was, it was going to grow only larger, when the rest of the levies Caesar had summoned arrived at Zeugma. However, this would be something of a test as well, Pullus and some of the more astute Primi Pili understood; exactly how many of the client kings who had been ordered to send their own troops would actually do so wouldn't be known until they had been in Zeugma for at least a week. Caesar had sent his orders well before he planned on staging at Zeugma, accounting for delays in transit and sickness while on the march, but Pullus wasn't the only man who harbored doubts that the entire complement required by Caesar would actually show up. That, however, would only become apparent when they arrived at Zeugma. Also waiting for them at Zeugma were even more supplies, specifically several wagons loaded with pre-cut pieces of lumber, in a variety of lengths and shapes, which Caesar had ordered fashioned as part of his preparations. To other military men, like Titus Pullus, this was an example of the difference between a true professional like Caesar and a man like Marcus Crassus, who was universally viewed by the men in the ranks as nothing more than a rich dilettante who thought his vast wealth and the fact he had once crushed an army of slaves qualified him to be in the same league as a Caesar. As Romans had learned from the small handful of survivors of Crassus' disastrous campaign, the former Triumvir had not thought it important to account for the lack of timber that would be available to his army as they marched across the vast expanse of wasteland that composed much of Parthia. Caesar, however, had been insistent on compensating for this dearth of usable wood, but he had gone even farther than that. Another dozen wagons carried nothing more than charcoal, which would be kept in reserve for the moment when all forms of firewood had been exhausted. As far as Pullus was concerned, while these seemed to be small details, it was also the reason why Caesar was alive and thriving, while Crassus' severed head was moldering on the parapet of the

Parthian capital, staring sightlessly out into the vast expanse of desert that Caesar and his army must cross to exact their vengeance.

The fact that Caesar's army spent more time at Zeugma than they had in Antioch was a source of frustration for most of the army, but none chafed at this delay more than Caesar. While he had recognized this was a possibility, given how easterners of all stripe regarded time, not viewing it as a precious commodity that couldn't be wasted but as a slowly moving river down which a man drifted, carried by the gentle current, when confronted with the reality of what this meant in terms of delay, Caesar's frame of mind was such that his subordinates only sought him out when it was absolutely necessary. The Dictator wasn't a man to lash out at others because of the mistakes or misdeeds of someone else, but it did mean his patience, never his strength, was even thinner than normal. Consequently, it didn't take much for one of his Legates, Tribunes, or Centurions to experience Caesar's displeasure when they committed some sort of error. And, as usually happened in such situations, this meant that the men even further down the chain of command suffered as a result, since a Centurion couldn't lash out at his general.

It was Pullus who put it best, when he remarked to Scribonius with a grim humor, "If Caesar's not happy, none of us are happy."

"At least he doesn't use the *vitus*," Scribonius replied, then nodded to one of the rankers in Pullus' Century who happened to be walking by, trying not to be obvious about the way he was nervously eyeing his Primus Pilus, and more specifically, the twisted vine stick that Pullus was tapping against his leg.

"No," Pullus agreed, then added dryly, "at least not yet. But if that fat bastard Herod doesn't get here soon, I can't make any guarantees that he won't start."

"It's not just Herod who's missing," Scribonius pointed out. "Polemon and his cavalry aren't here yet, either."

This, Pullus acknowledged, was certainly the truth, and he also understood that of the two missing forces, Caesar was more concerned with the Pontics, because of all the component forces of the army, cavalry was critical, particularly when it was composed and equipped in the same manner as the cataphracts of Parthia. However, Pullus was an infantryman at heart and held cavalry in low esteem. Especially the Pontic cavalry, because he was one of the relatively few men in Caesar's army who had faced them in battle, back when Pharnaces, the son of Mithridates IV, had decided to take advantage of the unsettled state of the Roman world because of the civil war between Pompeius Magnus and Caesar. That had been after Pharsalus, when Caesar had deemed it best to remove Pullus from the 10th Legion after his dramatic encounter with Domitius. The cause of the mutiny had been rooted in Caesar's desire to immediately continue the pursuit of Pompey, not recognizing that his army had reached the end of their collective tether, and he had been forced to rely on a scratch force consisting of two Cohorts of the 6th Legion, which had literally a couple watches before been fighting Caesar's army. Cut off from the rest of their Legion, these two Cohorts had been given a choice by Caesar; march for him as he pursued Pompey or risk an uncertain fate by relying on Caesar's mercy. They had chosen to march for Caesar, but in his usual way, the Dictator had effectively solved two problems at once by naming a man he knew he could trust in Titus Pullus as *de facto* Primus Pilus, which removed the giant Roman from his comrades in the 10th while passions were still running high. What resulted was an episode that already was famous throughout the known world, when Caesar had been besieged in Alexandria by forces loyal to the boy king Ptolemy XIV for seven months, during which time the general had managed to impregnate Ptolemy's sister and wife, Cleopatra VII, siring a son known as Caesarion. Emerging from this situation victorious, Caesar had then marched from Alexandria into Pontus to confront Pharnaces, culminating in a battle at Zela. As such things went, Pullus was always quick to point out, it wasn't much of a fight; in truth, Caesar's dispatch to the Senate of Rome, consisting of no more than three words, was in most ways more famous than the fight itself. It was his experience leading the 6th at Zela that fed Pullus' lack of regard for the mounted troops of the type they would be facing, but he understood that, his own experiences aside, Crassus' Legions had been whittled down and then soundly defeated by men on horseback. Still, he was not particularly worried, but the source of his confidence lay in the man who was leading them; in the parlance of the Legions, Marcus Crassus wasn't Caesar's bootlace as a general.

Thinking along these lines prompted Pullus to ask Diocles, who had just served the evening meal in Pullus' tent, "What about the Armenians? Any word on whose side they're going to be on?"

Diocles shook his head, answering, "No, but from what Apollonius told me, Caesar's not going to wait for them to make up their minds. Once Polemon and Herod get here, we're crossing the river."

This aligned with Pullus' sense of the situation, so he only responded with a nod, and dismissed this as just another matter that, ultimately, had no bearing on the men of the 10th Legion. Whether the Armenians, another force who equipped themselves in the same manner as the Parthians, were on their side or arrayed with the Parthians was beyond Pullus' immediate control, and, over the years, he had learned the folly of worrying about things over which he had no power to do anything about. Instead, he turned his mind to the more immediate and pressing matters, things that he could either control or influence.

This was what prompted Pullus to tell Scribonius, "As long as we're stuck here, I've got a favor to ask."

"You want me to spend more time with Gaius," Scribonius answered immediately, eliciting a grin from Pullus at yet another sign of how well Scribonius knew his Primus Pilus. "Don't worry; he's already gotten his share of bumps and bruises, just not from me."

"From who?" Pullus asked, slightly concerned that it wasn't Scribonius, but it didn't last long, when Scribonius answered simply, "I put him with Vellusius."

This caused Pullus to relax; if it couldn't be Scribonius tutoring young Porcinus, Pullus reflected, having Vellusius do it was close to a perfect substitute for the Pilus Prior. His faith in Vellusius' ability stemmed from two simple but salient points; like Scribonius, Publius Vellusius was Titus Pullus' longest-term comrade, and the last of the three remaining tent mates of Pullus and Scribonius. Unlike the two Centurions, it wasn't in Vellusius' destiny to rise through the ranks, but this was perfectly acceptable to Vellusius, who had no desire for the responsibilities and headaches that came from wearing the transverse crest. The other point stemmed from the other common thread running through the background and lives of these three men, and that lay in who their original instructor was back when they were fresh-faced *tiros* in Hispania, when the 10th was still a new Legion. These three had been in the First Century of the Second Cohort, their original Pilus Prior the famous Gaius Crastinus, who had fallen at Pharsalus as the Primus Pilus of what was now known as the 10th Equestris, Caesar's most famous Legion. Crastinus' Optio had been a man named Aulus Vinicius, and it was to Vinicius that Pullus, Scribonius, and Vellusius, if asked, would have credited with instilling in them the skills necessary to survive the most combat any Legion of Rome had ever endured in their first sixteen-year enlistment. The

37

fundamental basis for that skill lay in something that, when Pullus was first exposed to it, he instantly dismissed as trivial and unnecessary, until Vinicius had demonstrated in the most fundamental and powerful way the superiority of what had already earned the name the Vinician grip. Deceptively simple in concept, but somewhat tricky to master, the Vinician grip required the thumb to be wrapped underneath the fingers instead of the conventional grip where the thumb lay on top. The reason for this was based in the reality that, of the hand, the thumb is the weakest part, and when sufficient lateral force was applied in a violent manner, usually in the form of a sword slash, the pressure on the thumb was such that a sword held in the conventional manner was more prone to being knocked from its owner's grasp. Which, as Vinicius had pointed out, in his normal dry style, was a bad thing. Subsequently, every man who had been part of the First of the Second when Aulus Vinicius had been Optio was trained to hold his sword in this manner, and over the course of hundreds of fights, Pullus, Scribonius, Vellusius, and every other man trained in this manner had experienced at least one moment where their lives were saved because they managed to retain their grip on their primary offensive weapon. Tragically, Vinicius' time as Optio had been cut short when, during the 10th's first campaign in Hispania, while conducting their first assault on a town, had been doused with boiling pitch and was burned to death. The aftermath of this loss had enormous ramifications, although even the main recipient understood that Gaius Crastinus had no way of knowing how far-reaching his decision to make the young Titus Pullus the weapons instructor in place of Vinicius would turn out to be. As Pullus rose through the ranks, first as Optio, then as Secundus Pilus Prior, promoted after Alesia, he required every man under his command to learn and master the Vinician grip, a practice he continued when he rose to Primus Pilus. Now, here in Zeugma, having one of Vinicius' original students serving as tutor to his nephew put Pullus' mind at ease, even as he understood it meant that young Porcinus would hardly feel the same way. But, in this area, Titus Pullus wasn't only a Primus Pilus; he was an uncle of his beloved sister's only son, and he was determined that the youngster would not only survive his first campaign, he would acquit himself in a manner worthy of someone who Pullus was already considering as one capable of continuing the Pullus name.

It was a week after their arrival in Zeugma that the Prince Herod, son of Antipater and one of Caesar's most loyal clients on this side of

38

what Romans called Our Sea, arrived with five thousand Jewish infantry, just beating out Polemon and his contingent of cavalry by a day. It took another day to finish the integration of the rest of this force into the army, then all was finally ready. Not surprising to any man in the army, especially Titus Pullus, there was actually another arrival at Zeugma that preceded that of the last of the auxiliary troops, and although in terms of numbers it wasn't a huge addition, the identity of the party meant it was an even more notable event. Having followed behind Caesar from Rome, where she had been staying in a villa on the other side of the Tiber, Cleopatra's entrance into the town perched on a bluff overlooking the Euphrates happened with a pomp and style that Pullus had observed previously when he had been with Caesar in Alexandria. Adding to the occasion was the presence of another personage in what was ultimately more of a royal procession than a journey, and it was the identity of this person, actually a child, that caused a huge stir in the army.

"Did you know she was going to bring the boy?" Balbus asked Pullus, the pair standing side by side on the huge forum of the sprawling camp just outside the walls of Zeugma.

Their presence was a matter of happenstance; they had been attending yet another briefing that Caesar insisted on holding as they waited for the arrival of Herod and Polemon.

Pullus shook his head, replying, "I'm not surprised she showed up, but I didn't think she'd be willing to risk bringing the boy."

The "boy" to whom they were referring was Caesarion, the result of the union between Caesar and Cleopatra that occurred during the siege in Alexandria. He was now a toddler of three, but as the pair witnessed, Cleopatra had insisted on dressing the poor child in the full regalia of a Pharaoh of Egypt; the only small grace, Pullus thought, was that she had the ridiculous garb made for his size, but even from where he and Balbus were standing, he could see the boy was struggling to keep his head erect, the weight of the high headdress making matters difficult.

"That boy looks ridiculous," Balbus muttered, careful to keep his voice pitched low since they were actually standing no more than a dozen paces away from the small army of Cleopatra's retinue.

Pullus, as aware of their proximity as his second in command, nevertheless couldn't smother a snicker at Balbus' words, which elicited a glare from one of the heavily made-up, richly garbed courtiers. This was something Pullus wasn't willing to let go unchallenged, especially given what he knew about this creature.

"Did they let you keep your balls when they cut them off?" he growled at the eunuch.

Despite the heavy makeup, both men saw the courtier blanch, but more importantly to Pullus, he quickly turned away from the Primus Pilus.

"I guess not," Balbus remarked dryly, which was almost too much for Pullus' composure, and he was forced to turn his back to the scene taking place in front of the *praetorium*, which was a serious breach in itself, at least if Pullus had been Egyptian.

"You bastard," he mumbled to Balbus, then composed again, spun back about.

He was just in time to see Caesarion step from his mother's side to walk forward to where Caesar was standing, wearing his *paludamentum*, the red general's cloak, and wearing his ivy crown that the Primus Pilus knew his general wore as much to cover his bald spot than for any other reason. Pullus idly wondered if this was the same one he had dragged along with him in his teeth on the disastrous day in Alexandria when the general had been forced to abandon his ship when it was almost capsized by panicked soldiers who were fleeing from the Heptastadion, the huge causeway that bisected the great harbor of the Egyptian capital. Returning his attention back to the scene, Pullus watched as the boy reached his father, and one didn't need to know Caesar well to see the pride there as he looked down at his son. While Pullus could hear Caesarion speaking, his voice didn't carry enough for him to hear the words, but just the tone of it elicited a sudden wave of emotion in the Primus Pilus that was even stronger because it was so unexpected. In this moment, Pullus wasn't hearing the voice of Caesarion, but another three-year-old boy, a sturdy child with his father's size but his mother's coloring, his face smeared with honey and clutching a carved toy Legionary his father had brought with him on a surprise visit. The stab of pain and regret was so strong that it caused Pullus to gasp aloud, which prompted Balbus to turn sharply, his scarred face expressing his curiosity at this unusual behavior by his Primus Pilus. He immediately wished he hadn't, because Balbus instantly knew why Pullus had reacted this way, understanding that Pullus wasn't seeing Caesarion, but his own son Vibius, named for his then-best friend Vibius Domitius. The boy, along with Pullus' woman Gisela and their daughter Livia, had perished in a plague in Brundisium just a couple years before, and as one of Pullus' best friends, Balbus understood how the man beside him still struggled to cope with the loss. Moments like this, he thought, don't help at all, and for a heartbeat, he actually considered suggesting to Pullus they withdraw from the forum, then immediately thought better of it. Fortunately, this scenedidn't last much longer; their greeting done, Caesar beckoned Cleopatra and Caesarion to follow him into the *praetorium*, and they naturally obeyed. Not before Cleopatra, her head moving ponderously because of her own regalia, turned to survey the small crowd of Roman soldiers who had been in the area to witness her entrance, and in doing so, her eye naturally fell on the largest Roman among them.

"Titus Pullus," she called out with a melodious, almost languid voice that Pullus had discovered was part of her allure. "It's wonderful to see you again! Are you ready for this great adventure Caesar has planned?"

Despite the rush of heat to his face at this sudden show of not just attention, but royal favor, Pullus managed to remember the manner in which he was expected to behave, walking forward to bend down and take the Egyptian queen's hand, which she had proffered for the customary kiss.

"Yes, Your Highness." Pullus tried not to mumble and to sound confident and prepared for this moment. "We're all ready and eager to get started."

Her laugh was as mellifluous as her speaking voice, but because her face was so heavily made up, if one didn't hear the sound of it, they would have found it impossible to believe she was actually doing so.

"Pullus," her tone was teasing, "is that your way of warning me not to give Caesar cause to tarry here?"

The truth was this was exactly what had been on Pullus' mind, and as warm as his face had been, now he had the absurd thought it was about to burst into flame. He also reminded himself that, of all the people he had met, Cleopatra ranked as one of the smartest, behind only Caesar, and what would be surprising to many, especially Romans of the upper class, Sextus Scribonius. This meant he had to remember to curb his tongue and refrain from blurting out the first thing that came into his mind, a habit of his that had caused him more problems than he would have liked to admit. That Cleopatra was teasing him only served to embarrass him even more, but before he could think of a reply that would seem witty but not offend the

Egyptian queen, she was gone in a swirl of robes and perfume. Following immediately behind her were the eunuchs, including the one with whom Pullus had his exchange, but this time, he kept his eyes directly to the front as he disappeared into the *praetorium.* Balbus suddenly appeared at Pullus' side, his face twisted into the leer that was his version of a grin, clearly enjoying Pullus' discomfort.

"Shut up," the Primus Pilus growled, turning to return back to the 10th's area of the camp.

"I didn't say anything," Balbus protested.

"No, but you were about to," Pullus countered, then gave Balbus a playful shove.

This was something Balbus couldn't argue, nor did he try to as the pair returned to their Legion, as Pullus wondered openly how long they would be stuck in Zeugma now.

When the army departed two days after the arrival of Polemon and his contingent of cavalry, most of the men were shocked that Caesar chose not to tarry now that the queen had arrived. However, while Pullus was mildly surprised, he wasn't of the same mind as his comrades of all ranks in the army. As he pointed out to Scribonius and Balbus, of all the men in the army, he was one of the only ones who had been in Alexandria and witnessed the dynamics of Caesar's relationship with Cleopatra. Yes, Pullus admitted, Caesar had been beguiled by the young queen, almost from the moment they had met; although Pullus normally tried to avoid gossiping about his superiors, especially Caesar, even he couldn't avoid divulging how Caesar had gone to Cleopatra's private apartments the very first night and hadn't emerged until after dawn. While he was certainly no expert in such matters, Pullus' own calculations agreed with the men who claimed to know by virtue of the births of their own children that, in all likelihood, Caesarion had been conceived that very night, or in the week thereafter.

"But you always knew who was in charge whenever they were together," was how Pullus put it to his friends. "So, yes, I'm a bit surprised, but not that much if I'm being honest. Especially considering how long he's been planning this campaign."

This, both acknowledged, was certainly true; nevertheless, Caesar's refusal to linger provided a worthy diversion to men who, in just a matter of watches, might be engaged in battle, and Pullus was loath to stop the men from gossiping because of this reality. He knew from long experience that, if a man, particularly one who had never been in combat before, was left to his own devices, with nothing else to engage his imagination, the time immediately preceding a possible fight could spell the difference between the man responding in the manner in which he was trained or becoming paralyzed by fear as all the things he had been dwelling on came to fruition and proved to be much worse than he had imagined. Actually, to Pullus and his Centurions, with whom Caesar had entrusted crossing the pontoon bridge that remained permanently in position on the western bank of the Euphrates River, which served as the boundary line between the two great powers, the fact that their crossing was unopposed was a bit of a disappointment. The 10th was ostensibly a veteran Legion, but in reality, it had just finished its sixteen-year term of service almost exactly two years before, and its last action had been at Munda. Now, although about a third part of the men of the ranks had signed on for another enlistment, and a bit more than half of the Centurions had as well, Pullus had been hoping for a short but sharp action, not only to blood his green men, but to get a sense of the fighting quality of his newly made over Legion. While he was cautiously confident that, when their moment came, they would acquit themselves in a manner that brought no shame to the Legion, and most importantly to Pullus, to himself as its Primus Pilus, he also understood that he couldn't be absolutely certain until that inevitable day arrived. However, while the crossing, which was made after a contingent of cavalry, dragging heavy ropes that were attached to the pontoon bridge, swam the river, then used the power of their mounts to pull the boats across the water, wasn't contested, it was definitely observed. In fact, even as Pullus, leading his Legion across, was ascending the opposite bank, a band of horsemen wearing the distinctive pointed helmets of the Parthians sat watching from the low bluff overlooking the crossing.

When Pullus, as the ranking man on the eastern side of the river, snapped an order to the Decurion in command of the Galatian cavalry to engage with these enemy horsemen, the Parthians demonstrated a trait that, as much as it may have frustrated Pullus and every other Roman, they all understood would be the most common response, which was to simply gallop away, relying on the speed of their own mounts to take them to safety. And, as Pullus noted dismally, once they were safely out of danger, they resumed their posts, watching as the massive army began to cross in earnest. Naturally, the small outpost that the Parthians kept as an observation point on their enemy was deserted; Pullus assumed that whatever civilians who had eked out an existence there, servicing the small detachment of the Parthian military, had made their retreat almost as soon as the Roman train came within sight of Zeugma. And, he was fairly sure as his men performed a thorough search of the small cluster of mud-brick buildings, those mounted observers were the last of the Parthians who had been stationed here, probably carrying out the orders of their departed commander to track the movement of the Romans at least long enough to determine the likely avenue of approach they would use. That, Pullus thought with grim humor, is hopefully where Caesar's acumen showed itself. Whereas Crassus, in ignoring the advice he had been given, had taken the most direct route, Caesar actually believed that the counsel had been sound, and was in fact following it himself. Actually, the first part of the route that Caesar and his army were following could just as easily have been taken on the western side of the great river as they traveled north for a few days' march, before it swung to the east. Perhaps in some ways this would have been the more prudent course, since it would keep Caesar's army protected from an attack by whatever army the great king Orodes sent against them by the natural barrier. This was something a general like the late Pompey Magnus, the later version who had grown cautious, in all likelihood would have done, but Caesar was no Pompey, and certainly no Crassus. Despite his personal feelings towards both men; he actually had been quite close with the pair, albeit for different reasons and, Caesar would be the first to admit with a rueful smile, separately, since neither man could stand to be in the company of the other, Caesar didn't think much of their generalship. Now the only man left of what would become known as the First Triumvirate was crossing the river for the precise reason that it would expose his army to a possible attack. Unlike Crassus, who was operating under the assumption of most generals whose fighting experience was done from a couch as they read some treatise, inevitably written by another "expert" whose credentials were essentially identical, Caesar understood that simply marching across Parthia to assault and capture their ostensible capital at Ctesiphon would be meaningless. Parthia was the only nation whose territory actually competed with Rome in terms of its expanse, but unlike Rome, much of that space was uninhabitable by anything more than small groups of people, clustered around what was ultimately the scarcest and most precious resource of that region, water. Consequently, the society that was once known by another name, the great Persian empire of Darius, was highly decentralized, and while it was true that Ctesiphon was where the Parthian king Orodes resided, in itself this was meaningless, because the Parthians were a more mobile nation than Rome. This, Caesar had understood from the beginning, was a huge advantage for the Parthians, and because of that ability to cover distances more quickly, meant taking Ctesiphon wouldn't mean much, other than in a symbolical sense. Oh, he knew it would be a huge goad to the pride of Orodes, but in terms of strategic value, this was about all taking Ctesiphon was worth, at least if Caesar was going to accomplish his true goal. And as of this moment, his objective was known only to him; Caesar planned on doing much more than avenging the loss of the seven standards and the death of Crassus. By the time he was through, Caesar would be adding this vast nation to those already under the dominion of Rome and make it a province. To do that, he understood that it was the Parthian army that was the true prize, and of the two objectives, more important than taking a city. And to do that, Caesar would march his army and essentially put a river to his back in the event of an attack by Parthia, although he was sure that any such assault by these Easterners would be little more than a probe, a test of Caesar and his men to determine if he was ultimately another Crassus, or even a Pompey, despite his reputation. That, the Roman general thought with grim amusement, would be when they'd learn who Caesar was, and in what danger they were of losing their empire.

As smoothly as their assembly and embarkation went, things didn't go all Caesar's way. It was on the third morning after the river crossing that the general was roused by one of the Tribunes, the youngster visibly agitated, although it was more from the thought of rousing Caesar from his rest than any other reason.

"General," he tried to sound confident but there was no mistaking the quaver of excitement in his tone, "I've just been informed by Gundomir that," he swallowed hard and closed his eyes, not wanting to see Caesar's reaction, "that Cassius has apparently...." He stopped then, for the simple reason that he wasn't sure which was the proper term. Had the man deserted, since he was nominally a member of Caesar's staff? Or would it be more accurate to use the word "escape," since for all intents, he was a prisoner. Instead, he settled for, "...left the camp. And," he thought to add plaintively, "I don't think he's coming back."

Yet, while the Tribune had been expecting an eruption of Caesar's temper, which was almost as famous among his subordinates as his acumen and luck, the general's only reaction, seated on the edge of his cot, was to give his subordinate a small smile.

There was a silence for a few heartbeats, then Caesar allowed, "The only thing that surprises me is it took him this long. Although," he added with a rueful sigh, "I have a feeling my nephew is going to love having the chance to tell me he told me this would happen."

Despite Caesar's calm reaction—frankly, the younger Roman held a strong suspicion that the general had been expecting news of this sort—the Tribune still felt compelled to ask cautiously, "Do you think he'll go to the Parthians and tell them what he knows of our plans?"

Caesar's response was an immediate shake of his head, and he replied firmly, "No. I know he won't do anything of the sort. Cassius is many things, but a traitor to Rome isn't one of them. A traitor to

46

me," he granted, again with a tight smile, "yes. But he'd never throw in with the Parthians."

Although the Tribune didn't share the same strength of conviction on this point as his general, he did trust Caesar's instincts about the man, ignoring the inconvenient fact that Caesar had been surprised by Cassius' treachery once before.

"How much time before the morning call?" Caesar asked the Tribune, who replied that there was a bit more than a third part of a watch to go. Hearing this, Caesar stood, stretched, and said, "Then there's no point in going back to bed."

Taking this as a rebuke, the young man stiffened, offering his apology for waking his general on a matter that Caesar had clearly been expecting.

Dismissing the words with a wave, Caesar walked to him and clasped his shoulder, saying, "No need to apologize, Quintus! You did exactly the right thing in waking me."

Stepping past his Tribune, Caesar beckoned to the slave who had actually been the one to waken the general, and the man hurried to help Caesar dress. Which, unlike most patricians, meant that the slave just handed Caesar each article of clothing he demanded, whereupon he clothed himself. As the Tribune watched, he realized that by doing so, Caesar was actually prepared to face the day more quickly than if he had simply stood there, allowing the slave to do the work.

Making note of this, he still felt compelled to ask Caesar, "Where do you think Cassius is going to go?"

"Hispania," Caesar replied instantly, informing the Tribune that the older man had given this some thought. "His brother's governor there. And," he added with a grin, "it's about as far away from me as he can get."

By the time Caesar and his army arrived at Samosata, the capital of Commagene, the scouting parties that ranged ahead and out from the Parthian side of the river had been bringing back reports of increased activity and signs that Orodes was summoning the levies owed to him by his *satraps*. Samosata itself, which was located on a high bluff overlooking the river, and the Commagene king, Antiochus I Theos, now faced a decision when the vanguard of Rome's army came into view from the high walls of the city. Over the course of his reign, Antiochus had tried to steer a neutral course between Rome and Parthia but had been forced into an alliance with Parthia by Orodes, which included giving his beloved daughter Laodice to Orodes' house in a marriage contract. More problematically at the moment, despite the fact that Antiochus had been awarded the coveted *Toga Praetexta* as a Friend and Ally of Rome, the king had chosen to offer Pompey Magnus troops for his war against Caesar. Subsequently, for a brief period of time, as the Commagene king listened to his advisors argue about the best course of action, it appeared as if Samosata would have to be assaulted. To that end, Caesar led a party consisting of his Primi Pili, his *Praefectus Fabrorum* Volusenus, the Legates, and a select group of Tribunes on a reconnaissance of the city, circling around from its southern approach to its northern. What they saw, Titus Pullus didn't like, and he sensed his counterparts— Balbinus of the 12th and Batius of the 5ᵗʰ—being as vocal as he was about the prospects of taking the city in a quick assault.

"Why are the walls black?" Balbinus asked of nobody in particular; as usual, it was Caesar who had the answer.

"They're made of basalt," the general explained. "Some of the monuments in Egypt are made of it. Although," he granted as he stared up at them, made even higher because of the city's location on the bluff, "I've never seen so much of it in one place. All that I saw there were in the form of obelisks and a couple of small temples."

"Does it make the wall harder to breach?" Pullus asked, but for this, neither Caesar nor Volusenus had a ready answer.

"I'm not sure." It was Volusenus who admitted as much.

"We're not going to breach the wall," Caesar said with a firm shake of his head. "We don't have time for a mine." Sighing, he did glance over at the men, all of them in full uniform and wearing the white transverse crests that marked them as Primi Pili, and whose own men would have to bear the brunt of what was to come, and said quietly, "We'll have to use the timber to make towers and go over the top. It's too tall for ladders."

Pullus, at least, had suspected as much, but hearing his general confirm it didn't bring him much comfort, and he and Balbinus shared a resigned glance, wondering which of the Legions would get the "honor" of being the first over those black walls.

Fortunately for all parties concerned, at least Roman and Commagene, there was no assault on the walls, as Antiochus determined that it was better to appease the army camped at his walls than one that was still far away. That, however, wasn't his only consideration; speaking in relative terms, Samosata wasn't that far from Zela, making the exploits of the Roman general now camped outside his walls much more immediate than something that had happened to another Roman general far away at Carrhae less impacting. Caesar's name alone carried with it a weight that Crassus had never enjoyed, and while Pompey had once been considered a military man in the same class as Caesar, that had been before the civil war. Now, Caesar and only Caesar stood astride the vast lands under the control of Rome, meaning that, in all reality, the king had made his decision much earlier. However, in some ways, he was still trying to protect himself and his people, therefore capitulating with undue haste could prove to be problematic, particularly in the event this Roman didn't prevail in the coming contest. This, Antiochus conceded only to a trusted few, was unlikely in the extreme, and he spoke with a conviction that came from the visceral impact of standing on the battlements of his city, watching the horrible and mighty machine that was the Roman army come plodding stolidly, but inexorably, under his walls. From his vantage point, he could look down at the ordered rows of tents, each of them uniform in size, and laid out in in such a way that he had learned was the same, no matter where they camped. This Commagene king wasn't much of a warrior; he had accomplished all that he had by virtue of his skill at diplomacy, but even he could see the enormous advantages available to the Legions just by the way they constructed their camp. And he had only to look over at the encampment adjacent to that belonging to Rome, where the huge army of auxiliaries were located, to see the vast difference between the two. In all truth, the auxiliary camp was more familiar to him than the Roman, because it reminded him of the few times he had been out on campaign himself. The only real difference was a matter of scale; just the auxiliaries alone comprised an army vaster than anything the Commagene had seen, or even heard about. These sights made his decision, if not simple, at least rapid, and before night fell on the first full day after the Romans arrived, a rider carrying a flag of truce led the king out of the gates of his city. Such was his conviction in the might of Rome that he'd decided, in order to avoid even the slightest offense to Caesar, instead of sending an envoy as he normally would, Antiochus himself appeared before Caesar. Much to the king's surprise, and considerable relief, Caesar treated him with the utmost courtesy, bordering on deference, although the Commagene wasn't fooled in the slightest; from the moment he came into Caesar's presence, he knew who held the whip hand. If anything, his reaction was a kind of scornful amusement at himself as he thought, You believed Parthia could be more dangerous than this man? And, without understanding why he was doing so in a conscious sense, the Commagene allied himself with Caesar, for the simple but powerful truth that this Roman was *Caesar*. What the king did recall later, after he had time to reflect on the moment, was how the thought had come to his mind; here is another Alexander!

The submission of Commagene was bloodless, but more importantly, it had been vital to Caesar's plans, which he had yet to fully reveal to anyone, even Octavian. While Caesar saw much promise in the youth, it was still a bit early to tell just what kind of Roman he'd be, and more crucially to Caesar, if he was the right one to become Caesar's heir. This was yet another secret, although this was one he had kept only from Cleopatra, the fact that Caesarion, while he would certainly inherit a vast amount of wealth and prestige from both his parents, could never be Caesar's successor. That, the general understood, would be too much for Romans of all classes to bear. Perhaps, he reflected, if Caesarion's mother had been a Gaul, or even from someplace like Numidia. But not Egypt, never Egypt, especially because Cleopatra was a queen in her own right. It was a pity, really, although not one he dwelled on much; Caesar was never given to worrying about things that were outside his power to control, and it was another way in which he and Titus Pullus were alike. At least, he admitted only to himself, once I've made sure I can't actually take control of whatever it is. On the matter of Samosata, Caesar had needed the city to come of its own free will, or to appear to do so at any rate. He wasn't fooled by the blandishments of the king, another of those oily fellows whose hair gleamed and stank of perfume, and who had waxed on and on about Caesar's greatness as a man of justice, whose wisdom was equal to that of some ancient Eastern king named Hammurabi. No, Caesar understood that the Commagene's capitulation was grounded more in fear, made manifest once he'd gazed down from his high black walls at the might of what Caesar could bring to bear. That reality didn't matter; what did was the *appearance* that the king of the Commagene had chosen of his own free will, picking Rome over Parthia. Hopefully, if all went to plan, he would be just the first of many to submit without the shedding of blood, particularly Roman blood. Besides which, as Caesar also understood how his men would view matters, having to fight for every single city, starting with the first one, would be viewed as nothing less than an ill omen by the rankers of his Legions, and they mattered even more than the ranks of his auxiliary cavalry if his plans were to be fulfilled. Caesar understood that, in this one area, there were skeptics around him, and in his ranks he had no doubt, who believed his composition of this army was repeating the mistake of Crassus.

The Legions couldn't fight effectively against the horse archers of the Parthians, and neither could they stand the massed charges of the heavily armored cataphracts, whose ranks were composed of Parthian nobility and their personal retainers. This was accepted as a simple fact, by almost everyone, especially in the aftermath of Crassus' defeat at Carrhae, and Cassius had been one of those who had been trumpeting this "truth" the loudest after he finally returned to Rome. Because he had survived, his warnings were given instant credence, so that when Caesar mustered the Legions at Brundisium, there were those who muttered that he was making a huge and probably fatal error. Naturally, Caesar didn't see it this way, but not because he disagreed with the basic premises espoused by Cassius and others. Under normal circumstances, he also understood that his Legions would be at a huge disadvantage, first against the waves of arrows the Parthians were capable of firing with their compound bows, then against the thundering weight of horses and men, both rider and mount wearing heavy armor, the horses in particular wearing blankets with iron plates sewn on that only allowed their legs below the knees to show. But Caesar had twice as many cavalry as Crassus had, which he planned on using to keep the horse archers at bay. As far as the cataphracts, he had a two-prong strategy to counter their effectiveness, although one of those was the one over which he had the least control, and contrary to his outer appearance, he worried about a great deal. However, one thing that Caesar had perfected was the ability to appear unruffled and unworried, no matter what circumstances; only once, at Munda, had his composure cracked, but as things so often did with Caesar, this actually served as an advantage. His army, seeing their general so openly worried for the first time in all the years they had marched for the man, had responded by finding energy they had sworn was spent just moments before, assaulting the forces of the young Pompey entrenched on the hill outside Munda one final time, thereby ending the rebellion and firmly establishing Caesar as First Man. Even so, while it was a victory, it hadn't been without paying a high cost in the blood of his Legions, particularly the 10th, the Legion he had created as Praetor of Hispania. And, while Caesar would never publicly acknowledge this, of all the men he lost, it was one who almost perished that had troubled him the most, and not because replacing a Primus Pilus who had fallen, as Gaius Crastinus had at Pharsalus, always posed a vexing problem selecting a replacement.

The simple truth was that, as much as a man of Caesar's station could, he was extremely fond of the huge Roman who he had first decorated as an overgrown, immensely strong teenage boy after the 10th's first campaign in Hispania. It was impossible not to notice Titus Pullus, simply because of his size, but as Caesar had observed over the years, there was much more than just raw, brute strength and a ferocity in battle that had become legend among the men of the Legions embodied in Pullus. Untutored he certainly was, yet as Caesar had learned from his earliest days in the Subura, surrounded by those whom members of his class sneeringly called the Head Count, uneducated didn't equate to unintelligent. Pullus, Caesar had learned, was very intelligent, but more than that, he was curious about the world around him. It amused Caesar to think how embarrassed and uncomfortable Pullus would be if the Primus Pilus was aware of how much Caesar knew about a habit that Pullus kept secret from all but a select few of his closest friends, his love of reading anything and everything he could get his hands on. Going further, if Pullus ever found out that Caesar, having discovered this desire to improve himself, had entered into something of a conspiracy with Pullus' servant Diocles, whereby the Dictator "suggested" titles for the Greek to procure, Caesar knew Pullus would be mortified. This exchange between he and Diocles was done through intermediaries, of course; as secure as Caesar was in his position, he didn't need the kind of trouble that would come if it became known he was encouraging a man of the Head Count to better himself. That this resistance came from members of his own class didn't surprise Caesar; what had come as something of a surprise was that the hostility didn't just come from them, but from members of Pullus' class as well. More than one man of the Head Count believed what they were told by the priests, augurs, and frankly, everyone above them on the social ladder, that their status was ordained by the gods, and any man who strove to rise above that station was guilty of hubris. This, as far as Caesar was concerned, was utter nonsense; indeed, aside from the other qualities owned by his favorite Primus Pilus, more than any other, it was Pullus' naked and unapologetic ambition with which Caesar identified most. He knew very well about Pullus' goal of elevating himself, and most importantly, those who bore his name, into the Equestrian order, that part of Roman society that could be called the middle class, especially now that the distinction between patrician and plebeian had become so blurred through intermarriage and adoption. Contrary to Caesar's knowledge of Pullus' literacy, this was no secret, because Pullus had never hidden this as his goal; at least, at first, before he had learned how many of his social superiors bore him enmity for that ambition. Naturally, although Pullus was more circumspect, once uttered, these words were always out there, being passed from one malicious mouth to another. And it had been at Munda that Pullus' ambitions had almost seen their end, when in the climax of the fight on the hill, Titus Pullus had suffered a near-mortal wound. In reality, as Caesar sent his personal physician to minister to the Primus Pilus, any other man would have succumbed to a sword thrust that pierced his chest. But Pullus wasn't any other man, although he lingered with one foot in Charon's Boat, as rankers liked to say, for several days. He was unconscious, so Pullus didn't learn until much later that his general spent every moment he could spare at his bedside, as if by his very presence he could somehow transfer some of his own formidable will into this giant Roman who had served him so well. Despite the fact that Pullus had been alone with Caesar many times since, neither of them spoke of this period of time, both implicitly understanding it would embarrass the other, and their mutual regard made this a moment of which neither ever spoke. And since Munda, Caesar had never lost his composure, and his fervent hope was that, once he was done in this life, it was the only time he did so. The Parthians, he understood, would have some say in this matter.

Regarding the Primus Pilus of the 10th, although Pullus was unaware of it, his wounding had been the source of the first disagreement between Caesar and his nephew, who had come to Hispania too late for the battle of Munda, but was by the general's side during the whirlwind period where the victorious Dictator put matters in order in the province. It had been a heady period for the young Octavian because he had literally been at Caesar's side through every meeting with locals officials, conference with his Legates, and when Caesar had visited Pullus on his sickbed, after the Primus Pilus had somewhat recovered, to rebuild the 10th Legion now that its first enlistment was up. Over the course of two days, Octavian had observed how Caesar seemed to almost defer to the big Roman who, if Octavian had been forced to admit, intimidated the younger man thoroughly, even supine. On only a couple occasions did Caesar quietly, but firmly, overrule Pullus' suggestion for a particular slot in the sixty spots of the Centurionate, of which roughly half needed to be filled to replace men who were retiring. Otherwise, his uncle and Pullus seemed to be of a like mind in almost everything, but that wasn't the cause of Octavian's disagreement with his uncle. It had been on the morning they had departed back for Rome, where Caesar and Octavian rode in a small but very swift two-man carriage that was partially closed, thereby allowing the two to converse privately.

"What did you think of Titus Pullus?" Caesar asked Octavian, shortly after the journey began, and he was genuinely curious about his nephew's assessment; while the Dictator knew the boy had a first-rate mind, and a keen grasp of politics, he hadn't gotten a sense of his ability to judge other men.

"Very formidable," Octavian admitted, although Caesar noticed he was staring through the small opening on his side of the carriage, not looking at his uncle. "Even when he's lying in bed. He's clearly an immensely strong brute. I heard the physician tell you he had never seen anyone else survive such a wound."

Caesar found Octavian's depiction of Pullus both curious, and frankly, troubling, which prompted him to say, "Brute?" He shook his head forcefully, "Pullus is certainly strong, but he's also extremely intelligent."

This seemed to nettle Octavian, giving Caesar the sense that the idea there could be someone else his uncle considered on a level even approaching his own somehow threatened the boy, but just as he was about to rebuke Octavian for his mislabeling of Pullus, he remembered what it had been like for him as a lad. Being the smartest person in any given situation can be a heady feeling, but as Caesar had learned through experience, and Octavian clearly had yet to understand, being uneducated didn't automatically equate to being simpleminded.

Therefore, his tone was gentle as he advised the boy, "Nephew, I know that you're extremely quick-minded, but you still have much to learn. And this is a time you need to listen to what I have to say and heed it." Leaning forward on his elbows so that he could pin Octavian with the power of his ice-blue gaze, Caesar continued, "Just because a man hasn't been tutored in rhetoric, mathematics, history, and poetry as you have, that doesn't mean he's stupid. And," he pointed a warning finger at Octavian, "you should *never* underestimate men like Pullus. They have much to offer in both practical matters and in giving you a real insight into what those of his class are thinking. Because, make

54

no mistake, while men like Catiline, Clodius, and Milo used this for their own betterment and not that of Rome's, they weren't wrong in their understanding that it's through the Head Count that a man has real power."

Octavian listened, but while Caesar could tell he was absorbing his words, he also understood in the way the boy cocked his head that he wasn't quite willing to accept his uncle's counsel.

"But," the boy confirmed, "that's not really true. It's the army and its loyalty that gives power. It's what gave *you* the ability to become First Man."

Rather than being put off with his nephew's rebuff, Caesar actually smiled at Octavian, pleased that he had at least understood the basic truth of what Rome had become; however, that understanding was clearly incomplete.

"That's certainly true," Caesar granted, having to suppress a smile at the flush of pride that suffused Octavian's face at what the boy thought was his uncle's ceding the point. "But," as quickly as it came, Octavian's smile fled, "that's not all to the question. Where do those men who march for me come from?"

"From the Head Count," Octavian said slowly, but only after a pause, and his smile quickly changed to a frown.

"And the men like Pullus, despite the fact that they're in the Centurionate, are part of the Head Count. Despite how high they've risen in the ranks. Or," Caesar thought to add, "how wealthy they've become." The older man paused for a moment before he plunged forward to divulge one of his decisions that he had been keeping to himself. "That's why, as soon as the time's right, I plan on elevating Pullus and a select few other men."

At first, this didn't seem to faze Octavian, who indeed just shrugged his acceptance, offering only, "That's certainly not unheard of, men with the necessary qualifications elevating themselves into the Equestrian order."

Caesar understood then that Octavian had mistaken his meaning and, for a brief instant, considered letting the matter drop and letting the boy find out like everyone else, when Caesar actually did what he was planning. No, he thought suddenly, if this boy is going to be your heir, he needs to know *everything*, including this.

"I'm afraid you don't understand, Octavian," he said this in a quiet voice, but with just enough iron in it to give his nephew a fraction's time of warning, "I'm not talking about raising Pullus and the others up into the Equestrians. I plan on making them Senators."

Despite the jouncing ride, Octavian's body went rigid with shock, his jaw dropping in astonishment, which caused him to blurt out without thinking, "You can't do that!"

As he would do several months later with Antonius, Caesar's reply was non-verbal, just staring calmly at his nephew. Who, Caesar noted, didn't flinch from staring right back, which upped the irritation and regard of the Dictator for his nephew in almost equal measure. The silence stretched out uncomfortably, and as Caesar expected, it was the younger man who cracked first.

"Of course," he spoke carefully, "you can certainly do so as Dictator. I...apologize for speaking so intemperately."

Caesar's first instinct was to comfort Octavian with a smile and an assurance that there was nothing for him to forgive, but there was something in the boy's manner that troubled him. Instead, he gave a grave nod, deciding that a bit more silence would do the boy some good. Besides, he reasoned, there would be more than enough time to expose Octavian to Pullus and those other men; he was sure that once Octavian saw the qualities each of them possessed, his concerns would be answered.

Chapter Two

"Great King," the courtier announced to Orodes, "a courier has arrived from the outpost at Zeugma." The man paused, then said dramatically, "The Romans have taken Samosata! Without bloodshed. The city surrendered without a fight."

Orodes, seated on the ornate throne and smothered in the robes of state, shifted irritably, which came from two causes. This news, while not unexpected, was still unwelcome, although the second was more immediate; thrones of the Parthian king weren't designed for comfort, particularly when said king was suffering the indignity of a bad case of the piles.

Ignoring his discomfort, acutely aware that there were potentially unfriendly eyes on him, Orodes asked the courtier, "Where are the Romans now?"

"According to the courier, they're still traveling north, following the river," the man replied, whereupon he was dismissed with a wave by the Parthian king.

"I wonder how far north they plan on going before they turn in our direction?" Orodes wondered aloud, wincing despite himself, not because of the pain but from the knowledge that he had just shown what his sons would construe as weakness. Or, he corrected himself wearily, at least one of them would; of Pacorus, he had no doubt about his loyalty. But Phraates was another story, and even as he sat on the throne, he could feel the young man's eyes on him, giving Orodes the feeling even then he was measuring the dimensions of the throne and deciding if it would fit him. Well, boy, the king thought with grim amusement, you're going to have to wait for your time. Not just mine, but your brother's as well.

It was Pacorus, his favorite son, who answered for the courtier, since he had already thoroughly questioned the dispatch rider.

"Father, Molon is the commander of the *washt* that was at Zeugma and is the one following the army," Pacorus relayed, "and I know him. He is a good man, a steady man, and he thinks that the Romans' intent is to follow the Euphrates all the way to Arsameia before turning east and crossing to the Tigris north of Mount Masia.

After that?" The prince could only offer a shrug and finish, "Molon doesn't speculate."

Orodes considered his son's words, thinking about the area that Pacorus had just described, saying slowly, "That's technically Armenian territory, and Artavasdes is a sworn ally."

"So was Antiochus Theos," Phraates pointed out, and despite the fact that his father was sure he brought this up to embarrass Orodes, the king couldn't deny this fact.

"That's true," Orodes replied icily, not deigning to look in Phraates' direction, a calculated move designed to warn his younger son not to overstep. "But Antiochus was never a warrior. And," he allowed, "he had a Roman army at his walls." Deciding then that Antiochus' betrayal was something that could be dealt with later, Orodes continued, "And Artavasdes is related to our house by marriage. No," he announced, "Artavasdes won't be willing to allow the Romans to sack Amida without a fight. Not," he favored the small gathering around him with a grim smile, "if he doesn't want to risk our wrath."

Over the course of the next few months, Pacorus often wondered if he had spoken up then, how matters might have been different, because unlike his father, the crown prince wasn't as sanguine about the fighting spirit of Artavasdes. His doubts were well founded; he was, after all, married to the Armenian king's sister, and as a result, believed he had better insight into the mind of Artavasdes because the siblings had been close growing up. And his wife, Pacorus thought ruefully, was never loath to remind him how their marriage had been forced upon her, after her brother had remained aloof when the first Roman invasion under Crassus had been crushed by his father. From the prince's perspective, Artavasdes' alliance with his house was one of convenience, and he didn't share his father's optimism about the prospects of Armenia putting up much of a fight. Yet he remained silent, a decision that would have enormous ramifications, because if there was anyone who could have persuaded Orodes to be more objective in his assessment, it was Pacorus.

The subject of Orodes' judgment was indeed more of a warrior than his counterpart in Commagene, but he didn't take much longer than Antiochus had in concluding that his best recourse lay with Rome rather than against it. However, where Artavasdes differed from Antiochus was in not waiting until Caesar and his army arrived at the gates of Amida, but choosing to ride out from the city, only with his

58

royal bodyguard, to meet Caesar and his army several miles west of the walls. The two leaders met almost in the shadow of the large mountain called Masia, a dormant volcano that could be seen for many miles in every direction. As such things went, it was a low-key meeting, at least by Eastern standards, although Artavasdes had brought along an ornate golden crown that he offered Caesar. Who, unlike on previous occasions, actually accepted the gift, although he immediately turned and handed it to Aulus Hirtius, his second in command. Even so, the moment caused many of Caesar's senior leaders, all of whom had been assembled to bear witness of this meeting so they could take the news back to their men, to exchange uneasy glances. Titus Pullus was one of them; it had only been a few months before when Antonius' supposed prank of offering Caesar a diadem during Lupercalia had caused such problems. It was true they were far, far away from Rome, Pullus reminded himself, but this army was still Roman in composition, and more importantly, in mind, and like many of the Primi Pili, he was wary that his men might react poorly to the news that Caesar was behaving more in the manner of a king. However, as he quickly learned, this concern seemed only to be shared among the officers of the army and not the rankers, all of whom lustily cheered when their general accepted what Caesar thought of as a trinket but represented several years' pay for the Gregarii. And, Pullus admitted, it was certainly...*shiny*, the burnished gold and gems encrusted in crown catching the rays of the sun, making the crown itself hard to see because of the winking fire. None of the men of Caesar's army, of any rank, realized it yet, but this was just the first of many such tokens of submission that would be coming.

More important than a golden crown, however, was what else Artavasdes brought with him, or more accurately, promised to deliver. Because of the time of day Artavasdes had arrived, Caesar ordered camp to be made earlier than normal, with the walls of Amida still not visible on the eastern horizon. Once the huge tent of the *praetorium* was erected, the Dictator wasted no time summoning his senior officers to a meeting, whereby he relayed what ultimately was the most important aspect of the Armenian capitulation.

It was during the evening meal that night, in Pullus' tent, where the Primus Pilus relayed the news to his friends.

"We got a lot more than a crown today," was how he began, which predictably was met with interest, particularly by Balbus.

"You mean he's going to pay the rankers something as well?" he asked eagerly, his scarred face lighting up in a way that only happened when the subject was an impending battle; or, Pullus thought wryly, a new whore with special skills had arrived at one of the brothels.

"In a way," Pullus teased, turning to wink at Scribonius, who was spooning chickpeas into his mouth.

"What does *that* mean?" Balbus grumbled, but when he also looked over at Scribonius, the third member of the trio just shrugged.

"It means that what he's bringing to us is better than gold," Pullus explained, still not quite willing to divulge what he had learned; he was having too much fun tormenting his second in command.

Balbus stared for a moment, clearly trying to think of what could possibly be better than gold; suddenly, whereas before his face had been alight at the thought of money, now his battered features split as he grinned and said with an excited gasp, "You mean he's giving us his..." For a moment, the smile vanished, twisting into a scowl as he tried to think of the word. "...concubines?"

This was so unexpected that Pullus' reaction was to stare, open-mouthed at his erstwhile subordinate, who mistakenly took this as a sign he was in fact correct, and Balbus slammed his hand on the table in delight, hooting, "Ha! I was right!"

Scribonius was silent, but it was because he was trying not to choke on his meal from laughter. In this he was unsuccessful, finally forced to spit out his chewed mouthful back into his bowl as he roared with mirth.

Pullus finally found his voice, asking incredulously, "You think he'd give us his concubines? How many do you think he has?"

Balbus shrugged, saying offhandedly, "I've heard these Eastern *cunni* can have hundreds. Thousands even." He was still grinning, and finished triumphantly, "I was right, wasn't I?"

"No," Pullus sighed, his surprise replaced with the same level of amusement as Scribonius, "you're not right. You really think Caesar would call us to the *praetorium* just to tell us we're going to have camp followers?"

When put that way, the smile on Balbus' face faded, yet he wasn't quite willing to concede the point, insisting, "These aren't just any camp followers! They're fucking a *king,* aren't they? That means they wouldn't be your common whore!"

Shaking his head, Pullus quashed Balbus' short-lived dream of carnal pleasures, made even more memorable by the exotic skills plied by the women of the East that, as Pullus could attest from his time in

Alexandria, was an article of faith among rankers, whether they had actually experienced them or not.

"It's not whores," he said firmly. "What Artavasdes is giving us are ten thousand horse archers and five thousand cataphracts."

Scribonius managed a whistle, and while Balbus looked a bit crestfallen, even he had to admit, if grudgingly, "That's probably worth more than the concubines."

"You think?" Scribonius retorted dryly, prompting a scowl from Balbus.

"You can't blame me for thinking about women first!" Balbus protested. "It's been months since we've seen a woman!"

"Actually," Pullus corrected him, "it's been a few weeks. At most."

"Well," Balbus grumbled, "it feels like months."

"This campaign is just getting started," Scribonius laughed, "and if you're desperate for a woman now, I don't want to be anywhere around you a few months from now."

"I'm no Greek," Balbus retorted, jerking a thumb over at Diocles, who only rolled his eyes from his spot at his small desk; this had been a source of amusement and teasing from Balbus almost since the two had met.

Turning the subject back to what he considered the most important, Pullus continued, "We're going to be at Amida for a week. It will take that long for the Armenians to get here." Addressing Diocles in his role as Legion clerk, he commanded, "I want the men ready for a full inspection, first thing tomorrow morning." As Diocles scribbled this note, Pullus asked his subordinates, "What else can we do to keep the boys too tired to make much mischief while we're waiting?"

The pair considered, but since this was a matter of rank, Balbus deferred to Scribonius, since he commanded an entire Cohort, despite the fact that Balbus was second in command of the entire Legion. This was another Roman practice that had military men of other nations scratching their collective heads; even other Romans found the hierarchy and chain of command in a Roman Legion confusing to follow.

"I think we should work on Caesar's maneuver more," Scribonius replied without hesitation, causing Balbus to glance at Pullus with a raised eyebrow that signaled his wry amusement, as if to tell Pullus, "You asked."

Pullus wasn't quite so circumspect, grimacing at the suggestion, but he also knew Scribonius was correct.

"Oh, they'll love that," he sighed, then finished, "But you're right. That's something that we can never work on enough." Turning to Diocles, he nodded for the Greek to add this item to the schedule.

"How many days do you want to have them working on this?" Diocles asked.

Pullus considered for a moment, resisting the urge to answer, "Until they do it right," settling instead for, "Until two days before we leave. That way, I'll give them a day to rest."

"And Amida?" Scribonius asked, not needing to expand.

While all the Romans had been somewhat surprised to find Amida wasn't quite the dusty, dry outpost they had assumed it to be, but was in fact a city of some fifty thousand inhabitants, Pullus still shook his head.

"No, we don't need any trouble with the locals. Artavasdes is their king, and while he didn't come out and say as much, I think Caesar is a bit suspicious about how devoted an ally the Armenians will be. The last thing he needs is one of the boys to give them the excuse to break the alliance."

"I was talking to Batius," Balbus spoke up, "and he's letting the boys in the Larks have one night in town. What about that?"

The news that one of his counterparts was allowing this didn't make Pullus happy; he was even less so when he asked Diocles what he knew of the rest of the Primi Pili and learned that more than half of them were allowing their men out into the town.

Muttering a curse under his breath, Pullus normally wouldn't have backed down from his decision, but he could tell from both Scribonius' and Balbus' demeanors that they were leaning in the direction of Batius and the others. Besides, he reasoned to himself, there's no telling when the next time will come where the boys can let loose and have a little fun.

Finally, he offered what he thought of as a compromise that, he thought, might help solve two problems at once.

"Tell the Pili Priores," he instructed Diocles, "that I'll let the boys have the second to last night here on the town." He paused and then finished with a grim smile, "Provided I'm satisfied with how well they perform Caesar's maneuver."

It is a truism that oftentimes great or catastrophic results can occur from causes that, in the moment, seem to be trivial. As Pullus and the rest of the 10th would discover later, this was one of those moments, and would only add to the luster of the 10th. Outside the walls of Amida, however, the name of the Primus Pilus of the Equestrians was roundly cursed for the eight days his men were forced to perform a specific action that Caesar had devised, for a specific moment in battle. With the command *"Repitate"* ringing over and over in their ears, the men of the 10th suffered the added indignity of seeing their comrades of the other Legions cheerfully doing little more than loafing as Caesar's army waited for this new addition to their ranks. Every man, to one degree or another, understood how important these new troops would be; what they didn't know was to what degree. Only the moment battle was joined would their value be learned.

"We've been betrayed!"

Pacorus, completely ignoring courtly protocol, relying on his status as favored son and crown prince, burst into the private quarters of his father Orodes. His timing could have been better, although all Pacorus heard was a feminine shriek, a billow of silken sheets, then his father sitting on the edge of the huge bed, glaring at him.

"This better be good," Orodes growled, snatching the sheet from the young girl to cover his own nakedness, leaving her bare body to be viewed by his son.

Pacorus took the sight in with the same kind of appreciation as he did for horseflesh; his father, he acknowledged, albeit silently to himself, always did have exquisite tastes in both.

Turning his attention back to the reason he had burst in, trailing the two guards who were always stationed outside the Parthian king's private chamber, both of them looking very much as if they hoped the tiled floor beneath their feet would suddenly open and swallow them up, Pacorus said bitterly, "I wouldn't say that it's good, Father, but it is important."

When Orodes gave an impatient wave for his son to continue, Pacorus informed his father of the news that Artavasdes, like Antiochus, had judged the Romans under his walls to be more of an imposing threat than the Parthians. Pacorus had barely finished before his father, completely forgetting his situation, leapt to his feet, the sheet slithering down from his body so that the Parthian king's body, stark white when compared to the nut brown of hands and face weathered by years of exposure, was there to see. While Pacorus tried to avert his eyes, he was struck by the sudden thought, *He's an old man already, with a pot belly and blue veins on his legs!*

"Well, Father," a new voice sounded from behind Pacorus, causing him to whirl about to see Phraates standing; leaning, actually, against the doorframe, arms folded laconically as he commented, "I hope our subjects never see the King of Kings naked! Our *satraps* would be at our throats in no time!"

"Shut your mouth," Pacorus snarled, furious with his younger brother, who always seemed to know exactly what to say to antagonize their father. "This is more important than hearing your wit!"

Phraates unfolded himself, his face becoming guarded, telling Pacorus that he hadn't arrived in time to hear the news.

"What it is, brother?" he asked. "What's happened?"

Rather than answer, Pacorus pointedly turned back to Orodes, who had taken the time to at least snatch a robe from the floor, where it had been discarded at some point earlier, but the king gave a disgusted wave, grunting his permission for Pacorus to relay the information to Phraates. For one of the few times, the two brothers and father were allied in their feelings, although Phraates reacted a bit differently.

"We'll tie him to four horses and send them to the points of the compass," he said through clenched teeth. Turning to his father, Phraates warned, "Father, this can't go unpunished! If Artavasdes is allowed to get away with this kind of treachery, you'll spend the rest of your days fighting off challengers for our throne."

Pacorus instantly took note of his brother's use of the word "our" when referring to the great seat that symbolized Parthian power, but before he could take issue, his father snapped, "Don't you think I know that, boy?" Jabbing a finger at his younger son, he spat, "And it's *my* throne, not ours! Mine! Which means it's my decision to make about what to do about Artavasdes."

To anyone who didn't know him, Phraates would have appeared unruffled at this rebuke, but Pacorus knew his brother well, indeed, and he saw how the knuckles of his brother's hands went white as he clenched his fist, and the little muscle along his jawline was twitching, always a telltale sign Phraates was struggling to compose himself.

"Of course, you're right, Father," Phraates spoke smoothly, actually making a bow in deference to his sire. "Please forgive my presumption. I'm simply...distraught at how faithless Artavasdes turned out to be, even after you gave him your sister!"

This was a veiled jab in itself, because Phraates had been steadfastly against Orodes' decision to seal an alliance in the more diplomatic fashion of marriage, long a tool of the great houses as they sought to navigate the treacherous seas of shifting alliances and competing interests. As far as Pacorus was concerned, Phraates' objection had been based more in his desire to solve problems in the manner in which he was most comfortable; through fire, pillage, and bloodshed. And when his father had sought to punish Artavasdes for the first time, he had allied himself to the Roman cause. When the Roman Crassus had tried to invade, it had been Phraates who urged him to continue the slaughter instead of settling for a handful of sharp skirmishes and the taking of a couple of small towns that were put to the sword, which Orodes had done only to bring the Armenian king to the bargaining table. Orodes was either too distraught to make an issue of Phraates' sally, or deemed it less important to deal with what had caused the scene in the first place.

However, there was a measure of insult by the king when, without even acknowledging Phraates had spoken, Orodes turned to Pacorus instead and asked, "How soon before this *dasht* is ready to ride?"

Pacorus answered instantly, "Prydaxes informs me they will be ready to leave here in two days' time, Father."

"And what about the *dasht* from Adiabene? What news from there?"

"It has already left Arbela, two days ago," Pacorus assured Orodes. Then, before he could ask, he said, "And the one from Bezadbe should be within sight of Amida now." The prince thought a moment, then added, "Although I'm certain that by now the Romans are on the march again."

Orodes considered what his son had told him, and he realized that in his secret heart, he wasn't surprised that Artavasdes' nerve had failed him. And, he silently acknowledged, the Armenian king had been in a difficult spot, much like Antiochus of Commagene had been. Still, it was not only inconvenient, in one thing Phraates was right; this kind of betrayal couldn't go unpunished. As he considered, he realized that, if all went as his seers had claimed, Artavasdes' treachery could be repaid at the same time as this nuisance of another Roman invasion was crushed.

Turning to his oldest son, Orodes felt a swelling of pride as he looked at the younger man standing there, eagerly awaiting the order that both knew was coming. Yet, unlike Phraates, Orodes also knew Pacorus wouldn't utter a word, and would stand here all night if need be, waiting for the command, while Phraates would have stormed off and gone galloping away to rouse the hordes of Parthia on his own.

Placing his hand on Pacorus' shoulder, Orodes said quietly, "It is time for you to leave, my beloved son, and take your place at the head of our army. Crush these Romans, and avenge the perfidy done to us by Artavasdes."

With this simple command, the king of the only nation whose might matched Rome set in motion a series of events that would shake their world down to its foundations, and beyond.

While the information that Pacorus had relayed to his father was accurate at the time he gave it to Orodes, the distances involved were such that by the time he burst into his father's bedroom, the situation had changed, substantially. Caesar, and his army, waiting at Amida, had indeed resumed the march, but not with the promised force of Armenians. Four days after Artavasdes' agreement to side with Caesar and his army, the Armenian king came to Caesar in the *praetorium*; that the king saw fit to come to Caesar was the first sign that something important was taking place, meaning it was not long after his arrival that Diocles was sent to find out what he could.

When he returned to inform Pullus, the Greek's face was grim as he told Pullus, "Artavasdes told Caesar that there's been a plague that struck his army three days' march from here."

Pullus couldn't stifle the string of oaths, but before he could learn anything more, the *bucina*, the horn used to relay signals inside a Roman camp, sounded the series of notes that summoned all Primi Pili to the *praetorium*.

Sighing, Pullus grabbed his *vitus*, and said over his shoulder to Diocles as he left his tent, "Call the Pili Priores and tell them to wait. I'll be back as soon as Caesar tells us what's going on."

When he entered the *praetorium*, several of the Primi Pili were already there, and Pullus could tell by their collective demeanor that most if not all of them had gotten wind of this new development.

"Plague! What a load of *cac*," this came from Aulus Lanatus, the Primus Pilus of the 11th Legion, a relatively tall, gaunt man about ten years older than Pullus, whose defining characteristic was two missing fingers; that it was on his left, or shield hand, had kept him under the standard. "You know that *cunnus* had no intention of ever bringing those men here!"

"That wouldn't surprise me," Pullus agreed, somewhat half-heartedly, but then pointed out, "but I'm sure Caesar sent someone to check."

"And how long will that take?" interjected Balbinus skeptically. "Then, by the time they get back, and we learn one way or another. They're supposed to be three days away."

"A rider with extra mounts would cut that in half," observed Marcus Junius Felix, the Primus Pilus of the 6th Legion.

"True," Balbinus granted, then added grimly, "if they don't get intercepted. By," he dropped his voice to add meaningfully as he took a quick glance over his shoulder for the presence of any prying ears, "foe, or friend."

There was a silence as the small group took a moment to absorb this assessment; as Pullus thought about what Balbinus had said, he had to grant that, if Artavasdes was indeed playing Caesar and the army falsely, it would be in the Armenian king's best interest to make sure that anyone Caesar sent to check on the status of Artavasdes' claim never returned.

"But," Felix voiced the question that Pullus felt certain his counterparts were asking themselves, "why? Why would he do something that stupid?"

"I can think of one reason," Pullus surprised himself somewhat, being the one who spoke up. "He's playing for time."

"Time?" Felix cocked his head, then there was a flash of dawning realization, and he gasped, "You mean you think he's trying to hold us here to allow the Parthians to close with us?"

Whether or not that was the case, as the Primi Pili were curtly informed by Caesar, they were not going to stay and find out.

"I've decided that, given this piece of news from Artavasdes, and how long it would take to verify whether or not it's true, we are going to be departing as scheduled," the general announced briskly.

"But what about Artavasdes?"

The fact this came not from one of the Primi Pili, but Hirtius, informed Pullus of the high probability that this was a question the Legate had been prompted to ask Caesar, which the Primus Pilus knew was a favorite trick of his general to use.

"Artavasdes' sons," Caesar smiled grimly, "are going to come with us. As hostages for their father's good conduct."

There was a silence as the group digested this, and it wasn't long before the Romans were all smiling, their fears put at ease. And, as originally planned, the army departed from Amida, but while it wasn't with the extra forces Caesar had planned on adding, it was with a trio of Armenians, and their attendants, who were worth almost as much.

Chapter Three

The first clash between the two great nations was almost too insignificant to mention, at least in terms of the blood shed by both small contingents of cavalry. However, in other ways, it was a meeting that would have enormous ramifications for Caesar's army because of the manner in which matters unfolded. Caesar's force consisted of a detachment of twenty cavalry, acting as scouts, but more important than their numbers was that this party was composed of Germans, a portion of the remaining men from across the Rhenus who had been with Caesar since early in his Gallic campaign. It was because of their unfamiliarity with the type of terrain through which they were now traversing, some eighty miles east of Amida, and just a few miles south of the Tigris, that allowed a contingent of Parthians consisting of mostly mounted archers, to burst from hiding and catch the Germans by surprise. Conditioned as the Germans were to consider likely areas of concealment such things as thick stands of trees, or heavily forested slopes, the barrenness of the terrain around them lulled them into the mistaken belief that they were safe. They quickly discovered differently, when seemingly appearing out of nowhere, the Germans were beset by a swarm of lightly armed but highly mobile horsemen who peppered them with arrows, striking a half-dozen of the more heavily armed but less nimble Germans. Only after the Parthians disappeared, as quickly as they had appeared, did the survivors of Caesar's party understand that their foes had been able to approach by way of a fold of ground that, from less than a hundred paces away, was almost completely invisible because it originated at ground level, then dropped down below the horizon. This was so far out of their experience that a fair number of the German casualties, as relatively few as they were, came about as a result of delayed reaction as their benumbed minds tried to make sense of what their eyes were telling them. As they learned that day, and it was a lesson that was repeated on multiple occasions, despite the seemingly interminable and invariably featureless terrain that was what appeared to the naked eye, the ground was liberally broken and split with draws, gullies, dry watercourses, and even depressions large enough to be considered small valleys, none of which were visible until the observer was almost on top of them. This was one of the secret allies of the Parthians, yet despite learning from the survivors of Crassus' campaign about the terrain, it was one thing to hear about it, and as these first unfortunate German victims discovered, another matter entirely when one is faced with it firsthand. Not surprisingly, after a couple more incidents like this, involving some of Caesar's other mounted scouting parties, those men charged by the Dictator with being the eyes of his army became cautious, excessively so. While it was an understandable reaction, it also slowed the progress of Caesar's army significantly, which as Pullus and every other veteran understood, was the quickest method to rouse the fury of their commander. One of the many aspects of his generalship that made him the most respected, and more importantly, feared military man of his age was the rapidity of his movement, and when he was thwarted, as he was now, his closest subordinates were subjected to his ire. Yet, despite Pullus' discomfort at just being in the vicinity of Caesar's wrath, aimed at the Legate in command of his cavalry arm, Marcus Aemilius Lepidus, the Primus Pilus found it difficult to blame the cavalrymen for their caution. He had eyes, and the experience from his time spent during the brief campaign at Zela after Alexandria, so he understood how disconcerting it was when a large body of the enemy suddenly materialized as if out of thin air.

Despite this feeling of sympathy, the Primus Pilus also knew better than to voice such feelings when Caesar was in a mood like the one he was displaying now. Not that Pullus felt sorry for the Legate, who he'd never thought much of, going back to their time together in Alexandria. Of all of Caesar's Legates, Pullus wasn't alone in his estimation that Lepidus was the weakest militarily, but he also was aware of the man's bloodlines and understood that, to men of Caesar's class, this mattered. And, Pullus noted with some satisfaction, the Dictator had never placed Lepidus in command of any Legion, let alone his most veteran and trusted, the 10th. As diverting as it might have been, watching Caesar administer a tongue-lashing to a subordinate inside the *praetorium* after a day that saw the army cover less than fifteen miles, Pullus was also aware that Caesar's concern about the slow progress wasn't just because of the damage to his reputation. While Pullus was as much in the dark about Caesar's immediate tactical plans regarding the Parthians, he had marched with the Dictator for his entire career and understood how the idea of striking his enemy when the foe wasn't expecting it and was off-balance was an essential central tenet of his general's philosophy on war. And, Pullus acknowledged wryly, in politics as well, which was why the Primus Pilus understood Caesar had been so shaken by his near-assassination at Pompey's Theater. It had caught Caesar on his back foot, as they liked to say in the Legions, where he found himself in a position to react to events outside his influence and control. As Pullus knew from his experience with the man in Alexandria, it was a posture that Caesar loathed being in; he was only truly comfortable when he was the man plucking the strings of the harp, and it was to a tune of the Dictator's choosing. Now, because of their slowed progress, it gave the Parthians not only a better idea of the intentions of the invading army, but more time during which to prepare for a response. Even worse, Pullus knew, was the likelihood that they would be able to meet Caesar while he and the army were still traversing the more rugged terrain, where veritable armies could be hidden within a fold of the ground that was invisible to the naked eye, which the German cavalry detachment had discovered the hard way.

Leaning over the map spread out on the table in the largest room of the *praetorium* that served as a combination conference space and officers' mess, Caesar hissed in frustration, even as he understood that it wasn't through the fault of the map, or the man who made it, for that matter. Under the best of circumstances, maps never bore all of the information about a region that Caesar would have liked; here along the northern edge of Parthian territory, it was even more the case that what the map didn't contain was at least as important as what it did. His decision to cross the distance between the Euphrates to the Tigris north of Mons Aunis wasn't without controversy, and generated a fair amount of resistance from his Legates; that the strongest objections came from Aulus Hirtius and Asinius Pollio, two of his most trusted, and in some ways more importantly, experienced Legates, was something Caesar forced himself to consider.

"Not only is the approach down the Euphrates an easier march, it cuts the time it will take to get well into Parthia by a week!" had been Hirtius' argument.

"And much of your strategy rests on the rapidity of our movement, Caesar." Pollio had bolstered the other Legate's argument, who, it must be said, managed to remain fast friends despite their natural position as adversaries in the courting of Caesar's favor and approval.

It didn't help, Caesar had remembered thinking, that they both agreed on this point as well. Nevertheless, he had overruled them and the others who resisted the idea, and the army had marched directly east until they ran into the river. Now, he and the others were in his large tent, pitched in the center of the camp on the banks of the Tigris, with the starkly bare, imposing brown bluffs all around them. Making this more difficult, according to not only the maps, but the information from his scouts was that matters only got worse over the next forty miles, as the river flowed along a north/south axis, before the terrain eased. Which, as Caesar understood perfectly well, meant at least two days, probably three where he and his army would be in mortal peril. By this point in time, four days after the first brush with forces that were positively identified as Parthian, not just by their manner of dress but by virtue of the flurry of missiles that filled the air, Caesar had reports from more than a dozen different sources, informing him of sightings of the enemy. To this point, the largest contingent had been around a hundred mounted troops; Caesar knew the Parthians called this smallest unit a *washt*, while the others were of varying sizes. There were two common factors with all of them, however; to this point, none of the Parthians who had been spied by his scouts were cataphracts, but the more lightly armored and highly mobile archers. The second was of the most immediate concern, and that was the collective trails of these various bands were heading in the same general direction, to the south, the same direction he and his army were now heading. And, if it had been Caesar's decision to make as their general, the ground he and his army would have to cover over the next forty miles was ideally made for horse archers, making it almost a certainty that there would be a major attack coming. Perhaps the only blessing, he reflected dismally, is that the broken ground and low but steep slopes of the draws and gullies effectively ruled out the use of the cataphracts on the part of the Parthians. Caesar understood that, from the rankers' collective viewpoint, this was good news; to a man, there was a fear of the heavily armored mass of horse and man that served as a huge fist of iron that could punch through the line of the staunchest veterans, even Roman. Regardless of their feelings, however, Caesar was far more concerned with the wearing effects of the archers. Judging from what he had been told, not just by Cassius but a handful of the rankers who had survived the debacle a decade before, when the archers first appeared, the men of the Legions had reacted with great amusement, making jokes about how, between their armor, shields, and training, the missile troops posed about as much threat as the mosquitoes that appeared along the riverbanks in the evenings and mornings. And, akin to those vermin, the Romans were sure they could be swatted away, or more accurately, driven off by the mounted auxiliaries that were part of Crassus' forces. That, as Cassius had said grimly, was how it started. How it had finished had instantly become a source of inspiration to those nations with whom Rome still contended, a mark of shame to all Romans, whether they marched in the ranks or not, and for the general of the avenging army, a sobering and crucial concern. And, staring down at the map, Caesar was forced to admit that the opening of hostilities was closer in terms of time and geography than he would have liked.

Although Caesar's army had been marching in the configuration that indicated contact with the enemy was imminent, which meant that they wore their helmets at all times, and without the leather covers that protected a vital piece of equipment, their shields, from damage in the form of water, which could render them ineffective, this order had come two days before. As any veteran could attest, and Titus Pullus and his men were to experience once more, it is impossible for the human mind to maintain a state of constant alertness over a period of more than a few watches, at most. When the surrounding terrain is as seemingly barren as the stretch of ground over which the Romans were passing, even canny veterans could be lulled into the belief that the idea of a substantially armed enemy force being able to not only approach, but attack without sufficient warning was impossible. The spot where the Parthians attacked served as an example, this time to the wider army and not just a band of German cavalrymen, of how ingeniously the Parthians could use the terrain to their advantage. Choosing a point where the river changed from its north/south orientation to one where it ran east for several miles, the Parthian cause was unwittingly aided by a decision Caesar made when, based on information from his scouts, he ordered his men to take what was in essence a shortcut. Because of the way the river looped back on itself, whereas Caesar had made it a practice to keep his army in as close proximity with the river as practical, he made the decision to march directly east, while the river was still traveling south. It wasn't a particularly long stretch of ground; according to the scouts, as long as the Romans marched in a relatively straight direction, they would reconnect with the river about five or six miles later. That it shortened the distance his men would have to cover was a consideration, certainly, but like his men, despite his caution and how thoroughly Caesar prepared for this campaign, even he was lulled by the vista of unbroken and relatively level ground that lay before his eye that was the shortcut. Like all the senior officers, Caesar was mounted on the horse that was almost as famous as the general himself, but ever since he had been the Praetor of Hispania, almost a quarter century before, he spent almost as much time walking with his men as he did riding. It was just one of the things that inspired a ferocious devotion from his men, but more immediately important to Caesar was that this time spent with the rankers gave him insight into their collective mood. Consequently, he understood that aside from shortening the march, more than anything, the men wanted relief from the constant strain that comes when men on foot traverse undulating terrain. For a bit more than a full watch, Caesar thought, we'll be able to march like a Roman army again. Of all the questions that are inevitable after a battle, the one that Caesar was forced to consider was, if he had known about some key features of what lay ahead, whether or not he would have made the same decision.

"By the gods it's good to walk on flat ground for a bit." Publius Vellusius' statement was accompanied by a groan that seemed to his comrades' ears to be composed of equal parts relief and disgust that this respite was temporary.

"For now," the man next to him in the rank of the First Section, First Century of the Second Cohort of the 10th Equestris spoke with the sour resignation of the kind of man who always inspected a pot of honey, convinced there was a rat turd in it. "But we're going to be back to going up and down, up and down quicker than Pan."

"Oh, Pluto's cock," Vellusius growled, although he had been expecting this kind of response, "for once would you just enjoy what little blessings the gods give us?"

"For what?" his comrade retorted. "So that I can get my hopes up right before Fortuna drops a load of *cac* on me?"

"Just for once, would you both shut up and stop your arguing?"

Both men immediately complied, not just because of the words, but who had uttered them. Vellusius shot Scribonius an apologetic glance, mumbling an apology, although the truth was that the Secundus Pilus Prior was more amused than irritated.

74

From his spot just a few paces away, at the head of his Century, Scribonius called over his shoulder and asked neither man in particular, "Have either of you noticed that you essentially argue about the same thing? And," he added dryly, "have been doing it for years?"

Vellusius' face flushed, and he shot a glance at the man with whom he'd been arguing, a lanky veteran of the first *dilectus*, Gnaeus Figulus, who not only marched next to Vellusius, but was his close comrade, the holder of his will. He saw in Figulus' expression the same confusion he felt at Scribonius' observation. That he was disposed to reply was due more to his familiarity with his Centurion than any other reason; his relationship with Sextus Scribonius stretched back to a shared tent in Hispania, when both had been raw *Tirones*. But while Sextus Scribonius, on the strength of his keen intellect and martial skills that, while they might not have been in the class of Titus Pullus, were still formidable enough that he was not only alive, had risen through the ranks, Vellusius was perfectly content as a *Miles Gregarius* and part of the reason for that came from his recognition of his own shortcomings when it came to matters requiring more than a rudimentary amount of thought. In simplest terms, thinking was hard for Vellusius.

"Centurion Scribonius," Vellusius began, always remembering to address his superior in the proper manner in front of others, "I don't think that's true. We," he jerked his head, the only thing free, at Figulus, "may quarrel a bit, but it's never about the same thing. At least," he did think to amend, recalling that there were times when one of their sessions started one day and continued to another, "most of the time."

You started this, Scribonius remonstrated with himself wryly as he replied patiently, "I don't mean the details, Vellusius. I mean the subject is basically the same." Glancing back in their direction as he walked, he pointed his *vitus* to Vellusius. "You," he continued, "always try to make the best of a given situation and see the good side to it. And *you*," with a flick of his wrist, the twisted vine stick pointed at Figulus, "are determined to piss all over Vellusius' boots about it. The actual subject," he concluded, "doesn't matter."

Only when put in this manner did Vellusius realize that, as usual, his Centurion was correct, but his acknowledgment of this fact never happened. In an extraordinarily short amount of time, events occurred that would erase this as a topic for conversation and Vellusius would forget all about it, as would the rest of those who had been listening in on this exchange as a way to pass the time.

"Riders! On the right flank! They're...."

If whoever shouted the warning was going to provide more information, they were cut off in mid-sentence and what followed was a sound Vellusius and his comrades had heard too often before, a sort of gurgling, choked sound that was informative in its own way. Nevertheless, the fallen Legionary, one of the two sections of men arrayed along both flanks of their Century, did manage to alert the others before an arrow slashed down into his body and ended his warning, and his life. Publius Vellusius may not have been made of the material that was required of a Centurion in Rome's Legions, but he was a member of Caesar's most veteran Legion and a survivor of the most intense period of combat operations in Roman history. Consequently, to an observer, the length of time he hesitated as he turned his attention in the direction of this sudden threat, located what to anyone's eye appeared to be a swarming mass of horseflesh with men astride, then reacted in the manner in which he'd been trained took no more than one or two heartbeats of time. Meanwhile, the Parthians were seemingly boiling up out of the ground like an underground spring that suddenly finds a path to the world beyond, only instead of life-giving water, this fount contained nothing but death in the form of sheaves of arrows fired from the famed and feared composite bow of the Parthian horse archer.

"Drop your packs! *Testudo* by Centuries!"

While his lungs weren't as powerful as those of the Primus Pilus, Scribonius could still manage to bellow with a surprising amount of volume, and more importantly, his voice was pitched in such a way that the sound of his voice carried farther than normal. Moving into his assigned spot when a Century and Cohort changed from their normal marching column of eight men across, with perhaps half a man's width between each ranker, Scribonius repeated himself several times, but even before he had completed his first iteration of his command, the men of his Century and the Second Cohort were already fully engaged in the series of movements required of them. In their idle moments, Scribonius, Balbus, and Pullus often discussed their desire to somehow be transported above their commands in such moments so they could appreciate what, to them at least, was the beauty of the intricacy and precision with which each man in the ranks moved, in the manner of some complex machine that was composed of many parts, each with their specific task but every piece ordinated to a common goal. If the Secundus Pilus Prior had been so blessed to be given wings, on this day, he would have been prouder of the men under his command than at just about any other time because he would have been able to truly appreciate how quickly, confidently, and smoothly his men went from the march into the closed ranks of the *testudo*, a formation that was in its own way as renowned as the men now peppering the Romans with arrows.

But Scribonius was consigned to his spot on the ground, so he only had a bare sense of what was happening, his task made more difficult by the sudden increase of dust, raised by the hobnailed *caligae* of his men as they shuffled into their new position while raising their shields into their proper posture, which varied from one rank to the next. Those men now facing the Parthians in the front rank had their shields held in front of them, while the men of the second rank thrust their shields up and between the men of the first rank so the bottom of their shields just touched the top of those in the first rank; it was the men of the third rank and those farther back who held their own protection directly above their heads, presenting a relatively smooth surface of hardened wood to shelter from the rain of arrows. The Parthians, who had taken advantage of two different gashes in the ground that served to drain water from the sudden storms that fell on this plateau over which the Romans were traversing, now appeared to be a semi-solid but rapidly moving mass that was almost instantly obscured by the dust churned up by the thousands of hooves of their small but nimble ponies. This was simply confusing; what was now streaking towards the Romans in what appeared to be black, serried waves arcing through the air was a mortal danger. Even if Scribonius had needed to continue shouting his orders, his voice would have been drowned out by the sudden start of what could only be described as a horrendously loud racket, as iron-tipped arrows came plunging down to strike the raised wooden shields. The sound, akin to thousands of invisible beings hammering on blocks of wood, would have been bad enough on its own, but Scribonius' experienced ear picked out a few slightly different notes of the discordant and dangerous song the Parthians were singing, when, instead of the wood of a man's shield absorbing the strike of an arrow, the missile managed to slip between the tiny cracks that he knew were inevitable. Those made a different sound, and while it might not have been as loud as those rendered harmless by a shield, it seemed to Scribonius it was a more substantial, meatier sound, which inevitably was instantly followed by a sharp cry, as one of his boys was struck. Usually, the shout came from the wounded ranker himself; arrows wounded far more men than they killed outright, although Scribonius knew from bitter experience that some of those who survived this would succumb to their wound, caused by the corruption of the body. Nevertheless, sometimes the cry was issued by a man who had escaped being hit because it was his friend next to him whose legs suddenly collapsed from under him. While Scribonius knew that this reaction was usually prompted by the grief that comes when one sees a comrade and friend either seriously hurt or killed outright, he understood that it was just as much a warning to those in the immediate part of the formation that they were now in peril. Considering how quickly the average Parthian archer could loose arrows, it was crucial that the sudden gap in the previously unbroken wall of shields be closed. Unfortunately, because of his vulnerable position, Scribonius couldn't afford to take his eyes away from those same missiles that were even at this instant plunging down in his direction; he would have to rely on the men to respond in the proper manner, for which they had spent too many watches to count practicing.

This was a moment to rely on his Optio, who was positioned behind the Century, where he was not only in a more sheltered spot, but was in a position to see what was happening, which prompted him to shout, barely turning his head towards his shoulder, "Terentius! Who's down?"

Before the words were out, Scribonius was forced to make a sudden, hopping move to his right, and even with the overlying noise, he heard the soft, whistling sound made by the feathers fletching the missile as it streaked down past him to bury itself in the ground, and the Pilus Prior took notice of how it still managed to penetrate the rocky soil.

"We've got two!" his Optio, another solid veteran who had been part of the same group of *Tirones* as Scribonius, Pullus and Vellusius, bellowed back. "But I can't see who!"

The fact that either man could maintain the presence of mind to communicate at all as black, streaking death was hurtling down from above was a mark of not only their experience, but why they now held posts of such importance in the Legion.

"Don't worry, Centurion!" Scribonius recognized the voice as belonging to a man of the Third Section, which in their current configuration Scribonius understood put him in the third rank back, almost dead in the middle of the Century. "It's old Varus who's down, and I'm afraid he's done for, but we closed back up!"

At least, that is what Scribonius believed he said, because the last couple of words were drowned out by the next volley of arrows, which were now coming in waves that were packed so tightly together it was difficult to see blue sky. It was only then the Centurion became aware that not just one but several *corni* were blowing, although in his opinion they were only adding to the din.

"If they're not in *testudo* by now," he said aloud, but didn't aim it at anyone in particular, "there's no point in sounding the call because they're all dead and can't hear it anyway."

A relatively short distance away, towards the head of the column, immediately behind where Caesar, his staff, and bodyguards were riding, Titus Pullus had been the one to order his *cornicen* to sound the call that was instantly picked up by the *corniceni* attached to the rest of his Cohorts. As quickly as the call was sounded by each Cohort, the ranks of the Centuries belonging to it dropped their packs, and executed a right-facing turn in the direction of the attacking Parthians, their own shields moving into the *testudo* formation. While there were arrows flying in their direction, it didn't take long for Pullus to determine that the center of the Parthian attack was focused on the last Century of the First, and what looked like the entire Second. There were certainly a good number of mounted Parthians directly ahead of him and to his right, weaving between each other and somehow avoiding headlong collisions with their own comrades, but Pullus was sure they had been instructed to keep up the intensity of the missile assault to a point that occupied the First Cohort. Consequently, he didn't have to worry quite as much as his friend Scribonius, yet that was about to change, since the Primus Pilus' first instinct was to turn and begin trotting down the column in the direction of the Second, which was made even more difficult and dangerous because he had to keep a wary eye on the sky to his left in an attempt to track arrows the might prove to be a threat. This also allowed him to judge whether or not his Centuries had managed to form their own protective *testudo* in a manner that he found satisfactory.

Overall, he was pleased, although when he reached the Third Century, he bellowed, "Glabius! I don't care how tired your arm is! When I come back this way and your shield is still that low, I'll *flay you!*"

Despite everything that was going on, Pullus suppressed a grin as he caught the grimace of his Primus Princeps Posterior, Gnaeus Celadus, who was the offending party's Centurion, understanding that Glabius had a thrashing at the hands of Celadus coming. Provided nothing worse happened to him, of course. By the time Pullus reached the beginning of the Fifth Century of his Cohort, he was starting to have second thoughts about refusing Balbus' offer to accompany him, although he knew it was the right decision. One Centurion alone provided a tempting target; a man Pullus' size, and wearing the white transverse crest that marked his status as the senior officer of the Legion, meant that anyone near him at a moment such as this was in just as much peril as he was. Having his second in command fall at the same time and from the same cause wasn't a risk he was willing to run, and the thought flashed through his mind how Caesar would take the news that his two most senior Centurions had fallen because Pullus wanted company. By this time, he had reached a point where there was no practical way for Pullus to draw any closer without a shield. Even as it was, he spent several valuable heartbeats of time, jumping one way, then dodging another, sometimes with his entire body and others just by leaning.

"Primus Pilus!"

The voice was familiar to him, but like Scribonius, he couldn't afford to risk turning his attention away from the Parthians.

"What is it, Vistilia?" he asked his Hastatus Posterior, the Centurion in command of the Sixth Century.

"I'm coming to you and bringing a shield!"

"No!" Pullus shouted sharply, though not because of any hubris on his part. "I don't want one of the boys going without one!"

"It's already too late," Vistilia, like Pullus, had to speak more loudly than normal, but there was still a muted quality to his voice that required Pullus to make an effort not to turn his head.

"Who?" he asked instead just as he made a hop out of the way of an arrow that, rather than penetrating the hard ground, either struck a buried rock or at such an angle that it caromed sharply off the ground to go skimming an inch of the ground for several more feet, where it ⋅ bounced off the greave of one of the men in the first rank, signaled by the combination of metal striking metal and the gasp of pain from the stricken man

Before Vistilia supplied the name, Pullus heard him ask the unseen man if he was all right, but while he couldn't make out the man's words, it was clear that he was, if only because Vistilia then

80

answered, "Petrosidius, Primus Pilus. He took one in the eye in the very first volley."

Pullus cursed bitterly; Asinius Petrosidius was not only a veteran, he had been one of the men salted into the ranks from Pompey's 1st Legion when the 10th had been formed. Experience of the kind owned by Petrosidius was worth almost the man's weight in gold. But he had no time to mourn, particularly when he heard Vistilia's crunching footfall behind him, approaching from his left rear.

"Hold your hand out and I'll put it there," Vistilia called, and when Pullus complied, he sensed the bulk of the Centurion out of the corner of his eye, then their hands touched as the exchange was made.

Even as it was happening, Pullus' eye had picked out a streaking arrow that whatever part of a man's mind is responsible for such things had calculated would be a threat. Subsequently, to the men in the ranks it appeared as if Vistilia's arm extending, the handoff of the shield, then Pullus raising it straight up but remaining out from his own body was actually one movement. And the Primus Pilus moved just in time as the echoing dull thud of an iron point striking the hardened wood resounded around the pair, causing both men to flinch. From where Vistilia was standing, he stared up at the back of the shield held just above his head, trying not to think what the slightly gleaming head of the arrow now protruding a couple inches through the shield would have done to him. Before he could mutter his gratitude, however, Pullus had already moved the shield to a point directly in front of his own body to deflect yet another missile. This one made a vastly different sound, something more in the nature of a gong being struck, although it was not as clear nor did it reverberate, caused by Pullus catching this arrow right on the large metal boss of his shield.

"Get back with your men," Pullus hadn't yet turned to look anywhere near Vistilia or the Fifth's direction, and was already moving again, always to where the fighting was most intense.

"Where's the fucking cavalry?" Scribonius muttered, again aloud, except this time, it was to his Primus Pilus, who had appeared a few heartbeats before from his spot, the appropriated shield now studded with no less than a half-dozen shafts.

"Gods only know," Pullus answered, the two of them now able to bolster their defense by holding their shields side by side.

While this was better, Scribonius sourly observed, "You're so fucking big, you're taking up part of my shield too! Move over!"

"I am not," Pullus protested, although it was with a laugh. "You're so skinny I could take half your shield and it wouldn't matter!"

Just as this left his mouth, an arrow loosed by a rider who had managed to draw closer than his other companions, although it was still just out of javelin range, struck the right edge of Scribonius' shield, the impact strong enough it almost yanked the shield from his grasp. This caused Scribonius to glare at his friend, who moved his body a few inches to the left; grudgingly, it seemed to Scribonius.

"If only these *cunni* would get within range," Pullus complained, despite knowing his wishes would go wanting.

"If you were them, would you?" Scribonius shot back dryly.

"No," Pullus acknowledged, even as he strained to hear the sound of hoof beats coming from his right rear.

Admittedly, this was a huge army, and the Parthian attack had occurred near the front of the column, but surely a mounted rider could have galloped back and sent orders for the cavalry acting as rearguard to come to their rescue by this time.

"How much time do you think has gone by?" he asked Scribonius, who had just finished shifting his grip on his shield from his left to his right hand to give it a rest.

Scribonius considered for a moment, but could only shrug and offer, "Maybe a sixth part of a watch."

"That long?" Pullus replied doubtfully, but before he could say anything else, he was interrupted when an arrow came slicing at him to strike the very top of his shield with the same kind of force as had hit Scribonius.

What neither of them had any way of knowing, their vision obscured by both their shields and the massive amount of dust that was now almost a hundred feet in the air, was that the identity of the Parthian archer was the same man, who had galloped away only to return, this timedrawing even closer. The impact from the arrow was powerful enough that, even with Pullus' strength, the top was driven violently back in his direction. For a brief instant, the shield was almost parallel to the ground, leaving Pullus exposed from the shoulders up and from about mid-stomach down. Before he could bring the shield back to vertical, yet another missile, loosed by one of the original archer's comrades who was following the first man's lead, struck Pullus. Fortunately for Pullus, the 10th, and the army, the angle was not square, so it struck a glancing blow, and Pullus' cause was further aided by the tip of the arrow striking the broad leather *baltea*

82

around the big man's waist. Nevertheless, while it didn't penetrate, it knocked the wind from the Roman, which was released in a great, whooshing sound that Scribonius clearly heard over all the other noise. Instinctively, he moved as if he was going to drop his shield, but Pullus, who had maintained his grip and was even then bringing his own shield back to the vertical, shook his head, although this was all he could manage. With his free hand, he gingerly reached down, half-expecting to feel the shaft of the arrow protruding from his body. When his fingers fumbled and felt the deep gouge in the *baltea*, his first thought was that he would have sighed in relief, but he was still struggling to get air in, not let it out.

"You all right?" Scribonius finally managed, but while he saw Pullus was essentially unmarked, he was still concerned; after so many years under the standards, he understood the possibility that Pullus was bleeding inside.

It took him two tries before Pullus finally managed to draw in enough air to gasp, "I think so, but it hurts like Dis!"

"Those bastards are accurate, I have to give them that," Scribonius said wryly; now it was Pullus' turn to glare at him.

"Really?" he scoffed. "What gave you that impression?"

Scribonius was about to reply, but then, in a trick of the wind, for an instant, the dust parted like a pair of curtains being swept aside, and when he saw what lay beyond, the Secundus Pilus Prior didn't hesitate.

"Second Cohort!" he bellowed. "Prepare javelins!"

Later, Pullus would claim that the only reason it was Scribonius who gave the order was because he still hadn't fully regained his breath. Privately, he acknowledged that his best friend simply had reacted more quickly, but before he could make any kind of comment, Scribonius bellowed the next command.

"Release!"

Originating from behind Pullus, he only had a sense of the heavy, weighted javelins streaking over his head, then caught sight of them just as they were beginning their downward arc. Despite it being a matter of only a couple heartbeats, the momentary glimpse was gone, and all that lay before the Romans' eyes was an opaque curtain, behind which there was only the vaguest sensation of motion. Still, in the fraction of an eye blink after the javelins plunged into the thickest part of the roiling dust, Pullus and his men were rewarded by a series of sharp, shrill screams, issued by both man and beast, as the hardened triangular points punched into and through muscle and bone.

Even as this was happening, Scribonius had opened his mouth to give the command for the second volley, but Pullus reached out and grabbed his arm with his free hand as the Primus Pilus instead bellowed, "Second Cohort! On my command!" He paused for just an instant, then followed up with, "Follow me! *Porro!*"

Under normal conditions, this rapid change in the normal series of commands would have caused chaos, but this was one of the modifications that Caesar had instituted and in which the men of his army had drilled incessantly. Recognizing that the threat they would face in the coming campaign was going to be in the nature of this ambush, Caesar had instilled in his Centurions the need for a rapid reaction, but at the right time. Over a short distance, men can outrun horses, particularly during a moment such as this, which Pullus had recognized when the enemy had drawn close enough and were as disorganized as they were then in the immediate aftermath of the javelin volley. More times than any man of the Legions could count, they had been forced to go from their various formations, both for battle and the march, to a dead sprint, practicing dropping their packs, and in another wrinkle, just one of their javelins. Using the lesson of Pharsalus, where Pompey's cavalry attack on the right wing of his army had been shattered by the extra line of men that he had placed, prone in the high grass, with their javelins used not as missiles but as spears, Caesar had trained the army to do the same thing. The difference was that they would not be stationary, but instead would be relying on their ability to cover a short distance more rapidly, and it was because of this knowledge that Pullus hadn't hesitated, either in giving the order, or in dashing ahead of the men of the Second Cohort, confident that they would be hot on his heels. His action did catch Scribonius by surprise, but his hesitation wasn't more than a heartbeat, putting him just a couple steps behind his Primus Pilus and best friend. Since Pullus was leading the charge, he was the first to reach the outermost edge of the blinding, choking veil, but if he hesitated before plunging into it, from his position just behind, Scribonius certainly didn't see it. Even before this thought registered, however, he was following his Primus Pilus. Since Pullus was leading, he was the first to reach the point where he could somewhat make out the situation that lay before him, although it wasn't in the way he would have wished, barely avoiding running directly into a horse, lying on its side

84

with one of his men's javelins protruding from its chest. Somehow, he managed to hurdle the beast, which even then was in its death throes, its hooves thrashing feebly, causing Pullus to land awkwardly, taking a stumbling step forward. Fortunately for him, he had pulled his borrowed shield tight against his shoulder, so that when he slammed into the Parthian who, presumably, had been the horse's rider, it was the enemy who went caroming off, landing heavily on his back. Before his mind could even comprehend this new threat, the Parthian's life was ended with a short, brutal thrust in the throat from Pullus' Gallic sword, the blade that he had spent more than a year's salary on in the winter after his second campaign year in Gaul. Having regained his footing, Pullus' attention had already turned away from his first foe when he became aware of a movement behind him to his right. He only spared a glance, knowing that it would be Scribonius, then he was already darting to where a Parthian was struggling to control his rearing mount that, even through the thick dust, Pullus could see had suffered a grazing wound along its forequarter, the blood and raw meat somehow showing vividly through the swirling dust. Only at the last instant did the mounted Parthian realize there was a new threat much greater than a rearing horse, but he only had time to turn his head in Pullus' direction when, with a sharp upward thrust, the Roman's Gallic blade, already bloody, punched up under the ribs of the archer, who let out a choked, gurgling scream as his lungs filled with blood. Again, Pullus was already moving, even before the Parthian had hit the ground, while the horse, now freed from its burden, wheeled around and headed in the opposite direction from the charging Romans. Then, neither Scribonius nor Pullus were alone, as the men of the Second came charging up to where they had paused, bellowing their own challenges and curses, eager to exact vengeance on these men they considered to be cowards for standing off at a distance, instead of facing them like true warriors. Pullus paused, trying to get a better sense of what was happening, but quickly realized it was impossible to get more than the barest idea of the situation.

Scribonius, panting from the exertion of not just the short run but from the effort of bringing down a horse with a slash across its nose, then dispatching its rider, gasped, "It looks like they're pulling back, but I can't really tell for sure, can you?"

Pullus' reply was little more than a grunt, but from experience, Scribonius knew by the tone that his Primus Pilus concurred. Hawking, the giant spat out a mouthful of gritty phlegm, trying to clear his mouth and ease his breathing in preparation to actually say something, but before he could, there was a sudden, new explosion of sound from their immediate right. The choking air now filled with alarmed cries, shouted warnings and curses, but more than the fact that it was in their own tongue, what informed both Centurions was the sudden vibration of the ground underneath their feet.

"It's our own fucking cavalry!"

Scribonius gasped in response at Pullus' words, instantly knowing the Primus Pilus was undoubtedly right.

"They're charging into our own men!"

Not until Caesar's army finished their trek across the plateau to return to the river as it looped back on its north/south orientation, whereupon Caesar ordered camp be made despite there being more daylight, did the officers of the army gather to discuss the ambush. By the time the *praetorium* was erected, atop the plateau on the western side of the river, Pullus, Scribonius, and the Centurions of the Second Cohort had had the time for their initial reactions of what had transpired to harden into a cold anger. Not for the first, or last time, did Scribonius offer a silent prayer of thanks to Fortuna for keeping him in his post as Secundus Pilus Prior, and not Primus Pilus, because no matter the justification, what Pullus intended to do wasn't likely to be viewed with any favor by Caesar's Legates. But, as Pullus rightly pointed out, it was Caesar's reaction that was important.

This didn't stop Scribonius from issuing his own warning as the pair strode to the *praetorium*. "Remember," he admonished Pullus, "don't get angry. And," he thought to add, "by the gods, don't insult Lepidus!"

"Insult him?" Pullus regarded Scribonius with a raised eyebrow. "I'm not going to insult him. I'm just going to tell the truth."

"And you have a way of... 'telling the truth' that sounds like an insult to everyone else," Scribonius countered.

"I can't help it if some men have tender feelings." Pullus shrugged, but when Scribonius continued to glare at him, he finally relented. "Fine," he sighed, "I'll guard my tongue and just stick to the facts."

"If you do," Scribonius laughed wryly, "it'll be the first time."

They couldn't continue their conversation because they reached the tent, but as always, Pullus was immediately recognized by the men of the provosts who were assigned as guards to the *praetorium*. It was one of the perks that came not just from being a Primus Pilus, but from being one of the largest men in the army, but Pullus never failed to return the salute that was rendered. When the pair entered, the part of the tent that served as the army office was still being assembled, with clerks placing the small desks and stools that were always arranged in the same way, in the same spot. As Pullus, and all but the newest *tiros* knew, each desk represented a particular aspect of army business; one desk, usually manned by a freedman clerk, although there were slaves as well, served to take in the daily reports that, even on campaign, Caesar required of his Centurions. Another desk dealt with matters of supply, at least as far as the raw materials needed for items such as *caligae*, while the desk immediately next to it was concerned with rations. No matter where they stopped for the day, or the circumstances under which camp was made, a Legionary could go to the *praetorium* and unerringly find the right place to address their needs of the moment. Even with the flurry of activity, however, both Pullus and Scribonius could see a small knot of men huddled together in the far corner of the large office, next to the leather partition that marked the boundary between Caesar's private quarters and the headquarters proper. None of these men were wearing their helmets, but it only took a glance for Pullus to see that none of the men were Centurions and, in fact, Lepidus seemed to be in the center of the group.

"Looks like they're closing ranks," he muttered to Scribonius.

Despite the fact that Scribonius agreed this was the most likely reason for the impromptu conference they were witnessing, he still felt compelled to caution Pullus. "Remember, Titus," he whispered, "keep your head."

"I know," Pullus growled irritably, but the reality was that he did know he needed to tread carefully.

Whereas Pullus didn't worry about incurring Caesar's wrath, his Legates were another matter entirely, and despite his outward appearance of being unafraid to speak his mind, Pullus was acutely aware that there were men of the upper classes, and were represented in some of the officers of this army, who wanted to take Pullus down a peg or two because of their belief he was aspiring to rise above his station. Which, Pullus would be the first to acknowledge, was precisely the case, but while Caesar cared only about competence in the field and leadership qualities as criteria for advancement up the rungs of the strictly guarded social ladder of Rome, Pullus knew the Dictator was in the minority. Granted, he was the most important one, which meant that as long as Caesar was pleased with Pullus' performance, Pullus was mostly protected from the wrath and vindictiveness of those who didn't share Caesar's more egalitarian views. Mostly, he reminded himself, as he approached the small cluster of men.

"Caesar's orders are to wait in the mess," Aulus Hirtius informed the Centurions, but when the pair began moving in that direction and Hirtius and the men with him didn't move, Hirtius added, "We'll be there in just a moment, so go ahead."

Ignoring the glare Lepidus was giving him, which to Pullus seemed to be equally composed of defiance and worry, he led Scribonius into the large room that served as the senior officers' mess and the conference room.

"At least we can get seats at the table since we're first," Scribonius commented, which prompted a grin from his friend.

This was another example of Caesar's unique attitude; most commanding officers, all of them being high ranking on both military and social scales, would require their enlisted officers, even Primi Pili, to stand, at least in the event there were not enough places at the table. Caesar, on the other hand, rewarded whoever arrived early to his meetings, allowing them to remain seated while requiring others to stand, no matter what their rank.

"Maybe we should stand up anyway," Scribonius suggested, "considering how this is likely to go."

Pullus shot him a scornfully amused look and taunted, "You didn't hesitate following me into a fucking cloud of dust so thick we couldn't see our hands in front of our faces, but now you're scared?"

"Not scared," Scribonius rejoined, completely unruffled, "sensible. But then, I forget who I'm talking to about being sensible. So," he moved to a chair, pulled it back with a flourish, then dropped into it, "never let it be said I don't follow my Primus Pilus." He paused for a beat, then added, "Even when he's being an idiot."

Not unexpectedly, this drew a laugh from Pullus, and he nodded to Scribonius in a silent salute that he had taken the honors in this exchange. Besides, he thought placidly, it's not like he's wrong. Before another dozen heartbeats' time had passed, there was a commotion outside the mess, then Hirtius entered, followed by the others. Hirtius, long accustomed to Caesar's policy, didn't even notice the pair of Centurions; neither did Pollio, or Ventidius. But, as befitting his rank, the youngest of the group, Octavian, was left the odd man out because he was the last into the room, whereupon he stopped and frowned at the sight of Pullus and Scribonius. Pullus, for one, didn't miss the boy's consternation, but while he was amused, he wasn't disposed to give up his seat, particularly since, by rights, Octavian was barely even of Tribune rank; his official designation was as *Contubernale*, a junior aide to the general, and Tribunes were rarely included in meetings like this. That he was allowed to attend by Caesar wasn't lost on Pullus, but neither did it dissuade him from remaining seated, although he did manage to refrain from giving the youth a cheerful grin. Even without that, two bright spots appeared on Octavian's cheeks, but rather than make an issue of it, he clearly understood he would lose, so he sidled just a step or two out of the doorway, then stood next to the leather wall. He had just chosen his spot when, from the opposite direction of the main entrance, the heavy leather flap was thrust aside, and Caesar strode in, holding a wax tablet, and as usual, trailed by two of his personal secretaries. Without any preamble, Caesar turned to Pullus.

"Primus Pilus, what's the butcher's bill?"

That a man like Caesar used the rankers' term for the official list of casualties was just another of the small ways in which the Dictator emphasized his connection to the men who did the fighting for him.

Rather than answer directly, Pullus nodded to Scribonius, saying only, "Since almost all of the casualties came from the Second, with your permission, Caesar, I'll let Pilus Prior Scribonius answer first."

Waiting only long enough for Caesar to nod his assent, Scribonius, without consulting any notes, rattled off the cost of this surprise attack.

"First Century, three dead, seven wounded, two seriously enough to be litter cases. One," his tone turned grimmer, "isn't likely to last the night. If he does," he shrugged, "the *medici* say it's in the gods' hands after that." Waiting just long enough to see that the secretary Caesar had designated to record this meeting stopped and looked up in a silent signal to continue, he went on. "Second Century, two dead, nine wounded, but three of them are litter cases, although they're expected to survive." Another pause, then, "Third Century." Suddenly, he heaved a sigh. "Five dead," this prompted an intake of breath from more than one man in the room, "ten wounded, half of them litter cases, and two of those aren't expected to survive."

The only small blessing was that the Third's casualties had been the worst by far, but the final tally from this first brush with the Parthians were thirteen dead, more than twenty wounded, and a half-dozen men unlikely to march again. Once Scribonius was done, Pullus gave the figures for his own Cohort, and the one Century of the Third Cohort where casualties had been suffered, but their combined totals weren't anywhere near that of the Second, which bore the brunt of both the ambush, and the catastrophe that happened immediately following their charge. There was a silence after Pullus finished, as each man absorbed this information in their own way, while the Primus Pilus mentally counted the heartbeats before Caesar spoke and gave him the opportunity to broach the subject that he was determined to address at this meeting.

It was an article of faith among the ranks that Caesar had the ability to read minds; this was an example where it reinforced at least Pullus' somewhat half-hearted belief in his general's ability.

"And," Caesar spoke, "these were all from arrow wounds, I presume?"

Despite the size of the table, Pullus felt the sudden stiffening of Lepidus that seemed to pass through the men around him and circle it, but even as Pullus opened his mouth, he saw Caesar's expression and thought, he already knows the answer.

"No, sir," Pullus replied, stopping Scribonius, who had tried to answer, with a gentle but firm hand on Scribonius' arm. "Unfortunately not. Three of the dead were cut down by swords, and at least a half-dozen of the wounded suffer from some type of slashing wound."

"Really?" Caesar's tone was cool, and he leaned back in his chair, but his gaze remained on Pullus. "And, do you have any ideas about how this happened?" He paused for an instant, but before Pullus could answer, he added, "Were there some cataphracts in this force that ambushed us?"

Sensing that Caesar was aiding him, albeit discreetly, Pullus didn't hesitate, replying firmly, "No, sir. There were no cataphracts with the Parthians. At least," he allowed with a grim smile, "this time."

"You don't know that for certain!"

Pullus had to suppress a smile, recognizing that, as usual, Caesar had anticipated that Lepidus would be unable to restrain himself from prematurely leaping to his own defense. If only he'd been that fast in responding to the ambush, Pullus thought sourly.

What he said, however, was "You're right...sir." Out of the corner of his eye, Pullus saw Scribonius wince, and he saw Caesar's lips thin at this subtle but unmistakable show of the scant respect in which Pullus held Lepidus. "With the dust that thick, it's possible that there were some there that we didn't see. But," his voice hardened, "the cataphract's primary weapon is a lance, not a sword. And I can assure you, as the *medici* have assured me, that the wounds our men suffered are from swords."

Lepidus' face reddened; if he had been wiser, he would have at least changed his tactic, but while Pullus judged Lepidus as incompetent, that belief wasn't without grounds, which he proved now.

"Then perhaps some of your own men were the perpetrators," Lepidus insisted, and now there was no mistaking the change in the room, except this time, it was his fellow noblemen who began to shift uncomfortably in their seats. Seeming to sense this, Lepidus thought to add, "You know that men in the ranks will use incidents like this one, where there was so much confusion, to even scores between themselves!" Taking the shocked silence as a form of agreement, he pressed, "In fact, it wouldn't surprise me at all if we investigated that this is the case with every one of these casualties!"

Titus Pullus wasn't even aware that he had risen from his chair until Scribonius reached out and, in imitation of what Pullus had done a moment before, grabbed the Primus Pilus' arm.

Fortunately for Pullus, Caesar's voice was the next to be heard, and his tone was harsh as he glared over at Lepidus. "Lepidus, that's enough! I don't want to hear another word of that nonsense from you!" He was silent for perhaps five heartbeats, while Lepidus' mouth dropped open, closed, then opened again as he struggled to maintain a semblance of composure. Then, in a softer voice, but with the same undertone of anger, Caesar asked, "Would you care to give your own report, now? Perhaps you can explain why you and your cavalry were so tardy in coming to the aid of the 10th. Let's start with that, at least."

There was no mistaking the ominous meaning of his last sentence, and while Lepidus might have been inept on the battlefield, he was smart enough to understand that this was just the beginning.

Clearing his throat, he began, "Yes, well...I'll be the first to admit that the timeliness of our response to the ambush could have been better. But, sir," he looked at Caesar earnestly, "you know how...foreign these cavalrymen are! Every one of them is a barbarian!" He shuddered, presumably at the horrible toll being in proximity to such unwashed hordes was taking on him, "And they simply don't listen! I ordered them to advance, but they claimed they didn't understand me!"

91

Caesar was clearly unmoved, and Pullus understood why when Caesar pointed out, "Which is why I told you to learn the necessary commands in each contingent's native tongue. To avoid this very kind of delay between receiving and carrying out my orders!"

Lepidus' face flushed even darker, and he suddenly stared down at the table as he mumbled, "Yes, er, about that. I just haven't had the time. What with my duties and all."

"Ah," Caesar said simply, once more leaning back. "I see. So you're unable to fulfill the duties I've given you."

"No, sir!" This caused Lepidus to look up in clear alarm, and he shook his head as he tried to assure Caesar, "It's not that. Well, I mean…it *is* that I've had so much to do, but not because you've given me too much!"

Pullus had to drop his head to avoid allowing a snicker to escape his lips, understanding, obviously before Lepidus did, that the nobleman had just admitted that he was unable to handle the duties that came from being a Legate in Caesar's army.

"That's good to know." Caesar's voice was mild, but one only had to look at the glittering blue eyes to know he was struggling to maintain his composure. "Well," he sighed, "we'll certainly discuss that later. But now," he pointed again at Lepidus, "I need to hear what happened when you finally showed up. Because, based on what I just heard from Primus Pilus Pullus, it sounds very much like a number of his casualties came from men under your command."

"That's not true!" Lepidus protested. Just an eye blink after that, he amended, "At least, I don't believe that to be the case."

"You were there, weren't you?" Caesar pressed. "You were leading your men, weren't you? So, surely you should know with any certainty whether or not your men ran down some of their comrades."

Lepidus shook his head, clearly miserable now, and he refused to look at Caesar when he said dully, "No, Caesar. Because of the conditions, I deemed it best that I stay removed a short distance to have a better idea of how the situation was developing."

Caesar didn't reply, at least immediately; instead, he seemed content to nod thoughtfully.

"I see," he said finally. "Well, that's certainly…prudent." This was when Pullus' and Caesar's eyes met, and the Primus Pilus, despite his loathing of Lepidus, still felt a stab of sympathy for the man; his career was about to be ruined.

"Although," Caesar continued in the same contemplative tone, "with so much dust, obscuring so much ground, it seems to me that the only way to have the barest idea of what was happening with my command was to *be* with my command at the point of attack. Do you disagree with that, Lepidus?"

"No, Caesar," Lepidus replied dully. Pullus' sense was that Lepidus was now aware of the full extent of the damage being done to not only his career, but his *dignitas*. "I don't disagree with that."

"And," Caesar went on remorselessly, "because, by your own admission, you were nowhere near where the men of the Second who were wounded...or *slain* in the manner they were, your claim that it might have been from cataphracts has no real basis, does it? In fact," as Pullus sat listening, he imagined that every word uttered by Caesar was like a nail being driven into the hands of Lepidus as he was being figuratively crucified, "it's not only possible, but it's likely that it was men under your command who committed a terrible blunder, one that might have been prevented if their commander had been present. Would you disagree with *that* statement?"

The silence dragged out interminably, but finally, albeit in a very small voice, Lepidus allowed that he, in fact, didn't disagree with Caesar's judgement.

The Dictator's manner changed immediately, and he closed the matter by saying, "Good! I'm glad we agree. Now," he returned his attention back to Pullus and Scribonius, "I want to talk to you two about what happened. I want to hear what went right and what went wrong. Aside from what we just discussed."

Thus began a period of time where at least once during the day's march, but more usually two and even three times a day, some part of the column would suddenly find themselves beset by hundreds of Parthians, always archers, loosing swarms of missiles at whichever Legion happened to be in the wrong place at the wrong moment. Rather than continually attacking the leading elements of the army, as they had the first time, the Parthians would allow the bulk of the army to pass before they would move into position. Using their intimate knowledge of every fold, every crease, any terrain feature that allowed for cover, the enemy soon demonstrated their cunning because they would wait until the cavalry elements that Caesar sent to scour every possible avenue of attack had examined the terrain, then moved on. Only after this would the Parthians creep into position, walking their horses in single file up the narrowest defiles, moving into their attack points. Their cause was aided, albeit unknowingly, by the very size of

93

Caesar's army; if a stationary observer were to time their progress, it took well more than a full watch for the entire army to march past, and that was if they were marching over smooth, even ground. And in this part of their progress, the terrain was anything but smooth, and was seemingly endless in its undulations. In one similarity to the Crassus campaign, one of Parthia's most valuable allies was time; at this point, during what would become known as the opening phase of an operation that would compete with Caesar's conquest of Gaul, the Parthians were content to allow the Romans to continue their southerly advance without a concerted effort to stop them. However, there were two major differences, one about which the Parthians were aware, and one that, while they suspected, it was impossible at that moment to determine the scope of the difference. Whereas Crassus, by choosing the most direct route, also chose the driest, Caesar's decision to use the river, while it lengthened the time it would take, robbed the Parthians of the valuable ally of the thirst of both man and beast that had been one of the contributing factors in the collapse of discipline among Crassus' men. But it was the second that, while the Parthians understood in a general sense that Caesar was Crassus' superior in every way when it came to the command over his army, they still hadn't experienced the depths of that difference. That, however, was coming. In the meantime, the Parthians were content to whittle down Caesar's Legions, one or two men at a time, until the wagons designated to carry the wounded were filled to capacity. Still, the casualties weren't nearly as high as those Parthians who had been part of the effort to stop Crassus had inflicted a decade before, but despite this, none of the men or their commanders were particularly worried. Time, they reminded themselves and each other, was on their side.

Chapter Four

Crown Prince Pacorus, riding at the head of the equivalent of two corps of Parthian might, twenty thousand men total, arrived at last, more than a month after the news of the invasion first reached Ctesiphon. The spot Pacorus chose to serve as his combination headquarters and supply base was a town located at the junction of the Tigris and the river known by locals as the Little Khabur. Aside from its strategic position, the town was on the eastern bank, but had grown to number several thousand inhabitants and was situated at the base of a high, long ridge that ran along an east/west axis that gave anyone positioned on top a commanding view in every direction.most importantly, the view to the north and west, in the direction from which Caesar would come as long as he continued following the Tigris, extended for more than fifty miles. In essence, it would be impossible for Caesar to either approach, or more likely in Pacorus' mind, attempt to slip past without being detected. By the end of the first day of his arrival, Pacorus was well satisfied, believing that between the advantages provided by the terrain, and his belief in the superiority of his cataphracts, which numbered almost fifteen thousand of the twenty-five thousand fighting men he had brought, Caesar's army would advance no deeper into his homeland. Despite his optimism, however, the prince was still taking precautions and making further preparations.

The morning after he arrived, he sent dispatch riders, recalling every contingent of the Parthian army that had been engaged in harassing the Roman army. He had his noncombatants, both armorers and fletchers, set to work immediately, converting the raw materials that he had been forced to bring with him in his haste to get here, into spearheads, arrowheads, and full arrows. Under normal circumstances, this level of preparation would have been enough; the Parthians had become accustomed to using the terrain of their desolate, barren land without altering it in any way as their strongest ally, content to let the harshness of the environment do its part to wear down whatever force was invading. But, while they still hadn't determined Caesar's mettle in a definitive way, just by virtue of his

95

reputation, coupled with the fact that he was wisely foregoing speed for the benefits provided by the river as both a source of water and security for one of his flanks, Pacorus had made the decision to alter customary practice. Taking a lesson from his approaching foe, Pacorus endeavored to make alterations to the ground on either side of both the Tigris and along the northern bank of the Little Khabur. However, as he quickly discovered, and as his father Orodes could have explained beforehand if he had known Pacorus' mind, Parthian fighting men had no inclination towards the kind of manual labor that was required to fulfill Pacorus' designs. Very shortly after he ordered work to begin, Pacorus determined that, if he insisted that all of his men involve themselves in his plans and bend their backs like the men of the Legions did, he ran a very serious risk of mutiny; that segment of his army who were cataphracts were guaranteed to do so. Unaccustomed as he was to not just disobedience but disagreement from his generals, Pacorus nonetheless recognized the futility and danger in pressing his authority over men who were of noble birth themselves. It was true he was the son and crown prince of the King of Kings, and had been officially named *spadpat*, or supreme commander of this *spad*, the name for the entire might of the Parthian kingdom, but in many ways, Pacorus and Caesar had similar problems. In the case of Caesar, he had been dealing with the intransigence, excessive pride, and monstrous egos of the men of his class for many years, but this was the prince's first taste of the kind of stiff-necked resistance to his authority, based in the bedrock belief that using a spade or other such implement was beneath the dignity of men who had been raised for war. Consequently, he made a decision that, while pleasing to the men of his army, wasn't viewed with any favor by the inhabitants of the town, or anyone who lived within a day's walking distance.

Putting out a call for the civilians of the area to assemble, either voluntarily or by force, Pacorus conscripted them as labor to fulfill his planned defenses, and no one was exempted, unless they were too infirm; otherwise, even the children were required to do what they could to help, which usually meant they were consigned to carry pails of the spoil to where they were directed, or in the case of the youngest, carrying water for the laborers to drink. From shortly after dawn, with one long break during the middle of the day because of the intense heat, until dusk, the people worked, all while Pacorus sent out continuous patrols that kept him apprised of the Romans' approach. His decision on a static defense wasn't met with universal approval, but only after the prince revealed the full scope of his strategy did his generals finally cease their outright objection and contented themselves with grumbling among themselves in the privacy of their quarters. Part of their resistance came from the unfamiliarity with the very concept of standing and fighting; for longer than any man could remember, warriors of Parthia had preferred a fluid, indirect style of defense where ambush was the preferred tactic, and once resistance became stiffer and better organized, to melt away, disappearing down the draws, gullies, and creases that riddled their land. This style of fighting had become so famous that it had earned the term "Parthian shot," whereby an archer who seemed to be intent on nothing but escape suddenly turned his body to fire over the rear of hismount. As Crassus had learned, it was an overwhelmingly effective tactic, and if the truth were known, one to which Crassus' men never fully adjusted. Part of their inability was based in the frustration that came from fighting a foe that behaved in a manner that Romans universally found cowardly, so that their passions were so inflamed from the constant harassment that was identical to what Caesar's army was facing that they couldn't restrain themselves from plunging headlong in pursuit. And the archers belonging to the army commanded by the now-dead general Surena, who had actually been a distant relation of Pacorus, had perfected the art of drawing just close enough to the ordered Roman ranks that men on foot were sure they could dash out and strike their hated foes down. For years afterward, Parthian men would spend their idle time debating on what possessed the Romans to continue what they viewed as their senseless insistence on trying to catch a hated archer, despite seeing one comrade after another who attempted the same thing cut down in a storm of arrows. In truth, it was Surena's success that was part of the reason Pacorus made the decision to alter his own tactics, despite their success with Crassus and his army. It was a mark of the respect the younger man held for Caesar, or his reputation, since he felt fairly confident that Caesar would have prepared his army for a repeat of what had worked with Crassus. And, once Pacorus received the reports from the commanders of those detachments that had been harassing Caesar, he felt at least partially vindicated in his decision. While it was true that the Parthians had drawn first blood, it was equally true that his archers had suffered much higher casualties themselves at the hands of the Romans than had been lost against Crassus, although those losses had been negligible with Caesar's former colleague.

What was the most troubling to Pacorus, however, was that his men hadn't been cut down by other mounted men, which he could at least understand, but by the heavily armored Legionaries, who it appeared had mastered how to close the distance much more rapidly than their dead counterparts a decade before. While he didn't experience it as a conscious thought, it was this piece of information that had more to do with Pacorus' seemingly unusual decision. And, on the fourth day after his arrival, as he rode along the preparations he had directed be made, the prince was grimly pleased at what he saw. Naturally, there was more that could be done, but the scouts had reported that morning that Caesar was within a day's march, and indeed, by the end of the day, Pacorus could see the low hanging cloud of dust on the horizon that was the telltale sign of a large body of men and animals approaching.

No, he decided as he surveyed the fresh piles of rocks and dirt, this would have to do. And, he admitted only to himself, the cost hadn't been completely insignificant; more than a hundred civilians had dropped dead from their exertions, but frankly, this didn't trouble Pacorus greatly. They were peasants, and their sole purpose was to serve their king, and their prince, although the fact that more than a dozen children had been among the victims was regrettable, if only because of the incessant wailing of their grieving parents. It was quite tedious, and he could tell it was wearing on the nerves of those of his men whose position was nearby, but while he was tempted to allow them to deal with those peasants making the most noise, frankly, he didn't need the headache that would cause. He had already been forced to execute two of his archers who had been caught raping a young girl under circumstances where their guilt wasn't in question. Instead, he signaled his approval that the preparations met his expectations with little more than a nod to the general he had assigned to oversee the work, then turned and trotted away to his next task. For this, he had to labor up the slope; at least, his horse did, but when he reached the top, once more, he was arrested by the view. From this vantage point, the dust cloud was more clearly visible, although it was still much too far away for him to make out even a dark black line that he knew would be the vanguard of the Roman army. Tomorrow? he thought to himself. No, he decided; more likely the day after tomorrow that the Romans would draw near enough to see what awaited them. While it was true that the Romans could conceivably bypass Pacorus and his men, the prince felt quite certain Caesar wouldn't consider doing so, for the simple reason that the Roman general would then place an army in his rear. And from Caesar's viewpoint, it was not only likely, but probable that there was another Parthian force behind Pacorus farther south; at least, he hoped this was what Caesar would think. No, he assured himself, the Roman will see us, and he will come for us. And then, he will learn that they're not the only ones skilled at war and know more than one way to defeat our enemy.

"Are you certain?"

"Yes, Caesar," the Decurion in command, Decimus Silva, assured his general, who he'd found walking with the men of the 11th Legion on this day.

Silva was young to be of Decurion rank, but he had more than proven himself in the civil war; recommending him further was that the man had taken the time to learn the German tongue, which as Marcus Lepidus had learned, to his misfortune, was an essential skill when leading men whose command of Latin could only be charitably be called conversant and nowhere near fluent.

Caesar had stepped out of the marching column, leading Toes, who he took time to mount by vaulting into the saddle without help, a source of secret pride to a man who was already endowed with what some men would insist was more than his share, then said, "Let's go take a look."

Without waiting, he put his mount into a trot while Silva hurried to catch up. Moving rapidly, they outstripped the leading Cohort that had the vanguard that day as the *turmae* of cavalry that Silva brought with him formed into a protective cordon around the general. As they made their way in a southwesterly direction, Silva provided more details to his general about what lay ahead.

"They've dug a large trench paralleling the river for what looks like at least a mile, but," Silva explained grimly, "it's where they put it that's the problem."

"Blocking the only fordable part of the river would be my guess," Caesar replied, amused when he saw the startled expression of his young Decurion.

"Er," Silva fumbled, "yes, sir. Exactly. On this side of the trench, the river's too wide and deep, and on the south side, there's a sheer drop-off that we'd never get the wagons down." Glancing at Caesar to see how he was absorbing this, he then added the next piece. "But they've dug another trench, except this one's a bit harder to understand. At least," he added hurriedly, "to me."

"Well," Caesar replied genially, "let's see if I can't puzzle it out."

They rode in silence then, covering the miles at a rapid clip, while Silva's troopers rode far out in every direction, doubly alert, not only because it was their general, but the man who paid them very well for their service. Caesar had always been generous, yet he was even more so with those in whom he placed trust to help keep him alive, and these Germans returned it tenfold. The ridge had been clearly visible the entire day, and now Caesar was close enough to see the slightly different shapes that appeared to be at the foot of the ridge that he knew meant manmade structures. The terrain between the ridge and Caesar's position on the western side of the river was the flattest he had seen for days, making the ridge not only the dominant feature, but informing the general that the Parthian commander, whoever he was, intended to use it to his advantage About three miles from the ridge, the troopers galloped ahead to check the small cluster of mud-brick homes that lay between the larger town and Caesar's party.

"We checked to make sure they were clear when we passed through the first time," Silva explained to Caesar. "But I just want to be sure there's no...."

"Surprises," Caesar finished for him, then praised the Decurion for his prudence.

Silva flushed with pleasure, reminding Caesar how it was seemingly small things like complimenting a man for doing something in which Caesar approved that made it easier for him to ask his men to do something more unpleasant or more dangerous. They sat their horses, both to give them a breather in the event they had to rely on them to depart in haste, and to allow the troopers to thoroughly check the small village.

Seeing one of them wave the all-clear, they advanced, and Silva explained, "We didn't go much farther past this point, sir. And," he added with some apprehension, "I wouldn't suggest we go any closer than that."

Caesar glanced at Silva, amused, but seeing how nervous the Decurion was, assured him, "Don't worry, Silva. I just need to get close enough to see what you told me about."

Slightly assured, Silva nonetheless knew Caesar well enough that, if the general got it into his head, he'd ride right up to the edge of the river. And get us filled with arrows, he thought morosely, since there was no chance he wouldn't be at his general's side. Fortunately for both of them, once Caesar got to the other side of the village, which had partially obscured his view of the ground between the village and the river, he was content to stop.

Silva pointed first to the darker line of relatively fresh dirt that had been piled along the Tigris, but Caesar glanced at it only long enough to confirm what Silva had told him before turning to examine the second trench. And, as he saw immediately, Silva was right to be puzzled; it took Caesar the span of a hundred heartbeats before the first glimmer of the purpose for it came to him. Silva was aware that something had happened because Caesar suddenly sat up straighter in the saddle, as if by boosting his height a bare couple inches, he could more fully discern the intent of his enemy.

Only when Caesar let out his breath with an explosive sound did Silva realize his general had been holding his breath, but he clearly heard Caesar when he said, "That cunning bastard."

It was a relatively rare event for men in the ranks to hear their general salt his language with words more commonly heard around the fires, but he was even more unprepared for Caesar to burst out laughing. Understandably, Silva found his commander's seeming happiness at what, despite his relative youth, he could see was a formidable obstacle, more than a bit disconcerting. Caesar didn't seem to take notice, at least at first. It was only when, after he turned Toes about and began trotting away and Silva caught back up with him, that Caesar let his Decurion know why Caesar was laughing.

"Unless I'm wrong," he said amiably to the young officer, but with the kind of tone that informed Silva that Caesar was sure he wasn't, "my reputation has preceded me."

It took quite a bit of work on the part of the headquarters clerks, as directed by the *Praefectus Fabrorum* Volusenus; nevertheless at the end of that day's march, with the army now camped just north but within sight of the abandoned village three miles north of where the Tigris and the other river intersected, whose name Caesar still didn't know, they had managed to put together a surprisingly detailed model of the ridge and the immediate area around it. There was a slight delay as they scrambled to gather the materials, then make the miniature ridge and other prominent features that Caesar required, using both his prodigious memory and eye for detail, along with contributions from Silva. Subsequently, it was after dark and shortly before the call to retire sounded when the Primi Pili were summoned to the *praetorium* along with the senior officers. Waiting for them there was a large scale model of what awaited the men of Caesar's army, which had been constructed in place on the large table, the only spot big enough to hold it.

Pullus arrived with Balbinus of the 12th, Carfulenus of the 28th, and Spurius of the 3rd; the four exchanged glances as their eyes took in the sight before them, but it was Balbinus who spoke for the others when he told Pullus, "I have no idea what he's up to."

Although Pullus regarded Balbinus with some suspicion, having taken note of the attention he lavished on the young Octavian, the large Roman didn't sense any dissembling or evasiveness on the part of his fellow Primus Pilus. And, even if he was disposed to press further, Caesar wasted no time.

"Comrades," his use of the word instantly caught Pullus' attention, and he could see the other Primi Pili were no less startled; this was normally how he addressed the men of the ranks, "I've scouted what lies before us, and I've determined that whoever is commanding the Parthians has decided that continuing in his tactics of using archers to wear us down isn't producing the results he expected." While it was a guess on Caesar's part, it was also a shrewd one, and was exactly one of the reasons Pacorus had chosen to stand and fight. "And," Caesar added, "it's my belief that he's going to try and induce us to commit ourselves so there can be a decisive engagement." Pausing for a moment to allow this to sink in, he continued, "In order to accomplish this, he's prepared the ground in such a way that, if we behave as he expects, we'll be on ground of his choosing, and which favors not his archers as much as his cataphracts."

It was Batius, the Primus Pilus of the 5th Alaudae who raised his hand, but without waiting for Caesar to recognize him, blurted, "So there are cataphracts waiting for us?"

The general's only sign of displeasure at the interruption was a thinning of his lips, but his tone remained the same as he answered Batius. "While I didn't personally see their presence, Batius, given the configuration of the Parthian defenses, I'd be quite surprised if they're not present, in force." He waited a breath to allow this to sink in, then said, "Now, if I may continue." Pullus ducked his head to avoid being caught smiling at Batius' suddenly reddened face, while Caesar pointed to the large model. "The reason for my surmise is based on the location and position of this trench that parallels this smaller river that intersects with the Tigris." Pullus and the others followed their general's pointing stylus as they all gazed down at the tiny trench that, judging from the scale, Pullus estimated to be no more than a dozen paces from the southern bank of the smaller river, placing it between the water and the ridge. Speaking of the ridge, Pullus hoped that the mound of molded dirt wasn't exactly to scale as far as the height, but although he didn't know it yet, he was going to be given the opportunity to find out. "As you can see, there appears to be a gap between the two trenches, rather than them meeting at right angles to each other, as might be expected. I admit this puzzled me at first, but then I took a closer look at the ground on the other side of the river, between the ridge and the trench." Continuing to use his stylus, he indicated the miniature of the gap, saying, "Although it's impossible to measure precisely, my estimate of the distance from this part of the river, to," his stylus then moved towards the ridge, "where the slope meets level ground is no more than five hundred paces. And, if you look carefully, you'll notice that about halfway down the ridge to the east, there's a dry watercourse that has lessened the severity of the slope, along with allowing anyone beyond the ridge to the south to cross over the ridge without having to go the long way around either end. Where we are now is closer to the western end of the ridge, which as you can see is protected by both rivers. And our enemy has done what I would do; protect the easiest approach, using not just the river, but the added protection of that trench."

He paused for a moment, both to catch his breath and to allow his subordinates time to absorb his information. Of his Legates, he had only confided in Hirtius and Pollio his full intentions, but now he was waiting, judging the reactions of the others to see which one of his Primi Pili gave him an indication they were beginning to understand.

"They want us to cross through that gap so that they can loose their cataphracts on us with the advantage of starting uphill."

Despite the regard in which Caesar held the man, the Dictator had to admit to himself that Pullus was still capable of surprising him, because it was the Primus Pilus of the 10th who uttered these words. He had spoken slowly, but audibly enough that everyone else could hear, as the large man was still putting the final pieces of the puzzle together.

Caesar nodded in approval, agreeing with Pullus and expanding further, "That's what I believe to be the case, Pullus. The Parthians set great store in their cataphracts, and while to this point we haven't encountered any, there's been enough time for an army of them to march from the Parthian interior."

This moment was the first where Caesar sensed that not everyone present agreed, and he glanced over just in time to see his oldest Legate, Publius Ventidius Bassus, and the one Primus Pilus in Caesar's army whose age was roughly the same, Batius, exchanging glances that communicated their doubt.

"Yes, Ventidius?" Caesar preferred handling objections head on, and not waiting for them to fester. "I can see by your expression you don't necessarily agree."

"It's not that, Caesar," Ventidius replied cautiously. "But I do wonder if they actually have their cataphracts in place. Couldn't it just as easily be that there's the usual complement of horse archers, and whoever's commanding that lot are using the trenches to slow us down as their men riddle us with those cursed arrows?"

"That," Caesar granted, "is possible. However," he pointed back to that gap in the trenches, "how do you explain this?"

Now Ventidius looked uncomfortable because he knew Caesar didn't mind a certain amount of debate, but he expected those who resisted him to offer an alternative to what Caesar had proposed.

After a short pause, the older man shrugged and said simply, "I can't."

Seeing Ventidius had nothing more to offer, Caesar was about to return to his briefing when Batius interrupted once more, asking his general bluntly, "Did you actually *see* any cataphracts, Caesar?"

The general was forced to swallow his irritation, recognizing, grudgingly, that it was a valid question.

"No, Batius," he answered honestly. "I didn't, but if I were their commander, I'd have them hidden on the other side of that ridge and use that notch in the ridge to bring my cataphracts into position. And," he returned to the model, "as you can see, if they use that approach, they'll not only have the advantage of the slope, but if we cross the river in between the two trenches, we'll have to immediately pivot to the east in order to be perpendicular to the river and the ridge in order to avoid them hitting us in the flank. But," his voice turned grim, "I believe that's what he'll use his horse archers for, to harry us and make it difficult, if not impossible for us to make the changes we'd need to."

Once more, Caesar paused, yet despite his explanation, he was actually pleased to see his men look so grim now that they understood the scope of the problem. This, he realized, was always a favorite moment of his, when men were suddenly anxious that whatever they were facing might turn out at long last to be the insurmountable

104

obstacle in their path to victory, for the simple pleasure of giving them hope by providing the solution he had devised.

This time was no exception as he said, "As grim as it may seem, I believe I have the answer to this problem."

Over the next sixth part of a watch, Caesar laid out the plan he had conceived, mostly during the ride back to the army, then revising it after conferring with Hirtius and Pollio on his return. By the time he was through, while nobody was overtly joyful, he was reassured by the change in their demeanor; a couple men even had small, grim smiles, and Pullus was one of them.

Then, Caesar dismissed his senior officers, but as they were filing out, he called out, "Pullus, wait. Stay behind. There's something I want to talk to you about."

"When are we doing this?"

"Tomorrow night," Titus Pullus informed Servius Metellus, his Tertius Pilus Prior and the man who had asked the question.

Immediately upon his return to his tent, Pullus had sent Diocles to summon the Pili Priores, but not before he stopped at the Second Century to find Balbus and the First of the Second for Scribonius, sending them hurrying to meet with Pullus, giving the Primus Pullus some time alone with the pair of men he trusted the most, and whose counsel he valued above all others, at least in military matters. Not surprisingly, none of the Pili Priores had been hard to find, nor had they tarried, giving the three only a few moments during which Pullus did most of the talking, explaining the task that Caesar had just assigned the 10th.

Metellus, a swarthy, short man with a barrel chest who had been born in Narbonese Gaul, considered the answer given to him by his Primus Pilus, yet his demeanor was such that rather than look relieved at the extra day to prepare, he seemed troubled. But before Pullus could probe further, he took a quick check around his tent, where all the Pili Priores were gathered, and saw that, if he was judging by expressions, Metellus wasn't the only one who seemed more concerned. Catching the eyes, or eye, more accurately, of his Octus Pilus Prior, in doing so, Pullus not only saw he was one that seemed to share Metellus' viewpoint, but experienced a sudden rush of fondness and regard that made this man another of Pullus' most trusted advisors.

"Cyclops?" Pullus asked, not bothering with the man's formal name, which was Quintus Ausonius, nor his rank. "It seems like you agree with Metellus. And," he nodded in acknowledgement of the others, "you two aren't alone. So," he leaned forward, and put his elbows on his knees as he stared intently at Cyclops, "what's bothering you?"

The man who bore the name Quintus Ausonius yet had become commonly called Cyclops after losing an eye while fighting under the standard of Quintus Sertorius, did flush, but he didn't flinch. Of everyone, not just in the tent, but in the entire army, Cyclops had known Titus Pullus the longest, having met the then ten-year-old youth who, along with his best friend Vibius Domitius, had sought him out, begging for him to train them in the way the Legions of Rome fought. He had put the pair off for two years before, worn down by what he initially viewed as a surprising persistence, he finally relented. Almost from the first day, he had recognized that Titus Pullus was destined to become a great Legionary. Naturally, the boy's size hadn't hurt, and the fact that he had continued to grow until he was one of the largest, strongest men in the Roman Legions was certainly a factor that couldn't be discounted, yet as Cyclops learned very quickly, there was much more to Pullus than brute strength. Encased in a musculature that was the envy of others was a relentless ambition, and coupled with an intellect that, while untutored, was formidable in itself, Cyclops had watched Pullus climb the ranks, aided along the way by Caesar. Consequently, Cyclops was aware that Pullus expected brutal honesty, so he didn't hesitate.

"I wonder why tomorrow night. Why not tonight?"

Reflecting later, Pullus recognized that, while he was surprised in the moment, he shouldn't have been, although he felt a bit better in the knowledge that it wasn't just him but Caesar who thought the men of his army needed a rest.

Outwardly, Pullus replied, "Because Caesar decided we needed a day to prepare. At least," he amended, "I suppose that's why."

"My boys are ready now," Cyclops declared flatly.

His voice was soon overwhelmed by the cries of the other Pili Priores who weren't about to be outdone by the Pilus Prior of the Eighth Cohort. As Pullus sat listening, he was keenly aware that at least part of the motivation on the part of his Cohort commanders was based in the atmosphere of the fierce competition between the Cohorts for the honor of being considered the best. Nevertheless, Pullus also knew that, if the rankers weren't physically prepared, his Pili Priores wouldn't have put their Cohorts forward. Finally, he raised a hand for silence.

"Remember," he admonished them, "we're not the only piece of this. Caesar is thinking about the rest of the army."

"We have the hardest part," the Quartus Pilus Prior Vibius Nigidius scoffed, "and if we're ready, then what's their excuse?"

Even if the others hadn't raised their voices in a show of collective support, Pullus didn't need their cries; a look at the faces of his Centurions was enough. Still, he hesitated, and as he usually did in such moments, he looked to Scribonius for advice.

Seeing Pullus look in his direction, the lanky Centurion shrugged, saying, "I don't think it would hurt to ask Caesar." He hesitated for perhaps a heartbeat, then added, "And for what it's worth, I agree with the others. If we're going to do this, I'd rather do it tonight than tomorrow. A lot can change. And," he finished grimly, "now that we've shown up, I wouldn't be surprised if whoever's commanding those bastards is adding some new and nasty surprises for us."

This clinched it for Pullus, but rather than allowing the men to disperse, he tersely commanded they stay put while he went to the *praetorium*. Time was of the essence; it was already approaching midnight.

Sitting on his horse, Pacorus gazed off into the near distance to where the rows of flickering fires that marked the Roman camp lay. The outer boundaries of the camp were just barely visible as darker black lines against the unlit ground, and just the size of it had given the crown prince pause. He still believed his plan offered the best way to inflict grave damage on the Romans, however it was one thing to draw up a bunch of squiggling lines on vellum and totally another to bear firsthand witness to the might of Rome in the form of the ordered and neat rows of tents. Such a level of organization was inconceivable to Parthians, even those of high rank; a commander in the Parthian army's hold was, at best, tenuous, and as he had learned a few days before, if his men had balked at doing the labor required to create fortifications that would, conceivably, help them in their defense and by extension save their lives, the very idea of creating ramparts every single night was abhorrent to them. Unaware that the Roman general Caesar had divined his plans, Pacorus still felt confident that he was doing the right thing, no matter what his generals might say. That at least two of them were also related didn't help matters any, and they both had been vocal in expressing their doubts about the wisdom of the younger man's strategy. Regardless, he had insisted on holding to his course, although he had bowed to the pressure from his uncles, and agreed to position his infantry on the top of the ridge, not immediately behind the trench as he had originally planned.

"In the event that we're unable to stop the Romans from pushing across the river, there should be some kind of force placed along the brow of the ridge to slow them down," had been the argument.

To Pacorus, this smacked of defeatism; if he did as they urged and placed the infantry in a line just below the top of the ridge, and then their strength was needed, it would mean it was due to his force of cataphracts and archers being pushed back and not sweeping the Romans from the field as he envisaged. However, he had been forced to admit, extremely grudgingly, that having his foot-borne troops on the heights was preferable than on flat ground because of the greater momentum that came from charging down the slope. The concept of using the invisible force that pulled anything movable down a slope was the same for both beasts and men; it was simply a matter of scale and relative speed. Finally, when Pacorus relented, it was more out of exasperation and being worn down by the pair of generals than from any recognition in the wisdom of their counsel. Whatever the cause, the result was the same, with his infantry, armed with wicker shields and spears, moving into their positions after darkness and using the rocks littering the slope to create a bit of a barrier. When the moment came, Pacorus resolved that he would at least have his infantry ready to rush down the slope, hopefully to do little more than mopping up the remnants of the Roman army that had been shattered by his planned attack. He had no way of knowing that this last-moment decision would actually cause Caesar and his army more headaches than they would have created in their original deployment. Pacorus had been busy himself, and this was his last stop, about halfway up the slope of the ridge at the western end, directly above the open ground between the two trenches. As Caesar had surmised, the force of cataphracts were indeed on the southern side of the ridge, the bulk of it shielding the Romans' view of the sprawling camp that, in its own way, rivaled the size of Caesar's army, at least in terms of area. Completely opposite in comparison to the symmetry and order that was the predominant feature of a Roman army encampment, the men of Parthia claimed a spot of ground that was part of the designated area, except that their status was an important factor in exactly how much ground would be claimed. The Parthian "army" as such didn't exist, at least if the model of Rome was used for comparison purposes. Whereas the Republic had a standing army, which might fluctuate in size but was nevertheless always ready to march, the King of Kings had to rely on the older system whereby his *satraps*, lords of plots of land that varied in size, were expected to supply a certain number of men, of a certain military type, whenever called upon. Each *satrap* was responsible for the equipping, clothing, and caring for his own contingent of men, but it was the actual numbers of men involved that varied widely. Subsequently, the corresponding amount of space each *satrap* demanded was similarly different, although as Pacorus quickly learned, there were some *satraps* who had a much different idea of how much space each man required than his counterparts. And, he acknowledged with some bitter amusement, it was also a matter of pride for many of them. What it meant was that, before he ascended the ridge to view the rectangular outline and rows of tents, Pacorus had looked out on essentially the exact opposite, where despite the fact he currently had less men under his command than Caesar, the camp of the Parthians on the southern side of the ridge spread along the base of the ridge, and farther south, for more than a mile in Pacorus' estimate. This, he thought ruefully, is what I have to deal with, while this Roman Caesar only has to bark out an order and then can walk away, knowing his men will obey him to their utmost. Hopefully, all that would change within the course of the next couple of days; the only thing Pacorus felt certain about was that at least this night, he and the rest of the Parthian host could rest easily. There would be no action tonight.

In the mark of a truly veteran, well-led Legion, the men of the 10th Equestris were actually formed up and marching out of the camp shortly after the beginning of the midnight watch, barely a third of a watch after Pullus hurried to the *praetorium*. It shouldn't have surprised Pullus that Caesar immediately approved the request to move the 10th's task up a night, although none of the men of the other Legions were appreciative, since they would now be expected to play their roles a day early. Fortunately, they hadn't been roused to begin their own preparations, so Pullus and his men avoided being the subject of invective from more than just the guard Cohort when they left the camp. And, rather than leaving by the traditional gate of the Porta Praetoria or Porta Decumana, it was the side gate on the eastern side of the camp that the 10th used, accompanied by a handful of men tasked to guide them to where they were heading. No torches were allowed, and each man's *caligae* had been wrapped in rags, while care had been taken to separate bits of gear that might come into contact as the men traversed the rough ground. Nothing was said, aside from the muttered calls of the Legionaries who happened to be positioned around this gate, but even then, Pullus was sure they couldn't have been heard more than a hundred paces away. Stealth was absolutely essential this night; the way Pullus had described it to his Centurions was that, for a short period, this was a Legion of *numeni*, the invisible, disembodied spirits that every Roman knew inhabited the silent, dark places of the world. He had even ordered that the men take the further precaution of keeping the leather covers on their shields so there was no chance of a reflection off the metal boss catching the eye of an alert sentry. Aided by the light of a half moon, ultimately what worked in the favor of the 10th was that, as Caesar had observed, this ground was as flat and level as he had seen on the campaign. And the dark bulk of the ridge was clearly delineated by the stars, along with the flickering torches of the Parthian position. The town located at the base of the ridge was itself dark, without a single light, even a flickering candle, but Pullus was sure none of the houses were empty. Whether or not there were eyes watching out one of the windows, he didn't know, but tucked the thought away as one of those things that was outside of his control. What was within his power was to set the example, and he did so now, moving as silently as possible for a man his size. And, as always, he moved up and down his column of Cohorts, stopping just long enough with each Pilus Prior to offer a word of encouragement and softly calling out the names of some of the veterans in the ranks he had known since the first *dilectus*. The men, obeying their orders to the letter, didn't call back, but Pullus saw the dull gleam of teeth as those men he singled out replied with a grin and wave of their hand.

In most ways, it was a normal march, but Pullus did take the precaution of not running up and down the column, choosing instead to take advantage of his longer legs and quickened pace to get where he needed to be. The first obstacle was encountered very quickly, in the form of the Tigris river, which had to be crossed. This was where Silva's knowledge came in, since he and his men had scouted for fording spots prior to the army's arrival. The place he chose was where the river was actually wider than normal, but had a small island in the middle, formed over the years by the silt and debris that built up in this location. Despite knowing, even as much sound as a few thousand men made crossing a river, that the sound wouldn't carry the distance to

110

the nearest Parthian ears, Pullus nevertheless felt the tension of the moment, worrying that by some chance trick of the wind or night air, the enemy would be alerted. Once he crossed—the water never got above waist level on him, although this meant it was almost up to mid-chest on most of his men—Pullus stood, staring hard in the direction of the ridge, watching the tiny points of light that he knew were the torches that illuminated the area around each guard post, looking for movement of some sort. Anything that might warn him that the Parthians had somehow heard the din made by splashing feet, yet despite his eyes watering from the strain, nothing changed. Only after the last man was across did he breathe easier, but he didn't have the time to spare in celebrating this first small victory because the worst was yet to come. Once across the river, he marched his men at an angle that, while it roughly paralleled the ridge, also moved them closer to the smaller river. The spot he was aiming for was farther east of the Parthian position, past the easternmost edge of the trench where, at a glance, there appeared to be an undefended gap of open ground before the terrain became too rugged to be traversed. But what Silva had first determined, and Caesar had confirmed with his own eyes, was the telltale sheen sprinkled amidst what to the naked eye looked like solid ground. That sheen came from water, and it told Caesar that whoever was commanding the Parthians hadn't extended the trench across this stretch of ground for a reason. What neither Silva nor Caesar could determine was just how soggy that ground was, so it would be Pullus and his men who would be the ones to determine how solid the footing underneath their *caligae* would be. The irony of the moment wasn't lost on Pullus; while being his size conferred advantages, there were certainly drawbacks, and the fact that by virtue of his weight he would sink deeper into however much of a boggy mess was waiting for them was certainly one of those times. Using a dry watercourse that conveniently branched off the little river on the northern side that was the only wrinkle in the otherwise smooth, flat ground, Pullus and Silva led his men into the depression, only stopping long enough to allow the marching column to reduce itself from eight men across to four men to compensate for the narrower track. While only about three to four feet deep, it nonetheless lowered the profile of the men of the 10th, especially since none of the *signiferi* were carrying their standards aloft, instead holding them parallel to the ground. Almost immediately, Pullus discovered that there was a tradeoff for this extra bit of cover; the ground was littered with rocks of all shapes and sizes, and most of them were loose. No matter how carefully the men placed their feet, it was inevitable there would be a sharp crack of two rocks colliding, or a skittering sound as the men's feet struck a smaller stone and sent it rebounding. At first, this was compounded by the curse of either the man who caused the sound or one of his comrades who chastised him, but a few swipes with the *viti* from the Centurions soon muffled that part of the disturbance. Pullus thought it unlikely that the sound escaped the confines of the shallow gulch; still, he winced every time he heard the sounds behind him. Partly because of the footing, and they were now less than a mile from the little river, Pullus slowed the pace dramatically, and sent a makeshift section of men ahead a short distance, composed not of the normal tent mates but his stealthiest Legionaries. He hadn't seen anything on the approach that would indicate that the Parthians had placed sentries this far east, but he was a veteran of more battles than he could easily count, and there was a reason he had survived what was the longest stretch of fighting any Roman army had ever endured. Stopping intermittently whenever the scouts ahead either signaled, or disappeared from sight because of a slight bend, it took the 10th the same length of time to cover the last half-mile to the river as it had taken to get to this point from the camp. Finally, they reached the spot where the gulch, which had been growing shallower and wider, essentially ended, but it was the scouts who were the first to reach the boggy ground, and it didn't take more than fifty heartbeats' time before one of them came back to inform Pullus. The Primus Pilus didn't need more than the light provided by the partial moon to see that he and his men had reached their first major obstacle; his scout's legs below the knees were black from the muck that lay ahead.

"How far did you get?" Pullus whispered to the man, a veteran named Glabrio, who gave his answer with a grim shake of his head.

"Not even halfway to the riverbank," he replied in the same hushed tone. "And Primus Pilus," he added, "it looks like it's just as bad on the other side of the river."

"Can you see how far?"

Glabrio shrugged, then seeing the glare of his Primus Pilus that told him this wasn't an acceptable answer, hastily answered, "At least fifty paces, maybe sixty."

Pullus swore again, but he didn't have the luxury of time to think. As it was, he was acutely aware that the leading elements of his Legion were no longer even partially protected by the depression of the gulch, and while every man who was exposed was crouching down as he was, they couldn't risk staying long in one spot as exposed as this.

"Fuck it," he grumbled, then nodded to Glabrio to return to the advance section, then rose from his squatting position to a half-crouch, following immediately behind. "Time to get filthy."

The crossing of the boggy ground had one salutary effect, at least as far as Pullus was concerned. By the time the entire Legion had crossed, no man emerged on the southern side of the river on firm ground without at least their lower legs encased in thick, black mud. While he hadn't really thought about it before, only when the Legion was safely across did he realize that, if anything, they were harder to see with the lower half of their bodies now matching the darkened colors of the night. Tucking this away as something worth remembering, Pullus led the way, climbing what began as a gentle slope up from the river, but within two hundred paces turned radically steeper. Again, it was Glabrio who returned to Pullus to whisper that the scouts had found a cleft in the rock of the ridge, another dry watercourse that would provide cover. However, in what Pullus thought sourly was becoming a pattern, it didn't come without a cost, and this one was that it was only wide enough for two men abreast. That would stretch his Legion out to the point that, as Pullus was reaching the top, there would still be men exposed down by the riverbank, and while he had been dividing his attention between the ground before him and the torches of the easternmost sentry posts, which hadn't moved at all, he wasn't willing to take the risk.

"No, we're going to go straight up this bastard," Pullus whispered to Glabrio, then pointed to the bare slope, just to the right of the shadowed vertical crack that was the route Glabrio had just suggested. "Right now, speed is more important than cover." He glanced up at the moon, which had begun its downward arc, estimating, "We've got barely more than a full watch before it gets light. And we still have to cross the ridgetop to get in position."

Even if he had been disposed to argue, Glabrio knew it wasn't his place, simply nodding that he had understood his Primus Pilus before turning about to go alert his comrades scouting ahead of the changed route. As Pullus waited a few moments for Glabrio to reach the others, Balbus moved up from his spot, where the pair engaged in a whispered conversation, so it was left to Balbus to express his misgivings about Pullus' decision.

"How wide are we going to be going up?" he asked Pullus.

"Four men across," Pullus answered after a moment's thought. "It still gives us a longer tail than I'd like, but it's better than two across if we use that," he indicated the cleft with his head.

"True," Balbus agreed, but in such a way that Pullus knew his agreement was half-hearted at best.

Pullus opened his mouth to ask Balbus why he was hesitating, then thought better of it; this was the Primus Pilus' decision to make, and he had judged this to be better than the alternative. Once Balbus determined that Pullus wasn't inclined to probe further into the cause of his second in command's reservations, the scarred Centurion gave an abrupt nod, then turned to go.

Seeing this, Pullus felt compelled to reach out and grasp Balbus' shoulder, prompting him to turn around.

"If this goes wrong," Pullus told him with a grin, "I give you permission to say 'I told you so.'"

"Oh, don't worry about that," Balbus assured him, then turned back around, mainly to hide his own smile.

Pullus watched Balbus' retreating back, shaking his head in amusement, knowing the implicit sentiment that Balbus hadn't expressed; provided we survive. Waiting just a moment longer, Pullus took a deep breath, then rose and, without hesitation, resumed climbing the steepened slope of the ridge. From that moment on, the progress was slow but steady, with Pullus stopping just once for a span of no more than a hundred heartbeats to catch his breath. When he did, his vantage point gave him a better view of the Parthians' defenses down by the river, and he was relieved to see that there was still no indication that they had been spotted by the sentries that Pacorus had left posted along the length of the trench paralleling the small river. Of course, that was going to change at some point, but Pullus offered up a prayer to Fortuna that it wouldn't happen until the right moment. About a sixth part of the watch after he began the ascent, the entire Legion had ascended the ridge, and now Pullus did allow the men to catch their breath while he held a hurried conference with the Pili Priores. Because of their position on the ground, the one thing that neither Silva nor Caesar could offer was anything more than a guess about how wide the ridge was at the top. To Pullus' dismay, while the top of the ridge where they were standing appeared to be about five hundred paces across, which would allow the Legion to array itself in what would be close to their normal four Cohort front, as he peered west along the length of the ridge, he didn't need more light to see that

114

it narrowed dramatically, even before the dip that Caesar had pointed out as the most likely avenue for the Parthians to cross from the southern side of the ridge. He had seen the moment he reached the top that Caesar, as usual, had been correct; arrayed before him on the opposite side of the ridge were the glowing coals of what he was sure was more than a thousand fires, stretched out south and along the base of the slope, looking as if a giant had carelessly scattered a handful of rubies on the ground. The size of the camp alone was a daunting sight, but now that he understood the dilemma posed by the narrowing of the ridgetop, for the first time, he felt real misgivings about the wisdom of continuing with the plan. Not that it mattered, he reflected glumly, because we're already here, and there's no way to get word to Caesar, at least not by taking the same route we took to get here. Conceivably, he recognized, he could dispatch Silva to dash back down the ridge, but since Pullus had insisted that the cavalryman accompany the Legion dismounted, the only sure way to get a message to Caesar in the shortest time would mean he had to cut across the face of the slope diagonally. Even for a man on horseback, it would be a matter of rolling the dice, but on foot, the chances of him making it back to the Roman position and remain undetected would require him to move as slowly as possible. And if he hurried, Pullus felt certain that he would be spotted, and either captured or killed. It was no fit end for any Roman, let alone a man like Silva, who Pullus had come to regard as a good man, even if he was in the cavalry. Spitting in disgust, Pullus turned his attention back the Pili Priores.

"We're going to have to stay in column," he announced quietly, but since they all had eyes and had seen the same thing, there wasn't any comment made. "At least until we get on the other side of that dip. Then?" He shrugged and said simply, "We'll have to see what our options are."

There was nothing more to say then, and the Centurions returned to their Cohorts, while Pullus gave the signal to move. Even as they resumed, he gave a glance over his shoulder at the eastern horizon, wondering if the lightening of the sky was a figment of his imagination, or if it was really that close to dawn. Not willing to risk that it was actually the latter, he moved a bit more quickly than he would have liked. The practical consequence of his decision was that, inevitably, the increased pace meant men were more likely to trip or to dislodge a rock and send it bouncing across the ground. That was bad enough, but it was only afterward that Pullus and the rest of the

Legion recognized that what was about to happen turned out to be the kind of mishap that actually aided one's cause as much as it damaged it.

"What was that?"

The Parthian sentry, one of the pair who had been placed at the easternmost spot about a hundred paces beyond the end of the new Parthian infantry line along the top of the ridge, stared farther east, sure that he had heard something that wasn't part of the normal night sounds. His companion was older, and a veteran at that, which contributed to his sour frame of mind. Sentry duty of any sort wasn't something soldiers of any army looked forward to with any enthusiasm, but the veteran was doubly put out because he was being punished by his *satrap*. While it was true the veteran had neglected his main weapon, a long spear, so that the point had become too rusted and pitted to be deemed serviceable, he had been put on sentry duty every night because of it. This was enough of an insult, but being paired with one of the rawest youths that had filled out his levy was the worst part.

"What was what, boy?" the veteran snapped irritably.

"Didn't you hear that sound? It was like…" The youth kept his gaze east while he tried to think of the proper term. "…someone dropped something like a piece of metal on the ground."

"You're hearing things, boy," was the veteran's judgment, but his counterpart had as much pride as this man, and he had endured enough of the veteran's abuse.

"My name is Artostes," he replied hotly. "And I know I heard something!"

Heaving a deep sigh that the veteran, whose own name was Gaspar, hoped would communicate that he was only indulging the boy, he reluctantly pulled himself to his feet from where he had been sitting on a convenient rock just the height of a low stool. That he had been sitting down, Gaspar knew, was an offense in itself, at least technically, although in the three campaigns in which he had participated, he had never seen a man punished for it. Walking the short distance to where the younger Artostes was standing, who was leaning against his spear and with his wicker shield grounded, the older man looked over Artostes' shoulder towards the east as well. He gave no more than a cursory glance, but he did cock his head to the side to briefly listen to the night. Unlike their counterparts down below along the main defenses, the Parthian commanding this contingent, had refused to allow torches lit once they were in their new position atop the ridge, yet despite the fact that not having any light helped his night vision, Gaspar wasn't particularly appreciative.

"It's what I thought," he snorted, about to return to his spot. "You're hearing things. There's nothing out there."

Before he walked more than two paces, however, there came another sound, again from the eastern darkness, and this time not even Gaspar could pretend he didn't hear it. Still, he was neither alarmed, nor thought it worth sounding the alert about, knowing it would rouse his comrades. And if it turned out to be nothing more than some of those noble bastards and their horses using that low point to move into position earlier than they were supposed to, well, he didn't want to risk arousing their wrath for being the one who exposed what they were doing. While a Roman sentry wouldn't dream of remaining silent and thought little of raising the alarm, especially in Caesar's army, since even if it turned out to be false, he wouldn't be punished for it, other than perhaps a smack of his Centurion's *vitus*, the opposite was true with their Parthian counterparts. Since it was inevitably the lowest ranking members of their society, which was even more stratified than that of Rome's, who stood sentry duty, it had been an article of faith among them that it was a foolish, or insanely brave man of their class who sounded an alarm that roused their superiors from sleep, especially if it proved to be false. Despite this knowledge, there was enough of a soldier in Gaspar that, albeit reluctantly, he turned about and returned to Artostes' side. Together, they stared east, and this was the moment when they both realized that dawn was in fact approaching, as the eastern horizon had turned a sullen, orange-pink in color, signaling the start of another brutally hot day. It was thanks to this light that, when the scouts sent ahead by Pullus ascended the near slope of the depression, they were starkly outlined against the light. Still, neither veteran nor new recruit immediately responded, because their minds were running along the same lines.

"Maybe it's some of the cataphracts stretching their legs while they wait," was Artostes' suggestion, and somewhat surprisingly, Gaspar didn't immediately dismiss it.

It was as if neither of them could quite credit the idea that these were Romans, which meant their reaction was delayed by several heartbeats as they both stared with more curiosity than fear, at first. Then, immediately from behind the first men the pair had spotted, something seemed to come thrusting up from the ground, appearing to

117

rise up in a winking fire caused by the first rays of the sun catching the gilt silver of its outstretched wings.

Gaspar's mouth dropped open, intent on sounding the alarm, but nothing came out; that it was the raw youth who regained his wits first was something that neither Artostes nor Gaspar would have time to argue about.

"That's a Roman eagle!" Even as he said this, the boy was spinning around, dropping his spear so he could cup his mouth with both hands to yell louder than he ever had before, in a voice made shrill with shock and fear. "Romans approaching from the east! We're under attack!"

Glabrio froze, his eye catching the sudden movement in the gloom ahead, but even as he was turning to hiss a warning to Pullus and his *aquilifer* Aulus Paterculus, who were just behind him climbing the last few feet of the depression, they heard the shrill cry of a Parthian sentry whose name they would never know.

"Pluto's cock," Pullus snarled, both startled and suddenly fearful. "Where did that *cunnus* come from? There was nobody up here before the sun went down! We'd have seen them!"

Paterculus, obeying Pullus' order that he raise the eagle standard to its vertical position and had been the inadvertent cause of the alarm that was being sounded at that instant, said hopefully, "Maybe it's just a sentry they sent up here so he could see us coming out of camp after sunrise."

The amount of time it took for Pullus to hear, process, then begin to hope this indeed might be the case was the span of a heartbeat, but even before he could respond, Paterculus' optimism was shattered by the sounds of other voices shattering what had been a relatively quiet night.

"Doesn't sound like it," Pullus said bitterly, but as he was saying it, his legs had driven him back up to the top of the ridge, where Glabrio and the other seven comrades of the scout section had stopped and unconsciously arrayed themselves in a proper battle line, facing in the direction of what was rapidly becoming clear was a large body of men.

Drawing even with Glabrio, the wan light of dawn coming from behind him, while it outlined the Romans, did allow Pullus a glimpse of what lay more than twenty paces beyond where he was standing. And, while he couldn't make out any real level of detail, just the swirling motion that stretched back west along the ridge, well out of his range of vision, told him that it was not only more than a sentry, it was a sizable body of men that, somehow, had managed to move into this position under cover of darkness. They must have been moving in while we were making our way here from our camp, Pullus thought, although outwardly, he presented his normal, calm demeanor as he snapped an order to Valerius, the Legion *cornicen.* Now that they had been discovered, Pullus knew stealth was secondary to speed, and Valerius immediately sounded the notes that signaled the men of the First Cohort to assemble in their battle formation. Naturally, it wasn't that simple; they weren't in the forum of camp, but on an undulating surface of rocky ground.

"First of the First, rally to me!" Pullus roared, but even as he did so, he was moving to a spot on the ridgetop closer to the river, stopping only when he judged that the slope downward got too steep.

It was far from ideal; because of the curvature, even after the sun rose, he would be unable to see across to the farthest of the other two Centuries of the standard three-Century front. As he judged it, he might be able to see Balbus, but certainly not his Princeps Prior, Marcus Laetus, nor could he judge if there was enough space on top for any of the other three Centuries to align in a single line. Shrugging, he understood that this was one of the moments where he wouldn't have the luxury of time to order his Legion into a disposition that fit the circumstances and room available. Judging from the still rising tumult in front of him, the one thing Pullus did understand was that it was highly unlikely just his Cohort would be able to subdue whatever was out there. The only consolation, he thought, is that just from the sounds, they're more disorganized than we are. Then, there came the sound of a *cornu* that, not only from the direction but from the three notes played first, told Pullus his Third Century was moving into position. As much as was happening, and as rapidly, Pullus' estimate was that less than a hundred heartbeats of time had elapsed since the Parthian sentry had shouted the alarm, which meant that his Centurions were outdoing themselves in getting organized. The ambient light by this point was sufficient that, as he had suspected, it allowed Pullus to at least see the slight gap between his First and Balbus' Second, and that they were more or less settled into formation, although there was still a ripple of movement. Looking past the Second, however, was still fruitless, but there was no more time to waste. Better to attack now with what I have, Pullus decided, if only to keep those bastards, whoever they are, from getting organized.

Consequently, rather than have Valerius sound the notes, which would take a fraction longer, Pullus filled his lungs and bellowed, "First Cohort! Advance!"

It was ragged, certainly, but the men of the First, at least those who were in a position to do so, stepped forward, while those men who had been scouts immediately retreated a few paces to integrate themselves into their normal spots in their respective formation. Behind Pullus and on the opposite side of the formation, his Optio, Numerius Lutatius, was snapping at a couple of men of the Century who weren't aligned with the rest of the formation to his satisfaction, while behind him, the Fourth Century under the command of Gnaeus Celadus was taking advantage of the space provided by the advancing first line to assemble directly behind their First Century. Up front, Pullus could see what had been indiscriminate motion coalesce into tangible shapes of men, as the Parthians nearest the advancing Romans tried to gain some semblance of organization. Between the shortened distance and the growing light, Pullus was able to discern the outline of the rectangular, leather-covered wicker shields used by the Parthian infantry, telling him the nature of this unexpected threat.

"Cohort, halt!" Without taking his eyes off the hastily assembled line of the enemy, Pullus counted on the distinctive sound caused by his men crashing to a halt before he shouted, "Prepare javelins!"

Again, the Primus Pilus counted on the sounds that his experienced ears told him were his men thrusting their left foot forward while leaning back, their right arms pulled back as far behind their ears as they could stretch and pointing the hardened metal tip towards the sky. In the fraction of time between his commands, he heard Balbus' voice repeating his command, then the faint cry of whom he assumed to be Laetus on the far side doing the same. Even in the space of time, as short as it was, between the preparatory command and the one he was about to issue, more Parthians had scrambled to join what was still a woefully thin line that was the only thing standing between the 10th and what was still little more than a disorganized mob of Parthians, most of whom were still trying to understand exactly what was happening. Good, Pullus thought, that's just more of you to kill.

"Release!"

In a movement that looked like a rippling wave, the First, Second, then Third Centuries hurled their deadly missiles, and even with all the other shouts and noise coming from the Parthian mass, Pullus and his men distinctly heard the moan of fear from the target of this volley, but it was instantly drowned out by the racket caused by the javelins punching down from the sky to smash into shields and bodies. Even before the screams of those who had either misjudged the arc of the javelin that posed the greatest threat to them, or simply had too many Romans pick him as a target, Pullus was giving the preparatory command for the second volley.

"Release!"

What had been a steadily growing line of Parthian infantry coalescing into a somewhat organized resistance was wiped out in the space of time it took for two volleys of javelins to strike,turned into a heaped ruin of stricken men, their shields and bodies studded with the ash shafts used by Romans for their javelins. Not taking the time to savor the elimination of this fragile buffer protecting their comrades, Pullus, his sword already out, waved it over his head.

"Now, boys! Follow me! *Porro!*"

Even before he finished the order to charge, his voice was drowned out by the roaring answer of his men, as they went dashing forward, behind their Primus Pilus, as intent on creating havoc with their enemy as Pullus was. By virtue of his longer legs, and his status as Primus Pilus, Pullus was the first to reach the remnants of the shattered Parthian line, where less than a half-dozen men were still standing, and only two of them still had their shields intact and whole. While Pullus would never know it, the Parthian he had selected as his first target was the youth Artostes, who had managed to survive both volleys without his body or shield pierced. His former partner on sentry duty, Gaspar, had not been as fortunate, and it was his transfixed body, lying at his feet, that Artostes couldn't seem to tear his eyes away from, at least not until the last instant of his life when the huge Roman, the biggest man the boy had ever or would ever see, came hurdling over the corpses of Artostes' comrades. Only looking up then, Artostes' eyes met the Roman's, and he had an instant to understand that there would be no mercy coming from this giant, whose mouth was fixed in what could only be described as a snarl and whose eyes were mere slits. It was the sword, pulled back at shoulder height, that a part of Artostes' mind noticed was made of a darker metal than those he had seen before and caught the growing light in such a way that he even noticed the swirling patterns of the blade that, with a motion so ridiculously slow Artostes was surprised that he seemed unable to simply step aside and avoid, went plunging into his chest, while the boy could only stare dumbly down and watch as it took his life. Oddly, he didn't feel much pain, at least until, with a savage twist, the giant yanked the blade from the hard breastbone, but even then when he opened his mouth to scream, all he heard was a queer, gurgling sound as his mouth filled with a thick liquid that tasted salty and like copper all at the same time. He was still aware enough to feel his legs collapse as he toppled to the ground and landed on his side, while the giant Roman didn't even pause as he hurdled over Artostes. The last thing the youth saw, in one of those ironies of battle, was the face of Gaspar, whose own eyes were open but had gone dull in death; Artostes joined the veteran no more than a heartbeat later.

Battle on the Ridge

Chapter Five

"Your Highness! Please wake up! Something's happened!"

Pacorus, who had only really been dozing, came fully awake instantly, swinging his feet to the carpet and standing erect.

"What? What is it?" he demanded of his slave, a man he had known all his life.

"One of your generals is here, Highness," the slave explained, "and he says that there's something happening on top of the ridge!"

"Something happening?" Pacorus repeated, more to buy himself some time as he tried to think through the possible meanings.

He was about to snap at the slave but realized not only would it do any good, it would waste time, so instead, he grabbed a silk robe, wrapping himself in it as he strode past the slave and left the chamber that had been designated his private bedroom. Standing a few paces away in the next room was one of his generals; that it was also one of his relatives who had objected wasn't lost on the prince.

"Yes, Kambyses?" His tone was abrupt, but he frankly didn't care about the elaborate courtesies that were part of everyday life in the Parthian court; at least, not right now. "What's happening?"

That Kambyses hesitated only deepened Pacorus' sense of foreboding, as the older man finally answered, "Frankly, Highness, we don't know with any certainty. All we do know is that, judging from the noise, there's a battle going on."

"A battle?" Pacorus shook his head in equal measures of shock and disbelief. "But how? Why didn't the sentries along the river raise the alarm?"

"We don't know, Highness," Kambyses admitted frankly, yet there was an undertone of rebuke as he reminded the young prince, "but it doesn't matter right now. Does it?"

Pacorus felt the heat rush to his face, but he managed to quell the urge to put this general in his place, relative or not.

"No," he admitted grudgingly. "No, it doesn't."

Turning to his slave, he snapped his fingers and snapped an order to the man to bring his armor. While he waited, he turned his attention back to Kambyses, studying the older man's face for a moment. Yes, the man was a thorn in his side; he was also one of the most experienced generals under his command and had been under Surena's command against Crassus, distinguishing himself.

With this in mind, he found himself asking, "So what do you think is happening?"

To his credit, Kambyses didn't hesitate. "I think at least a Legion of Romans managed to find a way to get past our defenses and are trying to take the ridge."

While this had been Pacorus' first inclination, his stomach still twisted in knots, and he sought reassurance from Kambyses about the man commanding the Parthian infantry.

"Do you think Sosimenes is up to the task?"

Kambyses considered for a moment, then said carefully, "I don't know that much about Sosimenes, Highness. He's....untested."

Pacorus sighed, knowing this was nothing but the truth. There was no prestige in commanding the infantry of Parthia, so it inevitably devolved onto the most junior among the nobility, usually a second or even third son of a *satrap*. He supposed it was possible that this Sosimenes, who he had only spoken to on a couple occasions, was made of the right stuff, but there was only one way they would know. By this time, the slave had returned, puffing slightly from the effort of carrying the heavy armor, consisting of lamellar plates of metal, sewn onto a heavy leather vest so closely together that the spaces between each were less than the thickness of a fingernail. Aided by the slave, Pacorus pulled on the armor, strapped on his sword, then took the closed iron helmet with the nose and cheek pieces that protected most of the face.

Ready, he didn't wait for Kambyses, sweeping past him while saying, "Let's go find out what's happening."

What was happening atop the ridge was the slaughter of most of his infantry, at least those men who stood and fought. After the initial attack by the First Cohort, the subject of the conversation between Pacorus and Kambyses, Sosimenes had managed to array his men in a formation that lay athwart the ridge from north to south, with enough time for the ranks to run six and more men deep. And, since the Parthians were armed with spears, there was a brief period where their longer reach forced the Romans to stop their headlong charge and get themselves better organized as well. Unfortunately for Sosimenes and his men, the spot the young Parthian noble had chosen to make his stand was a sign of his inexperience because it subsequently allowed

Pullus to bring more of his Legion to bear. It was true that it would have been extremely difficult to make his men align themselves farther east on the top of the ridge, since it meant they were closer to the charging Romans, yet it had been the best of the bad choices available to Sosimenes. Instead, by falling back to the west for some breathing room, he was on the broadest, flattest part of the ridge, almost a full mile across, giving Pullus more than enough room to bring his entire Legion in a single line of Cohorts, but with a three-Century front, thereby giving him a second line. By the time Sosimenes had made his disposition, the sun was almost completely above the horizon, which as Pullus had understood when Caesar laid out his plan for the 10th's attack, meant that the blazing orb was another ally. Forced as they were to squint into the sun, once the rest of the Legion was in position, those Cohorts that hadn't expended their supply of javelins released their volleys high into the sky, forcing the men of the first two or three ranks of their enemy to try and spot the streaking missiles against the backdrop of a blazing sun. Not surprisingly, even more havoc than usual was wreaked on the leading ranks of the Parthian formation, and since they were facing one of the most experienced Legions in the 10th, whose Centurions knew how devastating the period immediately after javelin volleys were, they weren't given any time to regain their cohesion or recover their collective wits before the Romans slammed into them. After that, it was not much more than wholesale slaughter; only the men of the rearmost two ranks survived intact, at least from the Roman onslaught, but that was only because they turned and ran. However, a few hundred panic-stricken men, those to the left of the formation, putting them on the northern side of the ridge, forgot about the sheer drop-off, and while not all of them who went sprinting off the edge of the precipice, which was about twenty feet high, died, many of them did, while those who survived didn't escape without broken bones. By the time the sun had fully risen and there was a finger's width between it and the eastern horizon, the 10th was in possession of the ridgetop, whereupon Pullus immediately set men to building a fire, using the spear shafts and wicker shields of the Parthian fallen. This was the prearranged signal to Caesar that the first part of his plan was fulfilled and set the second phase into motion. Meanwhile, Pullus was absorbed in the normal tasks of a Primus Pilus immediately after a battle, even a victory as one-sided as this. His Pili Priores were gathered around him, each giving him their own butcher's bill, and the news couldn't have been better.

Once they were all tallied, it took Pullus a moment to absorb, and he shook his head, asking nobody in particular, "We didn't have one man killed? Not one? How can that be?"

"Because we're that good," Metellus spoke up, but while the words could have been considered boastful, his tone was matter-of-fact, just a simple recognition of a reality forged by rivers of blood of both friend and foe.

"That we are," Scribonius agreed, but then turned to more practical matters. "But what now?"

"Now," Pullus replied, informing his officers for the first time the second part of Caesar's plan. "We wait for Caesar. Or," he turned and stared down the southern slope at the boiling activity in the Parthian camp, "we wait for them."

"So how do you want us to shake out?" Scribonius pressed, using the slang term used by the Legions for deployment.

Pullus considered for a moment; this was a detail that Caesar had left up to Pullus' discretion, trusting his best Primus Pilus to determine the proper course once he had the advantage of the height of the ridge so that he could see all of the Parthian positions.

"It looks like they're trying to decide." He pointed down to a small knot of horsemen in the southern camp, distinguishable as the likely commander by the huge, flowing standard carried by a mounted man on the outer edge of the group. "But if I were them, I'd get the fuck out of here and live to fight another day. We've already given them a bloody nose. Although," Pullus acknowledged, "from what we've heard, they don't really think much of their infantry. So they might not think it's much of a loss. In fact," he considered, "they might actually think we did them a favor giving them less mouths to feed."

"And they can move faster now," Scribonius pointed out, which the others instantly accepted as a possibility. Pointing down at the Parthian camp, he added, "But it doesn't look like they're considering it."

Pullus, who had turned his back on the camp to survey the ridgetop with a thoughtful gaze, returned his attention and saw that Scribonius had been right; there was a mass of movement, truly enough, but not of tents being struck, but rows of mounted men forming up. At least, that was what he assumed because, fairly quickly, the dust raised by thousands of hooves obscured the scene. It was the dust that gave him an idea.

"They can't see us right now any more than we can see them." His tone went from thoughtful to urgent as he turned and gestured to one of his Centurions, the man with one eye that Pullus trusted implicitly. "Cyclops, I want you to double-time your Cohort, back along the ridge to the east."

If his Octus Pilus Prior was surprised, he didn't show it, although he rarely showed much emotion either way. But once Pullus explained what he wanted, his weathered features creased into what was a wolfish smile.

Saluting, Cyclops simply replied, "I understand, Primus Pilus, and I will obey."

Then, not wanting to waste any time, he spun about, bawling for the other Centurions of the Eighth Cohort. There was a lot for his boys to do and not much time to do it, but Cyclops understood how devastating a surprise this could be in the event these Parthians were stupid enough to try and knock them off the ridge. While Cyclops hurried off, Pullus and the rest of the Centurions remained as the Primus Pilus tried to decide what to do next. Before he could get any further with his instructions, the booming notes of a *cornu* came rolling across the ridge, relayed by Valerius, the First's *cornicen* who was still positioned closer to the northern edge of the ridge, along with Balbus and the rest of the First.

"Caesar and the rest of the boys have started their advance," Pullus remarked, needlessly, since every other Centurion knew the call as well as he did. "Which means we need to get in place."

"And?" Scribonius asked him gently. "You never got around to telling the rest of us where you want us."

Normally, Pullus didn't react well to rebukes, no matter how gentle, but it was different with Scribonius, both because he had a way of saying things that made it difficult to take offense, and he was inevitably right in bringing whatever it was up for consideration.

"Right," Pullus muttered, eyes narrowed in thought. He then pointed with his *vitus*. "All right. Scribonius, I want you to replace the First on the northern edge. I want my boys on this side since I think it's the most likely spot. But," he pointed in a different direction than would have been the normal spot, "I'm putting the First on the left instead of the right, nearest to the dip." Sweeping his *vitus* to the right, back in a westerly direction, he continued, "The Third is going to be next to us, while the Fifth is going to be next to the Third."

"Ah." Scribonius understood immediately. "You want the odds on the south and the evens on the north."

128

Although this was exactly what Pullus had in mind, he was still a bit nettled that his friend discerned his intent so easily, which prompted him to growl, "Not completely! If you'd wait, you'd know what I want."

"You're right, of course," Scribonius replied placidly, long accustomed to these little fits of temper by his friend. "Forgive me, Primus Pilus."

Pullus glared at Scribonius, knowing full well that his friend wasn't really asking his pardon as much as continuing to needle him, but there were more pressing matters.

"Right." He turned back to the east and pointed. "While you're right about that part, I don't want all of us there. I already sent the Eighth in that direction, but I want you, Glaxus, and your boys directly across from the Eighth. And," he added meaningfully, "you need to do the same thing as the Eighth and scrounge up all the javelins you can."

Marcus Glaxus, the Nones Pilus Prior, had once been Pullus' Optio, replaced by Lutatius when he was promoted. He saluted and began to move, but then was stopped when Pullus called to him again.

"While you're at it, pick up some of the Parthian spears as well." He shrugged and added, "You never know when they might come in handy."

The rest of Caesar's army arrayed itself as quickly as a force its size could manage, their deployment complicated by the fording of the Tigris to the eastern bank. Leaving his cavalry on the opposite side from the Legions, Caesar placed his auxiliaries on the same side as the cavalry, giving them the task of guarding both the Legion camp and their own. This, the Dictator had decided, would be a day for the Legions, and perhaps the cavalry. By choosing a static defense, the Parthian commander, whose identity Caesar still didn't know, had actually done Caesar and his men a favor, because it allowed the Romans to use their most potent weapon, the heavy infantry of the Legions. Still, even as experienced as the Legions under his command were, and as smoothly as they moved into their assigned spots, it still took well more than a third of a watch before they were even arrayed in the *acies triplex* that, while it had been used by Roman generals before, Caesar had made world famous. Only then did they begin their advance, marching at a steady pace that, when viewed from a spot like Pullus' vantage point, never failed to arouse an observer's emotions. Watching the ordered lines, maintaining as near as possible to perfect alignment as the thousands of men marched in step, their shields carried before them, was either met with an almost overwhelming fear, or in Pullus and the 10th's case, a swelling pride at this tangible demonstration of the might of Rome. And, as removed from the scene as they were, it appeared to Pullus and his men that this precision was happening without any real effort; the truth, they all understood, was vastly different. Down there on the plain, Centurions were shouting, Optios were cursing, and men were alternating between encouraging and chastising each other, all with the common goal of achieving this level of order and discipline.

Down below the ridge, just behind the trench, were the remnants of the Parthian infantry, those men who had chosen flight over death, but as they watched their foes slowly but inexorably close the distance between them, they all understood their reprieve had been temporary. Those troops that had been billeted in the town, composed of mostly the horse archers, had filled the streets of the village, hurriedly mounting now that it was clear that the Roman attack had begun in earnest. Too far removed to make out any detail, they nonetheless had heard the bare bones of the disaster up on the ridge, and more than one man among them glanced nervously at the tiny figures lining the northern face of the ridge, just above the precipice that extended for more than a quarter mile to the east. They argued among themselves about what lay in their immediate future, whether they would be expected to drive their mounts up the flank of the ridge and try to dislodge the Romans up there by launching waves of arrows, or move the relatively short distance, using the gap between the trenches, and, in effect, turn their backs to the Romans above, with the original intention of raining their missiles down on the main body of Romans, who would be slowed by the river and then the slope. However, there was more than one man among them who fervently, if silently, prayed for a third option, and that was the shrill, ululating call of the Parthian version of the *cornu*, sounding the command to make a hasty retreat and fight another day. Regardless of those feelings, that if any of them had possessed the courage to utter aloud, they would have discovered that their sentiment was shared by most of his comrades, that call never came. Instead, a small cluster of more heavily armored men, signifying their status as not only nobility but as officers commanding, came galloping into view around the curve of the ridge from the south where the main camp was located. The noble who was in command of this band of archers, some five thousand total, was unmoved, and apparently unimpressed from the sight to the right front, now a bit more than a mile away. Finding the equivalent of the Centurion of these archers, he wasted no time excoriating him for not having his men moving out of the village already, insisting they move into the positions selected for them by the prince. While they obeyed, it was in almost total silence, with none of the eagerness or banter that indicated they were looking forward to the coming fight, instead resigning themselves to whatever fate their gods had assigned for them this day.

If these men had been informed about what was taking place in the southern camp, it might have made them feel better, or worse, depending on the individual. Surrounded by his generals was Pacorus, who not only felt trapped in a physical sense, but in the most important way, as if his ability to choose was taken away from him.

"What do you suppose your father would say if we were to run away with our tails between our legs, like whipped dogs?"

Pacorus opened his mouth to answer Cyaxares, the general who had posed the question with a sneer, but before he could answer, Kambyses interrupted, his voice no less harsh. "He'd say that compared to the alternative, the prince exercised wisdom in choosing to disengage from a battle he's not likely to win. Or," Kambyses held up a mailed glove to cut Cyaxares off, which clearly infuriated the other man, "even if he did win, it would be at such a cost that every *satrapy* in Parthia would be in mourning for years to come!"

"Pah," Cyaxares snorted dismissively. "Spoken like an old man! No," he insisted, no less emphatic than Kambyses. "They'd be in mourning because of the shame brought by skulking away! It's a slur on our honor that will never be forgotten!"

Finally, Pacorus could take no more, and he snapped, "Enough! Both of you!" Glaring first at one, then the other, his voice softened fractionally as he continued, "I need you to be quiet so I can think."

For the first and only time, his two most senior generals were in agreement, but it was Kambyses who spoke for the both of them. "Highness, the one thing we don't have is time. You must decide now, before it's too late and the decision is made for you." He thrust his mailed hand out, pointing in a northerly direction as he added dramatically, "By our enemy."

Pacorus, despite bridling at the tone, knew that the words were true and couldn't be ignored. What would his father want him to do? he wondered as, for the first time, he began feeling the tendrils of desperation and fear, *real* fear reaching out to try and grasp him in an embrace that would paralyze him. Then, a thought came to his mind that spurred him to make his decision, and while this one was about his family, it wasn't his father whose face he saw in his mind. If I don't attack, how will Phraates use this to poison our father's mind against me? It didn't take much imagination for Pacorus to conjure up a vivid idea of the kinds of things his accursed sibling would whisper. Never directly; no, that wasn't Phraates' way, but there were more than enough men in Orodes' court who were willing to take his brother's gold in the hopes of coming out on the winning side in a struggle that was sure to come. For the sons of Orodes, it was never far from their minds that their father had slain his brother, Mithridates, who had deposed Orodes and forced him to flee. It had been none other than Surena, the same general who was the architect of Crassus' defeat, who returned Pacorus' father to the throne, and while Orodes hadn't swung the sword, it had been at Orodes' behest that his brother died. The fact that this was the excuse Orodes had used to order Surena himself executed was also never far from Pacorus' mind, but he had always been close with his father, something that Phraates well knew, and was just one cause of his hatred towards Pacorus. No, he thought, I can't hand Phraates that kind of dagger to plunge into my back.

Outwardly calm, he finally broke the short silence, saying, "We stay and fight." Turning to Kambyses, he said softly, "I understand your concerns, Kambyses. But I can't afford to run. So," he pulled himself erect, trying to exude the air of a confident commander for whom there was no doubt about the outcome, "this is what we're going to do."

It was Caesar's cavalry who drew and shed first blood. During the point where Caesar's men were most vulnerable, crossing the little river, Aulus Ventidius, the Legate who'd replaced Lepidus, who was now toiling as quartermaster and without a combat command, led his men in a sweeping attack that saw them thundering through the village. Accompanying Ventidius, as an aide, was young Octavian, who hadn't been terribly enthusiastic about the assignment his uncle had given him.

"I'm not a great horseman," he had complained to Caesar, but while the general was secretly amused, he wasn't willing to yield.

"You need to be experienced with all forms of command, nephew," he told Octavian in a tone that told the younger man there was no point in arguing. "And I don't think the cavalry is going to be heavily engaged. All they have to do is keep part of the Parthian army occupied while I move the Legions into position."

Now Octavian found himself gripping his saddle with one hand, surrounded by whooping, smelly barbarians, all of them eager to finally have the chance to engage with the hated, elusive archers on ground where the Parthians' superior mobility was negated by the natural barrier of the ridge, and the artificial ones of their own making. Boiling out of the southern end of the town, while the youngster wasn't at the very rear of what had quickly become just a rolling mass of flesh, both horse and man, he was sufficiently far enough back so that he couldn't see much more than the hindquarters of the horses directly in front of him. That was an annoyance, but very quickly, he felt the tightness in his chest that he had learned was the first sign of one of his wheezing attacks. Fighting the panic that was as debilitating as the ailment itself, he frantically yanked the reins of his horse, instantly dropping backward through the rest of the cavalry. Because of the dust and confusion, nobody noticed his sudden slowing, so that in the span of just a few heartbeats, he found himself alone at the southern edge of the village, whereupon he slowed to a stop. It was still dusty, but not as bad, and it gave him the advantage of being able to watch events unfold, as Ventidius and the leading edge of his troopers entered the Tigris River in a fantastic spray of muddy water, slowing slightly from the extra resistance. Because of their angle of attack, they actually had to cross both rivers, but there was about a half-mile of ground between the two, and Octavian saw that some of the bolder of the Parthian horse archers had crossed the small river to meet Ventidius' men on this small patch of ground. He could just barely hear the shouting of the cavalry; because of the distance, he actually saw what appeared to be tiny slivers arcing through the air to land in the midst of Ventidius' men but didn't actually hear the shrill screams of what he assumed were horses for another couple of heartbeats. It was a decidedly odd sensation, seeing men and beast suffering first, before hearing what was the epilogue to their lives, in the form of those last shouts of despair or calls for the gods' intercession. His breathing became easier and, for a moment, he considered resuming and hurrying to catch up with his commander, but decided he could learn just as much by observing from this spot as he could right in the middle of the fighting. After all, he reasoned to himself, this way, I'm out of the choking, blinding dust and can see more clearly what's going on. So, he sat his horse, watching the opening of Caesar's part of the battle.

It didn't take more than the span of a hundred heartbeats for the Parthian archers to recognize that, as Caesar had seen, they were essentially caught in a trap of their own making. If they didn't try and stop the cavalry and instead concentrated on loosing their arrows at the Roman Legions that were even then wading across the small river, they'd only manage three or four volleys before the cavalry came sweeping in from their left flank. However, effectively turning about and facing the cavalry to beat back their sortie that came thrusting up in the gap between the two trenches meant that they would expose their backs to the Roman infantry. That this was the case was the result of another decision made by Caesar in the pre-dawn as his men were preparing themselves. While his initial intent was to seemingly take the bait his adversary had dangled, in the form of that gap, counting on the 10th being where they were supposed to be, atop the ridge, after thinking about it, he changed the point of attack for his infantry. His reasoning was based on two aspects—one fairly straightforward, the other an example of the kind of insight Caesar had into the minds of other men, and subsequently, the best way to exploit any weakness on their part. Originally, he had decided not to use his cavalry, wanting to hold it in reserve, fresh and ready to exploit a breakthrough or in the event that, as Caesar hoped, the Parthian army was shattered. As formidable as cataphracts were, most of their power came from being in tightly grouped formations, where they relied on the sheer weight and mass of heavily armored horses and men. But it was because of that extra weight that the effective range of a cataphract at full speed was significantly shorter than his cavalry, and when they were fleeing, they were just as vulnerable to being run down from behind as a fleeing man on foot.

Still, it was ultimately the second factor that served to actually change Caesar's mind, and that was the shattering effect on Parthian morale that would result from the sight of his men negotiating that ditch, delayed a fraction of the time that he felt certain the Parthian commander had assumed it would take. Caesar also held little doubt that the commander had been assuring his men that, with these two ditches, the Romans would be forced to behave in a manner that allowed the Parthians to use their own capabilities to their fullest. Watching as the hated Romans marched up to the ditch and threw in the filled bags of forage and bundles of firewood that had been brought as part of the supply train, then essentially march across would be a shattering sight, he didn't doubt. The force of archers, now faced with these two choices, behaved in exactly the way Caesar had hoped, with confusion and indecision as whoever commanded them seemed to decide his best tactic was to face the cavalry, then either reconsidered, or some of his men became concerned at the sight of the Legions approaching the ditch. There was one extra benefit that Caesar hadn't foreseen; that with the incursion of his cavalry across the small river and onto the open ground that was supposed to be a killing ground for the Parthians, the archers didn't have their accustomed amount of room to maneuver and were unable to gallop in the large, looping circles that made them such difficult targets. The only space they were being allowed was too steep to be of any practical use, and robbed of yet another accustomed advantage, the confusion and disorganization that had begun with the appearance of Ventidius only deepened. Caesar sat astride Toes, just behind the first line of Legions who were now at the ditch, working together as the bags and hurdles were passed forward from the rear, where the men of the second line were carrying them. Now, Caesar thought with satisfaction as he watched his plan unfold, all that remains are the cataphracts.

"We're splitting the cataphracts," Pacorus ordered, "into two groups of ten thousand apiece."

Like Caesar, mounted astride his horse but facing the southern slope of the ridge instead of the northern like Caesar, he gestured to his left, indicating the shoulder of the western end of the ridge.

"We're going to send half of them around to the west." The prince turned and pointed to the low saddle midway down the ridge to the east. "While the rest we're going to send the original way." Turning to the pair of his generals who would be commanding the two contingents, he tried to sound confident as he said, "We're going to crush the Romans in between the two jaws."

Once more, the pair temporarily forgot their differences, exchanging a troubled glance, except this time, it wasn't Kambyses but Cyaxares who spoke for the both of them.

"Highness," he spoke carefully, aware that he had already aroused the ire of the younger man, "while I can see the wisdom of attacking from both sides, that only holds true under certain conditions." Hesitating, he decided to simply point up the ridge at where the Romans arrayed on the southern edge of the ridgetop could be seen in their neat, ordered lines. "What about them?" Suddenly, he thought he understood Pacorus' intent and shook his head, assuring his lord, "If you plan on pinning them down with our archers, the slope's too steep for them to get close enough without killing their horses. At least, for more than a couple volleys."

Pacorus listened politely but didn't seem in the least bit upset at being questioned, actually smiling slightly as Cyaxares spoke.

When the general was finished, Pacorus didn't hesitate in his reply. "No, I don't plan on using the archers. At least," he amended, "most of them. I do plan on using a thousand of them as part of what I have in mind."

"Which is?" Kambyses was growing impatient; the prince's seeming placidity only irritated him more.

"Which is," Pacorus' calm demeanor was calculated, partly because he could see how agitated it made Kambyses, who the prince was beginning to think either had ideas above his station, or more troublingly, had been given secret instructions by his father Orodes, "that I'm going to deal with the Romans on the top of the ridge." He took a breath, knowing what was likely to come next as he finished, "With my bodyguard."

For a brief moment, Pacorus thought he might not have to endure a tirade, but the silence of the other two men was more because they were too shocked to speak. Then, seemingly recovering their wits at the same time, both began speaking.

"You can't do that! That's not enough men to face a Legion!"

"Your Highness, you can't take a risk like that! You're the king's heir!"

Pacorus did listen for several more moments as each man gave his own list of reasons why this was a terrible idea. When they paused to take a breath, only then did he answer.

"While I appreciate your concern," he tried to keep his voice from reflecting his doubt about their sincerity, "I've actually thought this through. No, I can't hope to defeat a Legion with a thousand cataphracts. But these men aren't just any cataphracts, as I'm sure you know. They're all direct descendants of The Immortals," he didn't need to expand on the reference, "and my plan is to keep the Romans up there occupied, just long enough for our main forces to crack the main attack. Then," he smiled, "you'll both have the honor of coming to save your prince from the mess he's gotten himself into. And," he added, knowing that ultimately this would mean the most, "rest assured I'll let my father know that's the case."

Neither man spoke; they both could see that their prince was determined to go through with his plan. And, while neither of them would ever openly acknowledge it, the idea of royal favor was enough to quell any further objections, something that Pacorus understood perfectly well. Seeing their silent acquiescence, the prince went on to give more explicit instructions about what he expected, including the signal he planned on using should he and his bodyguard need help extricating themselves from the Romans occupying the top of the ridge. While Pacorus was set on this course of action, if he had been informed of the identity of the Legion awaiting them, which was in its own way as famed, and feared, as their commanding general, while he might not have altered his plan, he definitely would have seriously considered doing so. Now, however, his destiny was in the hands of fate.

"Here they come!"

The call, alerting the men of the 10th that there was finally movement out of the main Parthian camp, originated from the Cohorts arrayed along the southern edge of the ridgetop, which meant that the information had to be relayed across the width of the ridge. Pullus had opted to arrange his men along the northern and southern edges of the ridge, with his southern disposition at a point closest to where the ridge curved to the west, where it fell steeply away down to the Tigris. While the Primus Pilus wasn't overly concerned that the Parthians would attempt to ascend the western shoulder of the ridge with the river to their back, which was a bit more than a quarter mile away from the ridgetop, he had spotted a shallow depression that carried runoff from the sudden storms that were part of the weather of this region. When he examined it, he judged that it was too steep for men on horseback, but a determined group of men on foot could assail his position from that direction. Based on what he and the men had just experienced in brushing the Parthian infantry off the ridge, Pullus decided that just two Centuries would suffice to guard this unlikely approach. On the southern side, he had taken advantage of the precipice that crowned the ridge along its southwest edge for a distance of perhaps three furlongs to the east, only deploying his Cohort, along with the other odd-numbered ones, in a line extending from this point to just short of where the saddle was located, right where the ridge began to dip. He had left Balbus in command of this part of the Legion, deciding that his best course was to station himself, along with Valerius, his

137

aquilifer Paterculus, and two men he had designated as runners for him. What was slightly unusual was not the runners themselves, but that only one of them was the man he normally used from his own Century; the identity of the other was an example of the small but important ways Pullus tried to shield his nephew from harm, at least as much as possible without it being blatantly obvious to the other men. Not that Gaius Porcinus appreciated the gesture; however, he also knew his uncle well, and understood by his expression when he had come to the First of the Second and called his name that in this he wouldn't be swayed. Consequently, perhaps the most apt description of Porcinus' state of mind was that he was resigned to spend what was going to be an eventful day running back and forth. Part of his irritation was that, by virtue of their position on the higher ground, the 10th had been able to be little more than spectators as they watched the rest of their comrades come marching up, while the cavalry had made its attack.

The Centurions had given the men leave to sit, and although they had marched in light order, with only their weapons and canteens, being the veterans they were, most of them had secreted a small portion of their rations somewhere on their person; inside their tunic, where it was trapped by the *baltea* was the most common, and now it was something of a festival as they sat munching their food and watching all that was taking place below, and they wouldn't have been Legionaries worthy of the name if there hadn't been spirited wagering going on about what was taking place below. Ventidius and his cavalry, forced to labor slightly up the slope in between the gap of the trenches that somewhat slowed the impetus of their charge, had still managed to inflict a fair number of casualties on the swarm of horse archers that had, to this point, been the only force to meet them, although whoever commanded the remaining Parthian infantry who had, in the lack of other orders, had streamed down to their former position at the trench, albeit with half the number with which they had marched up the ridge, were relatively nearby. Ventidius' thrust wasn't without cost; there was a scattering of men among the wounded and dead lying on the slope who were dressed in the garb of Germans or Gauls, but they were relatively scarce, especially when compared to their foes. Despite the Parthian archer commander's original intent of driving the cavalry off with the storm of arrows, Ventidius' force had steadily driven those on the northern slope farther east until they were now roughly behind the trench the Parthians had dug along the small river. However in their near-panic and haste to do so, the retreating

138

archers had shattered the thin line of spearmen, numbering perhaps a thousand whose commander at least had the presence of mind to try and array his men in a line blocking the Roman cavalry, but who became little more than fodder for the reddened long cavalry swords of Ventidius' Gauls and Germans after being shattered by the retreating archers. Meanwhile, the remnants of the Parthian infantry, standing on the heaped earthen ramparts that, even from where Pullus' men were, they could see hadn't been smoothed or tamped down, provided little resistance to the bulk of the Legions that had already crossed the trench. With a speed that was only surprising to the Parthians themselves, the Legionaries down below had worked together, relaying the bags and sticks that were dumped into the trench to serve as makeshift bridges across it.

As Porcinus had been able to observe, before his uncle had come to fetch him, the real thing slowing down the Legions crossing the trench weren't the Parthians, but the fact that there were only two such passageways per Legion, creating a bit of a funnel. This was Gaius Porcinus' first campaign, yet he didn't need to be a veteran to see that, if the Parthian horse archers hadn't been otherwise occupied, they could have easily dismounted and, from behind the protection of the earthen rampart, they could have merely aimed for the general area around each of the makeshift crossings and be assured of hitting something other than dirt. Instead, while they were battling for their collective lives, the only barrier to the men commanded by Caesar were perhaps a shade less than four thousand men whose morale had already been shattered when they had been driven from their spot on the ridge. In yet another error made by a young Parthian prince, who had the right general idea, but without the experience, or the correct mindset to create an effective defense, not only was the earthen barrier not correctly shaped and packed down, the spoil had actually been set too far back from the edge of the trench, thereby allowing men to cross the ditch and have space to gather at the base of the barrier. With just one volley of javelins, any spearman in the area around the makeshift bridges was either struck down or found his wicker shield rendered useless, leaving him with only a spear and little else to defend himself as Legionaries clambered up the crumbling dirt slope; indeed, the footing quickly proved to be a bigger hazard than the Parthians themselves. This was something Porcinus wouldn't be able to watch, but he wisely didn't make any comment that might inform his uncle of his discontent, since at moments such as this, as Porcinus had learned, Titus Pullus was a Primus Pilus first and an uncle second. Once Pullus retrieved his nephew, he reached the spot of his makeshift command post, curtly ordering Porcinus to stay there with the others while he went trotting off again, this time in the direction of the southern side.

"I wonder how many miles he's going to end up running before this is all over?" Porcinus wondered aloud.

He jerked, startled when Paterculus laughed; he hadn't been aware he had verbalized this thought, but the *aquilifer* replied, "At least five miles, but don't worry. Your uncle can handle it."

Oh, I know that—Porcinus did manage to keep this contained inside his head—I just wonder what that means for me? He couldn't say he was scared, exactly—nervous, certainly—but he had participated in the skirmish with the archers, although he wouldn't have characterized it as such, at least not until he was assured that this was exactly what that day had been; a minor clash, earning little more than a line in the Legion diary. No, he decided; he wasn't frightened of whatever fighting lay ahead, but in the prospect of letting his uncle down and not fulfilling his duty in a way that Pullus would find acceptable. Little did Gaius Porcinus know that he was hardly alone in this sentiment among his comrades in the Legion, although his was certainly more personal.

Standing next to Metellus, Pullus shaded his eyes with one hand as he watched the Parthians below, south of the ridge, split themselves into two groups, with one exiting their camp and moving to Pullus' left, and the other the opposite direction.

"Looks like they plan on using the saddle and coming around the western end of the ridge," Metellus commented, then glanced over at Pullus. "Did you expect them to do that, Primus Pilus?"

"No," Pullus admitted, shaking his head while he searched for the largest of the Parthian standards, which he felt certain would belong to the commander. "I thought they'd want to mass their cataphracts together and just come up through the saddle together." He shrugged, not particularly concerned. "But they're still going to have to come at us through the saddle because the western slope is too steep for them to come up from that direction." Even as he said this, his mind was recalling the sight of that depression he had noticed at the western end of the ridge, and he felt the first stirring of unease. "At least," he admitted, "I think it is."

Not surprisingly, this got Metellus' attention, and he turned and examined Pullus' face to see if his Primus Pilus was truly concerned about this possible oversight, or if this was just more idle talk.

Realizing he had alarmed Metellus, Pullus shook his head again and said, "Even if they can get their horses up there, by the time they do, they'll be blown, and we can just reach up and pull them out of the saddle. Remember," he clapped Metellus on the shoulder, "it's the horses that are the most dangerous weapon. The men on them are easy to kill; all you have to do is get past the point of those long lances, then they're just fresh meat."

Metellus was certainly inclined to take his Primus Pilus' word for it, not only because Pullus was his superior, but like every other man in the 10th, he was aware that Pullus was one of the few in the army who had actually faced cataphracts when he had been the *de facto* Primus Pilus of the 6th at the battle of Zela. What Pullus hadn't related to his Centurions when he assured them that the cataphracts could be defeated by men on foot was that their attack had been shattered before the Legions could engage with the cataphracts, and that it had indeed been Caesar's cavalry that had run the fleeing cataphracts down. His reticence was calculated; part of his decision to withhold this bit of information was based in the tactics Caesar had developed for his Legions to use, but more importantly at this moment were the different circumstances due to the terrain, and the disposition of their respective forces by both generals. Pullus stood with Metellus for a few more moments, then moved down the line of the odd-numbered Cohorts, heading in the direction of the saddle. Despite his confidence in the soundness of Caesar's plan and the dispositions he had made with the 10th, which his general had left to Pullus' discretion, the giant Roman was still, if not worried, then concerned. This two-prong attack had been a surprise; Pullus had fully expected the Parthian commander to concentrate his most potent force to form what was ultimately one giant, mailed fist to punch across the saddle to the northern side, then to come smashing into the bulk of the army that, although he couldn't see them, he was sure had breached the obstacle of ditch and earthen wall by this point. The presence of the 10th had obviously changed the Parthian commander's mind, but what nagged at Pullus was the question; what did the Parthian intend to do about the 10th? Their commander had to expect, as they passed through the part of this saddle where the ground rose on both flanks of their advance, that Pullus and his men would do *something* to stop them.

Was the Parthian really that unconcerned about Roman infantry having the high ground above him, even if it was for a relatively short distance? Finally realizing that such speculation at this point was useless, Pullus continued to where he felt sure the most potent thrust of the Parthian counterattack would come, Ordering his Cohort to move from their spot arrayed on an east/west axis, instead he arranged his own Cohort in a line at the top of the rise on the western side of the saddle, turning his Cohort perpendicular between the other odd and even Cohorts. Because of the distance, he had been forced to deploy his Cohort in a single line, so that his Sixth Century's left flank was less than a hundred paces away from the second line of Centuries of his even-numbered Cohorts waiting on the northern side. In its conception, the 10th was forming the same kind of formation that had been used against cavalry for centuries at this point, a huge square box. Where it differed was that Pullus had arranged his forces in such a manner that all sides weren't equal in terms of the strength of the line forming it, since he had decided to keep just two Centuries positioned at the western edge of the box and only his Cohort on the eastern side. Another difference was that not every Cohort was part of this main formation; therein lay the surprise Pullus had prepared for the Parthians, and despite his nervousness about ostensibly weakening his square by their absence, he was reassured when he looked across the saddle to the far eastern side. Even from his vantage point, because the far side of the saddle was slightly higher than where he was standing, and aided by the fact that the opposite slope actually dipped back down, forming a slight bump, he could barely see where Cyclops and his men were lying down, waiting for their signal. When the 10th had first passed through the saddle, prior to their assault on the enemy infantry, it had been too dark to see clearly, so once the sun was up, as Pullus was deciding what to do, he had walked down to the lowest point of the saddle. Studying the eastern side, he had realized then that, even on horseback, the only thing visible was the top of the shallow slope, and that because of the bump, anyone positioned behind it couldn't be seen. Trotting south, he went as far as he dared in the direction from which he expected the Parthians to approach, examining the eastern side of the saddle. As was almost always the case, it wasn't perfect; if he ordered Cyclops to arrange his Cohort in the normal manner, even if they were lying prone on the rocky ground, the Parthians would see the two Centuries that would be the left flank of the Eighth Cohort. Whether it was luck, experience, or divine intervention, the fact that Pullus had taken the extra time to examine the terrain of his position more closely had allowed him to give Cyclops orders that avoided possible detection. Despite his confidence in both himself and Cyclops, the Primus Pilus had an almost overwhelming urge to risk dashing once more to the spot that offered the Parthians the highest chance to detect the trap, but before he could do so, the *cornicen* of the Third signaled that the leading edge of the Parthian formation had begun climbing the slope. Now, Pullus realized, It's in the gods' hands.

Those Parthian archers who survived their attempt to stop Ventidius' attack and hadn't gotten themselves trapped behind the trench had gone galloping along the face of the slope to the west, following the river as it curved around the western shoulder. Meeting the part of the cataphract force under the command of Cyaxares that was advancing from the western end of the ridge, after an understandably short but brutal chastisement of the surviving commanders of the detachment, the surviving horse archers were ordered to regroup.

"You're going to be given one chance to restore your honor," the Parthian general told the three men, each of them in command of a *drafsh* of a thousand men, although all three units were now less than their normal number. "You're going to lead the way, and you're going to order your men to loose faster than they've ever done before."

"But, general," one of the *drafshi* protested, "our mounts are close to foundering. And," he added earnestly, "the men are almost as exhausted!"

Cyaxares didn't reply, at least verbally. Instead, he turned to one of his personal guards, a man with a beard that was almost completely iron gray, with a seamed, hard face and a prominent scar that crossed the bridge of his nose, and gave nothing more than a slight nod. Kicking his horse, the graybeard moved the distance necessary to bring him alongside but facing the opposite direction of the protesting *drafshi*, who looked understandably nervous. Still, he clearly never expected that, without a word being uttered, and with a speed that spoke of many years of experience, the graybeard drew his sword and in one smooth but brutally powerful stroke, decapitated the *drafshi*, whose head went spinning over his mount's head, the shocked expression still on his face, while his corpse sat for the span of a couple more heartbeats, the stump of his neck sending spurts of bright, arterial blood at least a foot in the air before toppling out of the saddle. His mount, trained in war, hadn't reacted to the sudden movement caused by his rider's head tumbling end over end to land with a thud on the ground in front of it, but when it was relieved of its rider's weight, only then did it react, moving quickly forward, one hoof striking its former rider's head to send it rolling a few feet farther away.

"Now," Cyaxares said pleasantly to the two remaining *drafshi*, their expressions identical in their shock and fear, "was there anything else?"

Words came spewing from both of them as they assured the general that they understood perfectly the role they were to play.

Satisfied that he had made his point, Cyaxares instructed them, "I don't need you to do anything more than keep those Roman dogs occupied while we form up in The Fist. As long as we have time to do that, I'll forgive your pathetic performance thus far. Is that understood?"

Once more, the two surviving commanders talked over each other in their haste to let Cyaxares know that they comprehended him perfectly. Listening just long enough for them to get the words out, the Parthian general dismissed them with a disgusted wave, sparing them barely more than a glance as they hurried away to where their men were standing, dismounted, as they tried to rest their horses.

Turning to the graybeard, who had removed the scarf he wore around his neck to clean the blade of his sword, Cyaxares commented, "I wouldn't waste my time cleaning your blade, Khorshed. By the time this day is through, you're just going to have to clean it again."

Despite the example of the slain *drafshi*, Khorshed didn't seem intimidated in the slightest; that he was Cyaxares' kin, and he had been serving Cyaxares since they were both old enough to ride to war, served to endow him with a familiarity that made him shrug and reply, "It's a habit, cousin." Giving the other man a grin that actually made him look even more ferocious because his front teeth on both top and bottom had been knocked out, leaving nothing but fangs visible, "Besides, it's better to kill Romans with a clean blade and not with the blood of one of our own on it."

If there was a rebuke there, Cyaxares chose not to interpret it that way, and he grinned back with a smile that, despite the presence of his teeth, was no less wolfish in nature.

"And it's about time we started, cousin. It's about time we started."

Turning to the Parthian equivalent of a *cornicen*, he curtly ordered him to blow the call meant for the archers that signaled them to advance. The horn was long and curved only slightly, the sound it produced closer in pitch and tone to that of the Roman *bucina*, but no less piercing. As the pair of Parthian nobles watched, the archers, who had already mounted on the orders of their two remaining commanders, went trotting past, their eyes all averted and with uniformly sullen expressions. What would never be known was whether or not Cyaxares took notice of not only the condition of their horses, their coats shining with sweat and their mouths with the telltale white rings around them that told any horseman with eyes that the dead *drafshi* had been speaking nothing but truth, or the fact that the quivers carried on the backs of the men, along with the pair strapped to their saddles on either side were less than half full, if that.

Pacorus did his best to give his small force every advantage he could dream up. Rather than leading the column headed for the saddle on the ridge, he ordered his standard-bearer to remain in his normal spot in the front rank, with Kambyses riding in what would be Pacorus' normal spot, while the prince chose to place himself and his bodyguard roughly in the last third of the eleven thousand cataphracts under his command. In addition, he had ordered his men to strip themselves of the insignia they wore that identified them as members of Pacorus' guard, and to exchange their white horsehair crests with the normal black worn by the other men. While they complied, it wasn't without some grumbling, but the prince was too preoccupied to notice, nor would he have made an issue of it if he did; there were more important matters at this moment than the quality of their obedience. Finally, rather than place his men amidst the formation whereby they were arranged in ten ranks of ten men apiece, he positioned them in the four outermost files on the left side, with two hundred-fifty men each, from where, at the proper moment, they could turn to the left and begin the charge up the western slope with a minimum of extra maneuvering. This formation wouldn't have the normal depth, it was true, but it would be wider to cover the width of the navigable part of the saddle's western slope. Pacorus was acutely aware that the Romans on the ridge might choose not to wait for the leading edge of the column to pass through the saddle, but he felt sufficiently sure they would allow the entire force to pass so they could conceivably fall on the rear of his men as the leading elements began engaging with Caesar's main force that he felt it worth the risk. His reasoning was actually sound; men on foot, even Roman Legionaries, had little chance against cataphracts when they met face to face. At least, normal Roman Legionaries, led by a man like Crassus couldn't, but he didn't know that yet. When he saw the leading edge of his force reach the foot of the gentle slope and begin to curve slowly north in order to follow its contour where the grade wasn't as steep, the prince began to experience the kind of doubts that plague every commander once a plan has been put into action. He was on the outermost file, with his most trusted men immediately in front, behind and to his right, none of them looking eager for what was about to take place, which didn't help his frame of mind. They're worried about me more than the coming fight, he tried to remind himself, while he kept his eyes on the height above them, where the front ranks of the Romans arrayed on the southern edge were now clearly visible. Still too far away for them to be a threat, but just the sight of them stilled the low buzzing of talk around Pacorus as each man began his own, private preparations; some praying to Mithra, or Ahura Mazda, or one of the lesser gods their noble house had claimed as their own, while others occupied themselves with more practical concerns, like checking for the hundredth time that their swords were loose in their scabbards, and they had their lances gripped in just the right spot. Because of their enormous weight, the pace set by the men of the leading rank could be best characterized as a plodding gait, even as they ascended to within a half mile of the point that marked the middle of the ridge, which was roughly the point at which Pacorus planned on launching his hopefully surprise assault up from the bottom of the saddle.

Clearly within view just above the heads of the front of the column, Pacorus' heart quickened, not just at the recognition that the moment was approaching, but because he realized that, although he had been atop the ridge himself, and had examined the saddle and the ground they were traversing at that moment, he hadn't really studied what was ultimately the most crucial stretch for his plan. The fact that he hadn't conceived it yet didn't make him feel any better about this lapse, and he understood that this was a mistake based in his youth and relative inexperience, not that this would matter or excuse him if he failed. How steep was it on the western edge of the saddle? Fighting the rising surge of panic, Pacorus tried to visualize that stretch of ground that marked the middle of the saddle and was perhaps a half mile wide from north to south, which was more than wide enough. The distance from the bottom of the saddle to the top of the ridge, however, he wasn't sure about, nor how steep it was. While he was certain it wasn't as steep as the approach, despite his best attempt, he couldn't envision the ground in more than a general sense. He had judged that the distance up the slope from the saddle to the top of the ridge was between three and four furlongs; if the pitch over that distance wasn't more than a hundred feet, it shouldn't slow him and his men down significantly, although it did mean he would have to wait to go to the gallop a bit later than he would have liked. If it was worse than that— the thought made Pacorus visibly shudder, prompting a concerned glance from the bodyguard to his right. Before he could spend more time worrying about what was coming, however, the front rank entered into the figurative shadow of the ridge, although the sun was now directly overhead. Because of their helmets that, while protective, also restricted their vision, Pacorus saw the heads of the men ahead turning to gaze upward at the slope nearest to them. Pacorus followed suit, although he did glance across the formation up at the eastern side of the ridge, but gave it only a cursory glance. Perhaps if he had paid more attention, he would have spotted the small puff of dust, caused by one of the men shifting his prone body to a more comfortable position, but Pacorus wasn't the only one who missed it; not one Parthian took notice as they continued their slow, steady progress.

"Steady, boys."

Pullus was standing, as were all of his men, knowing that there was no point in trying to hide his men arrayed along the western edge of the saddle. Naturally, the tension grew as the cataphracts, still maintaining their slow progress, drew nearer. Then, as the leading ranks drew even with the Romans of the First Century, by their own accord, without Pullus giving the command, the low buzzing of conversation among the ranks stopped as the men stared down at their foes, waiting to see what happened next. This was the moment that Pullus was in a quandary about, wondering if the Parthians would turn and begin their charge up the slope as soon as they were deep enough in the saddle to do so, and, if they did, what form the attack would take. While he believed that, given their numbers, whoever was commanding this column of cataphracts would dispatch a large enough portion of his men that would allow them to try and smash through the First Cohort all along their line, Pullus also recognized the possibility of the commander choosing to focus his assault on a narrow front, choosing two, or maybe even one of his Centuries in the center in an attempt to punch a hole that allowed the cataphracts to pour through. If they did manage to penetrate on such a narrow front, they would count on the speed of their horses to spread out into the midst of the large box, whereupon they could then choose the most vulnerable side. Pullus had taken this possibility into consideration, having the men of the second line of Centuries of both the northern and southern sides facing inward, ready for such a development. That would be in the event that his primary plan failed, but as of this moment, the Parthians seemed content to ignore him and his men. Oh, they were watching; Pullus could see the visible part of their faces between the protruding cheek pieces and nose guards, but their horses continued moving in the direction of a confrontation with where Caesar's men were waiting on the northern side of the ridge. Because of his position, Pullus couldn't see down on the northern side to determine whether the other Parthian column had begun their attack, but that was out of his hands, and he trusted Caesar. As Caesar trusted Pullus, who kept his eyes on the large purple standard, carried by a man in the direct middle of the rank that was now twenty men across, riding with their thighs almost touching. While neither he nor any of the other officers of the Roman army held the Parthian infantry in much regard, their feelings about the cataphracts were more respectful, recognizing the amount of training and discipline it took to maintain a level of cohesion that only a Roman could truly appreciate. The purple standard was the largest, but it was far from the only one; from Pullus' quick count, there were well more than twenty banners arrayed down the center of the formation. His guess was that this marked the location and demarcation point between what passed for different units of the Parthian cavalry. Still, they showed no inclination to turn their horses or their attention on Pullus and his men, so that it began to feel as if they were spectators at a parade. Almost despite themselves, the waiting Romans began to relax, the whispering resuming as men started speculating that perhaps they'd actually be left unmolested. This feeling was reinforced by the lack of any kind of signal from the Cohorts further west that would signal that the other column was actually going to be the one to try and knock them off the ridge, from either direction. In this respect, at least, Pacorus' plan was well executed.

The attack began in earnest with the sudden move from the very rear of the Parthian column, where the archers Pacorus had appropriated had attached themselves. Using their superior acceleration and speed, even with the sloping ground, they burst out from the dust churned up by the hooves of the cataphracts to go galloping up the western side of the column to interpose themselves between the Romans and their own comrades. Still, the cataphracts continued their advance; the leading ranks were now almost through the saddle, beginning their downward progress onto the northern slope of the ridge. Even over the sudden din, Pullus heard the sound of the *cornu* of Caesar's command alerting the army of the approaching enemy. Which, frankly, Pullus thought was a bit silly, since there was no way to miss a force of ten thousand armored cavalry heading one's way. This was only a passing thought as he stared down at the galloping archers, judging the moment when they would come into range. When he saw the leading archers lift their bow arms, Pullus bellowed the order to form *testudo*, followed instantly by the clashing racket as men moved shields to their positions, bumping against their comrades' in the process.

Pullus had taken a shield from one of the wounded, who were now lying in the middle of the ridge, tended by the handful of *medici* that had accompanied the Legion. Because of their lower position, the first volley was correspondingly low, the arrows universally striking well short of the front ranks, most of them skittering along the rocky ground, although a few managed to stick. Neither Pullus nor his men had time to appreciate the miss, because, as was their practice, the archers were loosing their missiles before the first had struck. This time, their aim was better, but again because of the difference in height, most of the arrows had lost much of their force so that, while several shields were struck, almost all of the missiles bounced off instead of penetrating the wood. The next volley did better, as the archers galloped higher up the slope of the saddle, but even with the growing cloud of dust, Pullus could see the archers' mounts were already tiring. Adding to their difficulty was the lack of room in which to perform their normal, looping attack, hemmed in by the semi-solid wall of cataphracts lower downslope. Who, Pullus was still able to tell, were plodding north, although they were now almost all of the way through to the other side. Maybe, he thought, they *are* going to leave us alone. That thought hadn't even finished when, with a sudden lurch of movement, what appeared to be the last couple hundred ranks of the cataphract column detached itself, turned to their left and began moving at a ponderous trot, directly for the First.

"All right, boys!" Pullus shouted. "Don't break formation yet! But those archer *cunni* have to get out of the way for these bastards, so be ready for the change!"

149

As if he had commanded it himself, the archers made one more circling pass, launching their last missiles in a rippling swarm that, ironically, was the most effective. All along the line of Centuries, amidst the hollow, slightly echoing crack as the metal points punched into the wooden shields, interspersed among this sound were shouts and screams of pain, as an arrow somehow found a gap between the shields forming each *testudo*. As smoothly as was possible under the circumstances, the men around their stricken comrades shifted position, quickly closing the gaps as the last part of the archers went by across the face of the slope, heading south, presumably back to their camp where they would likely resupply and try to rest their mounts for as long as possible. Despite his own shield being struck three times, and twice that number of arrows surrounding him, some still quivering in the ground, Pullus peeked underneath the rim of his shield so he could time his next command perfectly. The bulk of the cataphract column had now left the area of the saddle, save for the last few ranks, narrower now that this force had detached itself. From this point forward, Pullus knew, timing was crucial, and in preparation, he turned and shouted an order over his shoulder for Valerius, his *cornicen*, to prepare himself for his part in what was about to occur.

Pullus' main concern was that the rear few ranks of the advancing cataphract main column, who were now to Pullus' left and had just reached the beginning of the downward slope onto the northern face, putting the rear rank less than a quarter mile away from where he was standing, were still too close for his comfort. If he had Valerius sound the call too early, and Cyclops' Cohort moved into their position, it was conceivable that the rearmost cataphracts would still be in position to react by turning around and come pounding into the right flank of the Eighth. Consequently, Pullus kept his gaze on what he deemed to be the biggest threat, and not in the opposite direction, back south towards the Parthian camp; he had seen the archers trotting in that direction, and he dismissed them as a threat. Admittedly, it was difficult for Pullus to keep his eyes on the main column and not on the line of armored horsemen, well more than two hundred men across on a front that would engage at least four of his Centuries when they began their attack in earnest. Fortunately, at least as far as Pullus was concerned, the Parthian in command was still content to have his men move at a sedate trot, and although the Primus Pilus didn't know exactly why, his suspicion was actually correct; Pacorus had underestimated the severity of the western side of the saddle, forcing him to hold his men back from going to the charge longer than he would have liked. It wasn't until the advancing formation had covered perhaps a third of the distance to the waiting line of Romans before Pullus felt confident that the main force was now far enough away that, even if the rearmost ranks did turn and come to the aid of their comrades heading up the slope, it would be too late.

When he turned, Pullus' command was actually not that loud and consisted of simply saying to Valerius, "Now."

Instantly, the *cornicen* drew a breath, then sounded a single long note, and even before he was finished, it was met with an answering note on the opposite side of the saddle, although it was drowned out by the roar of more than four hundred Legionaries who immediately leapt to their feet and began running forward. Flowing over the protuberance that had helped keep them hidden, Cyclops, as Pullus knew he would be, was at the head of his men, and they went streaming down the opposite slope. From his vantage point, Pullus could see the Parthians in the rear ranks awkwardly turn around, hampered by their heavy armor and with their vision limited because of their helmets. The noise level became even greater as those Parthians added their own voices, shouting their warning about the presence of this new threat, which was quickly passed up through the more than thirty ranks towards the front of their formation. Even as Pullus was watching, the slow but smoothly advancing Parthian formation came to an ungainly, ugly halt, and one man detached himself, actually galloping up the slope.

For an instant, Pullus thought one of these Parthians had lost his mind and was going to forge ahead to conduct a lone attack, but when the mounted Parthian spun around to look across the slope at where the Eighth was still streaming down to get into their position, Pullus quickly understood he was trying to determine the nature and immediacy of this new, and clearly unexpected threat. More importantly, it informed Pullus that this had to be the man commanding this attack. Instinctively, without any real thought of doing so, Pullus moved himself along the front of his Cohort so that he aligned himself directly in front of this Parthian nobleman. That he did so didn't surprise anyone in the ranks, and if Scribonius had been in a position to see, he would have undoubtedly muttered a curse and rolled his eyes. Since they had been young *tiros*, Pullus' almost insatiable need to distinguish himself had guaranteed that he placed himself in the most dangerous position and took the biggest risks in battle. The fact that he had survived, not without sustaining more than his share of wounds, one of which almost killed him after Munda, was a tribute to the giant Roman's prowess and the *animus* in him that possessed a ferocity that was a horribly wonderful thing to behold, as long as one was on his side. Nevertheless, while Pullus had marked this man as his target, not even he could imagine the impact his actions would have, not just in this battle, but in the entire campaign. His potential victim, having taken in the Eighth, whose leading ranks were almost to the bottom of the slope, clearly decided that they weren't a threat, provided that he order the advance to resume. In fairness to Pacorus, whose identity was still completely unknown to Pullus and his men, his reasoning was sound. Under normal circumstances, once the cataphracts went to the gallop, with the head start they had over the Eighth, and combined with having to ascend the western slope on foot, the Romans would be unable to have any real impact on the coming clash. These weren't normal circumstances, and in yet another of the tiny little moments of seeming inconsequence that ended up having an enormous influence on the outcome, Pacorus had trotted back and returned to his spot, his back once more turned to Cyclops and his men. Therefore, he missed them suddenly coming to a halt and doing something that, under any conditions, would have been not only unusual but confusing. There was a ripple of movement as the Centurions of the Eighth chivvied and shoved men into a formation whereby the men were more loosely spaced then their norm. As the Parthians resumed their advance, Pullus and his men made their own preparations for what was about to come, while Cyclops and the Eighth unleashed what could best be described as Caesar's secret weapon, one of the new innovations that were specifically designed to defeat the Parthians' most potent weapon.

In fairness, it was Aulus Ventidius who came up with the idea. And, as the older Legate would be the first to admit, he had stumbled onto this new weapon by accident, when he had been too impatient to wait for one part of the weapon to be properly prepared. Like many such innovative ideas, it was deceptively simple and relied on an implement that was perhaps one of the oldest in mankind's inventory of destructive tools. The sling had been used for more centuries than anyone knew, and while there were men of certain regions who had developed a proficiency over and above their counterparts in other parts of the world, the Legions of Rome had only used this weapon sporadically and, most of the time, it was at the whim of the Legate in command. In this case, it wasn't the sling that was the subject of the innovation, but the ammunition used. The most common type of missile used by slingers were rocks, although they weren't just any rock picked up off the ground, unless it was an emergency or the supply of rocks carefully selected and shaped had run out. However, Romans had begun using lead missiles and, over the years, had developed a shape that was formed in a way where its trajectory was consistent, thereby allowing slingers to aim with more precision, and with enough intrinsic weight because of the metal to inflict more damage than a rock. Ventidius, charged by Caesar with coming up with an effective weapon to handle cataphracts, had been wrestling with the problem for months before the beginning of the campaign. Using the armor taken as spoils from Zela, Ventidius had tried everything he could think of; adding even more weight to the round knob affixed to every javelin, at the base of the slender, soft metal shaft and the beginning of the wooden portion. While this proved able to penetrate the lamellar armor, these javelins had to be launched from a much shorter range than normal, meaning that a Legionary would have to be willing to expose himself to the massive impact of a galloping, armored horse and rider. Naturally, scorpions were ideal, able to penetrate the armor with ease, and from a distance of well more than a hundred paces. Unfortunately, as Ventidius learned through experimentation, the time it took for a scorpion to reload meant that even a proficient crew couldn't get off more than two shots before the cataphract reached the front line. The other problem was the number of scorpions it would take to have a meaningful impact on stopping a charge. While he tried using lead missiles, Ventidius didn't hold much hope. Then, one day, he became impatient with the armorer *Immunes,* who were tasked with the job of supplying the various types of ammunition, and ordered them to skip the final step in the preparation of the lead missiles. Each shot was created by pouring molten lead into a mold, then allowed to cool. When the reusable mold was opened, since the seal between the two pieces of the mold wasn't perfect, it was inevitable that small amounts of lead leaked out of the mold, creating an irregular, jagged shape. Normally, the *Immunes* then filed off the rough edges to smooth the missile, under the assumption that it would aid in the stability of the lead shot in flight. This day, when Ventidius snapped at the men to just throw the supply in a sack before they had been filed, he did so out of exasperation and not with any expectation of a different result. In all truth, this was the last day he planned on experimenting with projectile type weapons. To his shocked surprise first, then delight, the slingers sent this batch of missiles sailing at their target, a mule who had the misfortune to go lame, and who was staked in place with the armored blanket draped over its body. The damage inflicted was instant and horrendous, causing even these hardened men to feel a flicker of pity for the poor beast. Just as important to Ventidius and the army as the damage inflicted was that the inherent mass of the lead missile was such that its trajectory wasn't altered a huge amount by the roughened edges, meaning that a skilled slinger could still place a shot where he wanted it to go. Still, Ventidius wasn't completely satisfied, and ordered a new set of molds made, of a slightly larger size, with the edges of the mold slightly biased, so that the edges were still razor sharp, but more uniform than they had been by accident. When Cyclops and his men leapt up, dashed down the slope, spread out, and began whirling their arms over their heads to launch their first volley of shot, it was with these missiles loaded in the pouch of the sling.

Pacorus' first indication of this terrible new weapon was the dozens of horrific screams that, in addition to being completely unexpected, were so shrill in nature that it set the hair on the prince's neck to stand on end. He had just given the command to go from the trot to the canter, making his ability to twist in his saddle to see what was happening even more difficult. Nevertheless, he managed, and the sight behind him caused his heart to feel as if it had come to a sudden stop of its own volition. He was only dimly aware of the gasp that escaped him, drowned out by the pounding of the hooves of his and his comrades' horses. Able to spare no more than a glance, Pacorus spun back around, his mind whirling as it tried to absorb the full import of what he'd just seen in what had been nothing more than a heartbeat's time. His rearmost rank had been savaged; by his guess, he estimated that the gaping holes in the otherwise neat ranks totaled to at least a third of the men, with the bodies of men and horses, most of them writhing in agony, strewn carelessly behind his advancing formation. More importantly, his eyes had taken in the sight of the arms of several hundred men swinging in tight circles over their heads, telling him the cause of this sudden onslaught, at least partially. But, he thought with alarm, a *sling* did that much damage? Before he could turn his mind to this problem, a fresh round of shouts, screams, and whinnying of hurt and panicked horses informed him the second volley had landed. For several, critical heartbeats, Pacorus was in an agony of indecision, and he even entertained the thought of calling off

154

the attack. Then, the part of his mind that was still rational pointed out that, if those Romans behind him had slings, then it was almost guaranteed the enemy arrayed before them up the slope did as well. I led us into a trap, he thought dismally, but in the fraction of time he had, he didn't see any way to extricate his men, and himself, from what was about to come.

Therefore, taking a deep breath, he bellowed at the top of his lungs, dropping his lance as he did, "For Orodes! For Parthia! For our gods! For our families! Charge!"

With a sudden leap forward, and with a thunderous roar in answer to their prince that drowned out even the pounding of thousands of hooves suddenly brought to the gallop, the Parthians began their final charge up the slope, even as they saw the arms of their foes above them begin to swing around and around.

That the Legionaries Pullus had designated as slingers only loosed two volleys was by design, as the final piece of Caesar's new tactics came into play. Immediately after the second volley, which had been released by the men of the first two ranks, they quickly made a simple turn of their bodies, widening the spacing, thereby allowing their comrades behind them to go bounding down the slope.

"The way for the Legions to defeat the cataphracts is to do what we can to negate their mobility," Caesar had explained when he unveiled what he had planned. "In a small space, a man on foot can move more quickly, and is almost infinitely more agile than a man on a heavily armored horse." Waiting for his Centurions to absorb this, he had gone on, "There are two ways to accomplish this. The first is to force them to attack on ground that favors us, either by virtue of higher ground. Or," his lips twitched in a smile, "by drawing them into a heavily wooded area." As he expected, this drew a chuckle; not one man expected to find such terrain anywhere in Parthia. "Since this second alternative is so unlikely, we're going to have to count on the first. But there's something else we can do."

This was when he turned it over to Ventidius, who had brought as evidence, the bloodstained, punctured armored blanket, along with a handful of the jagged lead missiles to pass around. Seeing his officers were suitably impressed, Caesar continued to outline the plan, the first time it was being implemented this day, on the ridge. As Pullus had hoped, the two volleys of missiles, with the men who had proven most proficient having been placed in the front two ranks, were aimed not at the riders, but the horses. It was something that Pullus found distasteful; he would have been surprised to learn how many of his men of all ranks felt the same way, but this was something that was never discussed openly, for the simple reason that their comrades would mock them for being soft. From Pullus' perspective, it was as if a giant, invisible hand swept across the front rank of the charging Parthians, now roughly fifty paces away from reaching the Roman lines, sending first horses, followed an eye blink later by their riders, most of them pitched headlong over the heads of their mounts, slamming and tumbling into the hard, rocky surface. The din was so overwhelming that, even if he had managed to relay his order to Valerius, the *cornu* couldn't have been heard more than a few paces away. Instead, as he always tried to do, Titus Pullus led by example, breaking into a run that, between his long legs and the slope, meant he had a head start of more than a dozen paces as his men followed, careening down the slope, shouting at the top of their lungs.

"Caesar! Caesar! Caesar!"

Since Pullus had aligned himself with the man who he had seen to be the commander, he only had to adjust his angle slightly, because the Parthian, while one of the remainder of those who were still mounted, consisting of about half of the front rank, had been forced to yank his horse to the side in order to avoid the tumbling body of the man who had been to his immediate right. This was just one of Pacorus' problems; by altering his trajectory in this final phase of the charge, it inevitably meant he had to slow his mount down, and in doing what he was forced to do, the two men to his immediate left were left with nowhere to go. Rather than collide with his prince, the Parthian to Pacorus' immediate left yanked the reins of his mount with enough force that it jerked the horse's head to the left, as close to a right angle that the animal's muscular neck would allow. Naturally following its head, it smashed headlong into the flank of the second bodyguard's horse, which in turn caused a ripple effect in the immediate area, especially with the second rank. What had just an instant before been a neatly ordered mass of horse and rider, pounding up the slope with an accompanying thundering sound, saw the middle of its formation suddenly become a mess of human and animal wreckage. Even as he was about to slam into the Parthian commander, whose horsemanship the detached part of Pullus' mind recognized was nothing short of superb, Pullus witnessed the fulfillment of Caesar's promise that these tactics would be devastatingly effective. Then he was hurdling the body of a horse, blood pouring from its mouth, trying to avoid its thrashing hooves, which he managed to almost do, but was struck a grazing blow in his right calf that caused him to slightly stumble. A Parthian, on hands and knees and presumably the rider of the downed animal, was shaking his head, trying to clear it when one of Pullus' knees smashed into his side, causing Pullus to bellow in pain, and the Parthian to lose his air in a great, whooshing gust. Pullus' blow had been unintended; he had planned to plunge his sword into the man's body between his shoulders, but the glancing blow of the dying horse had sent him stumbling. Despite this, Pullus recovered first, regaining his feet underneath him, but just when he was about to end this first Parthian, who was now on his back, gasping for breath, a massive hoof from a horse in the second or third rank who hadn't been knocked down came plunging down and struck the cataphract fully in the face. Pullus had only a glimpse of the carnage caused by a thousand-pound animal putting its full weight onto the man's skull, but afterward, he would vividly recall the sound it made, even as he threw himself to the side, narrowly avoiding being struck by the animal as it thundered past. In doing so, however, he made himself vulnerable to its rider; the Parthian, however, hadn't quite comprehended the changed circumstances, so he still had his lance couched against his body, but on the opposite side from the direction Pullus had jumped. By the time he could shift it over the animal's head and even attempt to lunge with it at Pullus' briefly unprotected back, not only was he past Pullus, but the Primus Pilus' men had bounded down the slope and caught up with their leader. Again, Pullus could only hear the moment as one of his men, reaching this Parthian, darted underneath the point of the man's lance, then with a savage thrust upward, plunged his short, stabbing sword into the unprotected belly of the horse. Its death screams only added to the din, but Pullus barely noticed as he got his feet back under him and, without more than the fraction of an eye blink's hesitation, went charging after his original target, Pacorus.

The prince had managed to get his own mount under control, but was now turned perpendicular to the direction his men were attacking, presenting a broadside target for Pullus. All around them was a maelstrom of noise, the air filled with choking dust, as the more agile Legionaries came pouring down the slope to dart in between the now-shattered ranks of the cataphracts, almost all of whom had been brought to a stop by the devastating effects of the lead missiles that had raked the Parthian formation. What perhaps a dozen heartbeats before had been a thundering menace, where every member of Pacorus' guard had been confident that, no matter what their reputation, no men on foot could withstand the sheer power of the onslaught galloping towards them, had devolved into a scene of utter chaos, confusion, and the beginning of panic on the part of the Parthians. While Pacorus hadn't actually been in this close proximity to any Romans prior to this moment, as he struggled to get his mount under control, what he was sure was the largest Roman in their army, if not in their entire nation, came into his narrowed view, and he instantly understood that this Roman was heading for him. Fortunately for him, he had been forced to drop his lance, so even as he kept one hand firmly on the reins as he felt his horse come back under his control, he drew his sword in one smooth motion. Reacting to the sensation of his horse's body now back firmly underneath him, he kicked his horse, which he had named Xerxes in homage to the Achaemenid dynasty's most famous King of Kings, and to whom Pacorus' royal line traced their own lineage, and the animal responded instantly, leaping forward directly at this large Roman.

In a slightly odd twist, because of their respective reactive moves, the situation between Pacorus and Pullus was essentially reversed, with the mounted Parthian upslope, while Pullus was downhill, and now forced to face Pacorus. Speaking of Pullus, not lost on the Primus Pilus was the danger he had put himself in, since his back was now turned downhill, where the bulk of the Parthian formation still was located, trying to regain their lost momentum. However, this was a moment where Pullus' total faith in his men served him well, since they had gone past him down the slope to engage with the Parthians. It was with this confidence that he charged up the hill, his powerful thighs pumping furiously as his eyes, narrowed into slits, watched his foe react to his own sudden attack. Fighting a man on horseback was something that Pullus hadn't done that often, but he had done so, and he understood that, in this case, his very size was a factor against him. Caesar, understanding that the average height of the men of his army was five feet and around five inches, and their average weight was one hundred twenty pounds, and that was after a winter in garrison, correspondingly understood that this gave those men an advantage against the cataphracts of Parthia, as long as it was under the right conditions. Pullus was a foot taller and a hundred pounds heavier, but he still moved very quickly for a man his size. Pacorus had managed to get his horse turned so his sword side was facing Pullus, and the prince now tried to time his slash downward at the perfect moment.

One way in which the two men were more closely related than either would ever know was in their almost obsessive attention to the profession of arms, and Pacorus had spent countless watches of time practicing for every situation that his military tutors could think up. Facing a man on foot, armed with a shield, was one of those situations, and while mounted Parthians disdained the use of shields, they had developed their own tactics to compensate for that lack, and he availed himself of one of those now. With a combination of commands, consisting of pressing harder than normal with his left knee and uttering a word in Parthian, the horse Xerxes became a weapon in his own right as with a surprising nimbleness considering the bulk of the animal and the weight of his load, he swung his massive body while rearing back, so his hardened front hooves came slashing at Pullus from his unprotected side. Once more, the Primus Pilus found himself forced to throw himself to his left, which was precisely the direction that Pacorus wanted him to go, since it brought his foe within range of his sword, and the Parthian didn't hesitate. His sword, whose quality, as one would expect of a prince, was a match to Pullus' own Gallic blade, although Pacorus' came from his side of the world, slashed down in a blurred arc that Pullus was barely able to block with his shield. Because of the angle, he was forced to twist his large torso in one direction to bring his shield around, while his lower body was continuing in the opposite direction. It was an exceedingly awkward position, although Pullus managed to block the savage, and powerful slash with his shield, but along with the hollow sound caused by metal clashing with wood, there was a resounding crack that Pullus knew didn't bode well for his chances of having his shield much longer. Because he was moving away from the blow, it wasn't as powerful as it could have been, but Pullus was surprised at the amount of force this Parthian was capable of producing. He could see enough of the man's face to see that the Parthian was much younger than he was, with a jet black beard that gleamed from the oil Pullus knew was applied in liberal amounts to their hair. This was all he had time to notice, as the horse, with all four hooves back on the ground, suddenly reversed direction so that this time his massive hindquarters came swinging towards Pullus. Again, the animal moved quickly, and Pullus barely had the time to move his shield from its slightly raised position, where it had just blocked Pacorus' downward slash, to its more normal position protecting the left side of his body. The impact of the horse's armored hindquarter slamming into Pullus' shield would have sent any other Roman flying off his feet, where the horse's rider could make short work of finishing the job by simply leaning down and thrusting his sword into his supine foe. Instead, Pacorus experienced a surprise similar to Pullus' an instant before when, while it once more sent the Roman staggering, not only did he remain on his feet, he recovered more quickly than Pacorus would have thought possible if he wasn't seeing it for himself. As surprising as this was, it was nothing like the shocked surprise the prince experienced when the giant Roman used his shield, not for defensive purposes, but as a weapon, a move Pacorus had never seen before. But it was the Roman's target that proved not only to be more startling, yet devastatingly effective, as the Roman aimed the metal boss directly for the side of Xerxes' head. Because of the heavily armored headdress that not only protected the horse's head but restricted its peripheral vision, Xerxes didn't see the blow coming. While the armor scales did absorb much of the force of the punch, the fact that the Roman who delivered it was Titus Pullus, who had managed to get his feet underneath him and put his considerable weight behind it, meant that once more the horse's head suddenly jerked in the opposite direction. This time, however, it wasn't in accordance to its rider's command; that Xerxes was stunned meant that the normally sure-footed horse actually staggered as its front knees buckled. Pullus' blow, and the results it caused, happened so quickly that even as skilled a horseman as Pacorus was couldn't keep his seat in the saddle. The prince felt Xerxes' front legs collapsing, but before his mind could comprehend and send the command to his body to compensate, he was launched over his horse's head. For the span of less than a heartbeat, Pacorus experienced a sensation where he didn't feel the weight of his armor as his body flew through the air, yet before he could even draw a breath, the ground came hurtling towards him, and he barely had time to tuck his head and slightly twist his body so he took most of the impact on his shoulder. What little breath had been in his lungs was expelled from the tremendous force caused by hitting the ground, which was bad enough; it was the thousands of tiny lights that seemed to explode in his vision when his helmet slammed against an embedded rock in the ground of the slope that rendered him insensible. In these, the last few heartbeats of his existence, if Pacorus had the time, and retained enough of his wits to comprehend that, while his twisting to take most of the impact on his shoulder was understandable, it meant that rather than at least being unconscious and perhaps already dead, he would have just enough awareness to see the giant Roman standing over him,

160

he might have made a different choice. As it was, Pacorus had just enough time to roll over on his back, and even with the bleary vision caused by the blow to his head, he was aware enough to look up at Pullus, whose face was a mask of a barely suppressed fury, with his massive arm holding his sword pulled back, about to plunge into his face. The Roman, despite being focused on his own private battle, was also aware of what was going on around him, but while he trusted his men to protect his back, what his ears were telling him informed him he didn't have time to savor this moment. While he had ascertained that this Parthian at his feet had been the commander of this attack, if he had been aware of his identity, even he couldn't have said what he might have done. But he didn't know at this moment, so the point of his sword hovered for perhaps a heartbeat longer than it normally would, then plunged down into the gap between the iron cheek pieces, shattering the prince's teeth on its way down into the rocky soil underneath him. Pacorus' body went rigid for an instant, then a series of small tremors rippled through his body as his spirit departed.

Neither Pullus nor any of his men were really prepared for what came next; their first indication that the Parthian their Primus Pilus had just slain was not only their commander, but a man they considered to be the second most important person in their kingdom followed within a matter of heartbeats after Pullus slew him. Naturally, his specific rank wouldn't be known for more than a full watch, yet the sudden howl, issued from the hundred Parthian throats who were in position to witness the large Roman slay their prince, not only startled the men who were fighting them, but gave them the first indication that something momentous had just occurred. However, it was what the Parthians did next that, in its own way, caused almost as much damage to the Romans, who had penetrated deep into the Parthian formation, darting in between their rapidly disintegrating ranks. Suddenly, one of the Parthians with a horn, on his own initiative, began blowing the call that signaled retreat, for which one of his companions next to him, cut him out of his saddle. But since the call emanated from the front of the formation, the now-dead Parthian's counterparts, assuming this was a royal command, repeated the notes. And just that quickly, the Parthian's attack on the 10th disintegrated, as those Parthians roughly in the middle of the formation, safe from the raking lead missiles of the Eighth, and far enough from the front that the Legionaries hadn't cut their way to them, turned their horses and began heading either to the north to join their comrades in the attack on Caesar, or to the south, back to the camp, whichever provided the closest refuge. By this point, the Eighth had been joined by the Ninth, who had been designated by Pullus as the reserve and who had been positioned farther east on the ridge top, and they too were loosing the lead missiles as fast as their arms could release them. Ponderously, at least at first, the middle section of the Parthian column, believing they had been issued a royal command, or at least pretending to, began going whichever direction offered at least temporary safety the quickest. Once the outer ranks went to the gallop, the mass retreat picked up momentum, until there were no cataphracts left except for those who were already engaged and fighting for their lives, or those who had already been slaughtered. Pullus hadn't wasted any more time, and moved back down the slope to rejoin where his line of Centuries were located; the only real obstacle to his progress the heaped bodies of armored men and horses, the latter of which Pullus took the time to put out of their misery after a cursory examination. Caesar had issued explicit orders that those Parthian mounts that might be captured unharmed be kept as remounts, which was in Pullus' mind as he made his way down the slope. Before this secondary mission could be seen to, however, he needed to try and bring some sense of organization to what was now ultimately nothing more than a mass slaughter. Those Parthians who had been unable to escape had been isolated into small groups of three or four at most, while others had lost even that small security, and were now surrounded, alone, by Legionaries who circled them, each of them waiting for an opportunity to strike as the beleaguered cataphract swung his mount one way, then another, all while swinging his sword whenever a Roman got too close. The manner in which Pullus' men were finishing off the remnants of the shattered attack was accomplished in much the same way as a pack of wolves work once they have separated their prey from the larger herd, but on a much larger scale.

The sounds of this part of the battle were unlike anything Pullus or any of his men had experienced previously, and the disorganization was similarly unusual. Spread across the slope, Pullus saw the Century *signiferi*, but in nowhere near their proper orientation or position for the moment when Pullus called the order to reform his Cohort in preparation for whatever came next. It was this moment when he also realized that, in his own headlong charge, he had completely forgotten his larger role as Primus Pilus, meaning he had left Valerius and his runners standing on the top of the ridge more than four hundred paces from his current position. Cursing himself, he spotted Balbus who, much like his superior, had gotten into the spirit of the fight, so that even as Pullus watched, he saw the scarred Centurion make a slight leap forward while ducking under the wild swing of Parthian's sword. Without a shield, Pullus' friend used his free hand to reach out and grab the Parthian's boot, giving a powerful yank upward that sent the cataphract, who was already off-balance, toppling over onto the side of his horse opposite Balbus, where three Legionaries, men Pullus recognized as belonging to Balbus and with swords already covered in blood, were waiting. Before the Parthian hit the ground, his shriek of fear and pain was cut short, while Balbus had already begun moving the dozen paces to where, this time, there were three Parthians clustered together. Since he was moving away from Pullus, the Primus Pilus looked elsewhere for another of his Centurions.

The next man wearing a transverse crest he saw was his Hastatus Prior, Titus Vistilia; more importantly, he saw that unlike Pullus, Vistilia had kept his own *cornicen* nearby. Making his way slightly downslope and towards the northern side of the ridge, Pullus was forced to navigate around small knots of men, all of them in similar circumstances as Balbus and his Legionaries, finishing the business of butchering the remaining Parthians. By this point, enough time had elapsed that the majority of the men of the First Cohort had finished killing the Parthians who had been left behind, so that they were now engaged in the one activity that, for the majority of rankers, made the harsh life under the standard worth living, the looting of the dead. Despite his preoccupation with getting to Vistilia so his *cornicen* could sound the call that would begin to get matters organized, Pullus nevertheless found himself grinning at the exclamations of disgust as men discovered that their Primus Pilus had been telling the truth all along. For longer than Pullus had been under the standard, the men of Rome's Legions had heard tales of the fabulous wealth of the East, and one particular tale had become an article of faith, that the cataphracts of Parthia wore armor that was not just heavy in its construction, but ornate and decorated with gold leaf, while the hilts of their weapons were embedded with precious stones. As Pullus had discovered after the battle of Zela, while these tales hadn't been fabricated, they were highly exaggerated; the only men whose armor was bedecked in this manner had been the highest-ranking nobles. And as his men were discovering, there was a distinct difference between being a *satrap* or an eldest son, and a man of a minor noble house. In fact, there was only one body on the slope that had been wearing the kind of armor and carrying a sword fit for a king.

Unbeknownst to Pullus, the corpse of Pacorus was now being guarded by a young Gregarius who had been selected as a runner and had seen his uncle slay the Parthian from his spot at the top of the ridge. As Pullus had continued down the slope, Porcinus had followed but stopped at the corpse, staring down in fascination at the dead prince, immediately noticing the gold leaf of his armor. Sure that his uncle would want to claim these spoils for himself, Porcinus had stationed himself there, but it hadn't been without confrontation; he had finally been forced to draw his sword on some of the First Cohort men, convincing them he was sincere in his willingness to use it to keep them from looting what rightfully belonged to Pullus. He could easily have ended matters without resorting to this measure, but it hadn't even occurred to him to use his identity and the status it brought as Pullus' nephew. He was still standing over the body of Pacorus when the *cornu* call sounded for the First Cohort, and the men were forced to leave their looting as they made their way through the bodies of man and horse to assemble at the spot Pullus had designated.

Cyaxares, in command of the western Parthian column, never learned of the death of Pacorus, as he himself was slain, trying to hack a path through the men of the 12th Legion in a desperate attempt to reach Caesar, who had positioned himself a short distance away. The Parthian had gotten within fifty paces of where Caesar sat on Toes, seemingly unperturbed at the sight of a handful of Parthians who had used their heavily armored steeds to press deeply enough that the two generals could see their opposite number's face, if not quite closely enough for Cyaxares to see the ice-blue eyes of this Roman general. But Caesar's lack of concern was warranted, because in his savage desire to reach this hated Roman, while he and the four men who had managed to remain mounted to this point had struck down more than their share of Legionaries, the Parthian had essentially sealed his own fate. In the same manner a finger displaces water in a cup only as long as the finger remains, once the rest of the cataphracts who had answered his summons to charge the Roman line had been cut down, Cyaxares and his four stalwarts were isolated and, one by one, the men of the Third Century of the First Cohort of the 12th, avenging their comrades who had been struck down, made quick work of all but the Parthian general. Who, as even his enemies would agree afterward,

164

didn't go down without putting up a fight that, had he survived, would have cemented Cyaxares' reputation as one of the greatest Parthian warriors of his age. Instead, he finally succumbed, more from the sheer exhaustion of his mount, the beast finally collapsing onto its front knees. Although Cyaxares managed to stay in the saddle, it ultimately didn't matter, prolonging his life for the span of perhaps a dozen more heartbeats. This moment marked the high point of the attack from the western end of the ridge, but while it ultimately failed in its creator's goal of penetrating deeply enough into the Roman formation that Cyaxares' cataphracts linked up with the force led by Kambyses, they did manage to inflict serious damage to Caesar's western wing. The latter Parthian, who was unaware of his prince's demise, had brought his column of almost ten thousand men crashing into the line of Legions Caesar had positioned paralleling but on the ridge side of the earthworks. With Kambyses' men aided by the advantage of starting uphill, the men of the 8th, 28th, and 11th Legions sustained their own heavy casualties, but while the Parthians managed to penetrate past the second line of Caesar's vaunted *acies triplex*, they were still unable to capitalize on this by pushing their way to the west to achieve Pacorus' plan of uniting with the Cyaxares.

That Caesar's men hadn't used the advantage of the earthen barrier was a mistake that had two causes, and one of them belonged fully to Caesar, who had been overconfident in his belief that Pullus and his 10th would have sufficiently savaged this column that by the time it joined battle with Caesar's main body, their numbers would have been reduced substantially. In its simplest terms, Caesar hadn't foreseen that Pacorus would only use a portion of his force to neutralize the 10th atop the ridge. Still, the fact that this line of Legions had been positioned with the earthworks behind them, instead of using it as protection and to negate the height advantage of the cataphracts, was more of a mistake by the Legate Caesar had placed in direct command of this part of the army. Truly, Aulus Hirtius had been in an unenviable position; again, in basic terms, the Legions under his command hadn't had the time to clear the bodies of the remainder of the Parthian infantry from the rampart, and the fact that the Parthians, in their ignorance, hadn't properly prepared the barrier and smoothed the rampart in the first place meant that he deemed the footing too treacherous.

Additionally, while the Parthians hadn't smoothed and tamped the surface, they had at least created the barrier with a more gradual slope on the side facing the ridge in the expectation that the assault by the Romans would come from the opposite direction. Which it had, but neither Pacorus nor his generals had even contemplated the possibility that the Romans would penetrate the defenses so quickly and now be on the opposite side. And, when the Parthian column had materialized from the direction of the saddle, it had happened faster than Caesar had assured his generals would be the case, forcing Hirtius to make a hasty decision. It was one that would have serious consequences, at least in the sense of the casualties sustained by the Legions who bore the brunt of the assault. The fighting was as intense as any of Caesar's veterans had experienced, and was unlike any of their battles with the tribes of Gaul, or against their own brethren during the civil war. Proculus Lanatus, the Primus Pilus of the 11th Legion, fell trying to cut his way through a wall of armored horsemen who had managed to isolate the sacred eagle of his Legion; the 11th alone lost three other Centurions, while the 8th sustained the loss of their Tertius Pilus Prior, and three other men wearing a transverse crest suffered grievous wounds. While the cataphracts certainly inflicted a large number of casualties, they in turn suffered mightily themselves, particularly in the column commanded by Cyaxares which, once their leader fell, were further handicapped by either the inability or the unwillingness of one of the remaining members of the upper nobility who were acting as his subordinates to take control. In contrast, Kambyses, once he determined that he would be unable to fulfill Pacorus' orders to the level needed to have a chance at victory, began to behave more prudently. Unlike Cyaxares, who in using the formation the Parthians called The Fist, where the focus of their attack was on a much narrower front, Kambyses had paused only long enough to arrange his men in a formation five hundred men across. However, instead of aligning his command twenty deep, he had actually ordered a slight separation into two groups, five hundred wide but only ten men deep. Trailing the leading formation by a hundred paces, Kambyses gave his second in command, Teispes, orders to wait to see what effect the charge led by Kambyses had before committing himself.

"If you see we've punched through but need more weight to exploit it all the way before we can turn to the west, then don't hesitate!" he had instructed his subordinate. "But, if the Romans shift their lines to try and stop us, that will weaken another point in their formation. Stay higher up here," he indicated the spot a couple hundred paces down the slope but high enough Teispes would be able to view the action, "so you can see. If you see a chance, take it! Otherwise," Kambyses' mouth thinned into a line, "be ready to come help us."

Actually, Teispes ended up doing neither, but for a reason that Kambyses couldn't fault. Being closer to the saddle, where Pacorus' doomed attack had just been shattered, Teispes was hailed by a rider who was galloping his horse in a manner that told the Parthian that he was carrying important information. Such was Teispes' faith in his prince that he fully expected this messenger to be bringing the news that the prince had engaged the Romans on top of the ridge and had at least pinned them down. His first indication that this might not be the case came when, as he turned in his saddle at the shouts from his rearmost men that someone was approaching, he naturally looked past the approaching rider. Still, his first reaction wasn't more than slight puzzlement at the sight that this rider wasn't alone and was simply the first to reach his spot. Even as he watched, he saw what had to be at least a hundred more cataphracts appear from the saddle, but he noticed they were riding their mounts as hard as this first man, who was even now pushing through the ranks of his men. A sudden stab of alarm struck him, prompting him then to turn his mount so he could more fully view the top of the ridge. When he saw the neat Roman lines, clearly undisturbed and in the same spot he had first spied them once they had cleared the saddle and reached the northern slope, his stomach clenched, the alarm now turning into something else. Then the cataphract reached him, although since he was not wearing his insignia as a member of the royal guard he had to identify himself as such, but it was his expression and the clear aura of grief radiating from the man that gave the noble a hint of warning.

"Our prince," the man sobbed, his shoulders shaking as he made no attempt to hide his grief, "our prince has been slain!"

As shattering as this was, Teispes managed to retain his own composure, at least enough of it to ask, "What of the attack?"

"It's been crushed," the cataphract moaned, turning his head back towards the ridge and seeing his comrades, who were still streaming down the slope after him, added fear to his voice as he babbled, "They slaughtered us! We didn't have a chance! They had slingers!"

"Slingers!" Teispes' own mounting worry was arrested briefly by this, and he shook his head in disbelief. "Slingers have never stopped us before and they couldn't stop us now!"

"These slingers were different," the man insisted, and his horse, as near to exhaustion as it was, began hopping nervously as his rider's tension communicated itself. "I swear it to Ahura Mazda, lord! They cut us down like wheat!"

The noble fought his urge to argue about this, understanding that the specifics of what was clearly a disaster weren't important at this moment.

Instead, he said abruptly, "Follow me."

He then turned his horse down the slope, going to the gallop, intent on reaching the part of his force that had already managed to smash into the Roman lines and penetrate the first and second rank of Centuries. He had to reach Kambyses.

When Kambyses was informed of Pacorus' death, he didn't hesitate. Aided by his observation that he and Cyaxares would be unable to accomplish their prince's objective, he gave the order to withdraw his men. This, naturally, was easier ordered than accomplished, and not without a fair number of losses, but it was a mark of this Parthian's skill that he managed to extricate his men at all. While he did so, however, his troubles were by no means at an end because when he understandably chose the most direct route back to the southern side of the ridge and his camp, he found a Legion blocking his path, arrayed across the saddle. Pullus had wasted no time, once the attack on his position had been thwarted, recalling the part of his Legion that hadn't been involved in the fight against Pacorus and his cataphracts to join his Cohort. He left the Sixth Cohort in a spot where they could continue their observation of the activity on the western end of the ridge; the presence of nine Cohorts of Roman Legionaries was enough to dissuade Kambyses from trying to force his way through. It was true that, by virtue of his position, Teispes and his five thousand men were not only still fresh, but in a position to lead a charge, not only would it be another uphill assault, Kambyses had been sufficiently discomposed by the news of Pacorus' death that he had lost the stomach for more Parthian bloodshed. It was a good decision; the fact that he had yet to be informed of the lethal new weapon in the form of jagged lead missiles that had wreaked such devastation among Pacorus' bodyguard would have only strengthened his conviction that it was time to disengage and lick their collective wounds. He was only slightly mollified by the knowledge that his own men had managed to inflict a significant amount of damage on the Romans, but his desire to avenge his prince's death was dampened by the knowledge that it hadn't been without a huge cost to his own men. Consequently, he and the remnant of his command turned and rode along the slope to the west, closer to the top, with the intent on linking up with the remainder of Cyaxares' command, which had suffered much higher casualties and was even then disintegrating into smaller groups composed of two or three dozen riders. Because of his vantage point, Kambyses saw the mass of horsemen belonging to the Romans, who had pulled back across the river once the battle had begun in earnest, now moving back towards the remnants of Cyaxares' force. Going to the trot, Kambyses' intent was to aid in the fight that appeared to be coming with the Roman cavalry, who he could see were moving in a direction that told him their commander intended to at least attempt to block the Parthian retreat around the western shoulder. Aided by the Tigris on one flank, and the slope leading up to the ridgetop, this was exactly what Ventidius intended, but in one of the few bright moments for the Parthians this day, the contingent of horse archers, forced to retreat back to their camp to replenish their supply of arrows, now made themselves useful. Launching their missiles in waves, the archers drove Ventidius and his men back in the direction of the river, leaving the path open for the remnants of Cyaxares' command, who wasted no time in trotting past, heading for the southern camp. Kambyses led his force, the three thousand survivors of his attack, and the intact five thousand men under Teispes, across the face of the slope to the western end of the ridge, following behind Cyaxares' men.

The archers' activity had an extra benefit; while they had to make tighter circles than normal, the dust churned up by thousands of hooves provided a cover over and above that provided by the flying missiles that had driven Ventidius and his men back. They were the only Romans that could have offered any pursuit, and if they had been allowed to press their advantage, it was conceivable they could have prevented the Parthians from reaching their camp and regrouping. However, in what would prove to be the most crucial contribution to the Parthian cause this day, the horse archers kept Ventidius at bay, and it was not long after the tail of Kambyses' column disappeared around the curve of the western end of the ridge that Caesar, understanding this, sent a rider to Ventidius, ordering him to withdraw. The sun was now a hand's width above the western horizon, and this battle, the first major clash between the Roman invader and Parthian defender, was over.

Ultimately, what aided the Parthian cause at least as much as the interposition of the horse archers at a critical moment was that Caesar's army had been damaged sufficiently that, even had Caesar pushed them forward and over the ridge, it was unlikely that they could have pressed their advantage. At least, not without suffering even more horrific casualties. Caesar had seen that, while the Parthian's western column had been almost completely destroyed; his estimate was there were no more than three thousand men left from that force, the detachment that had come over the saddle was essentially intact. Neither he nor any Roman knew that the body of Pacorus was lying among his men atop the ridge, but even if he had known, he wasn't inclined to ask his boys for one last effort. They had suffered enough, had done enough for one day, and as he always did, Caesar was looking past just this day, to the next battle, and the one after that. No, he decided, as he sat astride Toes, watching his men in the aftermath of a hard fight, still panting from the exertion and nerves, while the ground around them, littered with bodies of man and horse, rippled with the movement of the wounded and dying. Underlying it, as always, was what to the human ear sounded like one keening moan, as if the voices of man and beast were somehow one large chorus, where every victim was singing their own part. It was the kind of sound that, once a man heard it, he would never forget, and it would haunt his dreams for the rest of his life, but Caesar was...*Caesar*, so he had to be above this, in full possession of himself and keep his *dignitas* intact by dictating instructions to his aides in the same way as if he was standing in the camp forum, issuing the routine orders of the day. And, even as he was doing so, the Centurions of his army began to take command, directing the *medici* forward from their aid stations to go help those wounded who hadn't been dragged to the rear for one reason or another, and ordering their men to start the process of cleaning up the battlefield, which was always performed in the same way. First, the rankers separated the bodies that were piled together, searching for their own, giving their attention to those comrades who still lived, signified by a sudden shout for a *medicus*. Those men who were, if not actually friends but comrades, but had already succumbed, were pulled from the Parthian bodies, and it was done with a gentleness that Caesar never failed to notice, nor did it ever fail to move him seeing Romans treat their fallen with a manner bordering on reverence, laying them out as neatly as possible before moving on. And, while he continued sending out one dispatch after another,

Caesar's eyes never left this scene before him, as he watched another example of Roman efficiency in action. Taking just long enough to glance at the sun, Caesar estimated a full watch was remaining before dark, which meant he had to make a decision about what happened next as far as his men. He knew full well that at least the men of the Legions under his direct command fully expected to march back to the camp, whereupon they would begin the ritual of the army on the night after battle, which was as important and sacrosanct in its own way as any ceremony performed by the camp priests. However, while he didn't think it likely, he couldn't dismiss the possibility that if they vacated this position, the Parthians might actually reoccupy it, requiring the same bloody business to be repeated all over again the next day. In his bones, Caesar felt certain this wouldn't happen, but he admitted, only to himself, of course, that he had been too confident in this first battle, and even from where he was, here at the western edge of what was a battlefield that stretched more than a mile to the east, he could see the Legions who had been on the southern side of the earthworks had paid a heavy price themselves. Pausing in his orders only long enough to heave a sigh, Caesar realized that he really had no choice in the matter; at least part of the army would have to stay behind to ensure that the Parthians didn't try to regain the ground they had just lost. Once he was finished issuing orders, he turned Toes and carefully guided his horse around the detritus of the fight. As he did so, the rankers in the immediate vicinity straightened from what they were doing, coming to *intente*, but it was a Centurion, the Nones Hastatus Posterior of the 12th Legion, named Manius Vibulanus, who thrust his sword in the air.

"*Ave* Caesar! *Ave Imperator* Caesar!"

Vibulanus hadn't finished his first salutation when the men picked it up, joining in to honor their commander in the traditional Roman manner, hailing him as *Imperator* three times. Because Caesar was moving, so too did the salute, as men heard the cries of their comrades, so that the sound of thousands of voices, made hoarse from battle, seemed to follow slightly behind him, awarding him the ancient honor as he passed by. Three times they shouted his name and the title, raising their own blades, some still bloody from the deadly work of the day, calling his name with a fervor that Caesar understood was as much a celebration at still being alive as any attempt to honor him. For his part, he rode past without looking in either direction, his only acknowledgement a slight lifting of his right hand, letting his men knew that he heard their cries. Frankly, one reason for Caesar's diffidence was in his recognition of his own mistakes, and the awareness of the cost in the lives of his men, but he also knew that this practice of hailing him as *Imperator* was as much for themselves as it was for him; warriors loved to march for a victorious general. And Caesar was once more the master of the field.

"How much you want to bet the old man is going to claim that for himself?"

Balbus indicated the heavy, bejeweled sword that Pullus was examining, given to him by his nephew.

"It's from the first Parthian you killed," Porcinus explained helpfully, but Pullus hadn't needed to be told.

Even in the moment of battle, Pullus had noticed the ornate blade, tucking the memory of it away. Now, he was examining it as they stood a short distance away from the corpse of Pacorus, having been joined by Scribonius, who had walked from his spot on the northern edge of the ridge. Down the slope of the saddle, the men of the Cohorts who had faced the Parthians had been freed to plunder the bodies of the enemy dead, while at the same time, round up a handful of Parthian prisoners who had been trapped underneath their slain horses, or were slightly wounded. It was from one of these men, who were forced to march up the slope of the saddle in a group, surrounded by a section of Legionaries, that Pullus, and ultimately the rest of the army, discovered the identity of the slain prince. He had been stripped of his armor and his helmet removed, which Balbus was holding, examining the inlaid seams of gold that outlined the edges of the helmet. While the lower half of the prince's face was obscured by the blood that had poured from his mouth, with the beard that had gleamed so richly earlier now matted with it and sprinkled with bits of his shattered teeth that appeared in stark contrast the raven's wing color, the prince was clearly recognizable to men who had been charged with guarding his person. Half-stumbling and half-limping, all of the prisoners had their faces averted, their collective gaze turned downward only partially because of the treacherous footing caused by the bodies and debris, until one of them happened to cast an apathetic glance to his left, just as he and his fellow prisoners reached Pullus and the others. It was actually the sword that Pullus was holding, studying the hilt as he and Scribonius debated on whether the gemstones in the hilt were real or just colored glass or perhaps similar-looking stones of no value, that drew the Parthian's attention first. Because he had been in the rear ranks and was one of the first exposed to the raking lead shot from the Eighth Cohort, this Parthian's mount, struck multiple times, had collapsed so quickly he had been unable to throw himself free. Subsequently, he had been consigned to a mostly auditory experience of the battle, both trapped and sheltered not only by his own horse but by the bodies of his fallen comrades and their own steeds as he lay there hearing the screams of men and animals in their death throes. Because of his early exit, neither was he aware that the crown prince had fallen, at least until this moment, when his eyes went from the sword, to the body that lay sprawled at the feet of a giant Roman. Pullus and the others became aware something was amiss when the Parthian suddenly uttered a low moan, laced with such despair that there was no need to translate the grief he was experiencing, which was so powerful it dropped him to his knees. More curious than alarmed; even if it had been a ploy instigated by this Parthian in a suicidal attempt to exact a form of vengeance by slaying him, it never even occurred to Pullus this cataphract posed a threat, the Roman instead noticed where the Parthian was looking. Still on his knees, he refused to move, despite the increasingly hard jabs with the tip of a sword he was enduring at the hands of one of his guards. It was when the ranker, uttering an oath, brought his sword back above his shoulder in preparation to strike the Parthian's head from his shoulders that Pullus stopped him with a simple lifting of his free hand.

"Hold there, Fusus." That the Primus Pilus of a Legion knew the names of every veteran who marched in his Legion was another reason why Pullus was so respected by his men. "Bring him here."

Only then did the Parthian seem to return to his senses, so that when Fusus gestured at him to regain his feet, he did as he was ordered, then tottered over to Pullus. Whereupon, without the Roman saying a word or indicating he gave the man leave to do so, the royal guard dropped back to his knees. This time, he reached out, and with a bit of difficulty, managed to maneuver Pacorus' corpse so that his prince's head was cradled in his lap. While he was doing so, Pullus and the others still stood, watching, more bemused than anything else.

It was Balbus who broke the silence, commenting, "Primus Pilus, I hope you don't expect us to do something like that if you get yourself killed." He shook his head, then the left corner of his mouth lifted in what to anyone who didn't know him would think was a sneer, as he joked, "I mean, we love you. But not *that* much."

That this brought laughter from the others, including the largest Roman, was ignored by the Parthian, who was actually muttering some words under his breath as Balbus was talking. Neither Pullus, nor any of the men around him, spoke more than a couple words of the Parthian dialect, but he didn't need to in order to understand that the prisoner was saying some sort of prayer for the dead. Content to let him finish whatever ritual he was conducting, Pullus stood watching, his face expressionless, while his large fist still held the sword that had been the subject of discussion, which he began swinging in slow, lazy circles.

Seeing the man finish, Pullus commented to the others, "He must have been important, whoever he was."

"This is Pacorus, son of Orodes of the house of Arsaces, the crown prince of the nation you call Parthia."

Gaius Porcinus, who had yet to be released from his status as runner, would long remember the shocked silence, and the expression of his uncle as he stared down at the prisoner. As far as Porcinus was concerned, the surprise stemmed not only from the identity of the slain man, but that the prisoner had spoken in Latin, heavily accented and hard to understand, it was true, but still the Roman tongue.

It was left to Scribonius to regain his voice first, and despite the fact he hadn't been forced to shout a command since earlier that day, his voice was still hoarse as he managed, "Well, Titus. If you were going to choose someone to kill, you couldn't have done any better than this."

For his part, Pullus, while just as rooted in surprise as his friends, wasn't quite as willing to believe the Parthian. Buried deep within him, and most Romans, were stories of Eastern duplicity, and it was an article of faith that these oily men were liars of the highest degree.

It was with this in mind that Pullus' voice was hard as he asked, "How do I know you're not lying to me?"

Even in his circumstances, surrounded by men who he understood would kill him without giving any more thought to the act than if he were a pig to be slaughtered, the prisoner's tone still contained a fair amount of scorn as he posed a question of his own.

"Why would I tell you that you had slain our prince if it wasn't true, Roman?"

Pullus hadn't been prepared for this, but after the slight moment of surprise, he actually considered the man's words. As he thought about it, he realized that he couldn't think of any reason why this Parthian would lie about it.

174

"So this is Pacorus," Pullus informed the prisoner he accepted the Parthian's word for it indirectly. Thinking for a moment, he found himself in an absurd position, trying to offer some reassurance to an enemy by pointing out, "But your king has at least one more son, doesn't he? What's his name?"

"Phraates." The prisoner's mouth twisted into an expression that seemed to indicate he had just tasted something foul. "Yes," he agreed bitterly, "the King of Kings still has Phraates." Shaking his head sadly, for a moment both prisoner and captors forgot their circumstances, as the Parthian said mournfully, "I pray to Ahura Mazda for Parthia with Phraates holding power."

Pullus and Scribonius exchanged glances, their minds running along the same lines; this was the kind of information that their general favored above all others, seemingly random and offhand comments that gave Caesar insight into the inner workings of his enemy.

"What are you going to do with his body?"

While Pullus certainly didn't feel any obligation to answer a prisoner's question, neither did he begrudge it being asked, and he responded with a shrug.

"I suppose we'll leave it here." He did give his captive a cold smile and added, "I don't think we're going to be here very long. I have a feeling your army is going to be on the move very quickly."

Then, nodding to Fusus, who had been standing there the whole time trying not to betray how bored he was, Pullus indicated that the captive be returned to the company of his fellow prisoners. The Parthian rose, but only after gently removing Pacorus' head from his lap, then just as gently laying it on the ground. Giving his prince one last kiss on his forehead, the Parthian allowed himself to be led away, not responding when Fusus shoved him so roughly that he stumbled. This earned Fusus a sharp rebuke from Pullus; the prisoner had earned a modicum of respect for his show of devotion to his fallen prince. Then, before the prisoner had gone a dozen more steps, Pullus reconsidered. Calling Fusus, who was wise enough to stifle the groan at the fickleness of Centurions, Pullus had him bring the Parthian back to where Pullus was standing.

"Sit down there," the Primus Pilus commanded, then said no more, leaving the Parthian to wonder what lay in store for him next.

It was shortly after this moment when Caesar arrived, accompanied by his usual trail of aides and secretaries, his ascent up through the saddle made more difficult because of the aftermath of the fight. He stopped long enough to examine the corpses of the Parthians strewn along the bottom of the saddle, those men who had been in the rear ranks and subjected to Ventidius' new innovation. He viewed the results with grim satisfaction, thinking to himself he had to come up with a way to reward the older man for his contribution, because one didn't have to be a military expert to see the carnage the jagged lead missiles caused. Once he was satisfied, he guided Toes up the slope, the horse long accustomed to the smell of death that even his owner could begin to smell. The hot sun didn't help, although it was now close to the horizon, yet even as Caesar navigated his way around the small piles, usually composed of at least one horse and one cataphract, the growing stench meant he was cognizant of what he would be asking of the 10th. Men of the ranks, particularly Romans, were a superstitious sort, and having them remain in the vicinity of a battle, where the departed spirits of the enemy they had slain would now, at least in their imaginings, be roaming through the night, wasn't a prospect the 10th would savor. Fortunately, finding the Primus Pilus of the 10th was never a challenge, Caesar thought wryly, as he spotted the Roman who towered over everyone around him, and who even then was directing men to do his bidding. Pullus, spotting Caesar, issued one more order, then stood and waited for his general to reach him. The remainder of his men had finished their grisly but financially rewarding task of looting the dead, and had moved back onto the ridgetop proper, rejoining the rest of their comrades in the 10th. This left just Pullus, Valerius, Balbus, and one forlorn, slightly unhappy Gregarius in Porcinus to greet their general who, it must be said, was a bit peeved that there weren't men present to add their own hailing of him as *Imperator* in the same way that the Legions down below had done. Putting this absence down to the fact that there weren't men available to do so, Caesar pushed Toes into a trot the last hundred paces to reach Pullus, who rendered a salute, which Caesar returned even as he was swinging down from the saddle. Walking to Pullus' side, for a moment, the pair were content to gaze down the slope at the carnage wrought by the Primus Pilus and his men.

Finally, Caesar said in a conversational tone, "Well, Pullus, it looks like Ventidius' idea worked."

"That it did, sir," Pullus agreed, then admitted, "A lot better than I would have thought."

"You weren't alone," Caesar replied, but didn't add anything that might indicate he was one of the doubters as well. "But, obviously,

176

those lead sling shots cause quite a bit of damage." Then, before Pullus could make any comment one way or the other, Caesar turned to him and asked, "And what does your butcher's bill look like?"

"Lighter than I would have believed possible," Pullus told him, then proceeded to give the shortened version of a casualty report, simply listing the number of men put out of action by Cohort, rather than breaking it down by Century.

When he was finished, he hesitated for a moment in such a way that it caused Caesar to notice.

"And?" Caesar asked mildly, but he was expecting to hear something negative based on the way his Primus Pilus was behaving, as if he was about to impart bad news. "What else is there?"

Rather than answering directly, Pullus turned and nodded to his nephew, on whose shoulders it had fallen to guard the Parthian prisoner. A man who Caesar hadn't noticed immediately, so when the young Gregarius that the general knew was Pullus' nephew dragged a Parthian before him, the general had to contain his surprise.

"So you captured a prisoner?" Caesar asked, somewhat amused, which caused Pullus' face to redden slightly.

But instead of addressing Caesar, the Primus Pilus turned to the Parthian and said simply, "Tell him."

Whereupon the Parthian did, only after being forced to his knees by Porcinus, informing Caesar in a voice dulled by the fatigue and emotional toll of the day of the identity of the stiffening body, even as the Parthian described him, at which Pullus pointed out. In retrospect, Caesar had cause to be grateful that he and Pullus were alone, because the general's reaction was such that, in the coming weeks of this campaign, Caesar knew full well could have caused him innumerable problems.

"And you killed him?" Caesar snapped, wheeling on Pullus after a brief examination of the corpse. "Do you know how much he'd be worth alive, Pullus? That if you had used your head, how many lives of our army, and *your* men," Caesar stabbed an accusing finger at the large Roman, "would be saved? But no," Caesar's voice struck Pullus like a lash, "the great Titus Pullus only saw an enemy to be vanquished, and didn't stop to *think*." Even as the words were tumbling out of his mouth, Caesar understood he was being unfair, but the truth was he was frustrated with himself because of those errors he had made during this battle. The fact that Pullus looked as stricken as if his general had physically slapped him only made matters worse.

Holding up a hand to cut Pullus off before he could say anything, Caesar said wearily, "Please, forgive me, Pullus. That was not only unfair, it was untrue." He heaved a sigh that only a man like Pullus could hope to understand, the kind of sound that comes from the crushing weight of holding the fates of thousands of other men in one's hands. "No, you behaved perfectly correctly. There was no way to know this was anyone more than just another Parthian nobleman. But," he admitted ruefully, "he was much more valuable to us alive than dead."

The truth was that Pullus was only partially mollified by Caesar's words, which had ignited in the giant Roman a smoldering anger that, despite knowing he couldn't show it, still prodded Pullus to respond in defense of himself. Fortunately, for both men, he managed to refrain, keeping his ire bottled up inside him, while his face was a mask of professionalism.

However, neither could he deny the sense of what Caesar had said, and he agreed, "I can certainly see that, sir. But," he shrugged, and added simply, "that's a jug that's been broken." Turning towards more immediate matters, he asked, "What are your orders now, Caesar?"

Caesar actually hesitated, perhaps moved by his unwarranted chastisement to reconsider what he had planned for the 10th, but Pullus, seeing this indecision, offered what could have been considered an olive branch of his own.

"I told the men they needed to expect to stay put at least for tonight," he began, absurdly pleased by the look of relief that flooded Caesar's features. "We don't want to have to fight for this ground twice."

"Thank you, Pullus," Caesar spoke quietly, then emphasized his gratitude by putting a hand on the shoulder of his favored Primus Pilus. "I'm glad you understood the situation. I was worried about asking your boys to spend another night up here. It won't be comfortable, and..."

His voice trailed off, but Pullus didn't need his general to expand, and he assured Caesar with a chuckle, "I won't have to order the men to be alert tonight. They're all going to be convinced there's *numeni* flitting about, waiting to take possession of them and drag them off to Hades."

Caesar's own laugh was tinged with the relief he felt that Pullus understood, and, in fact, shared his skepticism about such matters. Then, before anything more could be said, the relative quiet was shattered by the higher-pitched sound of a *bucina*, the horn used by Romans to send commands when in camp, such as change of watch. Or, as the notes sounded at this moment, that someone was approaching. That it came from farther west and on the southern side of the ridge gave both general and Primus Pilus the news that someone or something was approaching from the south, where the remnant of the Parthian army was still encamped. Caesar didn't hesitate, vaulting into the saddle, then snapped an order to one of his mounted secretaries to surrender his own horse to Pullus, waiting for him to clamber onto the back of the animal before the pair cantered towards the source of the noise, one of them with the grace of a natural horseman and the other with the grim determination of a man who just wants to keep his seat in the saddle. They left a small cluster of men behind to their own devices, wondering what they were supposed to do next.

The reason for the call was because of the appearance of a lone Parthian rider, bearing a symbol the Romans recognized as that requesting a truce, but the rider had ascended only partway up the ridge before he was stopped by a section of Legionaries belonging to the Fourth Cohort who were serving as an advance outpost a short distance from the brow of the ridge. They forced the Parthian to wait until someone of appropriate rank could make a decision about whether or not to accept him into their lines, or to fill him full of javelins. Nevertheless, none of the rankers dreamed that it would be Caesar himself who came trotting down from behind them, with their Primus Pilus alongside, also mounted and doing his best to appear as if he was comfortable. Seeing Titus Pullus astride an animal was a significant enough sight that the presence of their general didn't have the impact it normally would, although the ranking Legionary did remember to salute. Caesar returned it, but he didn't waste any more time, trotting the fifty paces so that he could converse with this envoy without having to shout. That he did so without any regard for his own safety meant that Pullus felt duty-bound to hurry his mount along so that he could at least draw within a dozen paces himself, in the event this Parthian had something in mind other than talking. But the Parthian, his beard oiled but an iron gray, clearly had other matters on his mind, because while his eyes never left Caesar, he made sure his hands were clearly visible and held out at his sides.

"Yes? What is that you come to ask of us?"

That Caesar spoke in Latin initially surprised Pullus, yet when he thought about it, he realized the same thing his general had, just much earlier; the Parthians wouldn't have sent an envoy who didn't speak Latin. The Parthian clearly wasn't expecting to be addressed in such an abrupt manner, and his swarthy features darkened even more, but Pullus saw the man take a deep breath as he briefly closed his eyes before he replied.

"My name," Pullus wasn't sure why, but he was surprised at how deep the man's voice was, perhaps because he judged that this Parthian was average sized for his people, "is Kambyses, son of Otanes. I'm currently in command of this *spad*, sent by the King of Kings, the great Orodes…"

Before he got any further, Caesar held up a hand, interjecting with a tone that is used by the conqueror when addressing the vanquished, "Yes, yes. I'm well aware of all the titles your king claims. I'm afraid I'm very busy, so please get to the point of this request."

Even encased in armor, Pullus saw the Parthian's body stiffen with rage, as his eyes first went wide in shock, then just as quickly almost disappeared into two narrowed slits, and for a moment, Pullus felt certain that the Parthian would do something stupid and try to attack Caesar. This was actually exactly what Kambyses was considering, as his blood ran so hot that all thoughts about his purpose in asking for a meeting were boiled away, so that his hand had started moving towards his sword even before he had conscious thought of doing so. Ironically, he was saved from himself by the juxtaposition of the giant Roman that, frankly, Kambyses had barely noticed at first, so focused was he on seeing this Caesar in the flesh for the first time. But when Pullus moved his horse, he placed it at such an angle that, even through his rage, Kambyses recognized that this Roman would cut him down before he got near Caesar. Meanwhile, the man who had issued the insult and was now the subject of this sudden drama sat unmoving and seemingly unconcerned on his horse, his eyes the color of the ice found only in the deepest crevices of the highest mountains in the vast lands Kambyses considered his home, and which never left the Parthian's own face. Pullus' action served as a bucket of cold water poured over the burning rage that had ignited at the slur uttered by this Roman, and it gave Kambyses the clarity to see that Caesar had not only expected his words to enrage him, but it was highly likely this was exactly what the Roman wanted. Once more, the Parthian took himself in hand, bringing his emotions back under control, while he did the same to his mount, which had begun to quiver and paw at the

180

hard ground as the tension of its rider passed from Kambyses' body into its own.

"As you say," Kambyses finally managed, "you know whom I serve. But what you may not know is that our..." He swallowed, feeling the bitter taste of the words that came next. "...prince was slain today."

For the first time, Caesar's manner seemed to soften, and he nodded his head as he said gravely, "Yes, we became aware that Pacorus had fallen in battle." What Caesar said next was a source of much discussion and debate between Pullus and his friends, and the general nodded his head in the other Roman's direction, who was still in position to fall on Kambyses, "This is the man who slew him."

Kambyses gasped, and Pullus immediately noticed how effortlessly the Parthian controlled his mount as, without using his hands but with what Pullus guessed was pressure from one knee, Kambyses turned his mount so that he was now directly facing Pullus. A space of no more than five paces separated the pair, which Pullus knew wasn't enough room for the Parthian to get his horse up to any kind of speed, although he wasn't comforted by this thought very much. For an instant, Pullus considered sliding off his own mount, his discomfort on horseback such that he would have rather faced Kambyses on the ground, even if the Parthian stayed in the saddle himself. But, instead of attacking, once more, Kambyses gathered what remained of his composure.

"What is your name, Roman?" he asked Pullus, his voice suddenly made hoarse from the internal strain of the previous few moments. "I would like to know the name of the man who slew our prince, so that I may tell his father at least that much."

"My name is Titus Pullus," the giant Roman answered, still wary that the Parthian might try something.

"You are of one of Rome's noble houses then, are you not?"

Kambyses indicated the white transverse crest all Primi Pili wore, mistaking its purpose, thinking as a Parthian would, that nobility and competence were one and the same thing. While he had no idea what to expect, the Parthian was completely unprepared for the giant to burst out laughing, but it was the sight of Caesar smiling that was the most confusing. More shocked than offended, Kambyses was beginning to suspect that all Romans were at least partially mad.

"Why is this so amusing to you, Roman?"

Pullus was still too consumed in mirth that all he could offer was a shake of his head, then he gestured in Caesar's direction as he wiped the tears from his seamed face.

"The reason my Primus Pilus is laughing is that, to answer your question," Caesar's tone belied his own amusement at this misunderstanding, yet underneath this seeming lightheartedness, the general sensed that he could accomplish something here, "no, Kambyses, Titus Pullus is not from one of our noble houses. In fact," if Kambyses hadn't already been so confused and discomfited, he might have noticed the manner in which Caesar's eyes seemed to take on a gleaming quality or the slight quirk at the corner of the Roman's mouth as he supplied to Kambyses the cause of their shared amusement, "Titus Pullus is a member of our Head Count."

"Head Count?" Kambyses repeated the unfamiliar term.

"What you'd call your peasant class," Caesar informed him genially. "He comes from roughly the same class as the men who are in your infantry."

Titus Pullus would take a great deal of joy in recounting this moment to his friends, and never tired of describing how Kambyses' jaw dropped in utter shock, and for an instant, the Parthian reeled in the saddle so precipitously that Pullus was sure that, no matter how good a horseman he might be, Kambyses would hit the ground. Of course, he did no such thing, although he did shake his head not once but twice, in the same manner as a man who has taken a blow to the head and is trying to clear out the cobwebs in his mind.

"Our crown prince was slain by a...a...*peasant*?"

While it was the case that Kambyses hadn't known what to expect when he approached the Roman lines, never in his wildest imaginings could he have conjured up this conversation. Even as he was still trying to grasp the full import of this last piece of information, Caesar was the one who corrected him, or at least seemed to do so.

"*Not* a peasant," Caesar's voice had turned hard and implacable, "a *Roman*." Suddenly, Caesar kicked Toes forward to close the distance between himself and the Parthian, drawing abreast of Kambyses so he could stare into the eyes of his enemy. "And you'd do well to remember that difference, Kambyses. No matter what class a man of Rome belongs to, he is a Roman first. And that means he is born to be a conqueror."

While Titus Pullus had no objection to Caesar allowing Kambyses to retrieve the body of his prince, nor did he object to

182

allowing a half-dozen of the captured Parthians serve as bearers of his corpse, including the royal guard who had provided the identity of the prince, he was not nearly as happy about Caesar's decision to return Pacorus' sword to Kambyses.

"Caesar, I won that in battle!" Pullus had protested when Caesar ordered him, or Porcinus, more accurately, since he was the one in physical possession of it, to hand the valuable blade over to Kambyses. "It's a spoil of war!"

Probably more than any man in the army, Caesar was aware that the term Pullus had used was neither an accident nor was it without significance in itself. After all, Caesar had extricated himself from the massive debt in which he found himself when he was awarded the post of Praetor in Hispania, and it was by virtue of the campaign he waged against the rebelling Lusitani that he become solvent again. Also, Roman society, more than any other of its time, placed a high value on the rule of law, and subsequently, had come up with a vast number of procedures regarding almost every facet of conduct in which an individual Roman could engage. Therefore, when Pullus invoked the term, Caesar knew that, strictly judged, Pullus would be considered in the right by a Roman court. That, however, was a secondary concern for Caesar at this moment; the facts were that they were thousands of miles from a Roman court, he was in command, and he had made the decision that his aims would be furthered with this gesture.

"Pullus," he had been gentle with his Primus Pilus, but he was intent on ensuring that Pullus understand that on this, his mind wouldn't be changed, "I understand that it's a valuable sword. But I'll compensate you for it and give you a fair amount."

It would have been impossible to say who was more surprised, Pullus or Caesar, but as the general was about to learn, the monetary gain or loss wasn't part of the Primus Pilus' consideration.

"Pluto's balls," Pullus burst out, forgetting to whom he was speaking, which as Caesar knew from experience was a habit of his, "I don't care about that, Caesar! I didn't expect to keep it for myself!" He gestured at the retreating back of Kambyses, who was leaving the ridge under the watchful eyes of the men of the 10th, leading the men bearing Pacorus' body. "But we shouldn't just...give it back!" Shaking his head to emphasize his disagreement, Pullus finished stubbornly, "It would be like if we left the ridge for the night and let these bastards take it back."

If this had been uttered by any almost any other of his Centurions, and certainly from any of his Legates, Caesar wouldn't have put much credence in their sincerity. Not so with Titus Pullus; there was something to be said for having known this man since he was a sixteen-year-old, overgrown youth who had lied about his age to join the Legions, and Caesar knew that Pullus viewed money only as a means to an end. This was a viewpoint the two had in common; truthfully, it had often occurred to Caesar that he and Pullus shared the same views on more subjects than Caesar did with most of his social contemporaries. This was one reason why Caesar was certain that Pullus was being sincere, and was a reminder to the general why he had plans for his giant Roman over and above life in the Legion. Provided, of course, that he was successful in this campaign.

"I understand," Caesar repeated, "but this is my decision."

Having marched for Caesar as long as he had, Pullus knew by his general's tone when he was serious, and that further pursuit of this matter would only end badly for one of them, and it wouldn't be Caesar. Satisfying himself with a sigh as his last token of resistance to Caesar's plan, he turned and watched Kambyses for a few moments, then turned and saluted his general.

"With your permission, I'd like to get the men bedded down and as comfortable as they can get for the night."

Naturally, Caesar agreed, but he was about to inform Pullus that now that the day was at an end, he planned on holding his customary meeting in the *praetorium* and expected Pullus to be there, then thought better of it. No, he conceded, we'll hold it up here; perhaps that would appease Pullus slightly. Besides, Caesar wanted to keep his eyes on the Parthian camp below. If his instincts were correct, there would be a mass Parthian exodus happening before the sun rose on another day, and he wanted to be there to see it for himself, and to see the final stroke he had prepared. Therefore, he issued orders to his aides to go find the Legates who had been involved in the day's events, along with the Primi Pili, and bring them to the top of the ridge. The sun was now only halfway visible against the backdrop of the same, stark western hills that, other than their location, were identical to the one on which Caesar and Pullus were standing. One aspect of this campaign and the conditions under which it was being conducted were the incredible swings in temperature, and even with the sun only partially obscured, Caesar could feel that the air was noticeably cooler. The wind, already stiffer up here than down by the rivers, was picking up as well, and this prompted Caesar to turn to his last aide, actually his personal secretary Apollodorus, who was the only man remaining of the gaggle of aides and secretaries that men like Pullus called the Ducklings, and issue a quiet order to him. While Pullus couldn't hear what was said, just by the secretary's reaction, he could see that what Caesar was requiring of him wasn't insignificant. Despite this, Apollodorus didn't hesitate, turning his horse and immediately going to the trot, away from his general and master.

Returning to Pullus, Caesar said, "Why don't we go over there," he indicated a spot right where the southern side of the ridge dropped away out of sight, "and see what's happening?"

Without waiting for an answer, Caesar trotted past Pullus, who turned and followed him, wondering what task Apollodorus had been sent to perform.

Pullus got his answer in the form of a train of mules, each one accompanied by a section slave, and led by his own clerk Diocles, who he had insisted remain behind in the camp during the attack and not serve in his normal secondary function as a *medicus*. While they didn't bring the section tents, each mule was loaded with the *sagum* of each man in its section, a portion of rations, and perhaps most appreciated by the men, charcoal that would provide heat for not only their rations, but to help dispel the chill.

"Considering how magnificently they performed today," Caesar explained to Pullus, "I thought this was the least I could do to show my appreciation."

For his part, Pullus was thankful that the sun had set so that his grin couldn't be seen much past where Caesar was now standing next to him, holding Toes' reins in one hand. Pullus' reaction was only partially based in the pleased gratitude he felt whenever his general praised his boys, because it wasn't lost on Pullus that Caesar had spoken more loudly than needed, considering Pullus was standing within arm's reach. His general's words were meant to be overheard, as both men knew and understood how quickly his words would be relayed along the line of Cohorts, that had now all been shifted to the southern side of the ridge. And, Pullus thought with some amusement, by the time Publius in the Tenth heard it, Caesar's praise would have been elevated to the level of a paean comparing the action of the day to the battles for which the 10th had rightly earned fame, like Alesia and Pharsalus. Still, while Pullus respected and admired Caesar for his canny insight into how the minds of his men worked, there was a part of him that had been growing increasingly uncomfortable as he became more aware of the true level of manipulation that men of Caesar's class exerted on those of his own class. In Pullus' deeply held opinion, no man worthy of being called one liked to be handled in much the same manner as the marionettes used in the puppet shows that were popular with Romans of all classes, and if he took time to dwell on it, Pullus would have been forced to confront the deep vein of resentment that ran through his soul, aimed at men of Caesar's class. And, while Pullus would never admit it, at Caesar himself, for moments just like this. Despite this deeply held feeling, what Pullus forced his mind to focus on was that, ultimately, what Caesar said, and did, served to the benefit of his men, and the rest of his comrades in the army. No matter what the true motivation might be, Pullus couldn't argue that Caesar was effective at creating a bond between himself and the men who did the bulk of the fighting, and dying, for him. Turning his attention back to the moment, Pullus gave Balbus the effective responsibility of overseeing the distribution of the supplies brought to them, then in a whispered conference with Diocles, sent the Greek on his own, private mission. Meanwhile, Caesar had kept at least part of his attention on the camp below and, suddenly, he reached out and grabbed Pullus' arm to get his attention.

"See there, Pullus." He pointed down to the south. "It looks as if the Parthians are on the move!"

And when Pullus did as he had been instructed, he too saw what was really little more than darker shapes shifting about on the dark ground below. There were no fires blazing in the middle of the camp; only those torches that provided a rough outline of the boundaries of the Parthian position remained, making it impossible to see any details, but as the pair watched, they saw the disappearance of the only objects that shared the same shape as others that Pullus knew were their tents. One by one, these darkened shapes seemed to shift their appearance, becoming smaller, and only if Pullus strained his eyes could he see the smaller dark shapes that were the men striking them. Every few heartbeats, a stray breeze would carry a sound up to the watching Romans, usually the neighing of a horse, and once or twice the shout of a man. As they were watching, Pullus was struck by a thought.

"Wouldn't this be a good time to hit them?" he asked Caesar quietly. "They're completely disorganized; all they want to do is get away, and we know they hate fighting at night."

186

Caesar didn't reply, verbally at least, but even in the gloom, Pullus saw the gleam of his general's teeth as he turned and gave Pullus a smile. Despite his age, Caesar still had excellent teeth, which some of the rankers pointed to as evidence of his being blessed by the gods; from Pullus' perspective, given his more intimate contact with his general, he thought it had more to do with how fastidious Caesar was in his personal hygiene habits. What was well known was how he had his own depilatory slave, whose only purpose was to keep every hair of Caesar's body from the neck down plucked before it could grow; what relatively few were aware of was how assiduously Caesar scrubbed his teeth with a coarse cloth after every meal. A reason Pullus was one of the few who knew about this habit was because he had been present when Caesar had been introduced to this practice by a young woman barely out of her teens. That she had been Pharaoh of Egypt, and according to those backward people, directly descended from one of their gods and therefore divine herself, hadn't hurt her credibility with the older, more cosmopolitan Caesar. And it was the sight of those still near-perfect teeth that Pullus got a glimmer that Caesar had something in mind.

However, all he would say to Pullus was, "Keep watching."

Which, of course, his Primus Pilus did; they were still standing there, watching as the Parthians hastily broke down their baggage, when the rest of Caesar's senior officers began arriving. Naturally, the Legates were the first to come clattering up, since every one of them were mounted. It was at about this time when Pullus caught a hint of what Caesar might have been teasing him about, by virtue of who was missing. Where, the Primus Pilus thought as he surveyed the men dismounting, tossing their reins to some of the Ducklings who had returned from their respective tasks, was Ventidius? But then he saw, arriving later than the others, the young Octavian, who Pullus knew had been assigned to the cavalry arm as well. Before he could take any time to explore this development by approaching the youngster, Pullus was stopped by the arrival of the first of the Primi Pili; Balbinus of the 12th was the leader, puffing from the exertion of climbing the slope, but following closely behind him was Carfulenus, then Spurius. One by one, Pullus' counterparts joined the growing knot of men clustered at the edge of the ridge, with the Parthians busy down below, each of them puffing and cursing under their breath in direct relation to their age, and where they had found themselves upon receiving the summons from Caesar.

Only when Caesar began speaking did Pullus realize that one of his counterparts was missing, as the general spoke somberly, "Before we begin, I wanted you to know I grieve with you, Tiberius Atartinus. The men of the 11th aren't the only ones in mourning. Losing a man like Lanatus is one that is grievous for the entire army." He paused for a moment, then said quietly, "But I have every confidence that you'll do your utmost to follow the example he set...Primus Pilus Atartinus."

Neither Pullus nor any of the other Primi Pili needed any light to see the effect Caesar's words, especially his last ones, had on the man who, up until earlier that day was the Primus Pilus Posterior, second in command of the 11th Legion, if only by virtue of Atartinus suddenly standing straighter.

"T-thank you, Caesar," Atartinus spoke, then winced at his expression of gratitude, but he was in the company of men who understood very well the decidedly unusual situation in which a newly promoted Primus Pilus found himself.

Every one of them had experienced a moment similar to this one, when they had seen their own careers advanced because of the demise of their superior, almost always men they, if they didn't admire, at least respected, making them a sympathetic audience to Atartinus' quandary. How does one express their gratitude and their grief at the circumstances at the same time? Caesar saved Atartinus from further embarrassment, although it wasn't for that purpose, as his voice became brisk, his own subtle signal that the time for mourning Lanatus would come later; there was still business at hand.

Turning his attention back down to the camp, the general said, "I'll take your full reports momentarily, but there should be something...interesting happening down in the Parthian camp at any moment."

Pullus experienced a moment of uncertainty, so he turned to peer closely at the faces of Caesar's officers, made easier not only by the fact they had all removed their helmets, but as usually happened, there was a natural division as Caesar's Legates sought the company of their fellow nobles on one side of the general, while the Primi Pili were on the other. Only after a careful study did he reassure himself that Ventidius was the only man of Legate rank missing; the presence of his ostensible second in command was a matter of curiosity that he tucked away to find more about later. Pullus considered speaking up, then thought better of it, knowing that Caesar wanted to be the one to introduce this surprise; if, of course, the others hadn't already guessed. This didn't seem likely, judging from what he could see of the

188

expressions of the men around him; he was sure they had noticed Ventidius' absence as well. The quiet settled over their shoulders as they all stared down at the Parthian camp, waiting for whatever it was Caesar had planned. And they continued to wait, until some of the more impatient among them started to fidget, and while Pullus was one of them, he managed to refrain from engaging in the muttered speculation that his counterparts started engaging in with each other.

The first indication that Caesar's plan was coming to fruition came courtesy of the shrill, wavering sound of a Parthian horn, which was quickly joined by first another, then one more. Even with the darkness, the Romans above the camp could see a further explosion of what they knew was movement within the confines of the camp proper. However, it was the sudden appearance of a large, dark mass that abruptly materialized from the observers' right, or western end of the ridge, that brought the first shouts of excitement and acclamation. The sound of the hooves of thousands of horses at the gallop took a few heartbeats to roll up to the men on the ridge, but that thunderous noise soon drowned out all others coming from the camp. None of the Romans needed to hear what they knew from experience would be the shouts of alarm, cries of fear, and shrieks of agony as Ventidius and his Gallo-Germanic cavalry came slicing through the hugely disorganized Parthian camp. Even as they watched, Pullus and the others saw that some of Ventidius' men had been carrying torches, which they now saw thrown by their bearers, the flames thinning out as the torches tumbled end over end, looking very much like blazing circles to the naked eye, before landing amidst several of the dark bundles that were the partially dismantled tents. Some of the torches either sputtered out on their own or were stamped out by nearby Parthians, but very quickly, well more than fifty caught fire to whatever they landed on, which in its own lurid way, helped light the scene more fully. Within a span of no more than of a hundred heartbeats, most of the fires were fully involved, thereby allowing Pullus and the others to watch as Ventidius' men broke down into several separate smaller columns, spreading out into the camp in every direction, although they were too far away and it was still too dark to see their flashing blades cutting down Parthians without any discrimination between combatants and those who fulfilled roles similar to Diocles or Apollodorus. Despite the lack of detail, what they couldn't miss was the noise of slaughter rising up from the ground below, with shrill screams becoming a sound almost as continuous as the thundering sound of the hooves of Ventidius' cavalry, slashing their way into the remnants of an already defeated army. So absorbed was Pullus in the scene of mobile destruction taking place nearest to where he and the others were standing, he failed to notice something, until Caesar pointed it out.

"Look farther south," his voice was calm, at least on the surface, but Pullus could hear the underlying sense of tense excitement, "it looks like a fair number of the Parthians are getting away."

Since the fires hadn't reached the spot that was easily almost a mile from where they were standing, all Pullus saw was what looked like little more than a large, black stain whose borders seemed to shift as it moved. As he watched, though, he could finally discern that it was indeed moving south, picking up speed.

"I hope Ventidius can see that," Pullus wasn't sure but thought that it was Pollio who commented, "because from the looks of it, he's on the opposite side of the camp."

"I told him specifically to send a flying column through the camp to cut off any escape to the south," Caesar replied, then after a pause said only, "but it doesn't look like he was able to do so. I'm sure he had a good reason."

He better hope so, Pullus thought with some grim humor, knowing full well that, while Caesar was forgiving when a man under his commanded erred in some way, it was only when the offending party could offer a good, or at least plausible reason for doing so, something that the demoted Lepidus could attest to as he toiled away back in the main camp, counting chickpeas. Caesar and his officers continued to watch for perhaps another sixth part of a watch, but Pullus knew that if he could see how many men managed to flee to the south, after the larger group had made good their escape, his general hadn't missed it either. Nevertheless, Caesar made no more comment about Ventidius' actions, choosing instead to start asking for the butcher's bill from his Primi Pili. Apollodorus had returned by this point, and Balbus came to report that the men were now settled down as comfortably as possible. Pullus was tempted to point out that Ventidius' attack had guaranteed the Parthians wouldn't try any kind of offensive operation against the 10th, but quickly realized that his men wouldn't appreciate being roused to march back to the camp now that it was fully dark. When it came to his turn to inform Caesar of his casualties, the Primus Pilus of the 10th did experience a moment akin to what he thought Ventidius might endure, but his discomfort

190

stemmed from the fact that it was the men of the First Cohort who suffered the most, although when compared to the other Legions, his own losses were negligible.

Once Pullus finished, Caesar didn't waste any time, asking pointedly, "And why are almost all of your casualties just in the First Cohort?"

"Because," Pullus maintained his composure but he felt his face heat up, "I only used the First to repel the cataphract attack."

Pullus wasn't particularly surprised at the sudden hissing as his fellow Primi Pili drew in a surprised breath, but it wasn't them he needed to worry about being displeased.

"What were your reasons for just deploying the First?" Caesar asked, seemingly truly curious.

"I thought the First would be enough to handle them," Pullus replied honestly. "And we still didn't know about your situation, or even whether or not that column we saw head west was really going to attack you, or try to climb up from that side to knock us off."

Caesar considered this for a moment, during which Pullus held his breath, before the general shrugged and said, "That makes sense. I might have been more prudent, but," by the change in his voice, Pullus could sense that Caesar had already dismissed this as an item for further investigation, "it was your decision to make. And ultimately it worked out to our advantage."

Pullus carefully let out the breath he had been holding, deeply relieved by Caesar's acceptance, and that he didn't seem disposed to ask Pullus the one question he had been dreading, about the practicability of the western slope for a force of cataphracts. Ultimately, Pullus' decision to have his lone Cohort, arrayed in a single line of Centuries rather than the standard double line, be the only one to meet the Parthian charge was based in the Roman's immense pride, in himself and the men under whom his command was the more immediate cause. It was true that Pullus commanded every man in the Legion, but ultimately, his closest association with men of the ranks was with those in his own Century, then his Cohort. He had complete faith in his boys, and he hadn't even considered the notion that any one of them would have wanted the help of other Cohorts in repelling the attack. And if this had been true before the first line of cataphracts came pounding up the slope at them, once the word that their Primus Pilus had slain a crown prince of the enemy, they would have been even more adamant in having the honor that came from standing alone. As all Centurions knew, nothing made men happier than the idea of killing a member of the nobility, no matter for whom he fought.

Chapter Six

Caesar and his army ended up spending three days in this location, but not without the general ordering the movement of their camp from its original spot, placing it more or less on the ruins of the Parthians' former camp. Only after, the men were allowed to comb through the debris and loot the bodies of this second phase of the battle, which allowed Caesar to achieve two objectives in one. By giving his men leave to thoroughly search the Parthian camp, he also had them perform a cleanup of the area, removing the bodies and charred remains of Parthian tents and wagons. The bodies were buried in a mass grave that it took one full Legion most of the second day to dig, although they weren't the men required to perform the grisly task of moving the bodies from where they had fallen and dumping them into this huge hole, which despite its size, quickly filled up. By the time the final tally of the dead was performed, the army of almost forty thousand combatants had been reduced by a bit more than twenty-five thousand. The contingent of Parthian infantry, whose numbers Caesar had no more than an estimate to begin with, was the hardest hit; some eight thousand spearmen had been slain, but whether it was from a force of more than ten thousand men, Caesar didn't know. Neither was this the part of the Parthian army that Caesar had hoped sustained the heaviest loss; there were at least ten thousand cataphracts total who had survived the initial battle, and only five hundred of those had been cut down in Ventidius' attack. From the reports of Ventidius and his Decurions, these men had either been ordered or chosen to stand and fight, thereby allowing a disturbingly high number of their comrades to make good their escape. It was a victory, and a clear-cut one, but it hadn't brought Caesar the decisive moment he had been hoping for, one that would mean the rest of the march to Ctesiphon was clear of any real resistance. Regardless, Caesar also recognized that this had been a hugely important battle, on a number of levels, and he and his army had garnered substantial gains, both tangible and intangible.

Perhaps the most important lesson learned was that the tactics devised by Caesar and the innovation by Ventidius with the lead missiles worked in concert to defeat cataphracts, although the importance of the terrain was bloodily underscored in the difference in casualties suffered by Pullus' 10th and the men of the Legions under

Caesar's command. Even with the use of the sling and the lead missiles, as the men of the 11th in particular learned to their detriment, on level ground, despite the fact that a cataphract and his horse at a gallop wasn't as swift as those Parthians armed with a bow, they still covered ground too quickly for slingers to get off more than two, or perhaps three missiles. But, as the slain Lanatus and his men had learned, attempting to loose one more volley meant that men weren't prepared to face the onslaught of armored horses and men. The first line of Lanatus' Cohort were still in the process of transitioning between acting as slingers and dropping into the proper position to brace for the inevitable collision, and they suffered accordingly. A result of this mistake was in the isolation and near loss of the sacred eagle of the Legion, for which Lanatus paid with his life, a major factor in Caesar's decision to say nothing to the surviving Centurions about what was ultimately an error of judgment by their Primus Pilus. In other ways, the evidence of the damage done by the jagged lead missiles was seen by almost every man in the army, answering what had been a subject of much doubt among men of all ranks prior to this battle. But they only had to see the jagged tears, the area around it always soaked in blood, in the armored blankets of the horses, or the armor of a dead cataphract, to understand their doubts had been unfounded. It was in the area of horses where Caesar counted himself fortunate; of the five hundred cataphract mounts who had escaped serious injury while their riders had been slain, only a handful proved to be trained to their former master's hand too well, lashing out at any Roman who tried to come near. The rest immediately became highly prized by all the mounted men of Caesar's army, but the smaller, more nimble mounts of those archers who had fallen were almost as valuable.

However, it was what Caesar did with eleven of the horses that not only surprised the recipients, it made more than one of them uncomfortable, and Pullus was one of those. It had been in the aftermath of the fight when Caesar realized that, with a battlefield that ultimately covered several miles, it made sense that his Primi Pili had a mount available for those moments when Caesar needed to confer with them. Subsequently, he gave each Primus Pilus his own mount, but not without a slave to tend to it, thereby removing their collective excuse that adding the caring for an animal to the already challenging array of duties performed by the most senior Centurion of a Legion would render them ineffective. Regardless, this didn't quell the grumbling discontent of men who had spent most of their waking

194

moments using their feet to get from one place to another, and the general antipathy in which infantrymen of all ranks held for their mounted comrades, meant that none of the recipients felt honored to receive this gift. But, as they all quickly learned, Caesar's foresight soon justified itself, saving the Primi Pili from extra miles when they were called to confer with their general. None of them used their mounts for any other purpose than to go galloping up and down the marching column, each understanding how the act of a Primus Pilus riding while his men marched would create many more issues that weren't worth the greater comfort that came from riding all day.

The one positive, at least from the viewpoint of the men of the Legions, was that as they continued in a southerly direction, the ridge marked the last of the hilly terrain, at least in the vicinity of the Tigris. This didn't mean that the ground was smooth; there were innumerable cuts and gullies that ran in a generally perpendicular direction to the flow of the river, but these were minor obstacles when compared to the constant climbing and descending that had marked the first portion of the march. Now that every man in Caesar's army had experienced how their Parthian enemies were masters at using the small folds and bumps that were a feature of this barren land, even in the wake of their victory, none of them relaxed their vigilance. Always aware of the possibility of an ambush, the fact that from all appearances the remnant of the Parthian army was in full retreat, none of them took it for granted that they were safe from the kind of sudden ambush that had been a feature of the opening days of the campaign. Although there were some muted complaints by the officers under Caesar about his decision to stay in place for three days, those sentiments weren't shared by the rankers, all of whom were universally thankful for the respite. It was approaching the height of summer, and even with water being in plentiful supply because of the Tigris, every day was still a trial that had to be endured, particularly the middle part of the day. Caesar was aware he was taking a risk by allowing the Parthians to retreat unhampered, so he did dispatch a substantial part of his cavalry to maintain contact with the rearguard of the Parthian column, only allowing Ventidius and his men a full day of rest before their pursuit. Kept in contact by a steady stream of dispatch riders, who would often pass each other at some point back and forth, Caesar was kept apprised of the Parthian movements. It wasn't without cost, though; the day that the bulk of the army resumed its march south, elements of Ventidius' cavalry force once more found themselves going from being seemingly alone to assaulted by a swarm of arrows, loosed from the still sizable force of horse archers. As they always had, they seemed to materialize from the very ground over which the cavalry was progressing, and while they were quickly driven away, it wasn't without a handful of losses. Fortunately, no trooper whose mount had been shot from under him suddenly found himself afoot, although when given the choice of a fresh horse from the supply of Parthian remounts, their region of origin played a strong role in their decision. For the Gauls, they preferred the smaller, more agile horses, while the larger Germans tended towards the cataphracts' mounts, who despite their larger bulk, they found more than adequate for their needs since no self-respecting German would think of draping a heavy, armored blanket on his horse.

Despite this harassment, Ventidius' troopers were able to keep up the pressure on the retreating enemy, not allowing them the luxury of stopping for more than a night. For the next week, a blind man could have followed the Parthian trail, just by the stench of the corpses left behind belonging to those Parthians who had survived the initial battle but succumbed to their wounds. Not surprising any Roman, Caesar made sure to point out how the Parthian dead were almost universally members of either the infantry or the horse archers, which were comprised of the two lowest classes of Parthians. He didn't need to belabor the point; very quickly, the Centurions picked up on this, reminding their men that whereas the Parthians didn't care about the fates of their lower classes, the Legions of Rome supplied medical attention to men, regardless of their social rank. If they didn't comment on the quality of the care a man of Caesar's class might receive compared to a Gregarius, this was understandable.

On the subject of his cavalry, the news wasn't all good for Caesar. While their performance under Ventidius was vastly superior to the man he replaced in Lepidus, Caesar had been made aware of the behavior of one of his officers that troubled him. That it was his nephew Octavian, whose actions, or lack thereof, in contributing to the cavalry's effort on the day of the battle, made the matter doubly distressing. Ventidius had been understandably hesitant to condemn the youngster for his lack of enthusiasm, so Caesar had been forced to interrogate some of Ventidius' Decurions, most of whom hadn't shared the reticence of their Legate. Caesar's Germans had been the most scathing in their assessment, but certain that their judgment was excessively harsh, the general had availed himself of the one Roman

196

Decurion, in whom Caesar had seen a great deal of potential. Decimus Silva had openly squirmed as he stood in front of Caesar's desk in the *praetorium* on the one night the entire army had been together, but ultimately, he had answered every one of Caesar's questions unflinchingly.

It wasn't until Caesar asked Silva for his honest assessment of the young Octavian's performance that the Decurion hesitated, finally saying, "Caesar, I wouldn't say the boy's a coward, exactly. But I just think some men are born for this, and some aren't." He shrugged and finished, "I don't think your nephew comes to this naturally."

Ultimately, this confirmed something that Caesar had suspected for some time. In and of itself, this wasn't an indictment of the boy's character, but Caesar also understood how crucial the performance of a young Roman nobleman in his first campaign could be to his future. While he never spoke of it, the slurs against him about his supposed affair with the King Nicomedes of Bithynia had dogged him for most of his life. It had an enormous impact on his behavior, as he sought to disprove the rumors in a manner that was subtle but unmistakable; his reputation as one of Rome's most persistent and profligate womanizers was not only well earned, it was a direct result of those rumors about his first campaign. Now, his nephew had behaved in a manner in which Romans naturally sneered at, not showing an enthusiasm for battle. In many other societies, perhaps this attitude was not only understandable, but wasn't considered unusual. Not in Rome, however. Nevertheless, Caesar had seen much promise in his grandnephew, aside from his lack of martial ardor, and he wasn't willing to make an issue of the matter; at least, not yet. Putting this aside for the moment, Caesar returned his attention to the task at hand, and that was to try and determine the best course of action for his army. More specifically, whether or not he should maintain his policy of marching with the river in sight, or if he should go to a more direct pursuit.

By his calculations, based on the information gathered from his scouts, the next section of the Tigris was tortuously winding, and actually flowed directly east for about ten miles, then returned to its southerly orientation, but only for a distance of perhaps five miles, then it went back to an east-west orientation for another ten miles. This was as far as his scouts had ranged, and now he had a decision to make. Caesar was reasonably certain that the Parthians he was pursuing would take the most direct route south; what was more of a question was whether or not they would stop at some point before reaching Ctesiphon. And, he mused as he stared down at the maddeningly incomplete map, if they did stop before Ctesiphon, where was it likely they would do so? Much of his decision, which depended on whether to continue following the river or to cross to the eastern bank and continue a roughly southern course, bearing slightly east, was based in Caesar's ability to think like the Parthian commander. The fact that Caesar had actually met him, in Kambyses, was unknown to him at this point, and would remain so for some time to come, not that a brief conversation talking about a dead prince and who had slain him provided much information. However, of all the military commanders, not just in Roman history but going back through the time of Alexander, Caesar's ability to observe and learn about another man in even a brief encounter was unparalleled. If he *had* known that Kambyses was now in command, it would have informed his decision, based on what he had seen during their encounter. Instead, he finally gave up on pursuing this line of thinking, turning instead to the more straightforward question of how much time would be gained by taking the action he was contemplating. From his nearest calculations, based on the information given to him, it appeared to Caesar to be the difference between forty miles to be covered following the twists and turns of the river, or by cutting across this section and reaching the river by the most direct route, cutting fifteen miles from it. Working in favor of shortening the route was the terrain; the Romans had left behind the most rugged part of the route, and he had been assured by his scouts, through Ventidius, that the twelve miles distance where they would be out of sight of the Tigris before briefly returning to the river during this meandering section was almost completely flat. This essentially made Caesar's decision for him, reasoning that the waterless stretch was much less than a full day's march now that the challenges posed by the ruggedness of the land had eased. Once he had committed himself to the decision, Caesar's mind eased, comfortable that ultimately, he had made the best choice. While he had entertained the possibility that he and his army might catch the fleeing Parthian remnant of what he understood was the first but not last army facing him, he believed it was a remote one.

Kambyses was in a similar turmoil, even if it was for different reasons. The first two days after the resounding defeat had been a nightmare, even for this general, hardened by years of campaigning and whose status and rank meant that his daily ordeal wasn't nearly as harsh as those under him in rank. Even taking into account the different levels of care provided to the wounded by Romans and Parthians, the toll on the wounded was horrific; Kambyses was struck by the grimly amusing thought of how the Romans could follow their trail using the bodies of those Parthians left behind in much the same way they would back in Roman lands. The difference was that the Roman markers counting the miles were made of stone, and these in Parthia were made of flesh and bone. Not until the third day, when they actually passed the entire time on the march without Kambyses being informed someone had died, did he start thinking about more than just the next mile, and to even consider taking some sort of offensive action. Only part of his decision to stop and fight was based in his desire to resume taking some sort of offensive action. If he had been pressed, Kambyses would have admitted that he was in absolutely no hurry to face his king and present Orodes with the body of his beloved son, which was the only corpse not discarded by the fleeing army. And it wasn't just due to the normal anguish that a man experienced when faced with such matters as informing his king that not only has he failed in his larger assignment, but he has been unable to save a beloved son. Never far from Kambyses', or any other Parthian noble's mind, was the example of Surena, and how Orodes treated those who displeased him. Ultimately, this was what moved the Parthian general to consider using the ruins of what he knew had been one of the greatest cities of the kingdom through which the house of Arsaces claimed descent. By the time Kambyses and his men reached this point, some seventy miles south of the site of their defeat, the city, whose name was lost to him, had stood abandoned for more than five centuries, after being sacked and destroyed in some long-forgotten war. While it was true that none of the buildings that remained could have provided more than the crudest of shelter, enough remained of the structures made of mud brick that it provided a change in what, to that point, had become the unvarying sameness of the terrain. It didn't occur to Kambyses immediately; he had already ridden past the site after crossing the Khosr River, which was a tributary of the Tigris, and was actually a mile past it before, without any conscious thought to do so, he found himself suddenly stopped. Because of his position, not only as the highest ranking Parthian remaining, but by virtue of his spot at the head of the column, he only became aware he had done so when he noticed that those around him had suddenly stopped their mounts.

Turning to his ostensible second in command, a noble from another house than the Arsaces, and whose name was Melchior, Kambyses said simply, "Come with me."

Trotting back along the column, which had come to a stop, Kambyses studiously ignored the remainder of his army, if only to avoid being forced to confront the stares of men who, if not outright hostile towards him, at the very least didn't look at him with any favor. This stung Kambyses; that debacle on the ridge hadn't been his doing, and he definitely felt unappreciated for his role in extracting what did remain of this *spad*, but a part of him also recognized that these men had lost friends and relatives, so it was a bit much to expect them to hold one of the men responsible for that in any esteem. However, neither did he have any desire to speak to Melchior, a man more than twenty years his junior, but because of his status as oldest son of the most senior house of that branch of Parthian nobility, neither could he be completely ignored. This was why he had even deigned to bring Melchior with him, but that was about as far as he was willing to go, which meant the short ride to the ruins passed in silence.

Reaching the outer wall, or at least the remains of it, Kambyses guided his animal through the partially destroyed gateway, riding down the dusty path that had once been the main road into this city from the south. He wasn't the superstitious sort, but he nonetheless felt a chill that seemed to make the hair on the back of his neck vibrate, and the thought flitted through his mind that there were eyes on him and Melchior, disembodied ones that seemed to regard the pair with a kind of mocking amusement. It doesn't matter what you do, Kambyses thought he heard these words in the rustling, whistling sound made by the constant wind that flowed across this barren land, because you will end up here, with us. Whether it's today or tomorrow, time is no longer important; you will learn this soon enough. So discomfited was he that Kambyses felt his earlier resolve not to speak to Melchior unless absolutely necessary start to crumble, and he shot a glance at the younger Parthian. When he did, Kambyses wasn't sure whether that had been a good idea or not because the younger Parthian's expression spoke volumes, that if he was feeling any anxiety at all, Melchior was hiding it wonderfully. I wonder, Kambyses thought suddenly, if I'm the only one who is hearing this message because I'm the one that will fall? The intense feeling of relief that flooded through him at this thought did more to scare Kambyses than any of his imaginings about disembodied voices; never before had he gone into battle not only prepared to die, but actually feeling that it might be better than the alternative to what faced him in Ctesiphon.

Swallowing hard, he heard the hoarse quality to his voice as he indicated the ruins that stretched before him for several furlongs, aided by the fact that the southern end of the town was slightly elevated, and he said to Melchior, "I think we can hide at least the remaining horse archers here." There was a slight pause before Kambyses forced himself to ask, "What do you think?"

If Melchior noticed the hesitation, or heard the grudging tone of the question, he gave no indication, instead surveying the area before him.

"I think," his voice had a mellifluous quality that, under other circumstances, Kambyses would have dismissed as the kind of tone a courtier would use when he was playing the sycophant, but he was sufficiently distracted that he didn't really notice, "that this is certainly something worth considering."

Kambyses had never been known for his patience, but never before had he found himself under such tenuous circumstances, and if Melchior had known the older man better, he would have picked up the anxiety Kambyses was feeling, if only by the way the older man didn't snap at him.

"That's why we're here," Kambyses replied, trying to remain calm. "To consider it."

For the first time, Melchior turned to examine Kambyses more closely, then he asked evenly, "And to what purpose do you propose to have the archers wait here?" When Kambyses didn't immediately answer, he added another question, "Is it to buy the rest of us time?"

"That," Kambyses admitted, then before he could stop himself, he said bitterly, "and we need to hurt those dogs more than we have." Shaking his head, he finished sadly, "It's bad enough that I'm returning to Orodes bearing his son's body. I just want more to show for it, to at least give our king that much."

And you hope that it will save your life, Melchior thought with grim amusement, but aloud, he said, "That's not only understandable, it's for a noble purpose." He hesitated, trying to frame his thoughts because, despite his recognition of at least part of Kambyses' motive in trying to strike the Romans again, he also knew it wasn't the only reason. Nobody had ever accused Kambyses of disloyalty, not only to his house of Arsaces, but to the collection of regions known as Parthia. This was what caused him to be as honest as he was willing to be when he said, "But how willing are our archers going to be to die to save our cataphracts more time to escape?"

Under normal conditions, Kambyses would have snapped that the archers would do their duty to their king, and if that meant to die, so be it; these, he recognized, weren't normal conditions, and he was also acutely aware that it had been the interposition of those archers that had allowed his portion of the cataphracts to escape with as relatively few losses as they had during the battle on the ridge. Truly, losing a bit more than two thousand of the cataphracts under his command, whose value to his king went beyond their tactical use and extended to the strategic and diplomatic domain because of their status as nobility, wouldn't have been a cause for any celebration. But I suppose I can thank Cyaxares for putting matters into perspective, Kambyses thought with a mixture of bitterness and, honestly, relief. There's barely a thousand of his men left, so in comparison, I look competent. Turning his mind back to the last question Melchior had posed, he considered for a moment.

Heaving a sigh, he replied finally, "I suppose you're right. It's a bit much to ask, given what's happened."

"Besides which," Melchior pointed out, "we don't know if the Eastern *spad* has made it to Ctesiphon yet. We may need these men to defend the capital."

That, Kambyses realized, was not only true, it was also an important consideration, perhaps the only real consideration he needed to keep in mind. Parthia's vastness was so great that, as far away as Ctesiphon was from the edge of what the Romans called their sea, it wasn't even half the distance to Nisa, which was actually the ancient seat of power for those called Parthians. And it was also why, as devastating as the loss of Pacorus was, and the fall of Ctesiphon might be, it wasn't the mortal blow Kambyses was sure the Romans thought it would be. The truth was that, if one was being strictly correct, the Romans hadn't even made it to Parthia yet, and that what they were experiencing now in the barren vastness as they continued along the Tigris was the equivalent of the small appetizer served before the main meal. Sitting there, considering what Melchior had said, Kambyses realized that, while this was a blow to his pride and to Parthian morale, the defeat on the ridge was just the beginning. And their most potent weapon wasn't in the cataphracts or in the horse archers, but in the land itself. More than one invading army had been swallowed up, never to be heard from again, most of their men falling not from an arrow, lance, or sword, but from thirst, starvation, and exposure. No, he decided, there will be no sudden attack; let the Romans keep coming, and driving deeper into this country, not realizing that every step they took was one closer to their inevitable doom. Kambyses would be content to let the land itself defeat the Romans.

"You're right," he said, then turned his horse and, without waiting, put it into a canter, making his way up the dusty street and out of a dead city, to reclaim his spot at the head of the army.

The Romans reached the ruins the next day, but that was as close as they would come in their pursuit of the Parthian army. Caesar, once again ignoring the more superstitious among his men, ordered the camp be built just on the opposite side of the river from the ancient city, and there was an easy fording spot that allowed those bolder men who were so inclined to go across to examine the ruins. Not, of course, until after it had been thoroughly searched by Silva and his command, but all they found were horse droppings that were at most a day old, a short distance from the ruined southern gate. Somewhat surprisingly, at least to the rankers, it was Caesar who seemed to be the most interested in examining the remains of what they could all clearly see had once been a fair-sized city. Not on the scale of Rome, certainly, but for this part of the world a good size, holding perhaps a hundred thousand people within its walls. Even more of a surprise, and somewhat of an annoyance, was that Caesar insisted on his officers and Primi Pili to accompany him on his tour. Pullus, for one, had been looking forward to a nice cup of wine and a good scraping by Diocles to get the grime of the day's march off of him, and he was far from alone. Still, knowing Caesar as he did, he showed up at the *praetorium* in a state of what could be called resigned cheerfulness, understanding that, as always, Caesar had something in mind more than just passing the time. They walked across, Caesar leading the way, or more accurately, two of his German bodyguards who had insisted on coming along did first. Since this part of the wall was still intact, the party had to walk around the perimeter of the stone wall, each of them examining it in the way military men do, as a possible obstacle to overcome, until they reached the northern gate. As with the southern gate, the heavy doors were long gone, but not only was the gateway intact, so were remnants of the wall on either side, so the Romans entered in the same way they would have been required to when the city was still alive. The conversation had been muted, but then Caesar, holding up a hand that brought them to a stop, turned to the others.

"If I'm not mistaken," he began, "these are the ruins of a city that Herodotus wrote about. It's name was..." He paused to think for a moment, then came up with, "...Nineveh, I believe." He encompassed the ruins before them with a sweeping gesture. "It was once the greatest city of its time, if Herodotus is to be believed, and belonged to the Assyrians. Then this region was invaded by the Scythians..."

"Scythians?" Pollio interrupted. "Are you sure it was Scythians, Caesar?"

Caesar normally didn't like to be interrupted, but in this case, he was unperturbed, saying only, "Yes, Pollio, I'm sure. I consulted the original of Herodotus in the library of Alexandria, and according to him, this region was actually held by Scythians for almost thirty years before they were expelled."

"I hope that's not one of the books that got burned up," Pullus muttered to Balbinus, which caused his counterpart to begin snickering, and in turn prompted Caesar to glance over, not at Balbinus but Pullus, letting the Primus Pilus know he had been heard.

"You never did learn how to whisper, Pullus," Caesar said waspishly, nettled at this reminder of an accident that he still didn't like to think about, when his attempt to extract his men from difficulty in Alexandria had gotten out of hand and resulted in a huge fire that destroyed much of the great library.

Glaring at Pullus for a span of another couple of heartbeats, making sure his message was received, Caesar returned his attention to the topic, confident at least that Pullus wouldn't be heard from again.

It was Hirtius, in an attempt to lighten the mood, who asked, "And how were they sent back to Scythia, Caesar? Was there a battle?"

"No." Caesar shook his head. "At least, not according to Herodotus. It was accomplished by trickery. Apparently, the king of the Medes, Cyaxares, invited the Scythians to a banquet and got them drunk, then murdered them."

"All of them?" Hirtius gasped. "But there had to be thousands of them!"

"Herodotus doesn't say," Caesar admitted, "but I believe that it was just their leaders. After all," with this, he turned back to Pullus, giving him a slight smile that let Pullus know he had been forgiven, "as we learned the other day, once you cut off the head of the snake, the snake is no longer dangerous. So," he gave a slight shrug, "my guess is that this was how it happened. Either way, once the Scythians

204

were dealt with, the Medes attacked the Assyrians and naturally came to their greatest city."

"And destroyed it?" Batius asked skeptically, looking around at the ruins.

"They besieged the city for three months," Caesar explained, "so, when it finally fell, well, you know what happens then."

Batius nodded, as did all the other men gathered around Caesar, because they all knew very well what happened to a city that resisted being taken. Pullus, Batius, Balbinus, Spurius; all of the Primi Pili gathered there understood the brutal rules of war, and indeed, had participated in the sacking and destruction of places like this, although not of this size. But when men were forced to endure conditions even harsher than normal while conducting a siege of any length, forced to stay in place that inevitably led to disease, and as had happened at Avaricum, pushed them to the brink of starvation themselves, once the object of the siege fell, it was a foolish commander who didn't allow his men to exact their own form of revenge. Inevitably, this meant the kind of destruction they were witnessing here, on a long-deserted street of a fallen city that, even after the passage of several centuries and its destruction, possessed a shabby grandeur that was apparent to all of them. While Caesar was interested in exploring further, Pullus, Balbinus, and a few other Primi Pili had lost their taste for touring what was an example of the kind of destruction these men brought to a city whose offense was in resisting their efforts to conquer it.

Walking the short distance back to the camp, the group was silent, but it was Balbinus who broke the silence and actually voiced the thoughts that had been running through Pullus' mind at least, if not the others.

"I wonder if this will ever happen to Rome."

In truth, Balbinus uttered these words actually hoping to have his fears dismissed by his counterparts, but he was shaken when, instead of mocking him, there was a thoughtful silence, where the only sound for several heartbeats was the crunching sound of hobnails on rocky ground.

"Well," it was Pullus who broke the silence, but his tone was reluctant as he said, "it did happen once before, when the Gauls took the city for, what was it?"

"About a year," Batius answered.

"And we survived that," Pullus pointed out. Glancing over his shoulder at the growing shadows cast by the walls and ruined buildings, he felt compelled to point out, "They could have rebuilt this place if they'd had the courage."

"Pullus," Balbinus pointed out, "I don't think they could because those Medes, or whoever they were, didn't leave anyone alive."

While nothing was said openly, Caesar's army was only too happy to break camp and leave behind the ruins of Nineveh; even Caesar, normally not prone to what he considered the superstitions of other men, felt a vague sense of unease as he walked the streets of the abandoned ruins. If he had known that Kambyses had seriously considered using these ruins for an ambush, he would have been doubly grateful to leave them behind, if only because of the uproar such an attack would have caused among the rankers. Fortunately, the army resumed its pursuit without incident, continuing south along the river. Another blessing as far as Caesar and his men were concerned was that the Tigris had stopped its sinuous looping, removing the need for Caesar to decide on leaving its security. This was even more important now that it was the height of summer; the day the army departed Nineveh was the Kalends of Sextilis. So brutally hot was it, even marching next to the river, that Caesar was forced to relent in his normal practice of requiring the men to wear their armor; the Primi Pili had prevailed on him to allow the men to carry their helmets and not wear them some weeks before. The concession Caesar had required from his Primi Pili was that the men start the day in armor, but then allowed them to take it off at the first break in mid-morning. Once they stopped for the day and began construction of camp, he required them to do so in armor and wearing their helmets; in this, Caesar was inflexible. Despite knowing their general was doing this for their own benefit, it wasn't without a fair amount of grumbling from the rankers, but it wasn't at a level that concerned the Centurions, silencing the loudest complainers with a few swipe of their *viti*. Nevertheless, there were other matters that troubled those men wearing the transverse crests, and as it normally was within the 10th Legion, it was the Secundus Pilus Prior who was elected to broach the topic with Pullus.

"How far is it to Ctesiphon now?"

Scribonius opened what he hoped wouldn't turn out to be a contentious discussion with Pullus on the fifth night after they had marched away from Nineveh, during the evening meal in Pullus' tent, shared with Balbus and, as always, Diocles, who had served them.

Pullus thought for a moment, then answered, "According to Caesar, about a hundred fifty more miles."

Scribonius silently calculated what that translated into in terms of days on the march, coming up with, "So, at least another week?"

"About that," Pullus agreed, then pointed out, "but that also depends on what the Parthians do. It seems like they're set on running all the way there, but," he shrugged, "who knows?" When Scribonius didn't reply, choosing instead to stare into his cup with a frown that Pullus had long before learned not to ignore, Pullus sighed and simply asked, "What is it?"

Instead of replying directly, Scribonius countered with a question of his own, a habit he had picked up when he was a youngster and son of a wealthy equestrian who had his own tutor, who had taught using the Socratic method; it was something that drove Pullus to distraction.

"What's our ration situation now? I'm not talking about us," Scribonius added. "I know how we're doing. But what about the rest of the Legions? And," he added pointedly, "the cavalry? The gods know we haven't found much forage."

"That's only because we're following the river, and the Parthians are ahead of us, picking everything clean," Pullus protested.

Now it was Scribonius' turn to sigh; he had expected his friend to become defensive. Pullus was intensely loyal to Caesar, and his normal reaction to anything that might be implied as a criticism was to bristle at the suggestion that his general had erred in some way.

"Titus," Scribonius replied wearily, "I'm not criticizing Caesar."

"Well, it sounds like it," Pullus shot back, sitting back and folding his arms in a posture that Scribonius knew all too well.

However, Scribonius also understood that, if he endured the bluster from his giant friend, then laid out his concerns in a clear, concise manner, he was confident that Pullus would not only take him seriously, but after a period of what Scribonius thought of as germination, his concerns would take root in Pullus' mind as well.

It was with this in mind that Scribonius continued patiently, "Well, I'm not. But it doesn't change the fact that, from everything I've heard, the cavalrymen are getting concerned because they're already well into the barley."

"And where did you hear that?"

Balbus broke his usual silence; normally, he was more of a spectator for these sessions, but if Pullus wasn't aware, his servant instantly noticed this and correctly interpreted it as a sign that the scarred second in command of the Legion shared Scribonius' concern. More importantly, Diocles observed, there was something in Balbus' tone that suggested this wasn't a random question, that there might have been a discussion between Pullus' two closest friends prior to this meal.

"From that Roman Decurion," Scribonius answered immediately, strengthening Diocles' belief that this was part of a plan. "Decimus Silva." Shaking his head, Scribonius finished quietly, "He's really worried."

"I can't imagine it helps that we have all those remounts now," Pullus mused, telling the others he was now accepting Scribonius' concern, albeit tacitly, as something to worry about.

"That's true," Scribonius granted, realizing with some surprise that, in fact, he hadn't thought about this aspect, and it was a reminder to Scribonius that despite the appearance he liked to give, Pullus was far from the muscle-bound brute. Going on, Scribonius added, "It's one of those things that you don't think about, but you're right. It's a good thing for us to have those extra horses, but at the same time, it means this issue of forage is even more urgent." Taking a breath, Scribonius asked, "I don't suppose you've heard Caesar mention anything about this?"

As he had feared, Pullus' initial reaction was to stiffen, but while Scribonius was expecting a surly retort, instead, Pullus answered somewhat grudgingly, "No. At least, not in our briefings."

"Someone needs to find out what he plans to do about it," Balbus spoke up again, although his words were muffled by the piece of bread he was chewing.

Pullus turned to glare at the third of this small triumvirate, although as usual, Balbus' scarred face was expressionless as he returned the stare, placidly chewing his bread.

"Fine," Pullus sighed in exasperation. "I'll try and find out. But," he pointed a finger, first at Balbus, then Scribonius, "I'm not just going to come out and ask him outright. I don't need that kind of trouble."

"Maybe," Scribonius suggested, "you should ask Ventidius. He *is* the Legate in command of the cavalry."

Pullus considered that, then nodded in agreement. For a few moments, there was silence, but unfortunately for Pullus' digestion, Scribonius wasn't quite through.

"Also," he began, ignoring his friend's groan as Pullus set his cup down on the small table and crossed his arms again, "what do we know about Ctesiphon itself?"

"What do you mean?" Pullus asked, but he suspected he knew.

"Is it anything like those ruins?" Scribonius asked. "What was it called?"

"Nineveh," Diocles supplied, but only when it was clear that Pullus couldn't remember immediately, although it still prompted a mock scowl from his ostensible master.

"Yes," Pullus said dryly. "What Diocles said. Ninever."

"Nineveh," Diocles corrected, which earned him a crust of bread, although it was thrown at him, not offered.

"Whatever," Pullus scoffed, "you want to call it." Returning his attention to Scribonius, he asked, "What's your point, Sextus?"

Scribonius shrugged and replied, "I know we brought siege equipment, but it will be mid-Sextilis before we get there. And if Ctesiphon has walls like that old ruin, it's going to be a tough nut to crack." Scribonius paused, both to take a breath and to emphasize his next and final point, "And we've already suffered more casualties than I think Caesar was expecting, at least this early in the campaign."

That was something else Pullus couldn't argue. From its inception, Caesar's planned campaign against the Parthians had been based in the assumption that it would take more than one campaign season. And, while the initial objective of the first season was now within grasp, much depended on how long it would take to capture Ctesiphon. However, Pullus knew that, as Scribonius had pointed out, the battle on the ridge had been more costly than any Roman had foreseen, and now much depended on how stiff the resistance was at Ctesiphon. As Pullus and the other Primi Pili had been informed during the initial briefing held by Caesar about the campaign, Ctesiphon was *a* capital of the Parthian empire, not the only one. And, while it was supposedly the seat of power for Orodes, not until they were outside the walls of that city would they know if the Parthian King of Kings was still there, or if he had retired even deeper into his heartland. Now, Pullus thought with some disquiet, Scribonius is reminding me that we might run out of men.

When the walls of Ctesiphon became visible on the horizon, Kambyses rode ahead alone, save for the horse he led and on which the body of Pacorus was draped across the saddle. Carrying the sword that the Roman general Caesar had given back to him, Kambyses rode at a slow pace, dressed in his best ceremonial armor, sure that he was riding to his death. Certainly, he reasoned, Orodes' grief would be so horrible to witness that dying would be a kindness; only if he was lucky would that death be swift. The thought of dying didn't trouble Kambyses overmuch; the consequences rippling outward from the death of Pacorus, however, had haunted his sleep. When they approached the gates of the city, they were thrown open without any delay, the sentries there having been warned of the return of the *spad*, but while none of the men standing guard said anything, Kambyses felt their eyes on him first before moving to the second horse. The horse itself wasn't one they recognized, but as uneducated as men of the lower classes may have been, they didn't need to be literate to somehow divine the identity of the cargo it was carrying. Kambyses didn't deign to acknowledge them, staring straight ahead as he guided his mount up the wide street that led directly to the palace. Aside from the guards, the people of Ctesiphon were going about their daily business; at least until they spotted one of their nobles, and like the guards, while they might not have known the exact identify of the body he was leading, their suspicions caused a low, keening moan to issue forth from the women. The sound started out softly, but very quickly, it built in volume as the citizens of Ctesiphon stopped in their tracks to stand, staring at Kambyses as he rode by, bearing his horrible gift for his king. He had sent one of his personal bodyguards ahead to warn Orodes of his arrival, but with strict instructions not to mention what Kambyses was bringing with him, a decision he was beginning to regret. This street ended a short distance away from the royal palace, which was located on the opposite side of a large plaza, and Kambyses could see figures exiting the palace to stand on the high stairs above the surrounding plaza and streets. Kambyses didn't increase his pace, which allowed the people who had been hurrying about to join what became an impromptu procession, trailing behind the horse carrying the corpse of their prince. Accompanying them was the low, keening moan of the women who were tagging along, although Kambyses had no way of knowing whether or not they actually had divined the identity of his charge, or if they just understood that it had to be someone of importance to be conducted to their king in this manner. What he was aware of is that it gave Orodes a fraction of time to prepare himself, but to Kambyses, it seemed that the longest part of his journey south was the final distance across the plaza, where his king still stood at the top of the stairs, waiting.

When he got close enough, Kambyses could see the pallor underlying his king's normally dark complexion, and he noticed that one of the palace eunuchs who served the King of Kings was standing discreetly behind Orodes, but with a firm hand on his king's elbow. That was troubling in itself; the sight of Phraates, standing just behind his father and the eunuch was even worse. Because of his position behind his father, Kambyses assumed that the second son didn't feel the need to guard his expression, and it was seeing Phraates' face reflecting what could only be described as hope that was the worst part of all this for the Parthian general.

Reaching the foot of the stairs, Kambyses slid from the saddle, then with heavy steps, ascended them to stop at Orodes' feet, where he dropped to his knees, bowed his head, and said, "My King, I have failed you."

"My father is resting now," Phraates informed Kambyses, perhaps a full watch later.

It wasn't lost on Kambyses that not only was the prince and now surviving son and presumed heir meeting him in the throne room, but the normal set of advisors to Orodes were conspicuously absent. The older man briefly considered refusing to participate in this meeting, yet as quickly as the idea came, he dismissed it. Frankly, he was somewhat surprised he was still alive; he had been expecting Orodes to order his summary execution, but the king had been so stricken when Kambyses confirmed that he was indeed bringing Pacorus home that something seemed to just…die in Orodes. Indeed, he had shown Kambyses little interest from that first moment, and now he found himself essentially alone with Phraates, who was doing a poor job of looking distressed at the death of his brother.

"As heavy with grief as my heart is," Phraates broke the silence, and Kambyses noticed how effortlessly the younger man sat upon Orodes' throne, carefully arranging his heavily brocaded robe, seemingly paying more attention to this than the other man, "we still must talk about this Roman incursion, and why my brother, and you, failed to contain it."

Kambyses bristled at this slight, offended for himself and Pacorus. It was certainly true that the older man had had his differences with the crown prince, but ultimately, Kambyses had respected Pacorus, especially when contrasted to Phraates. Regardless of his personal feelings, however, Kambyses realized that Phraates was baiting him, and that, despite the tone or the reason behind his statement, it was something that had to be discussed. And, Kambyses was forced to admit to himself, it was a subject on which he had spent a great deal of time thinking about on the retreat.

"Pacorus' tactics were sound," Kambyses began, then paused before he added reluctantly, "if our army was constituted more like that of the Romans. But our infantry isn't capable of standing up to their Legions. And," he sighed, "they've developed tactics that counteract the power and effectiveness of our cataphracts."

Now Phraates stopped pretending to be more interested in his robes. Looking up sharply at Kambyses, his eyes narrowed.

"Oh?" he asked, clearly skeptical. "How so?"

Rather than answer verbally, Kambyses reached down into the small pouch at his belt, retrieving a jagged lump of lead, even more misshapen than when they were first cast, and darkened from the blood of its victim. In a calculated insult, rather than walk closer to Phraates to place it in his hand, Kambyses tossed the lead missile, although he was slightly disappointed when the other man caught it adeptly and without seeming to take offense. Examining it closely, Phraates' mouth turned down into a frown, and when he looked up at Kambyses, his skepticism had turned to disbelief.

"This?" he asked incredulously. "You expect me to believe that this tiny piece of lead is able to stop one of our *cataphracts*?" Phraates shook his head, refusing to accept this evidence. "A horse archer, yes, I'd believe that. But the armor on a cataphract is too thick for something like this to penetrate!"

This reaction, at least, was something which Kambyses understood, because up until he had seen for himself the massive damage such a seemingly insignificant chunk of metal could wreak on its victim, he would have undoubtedly agreed with the prince.

"I thought the same thing, Your...Highness," Kambyses replied, "but I can assure you that I witnessed firsthand the kind of damage these things can inflict." Walking closer so he was within arm's reach, he pointed down at the sharp edges, saying, "I believe that it's because they don't file down the edges of the missiles, so it serves as a cutting edge." Shrugging, he finished, "Whatever the cause, it's sufficient enough that it can punch through armor of both man and horse."

"Very well," Phraates replied reluctantly, "I'll take your word for it. But," he either missed or ignored the flush that suffused Kambyses' features at Phraates' tone that made it sound as if he was conferring a royal favor, "even if these things inflict the damage you claim they do, how many volleys can they let loose before we're upon them?"

"That," Kambyses admitted, "is where their second tactic comes in. And," he was reluctant to add this because of the loyalty he still felt for Pacorus, "I think this is where our prince erred. A Roman Legion managed to take possession of the ridge that was the base of our line of defense, and Pacorus tried to dislodge them. He led his bodyguard up a slope, and it was steep and long enough that our men were slowed down to the point that their advantage was negated."

"Negated? Negated how?" Phraates asked curiously.

"Because by the time they got close to the Roman lines, their mounts were almost blown," Kambyses replied frankly. "And then the Romans attacked."

"Attacked? Attacked how?"

"Men behind the front ranks left the formation, and they used the advantage of being uphill to run down and get into the front ranks of our men," Kambyses explained. "Then they attacked the horses first, not our men."

"The horses?" Phraates recoiled and, again, it was a reaction Kambyses understood. "How so?"

"They got underneath them and used their short swords to gut them," Kambyses explained matter-of-factly, despite sharing his prince's distaste. "Then they pulled their riders down out of their saddles and butchered them. And," he added, emphasizing his words because he believed this was the most salient point, "they didn't work alone but as a team, several men surrounding each horse and rider."

Phraates didn't have a response to this, at least at first, seeming to concentrate on the lead missile in his hand, which he turned over slowly.

Finally, he said, "It seems that we have to choose our ground more carefully the next time, then." For a moment, just the span of a dozen heartbeats, Kambyses dared to think the worst was over, but then Phraates returned his gaze to him, his eyes narrowed in what seemed to be a permanent suspicion of anyone and everything. "Where were you during my brother's attack? Surely you were somewhere close to him."

"No, Highness," Kambyses answered, choosing his words carefully, "the prince gave me another task to perform."

"Which was?"

Kambyses went on to explain in detail Pacorus' plan, and how he and Cyaxares had led two columns to attack the advancing Romans from two different points. Phraates listened, only stopping him to ask a question a handful of times but otherwise allowing the older man to give the Parthian version of an after-action report. From a Roman point of view, it was typically Eastern, an account filled with florid details of the personal bravery of certain men in the Parthian host, belonging to families that Kambyses knew would resonate with Phraates; that these men were also personal retainers of Kambyses wasn't anything out of the ordinary. Indeed, in the Parthian world, not adding such flourishes that lavished praise on trusted subordinates was not only against the norm, it would have been considered a huge insult to those men, something that practically required them to respond in a manner that Kambyses knew could lead to a blood feud between his house and theirs that would last for generations. For Cyaxares, however, Kambyses was less fulsome in his praise, although he was also aware that, while not overtly friendly to the second son of the King of Kings, the dead nobleman had been on better terms with Phraates than most men of his station. Consequently, he was careful not to indict the dead man, although he couldn't quite bring himself to shower platitudes at the feet of his counterpart. Once he was finished, Phraates considered, or at least seemed to, all that Kambyses had told him, but the general couldn't quite shake the feeling that he had just wasted his breath telling Phraates something the prince had already known.

Finally, Phraates asked, "What was the ground like? Did my brother place you and Cyaxares in the same kind of untenable position that he put himself in? Is that why twenty thousand cataphracts couldn't cut through these Roman dogs? Or," he added before Kambyses could answer, "would you say that the cause for your failure was my brother's decision to split you into two groups? Rather than use your combined strength to punch through a line of wooden shields and flesh?"

So it won't be Orodes who has me executed, but Phraates, Kambyses thought dully. It was clear to him by the way Phraates was framing his questions that he was laying the full blame at Pacorus' feet, but doing it in such a way that made it clear to anyone familiar with the Parthian court that there must be a blood price paid. And Pacorus had already paid his debt, Kambyses understood, and so had Cyaxares. He was the only man of appropriate rank left, and

Kambyses wondered briefly who would be given command after he was dead.

Then, suddenly and without any warning, Phraates stood up, saying briskly, "Well, there's nothing that can be done about what's already happened. And I'm sure you won't make the same mistake again."

At first, Kambyses thought Phraates was making a cruel joke at his expense, thinking, of course I won't; dead men don't make mistakes, but when Phraates began pacing, hands behind his back as he continued to talk, the Parthian general felt an almost overwhelming sensation of confusion, mixed with a heady sense of relief as his mind coped with the fact that Phraates didn't intend to have him executed. At least, he thought as he struggled to keep his countenance impassive, not yet.

Either unaware, or more likely, uncaring of the internal turmoil of his general, Phraates said, "Now we have to decide the best way to defend the city. And," at this, he spun about, both to pace in the opposite direction and to face Kambyses, "how much of our resources we need to commit to it."

Trying to make the mental shift from being condemned to death to apparently being at least involved in the next attempt to stop the Roman advance meant that it took Kambyses a moment to collect his thoughts and concentrate on the subject introduced by Phraates.

But his first thought wasn't about the city, as he asked Phraates, "Shouldn't we wait until your father is sufficiently recovered to participate in this discussion, Your Highness?"

For the remainder of his days, such as they were, Kambyses would have cause to think of this moment, when Phraates finally favored him with a smile. It was the first and only time during his association with the prince that Kambyses could remember him looking so happy and pleased.

"That won't be necessary, Kambyses. You're the first to hear this, but my father has removed himself from the throne and named me as his successor."

Kambyses froze, his buffeted mind reeling yet again, the first thought coming unbidden to him being, Oh, Orodes, my cousin. What have you done?

Chapter Seven

The reign of the Parthian who would become known as Phraates the Fourth began that day, and his first official act as King of Kings was to remove himself and his court from Ctesiphon, taking the bulk of the remaining cataphracts with him.

"We're going to Susa and reorganize and refit," he had told Kambyses. "We're still waiting for the eastern *satraps* to arrive, but I've sent couriers redirecting them to Susa."

What Phraates was ordering was something with which Kambyses couldn't argue, but it pointed out one of the major differences between Rome and Parthia, and more importantly, the challenges facing Caesar's campaign. Because of the vast amount of territory that composed the Parthian Empire, their society was highly decentralized, and ultimately, their capital was mobile in the sense that wherever the King of Kings went, he brought with him most of the trappings and mechanisms of government required to keep the kingdom operating smoothly. This didn't mean that the Parthians didn't attach significance to the relatively few cities of any size in their sprawling kingdom, and Kambyses knew that Ctesiphon was important to Orodes because it had been founded by the first of his line to claim the title King of Kings, Gotarzes his name, the first of the house of Arsacid to ascend the throne. While it had begun as a military camp, across the river from the city of Seleucia, it had grown rapidly, and it had been this Orodes, the second of his name, who had been the most vigorous in pouring a vast amount of money derived from Parthia's strategic location on the main trade routes between the East and West into the city. Its growth had been explosive, very quickly encompassing Seleucia within its environs, bisected by the river that ran down the middle of what was essentially one city now. But as it quickly became apparent, Phraates didn't share the same sentiment with his father, not even considering staying to defend it. Regardless, that didn't mean the new king planned to allow the Romans to enter the city unopposed; he just had no intention of being personally involved.

"I'm giving you the opportunity to redeem your honor and save the good name of your house," Phraates had told Kambyses. "You're going to stay here and defend the city."

Kambyses had accepted this new assignment with a fatalistic calm; as far as he was concerned, he had been living on borrowed time, almost from the moment Pacorus had fallen. And, he had to acknowledge, he was tired of running. According to the scouts who were shadowing the Roman army on its approach, they were now three days away, which gave him precious little time to prepare the city. Fortunately for Kambyses and his cause, while Orodes had been waiting for word from Pacorus, the former king had been busy readying Ctesiphon for a prolonged siege, stockpiling supplies and strengthening strategic weak points in the city defenses. Perhaps the most important action he had taken, or had ordered to be done, was something that Kambyses would only come to appreciate in the coming months, and that was in the digging of several wells throughout both the Ctesiphon and Seleucia sides of the river. Because of the relatively high groundwater table so near to the river, the laborers didn't have to dig very deep into the ground before striking water, and as a result of this action, Orodes deprived the Romans from using a favored tool when conducting a siege, while removing one worry from Kambyses' mind. Nevertheless, there were more challenges facing the newly named commander of the city's defense, and it began when Phraates informed him that he was not only taking the cataphracts, which Kambyses didn't object to, knowing that his fellow noblemen would be more trouble than they were worth in a siege, and indeed Kambyses could foresee a fair number of them refusing to fight on foot at all, let alone man the walls. However, the new king intended to take the horse archers as well.

Kambyses had objected, pointing out, "We need trained archers to man the walls, Your Highness. I have more than enough infantry, and their spears will be useful on the walls, but they'll only be so once the Romans begin the actual assault. Before then, I need some way to hurt them when they're approaching. And," he felt compelled to add, "I plan on doing whatever I can to disrupt their work before the actual assault begins."

Somewhat to Kambyses' surprise, Phraates considered this, and actually amended his order, saying, "I'll leave half of the archers here with you, then."

Kambyses started to argue for more, but there was something unsettling in the way Phraates sat, just watching him, clearly expecting the general to object, which caused him to cut off his plea before he uttered it.

Instead, he gave what was at best a half-hearted bow, saying only, "I thank you, Your Highness."

"Besides," Phraates said suddenly, favoring Kambyses with a grim smile, "their horses might be useful as food."

As much as he hated to admit it, Kambyses knew Phraates was speaking truthfully; it was not only possible, it was likely that the defenders would be forced to resort to eating their animals. If, he thought, I do my job right and it takes the Romans longer to take this city than they're planning. Unbidden, he felt a flickering of hope at this idea, and before he could rein it in, Kambyses' mind had flown ahead to a future where the Romans were stranded outside the walls of Ctesiphon, and the Parthian winter came. Despite knowing how dangerous it was to indulge in such fantasies, Kambyses allowed himself this small luxury, savoring the vision of watching from the walls of the city as the howling winds cut through the Romans like knives, as their foraging expeditions returned empty-handed, or better yet, didn't return at all, swallowed up in the vastness of the barren landscape that was the feature of this land just a matter of a couple miles distance from the river. Even from the relatively low vantage point of the twenty-five-foot high walls, the river disappeared into the distance as a bi-colored ribbon, with the green of vegetation and the small farms on either side of the muddy brown river. Those strips of green extended out from the river at most a mile, before the light brownish-gray of the land surrounding it swallowed it up, extending from there as far as the eye could see. A native of this hostile environment, Kambyses understood that this was their secret ally, and provided Ctesiphon could hold out, their most potent weapon, because while he was plagued by many doubts, there was one thing, one article of faith that Kambyses held as an absolute truth. No matter how well this Caesar had prepared, no matter how many supplies he brought, Kambyses knew down to the marrow of his bones that no foreign army could survive an entire Parthian winter, not without the shelter and security a city provided. All he had to do was make sure Ctesiphon didn't fall for at least three or four months; if he could keep the city safe, the winter would do what Pacorus had been unable to do on the ridge. And if he could do that, Kambyses understood that he would salvage his reputation; whether or not he actually survived was a

218

matter out of his control. Always hovering in the back of any Parthian general's mind was the example of Surena, who had repelled Crassus' invasion and had been rewarded for it by having his head removed. That, however, was so far in the future that Kambyses barely gave it a moment's thought; first, he had to make sure he was in the position to worry about it.

Of all the men in the Roman army, of all ranks, only one had a true grasp of the importance and scarcity of what was ultimately the most precious commodity in their vast array of supplies and weapons. Caesar fretted constantly about the amount of time this campaign was taking, over and above what he had calculated would be inevitably expended in pursuit of his aims. First it had been the terrain during the early part of the march that had been more rugged than he had been led to believe, reducing the distance his army covered by at least ten miles a day from what he had planned. Every single day, Caesar and his army fell further in arrears, but to his Legates and Centurions, outwardly, Caesar displayed his usual air of confidence and, most importantly, the sense that nothing was happening that Caesar hadn't expected. It was only in the dark watches of night that the Dictator for Life gave in to his doubts, tossing and turning as his mind, normally his most potent weapon, became his most powerful adversary as it chewed away at his confidence. This was something new for Caesar, and while he wasn't prone to introspection, he was aware that this new appearance of self-doubt had been caused by the attempted assassination at Pompey's Theater. While a part of him had been aware that his enemies were up to something and wanted him removed from Rome's political scene, only in the aftermath had he come to the realization that he hadn't truly believed they had the will to go through with something as drastic as killing him. It had shaken Caesar to his very core, and he did worry about what was taking place back in Rome, especially now that Cassius had escaped. This was something about which he was having second thoughts; he had arranged for Cassius to do so, but while it had been to remove a man who was clearly a threat from his immediate circle, Caesar hadn't anticipated the gnawing doubt that accompanied his decision. Self-doubt and second-guessing were new sensations for Caesar, and he didn't like it a bit, although it did have one salutary effect, because for the first time, it gave Caesar some insight into how other men thought. Now, after the battle on the ridge which, despite being a victory, had been costlier than Caesar had anticipated, he was acutely aware of every delay, no matter how slight, and despite his tremendous self-control, his nerves began to show. Snapping at his secretaries, being curt with his Legates—it was actually young Octavian who bore the brunt of his uncle's ill humor, which he endured with a patience that came from his deep respect and affection for Caesar. But it was his interaction with his Primi Pili, and with one in particular, that was the beginning of a deeply held antipathy on the part of the young nobleman and favorite of Caesar for another of the general's inner circle. For reasons that Octavian could only guess at, Caesar's ill temper didn't extend to his senior Centurions, but it was only with Titus Pullus with whom Caesar displayed what Octavian was beginning to regard as his uncle's old persona. While Caesar was unaware of it, Octavian had observed the change in his uncle, and had correctly ascribed it to the plot against his life, yet that was the extent of the youth's insight. Now, whenever his uncle and the Primus Pilus of the 10th were together, and Octavian witnessed the easy familiarity and clear mutual respect each man held for the other, despite the vast social gulf between them, the young man felt a flare of jealousy, to which both men were oblivious. Diocles, and Caesar's most trusted slave Apollodorus, on the other hand, took notice, and in their own scant spare time, discussed their observation.

"I don't trust that boy," was Apollodorus' judgment as the pair sat in Apollodorus' personal tent that, while on a smaller scale, was every bit as luxurious as his master's quarters, with a wooden floor and carpets to cover them.

Indeed, the carpets had become a longstanding joke between the two friends because they had once graced the floors of the royal palace of Alexandria, where the two men had served their respective masters during the trying seven-month siege. Several of these richly embroidered and very thick carpets had made their way onto the floor of Apollodorus' tent, and frankly, Diocles was more miffed with himself because he hadn't thought to take at least one for his own use than he was with Apollodorus for having the foresight to snatch a few of the precious things.

Diocles sipped from his cup before replying, then asked carefully, "Oh? And why is that?" The Greek shrugged and added, "He's certainly very bright. In fact, I'd put him on a par with Caesar in that way. He looks like Caesar, and I've noticed that he's actually picked up some of Caesar's mannerisms. But that's to be expected with a young man like he is, isn't it?"

Apollodorus regarded his fellow servant, looking at him evenly as he tried to discern whether or not Diocles was actually speaking from conviction, or was either saying what the Greek thought was expected of him or what he believed his own master, Pullus, would want him to say. Sighing, Apollodorus realized, such are the times we're living in, when I question my best friend's real intentions.

"That," he answered finally, "is true, on both counts. But there's something…false about the boy." Shaking his head, Apollodorus frowned into his cup, trying to articulate his concerns. "Oh, I know he admires Caesar, but there's an…artifice about him. It's like he's trying to emulate Caesar in order to…" His voice trailed off, but Diocles felt certain that he understood where Apollodorus was heading, supplying his own answer with, "…to take Caesar's place?"

"Yes." Apollodorus nodded vigorously. "That's exactly it! I think he's trying to prepare for the day when he steps into Caesar's boots! As if he could." He made a dismissive gesture, but Diocles didn't immediately respond or indicate his agreement with Apollodorus' assessment.

"I don't know," Diocles finally replied. "I think Caesar has big plans for Octavian. So it's natural for the boy to want to model himself after Caesar."

"But is the boy willing to wait his turn?" Apollodorus countered.

"That," Diocles acknowledged, "is the question, isn't it?"

Phraates and the royal retinue departed Ctesiphon, taking his father with him. Kambyses had only seen Orodes the first day and on one other occasion, when the former King of Kings listlessly confirmed that he had indeed stepped down and named Phraates as his successor. His manner had been so disinterested that, when he told Kambyses that Phraates had been telling the truth, he could have been discussing a course on the menu for the evening meal. From Kambyses' perspective, he was witnessing a man who had lost all interest, not only in the demands that came from his status as King of the Parthian Empire, but in his very life. Physically, the man had aged, literally overnight; when Kambyses rode across the large plaza to face his king, while Orodes was of roughly the same age as Kambyses, he had exuded a rough vitality and behaved like a man half his age, particularly with his large pool of concubines. But when Kambyses laid eyes on him the next day, he was looking at a version of his own future, seeing a man whose body was failing him, and was beset with the trials and tortures that came from old age. Gone was any sense of vitality; what Kambyses was seeing was a man who was waiting to die. Still, despite his misgivings about Phraates, Kambyses was pleasantly surprised when the young King of Kings only offered some cursory guidance about the best way to defend the city, seemingly trusting the older, more experienced Kambyses to the details. Even more surprisingly, Kambyses found himself wishing that Phraates would have weighed in on what was ultimately the most pressing issue. Despite the preparations Orodes had made prior to Pacorus' death, from what Kambyses gathered, he hadn't given any indication about his plans for defending what was, in theory at least, the sister city of Seleucia on the opposite side of the river. In reality, however, the burgeoning population of Ctesiphon, which had become a beacon drawing all manner of people from the hinterlands of the far-flung empire, had long before spilled across to Seleucia. Indeed, there were three stone bridges linking the two, but aside from being home to Parthians or those who sought protection from the King of Kings, in the way that mattered they were still two distinct and separate cities. The only spot where the walls of Seleucia had been altered was where the bridges crossed the river, but so unthinkable was the idea that an invader would ever penetrate this deeply into their territory, the Arsacids had never deemed it necessary to construct fully operational gates between the two cities, at least on both sides. This made for a unique, but pressing, problem for whoever was charged with the defense of the Parthian capital. There wasn't enough time to construct any kind of protection for the bridges themselves, and additionally, the only accommodation that had been made when the bridges were constructed was essentially to tear holes in the walls of Seleucia where the bridges were located. While it was true that Orodes' predecessor had partially completed the process and there were gateways, along with huge doors, on the Ctesiphon side, neither he nor the man who deposed him, his own son, had finished the process of strengthening the walls on the Seleucia side.

Essentially, Kambyses found himself caught in the cleft of a hugely critical dilemma; how much effort and resources should he expend to keep Seleucia from falling? Not lost on Kambyses was that in order for the elements to do the work he and all Parthians wished them to do, the Romans had to be denied the shelter provided by a city like Seleucia. Should Seleucia fall, which at this point was extremely likely given the three gaping holes in its defenses, this hugely important advantage with the weather would vanish. It was true that the supplies contained in the stone granaries and warehouses of that city could be transferred fairly easily, and most importantly, quickly across the bridges into Ctesiphon, and there would still be the difficulty for a foreign army scouring the countryside for anything edible, but that wouldn't be enough, Kambyses was certain of this. He had experienced enough of the mettle of Caesar and his Romans to know that without both of the twins of exposure and hunger, his task became exponentially more difficult; indeed, it was near impossible. And yet, trying to hold Seleucia would be far more difficult than Ctesiphon, not to mention the problem of what to do with the more than fifty thousand inhabitants who occupied the older city, founded by one of Alexander's generals. However, neither could he allow it to remain unoccupied and just waiting for the Romans to inhabit it, but Orodes had either not gotten to this point in his planning for the defense of the capital, or more likely, he had, but kept his own counsel and not shared it with Phraates. After all, up until Pacorus fell, Phraates hadn't been viewed with any favor by his father, sharing his eldest son's distrust of the younger brother. Who was now King of Kings, but he hadn't provided any help on this dilemma either.

"I'm sure you'll come up with something," was all the young king had said, but his mind was clearly elsewhere, which Kambyses suspected was on making good his escape to Susa.

Regardless of his personal feelings for the young king, Kambyses recognized that Phraates was right to not devote too much energy or time to Ctesiphon and its fate; there was very little he could do to avoid whatever was going to befall it and its inhabitants. Better to make good his escape with the precious royal treasury, which traveled with the King of Kings wherever he went, and the even more important cataphracts, in whom Kambyses still had ultimate faith. As long as Phraates didn't repeat the same mistake as his older brother and chose the ground carefully, Kambyses was certain that this time, with the combined might of the easternmost *spad*, the Romans would be crushed. If, he thought grimly, I fail in bleeding them dry here first. And that was something he was grimly determined to do; it was the least he owed Pacorus.

The walls of the twin cities came into view while the Roman army was still a half-day away, only slowly growing larger with every step. Pullus and the 10th had been cursed to march drag today, behind the baggage train, meaning that all they saw was a cloud of thick, choking dust that made visibility so difficult it was impossible for the men to miss the animal droppings under their feet, let alone the walls of the enemy capital. Gaius Porcinus and the rest of the First of the Second had it worst of all; it was their turn to be at the very tail end of the column, followed only by the *ala* of cavalry, and the flanking outriders who moved ceaselessly up and down the long column, always on the alert for another ambush. Strangely, though, there hadn't been a sighting of more than a handful of Parthian horsemen since a couple days after the battle on the ridge, which actually served to make the rankers more nervous and watchful, not less so. Porcinus' close comrade, Vulso, had been complaining about how Fortuna was pissing all over them almost without letup; Porcinus was sure the only time he paused was to take a breath. Despite his fondness for the older veteran, Porcinus was still getting worn down by his friend's constant complaining. If he had been informed that he would be hearing essentially the same thing, with only minor variations, no matter where in the column he was located, perhaps he might have felt better. Then, there was a sudden flurry of activity, followed by the sounds of the *cornu* belonging to each Cohort relaying the command, rippling back past the baggage train. Thanks to his height, the one blessing Porcinus counted was his position on the outside file, but in moments like this, it also meant the other men of his section pestered him for information as he leaned over to peer ahead.

Finally, he had had enough and snapped, "Not only can't I see because of all the dust, I can't think because none of you will shut up!"

This had the opposite effect Porcinus had hoped, as the jeers and taunts of the others only increased, prompting the young Gregarius to offer up an obscene gesture as he declared, "Fine! I'm not going to tell you what I see now that the dust has settled!"

Instantly, his tentmates changed their collective tune, now singing his praises and declaring what a wonderful fellow he was, prompting Porcinus, who just didn't possess the ability to hold a grudge over such trifling matters, to grin.

"I think we're here," he told them.

"Where? At Cutisiphon?" Vulso stumbled over the hard-to-pronounce name.

"Yes," Porcinus laughingly corrected him. "Although it's Ctesiphon."

"I don't care what you call it," Vulso grumbled, instantly becoming the subject of his tent mates' taunting.

"And? What does it look like?"

224

This demand came from the middle of Porcinus' rank, from another veteran named Gaius Licinus, prompting Porcinus to take a small risk and move a couple steps to the side of the formation, using the momentary stop to his advantage. . Aided by a slight slope that placed the rear of the column a dozen feet above the front, Porcinus stared, hard, at the line of the walls of the city, acutely aware that he was the object of scrutiny from his tent mates in much the same way as he was examining what lay ahead.

"Well?" Licinus called. "What do you see?"

Frankly, Porcinus wasn't sure; he wasn't a veteran like the others, although he had been blooded, and not only was this his first campaign, this was the first city of any size he had seen since Samosata.

Understanding his friends needed to hear something, he finally said, "I...I'm not sure, but it looks like there's two separate cities, with the river running between them."

This prompted a collective groan, and it was another veteran, Titus Calatinus, who exclaimed, "You mean we're going to have to take two cities? Not just one?"

With a rapidity that, to Porcinus, at least, reminded him of a fire lit in a pile of dry straw, word of Porcinus' observation whipped forward through the ranks of the First of the Second, at least to begin with, although by the time the column resumed marching, the entire Second Cohort was abuzz with the speculation and complaining that, whether rankers wanted to admit it or not, helped while away the miles under their *caligae*. Unfortunately for Gaius Porcinus, his name was attached to his observation, made with the best of intentions, of course, but by the time Caesar ordered a halt for the day to begin what would be a stay of an indeterminate duration, the 10th was in enough of an uproar that the young Gregarius found himself standing in front of a visibly angry uncle. The problem for Porcinus was that Titus Pullus wasn't an uncle in this moment, but a Primus Pilus, and it was using what Porcinus thought of as his uncle's command voice that he addressed the young ranker.

"What the *fuck* are you doing, telling anyone and everyone that we're going to have to storm two sets of walls at the same time and in less than a week?"

Pullus raged at his nephew, who was standing at a rigid *intente* in front of the small desk that Pullus used for writing reports. It was lost on Porcinus in the moment, but the fact that his uncle had actually waited until the large tent that belonged to the Primus Pilus was erected, meant this tongue-lashing was in private. Standing next to Porcinus, his face immobile and not giving a hint about his personal feelings was Scribonius, although if Porcinus had been paying attention, he might have noticed the slight quirk of his Centurion's mouth.

When Pullus remained silent for a heartbeat, Porcinus sensed that, after absorbing his uncle's wrath for a span of at least fifty heartbeats but which seemed much longer, Pullus was actually at a point where he expected an answer, prompting the young ranker to stammer, "B-but I didn't say any of that, Un…Primus Pilus! At least," he thought to add with a mumbled, "most of it."

Pullus and Scribonius exchanged a glance, but since Porcinus' gaze was locked on the imaginary spot on the rear wall of his uncle's tent, he missed seeing them give each other a grin.

Heaving a theatric sigh, Pullus asked wearily, "All right, tell me what you *did* say."

Porcinus essentially repeated the description he had given to his comrades. When he was finished, Pullus gave a shake of his head, both amused and disgusted.

"So, of course, by the time we hear it, we're going to perform a task that rivals Hercules' cleaning out the Augean stables," he muttered, tossing the stylus he had been holding down onto his desk.

"And you're surprised?" Scribonius asked dryly, then, with a laugh, ducked the stylus after Pullus snatched it back up and flung it at his head.

"No," Pullus admitted, then began rubbing the back of his neck, a habit that both of the other men knew was a sign of their Primus Pilus' distraction. "I'm not surprised, but that doesn't mean it's not a pain in my ass." Returning his attention to Porcinus, he satisfied himself with a glare, but his tone was no longer angry when he admonished Porcinus, "I understand how these things happen, Gaius. But just be careful what you say, all right?"

Certainly Porcinus was relieved that he had endured his uncle's tirade relatively unscathed, yet he was also bemused, meaning that before he could stop himself he blurted out, "But I didn't do anything! At least, nothing different than anyone else does! They asked me a question and I told them what I saw, that's all!"

Pullus shifted uncomfortably, but instead of answering, gave Scribonius a look that his friend correctly interpreted, prompting him to answer Porcinus instead, and more gently, "That's because you're not just a Gregarius, Porcinus. You're his," he pointed to Pullus, "nephew, which means that anything you say your comrades are going to consider comes straight from his mouth."

"But that's not my fault!" Porcinus insisted, then pointed out, "And how could I have possibly known what he had to say about what was coming when I was stuck behind the baggage train?"

This prompted both men to chuckle, although it was Pullus who answered his nephew, "Gaius, you've been in the ranks long enough to know that if most of your comrades' wits were sparks, we wouldn't have enough to start a fire."

Despite his aroused indignation, Porcinus had to laugh at his uncle's characterization, knowing how true it was.

"And," Scribonius added, "you know that rankers love to gossip. They're worse than teenage girls gathered together at the fountain doing the wash."

"The worse it is, the better it is," Pullus agreed, still smiling. Then, he turned serious. "But Scribonius is right, Gaius. I understand why you're upset, but this is what comes from being connected to me. Your friends, the boys in your Century, Pluto's balls, even men you only know by sight, are going to pump you for information because of who you are. In fact," Pullus thought to add, "I can practically guarantee that you're going to be swarmed the instant you leave this tent by men who want to know what's about to happen."

Porcinus considered this for a moment, then decided if he was going to be in this position, he might as well take advantage of it, asking, "So, what *is* about to happen?"

Both his superiors burst out laughing, and Scribonius slapped Porcinus on the back, telling him, "Now you're thinking like a real Gregarius!"

Pullus paused to wipe his eyes, then, still chuckling, told Porcinus, "Even if I knew, I wouldn't tell you. But," he got himself under control, taking a breath, "I don't know, although I'm about to find out. Caesar's holding his briefing shortly. Now, go help your Century finish the camp."

And with that, Porcinus was dismissed, whereupon he learned firsthand how prescient his Centurions had been when he saw a couple of his tent mates loitering along the Second's side of the camp forum, having taken advantage of their Centurion's absence to slip away from their work doing their part to construct the camp. Stopping for a moment, Porcinus was amused, but felt a certain amount of chagrin at the same time, realizing that, despite their current status, both his uncle and Scribonius were rankers at heart, if no longer by rank.

While the rankers and the junior Centurions were busy building what would be the main camp, about a mile north of Ctesiphon, Caesar took his senior officers on a tour of the ground surrounding what they also saw were essentially two cities separated by the river. In what little time he had, Kambyses had thrown up makeshift barriers that extended from the corners of both walls nearest the river that ran down to the riverbank. They weren't much to look at, being ten feet tall, but they were manned with watching Parthians, and Caesar acknowledged that they did the job of preventing any easy access to the bridges, or the walls of either city that paralleled the river. Nevertheless, he marked them as the obvious weak points, although he was bothered by the fact they were overlooked by the city walls themselves.

"They can rain all manner of things down on top of us if we take those shorter walls," he mused as his party sat their horses a short distance away, just out of range of the Parthian archers.

"What if we used mantlets?"

Caesar glanced over at Octavian, who had asked the question, quietly pleased that his nephew had instantly deduced the proper solution for this tactical problem.

"That's exactly what we'll do, nephew," he said approvingly. "Although we're going to have to dismantle some wagons to make them, and we're undoubtedly going to lose some of them." Pointing up to the corner of the wall of Ctesiphon immediately above the smaller wall, he observed, "Judging such things from this distance is a problem, but I've seen enough city walls to know that these are thick enough that the rampart is going to be wide enough for them to emplace some sort of artillery up there. But since the Parthians don't use artillery," Caesar grimaced, "at the very least, they'll haul some large rocks that they'll be able to just roll off the top." Shaking his head, he finished grimly, "No, we're going to lose some of those mantlets, which means we're going to lose wagons."

"Then we better not fail." Pollio laughed, while the others either smiled or chuckled at this obvious truth.

"Caesar," Balbinus spoke up, pointing to the city on the opposite bank, "what are we going to do about that? Once we get over that short wall, we're going to be between those two, and if they're going to be doing what you say in Ctesiphon, aren't they likely to do that there as well?"

228

Pullus was happy that someone had mentioned the first thing that had popped into his mind when Caesar had indicated this as the likely spot for an assault. Of course, Caesar had already thought of that, or at least reacted in a manner that suggested he had; like everyone else who was in regular contact with him, Pullus could never tell when he had been caught by surprise.

"They are, Balbinus," Caesar agreed, then pointed in the direction of Seleucia, "which is why we're taking this first. And we aren't going to assault Seleucia from the river side, because it poses the same problem." Turning Toes' head, Caesar started to trot towards the river, calling over his shoulder, "Let's go look at their western defenses."

His move had been so abrupt that it caused his German bodyguards to go to the gallop immediately, pushing past Caesar to act as a screen, while the other members of his party scrambled to mount their own horses, then catch up. Which, naturally, meant that Pullus and his fellow Primi Pili were forced to put their animals to the gallop, and the giant Roman had to grit his teeth as his own horse, one of the largest from among those taken from the battlefield, stretched its legs. Holding on with the same kind of grim determination that made him so formidable in a fight, Pullus inwardly cursed Caesar for this new policy of requiring his Primi Pili to act like they were all equestrians. Yes, we'd be slower, he grumbled to himself, but at least I'd be able to sit down tonight and enjoy my meal. Still, the largest part of his displeasure came from this perambulating inspection of the Parthian defenses, because his experienced eye took in enough to know that this was going to be a tough task, if only because of the problem posed by the sheer scale of having to take, in effect, two cities and not one. They crossed the river; there was a natural ford a half-mile from the walls, where a small island of built-up silt essentially bisected the flow. Only on the eastern side was the water deep enough that the horses' hooves left contact with the riverbed, and then for only a distance of a dozen paces, something Caesar noted would have to be addressed. The small island itself was less than a hundred paces across, but as Caesar reached it, he realized it gave him an unobstructed view south straight down the middle of the river. Deciding on the spur of the moment to hold another small conference, he sat Toes, studying the gap between the two cities, taking in the presence of the three bridges. While it was impossible to tell with any precision, from his estimate of their relative positions, it appeared that these bridges were placed roughly equidistant from each other, with the northern, or nearest, bridge spanning the river what he guessed was at least two furlongs from the corner of the northern and western walls.

Once everyone had joined him, he indicated the bridges, pointing out, "They're made of stone, so we can't send some sort of fire rafts downstream, although even if they were wooden, I wouldn't do it." Glancing around at the others, his voice hardened as he emphasized, "Those bridges are the key to the success of taking Ctesiphon. They have to be preserved, and any attempt by the Parthians to destroy them has to be stopped."

Without waiting for comment, he kicked Toes and went splashing into the water on the opposite side of the small island, where he immediately learned that this part of the river was much shallower. Crossing to the western bank, Caesar continued at the trot, paralleling the northern wall, this one belonging to Seleucia. That the older city was also larger had been apparent on their approach, but it wasn't until he reached the northwest corner and had a vantage point for the entire length of the western wall that he got a sense of the difference in scale between the two. And, to his dismayed surprise, that wasn't the only challenge when, in the span of time it would take almost every other man just to comprehend this new difficulty, Caesar recognized it, knew what impact it had on his plans, and how he would have to modify what he had in mind for the taking of the Parthian capital.

"Of course! The King's Canal!" Scribonius slapped his forehead. "I should have remembered that! But you're saying Caesar didn't know?" he asked Pullus, curious but also somewhat doubtful.

In answer, Pullus shrugged and said only, "That was the impression I got, but you know how it is with him. It's impossible to know whether he forgot like you did, or he never knew." He regarded his friend with a half-amused, half-curious expression, then asked his friend, "But where would either of you have gotten the information that there was a canal?"

"That," Scribonius admitted, "is what I'm trying to remember. I think it might have been from my old tutor, actually."

While it was said casually, Titus Pullus instantly become more interested. He had known Scribonius for almost eighteen years by this point, over half his life, but while he considered the man his closest friend, Scribonius had always been notoriously close-mouthed about his background. Over the years, over the thousands of watches spent together, Sextus Scribonius had offered up snippets of his past like a miser, and only then offered in the form of an offhand comment that Pullus had long before surmised was done in such a way as to avoid further inquiry. Now, he had just provided Pullus with another clue to add to what precious little he knew about his friend and his most trusted Centurion.

Despite this rising excitement, Pullus managed to sound casual as he asked, "Oh? Who was that?"

Scribonius didn't reply, at least immediately; instead, he favored his friend with a small smile that Pullus correctly interpreted as Scribonius' recognition that this was a source of more than just idle curiosity.

Nevertheless, he did answer the question, saying lightly, "His name was Alexander, but he was known as Alexander of Miletus."

"Never heard of him," Pullus answered instantly, although it was a lie.

A small lie, but even so, it came from a desire to learn more about his friend. Scribonius, however, wasn't fooled in the slightest.

"Oh, really?" He laughed. "That's interesting, since you borrowed one of his works from me."

Pullus' face flushed at being caught, although he returned Scribonius' amusement with a grin of his own, cheerfully admitting, "Well, it was worth a try. Anything to get you to tell me more about one of my Centurions and where he came from. You know," he pointed out, semi-seriously, "you're the one man under my command who I know the least about."

"What can I say?" Scribonius grinned back. "I like being an enigma to you. It keeps you on your toes."

"That's an understatement," Pullus grumbled, then returned to the original subject. "But I don't remember reading about this canal. The scroll you gave me was just about the Chaldeans."

"No," Scribonius agreed. "It wasn't in that one. It was one of his I read when I was a teenager and he was my tutor."

"And?" Pullus pressed. "What do you remember?"

"That it was Seleucis Nicator, the Macedonian who was one of Alexander's generals and divided up all that Alexander conquered, who started the canal from the Euphrates. But he didn't start it from nothing. In fact, that's why I remember it, because Alexander claimed that he actually did more of an improvement on an existing system that was already there."

"Well, no matter where it started, Caesar wasn't happy about it being there."

"I can see why," Scribonius agreed. "It's one thing to try and cut off water from one source, especially when it's a river the size of the Tigris. But now?" He shook his head and said, "There's no practical way to try cutting them off now."

Pullus agreed, although he felt compelled to add, "It didn't take Caesar long to come up with an alternative plan, though."

"Which is?" Scribonius asked, but Pullus just grinned at him.

"You'll find out soon enough," he told Scribonius, but then he threw in, "unless you want to tell me more about yourself in exchange for me telling you now."

As Pullus expected, his friend demurred; what he didn't expect was Scribonius throwing a heel of bread at him in answer.

It was Melchior, who had chosen of his own accord to stay with Kambyses rather than accompany Phraates, who brought his commander the news.

"They've split their army and are making several camps around us," he informed Kambyses relatively early in the morning but only after the younger Parthian had answered the summons from the commander of the guard on the walls. Watching just long enough to determine what was happening, he had hurried to the palace, which Kambyses had appropriated as his headquarters. "From what we can tell, it appears as if they're going to create at least four camps. Two on the eastern side of the Tigris and two on the western side. While they haven't gotten that far yet, my guess is that they'll place a camp on the southern side and the other on the northern side of the canal."

Kambyses listened without comment; so far, nothing the Romans had done was unexpected, although he was slightly surprised that they hadn't begun damming the Tigris. He had hoped the presence of the canal would convince the Roman general that this would be a fruitless exercise, but this was a case where Caesar's reputation for his elaborate engineering in similar situations had preceded him. It was this renown that had convinced Orodes to dig wells within the walls, which now appeared unnecessary, but they would still be convenient. Despite the appearance that the Roman was positioning his men in such a way that it would be difficult for him to divine exactly where they would concentrate their forces in an assault, Kambyses still felt certain that it would be in one of two likely spots. While his conscripted labor force had done a creditable job under the circumstances, he wasn't sanguine that the makeshift walls could withstand a full-out assault by men who were the acknowledged masters in this kind of warfare. The business of a siege was something with which the Parthians had little experience, even when they did conduct them, they went about matters far differently. This lack didn't come from disinterest as much as the reality of the region in which they lived; there was a paucity of resources of the type that were required in the creation of such things like siege towers and artillery. Therefore, the Parthian approach to siege warfare was based in the same quality they exhibited in the other method of waging war, and that was to use patience. Essentially, a Parthian siege was one in name only because they simply outlasted the defenders, cutting off all supply routes, and occasionally going to the effort to stop the supply of water, but only if it was a relatively straightforward matter. This lack of familiarity with the precise nature of siege warfare was a handicap for Kambyses, but he felt confident that he had taken steps to educate himself in a relatively short period of time. Still, like with most things, choosing to access what was a valuable source of knowledge in the ways that the West waged warfare didn't come without some risk because Kambyses didn't learn from a text or scroll in the small library in the palace, but from some of the citizens of Seleucia.

Specifically, Kambyses had let it be known that there were riches to be made by a knowledgeable inhabitant from the large Greek population of Seleucia who still called this former capital of the Seleucid kingdom home. The hazard, Kambyses understood, was based in the question of where these citizens' loyalty still lay; it was true that they had been well-treated by their Parthian overlords, for the simple reason that the Greek population of Seleucia, some twenty thousand inhabitants, contained the vast majority of skilled labor, not to mention those men who were part of what had been a smoothly running bureaucracy, well before the house of the Arsacids claimed the city by right of conquest. It had been a shrewd decision by the first King of Kings of this house to treat the conquered Greeks with clemency, and choosing to leave them in all but the most important and crucial posts in the government. Regardless of this policy, Kambyses was aware that, until they were put to the test, he couldn't guarantee whether or not the Greeks would choose to stay loyal to his house, or would feel a stronger kinship with a people who, in all ways that mattered, had more in common with them. His hope was based in his experience that, while the Greeks of Seleucia may have shared a common culture with the men outside the walls, more often than not, men acted in their own self-interest. None of them had to possess military experience to understand that when a city held out for any length of time, those attacking the walls wouldn't make such fine distinctions should they manage to get into the streets of that city. Even a cursory knowledge of the time in which they lived meant that everyone alive and aware enough to appreciate the meaning had heard the tales and knew what happened to a city that fell by the sword. This was what Kambyses was pinning his hopes on when it came to the loyalty of the Greeks in Seleucia. However, he also quickly realized that he needed more than just their tacit cooperation, which was why he had sent out the call for any man of Seleucia who was skilled in the art of manufacturing implements of war, not the simple arrowheads, spear points and swords, of which the royal armory possessed in huge quantities already, but in the form of artillery. Specifically, pieces that could be mounted on the walls that would be sufficient in strength and size to rain all manner of death and destruction on the Romans, no matter how well prepared they were for this kind of warfare. Regardless, while he had hoped for a handful of men who claimed such expertise, even in his wildest dreams he had not expected the more than three hundred men who crossed the bridges from Seleucia and presented themselves at the palace. Oh, it had been quite hectic, but between Kambyses, Melchior, and two of his other sub-commanders, they had managed to set up a makeshift system whereby each applicant was posed a series of questions. Those who answered intelligently, or at least provided the correct reply, were courteously asked to wait in the palace, while the other interviews continued. Once the last man had been questioned, Kambyses was left with more than eighty men who had either demonstrated or been convincing enough about their ability to create the kinds of machines the Parthian general required. Unfortunately, that had been the easiest part of the battle; procuring the raw materials these newly appointed engineers required had been another matter altogether. But in another act of wisdom, Kambyses restricted his men from scavenging the pieces of seasoned wood, the ingots of iron, and the other odds and ends required to just the Parthian side of the river, in Ctesiphon. While he was heartened by this seeming show of loyalty, even if it was purchased, Kambyses wasn't willing to test this support by sending his men into Seleucia to break into those houses and small temples that contained the materials needed for construction of the artillery. This, at least, was his original intention, but when he learned that, even after conducting a house to house search, and a fair amount of destruction of property caused by ripping out timbers and iron latches, there was only enough to create a dozen artillery pieces, Kambyses was forced to rethink his decision. Most importantly, he had asked for two very large pieces, and while the Greeks had assured him that they could be built, after surveying the pile of wood that came from Ctesiphon, they unanimously pronounced that none of what was available would supply one machine the size he wanted, let alone two. It was actually after Kambyses, upon receiving Melchior's report, took a tour of the walls himself, spending a short period of time watching as the Romans first marked out, then began constructing not four, but five camps, that he made his decision.

Turning to the Greek he had appointed as the chief engineer, a man about Kambyses' age, with gnarled hands and a bent back, he told the man, named Anaxagoras, "I'm afraid we're going to have to search Seleucia as well. Do you think there will be trouble?"

Anaxagoras considered for a moment, but the best he could offer was a shrug, saying only, "I don't know. But," he hesitated for a moment as, unknown to Kambyses, the Greek offered a prayer to his gods asking for forgiveness, "I do know where you can find what we need."

By the end of the second day after their arrival, as Kambyses had observed, Caesar had settled his men into five separate large camps, more or less in a direct line out from the corners of the eastern wall of Ctesiphon, and from the western wall of Seleucia. The third camp, consisting of the auxiliaries, was erected near the canal, which bisected the western wall of Seleucia, where it disappeared underground about fifty paces from the wall, and according to Caesar's information, resurfaced in a large circular pool that then radiated out through the city with smaller waterways. While he had decided in the span of the first few heartbeats to essentially forego any attempt to cut off their water supply, Caesar still had plans for both canal and river, and indeed, this was why he chose the auxiliary camp to occupy the ground, about a mile from the walls. Along with his most accomplished *Praefectus Fabrorum,* Gnaeus Volusenus, who had been the man Caesar trusted to scout the coastline of Britannia in search of a landing site, among other contributions, they had performed a more thorough examination of the entire ground surrounding the twin cities. The small party, consisting of Caesar's bodyguard and the men who worked exclusively for Volusenus as pioneers and camp engineers, had taken almost a full half day, which was done while the rest of the army was moving into their designated positions. While he felt confident that the Parthians wouldn't attempt a sally, if only because of the flat, open ground that precluded any chance at surprise, he still had ordered a Cohort from each Legion to remain in formation, standing ready as their comrades toiled. And, as they quickly learned, depending on which camp it was, their task was more difficult than normal. Once a certain distance away from the river and the green ribbon of topsoil deposited along its banks after thousands of years, especially on the more desolate western side, the Legionaries found they were forced to use pickaxes first, dislodging and breaking down the rocky ground, before a trench could be dug. And fairly quickly, the Primus Pilus of the 7th, Lucius Aquilinus, mounted the horse Caesar had given him and sought out his general. Instead of Caesar, the first man that he ran into that outranked him was Octavian, who was actually spending time with the other youngest noblemen of the army, talking to his closest friend Marcus Agrippa as they performed their own lazy scouting trip around the cities.

After rendering the boy a salute, Aquilinus, a crusty veteran from Umbria who had first enlisted in Pompey's Second Legion, then transferred to the 7th when it was formed and had worked his way up the ranks to his current post, asked him with as respectful tone as he could muster, "Do you know where Caesar is? Have you seen him lately?"

"No," Octavian answered readily enough, but then asked Aquilinus the purpose for which the Primus Pilus was seeking Caesar.

Aquilinus hesitated, then decided it couldn't hurt, telling Octavian, "We've got a problem with the ground. If we have to dig the trench to Caesar's normal standard, it'll take us another day to finish the work. And," he felt it wise to add, "our wall is going to be unstable because it's mostly rock."

Octavian's initial impulse was to simply insist that Aquilinus go back and stripe a few men with his *vitus*. His viewpoint, such as it was, and still relatively uninformed, was that rankers of any sort would look for any excuse to avoid the kind of manual labor that, in every other segment of Roman society save the army, was reserved for slaves. Fortunately for him, his friend Agrippa, who had come to know Octavian quite well, anticipated this would be his reaction. While he didn't say anything overtly, he settled on a strategic cough, which was

236

enough to catch Octavian's attention. Glancing over at his friend, one of the few people in whom Octavian completely trusted, second only to Caesar himself, the youth had learned that, for reasons he chose to ignore, Marcus Agrippa seemed much better attuned to the men of the ranks than Octavian himself. Under normal circumstances, this would have been unacceptable to Octavian; he was nothing if not extremely competitive and hated to be bested at anything. The lone exception was in martial matters; in this, Octavian had long determined that, while he wasn't possessed of either ardor or skill in the arts of warfare, this wasn't the case with Agrippa. He had taken to the role; even through all the slightly belittling duties of a *Contubernales*, which was a status even lower than a Tribune, and in an army as veteran as this one and led by a man like Caesar, Octavian had still never heard Agrippa utter a word of complaint. Now, in an exchanged look that lasted perhaps two or three normal heartbeats, Agrippa managed to communicate to Octavian, which wasn't the first time something of this nature had occurred, nor would it be the last.

So, instead of what he had intended to say, Octavian surprised even himself when he assured Aquilinus, "I'm sure Caesar won't have a problem if you keep the ditch to its normal dimensions. Or even," this caught both Aquilinus and Agrippa off guard, "a bit shallower."

While Aquilinus was certainly relieved, he wasn't completely convinced that this permission, given by the lowest ranking of the senior officers of the army no matter who he was related to, would keep him from a chastisement from Caesar when he became aware of it.

"Thank you, sir," he said carefully, cursing himself for bothering to ask this boy and wondering how to extricate himself, "but…"

"You can tell Caesar that I gave you permission," Octavian replied coolly; while he understood the Primus Pilus' hesitance, it still nettled him.

Clearly relieved, which irritated Octavian even more, Aquilinus saluted, then before the youth could change his mind, turned his horse and went trotting back to camp.

"You did the right thing," Agrippa said quietly, once he felt certain Aquilinus was out of earshot. "And I'm sure Caesar won't mind."

"I hope not," Octavian agreed, then gave a rueful laugh. "But if those Parthians somehow overrun their camp, I'm telling him you talked me into it."

Agrippa laughed as well, then the pair resumed their own progress, which consisted of little more than watching the men of the Legions hard at work, beginning the process of hemming in two cities.

Caesar didn't have any issue with Octavian's judgment, and in something of a surprise, praised the younger man for having the courage to make the decision in his own name.

"I have Legates who wouldn't dare do that," was how the older man put it to his nephew, ignoring the flush of pleasure that suffused Octavian's features. He did so because he knew how Octavian was going to take what came next. "I'm sending you out with Ventidius again."

Octavian demurred at this, or at least tried by saying, "But I've already spent time with the cavalry. Isn't it time I'm attached to your staff?"

Caesar stifled a sigh; he had held out hope that Octavian would accept this assignment without hesitation, but although he didn't relish the thought of confronting the youth, he understood it was time for him to be frank with Octavian.

"You're not going to be attached to my staff until you've served in a combat capacity," Caesar began, holding up a hand when Octavian opened his mouth to continue protesting, in a gesture that was as commanding as any of his verbal orders. "And I've received reports from too many other officers in the cavalry that your contribution to the battle on the ridge was…minimal." Caesar decided on this gentler term.

Octavian's face reddened, his lips thinning into a bloodless line; Caesar was familiar enough with his nephew that he understood Octavian was struggling to contain himself, which was unusual enough that it suggested to Caesar that the boy was aware his conduct hadn't been noteworthy.

When Caesar stopped speaking and didn't resume immediately, Octavian took that as permission for him to speak, and he blurted out, "Who's saying this?" Before Caesar could reply, Octavian's lip curled as he said, "Is it that Decurion Silva? He's nothing but a low-born…"

"Nephew," Caesar cut him off, and while he didn't raise his voice, the tone matched the icy blue of his eyes that pinned Octavian in his gaze, "you need to carefully consider your next words." For a moment, the pair stared at each other in a silent battle of wills, but Octavian's resistance was short-lived, and he was the first to avert his eyes, prompting Caesar to go on, "But to answer your question, as it

R.W. Peake

turns out, while I did talk to Decurion Silva, he was the kindest in his assessment of your time with the cavalry."

As quickly as the blood came, it rushed from his face as the import of Caesar's words hit him; that it was Aulus Ventidius, at the very least, who had reported to Caesar about his actions during the battle meant that he couldn't do anything about it. But neither was it in Octavian's nature to forget a slight, whether it was earned or not, and he simply tucked this away as a matter to be dealt with later, when he was in a position to do something about it. Outwardly, Octavian looked down at the floor, unsure what to say.

Caesar, understanding that this was all he would get in terms of acquiescence from his nephew, who had more than his fair share of pride, continued to explain, "I know that you don't have the same...enthusiasm for battle that I do. But, Gaius," he actually leaned forward a bit so his eyes would be on the same level of Octavian's, who steadfastly refused to look at his uncle, "if you're going to fulfill the plans I have for you, you have to show the men you're leading that you're worthy of their trust. Because if they trust you to lead them in war, it makes it much, much easier to lead them in peace. Do you understand what I'm telling you?"

"Yes," Octavian exhaled, "I do." Only then did he look up at his uncle, and it was only with a partial sense of calculation that this was what his uncle wanted to hear that he continued, "And I know that I wasn't...exceptional in my behavior. But, uncle," he shook his head, his golden, tousled hair catching the light from the lamps as he did, reminding Caesar that his nephew was remarkable in more than just his mind, "I just don't *like* seeing men die and bleed. And suffer."

Caesar listened, saying nothing, even as he was aware that Octavian was telling him, at best, a half-truth. He wouldn't go so far as to say the boy was a coward; it was too early to make that kind of condemning judgment, especially when it was against his nephew, in whom he had such high hopes and ambitious plans. No, Caesar was sure, Octavian wasn't overly concerned about the suffering of other men, he was worried that he might end up being one of those who did fall in battle. Every Roman man worth his salt, at least in Caesar's view, wanted to go into at least one battle and emerge with some sort of wound that would signal his bravery to others, but not disfigure him. Or, he thought with some amusement, kill him. That, he felt certain, was what his nephew truly feared, and while it was something he understood, this fear wasn't something Caesar respected, which led

239

him to speak in soothing tones while at the same time imparting a harsh message.

"Gaius," he placed a hand on the boy's shoulder and gently but firmly exerted pressure on the youth to force him to look his uncle in the eye, "every man is afraid when he's in a situation where he could die. But while all men have fear, a Roman man doesn't allow his fear to control him. He," Caesar emphasized by squeezing Octavian's shoulder, "is the master of his fear. He is the one in control." He paused for a moment, then finished, "This is what it means to be a Roman, especially a Roman of our class. We have to set the example, and to do that, we must conquer our fear and make it the slave, not the master. Do you understand what I'm saying?"

"Yes," Octavian replied soberly. "I do, uncle. I truly do." To his horror, Octavian felt the sting of tears, and he had to swallow past the sudden lump that caused his voice to choke with emotion, "And I swear to you I'll learn how to master my fear."

"I know you will, Gaius," Caesar assured him; there was no need to add anything else.

The boy was bright, and Caesar felt certain that Octavian understood the ramifications to his own future if he was unable to at least avoid the appearance of being a coward, because Caesar couldn't afford to invest any more of his time, effort, or resources in his nephew if he was unable to do so. All of this was communicated in the look that passed between the two, and Caesar was heartened to see the sudden set of Octavian's jaw, recognizing this as the youth's sign of determination.

"Now," Caesar was done with this matter; there was so much more that required his attention, "you understand why you're going to stay with Ventidius?"

"I do," Octavian assured him. "And I swear on Jupiter's black stone I won't let you down."

Caesar nodded his approval, then went on to explain to Octavian what it would mean being with Ventidius. By the time he was through, the youth was already beginning to regret his oath.

The task Caesar gave to his cavalry was relatively straightforward; it was the scope of what he required of them that gave not just Octavian pause. Even Ventidius, who to his surprise was finding he enjoyed being a cavalryman a great deal, was, if not grave, at least sober when he listened to Caesar explain what was expected of him and the force of cavalry that came from no less than four distinctly different nations. Part of Caesar's decision was based in the recognition that, during a siege, the value of a good cavalry arm was greatly diminished. He would keep two *ala* of horsemen; the rest would go with Ventidius, who was charged with determining the whereabouts of the large force that had departed Ctesiphon a little less than a week before. Even away from the river, on the barren, rocky ground that was the predominant feature, the scars of so many horses' hooves and the grooves of wagon wheels was impossible to miss, extending in a dark swath moving southeast from the Parthian capital. To the naked eye, it vanished into the shimmering distance, pointing like an arrow at a slight angle away from the green ribbon of the river. It was into this barren land that Caesar was sending Ventidius, but in a variation from the standard practice, the cavalry was taking two hundred mules, loaded with provisions. This was done in anticipation for the time when, after following the river as it flowed in a generally southeast direction, Ventidius and his men were forced to cross a notoriously waterless stretch of land; the best estimates given to Caesar by prisoners and other sources was that it was more than seventy miles of ground that had to be covered without water. It would certainly slow Ventidius down, but his task was to locate the bulk of the Parthian army, since Caesar correctly guessed that there were few, if any, cataphracts penned up within either Ctesiphon or Seleucia. Correctly deducing the same thing that Kambyses and Phraates had implicitly understood, that cataphracts would be not only useless, they would be detrimental in the defense of the cities, Caesar's primary concern was that whoever led them away from Ctesiphon would be returning, just with a larger force. And, understanding that there wasn't anything nearby that would give his men the advantage that was absolutely essential to success against the heavily armored cataphracts, it was imperative to the general that he be forewarned of their coming in sufficient time to make proper preparations. To that end, once the camps were constructed, Caesar put the men to work diverting either the river or canal, a task that quickly proved to be more difficult than anticipated. The problem, as it had been with two of the camps, was the ground that had been baked under a sun for thousands of years to the point that men had to use pickaxes just to break the surface. Nevertheless, the men persevered, working in the same manner they had marched, where they toiled until it became too hot, then retired to their camps and the parlous shade of their tents, although most men preferred to sit outside of them, rigging up crude shelters from the sun as they got what rest they could. Then, a full watch past noon, they were trooped back out to resume their work constructing smaller channels that would supply their camps with fresh water. Only in one camp was the location close enough that, taking a lesson from his time in Alexandria, Caesar had his men dig straight down, whereupon they struck water in a matter of six or seven feet. The men of the 10th were ecstatic at their good fortune, as was Pullus, although as with all things concerning the army, it meant that they were required to remain in full armor, waiting to be summoned to repel any attempt by the Parthians to stop their comrades from accomplishing their own tasks. Not all the channels were equal either; the men of the 11th, 7th, and 15th Legions, who shared the camp on the southeast side cursed their luck, their Centurions, and most of all, Caesar, for giving them what was by far the most difficult task. Because of what Caesar had planned for the Parthians inside the walls, the Legionaries of these unfortunate Legions couldn't dig a channel straight from the Tigris on the southern side of the cities. Instead, they were forced to dig, and dig, carving a channel directly north, crossing a distance of almost three miles to the northeast camp, where instead of drawing water from the river, they joined their canal to the one excavated by the men of the 5th, 8th, and 28th. While the auxiliaries weren't as fortunate as Pullus and his men, they were still only required to dig from the canal, a distance of a bit more than four furlongs away, while the final camp on the southwest side copied their counterparts on the opposite side of the river, linking their own supply to the channel that came from the canal. Even so, this was still a distance of almost two miles, which meant that even with forty thousand men actually doing the labor, the system of small canals wasn't finished until the fourth day. While all this work was going on, other men, mostly the metalworking and woodworking *immunes* were also busy, assembling the artillery and other heavy equipment that would be needed for the siege. For the Parthians on the walls, while the camps were too far distant to make out anything other than the vaguest sense of movement within their enclosures, they could clearly see the line of men, pickaxes swinging, while others hauled away the spoil in large wicker baskets, piling it on the city side of each canal, making a rampart that could be used to protect the canals if this was required. It was Roman organization and efficiency, as practiced by the acknowledged master of this kind of warfare, and it didn't take the rank or experience of a man like Kambyses to witness this and be disheartened. Nevertheless, the Parthians were equally busy, as both sides prepared for the coming struggle.

Chapter Eight

Once his army's water supply was secured, only then did Caesar implement the second phase of this part of his plan for besieging the cities. It required a bit more digging, and this time, the 10th didn't escape the drudgery of manual labor, but when compared to what their comrades had been forced to do, while they weren't happy, they only did their normal amount of complaining, more out of habit than for any other reason. Their job was even more straightforward, and that was to dig another channel, but this one connected their latrines with the river, but downstream, closer to the cities.

"While we can't completely cut off their water, we can certainly foul it," Caesar had told his Centurions.

This was another common practice, so none of them acted with surprise, and with his usual thoroughness, Caesar had ordered the auxiliaries to essentially do the same to the canal. It wouldn't take long for the Parthians to realize what the Romans had done, but unknown to Caesar and his men, this wouldn't present the normal hardships, thanks to Orodes' decision to dig wells. Of course, this wouldn't be discovered immediately, but even if he had known, Caesar wouldn't have changed his decision. Having the effluvium of several thousand men flowing through the open channels that supplied the cities' water from the river and canal would be unpleasant at the very least. With this matter disposed of, Caesar turned the men to the next step in the methodical approach Rome took to siege warfare. However, because of the nature of the land, Caesar was forced to modify what was essentially the same approach he had used at Alesia and Dyrrhachium. Instead of hemming in the cities with a continuous line of earthworks surrounding them, Caesar ordered the construction of more small fortifications than normal, placing them close enough together so that the artillery pieces were within range of each other. Caesar had long been known for his love of artillery, boosting the complement of scorpions for each Legion, but in preparation for his campaign against the Parthians, he had gone even farther than normal. Given the lack of raw materials in making such pieces, Caesar had foreseen the need for replacement parts, requiring each Legion to add a wagon that carried nothing but extra pieces, ultimately giving each Legion another six scorpions and two ballistae over and above their normal complement. Recognizing the impracticality of creating an earthen barrier that

244

would keep the Parthians within the cities penned up, Caesar settled on creating these smaller outposts, each one studded with scorpions, arranged in such a way that any Parthians attempting to break through would be required to run a gauntlet, where they would be raked by streaking scorpion bolts from either side. Although he felt fairly confident that his Legions and their artillery would be able to stop a sizable force of Parthians, whether they were trying to break out or to link up with the city in the manner that Vercingetorix and his Gallic army had attempted at Alesia, this didn't end his worries.

With a ditch and earthen wall, it made it extremely difficult, if not impossible, for a single man, particularly a mounted man, to slip past the Roman defenses. This wasn't the case here; indeed, once Caesar had determined the practical impossibility of digging all the way around both cities, he had resigned himself to the probability that, at the very least, the Parthians would be able to communicate with whatever other forces were lurking out there, by virtue of single riders who possessed the cunning and stealth to slip past his outposts. It wasn't until the Romans had been in place for more than a week and their initial work was done in setting the stage for the siege that he was forced to modify his original dispositions. After a sleepless night, when the alarm had been sounded by the Century stationed at an outpost no less than a half-dozen times, and his men had been successful in stopping a Parthian rider from slipping past only one of those times, Caesar was forced to reassess their situation. Once more, he, Volusenus, and his complement of men, along with Caesar's personal bodyguards, went on a circuitous inspection of the Roman lines, stopping at each camp and most of the outposts. This was done with two purposes in mind; Caesar was afraid this was going to be a long siege, which meant morale would be crucial, so being regularly seen by his men was important to keeping their spirits high. More importantly, however, it also allowed him to view the ground from the vantage point of each outpost, which meant that it took almost an entire day for him to make the complete circuit of camps and outposts, spending time at each one, studying their placement. What he quickly saw was that, what appeared to be a solid ring of small outposts that seemed impossible to slip past undetected by more than a single man when viewed on a map, turned out to be little better than a bucket with several holes poked in the bottom. Subsequently, when he returned to his own *praetorium*, located in the northwest camp with the 10th, he issued another set of orders that would set his men back to the kind of work they hated the most under normal circumstances. Realizing that he still couldn't plug all the holes, for the same reason he had foregone having his men toil and battle the rocky ground, Caesar determined that he could plug some of them. In doing so, he could at least narrow down the array of choices for any Parthian sent out from the city, down from more than a dozen spots to three obvious choices, and one more that a truly skilled man might be able to negotiate undetected. His method was to take something of a compromised approach, where he, or more accurately, his rankers, created the more standard ditch and earthworks, but radiating out from both banks of the river and canal, extending as far as possible before the ground became too hard to work. Once it was completed, which took yet another two days, the charcoal marks denoting these new fortifications were added to the large piece of vellum that Caesar used, stretched out and hung from the wall of his tent behind his desk.

"It looks like he forgot to finish drawing a circle," Balbinus whispered to Pullus as they stood among the other Primi Pili examining the new dispositions. Pointing at the two open spaces, Balbinus asked Caesar, "Sir, how wide are those gaps?"

Rather than answer himself, Caesar turned to Volusenus, who consulted his wax tablet, where he had the appropriate figures written down.

Frowning, the *Praefectus Fabrorum* spoke reluctantly, knowing the answer he was giving wasn't the one these men wanted to hear, saying, "On the western side, because of the canal, there's actually two gaps, between the canal and northern side of the river, and the canal and the southern side of the river. The northern gap is a bit more than a mile wide, while the southern gap is wider than that because of the way the river curves east. That," he consulted his tablet, "gap is thirteen furlongs, so a bit more than a mile and a half." Glancing up, Volusenus took a breath before he continued, "It's on the opposite side where the news is worse, I'm afraid. Since there's not a canal that softened the ground on that side, that gap is more than two miles wide."

Since the burden to manage this gap fell on the men of the camps to the northeast and southeast, they were the Primi Pili to react most visibly, and more than one of the half-dozen men either sucked in a breath or uttered a soft curse. Caesar, at the moment content to let Volusenus relay this news, understood that what he was about to order would be even less popular, but he had considered the matter long and hard, knowing it needed to be done.

"We're repositioning the outposts slightly," he began, which wasn't unexpected, but then he added, "and we're going to have walking outposts."

For the span of a heartbeat, the silence was total as all the Primi Pili tried to comprehend this addition; then, utter chaos broke out, which was an unusual enough event in Caesar's headquarters that he delayed in reasserting control.

"Caesar! Having men out there in the dark? Outside of the outpost? That's too dangerous!"

"What if the alarm sounds? The scorpions are just as likely to skewer one of our men as one of those Parthian bastards!"

While this wasn't all that Pullus was able to pick out among the babble of voices, he quickly determined that his counterparts were essentially saying the same thing. Only Pullus, Spurius of the 3rd, and Balbinus of the 12th remained silent, although it was only Pullus who had been forewarned by Caesar, in a private meeting before this briefing, about the general's decision. Caesar had met with Pullus to gauge his most trusted Primus Pilus' reaction as a way to determine how the others might take this news, so Pullus had already raised the objections that were being voiced. This was why he remained silent; Balbinus and Spurius followed Pullus' example because he had warned the pair what to expect and had impressed on them that Caesar's mind was set on taking this step. Finally, Caesar had endured enough, but the Primi Pili were sufficiently agitated that, when he raised his hand for silence, they didn't immediately obey.

"*Tacete!*"

Caesar didn't use the full volume of his voice often; therefore, when he did, it carried even more impact, and as he expected, this was sufficient to stop the Primi Pili in mid-word. What didn't change were their sullen expressions, but this was something a wise commander chose to overlook at this moment.

"While I understand your concerns, and I share them," his voice had immediately returned to its normal level, "I know I don't have to impress upon any of you the need to keep the integrity of our lines and make it as close to impossible for any Parthian to break out. Like," Caesar's mouth turned down and his tone became grim, "what happened last night. For all we know, there are men riding for help." Taking another deep breath, he added the second part of this new change in plans. "Which is why we're repositioning the outposts in such a manner that they provide some protection. It won't be a contravallation like we had at Alesia, but now with these new ditches, it at least gives the Parthians only a couple of choices to try and penetrate."

He paused to allow the men to absorb and start to accept this change; once he judged, by way of their expressions, that they had come to terms with this modification, only then did he move on to give the full details. Despite the fact that these were necessary adjustments, all of the men present were also aware that this was extending the time they would have to spend actually besieging the cities, and that there were Parthians who had slipped past the night before, riding to summon help.

If Caesar and the rest of his officers had known the reality of the situation, it would have put their minds somewhat at ease. While it was true that Kambyses had sent men out to carry messages to his king, they weren't pleas for help, but merely updates on the defense of the cities. Whereas Caesar and, to a lesser extent, his Legates and some of his Primi Pili were aware that the Parthians didn't view their cities in the same light as Romans, Greeks, and, in fact, every other culture with whom Romans had any congress, it was still inconceivable to them that their Parthian enemies would be willing to sacrifice a city that was their capital. This ignorance, while excusable, was also a crucial mistake in the events that were to come, although even after all that happened, when Caesar, Pullus, or any man in the army looked back, they would have been hard pressed to see what they could have done differently. Nevertheless, what Phraates had ordered, and ultimately what Kambyses had agreed with his young king about, despite his personal feelings, was that Ctesiphon, and Seleucia were pieces in the great game that could be sacrificed without the Parthian cause suffering such a material loss it would be impossible for them to recover. That this sacrifice of thousands of civilians was considered, if not trivial then not seriously damaging, was based in more than just the sprawling nature of the Parthian empire. Certainly, some of it stemmed from the dismissive attitude Parthian nobles held towards their social inferiors, seeing them as nothing more than sources of labor that created wealth for their *satraps* and fodder for the swords of their enemies, but that wasn't all of it. While the Arsacids had founded Ctesiphon, originally as a military camp across the river from Seleucia when they were performing their own siege of the city, and it had been Orodes who had poured money and effort into creating it into the showcase for his house's dynastic ambitions, the truth was that it was

248

still in most ways a new city. Consequently, neither subjects nor the ruling families of the Parthian nobility looked at Ctesiphon with the kind of attachment that Orodes had, the former King of Kings seeing this as his legacy to his house's glory. But now, Orodes was no longer King of Kings; indeed, unknown to Kambyses at this point, a bit more than two weeks after he had last laid eyes on the old king, Orodes was dead. Even if Kambyses had known, it still wouldn't have changed matters all that much, especially since the general commanding the defense of the two cities viewed them with the same level of indifference as most other Parthians. With the exception of those now trapped inside the walls, of course, but while Kambyses didn't hold any real attachment to the city, nor it must be said, towards those he was charged with defending, he was absolutely concerned about his own reputation and the sting of the defeat in his last battle. This fueled his determination to break the Roman army outside the walls, and he understood that the best, really the only way to do that was to prolong the siege for as long as possible, thereby allowing the Parthian winter to arrive as his ally. It would be the elements that brought salvation, not a force of cataphracts and horse archers. This was why his dispatches to Phraates, if anything, understated the difficulty and challenges Kambyses faced, and not a plea for any succor. Orodes had provided the solution to the water supply; it hadn't taken long for the citizens of both cities to learn that the Romans were using their normal water supply as a sewer, although the stench was bearable as long as one wasn't near one of the waterways. The old king had ensured the granaries were not only full, but the warehouses of the city were bursting at the seam. According to Gobryas, one of the other nobles who Kambyses had appointed as quartermaster, there was enough food for six months of rations, for all of the people, and that was at the normal rate of consumption. Just by cutting back to three quarters of the normal added another three months, but Kambyses hadn't decided whether to take this step early when it was more in the nature of a prudent precaution, or to wait until it was forced on him. Ultimately, he decided to compromise; he would allow those inside the walls to receive their full complement of rations for the first month, then he would re-evaluate. Although this was certainly an important consideration, most of Kambyses' attention, and his time, was spent in the series of makeshift workshops, spread evenly between the two cities, where his smaller army of craftsmen were working through the watches to manufacture an array of artillery weapons that Caesar himself wouldn't sneer at possessing. Yet, as crucial as these implements would be, they were of secondary importance to what they would be hurling from the walls of the city. This was another thing for which Kambyses had cause to thank his former king for, because Orodes had been assiduous in stockpiling what the general felt sure would be his most potent weapon, and in a land where other resources were scarce, it was blessed with an abundance of this substance. With the artillery, which Anaxagoras had assured Kambyses would number more than fifty machines, including the two largest pieces, procuring the materials for the construction of them had created a huge headache for Kambyses, just as Anaxagoras had warned him. He had been made aware of this difficulty when a delegation appeared at the palace headquarters in Ctesiphon, and he had instantly seen by their mode of dress and their accents the delegation was composed entirely of the Greeks of Seleucia. More specifically, the leaders of the group were attired in the garb that Kambyses knew signified their status as members of the priestly orders, of which there were more than a dozen temples of varying sizes scattered throughout Seleucia. Even before the Greek Kambyses correctly deduced was the leader of the delegation opened his mouth, the Parthian had a suspicion he knew the purpose of this visit.

"Your...Excellency," the Greek, who appeared to be in his early sixties, and who sported a flowing beard that, unlike the Eastern custom, wasn't oiled, spoke with a cadence and diction that betrayed his many years speaking before others, "my name is Philocratos of Ephesus, and I am the high priest of the Temple of Zeus in Seleucia. I am speaking on behalf of myself and," he made a half-turn towards his compatriots, accompanied by an elaborate gesture, "my fellow priests, both of my temple and that of the others that have been desecrated."

Despite his suspicion that this was the purpose of their visit, Kambyses still stifled a curse; he didn't need more headaches than he already had, but he restrained himself from simply throwing these Greeks out and informing them the next time they showed their faces to him with their complaints, he would have their heads parted from their shoulders. Nevertheless, while this would certainly be simpler, Kambyses also was aware that he needed, if not the cooperation of the Greek community of Seleucia, then at least not to have to worry about their actively performing acts of sabotage that would help the Romans outside the walls.

It was with this in mind that Kambyses kept his tone, if not warm, at least polite, asking, "Desecrated? How so…?"

"Philocratos, Your Excellency," the older Greek reminded him, but he wasn't as successful at keeping his irritation at being forgotten so easily hidden. "As far as how this desecration occurred, the simplest way to put it is that the Temple of Zeus, *my* temple, no longer exists. And," now the priest made no attempt to hide his anger, "our information is that it was done at your order."

"Really?" Kambyses tried to sound puzzled. "I'm sure you're mistaken, Philocratos. I gave no orders to destroy any temples in Seleucia." Offering his audience an exaggerated shrug, he said, "I'm afraid that your information is incorrect."

Realizing that he had been neatly outwitted, the Greek tried to regain his composure, and even Kambyses had to admit he did an admirable job of it, as he kept his tone respectful and the volume of his voice was as if this was a normal conversation of no import.

Forgive me, Your Excellency, and you're indeed correct." Philocratos, it seemed to Kambyses, possessed the ability to be as falsely courteous as any Eastern courtier. "I'm well aware that you gave no such order. Please excuse my…mischaracterization. However," the Greek's voice hardened, just a fraction but enough for Kambyses to notice, "while you certainly didn't command my temple, and," he added in what sounded to Kambyses was an afterthought, an impression under which he wasn't alone judging from the expressions of a half-dozen of his fellow priests, "any of the lesser temples to be torn down, unfortunately, the end result of what you *did* order is the same, because they are no longer standing."

For a moment, Kambyses thought of summoning Anaxagoras and offering the man up as a sop and appeasement to this group of priests; perhaps seeing their fellow Greek executed would not only satisfy their outrage but send a subtle yet unmistakable message about who really ruled here. However, he quickly discarded that idea, thinking, No, I'm going to need him more than I need this bunch. He serves a useful, no, a *crucial* function to our cause. Still, he reminded himself of his original recognition; he didn't want to turn these Greeks into enemies.

More to buy time to think than for any other reason, Kambyses tried to appear as if he still wasn't grasping the full import of what he was being told, asking, "Could you please describe what happened, exactly?"

251

Although Philocratos knew by Kambyses' own demeanor the Parthian already understood, the Greek wasn't unskilled himself in the language of the Eastern court. After all, he had been high priest of his temple for twenty years, which meant that he had had multiple audiences with members of the Parthian court, and on two different occasions, with the King of Kings himself, Orodes.

Therefore, he patiently did as Kambyses asked, explaining, "While it's true that you didn't order the temple, or *temples*," he amended in response to the hiss of anger from one of the other Greeks, "to be destroyed, your requirement for seasoned timbers of a certain size meant that the only examples to be found were in the main support columns that were instrumental in the construction of our temples." Philocratos concluded by raising his hands and shrugging, saying simply, "And without those columns, our temples collapsed."

Kambyses didn't reply, at least immediately, then after a moment of studying the faces of the men standing before him, asked softly, "So, what is it you want, Philocratos?" Up to this point in his dealings with others, particularly his fellow countrymen, Kambyses had been careful to avoid not only sitting on the throne of the King of Kings, but standing anywhere near it. Until this moment, when he walked slowly to it, then in a seemingly casual way but which was fraught with a significance he was sure at least this old priest would understand, leaned on one arm of the throne as he continued, "If all is as you say, and I don't doubt that it is, the damage is already done, is it not?"

"Yes, Your Excellency," Philocratos agreed heavily. "We have three temples that were completely destroyed, and two that, according to what I have been told by men experienced in such matters, while they are still standing, are too dangerous to enter, and are beyond salvage. And," he pointed out, "as you undoubtedly know, that to rebuild the temples, in the same manner in which they were first constructed, requires columns like the ones your men took, which is not easy to do," he finished, needlessly as far as Kambyses was concerned.

He also didn't miss that when Philocratos described rebuilding as difficult, what he was sure the Greek meant was "expensive." Only along some of the highest mountain slopes at the farthest corners of the Parthian empire would trees of such a massive size be found. That there were parts of the world where this essential material in one form of construction was plentiful Kambyses knew, although only in an academic sense; his mind simply couldn't comprehend the idea of

252

forests, filled with huge trees that stretched for miles. And while such timber was available to the Parthians, the expense of retrieving and transporting of it was such that in the past, they had instead purchased it from the port cities nearest them. Now, in the throne room in Ctesiphon, Kambyses at least felt that he had a better idea of what this meeting was about.

"What you say about reconstruction is certainly true," Kambyses granted, then in another display calculated to send a message, he began drumming his fingers on the arm of the throne as he mused aloud, "I wonder how much such a project would cost?"

"As it happens, Your Excellency," Philocratos replied, yet as he did so, he turned around, extended a hand, and was smoothly given a wrapped scroll that he turned and held up in front of him, "we found in the rubble of the temple, from our archives, there survived an old but very detailed report of how much the Temple of Zeus in Seleucia cost to build. And," he added, this time because of something one of the Greeks behind him muttered, "as I've been informed, my brother priests who are responsible for the other temples that were destroyed have similar documents."

I just bet they do, Kambyses thought with grim amusement, but the ink's not dry on these "old" documents yet, which is why you didn't bring them. A part of Kambyses bridled at continuing this pretense, yet he placed sufficient value on keeping the peace inside his walls so that he reached out and accepted what he was sure was a new document that contained a highly inflated cost for rebuilding the temple. Which, he did have to admit, he had known full well was destroyed, and indeed, had been told by Anaxagoras beforehand that to retrieve those valuable pieces of timber would cause the destruction of the temples where they resided. That, however, wasn't something these Greeks needed to know. Now, Kambyses thought, after the delegation departed, all I have to do is make sure the city doesn't fall. Even then, the Parthian was keenly aware that the new King of Kings was likely to take a dim view of one of his generals making promises on his behalf, but that was a problem that could be dealt with later. First, there was the matter at hand, and it was with this in mind Kambyses left the palace to take his afternoon tour of the walls, trying to determine if the Romans had settled on a plan, and most importantly, what that plan was.

From the very first campaign under Caesar in which Titus Pullus had participated, he had learned to trust his general's plans and decisions. Not that there hadn't been times when Pullus found himself second-guessing one of the greatest military minds of not just Rome, but of his age. Still, none of those times compared to the ambivalence with which Pullus viewed Caesar's plan for taking first Seleucia, then Ctesiphon. On the table in the large conference room, a model even more elaborate than the hastily constructed diorama of the ridge and its defenses greeted the assembled officers of Caesar's army, while Caesar stood next to it with a long rod with which he used to point out salient features.

"After performing a thorough examination of the defenses, and taking into consideration the resources available to us," Caesar had announced at this briefing, the aim of which was to at last unveil his plan to assault the Parthian capital, "I've decided that this is going to be rather straightforward. At least," he allowed, "in the plan itself. The execution, however…" His face turned grim as he turned to take each Primus Pilus in his gaze, one at a time. Pullus and the other Primi Pili knew this was a favorite tactic of Caesar's at such moments, alerting these men of the gravity with which Caesar was treating this manner. In that glance, no more than a heartbeat's worth of time for each of them, and if they had been asked, each Primus Pilus would have said something eerily similar about how they interpreted that look, that their general was aware of the meaning of what he was asking, that it would come at a high cost in blood, and that Caesar wasn't making the decision lightly. When he thought about it later, Pullus decided this was the first moment his misgivings came to life in the form of a tight, fluttering sensation in his gut.

"Seleucia has three exterior gates, on the northern, southern, and western sides. And, as you've undoubtedly seen by now, there are three bridges on the eastern side that lead across the river into Ctesiphon. But, as I'm sure you've also determined, trying to force our way between the two cities would expose us to a murderous crossfire. So," he made a quick motion above that part of the model, dismissing the interior gates as an option, "we're not going to waste any time talking about that, at least until we take Seleucia and start our plan to take Ctesiphon." Moving the point of the rod to the southern side, Caesar continued, "The southern gate is well-fortified, but the biggest challenge is based in the fact that the defenders have destroyed the bridge across the river, which is within range of the walls because the city actually sits in a loop of the Tigris, which exits from the

254

section of it between the cities and turns almost directly west. Also," he added grimly, "while we haven't seen any signs that the Parthians have artillery, at least of a large enough size that it gives them the range beyond perhaps a hundred paces from the walls, and we do know that they don't favor its use anyway, they won't need much to make rebuilding a bridge, just to get to the gate, a bloody business." Caesar then indicated the northern gate, continuing, "As you've also no doubt seen, the northern gate is not only heavily fortified, judging from its appearance, it's actually a double-gated entrance. And I'm fairly certain that the passage between the two gates is designed in such a way that the defenders can simply tip over their cauldrons of flammables down onto our heads. So penetrating the first gate would only be half the battle, so to speak. And," he finished grimly, "I'm not comfortable sending men in there, knowing the likelihood they'll be burned alive. Without actually seeing that passage, it means this is a risk with your men's lives I'm not willing to take."

All the muttering and shuffling about as the Centurions conferred quietly among themselves or moved into a better spot to see the model had ceased by this point; Pullus noticed the heavy quality of the silence as each Primus Pilus absorbed Caesar's grim assessment, and Pullus could see that, like he had, they accepted their general's reasoning as the most likely outcome. Of all the things fighting men of any nation feared, burning to death was at the top of the list of the many ways in which a man could die in battle.

Seeing and understanding their silent acceptance, Caesar resumed by saying, "And, we don't have the ability to undermine the walls, for a number of reasons."

Pointing to the model of Seleucia, he indicated the southern wall. "As all of you have seen by now, of the two cities, in some ways, Seleucia presents a larger challenge, at least from the perspective of trying to undermine a section of its walls. Here," he moved the pointer along the length of the tiny southern wall, "as I've already pointed out, isn't possible because of the missing bridge. Only here," the tip slid to the spot where the river went from its east/west orientation along the southern wall back to its southerly direction, "is this gap where the river turns back south. While our hosts haven't invited us for a closer examination," as Caesar hoped, this prompted a chuckle from his assembled officers, "it's no more than a span of a hundred paces, perhaps one hundred twenty. But, although this would be the section of ground where it's close enough to the river we could theoretically dig, that's actually the problem. It's *too* close to the river, which means a tunnel, even if it's properly dug and shored up with support timbers, would flood." This in itself was enough to discourage, but Caesar wasn't finished, moving now to tap what represented the southwest corner of the Seleucia wall. "Even if we could solve that problem, we'd have to approach the wall so that the tunnel would go directly underneath the corner. Which I don't have to tell you, is the strongest part of a wall. So," he then turned to the western wall, and moved the pointer to indicate the tiny canal that flowed underneath the wall, "we examined the idea of using the canal in some way. It would be an easy matter to stop the water flow," Caesar acknowledged, "and in some ways, the Seleucids did us a favor by creating a tunnel under the wall already. But," Caesar glanced up so his men could read his expression more easily as he said, "I don't think I have to go into much detail about why this is unfeasible. Do I?" Seeing the men shaking their heads, Caesar turned away from the canal, which despite knowing it wasn't going to be an option, filled Pullus with relief. From the first day when he had examined the defenses, and understood as Caesar had that Seleucia would probably be the first target for an assault, Pullus had seen the canal as an obvious candidate for exploitation. Its greatest advantage was that any Roman charging down into the yawning darkness could be certain that the distance the canal covered under the wall would be well constructed and unlikely to collapse. Indeed, from just his cursory examination, he had seen that the mouth of the tunnel was constructed of tightly fitted bricks, held together with not just mortar, but by its own weight, making it stable and, under other circumstances, safe for passage. The canal was ten feet wide as it reached the wall, but Pullus judged that the tunnel wasn't that high; despite viewing it from a distance, he had been certain that a man his height would have to almost crouch. Although Pullus hated enclosed spaces, it was the fact that nobody knew exactly what lay on the other side of the wall that had convinced him this wasn't a good choice for an assault, and he was happy that Caesar understood this as well.

"The walls on the western side are clearly thicker than the wall that fronts the river across from Ctesiphon," Caesar was continuing, "which not only makes sense, it tells me that it was a later addition to Seleucia."

"How can you tell that, Caesar?"

That it was Pollio who asked the question, along with his tone of voice, informed those who knew Caesar well that this wasn't a random question, asked out of curiosity. And, while Pullus would never say so openly, he was one of those of Caesar's officers who felt certain that there was a level of vanity in Caesar's instructions to Pollio to pose this question. He does love to show everyone how much smarter he is than everyone else, Pullus thought, secretly amused at what he felt sure was his insight, unaware that more than one of his counterparts had deduced the same thing.

"Two ways, Pollio," Caesar answered, giving his lieutenant the kind of smile that made Pullus think that Caesar was acutely aware this was a performance he was putting on, "the first being the history of how these two cities came into being. When Seleucia was founded, there wasn't anything across the river, and a possible assault against the city could have come from any direction. Why would they bolster only the western wall?" Pausing long enough to gauge how this was being received, once he was satisfied that his officers accepted this logic, he went on, "And the second reason is that once Ctesiphon became a city, Seleucia had already been conquered by the Parthians. As we can all see, while they developed separately, for all intents and purposes, they're one city. None of the Arsacid kings have bothered to unify the defenses by creating one single wall that crossed the river along both northern and southern sides. Frankly, I don't think they have the wherewithal for that kind of engineering, although," he ceded, "the Greeks, who compose a large portion of the population of Seleucia, are certainly capable of doing something like this. No," Caesar finished, "they strengthened the western wall for the very reason we're assaulting from this side. It's the best option available to us." Silence filled the room, each Centurion, and Legate for that matter, absorbed in his own thoughts as he stared down at the model. Caesar had paused to take a breath, but he quickly continued, his tone returning to its normal brisk quality. "Still, despite the thickness, Volusenus has calculated, and I agree with his calculations, that we have enough heavy artillery, and enough ammunition of sufficient size, to breach that wall. But," his expression grew grave, "we have enough only to punch one hole in the western wall."

None of the men needed to be told what that meant; with only one point of the city's defenses being the focus of the Roman assault, the Parthian general had more than enough warning about where the assault was going to be taking place. More importantly, it gave him the ability to do something about it.

"How long do you think it will take to create the breach?"

The question came from Sextus Crispus, the Primus Pilus of the 22nd Legion, but while it was certainly a valid question, and one that Pullus and those Primi Pili who led the more senior Legions were interested in hearing, that didn't stop the large Roman from exchanging a glance with Spurius, the Primus Pilus of the 3rd, their thoughts running in a similar direction. The truth was that, while it was a good question, neither Pullus nor Spurius thought that the 22nd would be the first Legion through the wall. No, they both were sure, that will be us, one of Caesar's Gallic Legions, the men who had been through the most with their general, and in whom their general trusted the most.

"As you undoubtedly know, Crispus, that's very difficult to say," Caesar replied, but while he didn't sound evasive, he was clearly reluctant as he offered, "but our best estimate is that it will take a week. At least."

Instantly, a low chorus of mumbling conversation filled the room once more, as both Primi Pili and Legates were moved to comment. A week, as they all knew, was an eternity under these circumstances, because it gave whoever was commanding the defense the time to not just understand the nature of what was coming, but gave him the ability to do something about it. By the time the breach was created, what was likely to be waiting for the first Legionaries through the breach would be a far cry from what was there right now. Every man there, representing well more than two centuries of combined fighting experience, could think of easily a half-dozen different types of challenges waiting for the first through the breach. Caesar seemed content to let his officers discuss this piece of news with each other, but finally, he tapped the model again, increasing his force until it made a sharp enough rapping sound to arrest the conversations.

Once it was silent again, Caesar said calmly, "I understand your reaction, comrades. In fact, I share it." Once more, Caesar paused, which was unusual in itself, and didn't help Pullus feel any better. "Which is why we're going to have to keep our Parthian friends busy while all this is going on." It was only when he continued after yet another hesitation that Pullus understood why Caesar was so reluctant. "While this is the real assault, from the perspective of the Parthians, we have to convince them that this isn't our main effort. So we're going to be assaulting the walls, more than once and at different points, during the time we are working to breach the western wall."

Once more, there was a silence, but Caesar quickly saw that it was because his officers were trying to comprehend the full ramifications of what this meant.

Although it wasn't planned, ultimately, the eyes of those men wearing the white transverse crest looked unanimously to one of their own, which meant it was Titus Pullus who spoke, slowly, "That means we're going to lose a lot of men in these fake assaults that aren't likely to succeed."

It was a sign of how much Caesar respected not only Pullus, but all of his Centurions, that he didn't hesitate, or try to modify his answer and couch it in more palatable terms.

"Yes, Pullus," he replied calmly, making a point to look Pullus unflinchingly and directly in the eye, "that's exactly what it means. We're going to shed a lot of blood to take these cities."

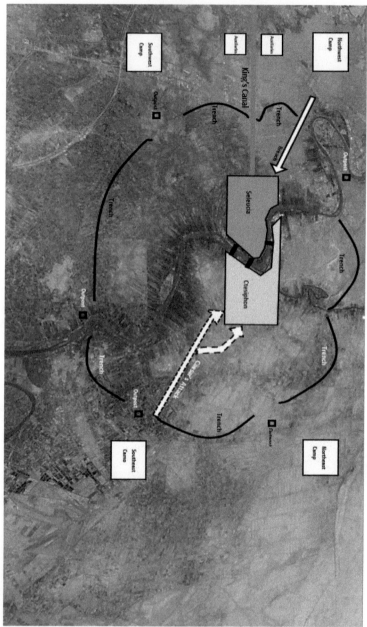

Siege of Ctesiphon/Seleucia

Chapter Nine

On the Ides of Sextilis, the siege of the Parthian capital began in earnest. Kambyses had only recently arisen when a messenger from the commander of the guard watch who had just galloped across the central bridge arrived at the palace. Despite the fact that Kambyses had been expecting news of this nature for days, when it finally came, he found that his breakfast, which he had been halfway through consuming, no longer appealed to him. Leaving his meal, he didn't bother donning his armor; he felt certain it wouldn't be needed yet. Snapping an order to a slave to have his horse saddled and waiting for him on the plaza, Kambyses dismissed the courier back to the commander with the assurance that he would be following behind shortly. Shouting for Melchior, on whom he had begun to rely more and more, even if he still didn't trust the younger man, Kambyses strode from the large room located roughly in the center of the palace, navigating his way down the wide corridor that led first to the throne room, then to the main reception area. The building was large enough that, when he reached the reception area, Melchior had come hurrying from his small room that had housed one of the resident king's favorite concubines. While Kambyses' choice for Melchior's lodging hadn't been an insult, exactly, it had been calculated to remind Melchior that, while he enjoyed Kambyses' favor, and he wasn't forced to reside in the officers' quarter of the cramped royal barracks, the young nobleman nevertheless depended on Kambyses' largesse. Although the Parthian commander had initially been reluctant to take on any of the trappings or avail himself of the benefits that came from, if not being the King of Kings, at least immersed in the luxury that came with the title, that had quickly worn off. Kambyses had sipped from the cup of ultimate power and discovered he liked the taste quite a bit. Once this ordeal was through, he had begun to think of the possibility of challenging Phraates for the throne; provided he survived this, of course. Doing that very thing was the foremost matter in his mind now as he waited just long enough for Melchior to hurry to his side.

Eschewing the normal ritualistic greeting that under other circumstances was very important to the members of Parthian nobility,

Kambyses related the news to Melchior by saying only, "It appears it's begun."

Unsurprisingly, Melchior needed no more than that, asking quickly, "Where?"

"The eastern wall," Kambyses answered, neither bothering nor needing to explain which eastern wall it was.

Waiting only long enough for Melchior's own mount to be brought, the pair then moved at a quick trot through the streets of Ctesiphon, heading to the eastern wall of the city to see for themselves in what manner the Roman assault would come. Their way was impeded by the rushing activity that the alarm had prompted, as the men of the various commands who had been quartered throughout the city answered the blaring sound of the Parthian horns sounding the call that, at last, it had begun. This was bad enough, but the civilians of the city had left their dwellings to come rushing out into the streets; seeing Kambyses, most of them recognized him as the noble who controlled their destiny, which prompted them to behave in a much bolder manner than normal.

"Great One, are the Romans coming at last?"

"Oh, Brave Kambyses! We beg you to protect our lives!"

"We are going to the Mithraeum right now to make a sacrifice to the bull slayer! He will guide and protect you against these Roman dogs!"

These were only those cries and pleas that Kambyses actually could make out amid the babble of the many voices calling to him, but it was the impediment the civilians caused that tried his patience to the point that he stopped trying to guide his horse through the crowd with a minimum of disruption. Giving the beast its head, Kambyses' mount responded in the manner in which it had been trained, suddenly moving straight ahead, plowing a path through the crowded streets, knocking the slow or stubborn aside. The calls for help and the shouts of praise quickly turned to cries of alarm and pain when someone wasn't agile enough to move out of the horse's path.

"That might stop some of them from making sacrifices to protect you," Melchior said with a laugh once they had managed to move past what seemed to be the worst of the congestion.

"Maybe that will teach them to stay out of the way," Kambyses growled, but then gave Melchior a tight grin.

Reaching the northeast corner of the city, where the covered stairs led up to the ramparts, both men dismounted, then hurried up the steps. Kambyses had seen the commander of the guard, a grizzled veteran who had a scarred, puckering hole where one eye should have been, but who Kambyses knew to be a fierce fighter, standing at the top of the stairs.

"Well?" Kambyses demanded, but while the guard commander was subordinate to the general, he wasn't intimidated in the slightest.

"Follow me," was all he said, turning and walking along the rampart to the northeast corner.

Naturally, Kambyses did so, followed by Melchior, yet despite mentally preparing himself, when he reached the edge and stepped into the gap between crenellations so that he could look down at the ground beyond the wall, he couldn't stop himself from gasping. Instantly realizing that as much as he thought he had prepared himself for this moment, actually seeing the might of Rome arrayed outside the walls of the city he was charged to defend was impossible to imagine. Not, he thought, until you see it. Despite the sudden chill that seemed to overtake his body, enough to make him visibly shudder, a part of Kambyses' mind admired the sight before him. Ordered lines of men, neatly arranged in groups of uniform size that Kambyses knew were called Centuries, without any haste or signs of anything that could be construed as betraying a collective case of nerves, the Roman lines moved slowly towards the eastern wall of Ctesiphon. They were still more than a half-mile away but clearly moving in Kambyses' direction.

Turning to Melchior, who was standing beside him, staring down with the same fascination as his general, Kambyses said quietly, "You know what to do."

The Parthian army wasn't as rigid in its customs as their Roman counterparts, so there was nothing Melchior was expected to say, or do, for that matter, to acknowledge his orders had been received, understood, and would be obeyed. Still, he did render the Parthian version of a salute, which was placing the knuckles against his forehead, then he turned and went sprinting down the northern rampart, heading to the western corner. Suddenly, Kambyses was acutely aware that he was standing there unarmored, so he turned to the commander of the guard.

"Send someone back to the palace to fetch my armor. I'm going to stay here to make sure we're ready for these dogs."

In an imitation of Melchior's gesture, the commander added a short bow, then turned and hurried down the stairs, bawling an order for one of the men sitting next to his horse, waiting for such a summons. Kambyses turned his attention back to the sight before him, and while he was confident of the outcome, he still realized that, in a small way, he had been outwitted by this Caesar. The surprise that Anaxagoras and his men had prepared were on the other side of the city, because Kambyses had felt certain that the Romans would focus their effort there, where the river separated the two cities. Even with the construction of those two smaller walls that closed the gap between the cities down to just the width of the river, Kambyses had been confident that the Romans would see this as the obvious weak point, which was exactly what Kambyses wanted them to see. However, he was an experienced warrior, perhaps not in this style of warfare, but it didn't take expertise in defending a city to know that one's enemy rarely behaved as one liked. One thing he instantly divined about why this Caesar had chosen the eastern wall came when he was forced to squint and shade his eyes because of the still-rising sun. It made it extremely difficult to make out any level of detail as the Romans closed the distance; they were now close enough that Kambyses heard the deep notes of one of their horns, and despite himself, he felt a stab of dread, reliving the battle on the ridge, the last time he had heard those cursed things. Swearing an oath at the glare, he continued staring at the advancing Romans, finally able to pick up the presence of what he knew would be ladders, which at this moment looked like dark, straight lines that began roughly in the second rank of the leading Centuries, and extended through the ranks.

"So they think they can scale the walls with ladders?" Kambyses muttered, hearing the skepticism he felt inside expressed aloud. "Surely they can't think it would be that simple."

From behind him, Kambyses heard the rhythmic slapping sound of sandaled feet, running up the parapet behind him, the bulk of the mixed force of archers and infantry that had been positioned, ready and waiting, in the northwest corner of the city. Melchior had obviously reached their commander, and Kambyses turned just in time to see the noble he had appointed to lead this group of defenders, another youngster whose *satrap* had been the late, non-lamented Cyaxares. What was his name again? he wondered.

Then it came to him, just in time for him to acknowledge the man, "I'm glad you and your men arrived so quickly, Sosimenes! But," he spoke loudly, meaning this to be heard by more than just his sub-commander, "tell me; are they ready to fight?"

As Kambyses expected, his answer came in the form of roar from the men who would bear the brunt of the actual fighting, prompting Sosimenes to just grin at Kambyses.

"Do they sound like they're ready, Lord Kambyses?"

"They do," Kambyses agreed, still speaking loudly, then he turned to face down the eastern wall where the men were still filing by and getting into their positions along the crenellation, "but now let me see your words put into action!"

This was met with another roar, as the men swore they would back up their words with deeds. Meanwhile, the Romans kept their slow, measured progress in their direction, and Kambyses was beginning to worry. However, when he turned to gaze down the length of the northern rampart, he saw the first of Anaxagoras' surprises being pushed by its crew, its wooden wheels making a deep, rumbling sound as they rolled across the stones. Allowing himself a grim smile, Kambyses turned and walked to the stairs, looking down for one man in particular, quickly seeing him among the small knot of Parthians waiting to do their part. Since this man was already gazing upward, Kambyses caught his attention easily.

"It's time," Kambyses called down, and the man acknowledged his general, the group of men immediately setting in motion.

Each of them hoisted a yoke, placing it across their shoulders, then began moving towards the stairs, where they were forced to ascend by turning sideways. To an uninformed observer, it would have been impossible to know much about their cargo, which looked like nothing more than a pair of medium-sized pots, one on each side, but the manner in which each bearer moved up the steps, clearly being careful not to swing or jostle their cargo, might have at least warned them it was something precious. Or, perhaps, extremely hazardous and volatile. One by one, the dozen men reached the top of the stairs, where Kambyses had another group of men waiting to relieve each man of his burden, whereupon the bearer immediately descended the stairs, still turned sideways to allow their comrades still making their way up room to move. In this manner, there soon was a stockpile of these jars, which were handled with as much care once they were unloaded, while the first artillery piece was rolled into position. As Kambyses had been warned, it was a tight fit, which was why the smallest piece had been brought forward first, but it was crucial to his plans that the surprise was as close to total as he could make it, which meant that the first three pieces had to be muscled across the interior corner of the wall so that it wasn't near enough to the exterior part of the wall to be spotted by a sharp-eyed Roman. The throwing arms of each piece were already cinched down, not only so they were instantly ready, but it made their profile that much lower. It was a hectic and extremely tense period of a few hundred heartbeats, yet somehow, despite Kambyses realizing that this entire operation hadn't been planned particularly well as far as the details, the Parthians managed to get everything as Kambyses wanted in time to give them a few moments to breathe. By this point, the Romans had stopped, now about a quarter mile from the walls, and just out of range of all but the last piece of artillery, the giant machine, although it was still quite a distance down the northern rampart, waiting for Kambyses to order it forward. He, however, was waiting for the Romans, except that, even after their ranks had been reordered, and their men were now standing in perfect alignment and motionless, as if they were on the parade ground, there were no horns, no dipping of standards, or any indication at all that they were about to resume their assault. By this point, Melchior had returned, still panting, and he stood with Kambyses, staring down at the even lines.

"What are they waiting for?" Kambyses muttered.

Melchior didn't answer, mainly because he didn't have any idea either. Shading his eyes, which were a bit sharper than his older general's, he stared beyond the rearmost line of Romans, where there were small knots of men. Because they had both been so intent on the leading ranks of the approaching enemy, it took a moment for Melchior to recognize that these small clusters of men were surrounding something larger than they were, and more importantly, they were moving. Slower than the Roman infantry had approached the wall, but with the main force motionless, it made it easier to see that these groups were, indeed, also moving.

"Look!" Melchior pointed past the rear line of Roman infantry. "I think they're moving their own artillery into place!"

Under normal circumstances this, at the very least, would have been a cause for great concern for the commander facing Roman artillery, but now Kambyses made no attempt to hide his smile. Temporarily forgetting their respective statuses, the older general slapped Melchior on the shoulder, his tanned, lined face showing real pleasure for the first time since he had taken command.

"This is exactly what we were hoping for," he crowed. Then, turning in the direction of where the crew of the final piece was waiting, he waved his arm, which was acknowledged by a return wave.

An instant later, the stones underneath their feet began to vibrate, followed an instant later by a sound that, while similar to the noise made by the lighter pieces, was much, much deeper. Kambyses turned to watch the men, roped into a harness much like those for beasts pulling a wagon, straining with all their might, while the man who oversaw these slaves cracked his whip with a skill that spoke of long practice. While the Parthian commander would have preferred to use animals, there had been no practical way to get them up on the parapet, and even if they had, it was not just impossible, it was almost certain that even if it wasn't, the animals wouldn't have reacted well to being so high off the ground. This was the next best thing, but it also meant the giant piece moved more slowly than he would have liked, so that it became something of a race between the respective artillery pieces to move into a position that was within their range. Unknown to the Romans, however, was not only the presence, but the existence of anything close to resembling their own ability to hurl large objects long distances. This they would learn the hard way, Kambyses thought with a savage satisfaction. The Roman artillery stopped in a very ragged unison, but Kambyses counted quickly: one, two, three, four, five, six. Six *ballistae* of sufficient size to reach the walls from their current range of four hundred paces and still retain sufficient velocity to inflict damage on not just any unlucky defender, but the wall itself. That Kambyses knew the range with such certainty was based in one of the preparations that he had made after his arrival. At first, he had considered simply painting rocks and arraying them at certain points where the distance was known, but quickly discarded that for the obvious reason that it removed the element of surprise. Instead, he had small pieces of highly polished brass embedded in the ground, making sure they were almost impossible to see from ground level; only from the vantage point of the wall could the defenders look down and see the tiny golden shine of each small disk, arranged at regular intervals. From four hundred paces down to fifty paces, all around both cities, the defenders could determine the exact range to their respective targets, and while the Romans would learn about this advantage soon enough, and in the mannerthat Kambyses had hoped, they remained ignorant of it at this point in time.

The grating sound stopped, and Kambyses turned to see that the final piece was in its designated spot, while the crew worked furiously to secure it, using heavy ropes to tie the piece down to a series of stakes that had been pounded into the stone surface of the rampart.

Anaxagoras was there as well, and it was he, dressed in armor of a sorts, consisting of an old-style breastplate once favored by the phalanxes of Greece, along with a pair of old greaves, who carried a tall wooden pole, marked with a series of painted stripes. As the final preparations were made, the Greek walked to the very corner crenellation of the northeast corner of the wall, and slid the pole through the iron loops that had been hammered into the stone. Since he was ignorant of such things, Kambyses had asked about this seemingly insignificant device, but Anaxagoras assured him it was essential.

"See that rod attached to the front of the piece?" He had pointed it out to Kambyses. "See how it's striped as well?" Kambyses indicated that he did, yet despite immediately understanding its purpose, Anaxagoras had still explained, "By aligning the stripes with the stripes on that guide pole, which in turn we've aligned with those embedded markers, it means that not only can we be precise with our shots, it won't take as long for us to find the exact range to hit whatever target you give the men." While this was certainly welcome news, Anaxagoras had also felt it necessary to warn, "Even so, much will depend on the time of day, and the weather." He shrugged. "Frankly, there are a number of different factors that come into play. Hitting the target the first time is very rare, even with all the precautions we're taking."

Rather than bridle at this display of what could be called pessimism, Kambyses had laughed and clapped the Greek on the shoulder, assuring him, "Remember, we're not hurling rocks, Anaxagoras. We just have to be close."

"You'll be close," Anaxagoras had assured him. "That much I *can* promise."

Now, Kambyses saw, it was time to find out. But just as he was turning to give the command to begin the preparations necessary to launch their surprise on the Romans, he was stopped by a new sound. Once more, a thin, wailing note cut through the air, except this time in the direction of the opposite end of the eastern wall, at the southeast corner.

"What now?" he muttered, but before moving down the wall to investigate, he strode over to a spot where he could lean out between the crenellations to peer down the length of the eastern wall.

The city wall was more than two miles long, which placed the Roman camp on that side another two miles distant from his position, which made for little more than a dark line made by a dirt wall that

268

was even lower than normal. At such a distance, it was impossible to make out any movement; at least, at first. As Kambyses continued to stare, his eye picked up the faintest ripple of motion, another dark line that was slightly separate from that he knew to be the camp. During the span of several heartbeats, he was able to see that the second line appeared to be inching away from the stationary camp, moving in the general direction of the far corner of Ctesiphon. Then, just as he was about to turn away, there was a tiny, winking flash, much the same in size and nature as those pieces of polished brass, except that this one was silver, its comparative strength and size to the markers made so by the distance.

"A Legion eagle," Kambyses mused to himself. Straightening up, he turned to Melchior and ordered, "Take your horse, go down there, and find out what's happening. Report back to me as quickly as you can!"

Melchior repeated his knuckling, but he hesitated for a fraction, long enough to prompt Kambyses to indicate he had noticed.

"Well?" he asked abruptly.

"If this is a feint, and that's the main attack, what do you want me to do?" Kambyses opened his mouth to snap that it was obvious, that Melchior was to alert him, but then Melchior added, "By the time I get there, see what's happening, then get back here and tell you," he took a breath, and finished, "then we have to move this artillery; they'll be under the walls and up the ladders."

To his credit, Kambyses instantly realized that his subordinate was right, but he suppressed the feeling of embarrassment at his own lapse, understanding that the time for self-pity and remorse was later.

Thinking rapidly, he turned and rapped an order. "Take the three small pieces and move them down the wall! But don't be seen!"

"That will only give you the large one," Melchior commented, but once more proving this wasn't just an idle observation of the obvious, he asked Kambyses, "Do you want me to summon the other smaller pieces to replace them? We could move the three we have on the Seleucian corner on this side to replace these three."

Kambyses grimaced, experiencing his first real taste of what it meant to be in supreme command of an effort like this; there were so many details!

"No." He shook his head. "I still think we need to keep those where they are. I think," he muttered this more to himself, although Melchior heard him, "they're going to be needed over there."

Before the sun had risen to its zenith, Parthian horns had sounded the alarm at all four corners of the dual cities under siege. Only the auxiliaries in the camp near the canal hadn't moved into an attack position, although they were formed up outside their camp. From all four directions, the Romans came, but ultimately, it was a demonstration, at least as far as Kambyses determined, because no real assault was made. No ladders touched the walls of either Seleucia or Ctesiphon, despite all four forces carrying them. By the end of the day, the only real material gains the Romans could claim was that they had emplaced their heaviest artillery within range of the walls, but despite the six pieces being within range of Kambyses' largest machine on the northeast corner, he never ordered it to send its load and expose not only its location, but its existence. It was a prudent decision, and one that would cause the Romans a fair amount of damage later because of this ignorance. However, across the river, on the western wall of Seleucia, while the Romans had arrayed themselves in the same manner, and their Legions idled their day away, there was other activity. Namely, the Roman artillery pieces assigned to that part of the siege began launching their missiles, although as Kambyses was quickly informed, their intent wasn't to wreak havoc with the defenders on the walls. Instead, apparently, their objective was the wall itself; when he learned this, Kambyses allowed a grim smile, reminding himself that he would have to thank his now-deceased King Orodes for having the foresight to strengthen the western wall. All in all, Kambyses had to admit that, despite the Parthians' relative indifference to the science of siege warfare, his former king had done a magnificent job of preparing Ctesiphon for this trial. It made sense, Kambyses thought to himself; this was Orodes' pride and joy, the showpiece of his house and of Parthia, and he would naturally do all within his power to defend it, despite the relative indifference the other noble houses of Parthia held towards it. Susa, on the other hand, as Kambyses well knew, was another matter altogether, which was why he had understood why Phraates had chosen to remove himself to the more ancient city. That, however, was all the thought he could afford to give to the new King of Kings. The first watch had been nerve-wracking, as the Parthians on the walls waited for their foe to make their next move, but then it had just become monotonous. At first, men only fidgeted, then, as they grew increasingly bored, began talking; finally, Kambyses allowed most of them to sit down on the parapet while sending men to draw water from the nearest wells.

Meanwhile, Kambyses paced, taking reports from the couriers sent by his officers commanding the other detachments, and despite his feelings towards the Romans, he again was forced to admire how they stood, in the hot sun, just....waiting. But waiting for what? This was why Kambyses found it necessary to pace, to release the tension that, while it had started to subside among his men, continued to mount in their commander. The only change in the Roman lines occurred when a train of mules came plodding out, led by what Kambyses correctly assumed were slaves, bringing skins of water, whereupon they moved through the ranks, behaving with the same kind of order and precision that he had witnessed with the Romans who would be doing the fighting. *Even their slaves behave in a more organized fashion than we do,* he thought dismally, but this wasn't more than just a minor observation, his mind still remaining focused on the larger intentions of his adversary. *What do they possibly have to gain by just standing there? Other than getting hot, and tired, beaten down by the sun?* Finally, he could take it no longer, descending the stairs and mounting his horse, intent on making an inspection of the other positions. The problem was, once he had done so, he was no more enlightened than he had been beforehand; if anything, it puzzled him even more deeply, because the Romans from the other camps, with minor variations, were behaving the same way. Only on the northwestern part of the wall of Seleucia was it different, but while Kambyses spent time there, mostly discussing with Melchior the meaning of what seemed to be a wasted day, he missed something. More accurately, while he noticed that Melchior had correctly reported this was the only place where Romans were more active by launching what appeared to be stones, albeit rounded and smoothed, he didn't think to count the number of pieces involved. Once he had given a cursory glance to the Roman positions, he had moved away from the crenellations, encouraged to do so by flying shards of rock from the smashed stone that slammed into the wall just a couple feet below the top of the wall.

"They're remarkably accurate," Melchior had told him, but Kambyses was initially dismissive.

"I just saw them waste a stone that went too high up," he scoffed, "so they're not *that* good."

Melchior shook his head, assuring Kambyses, "They're doing that on purpose." Seeing Kambyses' reaction, he explained, "It's to keep our men from spending too much time watching what they're doing." This was when he pointed down to a small shed, tucked against the northern wall and fifty paces from the corner. When he did, Kambyses naturally glanced that direction; then he understood, because he couldn't miss the bloody smear around the door. "I've lost three men so far, and a half-dozen are wounded," Melchior said quietly. "I put the dead men out of sight in that shed." While Kambyses nodded, he still looked sufficiently doubtful that Melchior felt compelled to point out, "Lord Kambyses, look around you closely. Not one of those missiles has overshot the wall. But they're hitting just below the crenellation by accident?" He shook his head, "No, they're trying to keep our heads down. And," Melchior finished bitterly, "they're doing a good job of it."

Kambyses ultimately did accept Melchior's explanation, but although he believed his subordinate, and it made him more anxious, he was unwilling to risk taking another look. Since this time, his first visit to that part of the wall, Kambyses found himself making the trip another half-dozen times as the day dragged on, but he never made another effort to look more closely. Unknown to Melchior, Kambyses, or the rest of the men on that section of the wall, none of them were given or took the opportunity to lean out and examine the outer part of the wall to assess the damage. In this, the Roman plan worked perfectly.

By the time the Romans turned about and marched back to their camps, the men of Caesar's army were exhausted. With the exception of a tiny segment of his force, the men had spent the day in place, their shields grounded, simply providing a presence that let the Parthians knew they were there. They were allowed to take off their helmets, but only after some men collapsed from the heat; however, this was an army with experience in such things. As their Centurions constantly reminded them, they had spent several days in a row in Hispania, when facing the Pompeian generals Afranius and Petreius; at Thapsus, they had done much the same. This was certainly true, but it wasn't lost on any man who had been there that the Parthian sun was hotter, the air drier, and while there was a constant breeze, it contained not a drop of moisture; if anything, it made the men hotter, not cooler. Nevertheless, they did their duty, just their presence causing Parthians to remain alert. It was the beginning of Caesar's strategic attempt to wear the defenders down, and while he was counting on the superior discipline and training of Rome's Legions, the bulk of his hopes rested on his certainty that, when all was said and done, his men were tougher than any man behind the walls. Over the course of the next three days, the Romans sallied forth in the same manner as the first, but only the first one saw the men from all the camps march forth. The next day, the Romans of the southwestern camp marched out, arraying themselves in the same manner, but this time, they marched a bit farther north, so that essentially, there was a sizable force consisting of three Legions and the ten thousand auxiliaries separated only by the canal. This prompted a stir of alarm inside the defenses as Kambyses hurried men to this point on the walls, while the artillery was once more manhandled into a position to defend against a possible attack. Meanwhile, the only constant in the Romans' actions was the almost rhythmic sound of stones cracking against the wall of the northwest corner. It had been on the second day when Kambyses, ordering a man to have a rope tied around his waist, then lowered over the side of the wall to examine the damage that the Parthian commander recognized the high probability this was going to be where the Romans focused their assault. Not the gates, as he had hoped, and for which he had prepared to defend, but the wall itself, although his initial pleasure that the Romans had chosen this section of the wall since it had been strengthened didn't survive sunset of that second day. It had been Anaxagoras, who had been present when Kambyses and Melchior had discussed— gloated would have been a more accurate description— about the extra layer of wall, who had warned them.

"You don't think that extra thickness of stones is going to make a difference, do you?" he asked Kambyses, his incredulity enough to make him forget to at least sound deferential.

Fortunately, for both men, the Greek had proven himself valuable enough to be forgiven a lapse that normally would have seen him whipped, but Kambyses' tone was stiff as he replied, "I did," he admitted, "at least until just this moment. What are we missing, Greek?"

Instead of answering outright, Anaxagoras beckoned to the pair, and they climbed the stairs to the top of the wall. By this time, they had disciplined themselves to remain far enough away from the outside of the wall to give the Romans any kind of target, and they looked down where Anaxagoras pointed.

"See that gap?" he asked them, rhetorically, because only a blind man could have missed it, and they both answered they did. Anaxagoras explained, "Whoever great King Orodes commissioned to do this work was either in a hurry or didn't know what he was doing, because this isn't anchored to the original wall."

Although he suspected he understood, Kambyses wanted to make sure and asked the Greek, "And what does that mean, exactly?"

"It means that once the Romans knock a hole through the original wall, it means that it won't take more than a couple volleys from their machines to knock this part of the wall down. And," he felt compelled to add, "nobody wants to be down there when it comes down, because it's likely to fall in one piece, more or less at least."

Kambyses and Melchior exchanged a glance, the junior officer's in a clearly questioning manner, while Kambyses rubbed his temples as he thought about what he had just learned.

Finally, he sighed and said, "So, if I understand you correctly, they're going to be punching a hole in this wall much faster than we believed."

"Yes, exactly," Anaxagoras replied immediately, then pointed out, "But I'm willing to bet they don't know that."

"So?" Melchior asked dismissively. "What does that matter?"

"It means," it was Kambyses who supplied the answer, "that when it happens, they may not be prepared to follow through."

Melchior understood immediately, but still wasn't entirely convinced. "So it means we *might* have enough time to set up a defensive position around the breach that would be extremely difficult for them to break through. But," he hesitated, then continued, "we might not. And," he argued, "it's just as likely that they're going to be standing there, ready to pour through this hole before we can stop them."

For a moment, the trio remained silent as Kambyses absorbed his subordinate's observation.

Then, he turned to Anaxagoras and sighed. "He's right. That's a risk I'm not willing to take." Addressing Melchior, he ordered, "Go ahead and start preparing for a breach here. Pull the artillery from the other positions so we can rain down on them and kill them like the dogs they are. And," he added, "go ahead and tear down those buildings," he pointed down to the stone structures that formed the first block nearest to where they were standing, "and use the rubble to form a breastwork."

This was when Anaxagoras interrupted with a conspicuous clearing of his throat, and Kambyses turned to the Greek.

"Your Excellency," he offered, "I think I might have a better idea."

For the next few moments, Kambyses and Melchior listened, looking to where Anaxagoras pointed down below to the street level. By the time he was through, Kambyses was smiling, but it was with a clear sense of anticipation and, Melchior decided, hope, which he shared with his commander once Anaxagoras was finished.

"Begin work immediately," Kambyses ordered, "and you'll have as much help as you need, and I'll give you as much authority as you need to get this done as quickly as possible. Now," he took a breath, "how long?"

The Greek considered for a moment, then answered, "If I start immediately, and have enough men to work through all the watches, I can have it done by this time tomorrow."

"Do it," Kambyses ordered, then turned to Melchior and said, "I'm appointing you as the commander of this effort. You have full authority, and if you run into any trouble, come find me immediately." Both Melchior and Anaxagoras stood straight as they gave their version of a salute, but before Melchior turned away, Kambyses added, "Melchior, you understand that the responsibility for this being done in time is on your shoulders. Do I need to remind you what that means?"

"No, General," Melchior tried to hide the bitterness at this blatant warning, "you don't need to remind me."

Without waiting for a reply, Melchior turned about and hurried down the stairs after Anaxagoras, who hadn't wasted any time. Kambyses watched the younger man's retreating back, smiling.

"There's something…odd happening at the northwest corner," Volusenus told Caesar that night at the evening briefing.

"Odd?" Caesar's eyebrow lifted, while the other officers stopped their own quiet conversations to listen. "How do you mean?"

Volusenus frowned, not replying immediately as he tried to frame his thoughts, finally admitting, "I wish I could be more specific than that, Caesar. But it's based in a couple observations. Murena alerted me to it," Volusenus named the ranking *immune* who had been given nominal command of the artillery emplaced at that spot, "and when he pointed it out, I noticed the same thing he did. So while I was there, I ordered him to cease loosing for a few moments," Caesar's mouth turned down in a sign every one of his officers had seen before and knew it indicated he was displeased, which prompted Volusenus to hurriedly add, "and that's when we heard something."

Caesar's expression changed instantly as he sat forward, his eyes narrowing as he said, "Go on."

"It started with Murena, who noticed that there wasn't any sign of movement, at all, on the wall…"

"But they'd stopped trying to peek at what we're doing a couple days ago," Pollio objected; that it was another of Caesar's lieutenants reminded Pullus of the fierce competition among the most senior leadership for the position of favorite with the Dictator.

"They did," Volusenus agreed, and none of the other men missed the coolness in his tone, "but they were still visible, moving about. Sometimes, you'd just see a man moving in between the crenellations, or we'd catch a glint off a helmet. But now, there's not even that."

Caesar considered, but he wasn't convinced this was as noteworthy as Volusenus seemed to think, yet he did trust his *Praefectus Fabrorum*, which moved him to prompt his subordinate, "Which leads us to this second thing you mentioned."

"Yes," Volusenus nodded his head, but then hesitated, grimacing as he went on, "but this is just my…speculation, based on what I heard."

"Which was?" Caesar was clearly growing impatient.

"While we had stopped our volleys and were watching, the wind picked up, but it was coming from the southeast."

The way Volusenus seemed to emphasize the direction told Pullus he thought this was meaningful, but it was Caesar who understood immediately.

"Which would carry noise from the city," he said, and Volusenus nodded.

"Exactly, and what I heard, and Murena can confirm, sounded like men busy at something." Volusenus tried to think of the proper description, settling on, "Like they were building something, but not anything small."

"What do you think it is that they're building over there?" Caesar asked Volusenus.

"Honestly, Caesar, I have no idea, other than it seems clear that they understand that it's likely we're serious about breaching the wall."

There was a heavy silence for several moments as all eyes turned to Caesar, who was turning this over in his mind. He had understood it was a bit much to hope that the Parthians would be fooled by the numerous demonstrations he had ordered, but he realized now that he had actually put more hope into this ruse than he had thought.

"Very well," he said at last, yet while outwardly he maintained his normal air that this wasn't anything unexpected, neither was he able to sound unconcerned as he gave an order that he had hoped to avoid giving. "We're now going to have to make a change in our plans and make a separate assault." Standing suddenly, he walked the short distance to the tabletop model, staring down at it, then, with his finger pointed, said, "We're going to have to make the assault at the farthest possible point from our real target, and we're going to have to convince the Parthians that we're serious about it, and it isn't the feint it actually is. Which means," now there was no mistaking his grave tone, "I'm going to shift most of the army to that side, and leave just three Legions at the northwest corner, and they're going to have to be enough to enter the breach and take Seleucia."

It was no coincidence that Pullus and Spurius were standing together, nor was it one that this was the first place Caesar looked. Pullus and his general's eyes met, but Pullus only answered with a grim nod, then Caesar looked to Spurius, who was on the short side of average height, meaning the top of his head came up to his giant friend's shoulder.

"My boys are ready, Caesar," he answered, and if anyone heard the hoarseness, they didn't comment.

"I know they are, Spurius," Caesar replied, but then turned his attention back to the larger gathering. "Now we have to decide when we do this."

"Murena thinks we're still two days away from penetrating the old section of the wall," Volusenus informed Caesar, "then it really depends on how thick whatever was added is."

"So we still have a bit of time," Caesar mused, except that Caesar was mistaken about that.

Moving a large body of men at night, even when the ground is level and relatively even, is a challenge; shifting them from three different camps, and doing it undetected by anyone watching from the walls, meant this was a testament to Caesar's organizational skills. More than this, however, it was the efforts of the Centurions and men themselves that allowed a massive maneuver such as the one performed that night to go as smoothly as any such similar movement they had done before. Aided by only a sliver of a moon, the Legions of the northeastern camp, the 6th and 22nd, marched shortly before midnight, heading south across the flat, four-mile expanse of distance in a bit more than two parts of a watch. This was much slower than normal, but Caesar had emphasized stealth over speed, and to that end, the men had taken care to cover all objects, like helmets, that might catch a glint of moonlight. Even with the distance from the walls, Caesar had deemed it necessary to take further precautions by having the men wrap their *caligae* in rags; even the keenest ears wouldn't be able to pick up the sound of hobnails striking rocks when it was a lone man, but multiplying that by just a bit less than the forty thousand *caligae* that would be moving into position on this night meant that Caesar wasn't taking any chances. Moving as silently as was possible for such a large body of armed and armored men, the contingent from the northeastern camp had the farthest to march by perhaps a mile, while the 5th, 8th, and 28th in the southwestern camp, departed later. Each Legion left a full Cohort behind, and when they marched, they were carrying only their shields and complement of javelins, while two sections per Century of the First and Second Cohort carried the ladders that would be used to scale the walls. Even if the Centurions hadn't issued strict orders for silence on this movement, the men weren't inclined for the normal banter they usually participated in when they were on the march. The reason for this self-imposed silence was simple; being the veterans they were, the men were more apprehensive than normal about this assault because they were restricted to using just ladders. While they all knew the reason Caesar hadn't ordered siege towers to be constructed—there just weren't enough raw materials to build one, let alone the three or more that would be required to take a city of the size of either Ctesiphon or Seleucia, at least not without completely dismantling most of the wagons —it didn't ease their anxiety about what was coming.

Scaling a ladder under the best of circumstances wasn't a method any man relished, but it was even worse for this assault because one single ladder simply wasn't tall enough to scale the wall. Therefore, Volusenus' engineers had been forced to lash two ladders together, but when he did this, they were too long; his estimate was that they would extend another five feet above the wall, which was just as bad as the ladder not being tall enough, and even worse in the sense that it gave the defenders the ability to push the ladders away more easily. Sawing the unneeded portion off the stout sapling poles, which had been carefully selected and trimmed before this campaign started, meant that there were less ladders per Legion than Caesar would have liked. And, while nobody spoke openly about it, there was the knowledge that while Ctesiphon and Seleucia were the first cities to be assaulted, they wouldn't be the last on this campaign. This was just one more thing that added to the tension of the men of the Legions; nevertheless, they stolidly marched along, prepared to do their collective duty. Leaving the southeastern camp, the new Primus Pilus of the 11th, Tiberius Atartinus, tried to keep his attention equally shared between watching his footing, his men, and the wall, waiting for some sign that a sentry had detected their movement, although only the gods knew how that could happen. The camp was less than two miles from the walls, which he could barely make out, and only then because the surrounding countryside was so flat that the walls loomed slightly higher than the black ground. No torches were on the ramparts, which Atartinus knew wasn't unusual; it might help calm a jittery sentry's nerves, but it made it almost impossible for him to see past the small ring of light a torch provided. Still, it wasn't until he heard the hissed warning from the pioneers attached to Volusenus who had been sent out of the southeastern camp to guide the incoming Legions to their proper spot that Atartinus felt relaxed enough to breathe normally. The 11th was in the lead, which made their bedding down on the hard ground the easiest, and they got arranged in a semblance of a formation outside the walls of the southeastern camp, where men tried to make themselves as comfortable as possible. It was this process of getting the men settled that actually proved the most troublesome, as whispered quarrels about one thing or another between comrades threatened to escalate into something much noisier, but the iron discipline of the Legions, as administered by Centurions who promised recalcitrant men a dispensation of future justice, of the nature meted out in the baths, in their own harsh whispers, prevailed upon those quarreling to settle their differences quickly and silently. The other two Legions,were also led to their spots, and just as they began their own process of settling down, the three Legions from the southwest camp arrived, having a shorter distance to march. That left only the Legions of the far northwest camp, but two of them had their own task, while the third, the 12th, was going to stay hidden in their camp, acting as a reserve. By the time this portion of the army had arrived from the southwestern camp, the eastern sky was just beginning to change color, first from a solid black, except for those stars low on the horizon, then a sullen gray, and finally, the first pinkish-orange color that marked the beginning of a new day.

Caesar arrived just before the dawn fully bloomed, and the Centurions of the eight Legions gathered outside the southeastern camp couldn't stop the sudden buzzing of men, who were heartened to see that their general had arrived. Atartinus, and some of the other Primi Pili, were puzzled by his presence, but they were the relatively few who knew, despite appearances to the contrary, that this wasn't the Romans' main effort. He had expected Caesar would want to be at the northwest camp, closer to where the crucial action was going to take place. Yet, while he didn't even consider asking, he nevertheless heard the reason for Caesar's presence, by way of overhearing Caesar speaking to Hirtius, who had originally been the man of Legate rank in overall command.

"If we want to convince the Parthians this is the main assault, then they need to see Caesar leading it," the general had explained to Hirtius.

Who, Atartinus could tell even in the semi-darkness, wasn't particularly happy about this new development. It was a reminder to the newly minted Primus Pilus about the ambition and hunger for glory all men of the Roman upper classes possessed, no matter who they served. This was all the attention he could pay to Caesar and why he was there, because the general gave the command, speaking loudly but not shouting, for the Legion to rise and make themselves ready. Before the men had finished climbing to their feet, Caesar and Hirtius had gone trotting down the line of Legions to relay the order to each Legion individually. It was because of this that Atartinus, standing in front of his leading rank and looking down the long line of Legions, saw them obey their general's command, one Legion at a time, looking to Atartinus like some huge beast that roused itself very, very slowly. The rippling motion caused by men standing up, Century by Century, Cohort by Cohort, and Legion by Legion, took a fair amount of time, and in the growing light, Atartinus, whose Legion was now anchoring the right, putting them the farthest along the eastern wall, grew more apprehensive with each passing moment. While the army was in essentially the right position and orientation to make the assault, Atartinus stared at the city wall, waiting for it to become light enough for him to spot the landmark that Caesar had given him, a stronghold in the form of a protuberance out from the wall. It was a standard feature of cities where the occupants were intent on defending what was inside. Since it was jutting out from the wall from above, Atartinus knew it would look like a square, large enough for at least one artillery piece, or about twenty men to line the three sides of the square. Working in their favor was that this strong point wasn't a fully enclosed tower, although the crenellations would provide the defenders some cover. This was why each Legion's complement of scorpions had been brought, broken down, with the pieces carried by the Legionaries designated as artillerymen who had exchanged their javelins for their part of this weapon, while other men carried bags containing the scorpion bolts. If all went to plan, once the Legions closed within range, the advance would halt just long enough to allow the artillery to be assembled, emplaced, and secured, whereupon the scorpions would begin the job of scouring the strong point clean of defenders or, failing that, kept up such an intense volley of streaking, deadly bolts, no Parthian would be willing to risk exposure for the length of time it would take to loose their own missiles at the men scaling the ladders. This, at least, was the plan; Atartinus might have been a new Primus Pilus, but he was a veteran Centurion, and like most veterans, he understood how rarely anything of this nature went according to the original concept. Finally, when the first solid rays of sunlight suddenly illuminated the walls as the upper rim of the sun poked over the horizon to his back, Atartinus saw the bulge of the strong point, and realized that he needed to reposition his Legion. This wasn't unexpected, and Caesar had accounted for the time it would take to shift his dispositions, but the general had pressed the need to do so without hesitation.

"The timing of all this is crucial," Caesar had explained, "because you need to be in place as quickly as possible, and give the Parthians the time they need to see our dispositions."

For this was Caesar's plan, and Atartinus wasn't alone in his struggle to comprehend this radical change from Caesar's normal behavior, where none of his men moved as quickly as he liked, and attacks always took longer than he wanted. While he had impressed upon his Centurions the importance of moving into the spot from where they would begin their respective advance on the walls, after that the actual assault would be conducted at what Atartinus and his counterparts would consider an almost leisurely pace. This was the first, and would be one of the only times where Caesar's normal speed of movement wasn't on display. Instead, he wanted to make the advance, then the assault, seem as ponderous as he could, giving their enemy not only the impression that the Romans were putting everything into this assault, but most crucially, give the Parthians the time to react. Caesar needed the Parthian commander to shift every available defender to this southeastern corner of the cities, as far away from the real assault as it was possible to get, thereby enabling a minimal force of two Legions to pour through one small breach. It was there on the northwest corner of Seleucia where speed was essential, but not until that wall came down. Volusenus had calculated that the original wall would come down well within a watch after the bombardment resumed, and that the addition would take perhaps a full watch after that. If all went as hoped, by the time the sun was at its zenith, Pullus would be leading the 10th from where they were hiding in the camp, and moving at the double-quick pace to the breach, followed by Spurius and the 3rd. Balbinus and his 12th would also be able to leave their tents, although they were to form up and move to a spot halfway between the camp and the breach, near enough where a *cornu* call from either Pullus or Spurius could be heard. Every officer in Caesar's army knew this plan wasn't Caesar's favorite; there were too many factors outside of his control to make him comfortable, the timing of both his movement and, more importantly, the Parthian reaction to the feint being crucial to success. And, as his Gallic veterans knew, these elaborate maneuvers consisting of separate elements separated by long distances that relied on timing their movements with each other reminded them, and they were sure their general, of Gergovia, one of the few defeats ever suffered by any army commanded by Caesar. Since that debacle, although no veteran would ever openly characterize it as such, their general had preferred to keep his tactical plans simpler, relying on speed of movement, and choosing the right moment, at the right point, with just the amount of force needed to accomplish his goals. Not this time; Caesar was acutely aware that every day spent here was a day wasted in pursuit of the real prize. That his goal—his true objective and not the one he had uttered aloud to his officers—was to subdue Parthia in one season, not the two he had stated when the initial plan was unveiled, Caesar hadn't shared, with anyone.

Originally, he had assured his officers, even those he trusted the most, he was taking a more prudent approach than the late Crassus had, as evidenced by his taking the long route down to where they were currently located. But he had always dreamed of subduing the Parthian capital, not this one, but what he understood was the *real* seat of Parthian power, as viewed by all but the ruling house of Arsacid, in one season. Susa, not Ctesiphon, had been his real objective, and every day spent outside these walls was wasted. Most important was Caesar's recognition that his army couldn't survive a Parthian winter under leather; they simply had to have the shelter of a city, but only Caesar was aware that he didn't plan on it being Ctesiphon and Seleucia. In order to fulfill his ambitions, however, Caesar's Legions had to take this city, today, and it did start out well. Atartinus' 11th had already begun shifting to the north, parallel to the eastern wall, whereupon the First Cohort, positioned on the far right, placed themselves so the strong point was directly to their front, about four furlongs from the southeast corner of the city. Next to them was the 15th, with the 7th, anchoring the Legions that would attack the eastern wall. Meanwhile, the other five Legions were shuffling into their positions, where the 8th was the last Legion arrayed along the southern wall, but well more than a half mile along it, about two furlongs away from the heavily fortified southern gate that was positioned in the traditional spot, roughly equidistant from each corner. When he gave his orders for the final disposition of this portion of his plan, Caesar had felt confident that whatever artillery the Parthians might have possessed wasn't of sufficient potency to pose a huge danger to the left flank of the 8th as they made their ascent. Although Caesar's belief in the paucity of Parthian artillery was understandable, it was still an error, perhaps not of judgment, but of information. While he was generally aware that the population of Seleucia contained a substantial number of Greeks, he frankly hadn't given much thought to how these Greeks would view the presence of a Roman army outside the walls of their homes. More specifically, he was ignorant that men like Anaxagoras, whose skill and experience in the manufacture and usage of the same kind of artillery on which Caesar relied so much would be available to the Parthian commanding the defense. The time to ponder all this, and the repercussions that came from it, was coming; now, the assault was ready to begin.

Kambyses was already awake and was actually on his way to the northwest corner to check on the progress Melchior was making in preparation for the inevitable collapse of the wall. Which, as he learned shortly after he arrived to find Melchior standing on the street next to the northern wall, would be happening in not much time after Kambyses' arrival. As the pair of Parthians stood watching as Anaxagoras and his small army of laborers hustled about, moving quickly but with a sense of purpose that was clear to Kambyses, there suddenly came a thunderous crashing sound that echoed between the stone wall and the buildings. Despite being well more than two hundred paces away, the sound made Kambyses and Melchior jump, although it was the junior Parthian who recovered first as they both watched the small cloud of dust come roiling up above the western wall.

"They've started back up," Melchior muttered, but even as he was finishing, another explosive crack sounded, and he had to yell as he finished, "and it's going to be like this until the wall comes down."

Kambyses nodded that he understood, then pointed at the top of the wall, where there were still perhaps a dozen men standing along the rampart. Looking, Kambyses thought with grim humor, very unhappy.

"When are you going to have those men get off the wall?"

Melchior, who had been facing Kambyses, more to aid him in hearing now that the resumption of the bombardment joined with the noise already made by Anaxagoras and his men as they finished their task, suddenly looked away.

"Actually, I wasn't planning on moving them," the younger Parthian said, loud enough for only Kambyses to hear.

Kambyses had just turned back to watch the wall, now almost completely enveloped in roiling dust and small pieces of stone, but this made him look sharply back at Melchior. His eyes narrowed as his mind grappled with what his subordinate had told him, and the thought flashed through his mind that perhaps he had underestimated Melchior, who was clearly willing to sacrifice men under his command without hesitation. That this gave Kambyses pause wasn't based in any regard or compassion for the men up there; they were Parthian infantry, meaning they came from a class far beneath either commander or lieutenant. Still, Kambyses felt certain about one thing; before this was through, he would need every spear, arrow, and body available to him to keep those Romans from taking either city.

"Have them come down now," Kambyses ordered, his tone making Melchior flush with what he considered the implied rebuke. Seeing Melchior's reaction, before the younger man turned to give the command to one of his own subordinates, who were standing nearby, trying to appear as if they weren't attempting to listen, Kambyses put a hand on the man's shoulder. "Normally," he explained, "I'd say leave them there. I'm not faulting your decision. But," his jaw clenched as if the words were too bitter to utter, "we're going to need every single man we have. We can't afford to waste anyone."

Melchior didn't reply, instead studying Kambyses' face before giving a curt nod of understanding. Turning, he shouted the command to one of his subordinates, a youth even younger than Melchior, but dressed in armor of a quality that told Kambyses this was another son of a *satrap*, perhaps a second or third son, but a noble nonetheless. The youth obeyed instantly, but he was forced to take a circuitous route to get to the men on the rampart; Anaxagoras' project made movement in this part of the city more difficult. This reality was a small consideration when measured against the value that Kambyses hoped this idea provided. By this point, the dust had begun settling down on the Parthian side of the wall, while the noise continued with a regularity that told Kambyses of the level of skill his enemies possessed at this aspect of warfare, as each crew moved with such a smooth precision that it reminded Kambyses of the heartbeat of some sort of giant, pulsing with a rhythm that was even and regular, which made it even more menacing. Kambyses had decided his place was here, which meant that the messenger who came galloping to the palace wasted valuable time searching for him, but as the pair of Parthians continued standing with their eyes fixed to the wall, no longer bothering to try speaking because of the noise, this allowed the courier to gallop up to them and get much closer than normal before either of them heard the pounding hooves. Once they did, they both whirled about just in time to see the rider vault from the saddle, then come running up to address Kambyses, where he dropped to his knees.

"Your Excellency," he gasped, making it difficult for Kambyses to hear him over the other noise, "Excellency Sosimenes sent me to report that the Romans are assembled at the southeast corner!"

Despite the urgency in the messenger's voice and the dire sound of his message, Kambyses actually smiled, because to him, this confirmed that the assault here on the western wall was about to start.

Consequently, he made a curt gesture for the man to rise as he said, "Inform Sosimenes that I thank him for informing me, but this is just another feint, and I expected it."

Rather than acknowledge the message, then turn and go back to his mount, the messenger, now clearly uncomfortable, still adamantly shook his head.

"Excellency," he said urgently, "Sosimenes told me that he's sure it's not a feint, that it's the assault!"

"And how does he know that?" Kambyses asked the messenger, more out of curiosity than any real belief Sosimenes was correct in his assessment.

His opinion changed with the next words out of the messenger's mouth.

"Because he said he sees that Caesar's with them. And," the messenger added, "he counts eight Legions!"

It was to Kambyses' credit that he didn't hesitate, but in acting as he did, he was essentially doing as Caesar wanted, which was his mistake. Fortunately, for Kambyses' cause at least, he wasn't alone in making errors.

"I'm going to leave you with a thousand archers, a thousand spearmen, and," he hesitated, knowing that Melchior wasn't going to be happy, "just the large piece. I'm taking the rest of the men and artillery with me." Before Melchior could object, he did think to add, "And I give you permission now to use the big machine at your discretion. I know we wanted to wait, but since I'm leaving you with less men, go ahead and use it."

Kambyses didn't wait for Melchior's response, hurrying to his horse, where those nobles who were part of his personal retinue and served as his staff were waiting. Ordering them to oversee the shifting of the defenses, he vaulted into his own saddle, turned his horse, and went galloping out of Seleucia, across the bridge and into Ctesiphon, intent on not just being present for the coming assault, but because he wanted to see this Caesar again. This time, he thought grimly, you'll be the one carrying a flag of truce and begging me for a favor.

"It's too fucking hot to be stuck in here," Balbus grumbled, seated at the small table in his Primus Pilus' tent along with Scribonius, waiting with Pullus for the sound of the *bucinator* stationed on the wall to signal the time to move.

While it was still early in the morning, despite the relative spaciousness of a Primus Pilus' tent, the air was stifling; that they were all wearing their armor didn't help. Even so, it was what these three veterans understood was coming that meant their body temperatures were elevated, along with their heart rates, even as their faces reflected none of the inner turmoil they were feeling. Pullus, with the most to worry about, was actually the calmest of the three, as Balbus started drumming his fingers on the table, which was a habit that Scribonius loathed.

Under normal conditions, the Secundus Pilus Prior tolerated it; this wasn't the case this day, prompting him to snap, "Would you stop doing that?"

"Doing what?" Balbus asked innocently, knowing full well this habit of his bothered Scribonius, which was why he kept on drumming the table.

Even with the tension of the moment, Pullus had to grin; oddly enough, this bickering between his two best friends was not only familiar, he understood it was their rough way of showing affection for each other.

"You know perfectly well what," Scribonius countered.

"Oh?" Because one side of his face was frozen from the severed nerves, Balbus could only raise one eyebrow, and he did so now. "You mean this?"

Whereupon he increased both the tempo and the force, making the sound of his fingertips striking the table even louder.

"Yes, that." Scribonius struggled to maintain his composure but was clearly having trouble.

"I really wish you two would get married," Pullus sighed, staring out of the open flap of the tent.

Across the northwestern camp, almost every tent was occupied, which was not normal for this time of day; what was even more unusual was that every occupant was similarly attired as their chief Centurions. Three Legions were hidden away but waiting to begin what would be as rapid a movement as could be achieved. In typical Caesarian fashion, nothing had been left to chance; the 10th would be exiting by the Porta Praetoria, the front gate that faced the city, because they were to be first into the planned breach. While the 3rd would exit the Porta Principalis Dextra, the side gate on the right side of the camp, only after the first two Legions were out of the camp, assembled and moving at the double quick to cover the distance to the city and assault the breach as soon after it was created as possible, would the 12th exit the camp and stand in reserve. This was the original plan, but just before Caesar departed, Pullus and Spurius went to Caesar, making a proposal that was a variation of this.

"There's going to be a period of time when the Parthians are either going to know the wall's about to come down and they'll move their men off the walls, or the dust is going to be thick enough that, even if they stay up there, they won't be able to see," Pullus told Caesar. "So we'd like permission to move early, once that happens."

There were a fair number of Romans of the patrician class who wouldn't have even considered a suggestion that came from a man from the lower class; luckily, Caesar wasn't one of them. After listening, he quickly agreed with this suggestion, but while he thought it was a good idea, he also was in a hurry to reach the far camp where the rest of the Legions were assembled.

It was after Caesar had mounted Toes, that Pullus, as was his habit, blurted out something that had been bothering him, asking Caesar, "I know your part of this is a feint. But what if you do get over the wall?"

Even in the darkness Pullus could see Caesar's teeth flash in a grin as he told Pullus cheerfully, "Well, then it'll be a race to see who can take their city first!"

And with that, he trotted away, leaving Pullus staring at his back, thinking ruefully, Of course, I should have known. It was in this moment Pullus realized that Caesar's effort was no feint. Contrary to what he had told his officers, he was set on taking both cities today.

The *bucina* call came shortly after Pullus had finally had enough of Balbus and Scribonius picking at each other and snapped at them to be quiet.

"Let's go," he said before the last note had even died down, snatching his helmet from the table as he strode out of the tent. All around him, men came boiling out of their own tents as Centurions began bellowing to their Cohorts and Centuries as they strode, along with their *aquilifers,* to their preassigned spots in the forum of the camp. To an uninformed observer, it would appear to be a chaos of scrambling men, shouting Centurions, and blaring horns, but was instead a highly organized and choreographed movement that would ensure that the Legion would be assembled and moving out of the camp as quickly as it was possible to do so. Pullus, letting his Optio Lutatius handle the First Century, was acting in his role as Primus Pilus, striding across the forum of the camp to bellow at the laggards about the striping that was in their future, where he found Spurius on the opposite side, doing much the same thing.

Seeing Pullus approach, Spurius called to him, "Pullus! Come here! I want to ask you something!" Curious, Pullus trotted over, and Spurius wasted no time. "I want my boys to go in first."

"What?" Pullus laughed, not thinking his counterpart was serious; then he took notice of Spurius' expression. Still, he shook his head, saying, "Caesar ordered us to go in first; you know that."

"I do, but if you say it's all right, I know he won't mind." Spurius grinned and added, "We all know you're his favorite!"

Pullus felt the flush rise from his neck, made worse by his knowledge that this was true, but he still wasn't willing to risk Caesar's wrath.

More to stall for time, he challenged Spurius, "And why should we switch anyway?"

"Because you lucky bastards were on top of that ridge, and you and your boys killed all those rich men," Spurius pointed out, "while my boys had to pick through those poor fuckers carrying spears!" This Pullus couldn't argue, yet he was still clearly reluctant, which prompted Spurius to add, "What if we give your boys a cut of whatever we take in the town?"

"How much?" Pullus asked, suspicious.

Spurius considered, then offered, "A tenth part."

"Bah," Pullus scoffed, "that's not nearly enough."

"All right," Spurius had known this would be spurned, countering with, "twenty percent."

"Twenty-five," Pullus pounced immediately.

This was the number Spurius had thought would be acceptable all along, and he thrust out his hand. "Deal."

Clasping his compatriot's arm, Pullus grinned and said, "Mars and Fortuna bless you and your boys. And let's pray there are a lot of rich people inside those walls."

Laughing, the two parted, with Pullus heading to his Legion, which by this time was in formation and ready to march, yet instead of using his *cornicen* to summon the Pili Priores, Pullus used the power of his lungs, which were almost as legendary as his physical prowess, bellowing the order for them to come to him. As soon as they arrived from their respective spots, he wasted no time.

"We're switching places with the 3rd," Pullus announced, and the consternation was as strong as he had suspected, so he allowed his Centurions to continue for a moment, then held up his hand, trying to suppress a grin as he explained, "We're going to get twenty-five percent of the 3rd's haul of loot."

As he knew they would, those same men who had been vociferous in their complaining and quibbling about their Primus Pilus' decision instantly began singing his praises. All of them were aware of the size of Seleucia, and that this was the older of the two cities. Adding this to their bedrock belief in the wealth of the East, about which they had heard so much, meant that every one of them began mentally spending the extra money that would come from

Pullus' deal. It was only later, after all that was about to transpire had happened, they would have cause to be even more thankful.

The wall finally came crashing down, but once the dust settled enough for there to be some visibility, both Pullus and Spurius experienced surprise, bordering on shock, when the very next volley of stones from the artillery knocked the unsecured addition to the wall down, toppling backward in more or less one huge piece as they stood watching. Confronted with a gaping hole much earlier than they had expected, their decision to leave the camp earlier than originally planned seemed to pay dividends, as they wasted no time. Separated by a distance of about a quarter mile, after the 10th marched out of the right gate, Pullus and Spurius were too far away for effective verbal communication, but with a wave, Spurius let Pullus know he had seen the same sight, and interpreted it the same way. This was evidenced by the 3rd Legion immediately beginning their approach, stepping out as if they were on a march, at least at first. Before they had gone a hundred paces, their pace increased to the kind of shuffling run that the Romans used to move more rapidly into position than normal. Because of their objective, the 3rd was arranged in a column of Cohorts; once Spurius got near enough, he would halt his men to adjust the width of his Cohort so that his men would fill the breach abreast, counting on his Pili Priores to follow suit. Waiting just long enough for the Tenth Cohort of the 3rd to move past, Pullus gave his own order, following behind the 3rd. If all went as planned, each Cohort of the 3rd would enter the breach a Century at a time, with the leading Cohort, naturally the First, leading the way and, hopefully, pushing defenders back from the breach, thereby allowing the following Cohorts room. It was a tactic that Caesar's Legions had learned and perfected in Gaul, but it had been a fair amount of time since the last such assault had taken place. The need for the attacking Legion to move quickly was paramount, counting on the shock and confusion that inevitably followed the collapse of the enemy defenses, because even when the defender knew it was inevitable, it was impossible for them to know exactly when it would occur. This was true for the attackers as well, but to a lesser extent; this time was the exception, as it happened more rapidly than any Roman was expecting. Now Spurius was leading his men at a trot, their hobnailed soles raising dust and quickly obscuring their lower bodies as they pounded towards the yawning gap that, even at the slower pace of Pullus and the 10th, grew ever wider in their view. Then, after Spurius and the First Cohort passed what to Pullus seemed to be some imaginary line, given how uniform the response was, suddenly the air filled with streaking arrows, fired from the ramparts, who were arrayed along the western wall, with the exception of where the breach was located.

"Pluto's cock." Pullus wasn't aware that he had uttered this aloud as he watched the first of what would quickly become an endless stream of missiles converging down, down, down into the First Cohort of the 3rd.

The black swarm of arrows seemed to form a shape that reminded Pullus of the Greek letter called Delta, except the point of the triangle was concentrated on the leading ranks of Spurius and his men, who were only now beginning to react to this threat to their cohesion and their lives. From ahead of Pullus came an added layer of the noise already made by the thousands of tramping feet, consisting of shrill screams, cries of pain and anger, and the sound of the Centurions who, before their *corniceni* could sound the command, began bellowing orders.

This prompted Pullus to thrust his own fist in the air, then as his men came crashing to a stop, shouting to his own Century, "Form *testudo!*"

Then he turned and ordered his *cornicen* Valerius to add his own notes to those that had just started sounding from the 3rd just ahead. With the practiced rapidity that spoke of the watches of training, the column of Centuries quickly transformed into a seemingly impenetrable wall of shields. Meanwhile, Spurius' Legion, momentarily stopped by the volley, now resumed their movement forward, but now gone was the ability for a rapid approach; it was impossible to move quickly for even the best-trained men when they were in this formation. Now, Pullus could well imagine how the two Legions looked from the vantage point of the wall, as if a huge, segmented beast moved slowly but steadily for the defenders, despite the rain of arrows that continued unabated. As the 3rd continued its advance, the nature of the noise changed to one that the men had heard before, albeit not as loudly, as the metal points of the arrows slammed into the overhead wall of shields. At the head of his own Legion, Pullus was still fifty paces away from the outer range of the archers on the wall, which was clearly marked by a veritable thicket of shafts sticking up out of the ground on either side of the Roman column. The sight of them carpeting the ground was daunting on its own; the bodies of those men of the 3rd who had been struck in the first few heartbeats of the volley made it even more so. More importantly, their bodies created something of a hazard, particularly as a good number of them were still moving, some writhing in agony as they clawed at the shaft that had pierced their body, while more were either limping or trying to drag themselves back to safety. With his men in *testudo*, Pullus realized it fell to him to guide them past the wounded, without tripping over them, or allowing them to compromise the solid wall of shields in some way. His only saving grace was that the archers, who seemed to have an inexhaustible supply of missiles, were at this moment concentrating their efforts on the 3rd, and when he glanced ahead, he was struck by the ludicrous thought of how Spurius' Legion had taken on the look of a huge porcupine, the arrows that had penetrated shields acting as the quills now bristling outward from every conceivable angle.

"All right, boys," Pullus bellowed, both for the sake of the stricken men immediately ahead and for his own, "we're coming through now! So I need you to stay right where you are, and when we pass, I'll have our *medici* come help you!"

Pullus' shouted promise wasn't based solely in his concern for the welfare of these unfortunates; he had long since observed that once a man was wounded, his only thought was to reach help, no matter what or who was in their way. If he could appease them with this promise so they didn't go staggering through his own formations, then this was what he would do, and he was pleased to see that, for the most part, it worked. One Legionary, however, was out of his mind with fear, an arrow protruding out of both sides of his neck. While gruesome, Pullus had seen wounds like this before, but unfortunately for this man, the Primus Pilus saw how the ranker was clasping his hand around the arrow where it exited the right side of his neck, the shaft between fingers that were completely red, while the spurting nature of the flow of blood told Pullus this wound was mortal. The wounded Legionary was clearly aware that, if he wasn't dying, he was very seriously wounded, and he came staggering towards Pullus, completely unheeding to the Primus Pilus' increasingly urgent commands for him to step aside. Instead, he held out his one free hand, plainly beseeching Pullus, staggering directly towards him, his eyes wide with panic.

"Primus Pilus," at least this was what Pullus thought he said, because as he spoke, a gout of blood came out of his mouth to run down his chin, making him gurgle the words more than speak them.

"There's nothing I can do for you right now, Gregarius," Pullus was now just a half-dozen steps away, and he shouted, "so you need to step aside!"

The man didn't obey, and as Pullus drew even, he actually reached out and grasped Pullus' right arm with a strength that clearly required his last bit of energy.

"Please," the Legionary's eyes were fixed on Pullus' face, who in turn forced his expression to remain a hard, cold mask, and he didn't hesitate to not only wrench his arm free, but then shoved the Legionary with his considerable power, sending the man staggering several paces to the side, where he collapsed.

"I'm sorry," Pullus muttered, only loud enough for himself to hear, yet he was thankful that he had managed to propel the man far enough out of the way that his own formation wasn't threatened.

He never gave the dying man a second glance; there were far too many other matters that required his attention, and when he did turn to glance back at his men, he did so in the opposite direction from where the Legionary had fallen.

"Dento, I can see your face, damn you! And if I can, those bastards on the wall can," Pullus snapped at one of his men in the first rank, square in the middle, who had allowed his shield to drop too much.

Otherwise, the *testudo* was holding well, so Pullus returned his attention to the front, trying to judge the moment when the defenders would no longer be able to loose their arrows on the 3rd because of the angle. That would be when it was the 10th's turn for this treatment, but Pullus, while he was alert and aware of what was coming, wasn't particularly worried. It had been Spurius' bad luck that some of his boys had been caught unprepared, but just to make sure, he gave another backward glance, this time stepping slightly out to the side of his column, kicking the shafts that had penetrated the ground out of the way as he did so, then looked down the length of it. The First and Second Cohorts were as far back as he could see because of the dust, yet he felt confident that his other Pili Priores had their Cohorts bunched as tightly as his and Scribonius' were, which was the key to an effective *testudo*. The only visible motion now was the legs of the men, except they were taking shorter, shuffling steps as they concentrated more on making sure their particular shield remained touching the others around it, while each Optio, who was trailing behind, walked in a semi-crouched position, looking through the only open end of this kind of *testudo*, the rear of the formation. As Pullus knew from his own time in that rank, this was the best way for experienced Optios to ensure the men were keeping their proper alignment and distance, because inside the formation, it was dark, at least much darker than outside of it. One lapse by a Legionary, one shifting of a shield too far in one direction was instantly exposed by a ray of sunlight, whereupon the Optio would immediately see it and shout to the offending man to correct it. This also meant the Optio was fairly well protected; the Centurions, however, were another story, and the Primus Pilus was the most exposed of all, which is why Pullus had, as all Centurions did at some point, scooped up a discarded shield from a wounded or dead man from the 3rd. In the back of his mind, he did wonder if the shield he was carrying now belonged to the poor bastard he had shoved out of the way, or whether carrying a shield with a different symbol on it brought ill luck, but he refused to let these thoughts linger for more than an instant. Up ahead, he could see that Spurius and his Century were about twenty paces short of the beginning of rubble pile outside the wall; this was when things got tricky, and despite himself, Pullus felt a stab of guilty relief that he had switched spots with his counterpart. Once Spurius reached the foot of the pile of rubble formed by the collapse of the wall, which almost always fell on both sides, although not equally, he would order his men out of the *testudo*. Oddly enough, by the time Spurius reached this point close to the wall, moving out of a *testudo* into a more open formation wasn't actually hazardous, at least from arrows. The instant the men dropped their shields—Pullus clearly could remember how much their arms would ache and the relief that came from dropping their shields, even if it was only momentary—they also had a javelin in their throwing hand, ready and poised to strike. If an archer wanted to try a shot, he would have to lean out from between the crenellations, and the chances were high that he would get a javelin in the face. Indeed, as Pullus watched, an even half-dozen Parthians tried this and every one of them was struck by a hurled javelin that, even at an upward angle, was thrown with enough force to penetrate their bodies. This seemed unusual to Pullus, thinking that even a boiled leather cuirass, when combined with a height of more than twenty feet, should be enough to keep the hardened iron point of the Roman javelin from punching through, let alone bury itself deeply enough in the body to wound. He got his answer why this was so in the form of one of the Parthians who, unlike the others who were either thrown or fell back and out of sight, tumbled forward, issuing a sharp scream that Pullus could hear even from his spot, cut short when the body hit the ground. Pullus couldn't actually see the Parthian impact the hard-packed dirt against the wall because of the men of the 3ʳᵈ were in between him and the spot where the body hit, but he got enough of a glimpse to recognize the distinctive garb.

"They're using their horse archers on the wall." This time, Pullus did think to turn around and shout this loudly enough so his men could hear. "So look alive, you bastards! You know how fast they can loose those fucking arrows!"

Turning back to the front, Pullus saw the short, wiry figure of Spurius, his white crest about the only thing Pullus could see, darting across the front of his Legion, making sure his men were properly spaced so that they filled the breach. Roman doctrine called for the men on the outer files to be no farther than the width of an arm's worth of space between the edge of the breach and themselves, measured from the elbow to the fingertips. While this was a simple concept, Pullus and his fellow Centurions had long since viewed this as something that was dreamed up by an armchair general who had never actually stormed a breach. The logic was sound, as far as it went; by ensuring that small of a gap, no defender could shove his way through to flank the breaching Century and attack from the side. What Pullus felt certain had never been taken into account was the footing and angle of the slope those throwing themselves through the hole had to account for, all while trying to keep from being stabbed. This was a rubble pile, made of broken bits of wall, and Pullus had seen that along with the pulverized remains of the stones, there were a fair amount of bricks that had collapsed as part of a section, the mortar still holding, so that corners and edges of the bricks protruded across the entire pile. Nevertheless, the momentary halt ended, and Pullus heard as well as saw Spurius lead his men up the pile, the Legionaries of the First Century, First Cohort of the 3ʳᵈ Legion roaring their collective promise to kill whoever dared stand in their way. Clambering up the pile, Spurius, as befitted a Primus Pilus, was the quickest up to the top, where Pullus saw a ragged line of what looked like the same kind of Parthian infantry they had faced at the battle on the ridge, waiting for the onslaught that was about to hit them.

"If that's all they have, this won't take very long," Pullus said, again aloud, although there was no way anyone could hear him.

Then, he could no longer pay attention to Spurius, whose Legion had resumed their own shuffling advance as the Second Century followed close behind the First. This signaled to the archers still on the wall to now concentrate their efforts on the next target, and Pullus' eye was drawn away from watching Spurius in time to see a ripple of motion as whoever commanded the Parthians to draw their bows. He caught just the barest glimpse of a long row of archers, spread along the wall save for the yawning gap of the breach, with the points of the arrows pointed skyward, just before they released the strings of their bows.

Moving his own shield up above him, Pullus bellowed, "Here it comes, boys! It's about to rain!"

Then it was the 10th's turn, and his words had barely died out when they were replaced by the hollow, wooden thud of hundreds of arrows striking shields. It was impossible to think, let alone try to give any orders, but Pullus counted on the men behind him to keep just enough space to see through the gap and watch for their Primus Pilus to resume his own movement towards the wall. Amidst the now-constant din that the men likened to invisible *numeni* banging on their shields with hammers came more metallic, clanging noises as iron tips struck metal boss, but also accompanying this were the sounds Pullus knew were inevitable, the same kind of shouts, cries, and calls for help that he had just heard from the men of the 3rd. And just like with the 3rd, there was nothing he could do, not now, except to move forward. Which, at first, seemed to be happening, after the First of the 3rd swept away the puny defending force who had tried to stop them in the breach, as the other Centuries of the First Cohort of the 3rd followed their Primus Pilus and his Century. Clambering up the pile, then disappearing behind it went the Second Cohort, followed as quickly by the Third. Then, the rest of the 3rd stopped, but Pullus was too occupied with trying to keep his shield up and in the proper position to block the missiles aimed for him to take more than passing notice. These things happened; there would be a stiffening of resistance, or there was a blockage of rubble that had to be cleared away before the forward movement could resume, but it wasn't until Pullus heard a series of screams that, even with all the battle he'd seen, made the hairs on his neck stand up, before he realized that whatever was happening wasn't normal. In a scene that would haunt his dreams for the rest of his life, a sequence of events occurred in such rapid succession that, no matter how hard he tried to later, he could never seem to put in their proper sequence with any confidence. From his later recollection, the screams were accompanied at the exact same time as a sudden flaring of a light that was over and above the sunlight, which was still not high enough in the sky ahead of him for him to see it above the walls. Then, without any order, verbal or by *cornu* that Pullus could hear, the men of the Fourth Cohort who had just ascended the rubble pile, suddenly turned and ran back down the pile, or at least attempted to do so, whereupon they ran into the Fifth Cohort at the foot of the breach. This was what a fair number of the Legionaries did, but as Pullus watched in astonishment, almost as many didn't attempt to do even that, instead throwing themselves to either the left or to the right of the breach, hurling themselves out of the way, and while it wasn't a great height, in the part of his mind that noticed such things, Pullus was certain that most of those men would be injured severely enough to be out of action. Yet that clearly seemed to be the better alternative to them, something Pullus didn't understand for the span of another heartbeat. Then, to his utter horror, at least a half-dozen men suddenly thrust themselves into view from where they had disappeared down to the street level on the other side of the wall, except they weren't running as much as staggering, moving with an odd gait and even odder gestures with their arms. What caused Pullus, one of the most veteran, hardened Centurions in Caesar's army to suddenly involuntarily retch, even while his arm continued to hold his shield in place as the arrows still came streaking down from the wall, was the sight of men, Legionaries, Roman men, burning to death in front of his very eyes. Only one of them moved with any haste, seeming to be aided by the downward tilt of this side of the rubble pile, which he suddenly ran down, uttering a scream so piercing that Pullus was sure even the men at the end of his column could hear it a few hundred paces away, trailing flame behind him as he hurtled mindlessly down the rubble pile. Thankfully for the men at the bottom who seemed to be frozen in place, he tripped before he reached the bottom, except his body quickly became a weapon for the Parthians as it tumbled down the pile. This finally seemed to spur the nearest men into action who, much like their counterparts just an instant before at the top of the pile, threw themselves out of the way. The other burning Romans had already collapsed, but it quickly became apparent that the suffering wasn't over, as Pullus' eye caught another sudden flaring of light from just inside the wall, quickly followed by another set of screams. Even as he struggled with all of this horror, the archers continued to loose their arrows as quickly as their arms could move, and as the Romans had learned in the first clash with them, Parthians could do this very rapidly indeed. Only later did Pullus recognize this was something of a blessing for his men; although they could hear something horrific was happening, their Centurions and Optios maintained their tight discipline, stopping curious men from compromising the integrity of their particular *testudo* and endangering their friends and comrades by issuing a snarled warning, or if within reach, a poke with the *vitus* as a reminder of what awaited them should they disobey. In this way, Pullus' men were spared, with perhaps the exception of the men of the first rank of the First Century, but even they only caught a glimpse, the only part they could see being the top of the rubble pile, since the lower part was obscured by the remaining Cohorts of the 3rd, now frozen in their tracks. That was enough, and Pullus heard the gasps of horror and moans of men who were forced to watch comrades die in the manner every man feared more than any other.

Nevertheless, Pullus gave his own warning, snapping, "Shut your fucking mouths, now! I don't want to hear another word, or by the gods, I will *make you watch!*"

As he hoped, this was all that was needed. Pullus, on the other hand, was at a complete loss. While it was understandable that the 3rd had come to a standstill, from where he stood, it appeared that the Centurions nearest the breach had lost control of the situation, because even as he watched, more men appeared like the most terrifying apparitions from a man's worst nightmare, fully aflame and out of their minds with a pain he couldn't even imagine. In response, the orderly formation that had been present just a matter of fifteen or twenty heartbeats before was disintegrating, at least with the rest of the 3rd, and he saw men suddenly break from their spots to run. And then, it was as if a spigot had been turned on, because the 3rd, one of Caesar's most veteran Legions, giving into the collective panic that swept invisibly through their ranks, turned and ran, right at Pullus and the 10th.

Chapter Ten

On the opposite side, the Legions under Caesar hadn't quite reached the same point in their own endeavor. They were now aligned to Caesar's satisfaction and had actually begun the advance. Completely unaware of the catastrophe taking place in the breach at Seleucia, Caesar sat Toes, watching as his men drew closer, almost to the point where they would stop once more, except this time, it was to allow the scorpions to set themselves up and make ready to start providing protection. Caesar knew this was the last of the easy part of this; to this point, they could have been performing a field maneuver in training, but he was also acutely aware of the likelihood of the number of archers probably contained in the city. He had received dispatches from Ventidius, whose advance scouts had finally visually spotted the Parthian contingent heading for Susa, and while there was no way to tell with any certainty, once he tallied up the number of casualties his men had inflicted during the battle on the ridge, and compared them to this report and what little he knew of the total numbers of Parthian warriors, his guess was that there was anywhere from three to six thousand archers missing. This made it highly likely they were inside the walls; if this was indeed the case, they were about to learn shortly.

Meanwhile, as he sat his mount, couriers from the two wings of his force, commanded by Hirtius and Pollio respectively, came galloping up at roughly the same time. Both his Legates wanted to report their progress, something that amused and irritated Caesar in equal measure; sitting where he was, he could see both wings perfectly well, and his eyesight, while not what it once was, perhaps, was still very keen. Besides which, these weren't the couriers he wanted to hear from the most, but he glanced over his shoulder at the sun and thought, *It's still a bit early for the wall in Seleucia to come down.* Consequently, Caesar was unconcerned, although this would certainly change. The scorpions were assembled quickly, and he watched as the nearest crews from where he sat began the final step of staking down the legs so that they would remain in place, while the Legionary who was the commander of each piece used a rod, placing it in the trough where the bolt would go, staring down its length to align it with their intended target. The nearest scorpions belonging to the 7th, to his right, on the short side of the assault, and the 5th to his left, were the first of the Legions along the southern wall to make their final preparations, and they signaled to their Centurion they were ready. Because of the distance along the southern wall, Caesar had to rely on the use of the horns to relay that the scorpions of the 8th, the Legion anchoring the left, were ready, and at last, it was time to begin the real work. Caesar was turning to his staff, specifically his own *cornicen*, and his standard-bearer, who held the red banner of Caesar that had signaled the start of so many battles, when Apollodorus, who was mounted on a smaller pony, suddenly broke in.

"Caesar, what is that?"

Irritated, the general turned, but as he did so, a movement caught his eye, high in the air and moving quickly. Caesar barely got his head around in time to see the object, not very large by any means, but trailing greasy black smoke, slam into the ground no more than a dozen paces short of the nearest scorpion to his right. Before his mind could register the meaning, a gout of flame erupted with a whooshing sound that he could hear even at this distance, as the men nearest to this suddenly appearing and unexpected fire shouted in alarm and leaped away.

"What...?"

Caesar didn't even get the question out before he caught sight of another smoky trail, except this one was more to his left front as it streaked away from the wall, sailing high into the air, leaving what might have been a careless, curving mark with a pen that left a black line in the sky. This one he spotted before it hit, although he wished he hadn't, because this one didn't miss its target. It wasn't actually a direct hit, but it didn't have to be, as once more a jar roughly the size of a small amphora of wine slammed into the ground and shattered into countless pieces, except those pieces were actually composed of little globules of flame, most of which splashed onto the wooden legs of the second scorpion to his left. This was bad enough, but one of the artillery *immunes* standing next to it was also doused, and immediately, the man seemed to erupt in flame, shrieking hideously as his comrades shouted in alarm. In their surprised fear, much like the men of the 3rd had done when their flaming comrades had emerged from the breach, the nearest men jumped away from a man that just a heartbeat before had been at the very least a comrade, if not a close friend.

300

Now, his body was dangerous just to touch, but although Caesar was as horrified as his men, he had the presence of mind to roar, "Someone put that poor man out of his misery!" It was left to the nearest Centurion, who sprinted up to the man and, without hesitation, plunged his sword into the burning man's back, driving him to the ground, whereupon he delivered a final thrust. That was the last moment of relative calm for several moments as the sky seemed to be filled with these jars of death, and it didn't take Caesar long to see they were hitting with what seemed to be uncanny accuracy. Within a matter of a hundred heartbeats, there were burning pyres dotting both wings of the Roman lines. Most of them were scorpions, the seasoned wood quickly catching, particularly since the fire seemed to actually stick to whatever it hit, but not all of these flames were fueled by wood. Men who were unable to dodge out of the way became human torches, although the one small blessing for them was that now nobody hesitated to put the tortured souls out of their horrific pain.

Caesar turned to give the order to his *cornicen* as he had a moment before, yet this time, his command was different as he said in a voice choked with an emotion that even someone who knew him as well as Apollodorus couldn't identify, "Sound the command to withdraw. We need to get out of range of those…things."

Caesar's Legions always obeyed his orders swiftly; this time was by far the quickest his men reacted to one of them. Despite the temptation to simply turn and run, the Centurions were responsible for their charges doing so in the same, measured manner in which they advanced; if the tempo they gave was a bit quicker, Caesar certainly didn't find any fault with this. Truthfully, he was as shaken as his men. How had he not known about this? And from where did artillery pieces of this much power come? These were just a few of his thoughts as he watched his shaken army move safely out of range. Left behind were the still-blazing scorpions that hadn't been removed quickly enough, and the smoldering corpses of those men who hadn't either. What caught Caesar's eye was the ordered row of scorpions, almost perfectly aligned with each other, now serving as beacons that sent a signal to both the men of his army and the Parthians.

"Sound the order for all senior officers," he commanded, once he was certain his men were out of harm's way.

There was much that had to be decided, but even as his mind began turning this new development over to examine it more closely, ultimately, he wasn't overly concerned. He felt certain that what he had just witnessed was the total arsenal of the Parthian artillery, which meant that the planned breach was safe from these fearsome weapons. And if the gods are good, he thought with a grim satisfaction, that wall is either down or is about to come down.

It had been almost too good to be true, and if Kambyses hadn't seen it for himself, he would have been hard-pressed to believe that what he had just witnessed could have happened. Any doubt he had, about either the use and value of artillery in general, or the abilities of Anaxagoras and his team of workmen in particular, had been wiped away in the amount of time it took to send more than fifty stoppered jars of the substance the Parthians called naphtha through the air, to crash into the Romans, and destroy almost every one of those accursed things the enemy called scorpions, along with at least three *ballistae*. It was truly a miracle, Kambyses thought, feeling so elated that he had to catch the stone crenellation he was standing next to on the wall because he was getting lightheaded. Down on the ground before him, the seemingly invincible Romans had been forced to withdraw out of range. For a brief moment, Kambyses wondered if he had been too hasty in unleashing this secret and potent weapon. Certainly, he had inflicted a huge psychological blow to his enemies and given the paucity of materials, which he had encountered firsthand in his own efforts to create an artillery force from scratch, the loss of those scorpions would undoubtedly hurt the Romans. But as he scanned the scorched, smoking ground, where even now there were still small patches of flame flickering stubbornly, by his estimate, they had only brought down perhaps forty Romans as well as the scorpions and *ballistae*. Perhaps if he had waited, allowed the scorpions to fire their bolts, then unleashed the naphtha missiles when the Romans were closer to the walls, he could have done real, substantial damage. Still, he was inclined to think he had acted wisely, and when he scanned the ramparts, watching the wild celebrations of his men, who were shouting something he couldn't quite understand at first, he felt certain he had done the right thing. When he finally listened closely and realized the men were shouting his own name, Kambyses felt a rush of excitement that he had never really experienced before as unbidden thoughts that he was sure he had long before repressed came out again, striking him with the force of a thunderbolt. How was it that it was Orodes' branch of the Arsacid house was King of Kings? Because the gods deemed this to be the way it should be, or because Orodes' great-

302

grandfather had been a cunning bastard who was bold enough to seize the throne? The men nearest him glanced at him in puzzlement when Kambyses suddenly shook his head violently, trying to banish these thoughts, at least for the moment. *Nothing good can come of this line of thinking,* he admonished himself; *not now anyway.* Later, perhaps, but first, he had to find out what was happening on the far side of the city.

Turning to Sosimenes, who he had thanked on his arrival and seen that his subordinate in charge of this side of the defense hadn't exaggerated, Kambyses said, "You'll know where I'll be. Send a courier the instant something happens."

Sosimenes placed his knuckle against his forehead, assuring his general he would do that very thing, but Kambyses was already bounding down the steps to where his horse waited, moving with an energy and purpose that had been missing for some time.

Titus Pullus was almost singlehandedly responsible for ensuring that the calamity that had befallen the 3ʳᵈ wasn't extended to his own Legion. As usual, his response to the sight of what was in essence a stampede of panicked Legionaries running directly for what he understood they saw as the safety of an intact formation had been done without thought, either about the danger or whether it was the correct action to take. Standing directly in front of his Century, Pullus had drawn his sword, facing the oncoming rush of men whose only thought was to get away from the horrors they had just witnessed.

"*Any of you come near us, I'll gut you like a fish!*" Pullus was certain he had never bellowed as loudly as he was doing at this crucial moment. "*Go around and get behind us! You'll be safe there!*"

Over and over, he shouted this, using his Gallic-forged blade as both a warning and a pointer that directed the panicked men of the 3ʳᵈ to run to one side or another of his intact formation. Even as he was doing this, Pullus was forced to keep his left arm up in front of him, holding the shield as the Parthian archers were offered targets whose only protection was their mail shirts as the 3ʳᵈ turned their collective backs. Sheets of arrows were still falling from the sky, and because Pullus' vision was partially obscured by his shield, which had already been pierced a half-dozen times, he sensed more than saw rankers of the 3ʳᵈ struck down by one of the arrows, slamming into the ground on either side of him and his men from the momentum of their flight that was suddenly arrested by a feathered shaft. Thankfully, most of the men scrambled back to their feet, even with an arrow protruding from somewhere on their back side, a fair number forced to limp or even hop because the arrow that had felled them was in one of their legs. As the 3rd streamed past, Pullus even saw men who had been struck more than once, but while he couldn't say they were still running, they were at least staggering past him. Even with the limited vision of the *testudo*, those of Pullus' men who could get a glimpse of what was happening naturally relayed this next development to their comrades inside the parlous shelter provided by their interlocked shields. Very quickly, a new layer of noise was added as the men of the 10th began shouting their own encouragement and, echoing their Primus Pilus, their admonition about not threatening their own safety. It was a moment that none of the men of the 3rd or the 10th would ever forget as the rankers of the 10th were forced to threaten harm to those comrades of the 3rd who were so panic-stricken their only thought was to force their way into the compact formation, seeking the cover provided by the shields of their brethren. Pullus would learn later that almost a dozen of his men, mostly the Optios but, in a couple cases, the Centurions, had been given no choice but to strike down men of the 3rd who hadn't heeded the warnings. This collapse of the 3rd, while understandable, was worse than what Pullus had witnessed at Gergovia, and what he had heard transpired at Dyrrhachium as, what was in reality a relatively brief span of time but in the moment seemed to last forever, the Centurions of the 3rd were no less panic-stricken than their charges. And as all of this was taking place, the Parthians continued the onslaught with their feathered missiles; Pullus had no doubt the Parthian bastards on the wall were reveling in this moment, shouting with glee and challenging their own comrades about how many Romans they could fell. Yes, he thought bitterly, they're going to be boasting about this for the rest of their days. Then, the moment was over, at least as far as the 3rd's retreat, leaving a detritus that provided anyone with eyes with the story of what had just taken place. Strewn in a swath that was roughly the width of the breach close to the wall but then fanned out in the direction of where Pullus and the 10th were still standing, the discarded shields, helmets, and the bodies of Legionaries related the failure of the 3rd to take the breach. The sight caused a temporary paralysis in Pullus, who, oblivious to the continuing sound of arrows alternately hissing past him or thudding into the shields of the men behind him, stared at the ruin before him, trying to comprehend it.

"Primus Pilus!...Primus Pilus!...*Pullus!*"

Only at the sound of his name was Pullus jerked from his daze, although he retained the presence of mind not to simply turn about and take an arrow in the back.

Instead, he turned his head to the side without moving his body, or more importantly, his left arm holding the shield, shouting back, "I hear you!"

"What do you want us to do, Primus Pilus?"

Pullus recognized the voice of his Optio, and a part of his mind noted by the location of his voice that Lutatius had moved from his spot at the rear. I'm going to have to talk to him about that, he thought dimly, but whether or not his subordinate was in technical violation of the regulations, his question was valid. And Pullus knew there was only one course to take; they had to retreat, then send word to Caesar and find out what the general wanted them to do in response. As unaware of Caesar's plight as the general was about that of Pullus and the rest of the men of both Legions, the only material difference in their situation was that Caesar had seen enough to deduce the cause of this setback. All Pullus knew was that there was a horrible new dimension to the Parthian defenses, one that turned men into flaming torches. But just as he was opening his mouth to give the order to begin the orderly process of withdrawing, his eye picked up movement at the very edge of his vision. Turning his head back towards the wall, Pullus saw a lone Legionary just as he started his downward dash, nimbly hopping over the protruding pieces of rubble, heading in his direction. When Pullus spotted him, he noticed that unlike the last men he had seen emerging from whatever was happening inside the walls, this one wasn't aflame. Because of his proximity to the wall, he was also ironically the safest he would be, yet the Legionary didn't hesitate even to catch his breath for the next part of his dash. While Pullus was trying to understand what he was seeing, the running Legionary reached the bottom of the pile, whereupon he was able to pick up speed because of the better footing, still heading in Pullus' direction. The Primus Pilus held his breath as the man reached the farthest edge of the beaten zone from where Pullus and the 10th were standing, marked in a clear but ragged line of arrow shafts sticking up from the ground. While the ground was better than the rubble pile, the dashing Gregarius had to negotiate a new set of obstacles: the bodies and discarded shields of his fallen comrades. For the span of a half-dozen heartbeats, Pullus dared to hope that the archers on the wall were so intent on punishing the 10th now that the remnants of the 3rd had fled out of range, that they would miss the sight of this lone man. Then, he saw the first arrow seem to magically sprout from the ground immediately next to the dashing feet of the Legionary. Pullus opened his mouth to shout a warning, but the Gregarius had obviously seen, or more likely heard the hissing sound of the missile as it passed, because he instantly changed his course, dodging to his right, away from where the first arrow had struck. He wasn't a moment too soon, because the ground where his feet had just been once more seemed to sprout arrows, two this time, but still having missed their target. The Legionary, who Pullus had immediately seen had not only discarded his shield, but had also shed his harness carrying sword and dagger in order to lighten his load, suddenly changed direction yet again, this time veering back to his left, heading more directly for Pullus. And just as happened an instant before, arrows came slashing down, dogging his footsteps, yet despite Pullus' conviction that some Parthian would adjust his aim, suddenly, the Gregarius came sliding to a stop, collapsing into a partial crouch at Pullus' feet, panting from the mad dash he had just made. While Pullus appreciated that the man had retained the presence of mind to stop as closely to the Primus Pilus as possible; in fact, his body struck Pullus' greaves with a fair amount of force, it meant that less than an eye blink later, Pullus' shield was almost jerked from his grasp as first one, then another arrow slammed into it. For the span of three or four heartbeats, Pullus' ears were filled with the hissing sound as missiles streaked down all around him and the Gregarius, the ground around them sprouting even more quivering shafts that joined with those already there. Pullus sheathed his sword and used his free hand to reach down and roughly grab the Gregarius by the neck of his armor, lifting the man to his feet with an ease that the Gregarius would recount to anyone who would listen for the rest of his days, boasting of the day the strongest man in the Legions picked him up like he was a newborn babe.

"Keep your feet and press your back to mine," Pullus ordered, forced to speak even more loudly because his shield was struck another two times even as he was relaying his orders. "We're going to back up out of range of these fuckers."

Although the man obeyed and he was still gasping for breath, he still blurted, "Primus Pilus, I have a message…"

"Save it," Pullus snapped, irritated at this disruption of his concentration. Without bothering to wait to hear the man acknowledge him, Pullus shouted over his shoulder the command to begin the withdrawal.

306

Waiting only long enough to hear the ripple of bellowed orders repeated from one Century to the next, then the inevitable sounds that followed as his men began their slow, measured backward steps, Pullus kept a firm grasp on the Gregarius' shoulder with one hand, protecting the both of them with the other, then began his own movement out of danger. Moving even more slowly than they had on their advance, the 10th retreated, moving out of range Century by Century, until it was just Pullus and the Gregarius, neither of them stopping until they reached the edge of the beaten zone farthest from the wall, as clearly marked by the line of embedded arrows as if there was another barrier.

At least, Pullus tried to stop, dropping his shield, which was studded with arrows, but the Gregarius saved the day when he whirled about to face the Primus Pilus, his eyes wide with urgency and fear, shouting, "No! No, Primus Pilus! We have to keep moving backward!"

"Why?" Pullus asked, but in dropping his shield, he had an unobstructed view of the entire expanse of the western wall for the first time in almost a third of a watch, and while he didn't fully comprehend, what caught his eye was enough for him not to wait for the Gregarius to explain. Whirling about so violently he knocked the Gregarius stumbling back, Pullus roared, "Open formation! Open formation!" And for the first time he could remember, Pullus didn't use a formal command, simply shouting, "Now, RUN!! Now! GO GO GO!" Even as he was shouting this, he had begun his own run away from the wall, just as the large arm of the large artillery piece was pulled down out of sight, ready to receive its deadly cargo that would be hurled at Pullus and the 10th.

It was the most ragged, undisciplined, and ungainly movement that the 10th had ever performed, but it was done quickly enough that the Parthians only managed to send one flaming missile after them, which landed just twenty paces short of Pullus and the Gregarius, who were now in essence the end of the column. Even so, Pullus felt the heat from the splattered, oblong patch of fire that extended from the point where the jar had impacted back in Pullus' direction, a stretch of some six or seven paces. The presence of the heat was disturbing enough; that every inch of that patch was on fire within the boundaries created by the shattering of the vessel was what alarmed Pullus. Anyone within that oval would be burned alive, he thought dismally, watching the shimmering air above the flames that distorted his view of the wall, where the single arm of the artillery piece stuck up from the parapet. Only later would Pullus become aware that, relatively speaking, he and his men were lucky, because this was the lone piece on this part of the wall.

Turning finally to the Gregarius, who had dropped to put his hands on his knees as he tried to catch his breath, Pullus asked, "Was that what you came to tell me?"

Somewhat to his surprise, the Gregarius shook his head, but explained, "No, sir. I mean, yes sir, but that's not all."

"I know you, don't I?" This was the first chance Pullus had to examine the Gregarius more closely, and while he didn't know the man's name, he added, "You're from the First of the First."

This time, the Legionary nodded, but his face was still hidden as he continued sucking air into his lungs. For a brief instant, Pullus considered snapping an order to the man to come to *intente*, if only so Pullus could see his face, but instantly dismissed the idea as churlish and ungrateful. This man, whether it had been his main intention or not, had saved some of his men from burning to death, maybe even Pullus himself. Therefore, he forced himself to be patient.

Finally, the man was sufficiently recovered to stand erect, and now he did remember to come to the proper position to render a salute, but without waiting to be acknowledged, blurted out, "I'm Gregarius Gnaeus Palma, and yes, I'm of the First of the First. I was sent by Primus Pilus Spurius to…"

"Wait," Pullus interrupted, but it was more from disbelief than hope he asked, "Spurius is still alive? How can that be?"

"Yes, sir." Palma nodded, then amended, "At least, he was when he sent me. And I think he still might be." When Pullus didn't reply, Palma took this as permission to continue, explaining, "This was a trap. They wanted us to breach the wall."

Although Pullus had deduced this, at least in a general sense, he was still prompted to ask, "How does Spurius know?"

"Because they built another fucking wall inside the city," Palma replied bitterly. "It's not as high as the outer wall, but it's high enough that we need ladders."

"And we gave our fucking ladders to the rest of the army," Pullus groaned, "so they could make enough that were long enough." Again, Palma's answer was a nod, but before he could say anything, Pullus said, "That doesn't explain how your Primus Pilus is still alive."

"Once we got inside, we saw that it was a trap, but then they started using that thing," Palma turned to indicate the large artillery piece, although its arm had been retracted, and there was no missing the anguish in the man's tone as he went on, "but it's apparently too big for them to move very far. So it's only covering the inside of the walls from the rubble pile to about a hundred fifty paces deeper inside the city. But because of their position, they can barely clear that inside wall they built next to the real one. So," Palma took a breath, "there's a section of their position where they can't drop that *cac* down on our heads."

While this was good news, Pullus wasn't clear on something that seemed obvious to him, prompting him to ask, "Can't they just use men to throw those pots down on your head from that inner wall?"

Palma shook his head, but while he was correct in his answer, it wasn't for the reason he thought.

"The inner wall is low enough that even if they threw small pots down, I'm sure that when they broke, it would send that stuff everywhere." Pullus didn't miss Palma shuddering as he undoubtedly remembered the sights he had been forced to witness, and the Gregarius looked up at him with eyes so haunted that it caused Pullus an involuntary shiver. "Primus Pilus," Palma asked plaintively, "what *is* that stuff? Greek fire?"

Although Pullus wasn't sure, based on what little he had seen, he felt confident enough to nod his head and say, "I think so. But," he was forced to admit, "I never knew the Parthians had it." And neither did Caesar, Pullus thought grimly, but didn't say so aloud; right now, there was no point. Turning his attention back to the more immediate problem, Pullus asked, "So what did Spurius send you out for? To get help?" The words tasted bitter in Pullus' mouth, but he still forced them out. "Because I'm not going to subject more men to that."

This clearly bothered Palma; these were his friends and comrades the Primus Pilus of the 10ᵗʰ was consigning to a likely horrible fate, yet he kept this from his tone as he replied, "Well, when I left, the Primus Pilus had some men working on something." Without waiting, Palma squatted down and began drawing in the dirt, explaining as he did so, "The Primus Pilus says the reason they were able to build that inner wall so quickly is that they're using what was already there." Drawing part of a roughly rectangular shape, he indicated, "Here's the northern wall, and there's the western wall," with a deft move, he rubbed out part of the line representing the side they were facing, "and

309

here's the breach. About fifty paces this way," Palma added a new line, sprouting from the western wall, "they've built that inner wall to block the street that's next to the wall. That's the one that big fucking *ballista* can barely clear. But then," he added a square, "there's a whole block of buildings. They're two stories, but they didn't tear them down; they just added what looks like a parapet on top of the roof so the men there can have cover. They're mainly archers," he continued, then amended, "at least they were, until a few of them took javelins in the face." His smile held no humor, but it did contain a modicum of a savage satisfaction at this, although he was now adding another rectangular block as he did so. "The new wall starts again and blocks this second street off that's," he had to think for a moment, "one street east of the main wall. Then there's this building," he pointed to the second structure, waiting for Pullus to indicate by a grunt that he understood, then added another line that extended from the edge of the second rectangle back to the line representing the northern wall. "The new wall joins at the northeast corner of this second building and goes to the northern wall. That part is lined with archers," he spat in the dirt, his spittle speckling the line representing their position, "and when I left, they were pouring it into the men who are," his now-filthy finger etched a roughly semicircular line at the junction of the second building and the new wall, "right here. The Primus Pilus has them in," Palma cocked his head as he tried to think of the proper way to describe it, "sort of a *testudo*, except it's like part of a circle, facing outward from that corner."

Pullus took a moment to absorb all that he had learned, both from Palma's description and from the drawing he had made in the dirt. Despite being somewhat heartened to hear that his friend Spurius had managed to keep some of his men alive and somewhat protected, he wasn't sanguine about how much longer they could last. This was when Palma supplied the last piece of information, which changed everything.

"The Primus Pilus doesn't just have them standing there trying to hold their shields up for as long as they can before their arms give out," Palma said, answering one of Pullus' most pressing questions before he asked. "He's got every man who isn't needed to keep a shield in place working on breaking through," Palma pointed to the line in the dirt that represented the northern wall of the second building, "right here. The building is stone, but the Primus Pilus is sure that the wall of this building isn't more than a single layer of brick, two at most." Now, Palma looked up at Pullus, his expression clearly

310

beseeching the Primus Pilus as he finished, "If they can get inside that building, they can hold out for a lot longer. That's why he sent me, to let you know that. They're going to hold out as long as they need for us to come get them."

Pullus didn't miss the use of the word "us" by Palma, understanding that the Gregarius would refuse to be left behind in any rescue mission. This was a large reason why Pullus didn't have the heart to inform Palma that, while his heart was with the Gregarius, his head told him that, at the very least, he had to wait for Caesar to tell him whether or not this was the proper course of action.

Instead, Pullus put his hand on Palma's shoulder and said with a voice made hoarse by both the yelling he had been doing and the emotion he felt for Spurius and his men, "Spurius clearly sent the right man. No matter what happens, I swear on the black stone that Caesar will hear of your bravery."

"Just get my friends out of there, Primus Pilus." Palma didn't even attempt to hide the fact he was begging as he looked up at the giant Roman who Palma knew was the best hope for Spurius and his friends. "Just…" His voice broke then, and tears started streaming down, his head dropping as he began sobbing.

If only he hadn't done that, Pullus thought.

"Do you think they'll come for us?"

Turning to the man who had asked the question, the Gregarius, a veteran on his second enlistment, reminded himself that this was just a youngster and one of the last-minute replacements that had been enlisted to replace the losses the 3rd incurred when a plague had swept the huge camp at Brundisium where they had been waiting for this campaign.

Consequently, instead of saying what he really thought of their chances, the Gregarius tried to sound hearty as he uttered what he felt sure was a lie. "Absolutely! We just need to hold tight, keep those bastards outside from getting in, and the rest of our boys will be here quick as Pan!"

"I wonder what happened to Glabrio," the younger ranker mused, and the older veteran took this is as a sign that his companion had accepted the fiction, albeit tacitly.

Gnaeus Glabrio was the Primus Princeps Prior, commander of the Third Century, and their Centurion. The older veteran hesitated, wondering if he should at least tell the truth with this; after a heartbeat's worth of thought, he decided that the boy would find out soon enough.

"He...didn't make it," was how he put it, unable to articulate anything more than this, hoping the other man would be satisfied with this.

"Did you see it?" the younger man pressed, causing his comrade to close his eyes and bite back a curse.

"Yes, I saw it," he snapped, his already-frayed nerves battered even more by being forced to relive what he had witnessed not long before. "What do you want to know? That he died burning like a fucking torch? Is that what you want to hear?"

As soon as the words were out, he regretted them, and even in the darkened interior of what was some sort of warehouse, he saw the younger man's composure start to crumble, his chin starting to quiver.

"I...I...didn't know," the youngster stammered weakly, then without another word, he dropped his face into his hands, trying to cover his weeping.

"I'm sorry, Terentius." The older man felt somewhat ridiculous reaching out to give his comrade an awkward pat on the shoulder. "My nerves are just raw right now."

Terentius didn't verbally reply, but he did nod his helmeted head, although he kept his face covered. Sighing, the older veteran tried to shift to a more comfortable position, and despite his personal misgivings about the possibility of rescue, there is always a part of every person that stays optimistic, refusing to accept defeat until the last breath is gone. All around him, crammed into this warehouse, conversations much like this one were taking place, as the remnants of what had been the First Cohort waited for whatever came next. Of the six Centurions, only Spurius was standing, although he was wounded, suffering an arrow in the calf that, fortunately, had been almost spent after caroming off a shield. The Primus Pilus Posterior was dead, but he had been luckier than Glabrio, taking an arrow through the mouth rather than burning to death; the other three Centurions were wounded to a degree that rendered them incapable of continuing in their duties. It had taken a third of a watch for the makeshift work party, protected by the wall of shields their comrades had provided and with only their swords and daggers as tools, to punch a hole in the wall of the building that was now their temporary refuge. In another small blessing, because of its proximity to the expected fighting, it had been emptied, at least on the first floor, while the second had apparently been the living quarters of what Spurius

312

assumed was some sort of merchant whose goods had been stored below. Not surprisingly, the upper floor had been deserted as well, and all but the heaviest furniture items had been removed. It was on the second floor that Spurius had directed the wounded be taken, where they were being cared for by volunteers from among the ranks of the survivors. Despite the chaos, and the inevitable shock that comes from seeing men you consider friends burn to death in the most horrible way imaginable, the Roman traits of discipline and order asserted themselves, with Spurius relying on the Optios of the other Centuries to step into the role of Centurion. Even as the last of the men who had been providing the protection with their shields backed through the jagged hole in the wall, Spurius had been busy, sending the wounded upstairs and taking a head count of the remaining men. He had known the situation was bad; once the count was done, Spurius was as close to despair as he had ever been in his entire time under the standard. While none of the Centuries had been at full strength, there still had been four hundred twenty men who marched out of the northwest camp what seemed like days before but was just a matter of a couple watches. Now he had less than two hundred men who weren't wounded, or whose injuries were, like his, not serious enough to keep them out of the fight. This was bad enough, but it was not just the number of wounded that were now sequestered upstairs, it was that more than fifty men were suffering from horrific burns and not arrow wounds. Even in the relatively short span of time it took to get things organized, Spurius had been informed that four of those men had succumbed, and the Primus Pilus understood that it was only going to get worse. Despite the separation, the men on the ground floor couldn't miss the heart-rending sounds that drifted down the wide set of stairs as men suffered through a pain that none of them could even imagine. That it wasn't even worse than it already was stemmed from Spurius' quiet orders to the men who were tending to these tortured souls, who surreptitiously ended the suffering of those unfortunates whose burns were the most severe. Despite all that was happening, Spurius' main concern was to keep the Parthians outside from gaining entrance, at least as long as possible, not necessarily because he held out any hope for rescue, but to do otherwise was simply unthinkable. Romans didn't surrender, and Spurius was determined that he wouldn't bring shame to Rome, to the Legion, and to Caesar by doing so now. Aiding him in this was the fact that his men were of the same mind as he was, which he knew just from their expressions and demeanor. Fortunately, there were only three possible entry points; the breach they had created at the northeastern end, a set of double doors on the southern side in the middle of the building, and a single door on the second floor, on the eastern side. There was a simple staircase up to that door, and Spurius had directed the men there to drag the few pieces of furniture left behind to block it. Of all the possible weak points, Spurius was least worried about this door; it would be next to impossible for any Parthian to ascend the stairs without making noise, and even if they did, the door wasn't wide enough for more than one man at a time to come through. The double doors were more worrisome, but they were stout and double barred from the inside. What worried Spurius the most was that the Parthians would use that horrible liquid fire and apply it to the door, and in an attempt to at least make this more difficult, he had men drag the stones they had knocked down to get into the building and stack them against the door. It wasn't to bolster it; he was acutely aware that they would simply be knocked over, but his hope was that it would provide a bit of insulation from the fire that he felt certain would be coming. That this hadn't happened yet puzzled Spurius, although he was thankful for every spare heartbeat he could snatch for his men. Only once had the Parthians tried to rush the hole in the northeast corner wall, but they had quickly learned that their spear-wielding infantrymen possessed neither the skill nor the resolve to throw themselves bodily into the gap. All it had taken were about a half-dozen javelins hurled into their midst for the Parthians to withdraw, and now matters were at a stalemate. Not without further cost to the Romans inside the warehouse, when one of the men of the Second Century stepped too close to the jagged hole and was almost instantly struck by three arrows loosed by Parthians up on the makeshift wall who were at the proper angle to see him. After that, Spurius had ordered that every man near the hole carry his shield with him and keep it up and in position, although after the first few moments, the rankers had settled down for the most part. Now, they were waiting for Spurius to think of something, for help to come, or to repel another attempt to penetrate the stone warehouse, all while trying to block out the moans and cries of their comrades a floor above, whose terrible burns created an agony that none of them wanted to contemplate.

Unknown to Spurius, the reason he and his men had been spared the fire was based in two simple but salient facts. When Kambyses had ordered the smaller artillery pieces to be moved from Seleucia and across the bridges to Ctesiphon, he had naturally ordered that all the ammunition for those pieces be brought. Since almost the entire arsenal consisted of the smaller jars of naphtha, with the more normal stone ammunition accounting for a quarter of the total stock, there were no small jars left in the vicinity of the northwest wall. That, however, was only part of the reason that Melchior didn't send a courier to his commander requesting a stock of the pots that were small enough for a man to hurl be sent back to his position. Ultimately, it was the same problem that had plagued Kambyses' attempt to build an artillery force from scratch; there wasn't much wood used in any of the buildings of either Seleucia or Ctesiphon. The stone warehouse that was now the refuge of those Romans who hadn't been burned alive or struck down by the volleys of arrows from the temporary wall offered little in the way of fuel, even for a substance as pernicious as naphtha. There was another factor, one that Melchior was less willing to acknowledge, and that was based in what he had witnessed shortly before this. Watching men doused in flames who, even for those who retained their wits and dropped to the ground to try and smother the flames, were completely helpless to stop as the clinging, viscous substance burned its way through its victims, impervious to their frantic attempts to beat the flames out, had made a huge impression on the young Parthian. Seeing this also reinforced the warning Kambyses had given him.

"We aren't the masters of this," he had waved at the rows of stoppered jars, "and you must always remember that. It's a powerful weapon, that is true, but don't ever think we are in control of it."

The prescience of these words were brought home to Melchior as he stood watching in horrible fascination at men who, despite the fact that they were enemies, he couldn't help feeling pity for as they ran in crazy circles, shrieking with a pain he found impossible to imagine, before collapsing to the ground as nothing more than smoking chunks of charred meat. When all was said and done, Melchior was simply unwilling to unleash the powerful but unstable weapon in a manner that wasn't strictly controlled, inside the city walls at least. The large artillery piece, staked in its position almost two furlongs down the western wall from the breach, had been able to lob its large vats of naphtha down into the enclosed area created by the temporary wall built by Anaxagoras, but it had been tested with vats filled with dirt to a level that approximated the weight of one carrying the naphtha beforehand. This had been done during the night before as part of the last-moment preparations for what the defenders of Seleucia knew was inevitable, so that when the piece started hurling the vats of naphtha, they had landed with devastating effect. Not without cost to the Parthians, which was another factor in Melchior's reluctance to have the piece pivoted from its orientation to align with the warehouse two blocks deeper in the city. There had only been one vat that landed short of its intended target, not clearing the lower temporary wall, but that had been enough; ten of his archers who had been arrayed on the section of temporary wall between the permanent wall and the first block of structures had been incinerated. Melchior, who had placed himself in the corner where the northern and western walls met, deciding this was the spot that gave him the best vantage point, had been close enough not only to hear those poor souls screaming in terror and pain, but to feel the heat, and even worse, pick up the smell of burning meat as the archers burned to death. No, Melchior decided, he would have to think of another way to root those Romans out of that building and to stay alert for another Roman attempt to get through the breach. That artillery piece was no longer a secret, and Melchior felt certain that even at this moment, his enemies were discussing how to neutralize this advantage. In the immediate aftermath of the Romans' first attempt to enter the breach, Melchior had dispatched a courier to Kambyses, both to inform his commander and to ask for further guidance. In this, he and his Roman counterpart were of the same mind, but in what was something of a reversal of roles, it was the man who was under the strictest discipline and respect for the chain of command who moved on his own initiative.

"We can't wait for Caesar," Pullus decided. "We're going to have to do something to at least get Spurius and his boys out of there."

Balbus, Scribonius, and the other Centurions were gathered in a knot of men, far enough away to avoid being heard by their men and the rest of the 3rd standing nearby. They had moved out of range of the large artillery piece, although whoever was manning the piece on the wall hadn't bothered to launch a flaming vat of naphtha but had instead sent some of their rock ammunition at the Romans. Using the scarred earth as the visible boundary of its range, the Romans had withdrawn more than a hundred paces beyond the farthermost dent in the ground. None of Pullus' Centurions argued Pullus' statement, yet neither did they look enthusiastic about the prospect of what their Primus Pilus was proposing.

316

Ignoring their silence, Pullus thought aloud, alternating between staring in the direction of the western wall, then back at their own camp, more than a mile distant, saying more to himself, "We don't have time to make mantlets that are fireproof, especially with whatever that stuff is." Turning back to his Centurions, he added bleakly, "You all saw how it behaved. Even men who rolled on the ground couldn't put the flames out. But," he spat in a combination of anger and frustration, "how did we miss that those bastards have Greek fire?"

As usually happened, it was Sextus Scribonius, by far the best read of the Centurions, not just in the 10th, but in the entire army, who supplied his guess. "I think it might be a substance they call naphtha."

"Naptha?" Pullus started irritably. "What in Hades is naptha?"

"Naphtha," Scribonius corrected, then went on, "but I've read about it. It's some sort of substance that bubbles up from the ground. It's thicker than water, sticky as honey and it's incredibly flammable." He reddened slightly at this statement of the obvious. "As you saw. But," he sighed, "it supposedly is only in this part of the world."

Pullus considered this, realizing that it didn't really matter where the substance originated, only how it behaved. Tacitly accepting his friend's assertion as being correct, he asked, "Did you read how it can be extinguished? Or controlled at least?"

Scribonius shook his head, his expression grim, and replied, "It has to burn out on its own. It can't be smothered. As we've seen," he said bitterly, "and it can't be doused with water. That just makes it spread."

Confronted with this reality, for the span of two or three heartbeats, Pullus considered the idea of conceding and leaving Spurius and his men in the hands of the gods, but this simply wasn't in his nature. His eyes narrowed, and he glanced over at the row of the largest *ballistae* that had created the breach. They had been withdrawn out of range, then their men had joined their comrades in the ranks in preparation for the assault.

"If we can't put that stuff out, then we have to figure out a way to keep them from using it." Turning, he scanned the faces of the assembled rankers, finding the one he was looking for, calling the *Immunes* who served as the chief artilleryman for the 10th. "Murena, get over here!" Naturally, the man obeyed, trotting up with his shield and javelins, stopping and coming to *intente* to render a salute, but this was one time Pullus didn't have time for the niceties, so he only nodded in recognition, immediately asking, "How much of the large ammunition do you have left?"

"Not much, Primus Pilus," Murena answered, then seeing Pullus' face darken at this vague response, added, "no more than ten stones for each piece."

"What about smaller ammunition?"

"That," Murena acknowledged, "we still have plenty of. But Primus Pilus," the *Immunes'* face clouded, and he involuntarily glanced back over his shoulder at the western wall, "we'd have to get closer to launch the smaller stones. And..."

"And you'd be in range of that *cunnus* throwing that fire," Pullus finished for him grimly. Murena had confirmed his fears, but Pullus had already begun thinking of a solution to this dilemma, so it was with barely a pause that he asked, "If we used two of the pieces and gave them the ten-pound stones, could your crews keep launching fast enough that it would make those bastards keep their heads down and not give them the chance to send that fucking fire our way?"

"We can," Murena answered, yet he was clearly hesitant. "But, Primus Pilus, that's about thirty stones for each piece, or a couple more. That won't be long enough to give the boys the chance to get to the breach, let alone to a spot where they won't be exposed like Spurius was."

Pullus shook his head, answering immediately, "We won't need that much time." Pointing to the *ballistae*, he said, "We just need time to move the other pieces close enough to throw the small ammunition. If we time it right, we can get them set up while those two pieces are keeping their heads down."

Murena considered this, slowly nodding, while the assembled Centurions exchanged glances with those men with whom they were closest, some of them nodding as well, while others shrugged, still not convinced.

"That," he conceded, "could work. Provided that we time it right."

"You need to make sure we do," Pullus told him, but rather than threaten or bluster, the giant Roman put a hand on Murena's shoulder, saying quietly, "And I have complete faith in you, Murena. I wouldn't be putting the 10th's lives in your hands if I didn't."

Chapter Eleven

On the far side of the two cities, Caesar was reorganizing his Legions; more importantly, like Pullus, he was trying to think of a way to neutralize the Parthians' weapon of Greek fire, or whatever it was. Like Scribonius, he was aware of the substance called naphtha, but unlike the Centurion, Caesar realized that ultimately, it didn't really matter whether it was a naturally occurring substance or the concoction that had been developed by the Greeks. What compounded Caesar's dilemma when compared to the one faced by Pullus was the presence of all but one piece of the Parthian artillery; which, Caesar reminded himself, he hadn't thought they possessed in the first place. This was more than just self-chastisement, it serving as a reminder to Caesar the danger of making assumptions when facing an enemy. Now, like Pullus, he stared at the walls of Ctesiphon, his mind working furiously, although as always, outwardly, he appeared as unflappable and calm as always to his subordinates.

"We could send for the rest of the scorpions," Caesar said, "but they'd just be subjected to the same thing as the ones we've lost already. Not to mention their crews." Turning to Volusenus, he asked his *Praefectus Fabrorum*, "How long to prepare the large pieces?"

"About a third of a watch." Volusenus had been expecting the question and had already performed the calculations in his head. "Although our stock of large ammunition is limited since we sent part of our inventory to the northwest camp to help create the breach."

Caesar shook his head, telling Volusenus, "I'm not going to waste the large ammunition." His mouth turned down into a grim line as he expanded, "We're going to fight fire with fire, so to speak."

Instantly comprehending where Caesar's mind was going, Volusenus warned, "That means we have to move those pieces closer than normal." He thought for a moment, then added, "We'd need a bit more time."

"How much?"

"No more than a sixth part," Volusenus answered.

"Then go ahead and get started," Caesar ordered, whereupon Volusenus turned and began trotting back in the direction of the southeast camp.

Caesar then issued instructions to the Primi Pili, who had used their mounts to come from their spots with their Legions, all of whom were standing safely out of range, but were still exposed to the blazing heat coming from the sun overhead and not the naphtha.

"Mus," Caesar turned to the Primus Pilus of the 7th, "I need to ask your men to make a sacrifice." The instant the words were out of his mouth, Caesar saw Mus stiffen, and he realized he'd made a poor choice with his words and hurriedly added, "Not of themselves," he assured Mus, "but since we're nearest your camp, I need you to send men to retrieve their *sagum*." He thought for a moment, adding the number up, and ordered, "Just from yours and the Second Century should be enough."

While he was relieved by Caesar's clarification, the Primus Pilus was confused, but he nonetheless saluted, then turned to hurry back to his Legion, which Caesar had chosen because it was the Legion closest to its home camp. As Mus bawled out orders for the men Caesar had designated to fall out and accompany him, Caesar turned to Lepidus, who hadn't been a total disaster as quartermaster, but who Caesar made sure was nearby at moments like this, determined to keep Lepidus from getting ideas in his head about giving orders during battle.

"I need you to take as many men as you need and bring back two dozen water barrels, full."

Lepidus looked confused, but like Mus, he began moving immediately, turning his horse to trot back in the same direction as Mus and his men, hurrying back to the camp.

"Lepidus!" Caesar bellowed, angry with himself as much as with Lepidus, who jerked his mount to a stop, further irritating the horseman in Caesar, looking back at his general. "Are you going to do that all by yourself? I said take men with you!"

For what was definitely the first, and would be one of the only times, Lepidus was actually thinking on his feet, and it was hard for Hirtius, Pollio, and the Primi Pili who were still there to tell who was the most surprised when the quartermaster shook his head and said, "I was going to use men from the guard Cohort in the camp since they're already there. This way, we don't have to wait for the time it takes them to run to camp."

While Caesar's officers were careful to look away, none of them would forget the sudden rush of blood to Caesar's face, which in itself was a momentous occasion that none of them would forget. However, it was also troubling, and was an indication of how rattled Caesar was by this surprise sprung on him by the Parthians. Despite the discomfort this knowledge engendered, such was their confidence in their general that they were equally sure that whatever he had in mind would counteract these new tactics and the introduction of this new weapon, as terrible as it was. With these orders given, there was a momentary pause, with the Centurions naturally congregating with each other, removing themselves a short distance from their superiors, while the men of Caesar's class essentially did the same. It was moments like these, Caesar observed, where the gulf between the classes showed itself, but he realized there were some things that were beyond even Caesar's ability to solve, and this was one of them.

"What do you think he has in mind?" Atartinus of the 11th asked the others.

"I'm not sure, but I think he wants to soak those cloaks Mus' boys are fetching, then have the artillerymen wear them when they're working their pieces," was the guess of Felix, the Primus Pilus of the 6th.

"But water doesn't put that stuff out," argued Batius, although this was more because he was naturally inclined to dispute any point made by another man.

"It may not put it out," retorted Felix, "but it's better than that *cac* hitting bare skin!"

That was something not even Batius could argue, and he didn't try.

"So let's say you're right," Clustuminus turned to Felix, "then what? What do you think he has in mind?"

"I think," Felix answered, his mouth setting in a grim line as he gazed at the walls, where he could see the Parthians lining it, "we're going to take those walls. Or," he sighed, "we're going to lose a lot of men trying."

Back on the northwest side, two of the largest *ballistae* had been pushed to a spot dangerously close to the marks left by the lone piece on the Parthian wall. Despite the fact the arm of the Parthian machine had been winched back down and was out of sight, its position had been well marked by the *immunes* of the artillery crews. Because of the paucity of the heaviest ammunition, accuracy was crucial, since the only way what Pullus had in mind would work was if the Roman artillery made it impossible for the Parthian piece to respond in kind. In the immediate aftermath of the repulse of the assault on the breach, Pullus had only been focused on the most pressing issue of rescuing Spurius and whoever survived, except in the intervening time, as they made preparations to do this, the Primus Pilus had another thought. And it was because of this thought that he made a decision not to send a courier to Caesar informing him of what had happened in their initial attempt to secure the breach. He was acutely aware of the risk he was running, but this was another moment where he was gambling that his status as one of Caesar's favorite Centurions would protect him if things went wrong. If what he had planned went as he hoped, Pullus was certain that Caesar would not only forgive him, he would endorse Pullus taking this level of initiative. However, he knew this had to work, and he spent his time as the others were preparing trotting back and forth to the northwest camp. Balbinus and the 12th had exited the camp and were standing roughly halfway between the ditch of the camp and where the 10th and the bulk of the 3rd were still arrayed.Pullus stopped briefly on his first trip back to the camp to explain to Balbinus what he had in mind.

"Are you *mad*?" Balbinus actually staggered a step backward, so taken aback by what he had just heard out of Pullus' mouth. "Caesar will crucify you!"

"If it doesn't work," Pullus agreed, but externally, he was unmoved. "But we can't leave Spurius and those boys to die."

Balbinus, as a Primus Pilus, understood in a way few others could, that what Pullus was saying was true, and that Pullus' decision wasn't just for sentimental reasons or based on his personal feelings for Spurius as a friend. If it had been just Spurius stranded, this would have been the kind of cold, clear-eyed decision that Pullus would have been more than happy to pass onto Caesar's shoulders because their general would possess the emotional distance required for making the best decision.Regardless, sacrificing the First Cohort, even not knowing how many of them were left, would be as crushing a blow to the morale of not just the 3rd, but to the entire army that would have tremendous implications which would reverberate for the rest of the campaign. What Balbinus didn't know was the other part of Pullus' plan, because if he had, he might have actually sent word to Caesar to stop Pullus from taking such a huge risk with his Legion. It was for this second part of his plan that Pullus rode his horse back to the camp, where he found the duty Centurion in command of his Tenth Cohort, Gnaeus Nasica, who had been left behind, a standard practice of Caesar's in the event that a Parthian relief column should suddenly materialize. Quickly explaining what he wanted Nasica to do, Pullus stayed only long enough to ensure that his Decimus Pilus Prior understood and was starting on his task.

"Bring them out where we are," Pullus ordered. "A Century should be enough to carry them."

Nasica, unsurprisingly to Pullus, looked confused, but he saluted and repeated his orders as the regulations prescribed. He did at least move quickly, Pullus saw, and that was enough for him, so he moved at the trot back to where the rest of his men were waiting. He arrived just in time to see the first large stone streaking away from the *ballista* that had launched it, tracking the round stone, or trying to do so, as it arced through the air. His eye never quite picked it up, although he clearly saw the shattering blow of the stone as it hit one of the crenellations, perhaps ten paces to the right of where he knew the Parthian piece was located, the actual cracking sound rolling across to him a heartbeat later. Cursing the miss under his breath, he sat on his horse, much like Caesar was doing at the same moment, watching as Murena shouted orders to the second crew, giving them the arcane information that Pullus had never understood but knew informed the artillery *immunes* what adjustments needed to be made. Within two heartbeats of Murena's correction, the second launched its stone, and this time, Pullus didn't even try to follow it, staring instead at the wall. This stone smashed into it, just below the gap between two crenellations, but hitting exactly where the Parthian piece was, prompting the men of both Legions to erupt in a roar of approval.

"Now, keep it up!" Pullus bellowed, then twisting in the saddle, waved to the men manning the other pieces, although his command wasn't needed; they had begun pushing their artillery as soon as they saw the impact.

Timing was crucial now, something that every man understood, but Pullus had done all he could at the moment. Without being ordered to do so, men in the ranks nearest to the moving artillery pieces broke ranks and ran over to help assist the *immunes*. Under normal circumstances, such a lapse in discipline as this would have been instantly and severely punished; Pullus cursed at himself for not thinking to order this earlier. A couple Centurions had started striding towards the men who had broken ranks, except they were stopped when Pullus held up his hand in a clear command to halt their intervention. Meanwhile, the two crews of the *ballistae* charged with ensuring their Parthian counterparts couldn't risk manning their own worked feverishly, with no waste motion and in a series of movements they practiced as relentlessly as the Centurions drilled their Centuries in the formation maneuvers. This meant that there was no more than a span of ten heartbeats between each heavy stone striking somewhere in the immediate vicinity of the Parthian piece. Even with a skilled crew—Murena had selected the two best from those attached to the 10th, which included his own—accuracy was a relative matter. Nevertheless, more than one stone missed the wall, sailing over it instead, but while most of them continued on until they hit the building immediately across from the parapet, Pullus just caught a glimpse of one that struck a Parthian who happened to be trying to move to a better spot. While it was too far away to make out any detail, even from where he sat, he saw a sudden explosion of red as the dark bulk of the Parthian's body disintegrated. There was a rousing cheer from the other men who saw it, but when a couple of the men helping the other pieces paused to look, Pullus roared at them that their fate would be similar if they didn't stop gawking. Rattling over the flat but rough ground, whereas Caesar had ordered his pieces to be placed evenly across the entire expanse of both the southern and eastern wall, Pullus had ordered his pieces to concentrate their emplacement into two spots. Those *ballistae* that would be responsible for maintaining the barrage started by the two pieces, now down to their last half-dozen large stones, were in roughly the same alignment as the larger pieces served by Murena, just closer to the wall. On their shoulders fell the responsibility to continue the relentless rain of stone ammunition, even if it was smaller. Once those pieces had been set up and could take over the responsibility of pinning down the Parthian artillery, Pullus had ordered four scorpions to move even closer to the wall, setting their lighter and more portable pieces up to provide more accurate support than the *ballistae*. The other scorpions, along with two larger *ballistae,* were being manhandled into position directly across from the breach; their responsibility would be to negate the archers that Pullus knew would be launching waves of arrows in the same manner that they had with Spurius. That was what? Pullus suddenly thought with some surprise, glancing up at the sun and realizing that it was now just past noon. Two watches ago? Pullus' musing was interrupted when he heard someone call his name, and he looked in the direction from which it had come, seeing Nasica at the head of a Century of men, hurrying from the direction of the camp. They were moving as quickly as possible, but their task was made more difficult because of the awkwardness that stemmed from carrying dozens of poles of varying lengths. Kicking his horse to the trot, Pullus met Nasica and his Century, pointing to where his own Cohort was standing.

"Take them to the boys in my Cohort," he commanded, then without waiting, trotted in that direction.

When Lutatius and Balbus saw him approach, they left their respective spots, as did the other Centurions, meeting at roughly the same time.

Hopping off the horse, Pullus said, "We're going to use the tent poles to make ladders."

"Ladders?" Balbus echoed, it taking a moment for the meaning to sink in. Then, without thinking, he stepped closer to Pullus, grabbing his friend by one huge bicep and whispered, "Surely you're not thinking of trying to take the city still? I'm all for going to get Spurius out of there, but…"

He didn't finish, yet there was no need.

"I just want to be prepared, Quintus," Pullus assured his friend quietly. "We're going to have to get inside the outer walls to get close enough for Spurius and his men to be able to join up with us." He shrugged and said simply, "And I'll decide then."

Balbus was not only the second in command of the 10th Legion, he was one of Pullus' two closest friends, and it was in this latter capacity that he spoke now, asking, "Are you sure about this, Titus? Because I can't imagine Caesar will…"

"No, he won't like it," Pullus agreed, then grinned at Balbus and added, "But I'll be dead if this doesn't work, so you'll be the one getting your ass chewed on by Caesar, not me."

Despite the grim subject, Balbus couldn't restrain a laugh, then shook his head.

"That's a pleasant thought," he groused. "Not only will you be dead, I'll be cleaning latrines for the rest of my life."

"If you're lucky," Pullus added, then he turned serious, his voice becoming intense. "I know I can count on you, Quintus."

"Of course." Balbus was shocked that Pullus felt the need to express the obvious. "To the death."

And, as Titus Pullus knew, this was no idle boast. Even with all that was happening and the daunting odds they were facing, Pullus had to swallow past the lump in his throat at this simple declaration by a man he thought of as a brother. However, it was Sextus Scribonius who, seeing his two best friends together, came trotting over and, when he heard Pullus' plan, offered more than just his pledge to follow his giant friend into whatever awaited them, not only because it went without saying, but he had a practical suggestion.

"You need to make sure the Parthians don't see we're carrying ladders," Scribonius had commented. "If they think that we're just going to try and get to Spurius, that can only help."

Pullus considered this, but when he glanced over at the men who were busily cutting and lashing a dozen ladders together, using the poles that had not long before held up the tents belonging to the senior officers of the three Legions, he wasn't convinced it was even possible.

"Palma said those walls are only about ten feet high," Pullus admitted reluctantly, "but if we want to hide those ladders, we're going to have to…"

"Start in *testudo*, all the way back here," Scribonius finished for him, sure this was Pullus' objection. "But right now, you've got the men working on the ladders on the opposite side of the formation, so it's impossible for them to see what we're up to. But," he hesitated, as aware as his friend what this meant, "we need to make sure they don't see it."

"The boys will be exhausted before we even get to the breach," Pullus argued, still unconvinced; it wasn't that the idea wasn't without merit, but as Primus Pilus, he had to think of every possible flaw.

"Maybe," Scribonius replied, "but they also know why we're doing this."

"I think Scribonius is right," Balbus interjected, although in keeping with the long-standing nature of their relationship, he had to qualify his endorsement by adding, "for once, anyway."

"Thank you so much," Scribonius retorted dryly, also falling back into his accustomed role, "I'll sleep better tonight."

"We'll all be sleeping tonight if this goes wrong," Pullus muttered, then relented. "All right. I see what you're saying."

Now that this was settled, Pullus wasted no time, having his *cornicen* Valerius sound the call for the Pili Priores, letting them know what would be expected of them.

"What are they doing now?"

Kambyses glanced over at Sosimenes, who had asked the question. They were standing next to each other on the parapet of the eastern wall of Ctesiphon, watching as their foes resumed their activity.

"It looks like they're going to try and keep their men protected as much as possible from what we're going to be sending them," Kambyses answered, then with a shrug he added, "Not that it will make any difference. You know as well as I do that water doesn't extinguish the naphtha; it only makes it spread."

For this was what had prompted the query from Sosimenes as they watched small groups of men rolling large barrels closer to the wall. Meanwhile, other Legionaries were shoving their own large artillery pieces back into a spot within range of the walls, yet even as the two Parthians continued watching, even when they reached a spot roughly even with one of the small brass disks that Kambyses knew marked four hundred paces from the wall, the Romans kept pushing their pieces forward.

"Well," Kambyses remarked genially, speaking loudly enough so the Parthian rankers nearby could hear, "we need to thank the Romans for making our job easier!"

As he expected, this evoked cheers from the defenders, although Sosimenes didn't seem to share their enthusiasm, instead leaning over to ask Kambyses, "Shouldn't we start now and not wait until they get those pieces into place?"

"Why?" Kambyses' eyebrow raised in surprise. "I think it will have more of an impact to allow them to think they have a chance." To emphasize his point, he waved a dismissive hand at the men rolling the barrels. "As if having water at hand is going to make a difference! No," Kambyses spoke firmly, "it will be better to let them get their hopes up."

Initially, Sosimenes was disposed to argue, but he knew Kambyses well enough to recognize by his expression that it wasn't wise to push the point.

Rather than continue in this vein, Sosimenes returned his attention to the Romans' preparations, content to watch as men pushed the small carts that Sosimenes knew contained the ammunition the Romans would be using. Yet, while the carts themselves were the same, there was something different about them that Sosimenes couldn't quite decipher, and his eyes began to water as he stared intently.

Finally, he couldn't refrain from blurting out, "What are those bundles on the carts? I've never seen them before."

At first, Kambyses' instinct was to dismiss his subordinate's question, yet as he had with Melchior, he had been forced to acknowledge the younger man was a competent commander in his own right. Consequently, he studied the scene, examining the nearest cart. The bundles appeared to be cloth of some sort, but it wasn't until the men pulled the bundles from the cart, then carried them over to the barrels that had now been placed just behind each artillery piece before Kambyses had the slightest idea.

"They're going to use those bundles some way…" he began, but by this point, the first of the bundles had been thrust into the barrel, and he saw the silvery glint of water as it sloshed out of the barrel, so he stopped to watch.

Once the first bundle was clearly soaked through, the man carrying it walked over to the artillery piece, whereupon he opened up the sodden bundle, still dripping water, then laid it across the front part of the frame of the *ballista*.

"Is that a cloak?" Sosimenes mused; as soon as Kambyses heard the other man's guess, he knew Sosimenes was correct.

Without waiting to see any more, Kambyses spun about and shouted orders to the crew manning the large artillery piece.

"Destroy that piece!" he roared. "Show them how they're wasting their time trying to protect it!"

Immediately, the men assigned to crew the largest piece began to muscle it into the proper orientation so they could fulfill Kambyses' command, and from that moment, it became something of a race between these two machines to determine which side would be the first to resume the struggle for the city. Sosimenes, with nothing to do but watch, moved his attention from one piece to the other as their respective crews hustled about. Subsequently, he was the Parthian who noticed that, once the cloth bundles now identified as the red soldiers' cloaks worn by the Legions had been removed from the top of the cart, the cargo in the carts didn't contain the racks of shaped stones that he had expected. In one of those small accidents that can have an inordinately large impact on the outcome of a battle, because there were more Romans than normal swarming around the cart and *ballista*, it took Sosimenes a fair amount of time to recognize that the bed of the cart was filled with jars, similar to but smaller than the one that even now his own artillerymen were carrying with great care to place in the basket of their own machine. It was actually the flare of fire, quickly accompanied by a trail of greasy, black smoke that informed him of what was coming. Turning towards Kambyses, he was sure that his commander had seen the same thing and understood the significance, but the older man's attention was turned away from the Romans as he watched the crew of the Parthian machine. In a corner of Sosimenes' mind, he was aware that the two opposing crews were at roughly the same point in their respective preparations to launch their own deadly cargo, and that it would be a race. Facing down the parapet meant that the Romans were to Sosimenes' right, while Kambyses was directly to his front, and the large Parthian piece was on the other side of his commander, but it was out of the very corner of his vision to his right that Sosimenes' eye picked up a sudden movement. Which, in reaction, prompted his own desperate lunge forward.

"They're using..."

Kambyses was only beginning to react, more to the feeling of Sosimenes' rush than actually seeing it, since his back was turned to his lieutenant, and had just started to turn his body when he was struck a huge blow from behind that sent him staggering forward towards the Parthian artillery piece. This was the last clear recollection he had of the next several heartbeats, as Kambyses' world seemed to explode, literally, in a blast of light and a heat so intense he felt it raise blisters on his exposed skin. But it was the horrific, gut-wrenching scream that Kambyses would never forget, despite the fact that he didn't know whether it came from his own throat or from someone else. Slamming into the stone surface of the parapet with terrific force, Kambyses had tried to get his arms out in front of him, except for a searing pain that consumed his right hand which meant that only his left was there to absorb some of the impact. The jolt of agony that shot up his left arm when he hit was as painful as his right hand, which he had somehow managed to thrust out to the side of his falling body, just of a different type. Then the rim of his helmet struck the parapet, causing his vision to fill with thousands of exploding stars, temporarily blinding him. Only in the immediate aftermath did he understand this was a blessing, because he didn't actually see Sosimenes, every inch of his body covered with the Greek fire contained in the jar hurled by the Romans and therefore blazing like a pine-knot torch, totter on his feet for what was no more than two or three heartbeats before staggering off the edge of the parapet to smash onto the paved street below. Kambyses heard, and even worse, smelled his subordinate's horrible end, while his own artillerymen seemed to be frozen in horrible fascination, staring down over the edge of the parapet to where a sizzling pile of flesh that had been a walking, talking man just a moment before lay, blazing away as the men down below were now shouting in shocked and fearful surprise. It was a testament to Kambyses' ability that he could regain his composure quickly enough that, even as the last of the stars went drifting out of his vision and he was struggling to his feet that he saw the smoking jar still in the basket of the Parthian *ballista* and most crucially understood what it meant if it was allowed to heat up and explode before it was launched.

"Yank the cord!" he roared, surprising himself at the volume he was able to muster. "Or we're all going to end up like him!"

This served its purpose, the chief of the piece reaching down and yanking the thin rope that removed the pin that kept the torsion arm in its down position. The sound of the heavy wooden throwing arm slamming into the crossbar momentarily overwhelmed the shouts of alarm still being sounded by the men down on the street, and Kambyses struggled to his feet, intent on seeing at least a measure of revenge that he felt certain would happen. Despite being woozy, he was still alert enough to turn and watch just as the smoking jar of naphtha hit the ground about five paces short of the Roman *ballista*, shattering into pieces that sent the sticky, flaming substance in a roughly oval shape that extended outward from the point of impact. He experienced a moment of a savage satisfaction as he saw a substantial portion of the flaming naphtha spatter onto the cloak that had been draped over the lower part of the Roman machine.

"Now those dogs will see how useless it is." He tried to keep the pain that was wracking him from his voice as he became more aware of the damage done to his hands. "They think a wet cloak will stop naphtha?"

Except that wasn't what the Romans intended, as instantly became clear when, instead of allowing the two forces represented by the naphtha and the sodden cloak to battle, two Romans leapt forward, one on either side of the artillery piece. Grabbing an edge of the cloak, which was now sending up clouds of steam as the flammable material still blazed away and evaporated the water soaked into the cloak, the men simply peeled it off the machine, then with an obvious and understandable care, dragged the cloak away several paces before laying it down in the dirt with the flaming side down. Even as they were doing this, Kambyses watched in something of a daze as another Roman hurried forward, carrying another sodden cloak that replaced the original. Meanwhile, the Romans who were clearly members of the permanent crew were performing their own respective tasks; while two men handled the winch that was used to lever the throwing arm back into position, another two Romans had trotted to the cart, perhaps fifty paces beyond the *ballista*, then with a bit more care carried another jar that Kambyses now understood was the Romans' answer to the Parthian secret weapon. Only once his benumbed brain had watched enough and absorbed this did Kambyses widen the scope of his attention. All along the eastern wall, and curving around to the southern wall, Kambyses saw small groups of Romans essentially performing the same series of movements he had just witnessed; the only difference was the stage each crew was in when he saw them. Shaking his head in an attempt to clear it, Kambyses couldn't stop himself from taking a couple halting steps over to the edge of the parapet to look down at what had just a moment before been Sosimenes.

"You saved my life." Kambyses' voice was audible but dulled from the growing pain caused by his scorched right hand and his broken left wrist. "I won't forget that, Sosimenes. I swear by Ashura-Mazda that you won't go unavenged."

Realizing he needed to do something to clear his head, Kambyses raised his right hand, staring at the huge, ugly blisters that had already formed on the back of it. Gritting his teeth, he clenched his fist with a convulsive power, and it took every bit of his will to keep from screaming aloud. Fortunately, it had the desired effect, meaning that when Kambyses roared his orders, his men reacted in their normal manner, leaping to their tasks.

"They want to try and burn us out?" Kambyses shouted, striding down the eastern wall in the direction of the southeast corner, where the smaller pieces of the Parthian artillery were arrayed. "Let's show them who can handle fire better!"

Before he had even finished, the air above Ctesiphon was crisscrossed with smoky trails made by flaming jars going in both directions. It would ultimately come down to a battle between the protection from fire provided by the stone walls and buildings of Ctesiphon or the makeshift defenses created by Caesar, and whoever had the will to see this most horrible method of warfare through to a conclusion.

Spurius and his survivors became aware that something was happening when they heard the shouts of alarm from the Parthians arrayed on the northern wall, directly across from their refuge. Peering through the gap between the two wooden shutters of the lone window on the northern side of the building, Spurius had seen that whoever was in command of this part of the defenses had kept more than a hundred archers positioned on the northern wall, a distance of no more than fifty paces from the warehouse. At this short range, the compound bow used by the Parthians was doubly lethal and powerful enough to penetrate a shield all the way through and continue on into the body of the man carrying it. It had been these men who had suddenly began shouting, prompting Spurius to cross over and peek through the crack between the shutters. He instantly saw that none of them were looking in his direction, but that their attention was collectively on whatever was happening to their right, in the direction of the breach in the western wall. It was not much later, just after Spurius roared at the men on the first floor to shut their mouths so he could listen, that they heard the cracking impact of stone on stone.

"I told you they wouldn't forget us, boys!" He had roared this at the top of his lungs within a heartbeat after his mind interpreted what he was hearing and added it to the reaction of those archers. "They've started the bombardment again! Help is on the way!"

Spurius had heard the term "shook the rafters" before, but this was the first time he witnessed that a noise could actually do that very thing, as the invisible force of sound issued from the men around him was powerful enough that dust started sifting down from the ceiling above him. After that, it was impossible for him to hear anything that might inform him of the progress of whatever was taking place, yet he quickly decided that it wasn't worth the effort to keep the men from talking and shouting excitedly about this first sign that they hadn't been forgotten. Over the course of the time since they had stumbled into this warehouse, Spurius had become increasingly concerned at the signs he was seeing that the spirit of his boys was ebbing ever lower; if this helped them keep the right frame of mind they might need in the event they had to fight their way out, then he was willing to overlook what was normally a lapse in discipline. Spurius didn't have to worry; fairly quickly, the men fell silent as they strained to listen to what was happening outside of their temporary refuge, trying to determine what their future held just by the sounds.

Melchior, who was standing in much the same manner as Kambyses was at this same moment, was puzzled.

"Why are they in their tortoise formation so early?"

Melchior asked this of Khortdad, who was subordinate to Melchior in the same way Melchior answered to Kambyses; unlike the relationship between Melchior and the general in overall command, Khortdad didn't enjoy the same level of trust from Melchior. That this was due to the simple truth that Khortdad was one of those Parthian nobles who, like their Roman counterparts in the patrician class, believed that their status at birth equated to competence in command, so consequently, he was naturally dismissive about any possible deeper meaning.

"Because they're scared," Khortdad sneered.

Melchior forced himself to take a breath and remind himself that he had, after all, asked the question. And, despite his instinct that told him otherwise, it was within the realm of possibility that Khortdad had uttered the truth, that after seeing their comrades burn to death in such a graphic manner, the Romans had been rattled. This didn't seem likely to Melchior, given all that he had seen to this point, and he regretted his lapse of self-discipline in asking Khortdad.

Still, he felt compelled to reply, "No, I don't think it's that."

He felt the eyes of his subordinate on him, reminding him of how he often had viewed Kambyses askance, thinking, "If only I were the one making decisions…"

And now that he was, even in a somewhat limited way, he felt a stronger sympathy to Kambyses than he had experienced previously. Ignoring the eyes on him, Melchior maintained his stare at the first of several formations of marching Romans, once more presenting a seemingly unbroken yet moving wall and roof of shields. Although he couldn't articulate why, Melchior felt certain that the Romans' choice of formation had nothing to do with the fear of being doused in the naphtha. This was especially true when Melchior understood the intent of the Roman artillery pieces that had been dragged to a spot even closer than the large *ballistae* was to pour an unceasing bombardment onto his own artillery, thereby stopping it from sending out its own cargo of liquid fire. Despite his shouted exhortations, the men who had been assigned to serve the only Parthian piece remaining on the western wall were unwilling to expose themselves to the hail of stones, and their shards, which were almost continually whizzing by above their heads. Consequently, the Romans moved unabated, slowly but inexorably, towards the western wall, and Melchior felt the inquiring eyes of the archers, who would ultimately be the first line of resistance the Romans would meet. Fighting the growing sense of desperation, Melchior tried desperately to think of some sort of counter that would put the Romans back on the defensive, as they had clearly been when he had unleashed the devastating surprise of the naphtha down on their unsuspecting heads once they had penetrated the breach. This was when the idea came to him, and to his credit, Melchior didn't hesitate, spinning about and pointing to one of the large vats of the volatile substance.

"Bring that vat to me!" he commanded, but it took him repeating himself twice before two men were willing to risk themselves to obey him.

Despite the shower of stone fragments that made a distinct whistling sound as they slashed past them, the pair followed Melchior down the rampart to where the first of the archers were waiting, their expressions expectant and concerned as the Romans continued their measured advance.

"I want each of you to get some rags, soak them in the naphtha, then tie them to your arrows," Melchior snapped, "then light them just before you loose them."

Instantly understanding and, more importantly, appreciating their commander's intent, the archers didn't hesitate, quickly getting organized into a line. Once he was satisfied that this was being done, Melchior wasted no time, hurrying back up the stairs to the rampart, just in time to see the first of the scorpion bolts streak across his front, but not before passing through the body of one of the archers without appreciably slowing down, trailing a fine red mist behind it as it left Melchior's range of vision as quickly as it had come. The archer's body jerked backward from the impact, except he didn't offer more than a low-pitched moan; Melchior decided it must have been because of the gout of blood that came rushing out of the man's mouth choked him. Before Melchior could take a step in the stricken archer's direction, the man's own staggering momentum carried him off the rampart, and he landed in the street, his body mingling with the charred corpses of the Romans who had been trapped earlier. This was the last of what Melchior would come to think of as the quiet time, as the air around him seemed to be composed of nothing but blurred lines of scorpion bolts and the slightly larger mass of the small rock ammunition. Very quickly, he learned that he had to carefully align himself with a crenellation in order to avoid being picked out by a sharp-eyed Roman scorpion gunner. Even so, he experienced a frighteningly close call, feeling the disturbed wind pushed aside by the bolt with all the force of a slap as it sought his death. Dropping into a crouch, Melchior was forced to navigate a winding path along the rampart, weaving around men who were huddled below the waist-high portion of the wall between each up thrust crenellation, careful to stay on his hands and knees as he made his way to the northwest corner. Not only would it provide the largest area of cover, it also gave him the widest vantage point to see what was happening, and even in the relatively short time it took him to crawl to the spot, when he risked taking a peek, he was dismayed to see that much had changed. Despite forming in what Melchior knew the Romans called the tortoise, which he thought was apt, much earlier than they had the first time, even with the slower pace, the leading Roman formation, led by what Melchior was sure was the largest Roman he had ever seen, was already within three hundred paces of the breach. Cursing, he scuttled over to the inner edge of the rampart and saw the archers surrounding the jar of naphtha, where they were carefully dipping what he assumed were strips of cloth they had ripped from their own clothing, then exhibiting an equal level of care, wrapped the strips around the shaft of an arrow. He had to fight the urge to shout at them to hurry up, knowing that as volatile a substance as naphtha was, they were moving with a combination of speed and prudence, not to mention the possibility that his command would startle them and cause an accident. Instead, he turned his attention beyond the section of temporary wall that was perpendicular to the northern wall and was attached to the corner of the second building, where he knew the surviving Romans of the first attempt still cowered.

Just as Spurius' men had discovered the danger in lingering anywhere near the jagged hole they had created in the northern side of the warehouse, the Parthians Melchior had insisted stay nearby were careful not to expose themselves to a javelin hurled at them through the same hole. For a brief moment, Melchior considered sending more men to the shorter temporary wall between the warehouse and the northern outer wall. Any Parthian standing on the makeshift rampart would be in a prime position, almost directly above the passage the Romans had created to get inside the warehouse, and their compound bows at that short range could do massive damage. If he did that, he could at least ensure that the Romans trapped inside who their comrades seemed intent on rescuing would be slaughtered, then he quickly dismissed the idea, although he couldn't articulate why he did so. After all, with this temporary wall hemming in any Roman attempt to penetrate the breach and drive deeper into the city, even if they had successfully neutralized the large artillery piece, once inside the outer walls, with this addition by Anaxagoras, the Romans would still be contained within what Melchior was determined to make a killing ground. The mute evidence of its effectiveness to this point lay strewn about on the ground level, a combination of charred or feathered corpses depending on whether the Roman had fallen because of the naphtha or from his archers. Those dead Romans who had at least one and usually more shafts protruding from their bodies had been the lucky ones, Melchior thought grimly before turning his attention back to the more immediate matter. For whatever reason, Kambyses' sub-commander decided that his best hope lay in doing what he could to keep this second Roman assault from negotiating the breach and gaining entry into the city. Despite feeling confident that this temporary wall would make sure this was as deep the Romans got into Seleucia, Melchior felt it was better to stop them outside the permanent walls. No, he decided, while he would keep the men that were already there in their current spots, he wasn't willing to draw strength away from the outer wall. And, returning his attention back to the situation outside the city, Melchior saw that the moment was rapidly approaching. Risking just a glance, he was only partially relieved to see that most of the men he had designated for his special task were either already back up on the rampart or were ascending the stone stairs, each of them clutching a number of arrows, the rags tied around them still dripping the sticky fluid that he hoped would be enough. Realizing he had done all he could do, Melchior took a deep breath, then stood up so he had a better view of the ground beyond the walls. Now, he thought grimly, we'll see how devoted these Romans are to their friends.

Contrary to his normal practice, Titus Pullus was marching closer to his Century than he usually did, and while none of his men commented on it, that he did so wasn't lost on any of them. Otherwise, he presented the same demeanor and attitude as he had hundreds of time before this; that he had picked up an undamaged shield wasn't unusual either. To anyone familiar with the Legions, like Titus Pullus, the *testudo* formations of the Centuries belonging to his and Scribonius' Cohort were slightly unusual in their configuration, but he felt fairly certain that the Parthians wouldn't notice. The reason for the difference was based in Scribonius' suggestion that the presence of the freshly made ladders be kept hidden from Parthian eyes. Consequently, Pullus had reduced the width of his formation to accommodate for the length of the ladders, but it was only by one file. Indeed, Pullus thought, there are Legates who wouldn't notice the difference, so the Parthians are even less likely to do so. Still, this was just one more factor added to his already taut nerves, which had been stretched even more tightly than a normal assault on a fortified city would be; every step he took, Pullus' thoughts were with his friend Spurius and whoever remained inside the walls. As he had promised, Pullus had found room for Palma, albeit in what would be the last rank of the First Century, aware of the difficulty of integrating a new man into a rank just before the fighting was about to start. At least this way, he had reasoned, Palma wouldn't be in the front. With the normal cadence, Pullus and the 10th marched in much the same manner that Spurius and the 3rd had earlier that morning, moving with a slow but measured step that brought them closer to the wall. This time, however, Pullus took comfort in the sounds of the artillery, both large and small pieces, each of them sending speeding missiles that, with any luck, would not only keep the Parthians' heads down, but would reduce the number of bows and spears facing them. Pullus had prepared his Centurions for the inevitability that they had already witnessed when Spurius' Legion had assaulted.

"I don't think it's likely that there are going to be less archers on the wall," Pullus had explained, "although it's possible that Spurius and his boys took down a fair number. But," his tone reflected his pessimism, "I'm not planning on that being the case. So, be ready."

And now, Pullus realized when he saw the serried line that marked the outer boundary of the range of the Parthian bow, we're about to find out. Yet, when the leading edge of Pullus' Century reached the clearly marked boundary and no sudden movement occurred that Pullus knew would be the signal the Parthians were loosing, he had to fight the flicker of hope he felt. No, he chided himself, they're just waiting for us to get closer. Maybe they're low on arrows; the optimistic part of his nature provided this happy thought, but especially in battle, Pullus wasn't particularly susceptible to such bouts of cheerful speculation. Nevertheless, Pullus and his men drew ever closer to the wall, still without any overt sign that the Parthians had even noticed their approach. Just when Pullus, despite screaming at himself, felt his body relax, there was a sudden blur of motion from the wall, but while his mind told him that it was the first wave of Parthian arrows, there was something different that took him an instant to identify.

"Fire!"

It was impossible for Pullus to know who shouted it first, but the cry clearly came from at least three of his men in the front rank who had been peering over the top of their shields and had seen the bright streaks that issued from the western wall on either side of the breach. Well, Pullus thought, at least it makes them easy to track, even as his left arm lifted his borrowed shield, while his eyes picked up the individual missiles that posed the greatest threat. Fire arrows had little effect on a *testudo*; at least, this was Pullus' experience, because the flammable material that was wrapped around each shaft quickly burned away, and the wood of the shield was protected by the painted surface. That, as he was about to learn, was only true under certain conditions. When the rags had been soaked in naphtha, however, the result was not only quite different, it was devastatingly effective. This wasn't apparent to Pullus in the heartbeats of time immediately after the first wave of missiles came slicing down out of the air, striking the First Century. Some arrows, hitting at an odd angle, skipped off a shield, which created a flare of sparks and fire before hitting the ground off to the side of the *testudo*. Far more struck squarely, hitting a shield, except while the metal arrowheads didn't penetrate far, they didn't need to do so. Despite the fact that the first of the arrows that struck his Century were several files away from Pullus, he felt as much as saw the flare of fiery heat as large droplets of flaming naphtha splattered onto the shields next to the one that was actually struck. This was alarming enough; while Pullus had been subjected to fire arrows before, they had never behaved in the manner he was seeing now as, rather than sputtering out, the flames actually seemed to grow in strength, and more horribly, spread across the stricken man's shield. Rather than the normal sound of hobnailed soles crunching on the ground, now Pullus heard the sounds of a growing concern, quickly reaching panic levels as the men around the Legionary with the now fiery shield began shouting their alarm. If this had been the only man, it would have been bad enough, but Pullus only had to turn his head slightly to the left to see that easily a half-dozen shields throughout his Century were in similar straits.

"Primus Pilus," Pullus barely recognized the voice of the man whose shield was now blazing away, "what do I do? What do I do?"

338

The reality was that Pullus didn't really know, and he wasn't given time to think as another wave of flaming arrows descended down with unbelievable speed, and he barely got his own shield up in time to block a missile that trailed fire behind it. In one respect, he was lucky because he actually twisted his left wrist outward at the last instant, depriving the arrowhead from striking squarely so that it struck a glancing blow before caroming off to stick into the hard ground. Regardless of this quick action, some of the naphtha transferred from the rag to the surface of his shield in the fraction of an eye blink's time it was in contact with it, leaving what, to Pullus, would have looked like a single streak of fire. While he quickly became aware that there was still a residue of the flaming substance on his shield by the heat he began feeling as it was transferred through the layers of wood, Pullus couldn't spare the attention to his own problems. Even as the words of the Gregarius were still lingering in the air, more shields of the men of his Century were struck, so that before the span of ten heartbeats, the many-legged but unified beast that was a Roman *testudo* had transformed into a fiery mass of uncoordinated movement as men began to give in to their fear of fire, which Pullus saw was in danger of becoming greater than their fear of him and Lutatius. Seeing this, Titus Pullus was as close to panic as he had ever been, and he honestly didn't know what to do.

Kambyses' frustration grew with every shattered fire-pot absorbed by the drenched cloaks that the Romans had devised as a defense. Regardless of the evidence before him, the Parthian commander insisted that his artillery continue flinging the fire-pots, but while they continued to shatter in spectacular but small explosions, the vessels didn't contain the bulk needed to inflict damage from their impacting on a target. And, while it didn't please any of the owners of the cloaks to see them absorbing the flaming naphtha, compared to the alternative, none of them were complaining openly about it, at least much. Caesar, still on Toes and at a safe remove, hadn't been sure this idea would work, but when it became obvious that it was effective, he allowed his mind to roam a bit farther out from the immediate situation. We're going to have to replace those cloaks before winter sets in, he thought to himself, and before he was absorbed in the next new problem that would inevitably arise, he looked over his shoulder and caught Apollodorus' eye. His servant quickly trotted over, scribbling down the note Caesar dictated, and then the general's attention was back on the action in front of him. Although it was true that this unusual usage of the cloaks had worked better than Caesar had hoped, his worries were far from over, and a short time later, when it became clear that the Parthians weren't willing to shift their own tactics, Caesar sent Lepidus back to supervise bringing even more *sagum* forward, as well as the replenishment of the water barrels. What nagged at Caesar was the same thing that plagues all commanders in the field, no matter how skillful they may be, and that is what they don't know. Specifically, what worried the Roman general was why his Parthian counterpart continued in his attempts to destroy the Roman artillery in the same manner as the first scorpions, when it clearly wasn't working. Caesar's primary concern had been based in the knowledge of what he would have done in the Parthian's boots and seen the ineffectiveness of what had worked before, which was to switch back to the more conventional ammunition, using stones. While it was certainly true that trying to strike a *ballista* with a stone ball, no matter how smoothly shaped, was a chancy proposition at best, if it *did* hit, it would do massive damage to the piece. Almost as effective, and slightly easier, was aiming for the members of the crew, although that was a matter of timing in catching them at a vulnerable moment when they were occupied with their own tasks and unable to dodge out of the way. No, Caesar thought with an increasing unease, this Parthian is being profligate with his most powerful weapon, despite that it was not as effective as it was the first time, and Caesar felt certain it was for a good reason. He had originally assumed, based on what little he admittedly knew about the substance, naphtha wouldn't be in unlimited supply. Yes, it bubbled up from the ground, but Caesar had only heard of two certain sources, while there was a rumor of a third, far, far away at the easternmost fringe of Parthian lands. However, if Caesar were to judge simply by the manner in which his enemy insisted on continuing to send firepots at them, it would strongly suggest that the Parthian's supply of the flammable material was much more plentiful than he would have thought. As Caesar was acutely aware, protecting his artillery, while important, wasn't nearly as crucial as what came next, when he sent his men forward once again with their ladders. He had pinned his hopes on the Parthians' exhausting their supply of naphtha before he sounded the order to advance, or coming close enough to it that they switched to their conventional ammunition. This should have happened already, Caesar felt sure; there should be rocks sailing through the air instead of these smoking fire-pots. Lepidus and the working party he had commandeered were returning by this point; the men carrying the cloaks ahead of those rolling the barrels of water. Despite the overall effectiveness of the doused cloaks, Caesar had been informed that his men had still sustained some casualties of the worst sort, when the Legionaries manning the artillery pieces had been struck, despite them being wrapped in a wet cloak as well as the pieces they served.

It wasn't until one such incident happened within Caesar's view that he understood what seemed unlikely to him, when a man of the 7th, the Legion nearest to his position, had been struck full force by one of the fire-pots. Even with the added layer of protection, the man was instantly consumed in flames of such magnitude and heat that the stricken man clearly panicked, while his comrades were unable to knock him down to at least try and get the flaming cloak off him. Instead, Caesar saw the man sprint in the general direction of the camp, running so quickly that he was beyond help before anyone around him could even attempt to help. In horror, Caesar, and the rest of the men within view, watched as the man, whose body was almost completely obscured by flame, slowed from his all-out sprint, to what could be called a staggering trot, before finally toppling over, still burning brightly. Swallowing the bile that had threatened to force its way up out of his throat, Caesar moved with a deliberate slowness as he returned his attention back to the walls. Still, the air was streaked with the smoking trails of naphtha, and it prompted Caesar to recognize that he could no longer delay.

"Sound the advance," he said to his *cornicen*, who hesitated, but only briefly, before filling his lungs with air, then sounding the series of notes that sent word to his men that Caesar's Legions were going to try again.

"We're down to a half-dozen pots for each piece," Kambyses was informed by another younger noble named Kariel, who had stepped up into the void of command created by the death of the unfortunate Sosimenes. When Kambyses didn't respond immediately, Kariel asked, "Do you want me to hold those in reserve? For when they're closer to the wall with their ladders?"

Kambyses considered for a moment, then nodded his head but didn't verbally reply. Kariel wheeled about and hurried to give the appropriate orders, and Kambyses didn't pay any more attention to his subordinate's actions, returning his gaze to the ordered lines of Roman Centuries who were clearly in the final preparations before advancing once more. This time, Kambyses knew full well that the Romans wouldn't be stopped from at least reaching the walls. Staring down the length of the southern wall, Kambyses watched as his men began to realize this on their own, with the archers, numbering about a third of the total force standing on the rampart, now stepping forward to a spot where they could have a clear path to the approaching enemy. Seeing that the sub-commanders charged with their particular contingent seemed to have matters in hand, he turned his attention to the shorter section of the eastern wall, expecting to see much the same. He did, but unlike with the scene along the southern wall, it seemed to Kambyses that these men were being subjected to a more intense barrage of scorpions and rocks, forcing them to move more slowly into their positions. This naturally caused Kambyses to move slightly so he could peer around the edge of the crenellation that was protecting him, yet despite having only the briefest spans of time before he had to jerk his head back when a sharp-eyed Roman manning a scorpion sent a bolt through the gap Kambyses' head had just been occupying, the Parthian had enough time to see the cause. For reasons that didn't immediately occur to Kambyses, the Romans had shifted more artillery from their positions facing the southern portion of the wall, yet while he knew this was meaningful, he found it impossible to decipher. Part of his problem was based in the almost continuous sound of whizzing bolts and the thunderous crash when a rock hurled by a *ballista* slammed into the wall, making it difficult for him to concentrate. The major part of his dilemma, however, was based in his inability to see any real advantage this shift gave the Romans. Despite all that had taken place this day that at least partially restored Kambyses' confidence that he and his men were a match for the Romans, not gone from his mind was the memory of the battle on the ridge. Therefore, the only certainty in his mind was that his adversary had a reason for making this change, no matter how nonsensical it may have seemed from a standard tactical viewpoint. By assaulting the shorter part of the wall, Caesar was giving Kambyses the ability to pull men from the southern wall, provided that the Romans' focus along that side continued to be evenly distributed. This was one of the few times where the Parthian infantry was, if not superior to the Legions, at least a match, because of the longer reach of their primary, in fact their only weapon, their spears. Climbing a ladder, the Romans had to grip their shields with one hand, the ladder with the other, then just before they reached the level of the parapet, draw their blades before leaping up and over the waist-high barrier. Knowing they would only choose the spots between the crenellations gave his men a virtual certainty about where their enemy would first appear, in between and framed by the two higher stones of the crenellation. But if Caesar was going to throw more of his men against the eastern wall, which seemed likely, why would he do that knowing it negated his advantage provided by the sheer length of the southern wall? Before Kambyses could think this through, the strange sound that he had learned were the Roman horns began blaring, the sound rippling across his front, down the eastern wall, then to his right along the southern wall, as each Cohort relayed a signal. Kambyses quickly understood its meaning when, at last, the Romans began moving in earnest, heading for the wall. Now, the Parthian thought, I'll find out what this Caesar is really up to.

"Drop the shields that are burning! Drop your shields! Drop them and follow me!"

Only much later would Titus Pullus rethink his decision, one that he made in a state of mind as close to sheer panic as he had ever experienced. Yet, somehow, he understood that the best, maybe the only hope for his men and himself lay in speed. He didn't wait for any kind of acknowledgment, just taking off at a sprint, his long legs and bulk making it more difficult to get up to speed, but once he did, his strides ate up the ground. Even with the wind now whistling between the flaps of his helmet and his ears, Pullus dimly heard the shouts of his men whose hesitation cost them a fraction of extra time, but he could clearly hear they were following him.

"Protect the men with the ladders!"

He bellowed this, over and over, even as he ran, yet he never looked back once he got to full speed, holding his shield up above his head as his long legs pumped furiously, propelling him across the hard ground, still studded with arrows and littered with the bodies of the Roman fallen serving as obstacles. This was part of the reason he didn't dare turn his attention away from what lay ahead of him, but ultimately, Titus Pullus was certain there was no need to check on his men to make sure they were behind him, and it wasn't just from their noise that seemed to propel him forward that gave him this confidence. He had been leading these men in one capacity or another for several years; he knew them and, more importantly, they knew him. What the men of the 10th understood was that Titus Pullus led from the front, and wherever the fighting was the thickest, he could invariably be found there, wielding his Gallic-forged blade with a combination of the enormous power that came from his size, but also with a skill forged by the untold number of watches he had spent since he was a young boy in Baetica, honing his craft. And that craft was dealing out death and destruction to the enemies of Rome, and as he had so often before, Titus Pullus was rushing as quickly as his legs could carry him to bring this deadly ability to the waiting Parthians. Arrows continued to streak down, but ironically, the fact that they were aflame made them not only easier to track, their flight was slowed to a point that made them easier to dodge. Nevertheless, even above the sound of his lungs sucking in huge gulps of air, Pullus could hear shouts of despair as men had their shields struck, which forced them to be discarded; worse than that were the shrieks of men, his boys, who had been unable to dodge out of the way while on the run and whose bodies were pierced by one of the flaming arrows. If he had stopped to think about it, to Pullus, this would have been a horrible fate; perhaps not as bad as burning alive, but close to it, having that nasty flaming substance thrust deep into your body to cook you from the inside.

Fortunately for Pullus, he simply didn't have the luxury of time, forced as he was to concentrate his entire being on weaving his way closer to the wall, choosing an erratic course that, while it made him more difficult to hit, meant he had much farther to run. To an uninformed observer, and if the truth were known, even to someone like Caesar if he had been there to witness it, this was the sort of headlong, foolhardy and, frankly, maddening kind of thing Titus Pullus was known for almost as much as his skill. To the men under his command, to his friends like Scribonius and Balbus, to his ostensible slave Diocles who was more his friend, Titus Pullus' behavior under such circumstances seemed to not just defy the favor of the gods, but was a challenge to them, as if the giant Roman were daring them to strike down one of those who, in his own way, was seen by others as beloved by them as was Caesar. By distancing himself, he provided a tempting target, and with his sudden changes of direction and speed, coupled with his obvious status as a Centurion of Rome, one that several of the Parthian archers on the wall chose to try to bring down. Although it was true that, even in their relatively ragged spacing, the rankers of the advancing Legion were an easier target, it was a matter of pride and prestige to these archers to be the man to claim striking down this giant Roman who dared to think he couldn't be killed. Which, contrary to what his friends, comrades, and men of the ranks thought, was very much a calculated move on the part of Titus Pullus. To be sure, there was a healthy streak of hubris in his makeup; he took a great deal of pride in his status, and even more in the legend he was building for himself, meaning his act wasn't entirely selfless. However, at the core of his decision was the bedrock belief that he, Titus Pullus, was the best man to offer himself up as the kind of tempting target that would help save some of his men, or almost as importantly, the use of their shields. Despite the serpentine nature of his advance, Pullus still closed the gap relatively quickly, getting underneath the effective range of the archers, but not before, like a large proportion of his Century, he had been forced to discard his shield when it got too hot to keep in his grasp. His shield was actually struck twice, but he kept it as long as he could, even as the intense flames of the naphtha-soaked rag melted the coat of paint and varnish away to begin eating into the wood. Gritting his teeth as the metal boss began to radiate its own heat as the naphtha that had splattered on it blazed fiercely, even after the second shaft struck it, he retained his grip. The sight this made, a huge Roman who was still advancing, holding his shield above his head, despite the fact it was now fully aflame, unnerved the Parthian spearmen who had been shoved and prodded up the interior of the rubble pile so they were now waiting in the breach. Finally, Pullus threw his blazing shield aside, the excruciating pain along the tops of his fingers that had been closest to the metal boss too much to bear; despite this, he barely broke stride. Then, without really remembering exactly how he got there, Pullus was at the foot of the rubble pile, facing a quadruple line of Parthians waiting at the top of the pile, their spears now jutting out from behind their wicker shields. In their own way, his lungs were as fully afire as his shield had been, his huge chest expanding to the point he could feel the stricture of his mail shirt, which kept him from fully inflating them. Because his breathing was so harsh, he could barely hear anything else, so it was with the corners of his vision that he sensed the streaking scorpion bolts, the gunners who had been saving their ammunition resuming their volleys now that he was close to the breach. Pullus didn't pause long, certainly not enough time to regain his wind, but he did risk a glance over his shoulder to see how close his boys were to reaching him. It was a piss-poor excuse for a formation; Pullus' instant thought was that his men looked more like a barbarian mob of warriors, but most importantly, they were within fifty paces of him. That was close enough for Pullus, and he began his ascent of the rubble pile, his sword now out, his face a mask of cold fury as he closed on the waiting Parthians.

Chapter Twelve

Kambyses got his answer about what Caesar had in mind, much sooner and in a more powerful way than the Parthian would have liked. The three Legions arrayed along the eastern wall, the shortest side of the coming assault, moved forward in their *testudo*, closing the distance much more slowly than Titus Pullus and the 10th were doing at roughly the same moment. As they did so, however, there was also movement along the half-mile of the southern wall, except it wasn't exactly what Kambyses had been expecting. While it was true that, like the Legions on the short side, the six Legions were advancing as well, it wasn't with their entire strength. As the front line of Centuries began their advance, along with the Centuries immediately behind them, the rearmost line of all six Legions also began moving, but not in following the advancing front line; instead, they moved parallel to the southern wall, heading in the general direction of the southeast corner. This maneuver confused Kambyses, if only for a moment, but he finally understood what Caesar was planning. It was at this moment that Kambyses learned one of the hard lessons all commanders in battle must face when orders are given, but for whatever reason, aren't followed. His recognition of this truth began with an innocuous thought: Where was Kariel? Suddenly, the Parthian commander realized that he hadn't seen his subordinate, thrust into the role of second in command with the death of Sosimenes, whose charred corpse was still within Kambyses' range of vision, for some time. So much had been happening that it took Kambyses an extra span of heartbeats to even remember why Kariel wasn't by his side.

Turning to the man in command of the unit of archers who were even then pointing their bows skyward as they drew their bowstrings back to their cheeks, Kambyses was forced to wait for the man to give the command to loose, then demanded, "Where's Kariel? Have you seen him?"

"No, Excellency," was the reply, but when it was clear he had nothing else to offer, Kambyses gave him a disgusted wave.

Finally, he was forced to send a runner down the length of the southern wall in search of his new second in command, yet even at this point, he wasn't worried, although this lack of concern didn't last long. Dividing his attention between the eastern portion of the wall and the southern, he waited for his artillery to send their last stock of naphtha down into the Roman formations. A half-dozen pots for each piece wasn't ideal, but that was still at least sixty of them, which he felt sure was more than enough to break this assault. When the only artillery missiles that issued from the walls were in the form of the stone balls, Kariel's disappearance took on a meaning much more important than just a subordinate vanishing. Unconsciously tightening his grip on the stone edge of the parapet, Kambyses stared down the length of the southern wall, trying to pick out the pieces there, but there were too many men crowding the parapet. Nevertheless, he tried to will the artillery to begin sending the deadly, flaming missiles down onto the raised shields of the Romans, except it never happened. Despite the evidence before him, the Parthian tried to maintain hope, yet when he shifted his attention outside the wall, it took him a moment to locate the partially buried brass disks, still catching the rays of the sun. Only then did he realize that it wasn't a matter of being in range for the naphtha pots, which was about a hundred paces shorter than the conventional ammunition. Even so, he counted the disks twice before his mind accepted that the Romans were now well past the third disk from the wall and within the range to rain fire down on them. And if that hadn't happened by now, Kambyses thought with a growing sense of dread, that meant it wasn't going to happen. Consequently, the reappearance of the runner, who had to thread his way past his comrades along the southern wall, was more of a formality that confirmed what Kambyses had already surmised.

"Excellency," the man gasped, not speaking until he had dropped to his knees and placed his forehead against the stone parapet, "I regret to inform you that Excellency Kariel has been killed."

It didn't really matter, but Kambyses was sufficiently curious to ask, "How did it happen?"

"He was struck by one of those accursed iron bolts," the runner answered unhappily, more out of fear that Kambyses would take his ire at Kariel for his inconsiderate act of dying than any feeling for another Parthian noble.

Fortunately for the runner, Kambyses wasn't like his dead counterpart Cyaxares, so the only thing the man received was a grunted command to rise and the order to remain nearby. Now that he knew there would be no more chance to use his most potent weapon, Kambyses began the grim process of trying to decide what the next best tactic was, although even as he did so, in his heart, he realized it was too late. Oh, he was sure that the stones would inflict casualties; even as this thought was going through his mind, he saw one of the leading *testudos*, about halfway down the southern wall, suddenly seem to fall apart as men went staggering or falling out of the normally tight formation, caused by a stone missile slamming right into its midst. Nevertheless, even as he watched, the Romans quickly reorganized themselves, and when they resumed their advance, there was what appeared to be only two men left behind, along with some objects that Kambyses couldn't identify, but he assumed were shields shattered by the stone. One of the stricken Romans was moving, albeit slowly, as he dragged himself back in the direction of the second row of Centuries that formed the first main line, while the other one lay still. This was certainly good to see, but Kambyses knew this wasn't going to be enough to stop the Romans from reaching the walls. Unlike Pullus, Caesar had made no attempt to hide the fact he was carrying ladders, and because of their higher than normal height, the ends protruded at least two feet from each end of their *testudo*. And as Kambyses counted, he discovered that each Century carried two ladders. He returned his attention to the shifting rear line, seeing that the Centuries closest to the southeast corner had already turned and were now moving into position behind the advancing Legions approaching the eastern wall. It was, Kambyses realized grimly, down to a case of mathematics. Caesar was gambling that his men could overwhelm those belonging to Kambyses, and although the Parthian was aware that, in this particular situation, his spearmen actually had an advantage over their enemies, who would be ascending a ladder while trying to avoid being struck by either a missile or a spear, what wasn't anywhere near certain to Kambyses was whether it would be enough of one to keep the Romans from taking the city. He also realized that this question would be answered, soon, one way or the other.

Pullus continued his headlong charge, this time up the rubble pile, but once more with a level of calculation that was at odds with the appearance he was presenting of a man lost to the bloodlust of battle. Unlike his dash to get under the arc of the deadly fire arrows, he ran in a straight line up the pile, his legs churning furiously to counteract the steep pitch. While not particularly far in terms of the distance that had to be covered, it was still far enough for the waiting Parthians at the top to estimate his speed and, most importantly, when he would come within reach of their spears. This was especially crucial to the two Parthians that Pullus was clearly aiming for, roughly in the middle of the line of spearmen who blocked the breach, and despite their relative lack of experience and training, killing this Roman, no matter how large, seemed to be a foregone conclusion. Unlike his normal practice, Titus Pullus didn't unleash a roar from his powerful lungs, for the simple reason he couldn't spare the amount of air it took, but his right hand was pulled back above his shoulder so the point of his sword was just inches from the rim of his helmet. While the Parthians couldn't have identified it as such, this was what the Romans called the second position, where the point of attack originated above an enemy's shield. Usually used as a feint by most Legionaries, this was due more to the fact that they tended to be shorter than their adversaries; this wasn't a problem for Pullus. Then, just when he seemed about to step right into the range where his nearest foes could simply thrust their arms out and this Roman would essentially run himself onto their spear points, with a remarkable amount of control, particularly for a man as large as he was, Pullus stopped his forward momentum. Not only that, he also dropped to one knee, in a sort of crouch that, for just the eye blink of time that was needed, confused the entire Parthian front line, all of whom naturally had their attention on what seemed to be the most immediate threat. The javelins that came slamming into them weren't in as great a number as Pullus would have liked, but they were effective enough as his two nearest adversaries were suddenly thrown back by the force of the missiles. Even throwing uphill, Pullus' men had managed to generate enough power that they avoided skewering their Primus Pilus and, more importantly, send those Parthians who had been their targets staggering back. Naturally, not all of the javelins struck fleshy targets, but the distinctive crackling, snapping sound that signaled the hardened triangular heads of the javelins had punched through wicker shields was almost as satisfactory to Pullus' ears. The Parthians who had been his most immediate threat had given way; one had been quick enough to get his shield up but had nevertheless gone staggering back a couple of steps, while the other one hadn't been as fortunate. He remained standing for the span of a heartbeat, his shield slipping from his hand as he stared down at the javelin embedded in his stomach, in the kind of shocked surprise that Pullus had seen more times than he cared to remember, just long enough for a javelin from the second volley to take him higher up in the chest. This swept him off his feet, and only then, knowing those men of his Century who had been close enough behind Pullus had expended both javelins, did their Primus Pilus rise back up to his feet. Except he didn't just rise; in one fluid motion, he took a large step forward with his left foot and, reaching out with his left hand, ignoring the flash of intense pain that came from flexing his blistered fingers, snatched up the wicker shield of the twice-hit Parthian, whose body was just crumpling to the ground. Pullus was never able to articulate, or really remember, how he was able to do such things, timing the rising to his feet at the precise moment that allowed him to grasp that wicker shield, even while it was still falling to the ground as it slipped from its owner's grasp. Despite managing to grab it, things didn't go entirely Pullus' way because he was forced to fumble with the shield a bit in an effort to turn it around so he could grasp its handle. The Parthian spearman whose shield had saved him managed to retain his wits, so that even as he went stumbling back from the impact, he managed to keep his eyes on the giant Roman. This particular Parthian was, as one might expect, given his spot in the front rank of the line blocking the breach, an experienced warrior, a survivor of the battle on the ridge, along with dozens of smaller battles, albeit against bandits, and when his *satrap* went marauding into the lands bordering his own. Seeing Pullus distracted, he recognized this was the best opportunity he would likely have to strike down a Roman, particularly one of their Centurions, and he didn't hesitate, lunging forward with his body as his arm thrust his spear out even further. The truth was that, with almost any other Roman, this Parthian might have been successful, but his gods didn't favor him when he placed him in the line facing Titus Pullus. Seeing the Roman's eyes flicker in the direction of the shield as he was forced to locate it visually, the Parthian's thrust was well aimed, but while the point of his spear drove straight and true directly for the Roman's heart, it never reached its target. As quick as the Parthian's thrust might have been, Pullus' sweep upward with his sword, originating just below his own waist, was quicker and had so much power behind it that the edge of the Roman's blade sliced through the thick shaft, just a matter of inches behind the point without appreciably slowing down. The consequence was that, while the Parthian did strike a blow, it was with just the shaft, while the spear point and a few inches of wood went spinning crazily in a downward direction. Pullus gasped in pain from the shock of the blow, as the part of his mind that managed to stay removed from the screaming fear of the moment acknowledged the power behind the Parthian's thrust. Unfortunately for the Parthian, who was now without a shield and armed with little more than a blunt pole, he wasn't given time to recover from the shock of seeing what he had been sure would be a killing thrust so quickly and definitively negated. Pullus' sword, now raised back above his shoulder from the momentum of his block of the Parthian's spear, wasn't oriented to allow for a proper thrust, which was always the preferred method of attack when using the short, stabbing weapon the Romans called the Spanish sword. It was an axiom that, first as a weapons instructor, then as Optio, and now Primus Pilus, Pullus had drilled into his men; the point always beat the edge. But while this was true in a general sense, Pullus and all other veterans had learned that, in battle, there were times when this didn't apply, and Pullus knew this was one of those occasions. With his blade out and parallel to the ground as it was, Pullus simply rotated his wrist, while he began to swing his arm at the same time, first moving it outward from his body before bringing it across his front. While his blade was still parallel to the ground, it was now at a perpendicular angle to where it had been less than an eye blink before. Even with his size, as this Parthian had already observed, Titus Pullus moved with the speed of a much smaller man, and it was with this speed that, within no more than a full heartbeat after his Gallic blade had sliced through the wooden shaft of the Parthian's sword, it was now slicing through something else. This time, it was a perfectly aimed blow that struck the Parthian, whose expression still showed the shocked surprise of seeing his attack thwarted with such ease, at the base of his neck, just above his shoulders. Once more, Pullus' sword barely slowed, powered by the muscles of his arm and aided by the twisting motion he applied to his entire torso, thereby adding to the force, and this time, it was the Parthian's turbaned head that went tumbling, in a gruesome mimicry of the spearhead just an instant before. The torso remained standing for perhaps a half-heartbeat, the hands still clutching the useless wooden shaft of the spear, but Pullus was already turning his attention to the Parthian he deemed the next greatest threat, to his immediate right. This Parthian was actually a man from the second line who had remained composed enough to step forward when the comrade directly in front of him had been killed in the second volley of javelins. That he had done so was commendable; that he had just stepped forward and didn't have his feet solidly underneath him meant that it was his destiny to outlive the man he had replaced by a span of only three or four heartbeats longer. Killing this Parthian with a more conventional thrust, Pullus had created a bit of a pocket of space for himself, but by then the first of his men came scrambling up beside him. Sensing this presence and correctly interpreting it was one of his men from the direction he appeared at the corner of his vision, Pullus recognized the voice of Dento, the veteran in the front rank who Pullus had chastised for dropping his shield not long before.

"We didn't want you to have all the fun, Primus Pilus!"

At least, that was what Pullus thought Dento said, although he was quite out of breath, but before he could answer, another of his men came to his side, this time on his right. Only then did Pullus risk a quick glance and saw that it was Balbus.

"What the fuck are you doing up here?" Pullus' tone was half-snarl, half-gasp of surprise.

"Making sure you don't do anything stupid," Balbus shot right back, although he was breathing as heavily as Dento.

Before anything more could be said, the Parthians of the second and third line were ordered forward, not by a shouted command or a blast from a horn, but by the crack of a whip. Because of his height, Pullus was the only one who, drawn by the sound, could see a heavily armored Parthian, just behind the rearmost rank, his beard gleaming like a crow's wing, as were the ringlets that hung from under his helmet. Their eyes met, and Pullus' lip lifted in a sneer, yet this was all the attention he could devote to the commander, a man who had to use a whip to get his men to obey. Despite this sign that these Parthians weren't as willing to engage as they perhaps should have been, they did come forward, their spear points bristling more than three feet beyond their wicker shields.

"All right, boys, you know how to handle these *cunni*," Pullus bellowed. "Get inside the points!"

Before his men could respond, the Parthians suddenly lunged forward in a ragged line, closing the last couple of paces between themselves and the Romans. Hoisting his appropriated shield, Pullus locked his elbow into the hollow just above his hipbone, then moved just a bit to his right to get closer to Balbus' shield. This wasn't the normal manner in which either Centurion was accustomed to fighting, at least for some time, but the habits of the Gregarius that had been drilled into them from their first days as raw *Tirones* didn't just go away. Instantly, both men's bodies responded to the training, and they worked as a team, Balbus protecting Pullus with his shield, while Pullus protected Dento. Taking the first spear thrust on his shield, the only thing that surprised Pullus was the sound the wicker shield made when absorbing a blow, but this was only unusual because it was in an actual, real fight. The shields Romans used for training were made of wicker, but were also heavier than the Parthian version, yet this one did its job, protecting Pullus from the spear point. When the Parthian recovered, pulling his spear back, Pullus' shield seemed to follow it, as if it was a beast tracking its prey to its lair, which wasn't far from the truth of the matter. In doing so, Pullus' shield reduced the space a spearman typically needed to generate power for a killing or damaging blow. With the man's offensive weapon thus negated, Pullus only had to get past the man's own shield, which he accomplished with a feint, once more from a high second position that caused his foe to raise his shield, even as the Roman's blade was whipping around and down before punching up, the point of the blade slicing into the groin of the Parthian. Emitting a high-pitched shriek of pain, the mortally wounded spearman staggered backward, dropping his shield and spear in a vain attempt to stem the blood spurting from the severed vessel on the inside of his thigh. Within the span of another fifty heartbeats, the Parthian spearmen had been swept from the breach, yet while this was certainly a welcome development, it also meant that the archers ranging the walls above, who had been withholding their volleys to avoid hitting their comrades below, now had no such obstruction. Before the last of the surviving spearmen, along with their whip-wielding officer, had turned to flee from the breach, dashing to the lone ladder that had been lowered for their use, the air filled with arrows once more.

"Get our ladders up here! And whoever's left with a shield! *Now!*" Pullus roared, once more repeating the same command over and over.

As he was doing this, the men of his Century, those surviving anyway, had gathered in the now-vacated space of the breach, the men still with their shields being chivvied up front by Lutatius. Their much-needed protection went immediately into service; now that the archers arrayed along the northern wall at a point where they could send their missiles down at the Romans in the breach no longer had to worry about their comrades, they wasted no time. Within a matter of heartbeats, the arrows were slicing down at them, moving so quickly now because of the reduced range that no man, Roman or otherwise, could have been able to pick the one out that was most likely to kill him. Which, of course, meant the shields were essential, except before Pullus could get his men organized, those shields belonging to the first Legionaries who had reached his side now had at least a dozen shafts protruding from them. This, more than anything else, goaded Pullus into acting more quickly than he would have liked. Crouched under the canopy of shields, Pullus glanced back just long enough to see that there were two files, of four men each, holding ladders.

"That'll have to do," he muttered, but only Balbus, who was squatting next to him, heard, and, more importantly, understood.

Reaching out, Balbus grabbed his friend's arm, shaking his head and saying urgently, "Wait! Not just yet!" Before Pullus could object, Balbus half-pivoted on his heels, then saw whom he was looking for about halfway down the length of the rubble pile. Bellowing with all the power of his lungs, the scarred Centurion shouted, "Valerius! Sound the advance!"

Pullus didn't understand why, but before he could press his friend, the deep bass notes, sounded in the specific pattern, rolled up past, and through them, the tone pitched so that Titus Pullus could feel the vibrations of them up through the soles of his hobnailed *caligae*. And then, no more than a half-dozen heartbeats later, he understood why his friend had done something that he realized, with some chagrin, he should have thought to do first.

"Do you hear that?"

This time it wasn't the youngster Terentius who noticed it first, but the veteran who had done his best to settle the boy's nerves down. His question went unanswered, verbally anyway, although the sudden rush of men leaping to their feet from their respective spots in the warehouse was eloquent confirmation that he hadn't been alone.

"You hear that, boys?" Spurius' voice, grown hoarse from his exhortations, suddenly seemed to possess a new strength. "I told you they wouldn't forget us!"

The answering roar from his remaining men was substantial enough that, once more, dust sifted down from the rafters. Even before it had drifted down to the filthy floor, the Primus Pilus of the 3rd was moving rapidly across the floor of the warehouse, shoving the few men who weren't quick enough out of the way. Reaching the makeshift hole in the northeast corner of the building, just before he reached it, Spurius slowed, knowing the risk of suddenly exposing himself.

"They're not paying any attention to us, Primus Pilus," ventured the Optio of the Second Century he had put in nominal command of the area immediately around the hole. "They're more worried about whoever's coming through the breach."

This confirmed Spurius' suspicions, but most importantly, it gave him the information he needed for his next command.

"On your feet, boys!" he roared, superfluously since every one of the rankers had scrambled to their feet at the sound of the *cornu*. "Form up on me! Quickly now! Hurry!"

It was to the credit of Spurius, his surviving Optios, and the men themselves that they instantly understood the futility of trying to assemble themselves in even an approximation of their normal spots, each of them knowing that the amount of time it would take to sort themselves out was too precious to waste., not to mention that, as large as the warehouse was, it was still too small to accommodate the men in a standard formation. The consequence was that in a fraction of the normal time, Spurius' men had shuffled into a rough semblance of a formation that was only five men across, thereby allowing them through the gap in the corner of the warehouse they had created more than two watches earlier. Meanwhile, as the men moved into position, Spurius was leaning slightly forward in an attempt to get a glimpse outside; although he believed his Optio, he was still being cautious, but he instantly saw that the Parthians who posed the biggest threat, those men either lining the northern wall directly across from the warehouse, or those who had been placed on the makeshift rampart of the temporary wall that intersected the northern wall and the corner the building he was in, all of them had focused their attention elsewhere. Specifically, whoever those fellow Romans were coming through the breach, although their identity was masked from Spurius because it was out of his range of vision. Those archers who had been making his men exercise caution whenever they came near the hole were now looking to Spurius' left, towards the breach. Most crucially, their arms were drawing back, holding for perhaps an eye blink, then releasing the taut string of their composite bow as they worked furiously in an attempt to stop the Romans advancing through the gaping hole in the outer wall.

Spurius turned and barked, "Are there any javelins left?"

The answer, when it came in the form of them being passed forward, was nowhere near the number for which Spurius had hoped. Cursing bitterly, Spurius was forced to rethink his next move. Because they hadn't been expecting the existence of an interior wall, his men hadn't been equipped with ladders and, in fact, they had been given to Caesar for his effort against Ctesiphon. There was a stone stairway that led up to the northern parapet, but it was located closer to the northwest corner and was nearer to the breach than it was to Spurius and his men. His initial thought had been to use that staircase to lead his men along the parapet and sweep the Parthians from the northern wall, but now he was dissuaded from this course by two separate yet salient facts. If he led his men out of the warehouse through the hole in the northeastern corner of the building, he would be forced to cross an expanse of well more than two hundred paces, back in the direction of the breach, then across the roughly thirty paces between the rows of warehouses and the northern wall, all while under the arrows of those Parthians directly across from him now. Even worse, he and his men would expose their backs as they headed for those stairs, no matter how quickly they moved. This in itself was bad enough, but it was the knowledge that, in essence, he would be leading his men in the opposite direction of whoever it was coming through the breach, and that could only end one way: badly. In the span of no more than three or four heartbeats, Spurius could envision the scene; his survivors running headlong into the men who had come to save them, colliding together while under the bows of their enemies above, who wouldn't even have to deign to descend to street level to slaughter them. Biting back another curse, Spurius didn't want his men to see him thwarted in this way; they had enough to worry about and had been through more than any Roman should have been forced to endure. Therefore, rather than say anything, he merely turned about, although his progress was impeded by his men, now formed up. Regardless of the obstacles they presented, Spurius moved quickly to the double doors on the side of the warehouse. Whereas before, he had discarded this as a possible exit for the simple reason that, while it would put him and his men behind the makeshift wall, they would have been exposed and, without support, they didn't possess the numbers to do anything ambitious like take the city. Now that help had arrived, however, Spurius' options had widened.

"All right, you bastards," while he spoke loudly, Spurius was still careful to modulate his tone in the unlikely event that some Parthian had his ear pressed to one of the wooden doors, "we can't go out through the hole. At least if we want to do any good other than soak up those *cunni*'s arrows." Nobody laughed, but there were a few grim smiles as he continued, "So, instead, we're going out this way. Except that instead of going right, into this fucking city, we're going to turn left." He paused for a moment to allow this to sink in before he finished, "And we're going to hit those cocksuckers standing on that new wall from behind!"

It was just as Spurius was relaying this command that Balbus ordered the 10th's *cornicen* to play the call that let the beleaguered men in the warehouse know they were coming. Almost as if it had been planned this way, which it most certainly hadn't, Spurius nodded to the two men at the double doors who lifted the bars that served to block entry.

Waiting only long enough to do this, then kick their half of the double door open, Spurius raised his sword and shouted, "Let's get out of here, boys! It's time to make these *cunni* pay! Follow me!" Then, he went running out into the sunlit street, followed by his surviving men, all of them shouting their promise to do just what their Primus Pilus had ordered.

With a *testudo* unlike any that Pullus had either ordered to be formed, or of which he had been a part of as a ranker, the protection provided by the men of both First and Second Century who still had relatively intact shields was crucial to the success of what Pullus had planned. The worst part was navigating the downward slope of the rubble pile that had spilled down onto the street that bordered the western wall. Just the treacherous footing alone would have made descending it with every man's shield staying in its proper position to provide the best protection from the arrows that were now slashing down from a devastatingly short range difficult. With the sheer volume of missiles, combined with the power that came from being just a matter of paces above the Romans, that Pullus' makeshift formation made it down to the street level at all, despite suffering a half-dozen men falling victim to the Parthian archers, was something of a miracle. Most crucially, it gave the men surrounding Pullus and the two files carrying the ladders a boost in confidence, offering them the first glimmer of hope that they weren't destined to die in this filthy street. Conditions were far from ideal, even accounting for the constant rain of missiles that quickly studded every man's shield with several shafts; although the footing wasn't as treacherous on the street, there were still innumerable obstacles lying in their way as they began moving parallel to the western wall, south from the breach. That those underfoot obstacles were the corpses of their comrades in the 3rd, and a fair number of them were horribly burned, ironically served to sharpen their concentration as they moved, as well as strengthen their resolve to exact vengeance. While their Primus Pilus hadn't had the opportunity to tell them what he had in mind, their faith in him was absolute, which was a good thing, because if they had known, the outcome might have been different. Pullus' plan, such as it was, required a level of coordination that would have been difficult under the best of circumstances; that his outline of what he intended had occurred in no more than a couple short sentences meant that Pullus and his men not only needed Murena and his artillerymen to serve their weapons more efficiently than they ever had before, the intervention of the gods would have been quite welcome. Instead of moving the short distance from the breach to the road paralleling the northern wall that led in the direction of Spurius and his men, Pullus was leading this small band away from the breach and the northwest corner of the large wall, instead moving parallel to the western wall, in between it and the first block of stone buildings. When the Greek Anaxagoras had offered up his idea to Kambyses about creating shorter walls blocking the street that Pullus and his men were now on, instead of aligning the temporary wall flush with the corner of the large warehouse, he had actually directed his laborers to construct it about midway down the length of it.

His reasoning for doing so, as he explained to Kambyses, was simply, "If we put it at the very corner, the instant the Romans get within a hundred paces of the breach from the outside, they'll be able to see it. We *want* them to keep coming, so we can get them into this killing ground."

And, to this point, Anaxagoras' plan had worked, if not perfectly, quite well; the corpses strewn within the confines of his deadly box testified to that. Now, though, Pullus and his men were moving, still in their irregularly shaped but compact formation of shields protecting the men with the ladders, all of them now so studded with arrows that it was difficult to see the wooden surface of the shields themselves. Although their initial objective was the short wall, this wasn't Pullus' ultimate target. Clearing this small wall would certainly eliminate the crossfire from the fifty or so archers standing on it, now drawing and loosing their missiles as fast as their arms could move, thereby saving the rest of his Legion from worrying about a threat to their right flank as they negotiated the breach, and it was to the trailing Cohorts the job of linking up with Spurius fell. Pullus knew, however, this wasn't enough; he also understood that he and his men were in a race against time, because as he had instructed Murena, now that they were inside the outer walls, his chief artilleryman had shifted the aim of every piece onto the Parthian's large *ballista*. And, to this moment, at least, Murena and his men had managed to bombard that spot along the wall so severely that none of the enemy artillerymen were willing to risk themselves to try and prepare their own piece. Regardless, as Pullus was acutely aware, ammunition of all sizes and types had been critically low, even before he had ascended the breach. Once Murena sent his last missile, it would take a few heartbeats for the Parthians to realize they were no longer in mortal danger, but then they wouldn't hesitate to resume lobbing those horrifically damaging firepots down onto the heads of Pullus' men. With Balbus and his Century as part of Pullus' force, it meant that Marcus Laetus would be leading the way for the rest of the First Cohort, followed by Scribonius and the Second. Because of his position inside the makeshift *testudo* that was almost an oblong shape instead of the neat, compact rectangle, Pullus was unable to look back to the breach to see how Laetus and the rest of his men were faring, although he could tell just by the sounds that they were at least in the vicinity of the breach. This was all the attention Pullus could pay to what was happening behind him; through the slight gap in the shields of the men to his immediate front, the dressed stones of the temporary wall filled his vision.

"We're almost there, boys!"

Even yelling, his words were almost drowned out by the hollow thrumming sound of the Parthian arrows, the archers delivering them now able to just lean over slightly and launch their missiles at point blank range. It almost sounds like it's raining; this was put forth by the detached part of Pullus' brain, although it was difficult to keep this thought in mind when the shafts were now punching through the shields and penetrating almost two-thirds of their length. Inevitably, men were being struck, mostly in the arms holding the shield, so that it instantly became a race between getting the two ladders up against the wall before the protection of their shields completely disintegrated. Adding to the urgency was the sounds of cracking wood that served to punctuate the constant drumming of the plunging arrows, further sign that his men's shields were being weakened from the pounding they were taking.

"Does anyone have javelins?" Balbus, who was crouched next to Pullus, shouted over his shoulder.

Neither of the Centurions heard anyone answer, but they both sensed some sort of commotion from behind them. What it was, and, most importantly what it meant only became apparent when a series of screams, choked cries and curses sounded from directly above them, but it was the two Parthian bodies who came crashing down, onto the upraised shields of the men nearest to the wall, that initiated a flurry of activity.

"Ladders up!" Pullus roared. "Now, boys, now!"

Only half of the original party carrying the ladders were the same men, yet they didn't hesitate, moving with a practiced speed, a man on either side holding the vertical poles, with the third man moving to the opposite side of the ladder, his back to the wall, while the fourth man began walking forward, moving his hands from one rung to the next, quickly raising the ladder. About a dozen paces in the direction of the warehouse across the street from the wall, the four men with the second ladder were doing the same. Without a word being spoken between them, Balbus had moved to the far ladder, while Pullus paused only long enough to snatch a shield that was offered to him, having discarded the wicker one earlier. This one had at least had the shafts cut away from it by its owner before he handed it to his Primus Pilus, but it was so riddled with holes that Pullus felt certain he could hold it in front of him without it completely obscuring his vision, or it providing more than the barest protection. Before he could dwell on this, however, he was ascending the ladder, with Balbus only a couple steps behind on his own, the two Centurions scrambling up as quickly as their already-fatigued legs could carry them. The surviving archers had continued loosing up until the last possible instant, but now their bows were useless, so they scrambled along the parapet, moving to the western rampart, both to get out of the way of the spearmen whose job it now was to keep these Romans from gaining ownership of this wall, and to give them distance to resume their own barrage of missiles. Neither Pullus nor Balbus had more than the barest sense of the construction of this temporary wall, so it was only in the instant Pullus' head cleared the top of the wall that he saw the parapet wasn't also made of stone, but was a wooden scaffold. It was just wide enough for men to stand directly against the stone of the temporary wall and still give others room to move behind them, as the archers who were fleeing the wall were doing now. Taking this in within the span of a heartbeat, Pullus' attention was focused more on blocking one spear thrust with his already-compromised shield, while dodging another spear thrust from the Parthian above him and to his right.

Throwing himself against the ladder, the spear belonging to the foe on his right still grazed him, skipping along the back of his mail *hamata*, although the point didn't catch in the links. Despite it not striking solidly, the thrust still had considerable power, forcing a gasp from Pullus as the blow knocked some air from his lungs. While his shield was in the right position to block the blow from the Parthian almost directly above him but slightly to his left, there was no missing the high-pitched, splintering sound that signaled his shield wasn't going to last much longer. Both Parthians, having struck at almost exactly the same time, were both forced to recover for another blow, which gave Pullus a bare instant of time where he could make his own move.

Using what he was sure was the last bit of spare energy in his legs, Pullus performed a move that he had learned quite by accident was deadly effective, if almost insanely dangerous. Springing up, he was forced to use his right hand, still clutching his sword, to provide the leverage needed to swing his legs up and over the parapet of the wall, then kicking out at the Parthian to his left. As he did so, to counterbalance himself and to provide a modicum of protection in the event the Parthian on his opposite side recovered his spear more quickly than Pullus wanted, he brought his shield up and across his body. For a matter of an eye blink, his body was almost horizontal, parallel to the top of the stone wall, but between the momentum and the sheer mass of his huge legs, the Parthian to his left was struck with such force that he caromed backward one, then two steps. His momentum from Pullus' kick was such that he teetered briefly on the edge of the wooden parapet, moving his arms in wild circles in a vain attempt to arrest his backward fall. The last Pullus saw of this particular Parthian was as he dropped out of sight, his shout of alarm mingling with all the other noise made by voices and weapons clashing. All Pullus cared about was that he no longer had a threat to his immediate left; the spearman who had been on the opposite side of the fallen man seemed to be torn by indecision as he held his wicker shield tightly against his body, while his gaze shifted quickly between the situation to his right, where the transverse crest that Pullus knew was firmly on Balbus' helmet was just poking into view, then to Pullus. Sensing this man's hesitation was more from a reluctance to engage, Pullus understood he was taking a risk by turning to his own right, thereby exposing his back to this spearman, but he also knew the Parthian was about to have even more to worry about, because another helmeted head had popped into view from the ladder Pullus had just ascended. He didn't take the time to see who had been following him so closely; it was enough that he knew one of his men would be doing that very thing. Secure in the belief his rear was thusly secured, Pullus punched out with his shield, although the Parthian spearman he was facing met the Roman's with his own, stopping Pullus from his goal of knocking his enemy backward at the very least. When his metal boss smashed into the wicker shield of his enemy, the Parthian naturally recoiled from the force of the blow, but he was bolstered by one of his own comrades who stood immediately behind him. Robbed of a quick victory, Pullus now lunged with his own blade, trying to come over the top of his and the Parthian's shields, as both men pushed against each other with all their might, but the Parthian managed to duck his head to his right and avoid being stabbed in the face. It was a testament to Pullus' strength that, while he was not pushing his adversary, braced as he was, neither were his own feet sliding backward, despite the added weight provided by the second Parthian, so that for the span of a heartbeat, the two direct combatants were in a stalemate, which Pullus sought to break with another overhand thrust. His attack was thwarted again, not by his nearest foe, but by the second Parthian behind the first, who just managed to raise his own shield to thrust it up and over the head of his comrade, barely in time, yet quickly enough that the tip of Pullus' sword plunged into the wicker instead of his enemy. Snarling in frustration, Pullus suddenly relented in his own pressure, not only because he was intent on shifting his point of attack, but he could feel the shield starting to give way through his left hand as the handle bowed under the tremendous pressure. Understanding it wouldn't be useful for much longer, his sudden release of tension against the Parthian's shield was followed by a slight pivot on his right foot, momentarily turning his back to the ladder side of the temporary wall. He hadn't held out much hope this would work, yet the gods favored him enough, because the Parthian, reacting to the sudden release of the enormous weight pressing against his shield, inevitably lurched forward before he could compensate. It wasn't much of a shift, just a slight but sudden lean forward, as if the man behind him had shoved him, which in a sense he had because the second man's reaction to Pullus' move was delayed even more, so that for less than an eye blink, the pressure he had been exerting to keep his comrade in place continued now that there wasn't a counteracting force. Consequently, the first Parthian's shield suddenly moved out from his body farther than it should have for, at most, the time it takes to draw in a sudden breath; it was enough for Pullus' blade. Striking

362

like a grayish-silver serpent, the point of the sword was the fang that punched through the layers of loose clothing, the leather cuirass worn underneath, and finally, the man's flesh and muscle to bury itself deep in the Parthian's gut. Pullus' blade was back behind his own shield almost as quickly as if it had never left its spot, and everything happened so rapidly that the now-dying Parthian's shield was pulled back against his body as the man continued to follow through on his recovery, in much the same way as a door slams behind an unwanted visitor. It was too late, however, which Pullus knew by the sudden widening of the eyes, the look in them full of the shock that comes from the moment when a man truly understands his mortality, although the Parthian didn't unleash the kind of scream that most victims of a stab wound to the vitals did, instead issuing more of a low, keening moan. Because the Parthian's body had shielded his comrade bracing him from seeing exactly what happened, Pullus heard the second Parthian shout what he was certain was a query about the first Parthian's status, probably asking why he wasn't making an offensive move. The second Parthian got his answer by virtue of the first Parthian dropping to his knees, and albeit in a slightly different way, the second Parthian's natural reaction to this event, his eyes briefly leaving Pullus to glance down at his dying comrade in an unconscious reflex, sealed his own doom. Like the first Parthian, it wasn't much of a lapse, but this fraction of inattention to the giant Roman cost him dearly when he was unable to bring the shield he had used to save the leading spearman just three or four heartbeats before back into position in time to save himself. He was ended by a thrust to the throat, and just that quickly, Titus Pullus was able to move away from his ladder, heading for where the temporary wall met the western rampart. It was a start, Pullus knew, but there was still a lot of fighting to do, so he paused just long enough for a quick glance over his shoulder to assess what was happening behind him. As he expected, Balbus, who wasn't perhaps quite as skilled as Pullus technically but more than made up for it with a ferocity that even Pullus, only to himself, acknowledged was greater than his own, was using it now to make progress for himself and the men who had followed him up his ladder. Pullus didn't spare more than a heartbeat's worth of time, but it was enough for his eye to take in the scene and understand that Balbus was well on his way to sweeping the wooden parapet clean of Parthians while heading in the direction away from the permanent wall, towards the stone building.

A crude doorway had been knocked out of the wall of the building that served as the opposite anchor point for the temporary wall, much in the same way Spurius and his men had done earlier, except this hole was a bit cleaner and opened into the second floor of the building. This was a mixed blessing; while it gave Balbus and the men who scaled the ladder closest to that end of the temporary wall shelter from the missiles of the archersand it would allow them to access the first floor and thereby spill into the street to continue their assault , there was no way to know whether Parthians were even then streaming into the building, climbing the stairs, and preparing to rush out onto the wooden parapet. At this moment, the archers were reorganizing themselves on the western rampart, preparing to renew the onslaught, sending their arrows the relatively short distance across the street to slash into Balbus and his men nearest to the building. This, Pullus understood, was in Balbus' hands; his concern was different, and ultimately, would play the largest role in the success or failure of his desperate gamble. Stepping over the bodies of the two Parthians he had slain, Pullus had the luxury of a bit more breathing room, as the comrades of the slain men had seen fit to withdraw all the way back to where the temporary wall met the permanent parapet. Standing now in a semicircle surrounding the heavy ladder that led up to the stone parapet of the main wall, well more than thirty Parthian spearmen waited for Pullus and the men who followed him in this direction. The distance was perhaps twenty paces between them but, although Pullus had more than his share of courage, he wasn't a fool, the fact that he still lived a testament to this truth. Understanding he would have to wait for more men to ascend the ladder, he at least saw who had been behind him—a Gregarius from the Third Section of his own Century who had just dispatched a Parthian Pullus assumed had been the indecisive spearman. If you don't choose, someone will choose for you; this was the thought that flashed through Pullus' mind, and in its own way served to remind him of his larger goal.

"Metellus!" The Gregarius responded by turning and trotting the short distance between himself and his Primus Pilus. Although Pullus had addressed him, his eyes weren't on Metellus; instead, he was looking in the direction of the permanent western wall but further down, south of the breach, and his gaze didn't waver as Pullus ordered, "Grab the first ten men who come up our ladder and bring them to me. And," only then did he shift his glance to Metellus, "be quick about it!"

Metellus sketched a salute, then ran to stand by the ladder to do as Pullus had directed while thinking to himself how unlikely it was that he would assure his friends and comrades that there was no hurry, although this thought remained tucked safely inside his head. Grabbing men as they climbed up, Metellus pushed them in the general direction of where Pullus was standing, facing the Parthian spearmen protecting the ladder up to the permanent wall. "Ladder" was probably not the right or correct term, because what Anaxagoras had built was more than a ladder, although it was also much steeper than a normal staircase. While Pullus had no way of knowing, the Greek engineer had been forced to create something that was a hybrid of both to compensate for the different heights of the respective walls. The temporary barriers, made by using part of the extra layer of stone that had been hastily and poorly added to the entire length of the western wall, were just ten feet high, while the walls of Seleucia were ten feet higher. Just like the permanent wall, the wooden parapet of the new wall was three feet lower than the top of the wall to provide protection, although Anaxagoras hadn't had time to add any crenellations. Like any expedient fortification, there were weaknesses, and he hadn't been able to prepare anything more elaborate, so the best he could manage was what Pullus was seeing. Twice as wide as a ladder, thereby allowing men to either ascend or descend side by side, it was nevertheless so steeply pitched that, especially if a man was in a hurry, he had to use his hands as well as his feet. Additionally, Pullus could see that coming down was much more difficult and hazardous than going up, which he hoped meant that the spearmen still up on the permanent rampart would hesitate to come to the aid of their comrades below. This stairway and the thirty nervous Parthian spearmen were between Pullus and his ultimate goal, which he had spotted farther down the western wall. More importantly, just in the span of time he had been watching, his heart began to sink when only three missiles, two scorpion bolts, and one of the smallest pieces of the rock ammunition had been launched by Murena from outside the walls. At this moment, the Parthians crewing the large piece weren't confident enough to poke their heads up above the level of the parapet to get a sense of what was actually happening, but Pullus knew this state wouldn't last. He had to get to that piece, before they could resume hurling those firepots, which he caught just a glimpse of through the open door of the small shed, where they were stacked on the opposite side of the machine, or more men would die the worst death imaginable. And, even worse for Titus Pullus, it would be his boys this time who faced being burned to death.

Kambyses had never felt so helpless as he did now, standing and watching as what appeared to be an endless row of ladders, extending for half of the southern wall, rose in a ragged unison, even as his archers poured arrow after arrow down into the tight mass of Romans clustered around each one. Even his spearmen were actively working, pairs of them picking up the large rocks that had been stockpiled at regular intervals, then dropping them over the parapet. As one would expect, these large stones did damage, but from where Kambyses stood, in the niche in the southeast corner, it appeared that his men were suffering almost as much in the exchange. Despite losing his scorpions and some of his larger pieces, Caesar had obviously shifted the javelins that were rightly almost as feared as the scorpion bolts, two of which each Legionary carried, from the supporting Centuries, up into the leading Centuries. Even while the ladders were going up, a few paces from the wall were roughly four ranks of Romans, each of whom seemed to have far more than two javelins, and these Legionaries hurled them up at any of Kambyses' men who exposed themselves between the crenellations. And because of the range, the only way his archers could try to stop their enemies at the foot of the wall was to risk leaning out between the protection of the stone crenellations, where they were as likely to get a javelin in the face as kill a Roman. It was even more dangerous for the spearmen dropping the rocks, because in order to inflict real damage, they had to not only expose themselves, but time their release so that the enemy below couldn't scramble out of the way. In doing so, they made themselves prime targets for the streaking javelins, and although Kambyses had no way of knowing, if he had been informed that the men selected to hurl these missiles weren't random choices, but had been specially selected for their strength and skill with the javelin, it wouldn't have surprised him. After watching for the span of two or three hundred heartbeats, Kambyses snapped an order to the courier who was still kneeling at his feet.

"Go tell Hystaspes to stop the men dropping the rocks," his words were hard to distinguish because his jaw was so tightly clenched, "we're losing more men than we're killing."

The courier hopped to his feet, staying only long enough to repeat the order, then dashed down the rampart, heading for the Parthian nobleman who had started the day as one of the most junior officers of Kambyses' commanders, but was now the fourth highest-ranking man in the chain. Kambyses turned his attention now to the eastern wall and, if anything, his spirits sank even lower at what greeted his eyes. While the expanse of the eastern wall of Ctesiphon that was under assault was less than half the distance of the stretch of the southern wall, the number of Romans was twice as many, the line of Centuries standing resolutely one behind the other, waiting to ascend the ladder, stretching back several hundred paces. This was a daunting sight; that Caesar had also concentrated his remaining artillery to cover the entire length of the eastern wall under assault meant that not even his archers dared to stand erect on the parapet. At this moment, the eastern rampart was packed with men, all of them crouching in terror as the cracking sound of the small stone ammunition smashing into the protective wall made an almost continuous din. Despite the hail of missiles, as Kambyses watched, one spearman, either with suicidal bravery or, more likely, panicked by the relentless nature of this bombardment, suddenly stood erect to stare out between the nearest crenellation, or at least, this is what he appeared to be doing to Kambyses. Before the Parthian commander could blink, the spearman seemed to explode, his upper body vanishing for an instant in a reddish-pink mist that was composed in almost equal proportion of chunks of meat that had an instant before been a man. Kambyses sensed the blurring motion of the speeding stone continuing through the spearman's torso, where it arced over the building nearest to the main wall, trailing a fine spray of blood and flesh. Not surprisingly, this example served to encourage the dead man's comrades from attempting to spy on the Roman's progress, and as Kambyses continued to watch, another man, who might have been more than a comrade but a real friend, kicked the bloody ruin of the dead spearman off the rampart. Despite the curtain of noise, Kambyses heard the sodden, thudding sound as the corpse hit the paving stones below, and despite all that he had seen and done in his decades as a warrior, he was forced to suppress a shudder. However, it did serve to convince him to give another order, this one to the second of the three men he had been using as a runner.

"Tell the archers to come down to the street." He had to shout to be heard, despite the man being within arm's reach. "I want the ones on the eastern wall to assemble over there." He pointed to a spot down below on the street level, about fifty paces away from the corner where he was standing but along the southern wall. "That way, they can send their arrows over the wall without exposing themselves and getting slaughtered."

This runner, also of the lowest rank, yet slightly bolder than his counterparts, repeated the order as expected, but then hesitated, not moving for a long enough period that Kambyses snapped at him, "Well?"

"Excellency, what do you want the spearmen to do? Do you want them to come down off the rampart as well?"

"No." Kambyses didn't hesitate, but while it was only an idle thought, he did wonder if this man had friends among the spearmen. "They need to stay up there and be ready to stab any Roman dog who shows his face."

Much to his benefit, the runner didn't hesitate, although Kambyses gazed at the man's back as he half-crawled his way along the eastern wall, relaying Kambyses' orders, who didn't have to watch long to see how readily and quickly his archers obeyed. Suddenly, the rampart seemed to come alive with crawling men, all of them heading to one of the two stone staircases that led down from the wall, but Kambyses had already turned his attention to the final runner.

"Go to the plaza," he ordered the man, "and tell Tallis to bring the reserve here. We," he finished grimly, "are going to need every one of them."

This runner had to fight his way through the crowd of archers who were still streaming down from the eastern wall and moving to the spot Kambyses indicated by a series of gestures and shouted directions. It wouldn't be very effective, Kambyses knew, just having the archers arcing their arrows over the wall to land blindly, but he hoped that the concentration of Romans would enable some of the missiles to inflict damage. Frankly, it was the only thing he could think to do.

Chapter Thirteen

In Seleucia, Melchior became aware of something occurring at the opposite end of the enclosed section of the city from where he was standing, but it wasn't until he saw a helmeted head wearing a white transverse crest standing on the parapet of the temporary barrier that ran from the northern wall before he understood that the Romans trapped in the building immediately next to it had somehow gotten out. Like Kambyses, his attention was torn between what was happening immediately in front of him as he faced down the length of the western wall, watching the smaller party of Romans climbing the ladders they had brought with them to scale the temporary wall nearest to the breach, led by a Roman that Melchior could see even from this distance was one of the largest men he had ever seen. Also like Kambyses, he had placed himself in a corner, this the northwest corner of Seleucia, so that he was almost exactly diagonally across from his overall commander across the river, separated by perhaps three miles as the crow flew. Now he had the Roman formations, these still tightly organized in the same attitude whereby their shields covered every Legionary from easy arrow strikes, moving directly underneath him, the first three formations already past him and moving across his front to his left. It was their movement in that direction that caused him to be looking in the general area of the far temporary wall, where he first saw Spurius. Even as he watched in growing alarm, several more men appeared on the parapet, next to the stone building, where they joined the first Roman he had seen in fighting for possession of the temporary wall. He saw his own men were resisting furiously, their backs now turned to the northern wall, although it was impossible for him to tell if they were organized at all, or were just standing there in a cluster. This was when matters partially fell into place for Melchior, as he realized the three formations were heading down the length of the street paralleling the northern wall to link up with the Romans who had just escaped from their refuge. What was still unclear to him was why the leading element of Romans hadn't done the same thing, but instead had made a right turn to ascend the temporary barrier, between the western outer rampart and the first row of buildings. While he had his archers maintain the steady onslaught of missiles on this first group, they had been temporarily restrained from continuing, as the Romans ascended their two ladders to the top of the shorter wall. As adept as Parthians were at archery, their skill was based more on the volume of missiles they could loose, not pinpoint accuracy, although they had managed to hit a handful of Romans as they were climbing. Once at the top of the temporary barrier, however, their arrows would be just as much of a threat to their comrades trying desperately to keep their foes from gaining possession of the parapet. Not, he thought glumly, that it appeared as if it would matter. He had exhausted his ready supply of naphtha; there were another two dozen jars of the precious stuff, but they were currently useless because the crew of the large piece was pinned down. It was the thought of the artillery piece that gave Melchior the answer to the puzzle about the intentions of the force led by the large Roman. Of course! The fact his stomach suddenly lurched so violently he was afraid he would vomit informed Melchior that he had stumbled on the real goal of this separate group. Following instantly behind this revelation was his understanding that he had essentially trapped himself, here in this spot in the northwest corner. He couldn't run across the rampart lining the western wall, because a hundred paces from where he was standing was the breach, and even if he had been on horseback, he couldn't have leapt across that section of collapsed wall. While he had known this very early in the day, Melchior realized he had counted on his ability to run down the northern wall, either crossing by the makeshift stairway down onto the wooden rampart and to the second building that formed Anaxagoras' box, then make his way between the two buildings to ascend the makeshift stairway to reach the western wall. Now, he understood that this was no longer possible; there were Romans on two sections of the smaller wall that he would have to negotiate. A feeling of helplessness paralyzed the younger Parthian; not for long, but for the span of several heartbeats, as his mind worked furiously. It was about this moment that Melchior realized that he no longer had any options left, that his time as a commander was over. Now, all that counted, he realized, was his sword. And, he thought bitterly, forcing himself to turn away from the western wall where the large Roman was even now leading a force of his men roughly equal to the spearmen who had either chosen or been ordered to stand on the lower wall to defend the stairway, there's only one place for me to go. There's nothing that I can do for them. Without wasting another glance, Melchior strode down the northern wall, heading for the only place he could have any impact, his eyes fixed on Spurius' white crest as he moved.

The Parthians defending the makeshift stairway proved to be some of the most stubborn warriors that Pullus and his men had encountered to this point in the campaign, at least of the lower classes. Fairly quickly, Pullus determined that at least part of this display of competent defiance was due to one of their own. Somewhat unusually, this Parthian was identified as the leader not by virtue of his finer armor, or his brandishing the long Parthian sword favored by the nobility, but by his actions and, most crucially, the example he set. Placing himself in the front rank, Pullus saw that the Parthian's face bore a long, white scar down the left side of it where it curved around, ending at his upper lip, of which a major chunk was missing, showing his bared teeth in something of a permanent snarl. More importantly, he handled his spear with a skill that Pullus hadn't faced before; regardless of his countenance, it was his constant exhortations and shouted commands that kept Pullus and his own men from simply sweeping them aside. It wasn't that the Romans weren't inflicting casualties; they were, but this Parthian was shouting commands at his men, and they were obeying him with such alacrity that the gap in the wall of spears and shields wasn't open long enough to exploit it. Pullus, or more specifically, one of his men, the veteran Metellus had learned this the hard way as he had tried to leap into one such gap, but was met in mid-stride by a strong thrust from the Parthian, who stepped forward to take his fallen comrade's place. The only blessing was that Metellus had managed to partially parry the thrust, forcing the spear point down and away from the center of his chest, but it still sliced into his thigh. Staggering back, cursing bitterly, Metellus had been roughly helped by his comrades, who grabbed the back of his harness and thereby removed him from the fighting quickly enough that one of the spearmen next to the Parthian who had inflicted the wound couldn't take advantage of him dropping his shield. Now Pullus had lost three of his men besides Metellus, while the Parthians had only been whittled down by just one more of their number than that. Their wicker shields were pressed tightly together, each man's spear resting on top of his own, which their owner jabbed forward as a way to discourage the Romans from getting too close. The men immediately behind each Parthian in the front line did essentially the same thing, laying their own spears across the top of the shield of the

371

man in front, made possible by how tightly packed together they were, creating a bristling wall that was difficult for the Romans to penetrate. Pullus was acutely aware that every beat of his heart where he and his men weren't ascending the stairway and sweeping down the wall towards the artillery piece brought him and his men closer to the moment when Murena was finally completely out of ammunition. Those of his men who were on the left side of this small knot of men but weren't in the front line directly opposite a Parthian had been forced to turn slightly and raise their shields, as the archers on the western wall near the large artillery piece began sending missiles at the Romans who had cleared the parapet. One of his men had fallen this way, but once they had adjusted, Pullus and the others felt secure enough to concentrate on their more immediate threat. Pullus had attempted several attacks, first by himself, then in concert with one of his men, yet the scarred Parthian had still proven to be a match for the Primus Pilus, thwarting his attempts. It was a consequence of this reality that caused Pullus to act in a manner that was reckless, even for him.

Immediately after rebuffing another attempt by the Romans, this time by the two Gregarii nearest the breach side of the temporary wall, it was when the scarred Parthian took his eyes off of Pullus, who was standing directly across from him, with the intent to check on those of his own men who had just weathered this latest attack, that Pullus made his move. Despite the Parthian shifting his attention for a bare instant, the Primus Pilus had been watching for any opportunity, and this was the one he chose, or was forced to, realizing this was likely the only chance he would get. Leaping not only up into the air, but at the same time hurling himself forward the two paces separating the two forces, and as he began his move, he had drawn his sword arm back over his head so that as his bulk descended, his sword was also slashing down. At the same time, Pullus drew his shield back far enough to cock his elbow before punching it forward with the same amount of power he had put into his sword slash. Moving at the same speed, but with the added force of the weight of the shield itself, as he intended, it struck the protruding spear points in the fraction of an eye blink before first his sword, then his body came crashing down onto his enemy. The scarred Parthian reacted in time, barely, Pullus seeing his eyes widen in surprise, yet there was no hesitation in his left arm bringing up his wicker shield to absorb the full force of the Roman's blow. And, unlike his comrade behind him whose vision was partially obscured, he also tilted his spear up and back out of the way of Pullus'

372

shield, while the second Parthian's spear penetrated the wood as Pullus thrust the shield forward, trapping the spear and rendering it ineffective. Even in reacting quickly enough, the scarred Parthian was still subjected to the enormous power that Titus Pullus was capable of generating with his sword, which sent him staggering backward, despite his intention of standing fast. In acting as he had, Pullus got inside the normal range of the Parthian spear, although he also was acutely aware that, as skilled as his adversary was, he had perhaps a fraction of a heartbeat of time before his foe adjusted to the change in effective reach. This was one reason why he violently threw his shield away from him to his left, which even in the turbulence of the moment, Pullus could hear the shouts of his own men who cried out in alarm at his precipitous move. However, the second Parthian's spear, still embedded in the shield, moved with it, and with enough force that it not only staggered the owner of the spear, but the shaft swung into the Parthian to the scarred man's immediate right, striking him a tremendous blow to the side of the head, something that Pullus barely noted out of the corner of his vision. With his left hand now free and ignoring the pain of the burns, which had blistered, then quickly burst, Pullus managed to grab the shaft of the scarred Parthian's spear, even as his enemy was beginning to recover from Pullus' blow, dropping the point back down while pulling his arm back before thrusting it at Pullus. At least this was what he was attempting, except for Pullus' fist instantly closing around the shaft just behind the point in an underhanded grip and, with every bit of his strength, pushed against the Parthian's thrust. As far as the Parthian was concerned, his spear might as well have been locked in rock, so solidly was it in Pullus' grasp. The Roman's hands were not only large, even considering the scale of his height and breadth, but he had also diligently performed strengthening exercises, prescribed to him when he was a *tiro*, by Aulus Vinicius. While every one of Pullus' tent mates, which included Scribonius and Publius Vellusius, had done as Vinicius had directed, they had performed the exercises exclusively with their right hand, to prepare them for the special grip favored by Vinicius. In one of the first demonstrations to his comrades that the young Titus Pullus was made of different metal than other men, he had been just as diligent performing the exercises with his left hand. And it served him in good stead now, as the Parthian quickly gave up trying to thrust the spear forward, instead giving it a good yank backwards toward him. Again, this was what Pullus had been waiting for, because the instant he felt his foe change the direction of his effort and try to pull his spear back, Pullus simply helped him along by shoving forward as well, although he used more than the strength of his arm. Once more throwing his body against the wicker shield of his enemy, the effect was the equivalent of two strong men suddenly throwing themselves bodily backward, directly into the man immediately behind him, who had only just regained his own footing, albeit only by relinquishing his hold on his spear, the point of which was still embedded in Pullus' shield, the bottom edge of it now havingfallen to rest on the surface of the parapet. Using his massive body as a weapon, Pullus' sudden charge forward, when coupled with his enemy's attempt to extricate his spear, sent the man behind the scarred Parthian not just stumbling backward, but knocked him completely off his feet, whereupon he crashed onto the wooden surface of the temporary parapet, landing heavily on his back, with a great whooshing gust of wind driven from his lungs. So too did Pullus' immediate foe, whose own momentum was even greater, unwittingly aided by his using the mass of his body in the attempt to yank the spear from Pullus' grasp.

For a sickening moment that seemed to last longer than it actually did, the Parthian felt himself falling backward, yet while he felt the instant when his balance tipped and thereby made falling inevitable, there was simply nothing he could do about it. Despite it lasting for no more than the span of two heartbeats, Pullus, still clutching the spear, had continued using his powerful legs to muscle himself forward, driving into this compact mass of flesh as if he was a battering ram. Although he knew it was inevitable, and indeed was what he intended, to Pullus, it seemed an even longer eternity than it had to the Parthian before his foe finally collapsed backward in a rough imitation of what had happened to the man in the second rank just an instant before. Meanwhile, even as he felt his foe giving way, Pullus continued pumping his legs until he felt them lift from the parapet as, at last, he came smashing down on top of his enemy. Despite facing in the direction he was falling, Pullus couldn't see anything more than the top of the wicker shield that was now being crushed between the two adversaries, along with the ravaged face of the Parthian, so while the impact stunned the men underneath his weight as he hoped, a sudden sunburst appeared in his own vision as his helmeted head whipped forward, caused by the sudden collision of both their bodies with the surface of the parapet. The iron strip above the brow caught the Parthian underneath him in the mouth, shattering the man's teeth. It hadn't been his intent to head butt the man, although he had used this

374

tactic before, but the terrific impact of his body suddenly coming to a stop as it crushed his enemy made his head whip forward with a force akin to that he would have generated on purpose. Pullus was only dimly aware of the sound created by bodies hitting the wooden planks of the parapet, although his ear did hear a distinct cracking sound, similar to when a shield had been weakened but with a much deeper pitch. The men around him, on both sides, had been taken by such surprise by this reckless move that there was actually a brief eye blink of time where those who were still upright just stood there, gaping down at Pullus. Then, Pullus had no way of knowing who it was, someone twitched, because instantly, he both felt and heard his men reacting as they leapt forward as well, not only to capitalize on what Pullus had done, but to keep their Primus Pilus from taking a spear in the back from the Parthian who had just an instant before been standing to the left the scarred Parthian. It was actually the hollow, thudding sound that cleared Pullus' mind of the temporary cobwebs, as his ears told him the story of one his men thrusting their shield above his body, just before a Parthian spear came slashing down to take him in the back.

"We've got you, Primus Pilus! Kill that bastard!"

This was all Pullus needed to hear, yet despite his adversary's heavy fall, and having Pullus' full weight on him, the scarred Parthian still had fight left in his body. With his left hand trapped between his chest and his shield, held there by Pullus' weight, and the pressure the Roman was putting as he bore down with all of his strength, the Parthian didn't even try to wrench his spear free from Pullus' grasp, knowing that it was useless in such close quarters. On either side of the two, their men were furiously engaged, the standoff that had stretched for moments before it was shattered by Pullus' leap onto the Parthian's shield now over, but while neither of them would ever know it, their minds were running along identical paths, as both of them realized this was the only fight that mattered. Because of the flowing robes favored by the Parthians, it took the scarred man an instant of fumbling to reach for the curved dagger attached to the belt at his waist, but the instant he released his grasp of the spear, Pullus felt the sudden relaxation and reacted quickly. Instantly divining his enemy's intent, Pullus also relinquished the spear, neither of them noticing it dropping to the wooden parapet with a clattering noise, but the Roman didn't bother trying to draw his dagger. He still held his sword in his right hand, although in this instance, while it wasn't as useless as the spear, it was still too unwieldy, and he was using his right arm to push against the Parthian's shield in order to add even more force to his weight. Instead, Pullus balled up his left fist, then aimed a series of blows at his enemy's face, with the intention of forcing the Parthian to stop trying to draw his dagger and protect himself. While the tactic was sound, because of the awkward angle he was at, and the fact that Pullus didn't dare relinquish one ounce of the pressure he was exerting keeping the Parthian not only pinned but relatively immobile, the Parthian didn't do what Pullus had hoped. Absorbing the blows instead, it was almost impossible for Pullus to tell if he was inflicting any damage on his foe; from his nose down, the man's face was a bloody ruin, with pieces of his teeth still sprinkled in his beard. Then Pullus sensed more than saw a sudden movement out of the corner of his eye, and of its own volition, his left hand swept away and down from the Parthian's face in an attempt to grab the Parthian's knife arm. Pullus did so, but not in the manner he would have preferred as he felt the blade of the dagger slicing across his palm, before his hand caught the Parthian's wrist. Letting out a howl of equal parts pain and rage, despite the further damage to his hand, it proved equal to the task, as once more the Parthian found his arm unable to move, clamped in a wet, sticky grasp that was nonetheless impossible for him to budge in any direction. Once more, it became a deadly contest of will as much as strength, as the Parthian, putting the last of his rapidly waning energy into the effort, tried to force his right arm to continue on its original trajectory, even if it was much more slowly than he originally intended. Pullus, however, was no less intent on keeping the Parthian from getting the point of his dagger close enough that, should his own grasp slip, it would punch through his armor and into his left side. He didn't have to glance over at the dagger to see that the Parthian had unerringly aimed for his heart, able to tell this just from the position of his own hand. Nothing else existed; if he had been asked in this very moment, Pullus wouldn't have been able to say what was going on anywhere outside his circle of vision, as it was reduced down to his enemy's face, which was contorted with the agony and desperation of a moment that both men knew would determine who lived and who died. All Pullus could hear was a roaring sound, but one that pulsed in a fast rhythm, sounding somewhat like waves rolling into shore, just at a much, much faster pace, and he was only vaguely aware of the fine mist of bloody sputum that came from his enemy, as the Parthian panted and tried not drown in his own blood filling his mouth at the same time. There would be no way for Pullus to ever estimate how long they were there, locked in this embrace, the point of the dagger quivering less than a hand's span from Pullus' side. What was important, for both of them, was that the point wasn't moving in any direction; at least, at first. But then, slowly, Pullus felt his arm begin to move, out and down, away from his body as he reversed the direction of the dagger, forcing it downward. Even if he hadn't felt it, he would have been able to tell just by the Parthian's expression, his eyes suddenly going wide and wild, the desperation growing with every heartbeat as his arm was forced back toward the parapet. Titus Pullus had been locked in bitter, hand-to-hand struggles before, but he would have cause to remember this one for the rest of his life, and it would be the expression of, if not defeat, then recognition that his enemy had lost his last and best chance to end this on terms favorable to him that would come back to Pullus later. His foe's strength finally gave out when his hand was just a few inches above the parapet, but Pullus had been exerting so much pressure that when the resistance against it suddenly disappeared, he slammed the Parthian's hand hard enough against the parapet that he heard, and felt, several bones snap from the impact. Even if he hadn't heard it, he would have been made aware by the sharp yowl of pain from the Parthian, accompanied by a drenching spray of blood, teeth, and saliva that coated Pullus face.

Understanding the Parthian's right arm was no longer a threat, Pullus released his grasp, but this time, instead of trying to punch the man's face, he moved his left hand over to a spot right next to where his right, still clasping his sword, had been pressing against the wicker shield. Transferring his weight from his right to his left hand, in doing so, Pullus quickly realized that, while he was still clearly stronger than his foe, that strength was waning, and he understood that he had to end this before the span of another twenty heartbeats had passed. Just as he transferred his weight, the Parthian, who recognized as clearly what Pullus was about to do as Pullus had when it had been the Parthian holding his dagger, gave one last convulsive heave of his body, trying desperately to extricate his left hand. His right, while unable to clasp the dagger, still flailed at Pullus, but it was too damaged to make a proper fist. This didn't stop him from hitting Pullus once, twice, then several more times, except now it was Pullus who grimly ignored this attempt. Raising his right shoulder up and twisting to his left gave Pullus just enough room to bring the point of his sword up, whereupon the Parthian switched tactics, using his mangled hand and arm to try and block Pullus' thrust. He was only partially successful; while he did block Pullus' sword, it was only for as long as it took for the razor-sharp point to slice through the meat of his forearm, on its way down to the man's throat. Using what he was sure was the last bit of his energy, Pullus pushed the blade down until he felt the grating vibration that he had long before learned meant he hit bone. The Parthian stiffened, his eyes going even wider as he stared up at Pullus, who watched as the dark black dots of the man's pupils slowly opened, and the last breath escaped in what sounded like a melancholy sigh. Collapsing on top of his dead foe, Pullus panted for breath, only gradually becoming aware of the wider world, and his tired body flooded with a weary sense of relief at the sound of his men shouting in triumph, accompanied by the pounding noise of footsteps ascending the stairwell that had just moments before seemed such an unattainable goal.

Sextus Scribonius, at the head of the Second Cohort, clambered up and through the breach before descending onto the street level of Seleucia. Like his comrades before him, the Pilus Prior had a difficult time tearing his gaze from the sight before him, despite the fact he had been warned of what to expect. Forcing his attention away from the grisly scene around him, the tall, lean Centurion stood in the lee of his Century's *testudo*, although there was no longer a blizzard of arrows slicing down at them. Celadus, or one of the other Centurions of the First Cohort, had led a Century directly for the permanent stairway positioned midway down the northern wall, whereupon they split into two groups, one moving east along the wall, while the other group were squeezing those defenders back in the direction of the northwest corner. Meanwhile, the other two Centuries had made their way directly towards the easternmost temporary wall where Spurius and his survivors were located, and were using the two precious ladders in their possession to ascend it. However, while it wouldn't be until sometime later that Scribonius learned the details, he could clearly see that the temporary wall already had Romans on it, so that the Century climbing up didn't have to do so while defending themselves. Most importantly, what the Secundus Pilus Prior saw was that the area of the northern rampart and eastern temporary wall was well under control. Since they didn't know what they would be facing, this had been the first priority Pullus had given his Cohort; now that he had seen this was handled by the rest of the First, in that instance, Pullus had left it up to his best friend as to the best course of action. While he didn't give his Cohort the order to change from their *testudo*, he

378

felt sufficiently secure to step away from the shelter of his men to stand near the first building as he pondered what to do.

This was where he was standing when a voice boomed out, "Oy! Why are you just standing there looking like a moonstruck calf? Are you composing a poem?"

Scribonius didn't need to turn to look to see who had called to him in this manner, knowing both by the sound of the voice and what he said it was Balbus.

"What do you care?" he scoffed. "You couldn't read it!"

"I wouldn't want to," Balbus retorted, stopping at Scribonius' side, where the friends exchanged grins.

"Where did you come from?" Scribonius asked, leaning over to glance curiously back in the direction from where Balbus had seemingly materialized out of thin air.

"While you were standing around out there, my boys not only cleared this building, but we killed all those fuckers on that wall around the corner." Balbus jerked his thumb over his shoulder, in the general direction of the building behind them.

Misunderstanding, Scribonius frowned. "I thought Titus was clearing that temporary wall, not you."

"I'm not talking about the first one," Balbus explained. "There's one in between these two buildings as well. And," he twisted and pointed at the second building, where they could see the ragged hole that Spurius had his men had knocked in the wall, "Spurius and his boys broke out of there and took that far wall."

"That's who I saw." Scribonius suddenly learned the identity of the men he had seen when he first entered the city. More importantly, his mind, which worked more rapidly than any of Pullus' Centurions, or any others in the army, something that Balbus, despite his barbed jests, was secretly proud that this was the case, instantly analyzed what this meant and, most crucially, what to do. "So it looks like we've taken care of this section of the town. If we control those temporary walls, that means we can move into the city."

"Titus was going to have Valerius sound the call when he took that artillery piece," Balbus added, instantly comprehending and accepting his friend's assessment. "But even if he hasn't done it yet, if we go down this block," he turned and indicated the narrow street between the first and second buildings, "we'll be hidden from view from those *cunni* on the western wall farther south from the breach." Balbus' eyes narrowed in thought, trying to visualize what was likely

379

to lie ahead, based on his extremely limited knowledge of the layout of the town beyond this small killing box created by the defenders. "We can follow this street south. It will take us deeper into the city."

"We can start," Scribonius agreed, although he held up a cautioning hand, "but we're not going to go farther than a couple blocks. Not until we hear from Titus and see what he wants us to do."

The scarred side of Balbus' face tightened; this went against his most basic instinct, but he also understood that, as he was with a maddening regularity, Scribonius was right.

"Fine," he agreed flatly. "But what about that way?"

Scribonius regarded the scene in the direction Balbus had indicated, although it was impossible for him to tell much beyond the easternmost temporary wall. He knew the overall dimensions of Seleucia well enough; from that barrier, it was perhaps three quarters of a mile to the far eastern wall and the river that ran between the two cities. What he didn't have any idea was whether or not the street that ran parallel to the northern wall continued for its entire length. His guess was that it did; he knew that this was a city originally founded by one of Alexander's generals, and that it had almost been an obsession of the dead Macedonian king that every city, town, and even military camp was laid out in a symmetrical, organized fashion. Indeed, Scribonius was one of the few men of the ranks in the Roman army who knew that the layout of Roman camps, and permanent installations, was a direct copy from the Macedonians. This was why he felt somewhat confident that any Cohort that went in that direction would be able to make it to the northeastern corner, which in turn would allow them to move south, yet in doing so, they would cut off the access to the bridges from any defenders in Seleucia, and vice versa for those in Ctesiphon. Whether or not there would be any resistance was impossible to tell because the temporary wall obscured his view, but that wasn't a problem. By this point, Spurius and his men had moved from the rampart of the temporary wall, ascending what was an inexact copy of the steep stairwell that Pullus and his men had just finished taking, and were now facing eastward down the northern wall away from Scribonius. While it was impossible for him to see, judging from their behavior, he felt certain Spurius and his men were involved in some sort of fight.

Scribonius turned to Balbus and asked, "Do you want to bring your boys with us? We might as well move down at least a block. That way, it will give the rest of the Cohorts some breathing room."

Balbus hesitated, not because he didn't think this was a good idea, but Pullus hadn't had time to give his second instructions that went past clearing out this first building next to the western wall. Thinking quickly, he shook his head and said, "I think I'm going to take my boys back towards the main wall." The mobile part of his scarred face split into a grin. "Maybe he'll need our help. That way, I can never let him forget it!"

Scribonius laughed, knowing that not only was Balbus speaking the truth, but how much their friend would hate having him rub it in if that was the case. He also saw the wisdom of Balbus' decision.

"Fair enough," he agreed, then added, "But don't come crying to me if my boys stumble onto the town treasury."

For a bare instant, Balbus hesitated, torn between the idea of doing his duty and the allure of the riches that Scribonius had planted in his mind, knowing fully well the effect his words would have on his friend.

"I hate you," Balbus grumbled. "Why did you have to bring that up?"

"Because," Scribonius laughed, then pointed at Balbus' frown, "I love seeing that look on your face."

"Fine." Balbus spat onto the ground next to them, then gave his friend a glare that contained equal amounts of amusement and disgust, the latter aimed mostly at himself for snapping so greedily at the bait Scribonius had dangled. "I'm going back to the wall. But," he warned, shaking a finger in Scribonius' face, "I'm going to figure out a way to get even!"

"I'd be disappointed if you didn't," Scribonius countered, again with a laugh.

He clapped Balbus on the shoulder, and the two men returned back to the grim business that was taking a city by storm. One of them would have cause to think about his decision for some time to come.

Once Pullus regained his breath, he scrambled up the makeshift stairway, leaving the corpse of the scarred Parthian behind, still lying sprawled atop the hapless spearmen who had been crushed under the weight of his comrade and Pullus, two in a scattered pile of bodies arranged in a rough semicircle around the stairs. Pullus' men had already begun engaging the defenders who stood between them and the large artillery piece, but there was still a distance of some two hundred fifty paces they had to cover to get to it, and every foot of space was filled with Parthians. The one small blessing that Pullus could see as soon as he reached the rampart, and aided by his height, was that the composition of the defenders was almost evenly split between archers and spearmen, although the bowmen were concentrated nearer to the large *ballista*, needing the extra space to be effective at all. Even so, the angle the archers needed was such that the points of their arrows appeared to be aimed at something high in the sky in an attempt to arc their missiles over the heads of their own comrades, who were now arranged in a series of lines across the parapet, about eight men across. Because of the overhead threat, once more, his men were forced to raise their shields above their heads, with those immediately behind the front rank of Legionaries using theirs to shelter their comrades who were just beginning to engage with the spearmen.

Slowing only long enough to get a sense of the situation, Pullus swore bitterly at the sight before him; this was the most organized he had seen the Parthian infantry. It was certainly the case that their cohesion was a matter of necessity, hemmed in on one side by the parapet of the western wall to their left and the drop on the opposite side, yet this almost didn't matter. Shoving his way through the space between files, which was even narrower than normal, Pullus made his way up to the fighting, forced to crouch beneath the sheltering shields, the sounds of arrows striking wood having become such a common sound that neither he nor his men took much notice. Then, just a matter of two ranks away from where he could see that the engaged rank at the front were the men of his Fourth Section, Pullus suddenly realized that he was once more without a shield; the last one he had used was still lying among the bodies on the wooden parapet with a spear transfixing it. Unwilling to deprive one of his men from their overhead protection, he was forced to reverse his course; it was a moment that would cause Pullus many sleepless watches as he wondered if his mistake made him the unwitting cause of what was about to happen. Turning about—at least this time, his men saw him coming and stepped aside just enough to allow him to pass—once he was clear of the last rank, he trotted back to the ladder. Standing for a moment, he surveyed the debris and wreckage of the fight for the temporary wall, composed of almost equal parts equipment and the bodies of the dead, then he spotted a shield that didn't appear to be too badly damaged. It didn't take long for him to scramble down, snatch up the shield, and return to his men, but it was enough time to set in motion the events that followed.

Shoving his way back to the front, as he always did, Pullus led by example, violently punching with his shield to engage the spearman directly across from him, while at the same time bellowing, "Stop standing about, you lazy bastards! We have to knock that fucking piece out of commission! NOW!"

Even as he shouted his orders, as he intended, the Parthian across from him took the bait of the proffered shield, thrusting his spear forward, where it struck squarely, the tip punching through just enough that, using his strength, Pullus was able to twist the shield to further trap his foe's spear. Simultaneously, he launched a hard feint that gave the Parthian the impression the Roman's intention was to bring his sword down on the shaft of the spear. In order to protect his only offensive weapon, the Parthian was forced to bring his shield across his body, precisely what Pullus intended, and while the spearman instantly realized his error, he was too late in bringing his only protection, besides the thick, padded undershirt he wore underneath his robes, back to block the third position thrust that was designed to come in from the side, behind a foe's shield. The Parthian to the doomed man's left did try to stop Pullus' thrust, but a spear doesn't move quickly enough against a sword, yet in doing as he did in his vain attempt to save a comrade, he gave the Legionary to Pullus' right the opening he needed, his blade moving so rapidly it was difficult for the naked eye to track. Just that quickly, Pullus and his Gregarius created an opening, and while it was Pullus who instantly pressed forward, the ranker didn't lag long enough to allow the Parthian of the second rank to step over the body of the first spearman. In doing so, both Pullus and the Gregarius, Appius Asellus, another veteran of the fourth section who was missing the last two fingers on his shield hand, exposed themselves to even greater danger, although the hazard was lessened by the nature of the weapons exclusively used by the defenders. Spears were good for keeping an enemy at bay, but once a foe got inside the reach of the weapon, they were next to useless. In reality, the greatest hazard posed to the two Romans came from the men of the second rank, but on either side of the foes they were directly facing and not right behind them, because their spears were jabbed at the Romans from an oblique angle. Regardless of this danger, Pullus continued pressing forward, using his shield to deal with the threat that came from the opponent directly to his front, while parrying the spear thrust at him from the Parthian to that man's left. Bringing his blade up, Pullus deflected the attack away from the center of his body and slightly upward, causing the spear point to go over his right shoulder, closely enough to his ear that he could hear the scraping sound of the wooden shaft against the edge of his sword. The momentum of his countermove brought his sword up to a perpendicular position, which enabled him to make a simple but brutally powerful downward stroke that was angled slightly outward from Pullus' body. Before the Parthian could recover from his thrust, the Roman's blade sliced diagonally through both the forearm and spear shaft, severing both and sending them to the stone rampart, which was already slick with blood. Before the stricken man could react, Asellus' own blade punched out, catching the Parthian in the mouth that was hanging open as his eyes stared down at the spurting stump of arm. Pullus hadn't even fully recovered his sword when, once more, his left arm thrust out, the boss of his shield smashing into the wicker of the Parthian's, staggering this man backward a full step, subsequently colliding with the shield of the man behind him and, just that quickly, Pullus and Asellus were now in the third rank. Behind and to their sides, the rest of the First Century was making their own bloody progress, either slaying or, as Pullus just had, forcing their foes backward, slowly but inexorably carving their way through the Parthians defending themselves and the artillery piece with a growing desperation. Risking an occasional glance over the heads of his enemies, Pullus saw the moment when one of the Parthians who manned the artillery, braving a peek between the crenellations, didn't immediately duck down, followed by a speeding missile from one of Murena's machines. Even worse, after that quick glance, he leapt over to the artillery piece, shouting at his comrades, all of whom followed suit, jumping to their feet.

"Pluto's cock," Pullus snarled under his breath; even as he did so, he renewed the fury of his assault, his sword moving in a blur of deadly motion.

It was now a race between Pullus and his men, cutting their way to the *ballista* and the frantically working crew, trying to send their flammable death.

It took Balbus longer than he would have liked to gather up his men of the Second Century, scattered about, either in the first building where, despite the fighting going on outside, they were taking a moment to regain their breath or were outside looting the corpses of the Parthians. At least, some of them; what stayed Balbus' wrath was the majority of his men were involved in a much different task. At the behest of Balbus' Optio, Tiberius Bestia, his men were the first to attend to the charred remains of their comrades of the Third Legion, moving them to the base of the northern wall and laying them in a row with a gentleness that was in harsh juxtaposition to the manner in which they had died. Balbus, despite his impatience at the delay, still felt a surge of pride, but there was still work to be done.

"That's enough, Bestia," he called out, a matter of perhaps fifty heartbeats after the Pilus Prior had stopped to watch. "I know those boys appreciate you looking after them, but we're not through."

It was only at this moment that Balbus remembered that Bestia had a cousin, the son of his father's brother, who marched in the First of the Third, and although many of these men were burned beyond recognition, Balbus wondered if Bestia had spotted his cousin among the fallen. Making a note to ask him later, Balbus, whose own *cornicen* was missing at the moment, had to use the power of his lungs to order his men to assemble in the street between the first and second building, next to the temporary wall that Anaxagoras had erected midway down this block so that it was roughly aligned with the one nearest the western wall on the other side of the building. His men came quickly enough, or so Balbus believed in the moment, although this didn't deter him from unleashing a swipe at some of the men who emerged from the building, bearing the guilty look any experienced Centurion knew was the most potent sign that they had been off fucking about somewhere. Nevertheless, his Century was assembled with their normal speed and efficiency, and if what was about to occur had never happened, Balbus wouldn't have had any cause to rethink his own actions and wonder if he had been harsher it might have changed things.

"We're going back inside, then out onto the wall," Balbus announced as soon as his men were assembled, "but we're not going to join the First on the western wall. Instead," the scar tissue that dominated one side of his face twisted in an expression that his men had learned from experience and observation was their Pilus Prior's version of a leer, "we're going to drop down on the other side of the temporary wall, then move down behind that fucking *ballista*. We're going to be the ones to get to it first, not those dozy bastards from the First! What do you say to that?"

As he expected, his words were answered with a roar of approval, but he was already moving, darting back into the building, and, this time, his men were close by, following on his heels as he ascended the stairs that led to the second floor and the hole the Greek laborers had made in the building to allow access to the temporary wall. Following the same example as his Primus Pilus, Balbus led the way, out onto the wooden rampart, inadvertently leading some of his men to disaster.

Titus Pullus' sword was almost black with blood that had crusted so thickly the sheen of the metal was barely visible. More importantly, despite the thousands of watches of training, his right arm had begun to tire. What this meant in a practical sense was that the speed that Pullus could normally call on, which was impressive despite his size, was no longer available to him, so that he was forced to rely on nothing but his sheer, brute power, and he used this to his utmost. Battering his way through the rearmost ranks of spearmen, if viewed from above, the First Century of the 10th Legion was nothing more than a wedge composed of iron, wood, and flesh, fueled by the fury and indomitable will of their giant Centurion. If those Parthians with the misfortune to stand in his path, in the last heartbeats of their collective lives, had been able to confer with each other in the afterlife, they would have concurred that while it was bad enough to die, to be slain by a man who barely looked at them as he thrust his blade into their vitals was a particularly ignominious fate. As strange as it was, it was nothing less than the truth; Pullus' eyes remained fixed on the crew of the large *ballista* as they laboriously winched the arm of their piece down, while two other men moved to the small wooden lean-to placed more than a dozen paces on the opposite side of the artillery. Just as he and the Gregarius who had replaced Asellus, the latter finally forced to step aside when he expended the last of his available energy in an ultimately vain attempt to keep pace with his Primus Pilus, cut through the final rank of spearmen, Pullus' growing sense of concern turned to alarm when he saw the pair of men returning to the piece. They each held one end of a wooden contraption that carried what to Pullus looked like little more than an amphora of wine but contained a much deadlier cargo, and the pair moved with a slowness and care that, under other circumstances, would have been comical. What gave the lie to the idea that this was simply an expensive vintage of wine was the presence of the man Pullus knew from observation was Murena's counterpart, who was standing next to the artillery piece. Regardless of the man himself, it was the smoldering taper he held in one hand, the smoke barely visible in the bright sunshine, that caused Pullus to feel as if his heart suddenly seized up, stopping for a span of time impossible for him to measure. It was true that they were through the most difficult defenders, and that most of the archers, all of whom were already at a handicap because they weren't on horseback, were now streaming past the artillery piece, while the Parthian holding the taper screamed what Pullus assumed were imprecations at them for fleeing as they pushed by him. Regardless of this positive development, from Pullus' perspective, what was equally true was that almost as many archers chose to stand as did those who fled, and while they didn't pose much of a challenge, they still had to be dealt with before Pullus and his men could reach the *ballista*. Realizing that pausing, even if it was to catch his breath, was time he couldn't afford to waste, Pullus plunged forward, stepping over the last corpse he had just dispatched. As he did so, he held his sword loosely, pointing down at the stone, as he swung the sword about so the tip made tiny, perfect circles in the air. It was an unconscious habit, but for the men behind him, it was a sight that was oddly comforting, even as it evoked a series of collective memories that, while different in particulars, shared the common result of pain, administered with a wooden *rudis*, at the hands of their Primus Pilus.

"You know, Silo," was how one Gregarius put it to the man next to him, both of them in the eighth section, "I almost feel sorry for those archers. It looks like the Primus Pilus is feeling bloody."

"Bah," Silo retorted; he would have spat, but his throat was too dry. "They deserve what they got coming!" Glancing over at the other man, Silo gave a savage grin and said, "I don't know about you, but I don't think he should have all the fun. Killing these *cunni* will be the easiest we've done all day!"

That, his comrade knew, was true, so he followed Silo, and the other men arrayed behind Pullus, as they caught up to their Primus Pilus. For his part, Pullus had reached the nearest of the archers who had chosen to stand; at first, anyway, except their initial resolve quickly dissolved as the blood-spattered giant Roman approached, his face a grim mask that was more menacing because of its relative lack of visible emotion. His nerve failing him, the archer nearest to Pullus suddenly threw down the long dagger he had been holding, then turned to join his more prudent companions; his fate was sealed when he saw that the relatively narrow space between the edge of the rampart and the artillery piece was now packed with his comrades, all of them intent on shoving their way through the bottleneck. Casting a terrified glance over his shoulder and seeing the giant Roman even then lifting his sword arm, the Parthian made the instant decision to choose what he saw as the lesser of two evils: throwing himself off the edge of the rampart. Despite his grim focus on cutting down any man who stood in his way, Pullus jerked in weary surprise, his eyes following the falling form of the archer, even as he knew he could have cut the next-nearest Parthian down because he was similarly entranced. Flailing wildly in the brief span of time he was in the air, the archer tried to adjust his body to land in a somewhat controlled manner; he was unsuccessful, striking the paving stones of the street on his side, hitting with enough force that even on the rampart Pullus heard the snapping of bones. Oddly, the mortally injured man didn't cry out, but Pullus barely took notice, already beginning to move towards the next Parthian, whose eyes were still fixed on the sight of his comrade, around whose body a pool of blood was slowly forming. This was how he died, only returning his attention back towards Pullus when the point of the Roman's blade plunged into his body, his eyes suddenly widening in shock, just before the dark parts of iris and pupil disappeared as they rolled back in his head. For a bare moment, just one, Titus Pullus felt a flare of hope that he would be in time, as a combination of events occurred that allowed him to move within striking range of the Parthian holding the taper. It began when the bottleneck suddenly cleared; whether or not the example of the archer who had chosen to risk falling to his death was the trigger, or it was just one of those coincidences, Pullus would never know, but from his perspective, it appeared that two archers, working in concert, began shoving their own comrades off the edge of the rampart. In rapid succession, in perhaps the span of two normal heartbeats, the pair dispatched at least a half-dozen of their supposed comrades in this fashion, the last of them just beginning to turn in recognition that the threat to their rear came not from the Roman, but two of their own. Whatever the cause, it enabled Pullus to advance to put the Parthian with the taper just within the arc of his sword, if he extended his arm out fully. Also, this foe had turned his full attention towards his task of lighting the oil-soaked rag that had been sealed into the mouth of the amphora with wax, so there was little chance of him dodging Pullus' thrust. All that remained was taking another half step forward, which Pullus had begun taking. What happened next was never really clear to Pullus, nor to his men who had now reached a spot just behind him.

On the side nearest to the crenellations, Pullus' Optio, Lutatius, was even then trying to clamber over the makeshift barricade made of barrels and filled sacks that the crew of the *ballista* had erected for the very purpose it was serving now, making it difficult for any foe to approach from that side. While none of them would ever understand exactly how it happened, the result was one they would be forced to live with for the rest of their lives, however long they lasted. Just as Pullus felt he had gotten within reach, and as his sword was even then beginning its downward arc, aimed for the outstretched arm of the Parthian, one of the pair of archers, who had only been intent on escaping, turned to see the giant Roman, his arm raised. Thinking that he was the target, in a blind panic, the archer reacted unthinkingly, lashing out with one foot, his sandal striking Pullus' left knee from the side. The angle was such and the force sufficient that it caused Pullus' knee to buckle, altering his aim just as his sword sliced down onto the Parthian with the taper, but not where he had aimed. In that span of time it took for Pullus' blade to descend, the smoking taper ignited the oil-soaked rag, bursting into flame even as the edge of the Roman's sword cut deeply into the back of the crouched Parthian, instead of severing his arm as Pullus had intended. Even as the scream of pain was leaving the Parthian's throat, the man on his crew designated to release the pin that held the *ballista's* arm in place yanked the cord attached to it. Faster than the eye could track, the arm of the *ballista* shot forward and, out of the corner of his vision, all Pullus saw was a blur of smoky flame hurtling out of the basket.

"Noooooooooooooooooooooo!"

While Pullus was only dimly aware that this came from his own throat, he clearly heard several of his men shouting the same word. Despite a part of his mind practically begging him not to do so, Pullus forced himself to turn around, but while he wasn't quite fast enough to spot the tumbling jar hurtling through the air, his eye just happened to fall on the temporary wall the instant before the jar impacted on the wooden rampart, exploding in a burst of flames and greasy black smoke that for a brief, blessed instant, obscured his vision of the wall as the liquid fire boiled outward from the center of the impact. It wasn't long enough, by any means, as the screams from easily a dozen throats punctuated the air, overpowering the other sounds of battle, and as Pullus watched in utter horror, he saw men of his Cohort, some of his boys, become blazing torches; if, that is, torches were able to stagger about and had limbs to wave wildly about in their ultimately vain attempts to stop the flames from consuming them.

"Isn't that the Second Century?"

At first, Pullus didn't recognize the voice, but when he turned in numbed shock, he saw Lutatius standing next to him, and Pullus took no notice of the sword in his Optio's hand, still dripping with the blood of the artillery crew. Then the words actually struck him, the meaning of them causing Pullus' heart to seem to stop for the second time in a short period, and he stared at the horror, searching for some sight of his friend.

"I...I don't see Balbus." Pullus managed to sound calm, although this was due more to the shock than any self-possession, as his eyes continued to scan the rampart, looking for a transverse crest, the only way to recognize a man from this distance.

His throat closed up, rendering Pullus speechless as his mind began to cope with the enormity of what he was seeing; there was no Roman on that wall, at least who weren't even then still burning to death, who wore the distinctive crest that identified him as a Centurion. Balbus, he was suddenly sure, was dead.

The reason Pullus was unable to spot his second in command and friend was for a simple reason, although it wouldn't become apparent immediately. As normal, Balbus led his men onto the wooden rampart, and he had been more than halfway across the temporary barrier, stopping right next to the spot where the ladder that Pullus and his Century had used was located, nearest to the western wall. Rather than order someone to do it, he had turned his back in the direction of the *ballista*, only after he had given a cursory glance and seen his Primus Pilus clearly within a pace or two of the piece. He was in the process of pulling up this ladder, with the intent of placing it on the other side so he and his men could descend down to the street level without risking injury by jumping down; this was the posture he was in when the *ballista* had loosed its deadly cargo, and he had just begun to turn when he heard the shouts of alarm from those men of his Century who had been closest behind him. Two of his men had already reached his side and were leaning over to lend a hand retrieving the ladder, and all three of them reacted to the sudden eruption of smoke-wreathed flame that roiled outward in both directions from where the jar impacted the wooden parapet, the sight of the flames and the sudden blast of intense heat so close together that they experienced both simultaneously. What saved Balbus and a good dozen of the men of the first two sections of the Second Century was that the jar smashed into the rampart closer to the building than to the western wall. However, it also meant that one of the men consigned to a fiery death was Balbus'

Optio Bestia; later, Balbus would learn that Bestia's cousin had, in fact, been one of those first men incinerated, meaning that the Bestia family suffered an almost unfathomably tragic loss in the space of a day. In the moment, Balbus' first thought caused him to rush *towards* the flames, not away from them, and in doing so, the Pilus Posterior suffered burns along his arms. A less painful result, but one that caused Pullus a fair amount of anxiety came when the intense heat caused the feathers on Balbus' crest to catch fire, which was only brought to his attention when, without warning, one of his men reached and tried to yank the helmet off his Centurion's head.

"Your helmet's on fire!"

Only then did Balbus realize that, while his entire body was experiencing the intense heat, it was the top of his head that, in fact, was even hotter, something he would have sworn was impossible before it happened. Fumbling with the leather cords that attached his helmet firmly to his head, he only managed to get it off with the help of the ranker who had brought it to his attention. While they were beating out the flames, the other unscathed men of the Second were doing what they could for their friends; tragically, this consisted of little more than ending their agony with a merciful thrust. Even this turned out badly, as a half-dozen of those who tried to intervene in this manner suffered burns themselves. Not all of the men who were hit by the splattering gobs of the sticky substance died; a number of men were struck in the lower extremities by small globules of the naphtha, and they quickly learned the difficulty of trying to extinguish the substance.

"Help them," Balbus snapped to the ranker who had been assisting him, pointing to two men who were in almost identical positions, sitting on the unscathed part of the rampart with their legs splayed in front of them, rapidly beating at the tiny, flickering flames that were barely visible but were cooking their skin, eliciting panicked shouts for help and screams of agony at the same time.

Responding immediately, the ranker moved to the man who was suffering the worst, with three separate spots where the naphtha had struck his legs, removing his neckerchief as he knelt. Meanwhile, Balbus beckoned to one of the other fortunate men who had been with him, indicating the other burn victim, yet even as he did so, the Centurion was moving in the direction of the building. The entire span of the temporary barrier was only about fifty paces, from the makeshift stairs joining the rampart of the western wall, to the spot where the roughly hewn hole gaped in the side of the first building, but the carnage was such that it took Balbus a moment for his mind to comprehend it. It wasn't the worst casualties his Century had suffered in terms of numbers; it was the nature of the damage that shook him to his core. The last of the men who had borne the brunt of the exploding flammable substance had just been dispatched by a comrade; later, Balbus would learn that it was even worse than that because this last fallen ranker had not only marched with the man who was forced to end his life, it was his close comrade, the holder of his will and closest friend who dispatched him. Such was the case here, but in the moment, Balbus was more concerned with reestablishing a sense of order; frankly, all thoughts of what lay on the south side of the temporary wall had vanished in the amount of time it took for that jar of naphtha to sail through the air and cause the devastation he was seeing. As if these problems weren't enough, it wasn't long before the smoke created by the naphtha consuming the tunics, and flesh of some of his men, grew thicker, as the wooden rampart, made of dry, seasoned timber that had been in a variety of other structures just a few days before, succumbed to the pernicious nature of the substance. More rapidly than Balbus could have believed, the dry timbers caught, and it seemed to him no more than a dozen heartbeats of time had elapsed since the initial impact before the wooden rampart was fully ablaze.

"Get off! Get off! Get off the rampart!"

Balbus roared this over and over, grabbing dazed men who were still trying to grapple with the aftermath of this catastrophe and what it meant, shoving them hard in the direction of the western wall, or as the flames grew, shouted at the men on the other side of the impact area to withdraw back into the building.

"Grab anyone who's alive and get off the rampart! It's going to collapse quicker than Pan!"

Despite their disorientation, Balbus' men reacted, even if it was more out of habit than any real thought, those who were relatively unscathed reaching down to grab men who, while alive, were in many cases still frantically trying to subdue the flames that were broiling their flesh. More than any other factor, it was the level and quality of the noise that was proving the most difficult for Balbus and the survivors to block out and keep from rattling them more than they already were. As it was with Quintus Balbus, the rest of those Romans who had been confronted with this awful Parthian weapon, the

392

screams of friends burning alive would haunt many a man's dream for the rest of their lives.

Chapter Fourteen

On the opposite side of the siege, at the southeast corner, Caesar had only gotten word shortly before about what had befallen Spurius and his men; as was so often the case, the event and the informing of Caesar about it was separated by a significant span of time, particularly in moments like this, making it difficult for any commander to decide the proper course. Consequently, the general seriously considered sending another of the Legions with him to Seleucia; after a moment's consideration, he dismissed this as impractical. The distance that had to be covered from this spot to Seleucia was more than seven miles, even using the most direct route, and while a Legion could cover that in a bit less than two parts of a watch, at that pace, it would take them time to recover from the effort, or they would be completely useless. As much as any other reason, it was the identity of the three Legions that persuaded Caesar to not only refrain from sending reinforcements, but from going himself. The latter part of his decision was based as much in the sight of men who at that moment were scaling the walls of Ctesiphon and what he could see was a furious battle taking place on the ramparts. Instead of going himself, he decided on something of a compromise, calling Pollio to his side.

"Go with this man back to Seleucia and see exactly what's going on," he ordered his Legate, and while his tone was calm, Pollio knew Caesar well enough to be alerted something was at the very least amiss on the other side of the twin cities. "Assess the situation, then send your report back to me. If you think Spurius, Pullus, and Balbinus need help, let me know how many Legions you think it will take." Pollio, as was the practice, repeated his orders, but just as he turned away, Caesar reached out a restraining hand. "Wait," he commanded as he thought for another moment, then slightly amended his orders by saying, "Instead of going back that direction," he indicated the vast expanse of open ground to the north, where the northeastern camp was visible only as a tiny dark line at the very base of the horizon, "go by way of the southwest camp. The auxiliaries are still standing by outside their camp. Or," he allowed, aware of the independent streak the petty kings and clients like Herod tended to exhibit, "they should be. No matter what you find, have them begin marching towards the northwest camp. That way, if you find they do need some help, they'll have some coming sooner rather than later. They're not the Legions," Caesar admitted, "but they'll be better than nothing."

As he expected, Pollio accepted this change with a nod, and another recitation of his orders before the Legate saluted, then turned and began trotting away, beckoning to the dispatch rider. Only then did Caesar realize he had missed something, but he was about to open his mouth when he saw there was no need, as Pollio commanded one of the pool of couriers that always waited near Caesar to switch out his fresh mount for the fatigued horse of the courier. Happy to see that someone else was thinking of the small details, Caesar returned his attention to the fight for Ctesiphon.

In his still-new role as Primus Pilus, Tiberius Atartinus was determined to be at least the first man of his Legion up the ladder and onto the wall of Ctesiphon, and he accomplished his goal, somewhat to his chagrin and much to his peril. Instantly surrounded by not just the spear-wielding Parthians, but two Parthian noblemen armed with swords, Atartinus ran the real risk of having one of the shortest tenures in his post in Roman history. Thankfully, he did manage to make enough space behind him for the men of his first section to join him and, with their help, he not only managed to survive a bit longer, he and his men forced the Parthians back towards the redoubt that housed the three artillery pieces that had been part of the force that wreaked so much initial havoc on Caesar's army, but had since been at least partly neutralized. This wasn't due to using the same method Pullus had employed with Murena and their complement of artillery, if only because there was more than just one piece placed in multiple spots along both the eastern and southern walls, in addition to this one large position. It had been Caesar, once more demonstrating his ability to think in unconventional ways, who at least partially negated the threat of the flaming jars of naphtha by having those Centuries within range not only drop out of a *testudo*, but to go to an even more open formation than normal. In doing so, the Romans not only gave the Parthians less opportunity to inflict multiple casualties because they were bunched together, it gave his men a better ability to track the incoming jars, which were easy to spot because of the black smoke that trailed behind them. Naturally, like any decision made under duress and when time is of the essence, Caesar's command didn't completely remove the risk, and there was a drawback, in the form of providing targets for the archers. Whereas a *testudo* was the best defense against massed forces of archers, by opening up their formation, men had only their shields, eyes, and reflexes to protect them from an arrow streaking down from the sky, moving much more quickly than the jars, and without a telltale smoke trail. But, while it may have been something of a brutal decision, no man of Caesar's army would have disagreed with the premise behind his orders, that if a man was fated by the gods to die, better that it was from an arrow than burning alive. As they would all learn later, this was affirmed by the horrible fate being suffered by too many of Caesar's men on the opposite side of the siege. So, while there had been more casualties from arrows than Caesar would have liked, far fewer men had been unable to leap out of the way of the naphtha jars, and now, Caesar was certain, the Parthians had run out of their supply. That this was so, at least to Caesar and his men, was made clear when the ladders touched the walls, and no flaming death rained down on the heads of the first men up their ladder, like Atartinus. This is not to say there weren't some tense moments, as Caesar and those souls who had either volunteered or been designated first up the ladders prayed to every god they could think of as they climbed. Even if their supply of naphtha had been expended, it was common practice to use boiling pitch, or in this part of the world where pitch was almost nonexistent, oil to dump down on the heads of the attackers. Whether or not the Parthian commander had placed his faith in the naphtha, or this was one of the myriad details that slipped his mind didn't really matter to Caesar or his Legionaries; what did was that none of the leading men scaling the ladders suffered a similar fate to their comrades in Seleucia. And, now that the Romans had achieved the walls, although the Parthians put up a fierce fight for the rampart, they were simply outmatched for this close-in type of fighting. However, this didn't mean the fight was over, by any means; the archers that the Parthian commander had ordered down from the walls were now on the street level, although some of them had climbed up onto the roofs of several of the nearest buildings, whereupon they quickly resumed the seemingly endless volleys of arrows that had been temporarily interrupted. Free from the risk of piercing one of their own now that those spearmen who had remained to fight were either dead or had withdrawn, the archers were posing such a hazard that for the time being, all progress on the Roman side of the battle had stopped as men formed serried ranks of shields and turned them in the direction of the archers nearest to them. Meanwhile,

396

Atartinus, followed by the first five sections of his Century, pushed north along the eastern wall, reaching the larger space of the redoubt, which was quickly taken, aided by the fact that the crews of the artillery pieces had fled without putting up a fight. Pausing to catch his own breath and allow his men to do the same, the Primus Pilus actually rested against one of the pieces, idly examining it. Although it was clearly recognizable, Atartinus, who had actually started out as an *Immune* assigned to a *ballista* crew before working his way up through the ranks, noticed some subtle differences in the design. Nothing that would stop them from being used by us, he thought, still not really making the connection. That happened on the heels of his last thought, and he slowly straightened up, staring down at the piece, studying not just its configuration, but how it was secured to its spot on the rampart.

"Caninus," he called to one of his men of the first section, "get the rest of your section and come here! I have an idea!"

Kambyses had made the prudent decision to withdraw from his spot on the wall, which was validated when he saw how quickly and ruthlessly the Romans swept all opposition from the ramparts. Now the only reason they were still up there and not down on the street level was solely due to the presence and activity of his archers. No Roman, or so it appeared, was willing to expose himself to the withering storm of missiles that would be practically inevitable when they attempted to descend the stone stairs. There was just no way for their shields, even as large as they were, to cover every part of the body when they were performing a task like going down the steps, and it would be a rare man indeed who could survive being pierced in his lower extremities while still retaining the presence of mind not to react naturally and drop their shield in reflex, thereby offering sharp-eyed archers a fatter, juicier target in the form of their upper bodies. But, as heartening as this was, Kambyses also was acutely aware that it couldn't last, especially since he had just been informed by the commander of this contingent of archers that they were now down to less than three full quivers per man. Should he save them, he wondered, and retreat in good order back to the central plaza, where Anaxagoras had prepared the last line of defense? Or would he be better served keeping the Romans up there on the wall for as long as possible before bowing to the inevitable? This line of thinking got him looking over his shoulder, wondering where the reserves he had ordered to come to him were, and why they weren't already here, ready for his orders.

This, more than any other factor, was what formed Kambyses' decision. Turning to the man who carried the long, thin horn used by the Parthians, he snapped, "Sound the order to retreat! We're going to move back to the plaza and wait for them there."

In the same manner that both Pullus and Balbus had experienced, what occurred next happened so quickly that Kambyses would never be able to sort it out in his mind, at least to a point that made any sense. His eyes were still on the horn player, who was lifting the horn to his lips, presumably to sound the series of notes Kambyses had ordered. The Parthian commander did have the barest sensation of movement out of the corner of his vision, although it was moving so quickly that he might have imagined it. What the object was only became apparent a heartbeat later, but the effect was such that, in a similar manner to when Kambyses witnessed one of his artillerymen trying to sneak a look at the advancing Romans, the horn player just...vanished. Of course, it wasn't that neat, and it wasn't all of him that disappeared, but this time, Kambyses couldn't escape the evidence of what a rock could do to a man, as he was suddenly bathed in warm, sticky fluid and what the exposed part of his skin could feel were warm chunks of matter that had, an eye blink before, been a man. Actually, it wasn't the entire horn player; the man's body from roughly the middle of his stomach down was intact, except that it now lay several paces away, thrown backward by the force of the missile that had eviscerated him. Shiny, slightly green loops of intestines were strung out around the ruined body, but while Kambyses, forced to wipe the blood and gore from his face in order to see anything at all, certainly took in this sight, it was the horn, lying more than a dozen paces away yet seemingto be perfectly intact, that made the strongest impression. In a daze, the Parthian commander was only vaguely aware of the shouts of alarm, disgust, and fear from the men who had been standing nearby, but he finally forced himself to tear his gaze away and look back toward the wall as his benumbed mind tried to make sense of what had just occurred. He got his answer in the form of another sudden blur of motion, followed less than an eye blink later by a second stone tearing into the ranks of his archers just a dozen paces away. This time, the single rock inflicted more casualties than the first one, as it tore the head off the archer in the front rank, barely slowing down as it smashed into the chest of the man behind him in an explosion of flesh, bone, and blood. Now slowed sufficiently that it didn't have the power to pass through the archer of the third rank, that was a faint blessing for this man, as it slammed into his stomach with the force of a dozen men punching him. In some ways, this man suffered a worse fate than his two comrades, who were at least now beyond pain, as he was destined to die in agony as his internal organs, ruptured by the force of the missile, hemorrhaged into his abdomen and body cavity. The third missile, this one in the form of an iron bolt, the lone weapon of this type that Anaxagoras and his men had constructed, did even more damage, something that Kambyses wouldn't have thought possible if he hadn't seen it with his own eyes, as the bolt sliced through four archers before embedding itself in the paving stones, dripping the blood and viscera of its victims. And just that quickly, any thoughts Kambyses had of an orderly withdrawal, fighting every step of the way back to the plaza, vanished in the length of time it took for the missiles launched by Atartinus and his makeshift artillery crews to shatter not only Parthian bodies, but their hopes.

Freeing the three artillery pieces had been the easy part of the business, as Atartinus discovered; the difficult part was sorting out men whose last turn serving as crews of artillery had been in their time as *tiros*, when they spent a few days learning the rudiments of what Atartinus knew was an arcane but important skill, particularly when a man marched for Caesar. Prying the iron stakes that had been pounded into the two rearmost legs of the pieces, Atartinus had taken the time to notice this seemingly minor but significant detail, because it was the mark of an expertise in the use of such machines that the Romans of all ranks had taken as an article of faith that the Parthians didn't possess. As Atartinus knew, while it would seem to make sense for a fixed piece to have all four points of contact securely fastened to whatever it was resting on, that would be a practical guarantee a particular machine would be available for perhaps a half-dozen volleys at most. Without the ability for the machine to move in response to the inevitable recoil caused by itself when its tension was suddenly released, the energy created by that recoil had to be absorbed by the wood of the machine, and if it was held rigidly in place, it wouldn't take long for it to shake itself apart. In the moment, it was just an odd thought that flashed across his mind like one of those random streaks of light that one sometimes saw in the night sky; right then, he had to give some of his men a quick lesson in what they needed to do once they muscled the three pieces so they were now pointing in the opposite direction. At the same time, the Primus Pilus was forced to send men to scrounge for material that could be used to place under the rear legs of the pieces to provide the proper angle. As these men were doing so, Atartinus gave a hasty lesson in the fundamentals of serving a piece.

"We're not going to be able to match what the boys over there can do," Atartinus jerked his thumb over his shoulder back in the general direction of where the Roman artillery was located, "but by the gods, we're going to be close!"

The men hustling to find the needed materials returned, a motley assortment of planks, a few bags that felt like they contained sand, and other odds and ends. Fairly quickly, each piece had been adjusted so they were tilted to what Atartinus could only hope was the right degree. In this, he was more successful than he could have hoped, as the first three missiles tore into the assembled ranks of archers who were arrayed in the street below, just within the minimum range of the artillery. And, before his men managed to winch each piece back into position, while other men hustled to bring the respective ammunition for each one, the Romans nearest the other pieces arrayed on both this eastern wall and on the southern one began following the example set by Atartinus. By the time Atartinus' makeshift crews released their second volley, the Parthians down below, those on both streets paralleling the eastern wall and the southern one, were subjected to a murderous crossfire. And, although these artillery machines weren't served with the same efficiency of those outside the wall, before each one had loosed their third volley, the hailstorm of arrows that had been pinning down their comrades on the ramparts, rendering them unable to advance, while not ceasing altogether slackened enough that the stalemate ended. The bolder Legionaries were, as usual, the first to move; it wasn't an accident that most of those were Centurions, since such was their nature and, indeed, why they were in these important posts. Leading their men down the stone stairs from both walls, these Centurions threw themselves at a thin, hastily assembled line of spearmen, no more than three ranks deep anywhere along its length, which curved from south to east, roughly following the contour of the wall, although the junction of the two walls was at a right angle. Some of the Parthians' officers, wearing the heavy armor that was much more comfortable to bear on the back of a horse, realizing this as the crucial moment in the fight, rallied their men to the best of their abilities. However, as all but one or two quickly learned, when men are constantly considered more annoyance than asset, and exposed to

400

the brutal treatment at the hands of these same men who were now calling for them to resist to their utmost, what little fight was left in these spearmen, the remnants of the force that had been arrayed on the rampart five ranks deep, was expended almost instantly. As it normally did, the backward flight started with the men of the rearmost rank, but at the far western end of the line of spearmen trying to keep the Legions who had surmounted the southern wall from going any farther, the Parthian noble who had assumed responsibility for this part of the defense was successful in stemming the flow, at least at first. His method wasn't unusual, and it was actually a practice shared by their Roman enemies, so that when the first man of the last rank turned to flee, the noble, his sword already drawn, nearly decapitated the infantryman with a single stroke of his sword. The man next to the now-dead spearman, who had indeed been turning to follow his friend, faced back to the front. As he did, he just happened to catch sight of one of his comrades, now with just one rank between them, take a sword thrust from a Roman blade through the mouth. The point of the blade burst through the back of the man's turbaned head, poking through the cloth in a tiny shower of blood and brains, and in that moment, the spearman's fear of the Romans was far greater than one of his own people, even if he was nobility and armed with a sword. This time, however, when the spearman turned to flee, before the nobleman could do more than raise his sword in a preparatory move to mete out the same punishment he had inflicted on the first man to try, the peasant executed a perfect thrust of his own, the point of his spear punching through the overlapping iron plates, penetrating deeply into the officer's chest. This was where the peasant left his weapon, barely noticing the nobleman, his lips suddenly flecked with bloody froth, tottering for a moment, the sword dropping from his hand, his body following immediately after. All that was in the spearman's mind was one simple thought: run. And when he did so, now that there was nobody inclined to stop him, his comrades in the rear ranks who were within sight of the scene quickly joined him. Before a span of thirty heartbeats had passed, the entire right, westernmost wing of this last-gasp defense of the walls collapsed. It didn't take a veteran Centurion to know to take advantage of this, and the Quartus Princeps Prior of the 8th Legion that had anchored the left of the Roman lines, and had been one of the first to lead his men down the stairs, didn't hesitate. Using a combination of his *signifer*, who thrust his Century standard aloft, then dipped it down so it pointed in the direction of the collapsing enemy right flank, and the power of his voice, the Centurion led the men of his Century as they went smashing into the remaining defenders, those spearmen who hadn't run. And by standing their ground, while their end was inevitable, it was hastened, especially when compared to those more prudent comrades who were now running through the series of streets that ran in a northerly direction, back to the center of the capital. What had been a desperate fight, but with a semblance of organized defense, quickly became a slaughter as more Centuries followed the example of the Third of the Fourth, and in the same way a barrier of sand is swept away by an incoming tide, so too were the last spearmen, although by falling, they gave their comrades who either abandoned them, or like most of the archers, had been withdrawn by orders, a brief respite. Before a sixth part of a watch had passed, the Romans had taken possession of the southern wall; now all that was left was to sweep northward, using the streets of the city to bring this siege to a close.

Fortunately for Kambyses, he had already begun his own withdrawal to the plaza. Meeting the reinforcements he had sent for, there were a few chaotic moments as he shouted at them to turn around and retrace their steps. While these men were rearranging themselves to reverse direction, Kambyses beckoned to one of the commanders of the force of remaining archers.

"Are you in command?" he asked peremptorily, realizing that this man, while wearing the armband that marked him as a commander of archers, was someone he only knew by sight.

"I...I believe so, Excellency," said the man, a young Parthian more than twenty years Kambyses' junior. "I haven't seen Hydarnes or Darius since the Romans threw their ladders up against the walls."

"No doubt they're dead," Kambyses said flatly; even if he had held any warm feelings for either of these men, this wasn't the time to indulge in maudlin behavior. "So that means you command the archers. How many are left?"

"I-I-I don't know for certain, Excellency." He then hurried on when he saw the older Parthian's mouth twist. "We haven't had the chance to make a count recently. But at last check, we had more than five hundred men." He swallowed hard before finishing, "Now? I'd be surprised if we have more than three hundred men left."

Gritting his teeth, Kambyses recognized this also wasn't the time to indulge in a fit of temper, so instead, he said tightly, "Very well. Here are your orders."

By the time he was finished, the young commander's face was ashen, yet he still met Kambyses' gaze with a resolute expression, his jaw clenched as he seemingly absorbed and accepted his new instructions.

"I understand, Excellency." He surprised himself with how calm he sounded. "We'll buy you the time you need."

It would have been difficult to determine who was more surprised when Kambyses said, "Thank you. I shall make sure the King of Kings knows that...." Suddenly embarrassed, he gave a short bark that might have been a laugh. "I don't even know your name."

"My name is Sarosh, of the house of Suren." Seeing the startled look, he added quickly, "I'm of a minor branch, Excellency. And I'm a fourth son."

"Well, Sarosh," Kambyses felt a hard lump form in his throat as he looked at this youngster who could have been a younger version of himself, although he had been a second son himself, "I know you will bring even more honor to the house of Suren."

Then, there was nothing else to be said; glancing over his shoulder, he saw that the reserve was now rapidly trotting back to the plaza. Not knowing what else to say, Kambyses turned and strode away, walking quickly. He would not run; the running for the day was over.

Sextus Scribonius found his Primus Pilus by following the sounds of the screams, issued by the poor, tortured souls who had the misfortune to still draw breath, despite their horrible burns. While Scribonius was the least superstitious of the men of the ranks, not just in the 10th Legion but probably in the entire army, he felt the hairs on his neck standing up as an involuntary shiver ran up his spine as, unbidden, the word *numeni* popped into his mind. At least, this was what he imagined *numeni* sounded like; nevertheless, he forced himself to continue walking, stepping over the bodies and debris, following his ears. It was when he turned the corner, back to the street running parallel with the western wall, that the combination of the sights and, worse, the smell of freshly roasted meat assaulted him so violently that, for the first time since he had been a *tiro*, Scribonius retched, as his stomach rebelled when his mind identified the meaning of the stench. The temporary wall still stood, but was smoking heavily, from something on the opposite side of the wall; Scribonius correctly guessed that it was the wooden rampart. Although this was the case, there were still more questions, except that, suddenly, Scribonius wasn't sure he wanted to learn the answers. Nevertheless, his feet moved, taking him towards the wall. Thankfully, those men who had been struck by arrows while they were scaling the walls were already being attended to by the *medici*, who, in their usual efficient manner, had moved in immediately behind the assaulting Legion. As Scribonius approached, he caught sight of the familiar face of Diocles, who was doubling in his role as a *medicus*; as the Greek liked to remind his ostensible master, anyone serving Titus Pullus had better learn at least the rudiments of patching a man up, although his skills in this area were still developing. Consequently, he was allowed to give aid to the less severely wounded, and this was what he was doing now, bent over a Legionary who was sitting on an upended crate of some sort. When he drew closer, Scribonius saw that Diocles was at that very moment sewing what the Pilus Prior could see was a puncture wound of the bicep as the Gregarius sat, trying not to wince. Although he didn't want to disturb the Greek at this task, he did need to find his friend, and it seemed a logical place to start; the times Diocles didn't know the whereabouts of Titus Pullus at any given moment were few and far between.

Clearing his throat once, then twice before the Greek looked up sharply, a look of annoyance on his face that disappeared when he saw Scribonius, although Diocles didn't smile, the Centurion did grin and said, "I hate to interrupt you, but I'm looking for your master. Any idea where he is?"

It was a moment that Scribonius would long remember, because Diocles' expression changed so rapidly, becoming so grave that for a brief instant, he felt sure the world had suddenly tilted. Scribonius couldn't summon the words, even in his mind, so unthinkable was it that Titus Pullus had suffered a serious wound, or worse. His momentary surge of anxiety didn't last long, fortunately, as Diocles pointed in the direction of the wall.

"He's on the other side of the wall." Diocles paused, seeming to search for words, which was singularly unusual in itself. "Helping out."

Under normal circumstances, this would have prompted a laugh from Scribonius, followed by a witty remark about the low likelihood that the Primus Pilus was getting his hands dirty, but just the expression on Diocles' face arrested any such thoughts.

"Helping with what?"

Diocles still didn't answer, then finally closed his eyes and said, "Honestly, Master Sextus, I don't even really know where to begin. But it involves the Second Century. And," Scribonius saw the hard knot of the Greek's throat bob, "it's bad. Very, very bad."

As quickly as the relief had come at the realization that Pullus was undoubtedly alive, and probably unharmed, proven by the Greek's presence on the opposite side of the temporary wall, it was swept away by a thought almost as horrible.

"Balbus?" Scribonius' voice sounded strange to his own ears, as if someone had grabbed him by the throat just as he spoke.

Understanding where Scribonius' mind had gone, he held up a hand in a placating gesture, assuring the Centurion, "No, Master Sextus. Master Quintus is fine. But his Century," his mouth twisted, but he forced himself to continue, "they were crossing to get to the rampart and the Parthians were able to get one last volley from that *ballista*."

Everything fell into place for Scribonius then; the screams, the smells, and the smoke. Before Diocles could utter another word, he began running for the ladder still leaning in the same spot where Balbus had been about to grab it.

"No! You can't go that way!" Scribonius stopped, and Diocles explained, "That smoke you see is from the rampart. It's almost completely destroyed."

Somewhat embarrassed by this lapse, Scribonius merely nodded, consoling himself that his shaken state of mind had made him forget the first thing he had noticed. Pausing for a moment, he then resumed heading towards the ladder while, this time, ignoring Diocles' query about why he was doing this when he had just been informed of the danger. With some effort, Scribonius manhandled the ladder so it was now leaning against the permanent wall, the top of it still about three feet short of the rampart. This was enough for him to pull himself up, so he scrambled up quickly, both out of concern for his friends and because there was still a battle going on, and a horribly disorganized one at that. Once atop the rampart, Scribonius only had to walk a couple paces before he had a clear view of the other side of the temporary wall, and he immediately wished he hadn't done so. The remnants of the rampart had collapsed, burned through, but among the blackened timbers, some of which were still blazing away, he saw what looked like twisted, charred sticks that he instantly knew were no such thing. They were the arms and legs of men, presumably of the

Second Century, and to Scribonius, one bony hand in particular seemed to point an accusing finger skyward, directly at him. Shaking this off, he hurried down the rampart, moving as quickly as he could by stepping over the piled bodies of the Parthians who had died and in doing so, gave the *ballista* the time to deliver one more volley. So many questions flooded through his mind, yet Scribonius was forced to shove them aside as he carefully stepped over the corpses to descend the stone stairs. There were men standing near the still-burning remains of both men and rampart, but Scribonius didn't see Pullus there. Nor did he see Balbus, then one of the men turned, and on seeing Scribonius, simply pointed to the building. The permanent double doors that, under normal conditions, were wide enough to allow all manner of goods inside, still hung there, barely, but they were open. When he entered, he was further assaulted by the stench, grown infinitely stronger because of proximity, and he instantly understood this was where the survivors had been taken; and, he thought grimly, wincing at the noise, from where the screams had come. It was dimly lit, so it took him a moment for his eyes to adjust, although he found Pullus readily enough, standing in a corner, talking in low tones to a man who wasn't in uniform—a military one, anyway—and Scribonius recognized him as the chief of the *medici*. Scribonius just caught the very end of the conversation, but it was enough.

"The men we have placed over in the far corner are the ones who have no chance to survive," the *medicus*, whose name was Stolos, was saying. "And I ask your permission to administer them more milk of the poppy."

"Of course I give permission," Pullus snapped, and Scribonius didn't need any lighting to know his friend was close to losing his temper. "You shouldn't be wasting time asking!"

"Primus Pilus," Stolos, unlike Pullus, remained composed, something that secretly impressed Scribonius, knowing how difficult that could be when standing next to a man who towered over you, "I apologize for not making myself clear. I said *more* milk of the poppy."

In the darkened interior, Scribonius sensed more than saw Pullus' body relax, as he replied softly, "Ah. I see." Taking a deep breath, Scribonius heard the throbbing intensity in his friend's voice as he asked, "Are you sure none of those men can be saved?"

Scribonius expected Stolos to assure Pullus that they couldn't, but the *medicus* actually hesitated before he answered, "I won't lie to you, Primus Pilus Pullus. It's *possible* that one or perhaps two of those men could survive. But that would require constant care, and we are

406

on campaign. And even if they did manage to survive, they would be so horribly scarred that it's unlikely they could function in the ways that are important to men. Their lips, their ears, their noses..." Stolos didn't finish, but he didn't need to; Pullus understood then.

"Go ahead then, Stolos," Pullus said, his voice heavy with the pain of the moment.

With a slight bow, Stolos departed, and Pullus turned, squinting at Scribonius. Recognizing him, he gave little more than a grunt of recognition.

Knowing he wasn't likely to get more than this, Scribonius asked, "Where's Balbus? Is he all right?"

The laugh that came from Pullus had no humor in it, "Oh, he's fine. He's a Gregarius again, but other than that," Scribonius could barely make out his friend closing his eyes as he added, "he's about as good as can be expected after watching some of his men, including his Optio, burn to death from that...that..." Pullus' mouth twisted into a bitter grimace, yet as gifted with invective as he was, Titus Pullus couldn't summon the right words to describe the horrible weapon that had caused the carnage. Then, completely unexpectedly, Pullus blurted out, "Caesar should have known they had something like this!"

This, perhaps more than anything he had seen or heard, rocked Scribonius to his core, because it was the first time since he had known Pullus that his friend hadn't gone out of his way to mute any criticism of their general by adding some sort of qualification that, implicitly anyway, excused one of Caesar's errors. Granted, they were few and far between, but when they did happen, they were costly in terms of lives.

"Titus," Scribonius spoke carefully, not only because he didn't want to upset his friend more than he already was, but also because it had become clear to him that, at least for the moment, his friend had lost sight of the job at hand, "this isn't the time for that. And if you want to speak to Caesar about what happened, and why it happened, I'll stand there with you as you do it. But right now, we need you to be our Primus Pilus."

For the span of three or four heartbeats, Pullus stared at Scribonius, his expression hard and unyielding, and despite his relationship with his friend, Scribonius wasn't blind to the fact that, just underneath his exterior, Titus Pullus harbored a volcanic rage that, when truly unleashed, was something that Scribonius had witnessed firsthand, and still shuddered when he thought about it.

Expelling a harsh burst of air, Pullus gave an abrupt nod, then said simply, "You're right."

Then, without saying anything more, he began walking towards the open doors, Scribonius following. A sudden movement from the darkest corner of the building attracted the Pilus Prior's eye, but when the man got close enough to the open doors to make out more than just a black shadow, Scribonius' first impression was that it was a ranker. It took him a heartbeat longer than normal to see that it was in fact Balbus; this was the moment when he not only realized why he hadn't immediately known it was the third friend of this trio, but why Pullus had referred to the Centurion as a Gregarius.

"What happened to your crest?" Scribonius asked.

While it may have seemed odd, this was exactly the best thing Scribonius could have said at this moment, because in its own way, it returned Balbus to the present, yanking him out of a despair that he had never experienced before. This certainly wasn't the first time he had lost men, and while his casualties were heavy in numbers, he had gone through this before as well; what had never happened to him before was the way in which those men had perished.

In reflex, he reached up to his helmet, his fingers breaking off the charred remnants of the feathers, which crumbled into fragments that sifted down on his already scorched and blackened helmet.

"Pluto's cock," he mumbled, "that's what he meant."

"What who meant?" Pullus asked, causing Scribonius to begin regretting his distracting question, but Balbus shook his head.

"Doesn't matter," he muttered, then he turned his attention to Pullus, asking in a voice that, despite its formal tone, echoed the shock he was still feeling, "What are your orders, Primus Pilus? I don't have as many of my boys available as I'd like, but we're still ready to fight!"

Pullus swallowed hard, trying to stop the welling of emotion, and he placed a gentle hand on his subordinate's shoulder, shaking his head as he said softly, "You and your boys are going to stay here, Quintus. You need to be with them right now."

Balbus recoiled, insisting, "You can't take the First back out there without the Second Century!"

Pullus took a deep breath, then replied, "I'm not taking the First, Quintus. The Cohort is done for the day. We have nine other Cohorts, and a city to take." Before Balbus could protest further, Pullus turned to Scribonius and said, "Let's go."

The pair strode back out into the bright sunlight, leaving Balbus to continue offering what little comfort he could to his suffering men.

For Pullus, this had become personal; he was going to lead the other nine Cohorts of his Legion over these walls boxing them in, and take this city. And he was going to put everyone he found to the sword as punishment for using such a foul means to defend this place. If Scribonius had been aware of Pullus' terrible resolve, he probably would have at least tried to stop him.

Sarosh, the young Parthian and only surviving commander of the contingent of archers who had been tasked with the defense of the Ctesiphon side of the two cities, was good to his word; he bought Kambyses and the remaining defenders perhaps a sixth part of a watch. That all but a handful of the archers, Sarosh included, perished in doing so was a minor tragedy compared to the growing reality that Kambyses was forced to recognize, that his defense of Ctesiphon was failing. The only bright spot in an otherwise dismal situation was that the last report he had received from Seleucia was that the Romans were still trapped within the killing box created by Anaxagoras. That he hadn't heard this directly from Melchior wasn't unduly alarming; the older commander assumed that he was either too busy directing the defense or he was dead, which didn't matter. What did was that, if this effort to stem the Roman advance into Ctesiphon failed, looking extremely likely at this point, he still could retreat back across the bridges in good order and Seleucia would still be able to hold out. Anaxagoras had his crews of workmen standing ready, divided between the bridges, prepared to hastily block the passages with a variety of material; frankly, he had been too exhausted to ask for details about how the Greek would accomplish sealing these weak points. However, to this point, the Greek had proven to be steadfast in his efforts to help the Parthian cause, despite the seemingly stronger ties he and his fellow Seleucians had with their Roman cousins. The odd thought struck Kambyses that he actually trusted the Greek more than he trusted most of his fellow countrymen. Forcing his mind from a line of thought that had little bearing on the moment at hand, he surveyed the large square, recognizable now only because of its location at the foot of what had been Orodes' palace. The palace complex itself had been cleared out of the civilians who, in their terror, had run to the place that in their mind represented the best place to take refuge. It had been an ugly scene, and Kambyses had been forced to order his spearmen to turn their weapons on the refugees, driving them not just from the steps of the palace, but all the way out of the central square. Only fighting men were allowed inside the ring of breastworks that had been created, a motley collection of overturned wagons, large wooden boxes that had been emptied of their original content and filled with dirt and rocks; essentially, anything deemed large and sturdy enough by Anaxagoras and his men had gone into making this last-ditch defense. Lining the barricade was a makeshift parapet, but the height advantage was minimized because the barricade itself was only about five feet in height; in order to provide some protection for the beleaguered defenders, Anaxagoras and his men were forced to use crates and even upended pieces of furniture that were only about two feet in height. Ultimately, this was the best that he could do, so most of the spearmen stood waiting for the Roman onslaught exposed from mid-stomach up. When Kambyses arrived, he felt an initial flare of anger at seeing this scanty protection, but between his weariness and the realization that this was a hastily constructed set of defenses, he gave Anaxagoras, one of the few civilians allowed to remain within the barricade, a grudging nod of acceptance.

"It will have to do," he muttered, watching as the Parthian equivalent of Centurions, who were nowhere near the Roman version in terms of responsibility, and more importantly, leadership abilities, shoved their respective charges into a spot on the barricade.

As the defenders made their last-moment preparations, terrified civilians, many of them out of their minds with panic at the sounds of tromping hobnailed soles echoing up between the buildings, still ran back and forth all around the barricade. Some of them, made bold by their desperation, tried to clamber up the barrier, but once a handful were dealt with by a spear thrust into their bodies, these attempts ceased. All along the barricade, men began wiping their palms and re-gripping their spears, the sound of the Legions of Rome growing louder, in the form of the pounding, slightly crunching noise created by thousands of hobnailed feet, marching in unison up every street that led to the square from the southern side of the city. Kambyses had remounted his horse, more to give him better visibility over the square than from any idea that it would give him an advantage in the coming battle; unless, the thought suddenly shot through his mind, *it gives me a chance to escape.* However, it wasn't cowardice, or even the normal sense of self-preservation that prompted the idea. Kambyses was truly torn by competing emotions, the shame he felt because he feared that his defense of Ctesiphon was doomed to fail, and the combination of resolve and hope that something could still be salvaged by a successful defense of Seleucia. If he could salvage one of the cities, there was a chance that Phraates would return, with not just the strength of the existing force of cataphracts that had left with him for Susa, but the armies of the east that he felt sure were, if not already in the old capital, nearby and would be joining forces with Phraates soon. Even more than the actual numbers the eastern army would offer, it was the composition of that force that, belatedly, Kambyses now understood gave the Parthians the best chance of crushing these Roman invaders. But, he thought dismally, even if I survive this, and even if I hold Seleucia, what am I going to tell Orodes? This was the pervasive idea that kept crowding its way into Kambyses' mind; following closely behind was how, even if Orodes forgave him for losing the city that was more important to the old King of Kings than any other scattered throughout his vast holdings, he felt certain that Phraates wouldn't be as understanding. And, he reflected bitterly, it has nothing to do with the new king's tender feelings he shared with his father about Ctesiphon, and all about the chance to remove a man whose first loyalty was to the father and not the son. Shaking his head in an attempt to banish this line of thinking, Kambyses made the decision that this was something beyond his control in that moment; all he could do now was fight, and keep his head, literally and figuratively. Thus resolved, he returned his attention to the situation at hand, just as the first Romans appeared down the street nearest from his position. While they were still more than two hundred paces, and partially obscured by the buildings overlooking the street, he could see that the shields of the men of the leading rank bristled with arrows. In between the barricade and Romans, a handful of archers were walking backwards, their arms still moving as they drew their bows, paused for a fraction of time, then released. As he watched, he was grimly pleased to first see one of the leading Romans stumble, then the man's shout of pain rolled up the street to him, but despite there being a slight bobble in the leading rank, he was quickly replaced by the man behind him, while the wounded Roman was grabbed and, none too gently from what Kambyses could see, pulled out of the path of the oncoming Centuries that were following the first. Since he was stationed roughly in the middle of the open square behind the barricade, his only clear view was the street directly across from where he sat his horse, but he was alerted by the shouts of the spearmen on the barricade farther down that they, too, had the Romans in their sights. So, he thought, it begins.

It took the combined labor of both Legions involved in the initial assault to knock down two of the temporary walls in Seleucia to allow access to the city beyond. Because of a lack of heavy tools, the Legionaries under Pullus and Spurius were forced to scrounge up materials that could be used to achieve that result; the task was made even more difficult by the efforts of the remaining Parthian defenders, particularly those archers who had chosen to flee when Pullus and his men took the *ballista*. Unlike Atartinus, it didn't immediately occur to Pullus to devote manpower to muscling this piece into a position whereby it could bombard the city beyond the temporary walls. Then, as he was standing on the main rampart, above the scorched temporary wall and watching his men batter at it with a motley collection of scavenged pickaxes and hammers, a thought came to him. Walking down the wall, Pullus stepped over the bodies of the Parthian artillery crew to the small shed, from where he had seen the two men, whose bodies now lay at his feet, carrying the jar of naphtha that had wrought so much damage on Balbus' men. Leaning over to peer inside, his jaw tightened at the sight of the remaining jars, each of them surrounded by straw, serving as a grim reminder of the volatility of this substance.

Turning, he beckoned to Valerius, telling the *cornicen*, "Go down and find Lutatius. Tell him to send Glabrio to go bring Murena and his boys here. I have a job for them."

Once Valerius was gone, Pullus returned his attention to the scene inside the walls, but instead of watching his men working, he surveyed the city stretching before him. Despite being on the wall, since most of the buildings of Seleucia were at least two floors, it made it almost impossible for him to see down to street level, except for a few spots where, for reasons he couldn't determine, there was a break in the line of rooftops that allowed him to see a random intersection. But even with this limited view, there was no missing the movement of people that Pullus could see were civilians, undoubtedly citizens of the city, who were now fleeing. Although it was impossible to know with any certainty, Pullus got the strong impression those civilians he could see were heading in an easterly direction. They probably think they'll be safe across the river, he thought, feeling his lips pulling into a smile that held neither humor nor any tender feelings. The reality was that something inside Pullus vanished when he been forced to watch some of his men burn to death, scorched away from his soul in the same way their flesh had been consumed by the pernicious flames of the naphtha. Unlike a fair proportion of his men, Titus Pullus

412

was able to delineate between those who fought him in battle and those whose presence in the middle of a fight was a matter of unhappy circumstance, and while, like most men, he had been swept away by the bloody madness of battle, he was usually able to rein himself in more rapidly than some of his comrades, like Balbus, when it came to putting civilians to the sword. It was this sensibility that had been burned away, while at the same time, what had been a random thought began to coalesce and harden into a resolve. Encased in this large, muscular body was a first-rate mind, capable of picking up seemingly unrelated strands and piecing them together to give him a fuller picture of what had been a mystery just moments before. While he was standing there, two seemingly disparate facts coalesced together; the first was the knowledge that Parthians never availed themselves of the kind of artillery that had savaged his men and those of the 3rd. The second was the recognition that if the Parthians didn't use this type of artillery, it was highly unlikely they had men who possessed the expertise to create a piece like the one standing idle a few paces away. Pullus' mind turned this over in his mind, but it was a movement out of the corner of his eye that attracted his attention that allowed the final piece to fall into place. Naturally reacting to a sudden darting movement, Pullus turned and looked down the length of the western wall, facing south. Running down the street next to the wall was a single man, and Pullus instantly saw he wasn't a warrior, but a civilian, one whose origins were plainly visible by his mode of dress.

"A Greek," he exclaimed aloud; the sound of his own voice startled him, but it also was the catalyst for what came next. "Of course." Rather than experience a sense of relief that this puzzle had been solved, or so he believed, Pullus felt a stab of chagrin that it hadn't occurred to him more quickly.

Seleucia was, ultimately, at its heart and in its origins a Greek city, something that Caesar had emphasized before they reached its walls and had taken just one glance by Pullus and the other Centurions to confirm, just by its architecture. And, while he wasn't aware of the specifics, Pullus was generally aware that much of the Roman knowledge of artillery had come from the Greeks, although Rome had made further advancements and refinements, like the scorpions that Caesar favored so much. Consequently, where would whoever was in command of the Parthian defense of this city find men with the expertise to create these pieces?

"Fucking Greeks," Pullus spat. "I should have thought of that earlier."

Well, he didn't say this aloud, but the emotions behind the thought were no less raw and real, they're going to pay a heavy price for that.

"Primus Pilus?"

Pullus spun about, startled by the sound, to see Murena standing there, panting slightly, but otherwise none the worse for wear.

"Come here, I want to show you something," Pullus said after returning the salute. Pointing down to the jars after Murena reached his side, he asked, "How far do you think those can go?"

Murena scratched his jaw, then glanced in the general direction of the eastern wall of Seleucia, which was just visible above the rooftops but more than six hundred paces away, mentally judging the distance.

Turning to Pullus, he asked, "Are you talking about using this piece? Or one of ours?"

"This one," Pullus answered immediately, "because we don't have the time for you to drag your pieces and get them set up."

Murena didn't answer immediately, instead walking to the piece, crouching down to examine it more closely, grabbing one of the metal stakes protruding from the stone rampart, testing it with a tentative wiggle.

Standing up, he returned his attention to the eastern wall, squinting at it, then said finally, "With this piece, I can't guarantee we can get all the way over into Ctesiphon, but we should be able to get fairly close to the eastern wall. But," he glanced at Pullus, indicating the far wall with a jerk of his head, "even if we could reach the wall, I don't see any men over there, Primus Pilus. It looks like they've given up the walls, at least."

"I don't want to hit the walls," Pullus replied immediately, then pointed to three different spots. "I want you to get close to where the bridges cross over to Ctesiphon." Murena would have cause to remember the look Pullus gave him as he said savagely, "I want to trap every fucking person we can inside these walls. They're going to pay for helping these Parthian bastards for burning our boys."

Titus Pullus was good to his word; with the help of Murena and his men, tumbling jars of naphtha arced over the rooftops of Seleucia to go smashing against the roofs or walls of the line of buildings as close to the eastern wall as possible, raining liquid fire down onto the heads of people who were, indeed, fleeing towards Ctesiphon. It was a testament to the ability of Murena and his men that, after sending a few missiles of roughly the same shape and weight as the precious jars, they were able to drop their flaming missiles down in close enough proximity to each of the bridges that they were effectively blocked off by the substance, sticking to anything flammable, like the heavily laden wagons that Anaxagoras had planned on pushing up the street leading to each bridge. It was only after the fact that Pullus and the men assaulting Seleucia learned that, even if the civilians in Seleucia had managed to flee across the bridges, they would have been met by the stampeding flood of civilians of Ctesiphon who were at that moment fleeing from Caesar's part of the assault force. As it was, both cities were effectively sealed off, for both groups of people whose only crime was to be unfortunate enough to be occupants of either one, although there was one man in particular who didn't view the citizens of Seleucia, the Greek ones at least, as being innocent bystanders. In another example of leading from the front, it was Titus Pullus who, once the temporary barrier between the western wall and the first block finally came down almost a third of a watch later, when the sun was a hand's width above the horizon, led his men on a mission of vengeance as they made their way through the streets of Seleucia. Meanwhile, it was Spurius who led his Legion, in a similarly vengeful frame of mind, along the street that bordered the northern wall until they reached the northeast corner. Then, in a movement that roughly paralleled that of the 10th, who were advancing south, the two battle-hardened, vengeful Legions moved into Seleucia, and there was no mercy to be had at the hands of Legionaries who had either been forced to witness, or had learned of the horrible deaths of their comrades. Panicked civilians were quickly joined by the men who had been charged with protecting them, their own cohesion and morale shattered by the ferocity of the Romans who cut, hacked, and slashed their way down the streets. Even in this chaos there was the order that was a hallmark of Rome, as Spurius, Pullus, and at last Balbinus, who had brought the 12th through the breach, gave orders to their respective Pili Priores to spread out among the streets of the city. In doing so, they created a net whose individual strands were composed of armored men that swept methodically south, building to building and block to block. The consequence of this advance was that, not much longer after the last of the naphtha that had served as a curtain of flame barring passage to the illusory safety of Ctesiphon flickered out, it was replaced by the more substantial forms of Roman Legionaries. Before the passage of a full third of a watch, when the lower edge of the sun was just touching the western horizon, Seleucia was effectively taken and under the control of Caesar's most veteran Legions. Only then did the real slaughter begin, led by two hard-bitten Primi Pili whose raging sorrow that stemmed from bearing the ultimate responsibility for sending men to the most horrible of deaths fueled their thirst and almost frantic desire to appease the shades of those lost men. Before the sun disappeared, the fading natural light was replaced by the fires set by Legionaries, created by dragging all flammable materials out into the street, usually an intersection, thereby giving the necessary light to slaughter those who resisted, and those who didn't.

Under normal circumstances, Spurius would have pressed the advantage of taking the bridges over the Tigris that led into Ctesiphon, but these weren't normal circumstances from his perspective. Subsequently, rather than lead his men into the city across the river, the Primus Pilus decided his men had suffered enough, and deserved the chance to vent their rage and sorrow on the people of Seleucia. And, in some ways more importantly, give his boys the opportunity to behave in the manner of all armies who take a city by the sword, and all that came with this event. Although neither Primus Pilus had conferred with the other in any way, not even by sending a runner to determine their next course of action, their minds had run along similar lines; Parthians didn't use artillery, so it was unreasonable to think that it had been the Parthians who lived in either city who built the machines that had brought so much pain and suffering. This left only one group, and it was on these civilians that both Spurius and Pullus turned their wrath, made even more potent because it was shared by men of every rank, in both Legions. Only the section of Seleucia that was secured by the 12th, roughly a swath running through the middle of the city from north to south, did any citizens fare better than those who found themselves trapped, either by circumstances or by virtue of their living in that part of the city, where the 3rd and 10th were seeking vengeance. This didn't mean that the bridges were left unsecured; Spurius stationed two Centuries apiece at each of the bridges, following the normal practice of designating the Ninth and Tenth Cohorts to this duty. What was unusual was the fact that these Centuries found themselves forced into a fight to hold their position, when a combination of frantic citizens of Ctesiphon and the reeling remnants of Kambyses' last stand in the square came fleeing across the bridges. Ultimately, the hapless Parthians, both civilian and military, were squeezed between two bloody jaws, as Caesar's Legions, after a savage but brief struggle with the Parthians behind the makeshift breastworks in the city square of Ctesiphon, made their own inexorable sweeping advance.

While the overall result was the same for both Roman forces, there was a material difference between the subsequent actions of the Legions under Caesar's command when compared to the wholesale slaughter that was taking place a short distance away across the river. Much of this difference stemmed from the fact of Caesar's presence inside Ctesiphon, as he and his staff came galloping through the now-opened gates of the capital, quickly establishing order among his victorious men. This didn't mean he immediately put a halt to the looting and rapine; it was an unwise commander who tried to curb the baser tendencies of the men who fought for him, particularly in the immediate aftermath of what had been a difficult assault, when their blood still ran hot from the madness that was a practical requirement if a man wanted to survive to see another sunrise. Nevertheless, when compared to what was taking place in Seleucia, order was quickly restored in Ctesiphon; it was only when Caesar, after a brief stop to survey the scene at the square, and dispatching some of his Germans to secure the palace itself, went trotting towards the bridges that he got the first indication that something different was taking place in Seleucia. It came from the confusing sight of a rolling mass of humanity which, despite the fading light, appeared to Caesar to be composed in almost equal proportions between Parthian civilians and the remnants of the defenders of the city, came running back up the street from where the centermost bridge over to Seleucia was located. Still mounted, Caesar and his staff happened to be on this street, which bordered the southern edge of the square that was now a pile of wreckage, composed of both the makeshift breastwork and the bodies of those men who fell where they were standing behind it. Unlike Seleucia, Ctesiphon wasn't laid out in the same grid fashion, so this street, while it led directly to the gate and bridge beyond that led to Seleucia, curved just enough to deprive Caesar of a clear view of the cause of this reversed tide of fleeing humans, who, by rights, should have been trying to get away from Caesar's Legions. What Caesar could see above the heads of the terrified Parthians who were just then reaching the semi-solid wall of two Centuries, having been hastily arrayed across the width of the street to stop them from reaching their general, was the lurid glow of fire. Although it was difficult for him to tell with any certainty, his sense was that the telltale sign that something was already burning was farther away than the western wall of Ctesiphon.

"What are they doing over there?" he wondered aloud, which prompted a guess from Pollio.

"It looks like they've set something on fire," he replied helpfully, prompting an irritated scowl from Caesar.

"Yes, thank you Pollio," he snapped. "but what I don't know is why. I gave all three Primi Pili explicit instructions that I didn't want either city burned to the ground."

Only partially rebuked, Pollio shrugged and said carelessly, "You know how it is with rankers, Caesar. Some of them just like to see things burn."

That this was an elemental truth didn't appease Caesar in the slightest, but if the truth were known, the irritation he displayed towards Pollio was caused in good part by his realization that he had neither heard from, nor attempted to contact the three Legions across the river for well more than a full watch. He had become so absorbed by the chain of events that occurred during the part of the assault over which he had taken personal command, he had forgotten that the original plan called for Pullus, Spurius, and Balbinus to be designated the assaulting force that was supposed to be the main effort, and that Caesar's part, no matter how elaborate or how many Legions were involved, had been a diversion. But, when he had gotten word by courier of the trap that had been laid in Seleucia in the form of those inner walls, he had shifted his focus, and in doing so, had relegated Pullus and the rest of the men fighting for Seleucia to a secondary role. What chafed at him was that in all of the tension and drama of the moment, he had neglected to send a messenger informing Pullus and Spurius that this was now the case, and they were no longer expected to continue their struggle in what was no longer the main effort. That this was the situation, he recognized, was entirely his responsibility, and he felt a certain heaviness in his heart that there were men who had undoubtedly fallen in the pursuit of a goal that was no longer their responsibility to attain. He had no way of knowing in the moment that this was the best he would feel about what was happening in Seleucia. Realizing that he needed to at least get a better idea about what was taking place in the city across the river, he also understood the impossibility of using the street he and the others were currently on because of the human barrier that was blocking the way. Most of the fleeing Parthians had come to an ungainly, stumbling halt at the sight of the line of shields, each of them held by hard-eyed men who stood with their swords held low and ready. Not all of the Parthians stopped, however; some of these trapped souls were so out of their minds with panic that they continued their headlong flight, trying to smash their way through the Legionaries in their path. The consequence of their action was borne out by the mute testimony of the small pile of bodies, some still twitching and others emitting low moans, that lay at the collective feet of the Roman Centuries blocking the street. Seeing the demise of their fellow citizens took away what little fight was left, and there was a din created by the clattering sound of spears and bows being dropped to the paving stones, as the soldiers mixed among the civilians signaled their surrender.

Before he trotted away to find another avenue to at least get closer to Seleucia, Caesar nudged Toes forward to where the Centurion in overall command of these two Centuries, was standing next to his *signifer*.

"Take these people prisoner," Caesar ordered, "and divide the fighting men from the rest of them. And," his tone changed subtly, but it was unmistakable to the Centurion, who was the Sextus Hastatus Posterior of the 8th Legion and, more importantly, he understood that Caesar was serious about this command being obeyed to the letter, "no unnecessary bloodshed. Do you understand, Lentulus?"

Despite feeling the flush of pleasure that Caesar remembered his name, Lentulus immediately came to *intente* and replied crisply, "I understand Caesar, and I will obey."

Nodding his own acknowledgement, Caesar turned Toes about, but in doing so, he saw that other Centurions, knowing their general's particular quirk in such matters, had already tasked men with dragging the makeshift breastworks away from the edge of the square, while other Centuries had almost finished dragging Parthian bodies into a huge pile, roughly in the middle of the square. While Caesar approved the initiative, the corners of his mouth turned downward at the sight of the corpses. Did they have to drag them into the middle of the square? It would have been less unsightly and out of the way, but before he uttered this aloud, he decided it wasn't worth the time. Guiding Toes through the opening that had been created in the barricade, then steering him past the bodies, Caesar noticed a small knot of his men, and even in the poor light, he saw they were surrounding a prone figure. Under normal circumstances, he would have ignored the sight; there were some things that, as the general of the army, he didn't need to witness, if only to be able to plead ignorance with the inevitable line of citizens that would claim some outrage had been done to them once the city was secured and the proverbial dust had settled. He would never be able to articulate why he didn't keep on riding; he still needed to get at least a better look at Seleucia, or better yet, send a courier across one of the bridges. Instead, he nudged Toes over to where the Legionaries were gathered, maneuvering so he got a better look at the prone figure, whose body was lying partially on the lower steps of the palace, face up but with his eyes closed. Even with the bad light, Caesar recognized the man, and before he had time to think about it, he had swung out of the saddle, landing on the paving stones and quickly striding towards the Legionaries. They had been so intent on what, to Caesar's ears, sounded like a furious debate, probably about how to divide the spoils represented in the gold-inlaid armor and bejeweled sword that they didn't realize their general was just a pace away. Then, one of them caught the movement and spun about, his mouth twisted into a snarl as he prepared himself to tell whoever this interloper was to fuck off, only to see not just a Centurion, but Caesar himself.

"*Intente!*"

Fortunately for the other five Legionaries, the habits drilled into them from their first day under the standard served them well as they immediately stiffened to the proper position without hesitation or argument.

Returning the collective salute, Caesar gazed down at the Parthian and asked, "Is he alive?"

"Y-y-yes, Caesar," stammered the Gregarius who had been the first to spy Caesar's approach, then tried to explain. "The boys and I were just discussing what to do about him." Pointing down at the man's helmet, which was next to his head, although Caesar didn't know if one of his men had pulled it off or it had been knocked off. "We could see he was one of their officers. So we weren't sure whether or not to…"

His voice trailed off, but Caesar wasn't fooled in the slightest; however, he deemed this wasn't the proper moment to let them know he knew they were arguing over the spoils that would be offered up by this Parthian, after he was dead, of course.

Instead, he commended the men. "That was very good thinking, because you're right. He's one of their officers. But," at this, Caesar actually squatted down, alerted by the fluttering eyelids that the

Parthian was returning to the land of the conscious, "he's much more than just an officer." Just then, the man's eyes opened, and while they were bleary and unfocused, his daze didn't last long before his eyes widened and began darting around, flitting from one downturned face to another.

"Well, Kambyses," Caesar's voice jerked the Parthian general from his examination of the rankers still standing above him and their eyes met as Caesar finished, "this is the second time we meet, and the second time after your defeat. It appears your gods have a sense of humor."

Chapter Fifteen

Kambyses' role in the defense of the capital came to an abrupt and somewhat ignominious end, when his horse reacted at the sudden movement caused by the first Romans surmounting the makeshift barricade. The Parthian was understandably intent on what would be the first of several breaches, so that even as experienced a horseman as he was, when his mount suddenly reared in what was ironically enough an action that it had been trained to perform, Kambyses suffered through that moment all horsemen, no matter what their ability, undergo, a brief instant where he no longer felt the pressing weight of his armor as he flew backward off his horse. He did catch just a glimpse of his horse's front hooves lashing out and catching a shouting Roman, his sword held low and out to his side in what Kambyses assumed was a preparatory thrust to his horse's vitals. One hoof struck the Roman's helmet, while the man crumpled to the ground, and in one of the odd little moments that occur in battle, the thought that ran through Kambyses' mind was how the Roman hit the ground before he did. Then, his heavily armored body slammed onto the stones of the square, and while he felt the tremendous impact, the back of his helmet colliding with the paving stones meant that he was unconscious before his body could register the inevitable pain of the impact. His next memory was a ring of faces peering down at him, but none of them belonged to his men, and if he was any judge, there was no mercy to be had from any of the Romans who surrounded him. Kambyses' first emotion when his mind at least partially caught up from its period of unconsciousness and his eyes focused enough to comprehend the identity of those who surrounded him, was the bitter ashy taste in his mouth as he recognized the meaning of their presence, that he had failed. Following immediately behind this disappointment was a feeling of relief at the idea they would put him out of his misery, yet as he quickly discovered, this was an illusory emotion, washed away in the amount of time it took for the Roman general Caesar to appear within his vision. What made matters even worse was the expression on Caesar's face, if only because it was in such stark juxtaposition to those worn by his Legionaries, who continued to stare down at him with a cold hostility that he could at least understand,

422

which was the same look he had bestowed upon his own enemies as they lay at his feet, when they understood that their lives could now be counted in the number of breaths they took. But this wasn't how Caesar was gazing down at him now, instead regarding him with the same kind of amused contempt that Kambyses had first experienced when he had been forced to come up the ridge, as a supplicant, to beg for the body of his prince. The expression Caesar bore was bad enough, but there was something else in the Roman's demeanor that cut Kambyses more deeply than any blade could, and that was how supremely unsurprised Caesar looked at seeing the man who had been the commander of the forces opposing him and his Romans lying at his feet. He never expected any other outcome, Kambyses realized with a rush of such bitterness and grief that, for a horrible instant, he was afraid his eyes would fill with tears.

"Can you move?" Caesar asked him, finally, after his examination of this prize was done. "Is anything broken?"

"Why? Why do you want to know?"

Kambyses barely recognized his own voice, which had been reduced to a harsh croak, made so by the combination of a lack of water, and the fact he had been bellowing orders for…how long? he wondered.

For the first and only time, Caesar seemed to be surprised. "Why?" he repeated, then replied in a tone that told Kambyses the reason was so obvious it didn't really need to be answered, "So I can have my physician come and examine you! He's Greek, it's true, but he's very, very good at such things."

Suddenly, a sense of befuddlement swept through Kambyses, washing away the vestiges of the bitter recognition of his failure, and he grew as confused as he had ever been in his life. In that moment, the realization that these Romans were truly different from anything he had experienced just added to the stew of emotions that threatened to overwhelm him.

"Why would you want to have this physician treat me when you are just going to kill me?"

Caesar smiled, although it was without a hint of warmth, and he countered, "Who said I was going to have you put to death?" He made a casual gesture at the men around him, all of whom were still glowering down at Kambyses, while two of them still held unsheathed swords that were crusted with blood that showed as black as ink, made so now that it was almost completely dark. "Oh, my men would be more than happy to do that. And," Caesar's expression hardened, "it would happen if I lifted my finger." As he said this, the Roman general extended his hand, as if to demonstrate the actual gesture he would use. But the hand remained still, hovering above Kambyses in a silent message that the Parthian correctly interpreted. "But that's not what I desire. At least," Caesar's voice became even colder, "not yet. Much of it depends on you."

"I will never divulge any information that you can use to hurt my kingdom!" Kambyses desperately wished his mouth hadn't been so dry so that he could turn his head and spit on this arrogant dog's boots.

But once more, Caesar seemed surprised, and this time, he actually chuckled as he assured Kambyses, "I have no doubt that's true, Kambyses. And I wouldn't waste the time and effort of my torture detachment in trying. No," Caesar shook his head, "torturing you doesn't suit my purpose." Returning to the original subject, he asked, "Now, are you injured? There will be more than enough time to talk about what your future holds, but as you can see, there is quite a bit going on and I've already spent too much time with you. For now."

Grudgingly, Kambyses began moving, first his legs, then his arms. Finally, with the assistance of two of the Romans, whose hatred seemed to radiate from them in a blast of such force that Kambyses felt certain he could feel its heat, he was pulled to his feet. This was difficult under normal circumstances; the armor worn by Parthian cavalrymen was bulky and heavy, but when it belonged to a man of Kambyses' status, it was even more so. Nevertheless, he made it to his feet, whereupon he began weaving around as his head spun, and this was the first moment where Kambyses actually became aware of the pain he was feeling throughout his body.

Seeing that the Parthian was vertical and essentially unhurt, Caesar wasted no more time, saying only, "You men guard him. If he needs to sit down, he's allowed to do so. If he asks for anything within reason, give it to him."

By the time the Roman general was through, he was vaulting into the saddle, then as quickly as he had appeared, he was gone, clattering across the square with a number of other Romans trailing behind him, leaving Kambyses with the same sets of hostile eyes upon him that he saw when he first opened his own. Sighing, he took a tentative step backward, then collapsed onto the stone steps of the palace. This was where he stayed as he watched the Romans sack Ctesiphon.

424

It wasn't until it was close to midnight before Caesar was informed by the Centurions responsible for the western wall of Ctesiphon and the three bridges that they had sent men across them and discovered that Seleucia had fallen as well. Wasting no time, Caesar moved at the trot, forcing his bodyguards to scramble to catch up, their way lit by the fires created by the flammable objects that had been dragged outside from the buildings. This was common practice, and served two functions; it helped illuminate the area, and it also gave Centurions and Optios visual confirmation that the block had been searched. And thoroughly looted, of course, while in Ctesiphon at least, the rankers were kept equally busy between grabbing all manner of items that might prove valuable and rounding up the civilians and herding them towards the center of the capital. This included women, although their ordeal included being forced to endure the brutal attentions of the conquering Romans, something that Caesar studiously, and deliberately, ignored as he made his way across the bridge. What greeted his eyes once he moved inside the walls of Seleucia was both disturbing and alarming to Caesar. In his usual thorough manner, he had given explicit instructions to his Primi Pili that, aside from the normal mayhem and rough handling of civilians that was an inevitable part of a city that fell by the sword, particularly when it came to the women, that the citizens of both cities were to be left alone. Provided, of course, they didn't do anything inherently stupid, like try to fight an armed Legionary for one of their former possessions. But what Caesar was witnessing was something completely different as, no more than a dozen paces away, he saw a Legionary standing over a man who, by his dress, was one of the Greeks of the city, and had clearly acquiesced and was on his knees. Without a word, at least that Caesar could hear, he caught just a glimpse of the Legionary's blade as it thrust out and down, the point plunging into the soft spot at the base of the Greek's throat, whereupon the man toppled over, again without making a sound.

"Gregarius!" Caesar roared, kicking Toes, who leaped forward and closed the space, as the ranker spun about, a look of sudden terror on his face at the sight of not just a Centurion but his commanding general approaching, Caesar's face a mask of cold fury.

"What by Cerberus' balls do you think you're doing?" Caesar roared, pointing down at the body of the Greek, the pool of blood still expanding out from his body as his sightless eyes stared up accusingly in the general direction of the Legionary.

The Gregarius had come to a position of *intente*, but even with just the light of a bonfire that was blazing away down the street, Caesar saw the man was literally shaking.

"Who's your Centurion? What Legion and Cohort do you belong to?" Caesar snapped, glaring down at the ranker.

"S-S-Sextus Princeps P-Prior Agricola, s-sir! T-Third Legion!"

The instant Caesar heard the identity of the Centurion in command of the Third Century, Sixth Cohort, he knew both ranker and Centurion belonged to Spurius, but just as he was about to turn to one of the secretaries with him to have the man's name recorded, he was struck by a sudden thought.

Still staring down at the terrified ranker, his voice only softened fractionally. "Didn't your Centurion instruct you that the civilians were to be unharmed if they didn't put up any resistance?"

"Y-yes, sir," the ranker answered, swallowing so hard Caesar saw the bony lump in the man's throat move up and down. Since this seemed to confirm that this man was indeed disobeying orders, Caesar did look back over his shoulder to issue instructions for the man's punishment, when the Gregarius spoke up. "But that was before, General."

This made Caesar return his attention to the man and stare down at him sharply. "Before what?"

"B-before," the man's chin began to quiver, and then astonishingly to Caesar, he saw the sudden shimmer to the man's eyes as the ranker finished, "Before those...those...*savages* did what they did to our boys in the First!"

Suddenly wary, Caesar would have cause to remember the slight fluttering in his stomach as, remembering what had happened to some of his men earlier in the day when the Parthians had unleashed their surprise of naphtha, he had a premonition.

"And," now his tone was gentle, attuned to the Legionary's obvious distress, "what was it they did, Gregarius?"

"They roasted them like chickens on the spit," the ranker replied with a vehemence born of hatred and grief, in seemingly equal parts. "That's what they did, Caesar! So," for the first time, the Legionary, obviously emboldened by his rage, looked up at his general, and there was a tone of defiance that was impossible for Caesar to miss, "Princeps Prior Agricola told us to make these fucking bastards pay for what they did!"

Caesar didn't reply, immediately anyway, then finally, he heaved a deep sigh, and his voice was no longer harsh, although it still carried the tone that any man in his army knew meant it was a command that was disobeyed at the risk of a punishment that carried a death sentence, as he said, "Very well, Gregarius. But from now on, if these people don't resist, you're to treat them with clemency and do only what's necessary to make sure they're secured. Is that understood?"

In a sign of how deeply emotions were running this night, rather than just be relieved he had escaped some form of punishment, the man actually hesitated, and although he rendered a salute, it was given so grudgingly that Caesar was tempted to make an issue of it. Then, he thought better of it; first, he needed to see just how bad the situation was before he meted out punishment to a Gregarius because of the quality of his obedience. Without another word, he turned Toes and started making his way towards the northern wall, in the general direction of the breach. As he and his retinue moved, those sounds that Caesar had initially associated with just the normal chaos and mayhem that resulted in the falling of a city took on a different meaning, and he realized that the shrieks of terror weren't just coming from those woman who were being roughly handled, but were equally the province of male throats. Since he was now moving along the street that bordered the wall on the river side of Seleucia, there wasn't very much activity in his path; the majority of whatever was taking place was happening deeper in the city, to his left. As he moved from one block to the next, he only paused long enough to gaze westward along each cross street, trying to catch sight of the Legion eagle of the 3rd, but what met his eyes were things he instantly regretted seeing, if only because these actions were in such flagrant disobedience to his orders. With only the light of the same fires, Caesar saw small heaps of bodies, roughly arranged outside the buildings along the street, as far west as he could see, and with every passing block, Caesar's anger deepened.

On the opposite side of Seleucia, much the same was taking place, as the men of the 10th, like their comrades of the 3rd, vented their rage and grief on the inhabitants of the city. Leading the way, literally and by example, were Titus Pullus and Quintus Balbus, the two Centurions whose loss was the most immediate and agonizing. Striding together up the streets, block by block, they kicked in doors, entered into homes and shops, dragging the occupants out, most of them usually kicking, screaming, and begging for mercy in a babble of Greek, Parthian, and sometimes even Latin, all to no avail. The only civilians who were spared from either a brutal thrust into their bodies or a slicing motion across their throats were the women, and somewhat surprisingly to their men, the children, who were largely left unmolested, at least by Pullus. If, that is, watching one's father be slaughtered in front of you while your mother was being repeatedly raped by laughing, shouting, and celebrating Romans qualified. That this was the case was due solely to Titus Pullus, and actually occasioned a tense moment between him and Balbus, who had no such compunctions, and it stemmed from a long-standing, recurring nightmare that Pullus suffered, one that he never divulged the cause of even to his closest friends, although Scribonius had been nearby for the actual event. And, since Pullus never spoke of it, he didn't know that Scribonius suffered eerily similar moments, waking in the night in a cold sweat, his heart racing from the terror that came from reliving his own moments that he wanted to forget. In Pullus' case, his personal nightmare came from the slaughter of two Gallic tribes, the Usipetes and Tencteri, which took place during the Gallic campaign, when Pullus was still a Gregarius in the ranks. Caesar had been as explicit in his orders then as he was now concerning the citizens of both cities, except it was the exact opposite; no member of either tribe was to be left alive, supposedly as a punishment for their tribal leaders violating the terms of a truce. Those orders were what caused Pullus to pursue a young woman, carrying what he thought at the time was a bundle of clothes, but when he cornered the woman at the edge of the river next to which the two tribes had camped, in a last-ditch appeal, the woman whirled about and thrust out the bundle at Pullus, which was when he saw a pair of bright blue eyes and a thatch of red hair that was an exact match to Pullus' quarry peering out at him from the bundle. Regardless of this heart-wrenching sight, Pullus' orders had been specific and weren't subject to interpretation; this was what Pullus had told himself as he plunged his sword through the infant, pinning it to its mother's breast, where they both died, alongside a river whose name Pullus never knew. Since then, however, Pullus had gone to great lengths to avoid being put in the same position, not wanting yet another face added to the parade of those who haunted his nights.

Subsequently, the streets outside each building soon became clogged with hysterically screaming children and sobbing women, many of whom were forced to endure being spotted by a passing Legionary, then being ravished yet again. Sometimes, the Legionary in question, not wanting the discomfort of being watched as he raped a woman that he was aware was likely to be the mother of at least one of those squalling children, would drag her inside, away from their eyes. This was more the exception than the rule, on this night anyway, as the Legionaries expressed their own grief at the loss of comrades in such a foul manner, which had quickly become common knowledge throughout the 10th. Instead, they would simply knock the woman to the street, climb atop her, and rut away, in clear view of those children who were earning their own nightmares that would haunt them for the rest of their collective lives. Meanwhile, Pullus and Balbus, neither of them ever sheathing their swords, strode from one building to the next, exacting their own vengeance, slaughtering all the male occupants who were of military age, accompanied by rankers from their Centuries who, without any order being given to that effect, joined their Centurions. Even fueled by their rage, both Pullus and Balbus were operating near the end of their respective tethers, which triggered Pullus' decision to become more selective and slaughter only those whose dress and accent betrayed their Grecian heritage. These, he reasoned, were the bastards who either taught the Parthians how to make those machines, or as he believed to be most likely, actually constructed the pieces themselves. Under normal circumstances, without the goad of being forced to watch his men perish in a horrible way, Pullus would have acknowledged that, even if they hadn't been forced by the Parthians to create these destructive mechanisms, that they might do so willingly was understandable. This was their home, after all, but these were conditions that were far from the norm, and Pullus wasn't sitting in his tent, back in camp, calmly and rationally discussing the matter with Scribonius and Balbus. Speaking of the former, even the normally levelheaded and pragmatic Secundus Pilus Prior had allowed himself, or more accurately, let his men vent their rage; despite feeling the same sense of outrage at the cause of this killing madness, Scribonius just wasn't made of the same hard iron as either Pullus or Balbus. Consequently, while he had led the way as his own Cohort spread through the streets, and he had blood on his sword, in his case, he was more swept along on the tide of the killing madness, trying to stay in control of his men. Once he saw that the initial fury had begun to ebb, only then did he feel it safe to leave his men in the command of his Optio, and went looking for Pullus. If he had been asked, Scribonius would have simply said that he was behaving in a normal manner, seeking out his commander for further orders; the reality was quite different. The conversation he had held with Pullus in the immediate aftermath of the loss of so much of his Second

Century was still in his mind, and Scribonius was also aware that, at some point, there would be an appearance, if not by Caesar himself, then one of his Legates. Although it took him some time, he found Pullus, standing in the intersection of a part of the city that seemed to be home to the skilled artisans of the city, judging by the bodies the Pilus Prior encountered during his search. The Primus Pilus was wiping his sword down, and the firelight coming from the pile of burning furniture nearby cast Pullus' face in a contrasting mix of light and shadow that, to Scribonius at least, only emphasized the crushing fatigue and sorrow that his friend was experiencing. Despite being surrounded by his men, each of them involved in some sort of business that came with the sacking of a city, whether it be looting a corpse, staggering slightly as they guzzled the caches of wine they had found, or grunting and thrusting on top of a screaming woman, Pullus himself seemed oblivious to it all. So absorbed in cleaning his sword was he that it wasn't until Scribonius stepped between Pullus and the dancing firelight, casting the object of Pullus' attention into darkness, that the Primus Pilus even noticed his friend.

Looking up quickly, Scribonius saw Pullus' expression, knowing that he was about to issue a rebuke, then when he saw Scribonius, he relaxed slightly, grunting, "Oh. It' just you."

"Yes," Scribonius laughed, but it sounded forced to his own ears, although Pullus didn't seem to notice, "just me." When this earned the shadow of a smile from Pullus, he felt encouraged enough to say softly, "Titus. What are we doing?"

Instantly, the lines delineated so starkly by the fire deepened even further as Pullus' normally hard features became even more so, but it was the sudden set of the jaw that told Scribonius he had erred.

"What do you mean, 'what are we doing?'," he demanded, then waved a muscular arm around the both of them. "We're taking this fucking city, that's what we're doing. Do you have a problem with that?"

Sighing, Scribonius shook his head, yet he was one of the few who was unintimidated by Pullus; they had simply known each other too long, and Scribonius had intervened far too many times in saving Pullus from himself to be deterred now.

"You know what I'm talking about," he countered quietly but firmly. Mimicking Pullus' gesture from an instant before, he indicated the small heaps of bodies as he pressed, "You know Caesar's orders specifically forbade this."

"Don't tell me what Caesar's orders are," Pullus snapped. "I know very well what they are. But," Pullus' savage expression suddenly changed again, his features twisting in a grimace of hurt and frustration, "he wasn't there! And he didn't know!"

"Know what?"

That this didn't come from either Centurion, and indeed startled the both of them, caused them to whirl about in the direction from where this new voice had come. By the time they did so, Caesar had already slid off Toes, but while he was walking towards the pair, his eyes were fixed on the carnage around him, and his expression was, if anything, more severe than the one worn by Pullus.

In a further sign of his agitation, Caesar didn't bother returning the salute of either man, instead pointing down at the nearest corpse and demanding, "What is the meaning of this?" Before Pullus could answer, Caesar snapped, "Did you forget your orders, or did you just decide to ignore them?"

It was a moment Sextus Scribonius would long remember. Rather than cow his Primus Pilus, Pullus was instead visibly angered, to the point where he acted in a manner that Scribonius was sure, in this moment anyway, would ruin the special consideration Caesar had always shown towards the large Roman who had been his favorite Primus Pilus.

"Come with me," was all Pullus said, then without waiting for his commander to acknowledge that he had heard, or even if he had that he planned on obeying, he began striding back north, in the general direction of the breach.

For a span of time that was perhaps a half-dozen heartbeats but Scribonius was sure was much longer, Caesar only stared at Pullus' retreating back in open astonishment.

"Caesar," Scribonius broke the silence, vaguely aware that all activity around them had ceased, "I'm asking you to trust Pullus in this. I think you'll understand if you follow him and look at what he wants to show you."

Caesar didn't reply, choosing to regard Scribonius with his cool blue eyes for another few heartbeats, then, without a word, gave the Pilus Prior a curt nod, walked over to Toes, threw himself into the saddle, then moved at a trot to catch up with Pullus. Leaving, it must be said, a hardened veteran of countless battles with knees shaking as badly as a *tiro* facing his first battle.

"I...understand," was all Caesar could think to say, at first anyway. Standing inside the building next to the breach that had been turned into a combination mortuary and aid station, where the *medici* were still working, some of them close to exhaustion as they did what they could for the suffering men, Caesar regarded the scene with dismay, and a grief that was close in intensity to that Pullus was feeling at being forced to return to this place.

One change was that, after finally conferring with Spurius, his own burn victims had been carried here to this building, so the efforts to save as many men as possible could be combined. Even so, many of the *medici* were weaving about in much the same way men of the Legions out in both Seleucia and Ctesiphon were, albeit from completely different causes.

Pullus was standing next to Caesar, and to this point, the Primus Pilus had barely spoken a word to his general, something that was extremely unusual for both men. Fortunately, Caesar's growing anger at what under any other circumstances would have been gross insubordination on the part of a Centurion who had never exhibited such behavior was doused the moment he entered the building and viewed the human wreckage.

Closing his eyes for a moment, Caesar's lips moved as he offered up a prayer for the dead, but especially for those men who were still suffering and whose low moans caused by a pain he shuddered to try and imagine provided a backdrop of constant sound.

"Did you know they had this..." Pullus' voice trailed off, his own voice barely audible over the keening and the quiet calls for more poppy syrup from one *medicus* to another.

"No," Caesar admitted, "at least, not until today." Glancing over at Pullus, he found himself in the unusual position of hoping that one of his Primi Pili believed him, which was what prompted him to say, "This was a complete surprise, Pullus. And we suffered losses as well. But," he added hastily, "nothing like this." They both remained silent for some time, each of them grappling with the deeper meaning of this conversation, as brief as it was.

Before either of them could speak, the chief *medicus* of the 10th, his face drawn and haggard, approached the pair, and, without preamble, said, "We're out of poppy syrup."

Caesar replied instantly that he would send someone back to one of the other camps, but when he turned to call for one of the men with him, he discovered they were nowhere near. Swallowing his irritation, he correctly guessed why, and strode outside to see all of his secretaries and even his bodyguards huddled in a group, talking in low tones. He didn't need much light to see they were all shaken, and he realized that they had followed him inside but couldn't force themselves to stay. Rather than chastise them, he called to Apollodorus, quietly ordering him to hurry to the other camps and procure whatever stock of poppy syrup they could spare.

"Except for the southeast camp," he told Apollodorus. "They have their own casualties to care for, and you saw some of them are men like this."

With a haste that under different conditions Caesar might have found amusing, the Greek secretary hurried to the others, and before he was back inside, they left with a clattering of hooves on the paving stones. Before he returned, Caesar glanced up at the moon, trying to guess what time it was, estimating it was now a full watch past midnight. At least, he thought grimly, it certainly seems that late, feeling every one of his years, which was something of a rarity. Pushing such thoughts aside as fruitless, Caesar rejoined Pullus, where they both continued what Caesar sensed was a silent battle, as he could feel the volcanic rage just under the surface of the Primus Pilus, and sensed that Pullus was struggling mightily to keep it contained.

Sighing, Caesar decided that it was better to deal with this now, rather than let it fester, and while he spoke softly, Pullus clearly heard him say, "I should have known they had naphtha. This is my fault."

Even if he couldn't have articulated why, Caesar had correctly sensed that, of all the things he could have said to Pullus, this would not only have the most impact, it would effectively render inert what had been building up inside Primus Pilus, thereby smothering the coming explosion of anguished rage before it could erupt and put both of them in an untenable situation. No matter how highly Caesar regarded Titus Pullus, no general could allow the kind of insubordinate behavior that Caesar intuitively understood was lurking in the breast of the Primus Pilus. And, while this was certainly neither time nor place to say so, Caesar was secretly amused at the sight of the other Roman, whose mouth opened, then closed, then opened again as his confused mind sought the best response.

"I...I was too late," was what finally came out, and Caesar looked away at the sudden show of emotion on Pullus' face. "We were trying to get to that last piece, and the shield I was using had split, so I went back and got one from one of the wounded." Shaking his head, Pullus closed his eyes as he vainly sought to banish the images as he relived the moment, but they were too fresh and raw to be so easily thrust aside. "I should have grabbed one from one of the boys in the rear rank. Then this wouldn't have happened!"

Without thinking, Caesar reached up and placed a hand on Pullus' shoulder, admonishing him gently but firmly, "No, Pullus. The fault is mine, and mine alone. As your general, I'm supposed to know what the enemy is capable of, and in this, I failed. We suffered our own losses on the other side from those…" his lip curled because, like Pullus, he shared the contempt for a foe who would use a method they considered cowardly and underhanded. The one slight difference was that, even in this moment, Caesar was not only aware that if the roles between him and Kambyses had been reversed he would have done the same thing, he was also tucking this knowledge away as a possibility to be exploited later; all he had to do was discover the source of this naphtha. Then, he thought grimly, we'll see how they like the taste.

"Was it this bad?" Pullus asked dully, but wasn't surprised when Caesar shook his head.

"We lost quite a few artillery pieces," Caesar replied, "along with a fair number of their crews. But, no, nothing like this."

Before either man could say more, there was a disturbance outside the building, over and above the shouts and raucous laughter of Legionaries who had been allowed to run rampant throughout the city, something that Caesar had decided to overlook the instant he stepped inside this chamber and seen the horrors it held. Both turned just in time to see Pollio enter, followed by a Centurion, and by just the way the man carried himself, Pullus recognized Spurius.

"I found him, Caesar." Pollio rendered a salute, but while it was correct in its presentation, Pullus saw the Legate reeling from the twin shocks of what his eyes beheld and what his nose smelled. "By the gods," he gasped, forgetting himself, and he actually staggered back a step, thereby colliding with Spurius.

Who, Caesar saw, was in a similar state of mind, and under the same pressure that Pullus had been when Caesar found him, which prompted the general to cross over to Spurius, and as he had with Pullus, placed a hand on the man's shoulder, the armor covering it still scorched from his proximity to the surprise of the naphtha.

"I grieve with you, Spurius," Caesar began; before he could get another word out, the Primus Pilus of the 3rd made a snorting sound that was impossible to misinterpret.

Then, before he could commit a blunder even more serious, Pullus walked to Spurius, and while he also reached out and clasped his counterpart's other shoulder, his grip wasn't nearly as gentle as Caesar's, and he returned Spurius' glare up at him without flinching.

"Caesar has already taken responsibility for what happened," Pullus said quietly, yet with an underlying tone that Spurius correctly interpreted as a warning that, if Spurius pursued his planned remonstrance, he would find that Pullus had reassumed his mantle as Caesar's staunchest defender among the ranks of the army.

And, despite Spurius' smoldering anger, the 3rd's Primus Pilus knew he was no match for Pullus. Swallowing hard, he only gave an abrupt nod, then turned to Caesar, his mind now on more practical matters.

"My Cohort is no longer effective," the Primus Pilus said flatly to Caesar. "I've got less than half the First and Second Century still standing, and the Third Century is almost as bad. My Fourth is down by a third. The other two Centuries," he finished with a shrug, "are the best I've got left, but they're at three quarters' strength."

Spurius gave a bitter, humorless laugh,and despite suspecting this was the likely case, Caesar still couldn't smother a gasp of shock at hearing it put so baldly.

Only Caesar would know the effort required of him to retain control of himself so that to his subordinates he presented the same demeanor as always, asking coolly, "How many of those losses are from burns?"

"Less than half," Spurius admitted, which was also a surprise, albeit a happier one. "Most of my boys who were killed or wounded by a spear or an arrow happened either at the beginning or in the last watch or so." His mouth turned down even more as he explained, "After we tore down the temporary wall and moved south, the farther we got, the harder the bastards fought." Shrugging, he finished, "I can understand why, since the bridges over to Ctesiphon were on our side, and I suppose they thought they needed to protect them."

"That," Caesar offered with a grim smile, "was *their* mistake."

Chapter Sixteen

Despite the fact that Caesar had accomplished his goal of taking both cities, and he had done so early enough in the campaign season that it was theoretically possible for him to take his army on to Susa and reduce it before the harsh Parthian winter, the reality, however, was far different. Caesar's army had been hurt, and badly, by the defense put up by Kambyses and his men. More importantly, it was the type of wounds suffered by Caesar's Legionaries that created a situation that, by the time the sun set on the day after the fall of both Ctesiphon and Seleucia, the general recognized that the campaign season was effectively over. While men suffering a slash or even a puncture wound caused by a spear or arrow could heal in a matter of weeks, or even days, this wasn't true for the men who had been subjected to the gruesome effects of the naphtha. More importantly, since a significant number of those men who suffered from naphtha burns were the *immunes* who served as artillery crews, it also meant that the very weapon that Caesar most needed to fulfill his ambitions of taking the third of the four most important cities in Parthia was unavailable to him. Regarding the artillery that had been destroyed by the Parthians' surprise use of the naphtha, there was some good news; most of the pieces constructed by Anaxagoras had survived intact and at least those that were *ballistae* of roughly the same size and power of the destroyed Roman pieces would serve as replacements. It was the lost scorpions that troubled Caesar, and by extension, his men the most; while it was widely known that this was Caesar's favorite artillery, there was a solid reason behind his fondness for the weapon. During an assault on a fortified position, especially a walled city, these small, portable weapons had proven their worth time and again, forcing the defenders to seek cover and thereby hampering the ability to rain their own missiles down on the assaulting force. With its relatively rapid reloading, a scorpion was able to send the iron-tipped bolts at a rate that gave a defender the span of perhaps ten heartbeats between each volley, and that was with a single scorpion. Now, with more than half of the army's entire complement of these weapons destroyed, Caesar was forced to recognize that pushing forward to Susa was simply not prudent, although his decision wasn't based solely on the dearth of scorpions. The cost of taking both cities in terms of the lives of his men had been steeper than Caesar had foreseen, yet even so, his army's strength hadn't been so crippled that, had other factors not come into play, marching on to Susa was out of the question. What had been seriously damaged, at least temporarily, was the morale of his army, and of his most senior and trusted Legions at that. It wasn't confined just to the 3rd and the 10th, either; indeed, most of his army had been shaken to its core by the horrors introduced in the form of tumbling jars of flaming naphtha. Nevertheless, it was the knowledge that the men of Caesar's army were practically guaranteed to encounter this weapon again that their general understood was a large reason for their collective state of mind. Consequently, Caesar instead turned his attention to those decisions and actions that had to be taken to prepare for wintering in Ctesiphon and Seleucia. Perhaps the most important decision, and one that would prove to be extremely controversial with the men, and not just of the ranks but throughout all levels of the chain of command, was born out of Caesar's recognition of the new circumstances caused by what had taken place. It was a mark of Caesar's awareness about how this new directive would be greeted that he actually withheld this for more than a month, allowing his army not only to heal, but to become more fully aware of the circumstances surrounding that decision. In another sign of how deeply affected and shaken his men were, when Caesar made the announcement that the campaign season was effectively over, this was met with, if not enthusiasm, then a ready acceptance that was telling in itself. It was during the first full week after both cities fell that Caesar was at his busiest as he organized the new administration of the recently conquered cities. Somewhat unexpectedly, he determined that it was actually the citizens of Seleucia who were the most resistant, but Caesar quickly ascribed this to what had taken place at the hands of Pullus, Spurius, and their men. Indeed, this was the first challenge he faced, within a day after he had the announcement made that there would be no further reprisals against the populace, provided of course they cooperated with Caesar and his men. Acutely aware of the tremendous psychological blow his men had absorbed, he was also cognizant of the rampant speculation among the men of the ranks, most of whom were confined to their respective camps, while one Legion apiece was assigned to man the city defenses and patrol the streets of both Ctesiphon and Seleucia. The subject of the gossip around the fires was focused almost completely on not just the use of naphtha, but its availability, and Legionaries wouldn't have been worthy of the name if it didn't quickly become accepted as an article of faith that this horrible substance was more readily available to their Parthian foes than water. This, as Caesar well knew, wasn't the case, or even close to the truth, yet that didn't matter, meaning it was just another reason that prompted his decision, thereby giving himself and his officers the time to combat a rumor that was proving to be as pernicious as the substance itself, and almost as damaging. The method by which he went about damping down the growing conviction that this campaign would be an endless series of assaults and battles where fire would rain down on their collective heads was one that he had resorted to before, although it wasn't something he did lightly. As any man who had marched for Caesar since Gaul knew, those men who had the tendency to talk the most, the loudest, and most importantly, in a manner that could be considered detrimental to the morale of the army tended to disappear with a frequency that, while it didn't go unnoticed, was never the subject of comment after the fact. What *would* change afterwards is that there was no longer talk of the type that Caesar considered damaging to his army; and, if he were to be honest, to his *dignitas*. Which one was more important to Caesar only he knew.

As part of his decision, Caesar sent word to Ventidius, recalling the bulk of his cavalry arm from their camp near Susa, where they had been watching the main part of the Parthian army and its activity . While every member of this contingent was happy to return to at least a semblance of civilization, none were more so than the youngest among the officers. Almost every day, Octavian would rise from his hard bed, convinced that he was dirtier, sorer, and more tired than he had ever been in his life, only to ruefully recognize by the time the sun had set that he had been wrong. The watches spent in the saddle, as the sun beat down mercilessly, with his horse plodding under him in a monotonous rhythm that threatened to lull him to sleep in the saddle had been punctuated by the sudden eruption of noise, sometimes accompanied by the shrill scream of a horse, or worse, a man, who had been struck a blow, usually from an arrow, as their Parthian foes came boiling out from the cover they had used to wait as the Romans drew near. Although it wasn't a daily occurrence, it nevertheless did happen several times a week, and on a couple of occasions, more than once during a day, just enough to keep not just Octavian, but every man, alert and aware of how quickly the monotony could transform into

438

terror. In terms of hardship, the most difficult part of their dogged pursuit of Phraates had occurred when they were forced to turn to the east, leaving the Tigris. Despite the preparations Caesar had ordered, with the complement of mules whose only cargo were skins and skins of water, it had been a trying ordeal, although it was more so for the men than the animals. That this was the case was due to Ventidius' orders that the mounts be given the priority when it came to watering, but while the men understood this, this was before lips began cracking and bleeding from the lack of moisture, and throats became so parched that any attempt at conversation among comrades sounded akin to a marsh full of croaking frogs. It was on the second day of the waterless stretch when Octavian faced his first real challenge to his authority, when he witnessed two of the Germans clearly violating Ventidius' orders, guzzling water from a skin before pouring the rest of the contents into one of their helmets for their mounts. They were unaware that he was nearby; or, he thought bitterly, They saw me but don't care because I'm...Even in his mind, he couldn't force himself to utter the word that he knew some of the troopers were muttering whenever he passed. The fact that his uncle had broached the subject of his possible cowardice before he left with the cavalry made it even worse. Somewhat to his surprise, Octavian experienced a stab of anger, real anger at recalling this slur, which he decided later must have prompted his next action. Kicking his mount, he headed towards the pair at the trot, clearly catching them by surprise, judging from their expressions. What was most telling to Octavian, however, wasn't the look on their faces, but the fact that neither of them made any attempt to hide the skin, which was dripping the precious liquid onto the rocky soil, where the dark spot it made disappeared so quickly that one might have wondered if it had ever been there at all.

"You two," Octavian began, and in an unexpected and slightly odd way, the dryness of his own throat gave his voice a deeper, gravelly quality that made him sound older than he was, making him feel more authoritative when he finished, "are on report. Who's your Decurion?"

The youth wasn't all that surprised when one of them, slightly larger than his comrade, gave him an insolent grin, made even more so by the trooper's split lips which made thin vertical lines that were slightly bleeding and tinged the man's mouth in red, although he did not reply.

His comrade did speak, but with a thick, Germanic accent that Octavian felt certain was exaggerated, saying cheerfully, "Tancred no does speak Latin, young Master."

Turning to face this man, Octavian struggled to maintain a cool, composed manner as he countered, "He may not, but you obviously do. What's your Decurion's name?"

The German, whose beard was plaited and had small bones tied into it that Octavian knew were supposedly the knucklebones of the men this trooper had slain, or claimed to at any rate, tilted his head and repeated the title as if he had never heard it before.

"Decurion?" At this, he turned to his comrade, saying a few words in their guttural native tongue, which prompted a laugh from the first German. Turning back to Octavian, the second German dropped all pretense at obsequy as he said harshly, "What you need know Decurion for?"

"Because," Octavian snapped, oddly relieved that this brute's insolence had ignited his anger to the point it overrode his innate sense of caution, "I just saw you guzzle water that's supposed to go to your animals first! You know that's a violation of orders, and I am reporting your disobedience to your Decurion!"

This elicited a growl from the German identified as Tancred, giving the lie that he didn't understand Latin, yet it was actually the second German, the grin instantly replaced by a scowl, who walked menacingly up to Octavian, glaring up at the younger Roman. Not lost on the younger man was how this German had approached him from his weak side, effectively putting the bulk of Octavian's body between himself and Octavian's sword.

"You no should talk like that, *boy*," the German growled, and as he did so, he extended a hand that, while he didn't actually touch Octavian's ankle, hovered there in a clear threat. "Boys," he continued, "*Roman* boys, they not good horsemen. Fall off all the time."

How Octavian retained his composure he would never know; that he did was a valuable lesson to him, and would be a trait he would exhibit many more times in his life. Looking slowly down at the German's hand, still inches away from his booted foot, Octavian regarded it for the span of a heartbeat before returning his gaze to the German, regarding him unflinchingly with eyes that were a bit grayer than Caesar's icy blue, yet there was still something in his look that caused the German to shift nervously. Then, as the silence drew out, he dropped his hand; his final acquiescence came by dropping his eyes, breaking the gaze between the two.

"What is your Decurion's name?" Octavian repeated, still speaking softly.

Swallowing hard, the German, ignoring the glare from Tancred, muttered the name of the fellow German who commanded his *ala*. There was another silence then, drawn out by Octavian, both to increase the tension the two Germans were clearly feeling, but also to savor what he saw as a victory.

"I've decided," his voice made the pair jump slightly, which made it difficult for Octavian to retain his grave expression, "that I'm not going to report you. This time." Both men, who had been so defiant before, sagged in obvious relief, yet it was short-lived. Leaning down so his face was closer, Octavian spoke even more softly, except this made his words even more impactful. "But if I *do* fall off my horse, for any reason, just be aware that I'm going to write a letter. In fact, I'm going to dictate it right after I leave you two, and if anything happens to me, that letter will go to my uncle. You *do* know who he is, don't you?" This time, it was Tancred who answered, albeit with only an unhappy nod. Accepting this confirmation, Octavian promised them, "So you know that by the time he's through, not only will you be punished, both of your families will be as well. Do you understand me?"

When they both assured Octavian that they did indeed both understand and accept that he was speaking truly, without anotherword,, the young Roman turned and trotted away, choosing to go in a direction where they couldn't see the broad smile he wore on his face at this victory. Over the years, Octavian would look back at this moment and think of it as the first where he exhibited traits worthy of being called Caesar. Even so, this was also an insult that he wasn't going to forget.

"All in all, Caesar, the boy did very well."

Ventidius paused to sip from his cup, the lines on his already seamed face now etched even more deeply because of the month of exposure to the harsh, unrelenting Parthian sun on little water. He was seated in front of Caesar's desk, but in a somewhat unusual move, the Dictator had roused himself from behind it to take the other seat next to Ventidius and was also sharing a cup from the amphora.

Seeing that Caesar was actually expecting more, the old muleteer cleared his throat and continued, "Yes, well, as I said, he performed admirably. In fact," Ventidius acknowledged as he thought more about the subject Caesar had broached, "I'd have to say that he outperformed all but Silva. He volunteered for every patrol, and the times we experienced some mischief from those bastards, he was always right in the thick of it." Ventidius gave a hoarse chuckle, and he waved a hand that was beginning to show the effects of the arthritis that plagued men his age as he qualified himself, "Now, I'm not saying the boy *loves* getting his sword wet. If anything," he mused, "the best I could say is that he was resigned to it but was doing the best job he could do." This news satisfied Caesar, and he thanked Ventidius, who repeated the waving gesture in reply, saying, "There's no need for that, Caesar. Besides, that boy proved very useful. He has quite a mind, I must say. He made several suggestions about our situation that proved quite valuable."

Although Caesar was certainly interested in hearing about what those suggestions might have been, he had more pressing concerns, and he asked Ventidius, "What of the Parthians? Were they reinforced?"

Ventidius grimaced in response, then nodded his head.

"Yes," he replied, "they were. By two different forces, actually. Both of them came from the east. The first arrived two days after Orodes and his bunch got to Susa. Or," he amended, remembering the one piece of news he had learned from the unfortunate Parthians who had been captured, "we thought it was Orodes. But I'll tell you more about that in a moment. Anyway, that first force numbered about eight thousand, but is composed of mostly archers." Consulting the tablet he had brought with him, Ventidius squinted at the figures, then supplied them. "About five thousand worth of archers, according to our count. The remainder is spearmen." Taking a breath, he went on, "It's the second force that concerns me, Caesar, for a number of reasons."

"Oh?" Caesar instantly became alert at the subtle but unmistakable change in the Legate's demeanor. "In what way?"

"Because they're twelve thousand strong, for one thing," Ventidius explained, "and hardly an archer among them."

Caesar sat back, yet, while this was sobering news, given how well the tactics that had, in part, been developed by the man across from him, he wasn't overly concerned. Ventidius correctly interpreted his general's nonchalance, and in partial reply, he shook his head grimly.

"Caesar," the older man's tone matched his grim demeanor as he explained, "there's something you need to know about this second force. They don't have archers, that's true, but that doesn't mean they're cataphracts. At least," he amended, "mostly cataphracts. Oh, there's a fair number of those bastards," glancing back down at the tablet for the numbers, Ventidius continued, "about five thousand, more or less. But the rest are infantry."

Rather than clarify, this served to send Caesar's mind in the opposite direction from which Ventidius intended to send it.

"So they're bringing seven thousand more infantry?" Caesar scoffed. "They worry me less than the cataphracts!"

"It's not the numbers that are the problem," Ventidius countered quietly. "It's *who* they are that is."

He fell silent then, yet kept his gaze on Caesar as he, correctly, guessed that his general would be able to work this out for himself. Granted, it did take a bit longer than Ventidius would have thought, but watching Caesar's face, as the realization of the full import of Ventidius' words dawned on him, and when they did, it elicited a gasp from the normally unflappable Caesar.

"You mean," his voice had gone hoarse in that brief instant of time, "those are *Crassus'* men?"

Almost from the moment the first survivors of Crassus' failed campaign into Parthia returned to the part of the world where Roman ears were there to hear about it, there had been much speculation about the fate of the large number of Legionaries who, at least according to Cassius and his fellow escapees, had survived and been captured by the Parthians. That there had been men who suffered this ignominy wasn't in much doubt; what was a topic of debate were their numbers, as a sizable group of Romans, namely Cicero, and Cato while he had been alive, had insisted that no Roman would opt for a life as a prisoner, choosing instead an honorable death, a *Roman* death. Caesar, on the other hand, hadn't been as sanguine about this conviction, but it was one of the relatively rare subjects about which he kept his own counsel. Between his extensive experience with the Roman lower class and his observation of men of every known nationality and status, Caesar had long concluded that what a man would boast while sitting in a tavern, or around a fire, surrounded by his friends, about

443

how they would rather die free than live as a slave, wasn't necessarily the case when that individual was actually faced with making that choice. And, even further, he didn't think Roman men were immune to this reality. Now, sitting in his office, which had been relocated to the throne room of the palace in Ctesiphon, Ventidius at least seemed to be confirming his belief.

"They're not wearing their old armor, so we couldn't be sure at first," Ventidius had explained. "In fact," he frowned, "what they're wearing is a type of armor I've never really seen before. It's *similar* to the kind the cataphracts wear, but the metal plates seem to be overlapping more than that. But," he added, "their helmets are almost identical to the ones worn by the cataphracts, and they carry wicker shields."

"Did you or your scouts get close enough to actually see their faces?" Caesar pressed; despite his trust in Ventidius and his scouts, there was a part of him that didn't want to be right, that wanted Cicero and his Boni to be the ones whose judgment proved correct, if only in this one instance.

"No," Ventidius admitted, then before Caesar's mind could make something significant out of this omission, the older Legate assured Caesar, "but we didn't have to. They marched in the kind of formation that only we use, for one thing. And while they carry wicker shields, they're not carrying spears. They're carrying javelins. Not," Ventidius held up a hand, "exactly like ours, with the counterweight and thin neck. But they're not heavy spears like the rest of their infantry uses. And they were wearing swords, although they looked a bit longer than the Spanish sword. No, Caesar," Ventidius' tone was not only sober, but was tinged with what sounded to his general like sadness, "they're Romans. But, Caesar, as disturbing as that is, there's something that bothers me even more."

"Oh?" Caesar's tone was light, yet there was no missing the tinge of bitterness. "What other piece of news do you have to ruin my day even more?"

To his credit, Ventidius didn't hesitate, knowing that prevaricating, especially with what he considered bad news, was something Caesar didn't appreciate.

"They had a tail," Ventidius said quietly.

Caesar didn't react, at first, which was telling in itself that Ventidius had managed to shock his general again, despite Caesar's own silent resolution that nothing more his Legate said could surprise him. That Ventidius used the rankers' slang word for the part of a

Roman army on campaign that every commander, with any wisdom at least, chose to ignore, provided it didn't hinder or slow the Legions in any way, made his words no less impactful. This "tail" was made of flesh and bone, it was true, but was composed of those women commonly referred to as camp followers by officers, and as wives by the rankers, despite the fact that no man of the ranks was legally allowed to be married. That these unions weren't legally sanctioned had absolutely no bearing on how most men viewed these women, or the offspring that inevitably followed. Now, if Ventidius was correct, and there was no reason to believe he wasn't, the presence of this tail meant that these men, these Romans, had integrated into Parthian society to a point where their ostensible captors allowed them to form attachments with their Parthian counterparts of their own class. Once he accepted that Ventidius was right in his observation, which happened almost instantly, Caesar's mind had run with this fact and examined its deeper meaning. Grudgingly, he had to salute the Parthian, presumably the King of Kings, who had allowed men who were technically their captives to integrate into their own society. In doing so, they now gave these Romans something for which to fight, and die, over and above avoiding the taste of the lash of their captors. And, he recognized, it freed up Parthian resources from guarding these men; allowing them to bring their women and families could also be viewed in two ways. As he thought more about it, in the span of the dozen heartbeats' silence between the two men, Caesar realized that there was still a fist of iron hovering above the heads of these Romans, as he understood that by having their families with them in Susa, the King of Kings still exerted control over them. If, by being in the proximity of their former countrymen, Crassus' Romans began thinking of their old homes and thoughts of returning to the ranks of their former comrades, Caesar had little doubt that their Parthian families would be the ones who suffered, and that their end would be too horrible to contemplate for most of those men to seriously consider returning to Rome. Oddly enough, this recognition actually served to deepen Caesar's conviction that his ultimate goal, not just of conquering the Parthian armies, but adding this vast expanse to the holdings of his beloved city, was not only desirable, it was the only way to ensure that these lost men, and their new families, would be protected. It was the least he could do for those men who had suffered so much; this, at least, was the fiction that Caesar would use as pretext for his ambitions.

Ventidius intruded on these thoughts when he broke the silence, asking, "What do you think the men will do when they learn about this?"

"That," Caesar replied, his face grim, "is a good question. And," the look he gave Ventidius was more than enough warning, "that's not something I want to worry about. Not yet." Shaking his head as if to banish the problem Crassus' survivors posed, Caesar returned to something Ventidius had mentioned, in passing, asking the older man, "You said there was something else?" When Ventidius' expression became confused, Caesar prompted gently, "It was when you were telling me about Crassus' men, how they arrived not long after Orodes...?"

"Ah," Ventidius interrupted, and he was embarrassed at this lapse in front of his general, "yes, that. I'm sorry, Caesar; I must be getting old!" Ventidius laughed at his own joke, then went on, "It does concern Orodes, in a way. We captured a handful of Parthians, as I'm sure you surmised." Glancing down, he fumbled with another tablet, opened it, and ran a stubby finger down the incised wax before he found what he was looking for, and continued, "Fifteen, to be exact. Four of them were infantrymen who fell behind on their march to Susa, and nine of them were horse archers. The other two were cataphracts." Caesar was about to interrupt to remind Ventidius that he didn't need this level of detail, but before he could do so, Ventidius gave his reason for doing so by explaining, "Caesar, those two cataphracts were hard, tough bastards. I was there for their questioning, and neither of them ever cracked before they died. And," as hard a man as Ventidius was in his own right, the memory still made him shudder, "both of them died an ugly death."

Glancing up through his bushy gray eyebrows, the older Legate studied Caesar's face, seeing that his general understood the significance of this seemingly random bit of information.

"So we can expect men of their class to fight to the death," Caesar mused aloud, "or, most of them anyway."

"It seems that way," Ventidius agreed, then continued, "No, what we learned about the late King of Kings came from the others. And most of them sang the same tune, or near enough that I'm certain this is the truth."

"'Late' King of Kings?" Caesar pounced immediately, as Ventidius had assumed he would, "Are you saying that Orodes is dead?"

"Yes," Ventidius nodded, then added hurriedly, knowing Caesar would want this specific detail, "but he didn't die as king."

"Didn't die as king?"

Now, Caesar was momentarily confused, which was precisely why Ventidius had thrown this out there; it was petty, he knew, but it was a small measure of revenge for all the times Caesar had put his muleteer on the back foot.

In answer, Ventidius shook his head, yet while he was tempted to not add anything to this, in order to savor the moment, instead, he explained, "No, Caesar. When Orodes learned of Pacorus' death, apparently, he immediately abdicated, either the day his son's body was returned to him or the day after. Now his other son, Phraates, is King of Kings. And Orodes died sometime after that." Glancing down one more time, he found what he was looking for, and finished, "None of the men we...questioned knew exactly when he died, but apparently, it was somewhere along the way to Susa."

Caesar sat, listening, then when Ventidius finished, he still remained silent, thinking.

Finally, he said, "It looks like I have some things to discuss with Kambyses."

Every morning Kambyses woke, he was a bit more confused than he had been the morning before. And, while he sensed this was the Roman general Caesar's goal, what furthered his disorientation even more was why it was happening. The Parthian was certain he had made it clear that he had no intention of cooperating willingly; indeed, he had expected to be hauled off to be tortured moments after he had made this defiant statement to Caesar. Instead, however, nothing of the sort had happened. Even more unsettling were the circumstances of his confinement, although the irony of it wasn't lost on him. He hadn't been moved far; in truth, it was really a matter of feet, as he and his possessions, minus weapons and armor of course, were transferred into the room that Kambyses had assigned to the deceased Melchior. Otherwise, he was still in the palace, but he did feel certain that the primary reason for Melchior's former room being used as his cell had to do with the fact it was an interior room, without windows and only one possible escape route. Which, he acknowledged, was heavily guarded with not one or two, but four men, all Legionaries by the look of them, and Kambyses took an odd comfort in the cold hostility that radiated from these Romans, even as he marveled at their self-discipline. None of them ever touched him, at least in a manner that Kambyses knew a Parthian would, no matter what their orders were, and it was another sign to Kambyses of how these Romans were unlike those that had marched for that puffed-up nobleman Crassus. While Kambyses' grasp of Roman society and their class system was, at best, rudimentary, he was aware that Crassus and Caesar were of the same social standing, although the one thing that the whole world knew was that Crassus was said to be the wealthiest man of his day, even more wealthy than the King of Kings. Which, Kambyses knew very well, had been a huge source of irritation to Orodes. In his heart, Kambyses had always believed that this was the true reason Surena had lost his head, because Crassus hadn't been captured alive so that Orodes could exact the elaborate and, even to a Parthian, extraordinarily cruel fate he had conjured up for the Roman general. So imaginative was it that, despite Orodes never getting the opportunity to use it on Crassus, he used the highest ranking surviving Roman as a substitute, having molten gold poured down the man's throat. When the rumor began circulating that it had in fact been Crassus, which Kambyses knew was not only encouraged but had been instigated by agents who worked for Orodes, no Parthian who wanted to remain in the land of the living refuted it. When Kambyses had what would be his third meeting with Caesar, two days after the fall of the cities he had been charged with defending, the Parthian general wasn't certain it would happen, but he tried to prepare himself for Caesar not only mentioning this incident and trying to determine the truth of the matter, he half-expected being told by the Roman he would be consigned to suffering the same fate in retaliation. And yet, nothing of the sort happened; instead, Caesar had treated him with the utmost courtesy, not requiring Kambyses to wear chains or indicating in any way that the Parthian was anything other than an honored guest. Regardless of this treatment, Kambyses wasn't fooled; he could hear the shuffling sounds of guards stationed just outside the large room, even as he and Caesar conversed pleasantly. Nevertheless, despite his inner resolve, Kambyses found it difficult to remain guarded in Caesar's presence. Part of it stemmed from the regard one fighting man held for another, even if they were on opposing sides; even more disturbingly, however, Kambyses discovered he actually enjoyed being in Caesar's company. It was a profoundly disorienting feeling, especially when Kambyses considered that it had been at his orders that he had unleashed the fiery naphtha down on Caesar's men, yet the Roman had only made one reference to it.

"My men hate you and want to flay you alive," Caesar had said, speaking in a manner as if they were discussing nothing more significant than the weather, "and I confess it would probably make them feel better about what happened." He paused then, and it was a moment Kambyses had cause to remember, as the Roman regarded him with those icy blue eyes he had first encountered when he had retrieved Pacorus' body, just a couple months before. The depth of those eyes seemed limitless, and Kambyses felt acutely uncomfortable for the span of the three or four heartbeats of silence before Caesar continued, "But if I had been in your position, I would have done exactly the same thing. I would have used every weapon at my disposal to keep my enemy from taking either of these cities."

What accosted Kambyses that moment was a queer mix of emotions, even as he knew he shouldn't be experiencing some of them. Most disturbing was the feeling of gratitude that washed through him, although later, he told himself that it was because of the punishment that Caesar had ascribed to his men and their desire to inflict it on him; he had seen more than one man whose skin was carefully peeled away from the underlying musculature, and knew that a skilled torturer could make this last for days. He had no doubt that there were such men in Caesar's employ, so he comforted himself with the recognition that a large part of his feeling stemmed from the happiness that came from avoiding that fate at least. It was the pride that he had felt, swelling up through him as Caesar essentially endorsed his use of the naphtha that was the most confusing, because ultimately, he had failed to keep the Romans from that very thing; they were now in firm possession of both Ctesiphon and Seleucia. So, he wondered, why wasn't he more upset, and why did it please him to receive Caesar's recognition for doing his utmost to keep both cities in Parthian hands? This turned out to be just the beginning of an unlikely relationship; rarely a night passed without Kambyses being summoned into Caesar's presence, but on none of those occasions did Caesar press him for information about the Parthian defenses at Susa, where other strongpoints were located, and the likelihood of the Parthian empire having the ability to draw on even more trained fighting men. Instead, Caesar asked about innocuous things, like the customs of the Parthian court, or what the daily life of a man of Kambyses' station held for him, and even more surprisingly to Kambyses, Caesar seemed particularly interested in the lot of those people who, as Kambyses had been informed on the ridge, were of roughly the same status as those the Romans called the Head Count. Why Caesar wanted to know this was beyond Kambyses, but he certainly saw no harm in providing the Roman with this information, since he could avail himself of it simply enough by grabbing one of the men from the ranks. It wasn't until much later, when it was too late, that Kambyses realized that everything Caesar did was with a larger purpose in mind, and in dealing with this Roman, there was no such thing as an innocent question. The first tense moment occurred when, although Kambyses had no way of knowing this, Ventidius informed Caesar of the shift in Parthian leadership.

"Tell me about Phraates," Caesar began, after the two exchanged the pleasantries that had become part of a ritual.

Kambyses' hand froze, the cup in it inches from his lips as he asked cautiously, "Phraates? Why would you want to know about him?"

"Because he's King of Kings," Caesar replied calmly, studying the Parthian's face as he continued, "When Orodes abdicated after he learned of Pacorus' death." The Roman hesitated for a moment, then added, "But you already knew that, because you were the one who brought Pacorus to his father."

It was a guess, but it was a shrewd one, and Kambyses gave an involuntary grimace that both men instantly understood betrayed the truth of the matter.

"Yes," Kambyses finally answered grudgingly, "that is true. I am the one who brought the prince home to his father." The memory of it prompted him to take a deep gulp of the cup that had still been hovering in front of him, and as he slammed it down, he finished bitterly, "I was the fortunate one to have to tell my king that I had failed in protecting his first son and heir."

While Caesar still regarded Kambyses as an enemy, not all of his elaborate courtesy and show of cordiality was feigned; indeed, if he had been able to peer into the Parthian's mind, he would have found its state to be a close match to his own when it came to the growing regard he held for the other man.

And now, he felt a stab of sympathy for Kambyses, prompting him to say, "I can't imagine how painful that must have been." Using the expression of mingled surprise and gratitude on the Parthian's face, Caesar repeated his original question, "But, tell me about Phraates. How did he take his brother's death?"

This elicited a scornful laugh from Kambyses, who countered, "How do you think he took it? It was the happiest day of that snake's

450

life seeing me ride up to the palace with his brother's corpse. Not," he allowed, barely refraining from spitting on the floor to show his contempt, "as happy as the next day was, when Orodes abdicated." Sighing, Kambyses finished with, "I just hope the king, the *real* king comes back to his senses and puts Phraates in his place."

"Ah," Caesar answered, his voice suddenly softer, "you don't know, then."

Kambyses' head shot up from his examination of his cup, eyeing Caesar sharply, suddenly suspicious.

"Know what?"

"Orodes is dead," Caesar replied evenly, but without any hesitation, telling Kambyses this was likely the truth.

More important to Kambyses than Caesar's demeanor was the small tightening sensation in his gut that he had long before learned to heed, informing him that Caesar wasn't lying to him.

"Of course," he sat back suddenly with a groan of realization, "I should have known that would happen!"

There was a silence then, both men absorbed in their thoughts, then, surprising not only Caesar, but himself, Kambyses asked dully, "What do you want to know about Phraates?"

Chapter Seventeen

By the end of the second day of an occupation of the two Parthian cities that would turn out to last much longer than anyone, with perhaps the exception of Caesar, expected, the building that had once served as the royal palace of the Seleucid dynasty had been converted into a hospital. That this building was so chosen had nothing to do with symbolism and everything to do with size, and this alone served as a sobering reminder to all the men of Caesar's army of the cost in blood that had been incurred. Not lost on any of them was the recognition that the campaign to subdue Parthia wasn't completed, and it was a sign of the overall mood of the army that, when the announcement was made that there would be no further offensive operations involving the entire army, while the men didn't cheer, neither was there a word of complaint. In the new hospital building, one entire wing was devoted to those men who had suffered from the use of the naphtha, and it was one of the grimmest places Titus Pullus had ever seen. Regardless of their personal feelings, both Primi Pili whose men suffered the most forced themselves to visit their men frequently. However, despite the ministrations of not just the *medici* but Caesar's personal physician, men continued to succumb at a daily rate, usually from some sort of infection that their bodies couldn't fight while trying to heal from within at the same time. Still, there were survivors, men whose burns were severe but not to the point where it killed them. Unfortunately, precious few of these survivors were fit for full duty, even after they had completely healed, most of them suffering horrible scars in the process that inhibited their ability to perform all but the simplest tasks. These men were given a choice by Caesar; if they so chose, they would be allowed to return to their homes in the Republic, with a full pension and payment of their passage, or to remain, if not with the army, then as part of the garrison that Caesar intended to leave behind when the army resumed its campaign. When those men unanimously elected to remain with the army in some capacity, the only men who were surprised were a few of Caesar's senior officers, along with some of the Tribunes, and one *Contubernales*, Octavian.

It was Octavian's friend Agrippa, more attuned to men of the ranks than Octavian, who explained, "The lower classes view any deformity or injury that leaves men disfigured as a sign that they're cursed by the gods. I suppose that none of them wanted to face their families and run the risk of being shunned."

When explained this way, Octavian not only understood, he sympathized, at least as much as he was able to when it came to men of the lower classes; he was acutely aware that there were men of his own class who whispered that his infirmity of wheezing was much the same thing. Although, he thought bitterly, in their case, they don't really believe it; they just use it as an excuse to slander me. Never following far behind his thoughts of this nature was the image of the face of Marcus Antonius, who had been the one man who never bothered to lower his voice when he repeated such things. Indeed, Antonius seemed to take a great deal of pleasure in saying this in front Octavian, although he was careful to couch it in terms that suggested he was merely repeating what other men said about his distant relative. It was something that bothered Octavian a great deal, and he had long before vowed to find a way to repay Antonius in kind for every slur the man had uttered against and about him. As far as Octavian's own fortunes were concerned, as he discovered to his great relief, his own conduct during the time spent with Ventidius had restored him to his uncle's good graces, and as things became more settled and Caesar's plans for the immediate future firmed up, the Dictator had begun dropping increasingly broad hints that he had an important role for his nephew to fulfill.

"Before that," Caesar had replied when Octavian, growing impatient, had pressed his uncle for details of his new and expanded role, "there are still things we need to take care of with the army."

While this delay chafed at Octavian, he also understood that Caesar was speaking nothing but the truth. Despite it still being too early to tell with any certainty, Octavian, being present at every daily briefing, knew how pessimistic the outlook was about how many of the wounded would be returned to full duty.

It was only when Caesar's personal physician, who the Dictator had summoned to give his assessment to the officers assembled in the palace for one of the twice-daily meetings, that the full scale of the likely outcome was made apparent.

"Even if every man we have left in the hospital were to somehow not only survive, but return to full duty, our losses across the Legions are ten percent. But," Caesar added grimly, "as we all know, the losses aren't equal. We'd have to do an incredible amount of shifting about, not only between Cohorts, but between Legions, just to reach this state where every Legion is operating at ninety percent."

Of all the assembled men, the two Primi Pili of the Legions hardest hit were acutely aware that this was not only the case, Caesar was putting the most optimistic face on their situation. Specifically, it wasn't just a matter of quantity; it was the quality of the men who had been lost that concerned Pullus and Spurius the most. Putting it in its simplest terms, both the 3rd and 10th had lost a substantial number of their most experienced and skilled veterans, which meant that the only way to restore the balance was to rob the junior Cohorts of their own complement of veterans. Although it was true that there was a preponderance of the best fighters in the First Cohort of each Legion, and of the Centuries of the First, the first three Centuries were filled with a larger percentage of these valued fighters than the other three, Caesar had long before learned the folly of packing all of the seasoned veterans into the most senior Cohort. Consequently, each Cohort and their Centuries had men whose skill and experience alone qualified them for service in the First Cohort of their Legion, but had been deemed too valuable to lose to the First because it would seriously compromise the fighting capability of that Cohort. Now, as Caesar was explaining the problem, Spurius and Pullus exchanged a glance, sharing their intense concern and their corresponding interest in how the general was planning to solve this issue. When they discussed it immediately afterward, neither of them, nor any of their counterparts, were even remotely prepared for what came out of Caesar's mouth.

"I think he's lost his mind," was how Pullus put it that night to Scribonius and Balbus.

They were sitting in Pullus' quarters for the evening meal as usual, but the quarters themselves were a radical change from Pullus' tent, spacious as it was. Each Primus Pilus had been given the use of one of the buildings surrounding the palace and that, from the appointments and furnishings that had been left behind, had obviously once been the homes of the various courtiers that attended the King of Kings. As a result, the three Romans and lone Greek were sitting in a spacious dining room, the table made of precious citrus wood that, despite his relative indifference to such things, even Pullus had taken the time to admire. Diocles had just finished serving the evening meal, and Pullus had forestalled the topic that was gnawing at the edges of his mind for the period of time it took them to eat their food, which had been prepared by the same slaves as always. It was true there was a plethora of newly captured Parthians and Greeks, many of whom, in their attempt to lighten their impending burden in bondage, had touted their abilities as cooks, scribes, and all manner of useful trades. Some of them were even telling the truth, Pullus was sure, yet when he approached Diocles about the idea of taking on one of these new slaves to relieve Diocles of one of his many duties, he was not only resistant, he was adamant that this not happen.

"What," he had scoffed, "and let one of them poison you? I don't think so!" Suddenly, the Greek's expression grew concerned as he asked warily, "And why would you want to? Do you not like my cooking?"

Pullus had laughed at this, clapping Diocles on the back as he assured him that, no, he was perfectly content with the fare his Greek provided. That Pullus was largely unconcerned with food, other than as a means to fuel his body, was something he didn't think Diocles needed to know; as long as the Greek managed to procure his larger portion of meat that almost all of his fellow Romans turned away, he was happy. Now Pullus had just shoved his plate away in a silent signal that it was time to talk business, which was prefaced by his pronouncement on Caesar's mental state.

"Why do you say that?" Scribonius asked, although he wasn't quite finished, but he had never seen anyone who consumed food as quickly as his friend.

Taking a deep breath, Pullus broached the topic at last, and while he had been mulling over the best way to bring it up, as he almost always did, he allowed his impatience to overrule his sense of decorum, blurting out, "Caesar has decided that we're going to hold an impromptu *dilectus* to plump us back up."

Balbus, who had just taken a deep draught of his watered wine, set his cup down with a care that was clearly exaggerated, and equally as carefully said, "I don't think that's a bad idea, but you obviously do." Staring intently at Pullus, as if trying to divine what part of this news had his Primus Pilus so troubled, he clearly didn't find the answer, prompting him to ask, "So what part don't we know?"

Pullus didn't reply immediately, instead choosing to frown down into his own cup, then he said, finally, "Because it's not going to be held anywhere in the Republic."

"Not in the Republic?" Scribonius echoed, and his expression caused Pullus a moment of a certain satisfaction at his friend's bewilderment, thinking, it's nice to see him looking like that for once instead of the other way around. "But where else is he going to find Roman citizens?"

In answer, Pullus didn't actually verbally respond, instead gazing steadily at Scribonius, understanding that while he had caught his friend off guard, it wouldn't take long for him to work it out. Indeed, no more than three or four heartbeats of time passed before Scribonius' expression changed from confusion to realization, then to shock as he suddenly sat back in his chair.

"You don't mean…" he breathed, to which Pullus only gave a grim nod.

Balbus, meanwhile, was growing more agitated, which wasn't unusual at moments like this, as he was inevitably the last man of the trio to catch on to these unspoken exchanges between the other two.

"I'm happy that you understand what he's fucking talking about," he snapped at Scribonius, while glaring at Pullus.

Under normal circumstances, Scribonius wouldn't have missed the opportunity for some fun, tormenting Balbus by drawing out his ordeal of being the last to know, but not this time; this, Scribonius realized, was too important a moment to make a joke, and while he would never say it openly, his own heart ached for the grief Balbus was experiencing. Who else better to understand what it meant to a Centurion to lose men, especially so many at one time, than one of his counterparts?

"If I'm understanding Titus correctly," Scribonius' tone was almost gentle, because he knew how raw Balbus' emotions still were, and what kind of impact this news Pullus was relaying would have on him, as he explained, "Caesar plans on enlisting new meat from the Parthians that we captured."

Because of the scarring, Balbus' face was difficult for others to read, but these two men, his best friends, had been together for too long for either of them to miss the shock that quickly transitioned to anger. Nevertheless, both jumped when, without any warning, Balbus' powerful hand crushed the cup he was holding, sending shards of clay and blood-red wine everywhere.

"*Cac*," Balbus mumbled, looking down at the gash in his palm from one of the shards.

Oddly enough, this seemed to dampen the rage that the other two men had seen was about to explode, and both of them heaved quiet

456

sighs of relief; Pullus in a rage was a terrifying sight, but there was something in Balbus that gave even his best friends pause about rousing his ire.

Taking the rag that Diocles had hurried into the next room to retrieve, Balbus applied it to his palm, although not before some blood dripped onto the table, and he mumbled, "I need to clean that up."

"Don't worry about that," Diocles spoke up, standing just behind Balbus, and over the scarred Centurion's shoulder, Pullus saw by Diocles' expression the Greek was as concerned as he was.

"At least we match now," Pullus joked, holding up his own hand, where the stitches had been recently removed.

"So," Balbus still seemed more absorbed in his own palm than anything Pullus had said as he spoke, "how is that supposed to work?"

"That," Pullus admitted, "is still being debated."

"Debated?" Scribonius asked doubtfully, shaking his head at this idea. "How's that possible? I've never known Caesar to give an order, then allow us to debate about it."

"That should tell you how his plan went over with all of us." Pullus gave a sour smile at the fresh memory of the huge uproar that happened immediately after Caesar's announcement. "I swear by the black stone, it was almost as noisy as any fight I've ever been in. Every one of us jumped to our feet, and we were all shouting at him about what a horrible idea it was."

Scribonius' gasp of surprise was only drowned out by the exclamation of Diocles, and the grunt from Balbus. Not lost on any of these men was the memory of all that had transpired just four years before, when a significant portion of Caesar's army, immediately after the battle at Pharsalus that had brought about Pompeius Magnus' final defeat, simply refused to march another step in pursuit of the fleeing Pompeius and the ragged remnant of his huge army. And Pullus, better than the other two, knew how deeply imbedded the resentment Caesar felt at what he saw as a betrayal on the part of an army that he had once commanded so seemingly effortlessly and to such great effect. Still, it was the 10th's refusal in particular that rankled Caesar the most, and had resulted in a period of extremely cool relations between the Dictator and his once-favorite Legion. It was during this period of time when Pullus had been with Caesar in Alexandria and the East, serving as the *de facto* Primus Pilus of the two Cohorts of the 6th Legion that had chosen to serve the man who conquered their own general. What was never lost on Pullus, or even far from his mind whenever he was in Caesar's presence, was that, while Pharsalus marked the lowest point in Caesar's hold over the army, in direct contrast, it secured Pullus' own status as a man Caesar could trust. Regardless of this advancement, it was in the dark watches of the night, as Pullus tossed and turned, examining all the twists and turns of a life that had taken him from a ramshackle farm in Baetica, to the post of Primus Pilus and to being one of Caesar's most trusted Centurions, that he remembered what it had cost, in the form of an almost lifelong friendship with Vibius Domitius. It was only when he was alone with his thoughts that he allowed his resentment of Caesar to occupy him, for what he ultimately viewed as his general's unreasonable expectation of not just his own Legion, but of the entire army that had given him his victory, especially since it had been won at a huge cost in blood. As Pullus well knew, the refusal of his army to budge wasn't based in anything other than sheer exhaustion and not out of any lack of regard for their general, but Caesar had clearly taken it personally, which had created a huge rift that only recently had healed. Now, Pullus was afraid that Caesar's plan to enlist Parthians into the Legions was going to rip the army apart, and he said as much to the two men he trusted the most.

That it was Diocles who spoke next would have surprised only those who weren't aware of how he was viewed by Pullus, and he asked, "So, Master Titus, what's your alternative? What do you think needs to be done?"

The silence that followed stretched out for a seemingly interminable amount of time, but Pullus' silence, or Scribonius' or Balbus', wasn't from shock that a slave had dared to speak; instead, it was precisely for the reason Diocles had spoken up, to allow his master to fully contemplate the issue at hand. As Pullus had learned in the four years Diocles had been in his service, plucked completely at random from the prisoners captured at Pharsalus and based on the Greek's half-fiction that he was experienced in attending to the needs of a high-ranking Roman officer, both Pullus and Diocles were the better for the Roman's choice of the man he called with increasing fondness his "little Greek." However, while it was true that, especially compared to Pullus, Diocles was diminutive in stature, standing just a shade over five feet tall, there was nothing small when it came to his intellectual prowess, nor his education as a tutor, the occupation for which he had been trained before circumstances found him in a state of bondage. Not surprisingly, it hadn't taken long for Scribonius to get a glimpse of the hidden depths of this Greek, and he regarded Diocles with a respect, and a fondness similar to Pullus', which meant that he was just as quick to grasp the underlying point Diocles was making. Finally, Pullus opened his mouth, yet it took him a bit longer to begin speaking, and when he did, it was very slowly, a mannerism that his friends and slave knew that, ironically, indicated his mind was working more quickly than his words would lead one to believe.

"That," he conceded, "is a good point, and it's not one that I thought of, at least from that viewpoint. What other choice does he have?" Shrugging then, he offered something up, although he was sure of the response when he offered, "We beat Pompey at Pharsalus when we were at half-strength. While it's true that we just lost a fair number of men in the First, we're still better off than we were then."

"And," Scribonius asked quietly, "do you want to go back to that?"

Pullus grimaced at this idea, and he wasn't alone; neither Balbus nor Scribonius recalled that period of time with any fondness. Putting it in its simplest terms, having half the men meant they had to work twice as hard in conducting the business of the Legions, and as all veterans, especially in Caesar's army understood, this meant such tasks as constructing marching camps, along with foraging and a number of other duties where more hands made for lighter work. As each of them could attest through experience, Caesar's expectations didn't lower in a manner corresponding to the relative strength of his Legions; his ditches were still deeper and wider than any other general's, and he still moved his men faster as well, while carrying the same load, one that was only partially distributed on the Legion's complement of mules.

"No." Pullus shook his head, pursing his lips as he continued the process of examining Caesar's plan more deeply. "I know nobody wants that. But...Parthians?"

"Did he say who he plans on drawing from?" Scribonius asked, then clarified at Pullus' look of confusion, "I mean, from which class of the Parthians he's going to recruit?"

Pullus' face cleared, and now his head nodded as he answered, "Yes, actually, he did. He's not going to bother trying to convince any of those Parthian nobles to join us. Not only would it be a waste of time, he knows we wouldn't trust them. Besides," he chuckled with heavy humor, "they'd expect to come in as Centurions or Optios, and that's not happening."

"Well," Scribonius replied thoughtfully, "we've seen for ourselves how badly they treat their rankers. We're harsh, it's true, but nothing like the kind of life they're living with these *satraps* ruling over them."

"But what's in it for them?" Balbus broke his silence, and as usual, in his own blunt way, revealed another consideration, and one that showed that Balbus wasn't lacking in intelligence, no matter how he phrased his point.

"You mean, other than not being sold into slavery? If they're lucky?" Pullus joked before quickly turning sober, knowing the likely reaction that was coming. "If they fulfill a full enlistment, they'll get the same thing we all get: a bonus and some land. And," he took a breath, "they'll be made citizens." The only one who was surprised at this announcement was Pullus, except that it came from the reaction, or lack thereof, from his two friends, which prompted him to blurt out, "Why aren't you two howling like Cerberus about that? I can tell you that's what the Primi Pili were most up in arms about when Caesar told us."

"Because," Scribonius countered dryly, "we're not quite as thick as you and your fellow Primi Pili. At least," he glanced over at Balbus with a grin, "not me or Diocles. Him, I'm not so sure about." Leaning over in an exaggerated manner, Scribonius spoke slowly, as one does with someone who is dim-witted, "Did you understand that, Balbus? That these Parthians would become citizens? Just like you?"

Balbus scowled at Scribonius, growling, "I figured it out too, thank you. I'm not nearly the idiot you think I am."

"Oh, I wouldn't be so sure about that," Scribonius shot back. "Anyone whose lifelong ambition is to cut a man's balls off so he can use the sac as his coin purse isn't disputing with Socrates."

"Quiet," Pullus growled. "I'm trying to think." Under normal circumstances, he not only accepted but enjoyed the banter between his friends. This time, however, wasn't one of those occasions. "I think," he said, "this may not be quite as bad an idea as we thought at first."

And, so it was that, of all the Primi Pili, it was Titus Pullus and the 10th who was the first to signal their acceptance of Caesar's plan, which created a whole other set of problems and challenges, both for Pullus and Caesar. Nevertheless, by Pullus' acquiescence, not only did it send a powerful message to the rest of the Primi Pili, in doing so, Pullus was assured by Caesar he would have first choice from the pool of potential enlistees. As his plans went, it was up to Caesar's normal standards, except for the one obstacle that Caesar apparently hadn't foreseen. When the announcement was made, through an interpreter from Seleucia who was Greek by birth, but spoke all three languages required in any communications of this sort, the response was decidedly unenthusiastic. By the end of the first day after this offer, not one Parthian had broken from the ranks of his comrades to step forward; by the end of the first week, it was hard for those of Caesar's Legates who had strenuously opposed this move to keep from openly gloating in Caesar's presence. In an odd way, seeing Caesar so discomfited amused Pullus as well, despite having thrown his lot in with his general, meaning that his own standing and prestige, albeit on a smaller scale, was at stake along with Caesar's. In his case, it was just with the men of the 10th that Pullus had to worry about, whereas with The Dictator, it was with every man under him, of all ranks. On more than one occasion, as Pullus watched men like Hirtius, Pollio, Ventidius, and, unsurprisingly, Lepidus gloating and snickering whenever they thought Caesar wasn't looking, the Primus Pilus was struck by the thought that, perhaps, this was actually good for Caesar. Maybe if he experiences a failure every so often, it might make him a bit less...*Caesar*, was the only word Pullus could summon that adequately described the state of being that he was trying to associate with his general. As he had quickly come to sense as a raw *tirone,* long before he could articulate why this was so in his mind, Titus Pullus had recognized in Caesar a truly singular soul, a man who, while he was mortal, was somehow more than that, just by virtue of the sheer prodigy of his talents, which were so numerous that Pullus recognized that he, and the others, had taken them for granted. Now, seeing Caesar thwarted in this way reminded Pullus that his general was, after all, a man like any other; a truly remarkable one, but still a man. Why he did what he was about to do was something that Titus Pullus would never really understand himself, so that when he was pressed by Scribonius, Balbus, and all of his Primi Pili counterparts, the best he could offer was a shrug and a vague response about doing what was best for the army.

"You want to do what, again?"

"I said," Pullus explained patiently to Diocles, "I'm going to offer every man who enlists in the 10th a cash bonus."

Diocles, who was standing in front of Pullus' desk, which had been transferred to the house near the palace in Ctesiphon, bore an expression of equal parts puzzlement and concern.

"So," he asked cautiously, "Caesar approved this?"

Pullus hesitated, then shook his head, and said simply, "No. This is my idea."

"Then where are you going to get the money from?"

Pullus didn't reply, but the look he gave Diocles gave the Greek his answer, eliciting a gasp of shock.

"You're going to pay for it yourself??"

"Well," Pullus smiled, both amused and touched at his Greek's alarm, "I *do* have a fair amount of money, don't I?"

Relatively early into their relationship, once Pullus sufficiently trusted his Greek slave, and had witnessed firsthand his shrewd sense of his management of what had become a substantial amount of money that Pullus had accrued, as had every man who marched for Caesar through Gaul, he had turned over the responsibility for his fortune to Diocles. Unlike a fair number of his counterparts, Pullus' desire for money wasn't based in the idea of wealth for its own sake; since he could remember, he had fostered an ambition to elevate himself, and his heirs, to the status of the equestrian order. This had been the fuel for the ambition that burned as brightly as that of the patrician Pullus had chosen as the most likely man to help him achieve those aims, in the form of Caesar.

"How much are you going to offer?" Diocles asked him, almost afraid of the answer; it turned out to be even worse than he feared.

"Five hundred *sesterces* per ranker," Pullus answered calmly, "and a thousand for men who have a skill that fits with any of our *immunes*."

"*Five hundred?*" Diocles visibly recoiled, as if Pullus had just landed a physical blow. "That's…"

"A lot, I know," Pullus replied, still remaining placid despite Diocles' growing agitation. "But what I need to know from you is, how many men can I afford to pay that bonus to?"

"Do you mean, of your entire holdings, or just how much we brought with us?" Diocles asked in response.

"Both."

Seeing that his master was clearly set on this course, Diocles discarded all the arguments he had summoned to lay before Pullus, instead performing some quick calculations in his head. The truth was that Diocles had disobeyed his master in one particular; before they set out on this campaign, Pullus had instructed him to only bring five thousand *sesterces*, which was still a considerable sum. It was at this moment that Diocles realized something; his master had actually asked how much ready cash was available, but he would, or should, have already known this.

This recognition was what prompted Diocles to ask sheepishly, "How did you know?"

Pullus laughed, then wagged a finger playfully at Diocles, saying, "Don't think I don't know you, you little pederast! I knew that if I told you five thousand, you'd bring at least double that, maybe more. So," now he turned serious, "how much did you bring?"

"Double that," Diocles admitted.

"So, the best I could do was enlist twenty men, and those are all unskilled in an *immune* trade," Pullus mused, then grimaced. "That's not nearly enough."

"Not necessarily," Diocles countered, having committed himself to serving Pullus in this matter to his utmost in the course of this conversation. "There's two different approaches you can take."

And, for the next several moments, Pullus listened; once Diocles was finished, Pullus felt much better than he had shortly before.

The bounty offered by Titus Pullus for Parthians to volunteer to enlist in the Roman army served to break the stalemate, but that was just one in a series of problems that, in any given moment, anyone in Roman uniform, no matter what the rank, would have sworn were insurmountable. It was a Parthian named Mardonius, a young man in his early twenties, who was the first to step forward, and while he would go on to prove to be an exemplary Legionary, his decision was based in a simple premise.

"Did you know that the Parthians don't pay their infantry?" Pullus asked this of Caesar, who, in truth, was unaware of this. "They're given an allotment of food, and they're supplied their spears and shields, but otherwise, they have to fend for themselves. The only way they can improve their situation is by whatever loot they take after a battle."

Caesar was, putting it mildly, surprised, and he sat back in his chair, tossing his stylus onto his desk in order to fully consider this.

"That," he concluded, "practically guarantees that their men are going to steal from anyone, no matter whether they're friend or enemy." The general frowned, shaking his head as his highly ordered mind tried to contemplate the deeper implications of what he had just learned from Pullus. "And it explains why we've been unsuccessful in luring them into joining our ranks. If they don't get paid by their own people, how are they going to trust us when we tell them we will?"

This was the opening Pullus needed, and he didn't hesitate, although he still felt a fair amount of trepidation.

"Actually, Caesar," Pullus began, "that's why I asked to see you. It's about that."

"Oh?" Caesar's eyebrow lifted, but he was joking when he asked, "Have you come to tell me that you've solved our problems?"

Pullus felt the flare of anger that was always lurking there, waiting to be ignited by what Pullus saw as an insinuation that he wasn't capable of solving thorny problems on those occasions when killing wasn't the preferred solution.

"Yes, I have," he replied stiffly, and it was a struggle to keep his tone neutral as he added, "and, in fact, I wanted to tell you that the 10th has almost completely filled its complement of new *tirones*."

Whereas Caesar was surprised before, now he was shocked into silence, his body going still while his eyes, narrowed and piercing, examined Pullus' face.

"Is this some sort of joke, Pullus?" While Caesar spoke lightly, Pullus didn't need to be warned of the jagged ice that was just beneath the seemingly placid exterior of Caesar's face, nor the danger despite the quiet tone.

"No, Caesar," Pullus assured him, then with what could only be described as a flourish, he handed over the three tablets he had been carrying, "Here are their names, and the Centuries into which they're being put. And," he hastened to add, "as we agreed, none of them are in a Cohort higher than the Eighth."

Caesar seemed almost reluctant as he reached out and took the tablets, although he did take them, opening each one to scan them quickly, as Pullus stood there, watching the small muscle in Caesar's jaw twitch, which he had learned to use as an indicator for what might be about to follow.

When Caesar looked up, Pullus tried not to openly sag in relief at the smile, but he also cautioned himself, He doesn't know all of it yet, Titus. Let's not get ahead of ourselves.

"Well, Pullus," Caesar's smile had broadened even further, revealing that set of teeth that were in much better shape than a man his age had any right to claim, "I congratulate you on the 10th once more leading the way! But, I expect you to share your secret about how you did it with the rest of the Primi Pili."

"That," Pullus replied, thinking, Here we go, "is what I wanted to talk to you about, because the idea I came up with is…unusual."

Caesar's good humor, although it didn't vanish, did visibly dim, and his tone was cautious as he asked Pullus how he had accomplished this heretofore seemingly impossible task.

"I offered them a bounty," Pullus replied, allowing time for Caesar to take this information and digest it.

"That," Caesar said after a moment, "is actually a good idea, and one that I should have thought about. How much? A hundred *sesterces*?"

Now, it was Pullus' time to swallow the hard lump and answer, "No, Caesar. Five hundred per man." Caesar's jaw dropped, but before he could reply, Pullus hurried on, "That's for straight Gregarii, though. For men with an *immune* skill, I offered a thousand."

Without saying anything, Caesar snatched one of the tablets back up, opened it, and began running his finger down one side, then the other.

Pullus realized what Caesar was doing, so he supplied the answer, "We enlisted three hundred men, Caesar. Then stopped there. It makes us still about twenty men short per Cohort, but we can live with that."

"Who's paying for this?" Caesar asked quietly, although he had already deduced the answer.

"I am, Caesar," Pullus replied firmly, even as it made his stomach lurch to think about it.

Caesar stared at Pullus for a long moment, then he offered Pullus a smile that held no warmth whatsoever, his tone suddenly going flat as he guessed, "And now you're here telling me this, hoping that I'll save your fortune for you and offer to pay out of my own purse."

Now it was Pullus' turn to be shocked, his jaw dropping, then that flicker of anger he had felt earlier came roaring back; this was the only excuse he could have offered when he snapped, "I expected no such thing, Caesar! I made this decision without ever considering the idea of asking you to reimburse me!"

As the words tumbled out, so did Pullus' ire, and before he knew it, he had moved closer to Caesar's desk so that their respective difference in size was brought into sharper juxtaposition, and while this wasn't the only time Pullus had lost his temper in front of Caesar, it had been far enough in the past that Caesar realized just how towering and menacing a presence Titus Pullus in a rage could be. But he was Caesar, so it wouldn't have been accurate to say he felt fear; a healthy, cautious respect for the damage he understood his giant Primus Pilus could inflict was a better way to put it. At the same time, Caesar understood he had erred, and it was this that caused him the most discomfort; of all the men whose sincerity he could question, Titus Pullus wasn't one of them, and while he knew that, he also recognized he had forgotten this fact. This was what made him lift both hands up in a placating gesture as he rose to his own feet, his eyes never leaving those of Pullus.

"*Pax*, Titus," Caesar's tone was in direct contrast to Pullus' who, while certainly not unleashing the roar he was capable of, had been raised to a point where even those who had never laid eyes on the man would know he was angry. "Please, forgive that remark. I sincerely apologize for questioning your motives."

There was a silence then, at least of a sort, the only sound the harsh, rapid breathing of Pullus as he struggled to shove the monster of his rage back down into the dark corner of his soul where it normally slumbered.

Pullus' own glare softened, gradually, then suddenly, his shoulders slumped, and he seemed more embarrassed than anything as he mumbled, "No, Caesar. Forgive me. You have every right to ask that question."

"Not of you, my giant Pullus," Caesar said softly. "Of others, yes. But I never should have doubted that you did what you did without any thought about somehow being rewarded for it."

Although Pullus wasn't altogether sure he liked the way Caesar put how he had acted without thought, he also understood that this was as much of a peace offering as his general could allow himself to give while still retaining his own towering *dignitas*. After all, Pullus reasoned to himself, he started a civil war that cost thousands and thousands of lives because his *dignitas* was threatened; the fact he's apologizing is enough.

"Well," Caesar's voice broke the tense silence, but it was his tone as much as his words that signaled this was an episode now in the past, "at least I know you won't leave the army anytime soon." Waiting just a heartbeat, he finished, "You're too poor now to go anywhere!"

With any other man, this might have served to rub salt in an open wound; instead, Pullus instantly began roaring with laughter, his general joining in.

Caesar had been caught by surprise; the other Primi Pili were not only surprised, there was a fair amount of anger, and all of it was aimed at Titus Pullus.

"Just because that bastard's rich as Crassus doesn't mean the rest of us are!"

This was the sentiment expressed verbally by Gnaeus Clustuminus of the 8th, yet he was far from alone. However, while the anger was real, it was also somewhat muted, not only because each Primus Pilus ultimately understood the necessity of this action, given how singularly unsuccessful they had been in enticing Parthians to join, but they soon learned that Pullus hadn't been as profligate as it sounded. While it was true that the total amounts offered to each enlisting Parthian were the sums Pullus had decided on, it was also the case that he didn't actually pay them that amount. Once he and Diocles had performed the necessary calculations, they quickly realized that the sum contained in the locked strongbox that was secured in the Primus Pilus' personal wagon wouldn't be nearly enough if each man was paid in full, which is what prompted Diocles' suggestion. Consequently, the men like Mardonius who enlisted were given fifty *sesterces* when they made their mark on the enlistment document, which when converted into the *drachmas* of the local currency, was still a huge sum to Parthian men of their class, whereupon they were told they would receive another hundred at the end of each year of this campaign. When the campaign was over, whatever amount was still owed would be paid then, but only on completion. Although it had been Diocles who offered this idea, Pullus instantly saw how this would enable him to actually put silver into men's hands, which he understood had a powerful allure all its own; it was only later he also recognized the shrewdness displayed by the Greek.

This was how Pullus summed it up to his friends, saying, "He knew that a fair number of these men are likely to die, a lot of them by this time next year. If," Pullus felt compelled to add bitterly, "taking Susa is anything like taking this fucking place."

Balbus' mouth tightened at this reminder of a tragedy that was still too raw and fresh, yet despite the pang of anguish Pullus' words evoked, ultimately, he was a professional Centurion, which compelled him to point out what he viewed as the most glaring flaw in this whole endeavor.

"Which is why I think a fair number of those fuckers are going to end up getting their throats slit," he declared flatly, "but not by a Parthian. By one of us who lost a friend, or worse."

This wasn't the first time Balbus had broached this idea, yet despite his growing impatience at hearing it, Pullus reminded himself that it was both valid, and that Balbus was still grieving the loss of so many of his men, especially his Optio, Bestia, who Balbus was still wrestling with the problem of replacing.

"I know," Pullus replied with a forbearance he didn't feel, yet neither was he willing to continue to indulge Balbus in what he saw his as his friend's petulant obstinacy, which prompted him to press the point, "but you agreed this is the only way we can get back to fighting strength. If we wait for a *dilectus* in the Republic, by the time they get here, and we get them trained, we won't be marching for more than a year, and you know that's true."

"I do," Balbus agreed, closing his eyes even as he did so. When he did, the slightest glisten of tears showed in the corner of his eyes, prompting both Pullus and Scribonius to look away when Balbus added, "But I don't like it. Not a bit. Having Parthians marching with us? It's not...natural."

As Pullus listened, he realized that this was one of those times when his heart agreed wholeheartedly with his friend, but his head was what ruled him here.

"Well, you better get used to it," Pullus replied grimly, "because for some reason, I have a feeling this is just the beginning of seeing strange faces marching with us."

Not surprisingly, this got both Scribonius and Balbus paying closer attention, the pair exchanging a glance in a silent query to the other about what they knew.

"Why do you say that?"

It was Scribonius who posed the question.

"No reason, really," Pullus answered, but since he was staring down into his cup, he missed how intently the two were regarding him, trying to determine if their friend was hiding something from them.

As both of them would attest, it wouldn't be the first time Pullus had been sworn to secrecy by Caesar, and despite his close relationship with these two men, he had never once betrayed that.

When Phraates, safely ensconced in Susa, received the news that Ctesiphon and Seleucia had fallen and were now firmly in Roman hands, he was neither surprised nor that distressed. Contrary to what

Kambyses thought, however, his lack of emotion at this development had little to do with his antipathy for Ctesiphon because it had been so important to his father. Putting the matter in its simplest terms, the new King of Kings had recognized relatively early that a Roman army commanded by Caesar was a completely different animal than one commanded by Crassus. Privately, he thought both his father and brother were mistaken in engaging the Romans so soon after they had crossed the imaginary line that marked the Parthian holdings. From Phraates' perspective, those cities were on the outer fringes of where true Parthian power resided; additionally, the moment they learned that the Romans were taking the more circuitous but well-watered route that followed the two rivers into the interior of the empire, Phraates was convinced that the cumulative toll exacted on the advancing Romans wouldn't sufficiently weaken them. Only if they had chosen the same route as Crassus, mistakenly thinking that the shortest way was the best, would his father and brother's tactics have borne fruit. Now that they had possession of the two cities, they would avail themselves of all the supplies his father had thoughtfully stockpiled for them, although he had meant them to be used by the defenders of his beloved capital. And, he guessed correctly, the Romans would probably be content with the progress they had made to this point, choosing to winter there rather than take the risk of marching on to Susa. Although it was true that the campaign season wasn't over yet, there was only about a month left before the weather began changing, and as all who had been born and lived their lives in this part of the world knew, not only did the change occur rapidly, it was wildly unpredictable. This, Phraates felt certain, would be something that this Caesar would have been told about, and for which he would account in his calculations about whether to continue marching on to Susa. Regardless of his belief, Phraates made sure to keep the Romans under constant observation; just, he thought with a somewhat bitter amusement, like the Romans keep eyes on us with their cavalry. While the bulk of the Roman cavalry that had been lurking in the vicinity in Susa, swooping down on the patrols Phraates sent out from the city, had since disappeared, Phraates held absolutely no doubt that there were still eyes out there, watching the city and all the activity. There was one thing that nagged at Phraates, although he felt somewhat confident that he had taken the appropriate steps to prevent any surprises from the men that were now in a camp, outside the walls of Susa. This force, exclusively composed of infantry, was unique among the entire array of Parthian forces, but they also were the men Phraates worried the most about when it came to what might happen at the decisive moment when they came into contact with their former countrymen. Known simply as *Crassoi*, these men, now numbering a bit less than seven thousand strong, had seemingly been assimilated into the ranks of the Parthian army. Despite his feelings for his father, Phraates had to acknowledge that Orodes had been extremely shrewd in both his treatment, and even more importantly, his placement of these men in the farthest eastern reaches of Parthian holdings, where they protected the tenuous border between Parthia and the *Tokharoi*, a fierce, warlike people who had swept in from the east and taken control of Bactria and who, as Phraates had been reminded over and over by his father, were even more of a threat to the King of Kings than Rome. While the Romans had been treated as captives for almost the entire first year, mainly because this was how long it had taken for them to march from Carrhae to their base in Merv, the most commercially important city in the Parthian empire, once they were there, Orodes ordered their status as prisoners end. His decision wasn't based in any magnanimity, but the recognition of the reality of the grueling nature of the march; while some twelve thousand men from Crassus' seven Legions had been captured alive, by the time they arrived in Merv, their numbers had been reduced to a bit under ten thousand. Once they were settled into a permanent camp outside the walls of Merv, while they were allowed relative freedom, the standing garrison and complement of cataphracts and archers who belonged to the *satrap* of Merv kept a careful eye on them, and as Orodes expected, over the course of that next year, the Romans seemingly accepted their fate, understanding the practical impossibility of marching and fighting their way back west across the vast expanse of mountains, desert, and barren lands that had claimed more than two thousand of their own on the journey to Merv. It wasn't until their third year, and after they had acquitted themselves with great distinction against an incursion by the *Tokharoi*, that as a reward for their fidelity, Orodes allowed them to begin mingling with the native populace, and as he expected, following a bit more than nine months later came the first of the infants that, as the King of King well knew, would provide a stronger tie to the Parthians than any oath.

And now, those *Crassoi* were here, in a marching camp that they had created in the same style as Caesar's army, and bringing their families with them, at an expense that Phraates admitted had made him wince because the women and children had ridden in wagons provided by the *satrap* of Merv. The *satrap* had demanded an exorbitant amount of money, arguing, with some justification, that by doing so, he was temporarily crippling the commerce that was so important to the Parthians by expropriating the means of transport for most of the merchants in the city. This, Phraates had decided, was worth the expense involved, and the impertinence of the *satrap* could be dealt with at a later time, once these Romans were dispatched. Naturally, the families of the *Crassoi* had moved more slowly than their men, particularly the children, so while a fair number of the women had marched behind the *Crassoi*, those with small infants, or who were pregnant, rode in the wagons. These laggards had finally arrived a week after the men, and now all of them were safely inside the walls of Susa, under "protection" by the garrison, composed of Phraates' personal bodyguard, men whose loyalty was never in question, for the most part anyway. But, whereas any Parthian who attained the title of King of Kings had to keep a wary eye on everyone around him, Phraates knew in this he could trust his men to carry out his orders, should they become necessary. As part of his plan, the bodyguard commander had been given very explicit instructions, which Phraates had then ensured were whispered in places where the *Crassoi* would hear, so that they were under no illusions about the fate that awaited their loved ones should they experience qualms in facing their former comrades. That was in the future, however; all in all, Phraates was pleased with his preparations, and was content to wait until the next year for that moment. Of all the traits of the East, patience was the cornerstone of every endeavor undertaken by Parthians, and Phraates, despite his feelings for his father and brother, was Parthian to his core.

Outside the walls of the twin cities of Ctesiphon and Seleucia, the arduous process of integrating new *tirones* into the rank of the Legions began a bit more than a month after both cities fell. Under normal circumstances, the task of training a new man to the point that he reached Caesar's exacting standards wasn't easy; with men who almost universally were ignorant of the Roman tongue, it meant there were times when even Titus Pullus despaired that these new recruits would ever be competent to stand in a Century line.

"Oh, they're willing enough," was Cyclops' judgment, who had become an even more frequent guest of Pullus' during the evening meals, accepting the responsibility that came from being the highest-ranking Centurion responsible for training the Parthians without

Pullus ever saying this aloud. The one-eyed Octus Pilus Prior was seated at the fourth side of the table in Pullus' quarters, and he finished chewing his bread before he resumed speaking. "And, honestly, they're not as unskilled as I thought they'd be, given how poorly they performed against us. But that," he spat out a kernel of wheat, "is because they weren't well-led."

"They weren't 'led' at all," Pullus pointed out. "We all saw how they were treated." He thought of the Parthian nobleman with the whip that he used to force the spearmen into the breach when Pullus led the second attempt. "When you're treated as nothing more than fodder for our swords, that's all you're going to get."

"There are no bad Centuries," Scribonius spoke up, beginning a truism that was often heard in the ranks, although it was Balbus who finished, "Only bad Centurions."

All four men nodded their agreement, then Pullus glanced back at Cyclops, indicating with a nod for his former tutor to continue.

"But this language thing," Cyclops grimaced, "*that* is something I don't know how to overcome."

There was a silence then, for several moments, as each Centurion at the table considered what they had understood would be an issue, but honestly, none of them had correctly assessed just how much of a challenge it would be.

As usual, it was Scribonius, the frown firmly fixed on his face that Pullus had long since learned meant his friend's mind was furiously gnawing away at a problem, who broke the quiet by saying, "Are there any of them who seem to be picking up the language more quickly than others?"

Somewhat to Scribonius' disappointment, Cyclops shrugged as he answered, "I suppose. I haven't been paying attention to whether any of these bastards have a nimble tongue. I just want them to obey quickly, and when they don't understand a fucking word, they don't do that."

"That's why I brought it up," Scribonius replied impatiently. "Because the way we're doing things now obviously isn't working. So," he went on, "I was thinking that if we found some of the new *tiros* who are quick studies, we pull them from training to teach them our tongue instead."

"But then they'd be behind the others learning the things that are important," Balbus objected.

472

Much to Balbus' delight, this caused Scribonius to flush, and he said defensively, "I didn't say it was a perfect plan! I just think it will be better than how we're doing it now."

"Why does it have to be from the ranks of the *tiros*?"

All four men turned at the sound of Diocles' voice, and being the subject of their scrutiny seemed to make him hesitate, but Pullus assured him, "Tell us what you're thinking, Diocles."

"Yes," Balbus added, "let's hear what your shifty Greek mind has conjured up!"

While it was certainly barbed, Diocles also was accustomed to this kind of heavy-handed attempt at humor, and under normal circumstances, he gave back as well as he received; this time, he wasn't willing to waste the time in banter.

"Actually, Master Quintus," he did reply tartly, "it's funny you should mention Greeks, because that's who I'm thinking of that might solve the problem you're discussing."

This was how, unknown to the Romans, the Greek Anaxagoras; indeed, a fair number of those men who had been part of the workforce that created the artillery that had done more to slow Caesar's progress than any other factor, and who had managed to survive the slaughter, became interpreters for the new *tiros*.

"What do you expect me to do about it? In here?"

Kambyses gave a disgusted wave at his quarters, which had long before lost their charm. They were comfortable, certainly, and the Parthian couldn't deny that his needs were attended to, within reason, of course, yet despite all this, it was still a jail cell, in effect if not style. Consequently, the announcement that he had a visitor surprised him; the fact it was allowed was even more so. That it was Anaxagoras was downright shocking, yet here he was, standing in front of Kambyses, who was trying to look dignified sitting on a couch that had been made for the comfort of one of Orodes' many concubines. The cushioning was so soft it made something as simple as sitting on it a precarious proposition, but Kambyses tried to ignore this as he regarded Anaxagoras, along with trying not to think about what kind of activities between the dead King of Kings and this concubine had taken place on it.

"Excellency," Anaxagoras had been allowed into his quarters only after being thoroughly searched, and it nagged at Kambyses as to why Caesar had allowed him this visitor, but no others, not even a woman. "I don't know what to do! I was approached by the Romans yesterday and asked to take a position interpreting for the new men."

It was a mark of how carefully isolated Kambyses had been kept that he had no idea of the circumstances surrounding Caesar's decision to strengthen his ranks with Parthians, which caused him to misunderstand the Greek and had prompted what followed after his initial remark when Anaxagoras said he needed aid from Kambyses.

"I didn't know you spoke Latin," was all he could think to say, still not truly understanding why Anaxagoras had sought his help.

"I don't," Anaxagoras replied.

Now Kambyses went from mildly puzzled to confused, prompting him to stand up, while Anaxagoras shifted uneasily on his feet, as if worried that the Parthian would attack him.

Giving a harsh chuckle at this, both pleased that at least one man still considered him dangerous, and disgusted that, ultimately, he was impotent to do anything substantial even if he had desired, Kambyses began pacing while he regarded Anaxagoras, thinking aloud, "Now, why would they need you to interpret, Greek? If you don't speak Latin…" His voice trailed off, his eyes narrowed, and there was an undercurrent to his voice that made Anaxagoras even more nervous than he had been when he walked in, as Kambyses asked softly, "Why don't you explain to me *exactly* what your duties entail? Or," he added, "more importantly, *whose* tongue are you going to be translating?"

This was how Kambyses learned of Caesar's plan; once Anaxagoras was finished, the Parthian found himself staggering back to the couch, barely noticing how deeply he sank into the plush cushions.

"That…that…*dog*, that *minion*," Kambyses gasped. "He's using our own men against us?" Looking up at Anaxagoras, the Greek knew the Parthian well enough to recognize the mixture of confusion and hurt as he asked Anaxagoras plaintively, "But why? Why would our own turn against us?"

The Greek hesitated as, before he answered, his eyes swept the room, looking for anything that Kambyses might use as a weapon if what he was about to tell the Parthian turned his bewilderment into rage. Fortunately, the Romans had been extremely thorough and there was nothing that could be converted into a deadly object, at least with any ease or speed.

Emboldened by this observation, Anaxagoras was nevertheless still careful to modulate his tone as he answered, "Because, Excellency, the Romans are paying men to march with them. And,"

Anaxagoras paused for a heartbeat, "they're paying very well when compared to what your *satraps* pay. Which, as you know, is nothing."

"Our *satraps* don't pay those men because it's their duty to serve us," Kambyses snapped, "and their needs are provided for by their *satraps*! The food they eat, the clothes on their back, their weapons are all provided for by their *satrap*! They are allowed to live on *our* lands, and all we ask in exchange is for their faithful service!"

"And what about their families?" Anaxagoras countered, still speaking quietly. "How do they feed their families?"

Kambyses didn't reply, and the silence stretched out for long moments; Anaxagoras was about to add, and you *satraps* would starve if those men didn't do work your lands, since you don't lift a finger at any labor you consider menial and beneath you. Wisely, this remained inside the Greek's mouth. Finally, with an explosive grunt, the Parthian waved a disgusted hand.

"Well," he concluded, "it doesn't really matter why they're joining the Romans. That they're doing it is enough." Returning his attention to the reason for Anaxagoras' visit, he asked bluntly, "So why are you here? To ask my permission to take Roman silver?" Repeating the wave, he said disgustedly, "Why shouldn't you? You're not Parthian, and if our own men can be bought so cheaply, then there's no reason why you shouldn't as well, I suppose."

Although the pair was ostensibly alone, Anaxagoras was as aware as Kambyses that there was at least one ear pressed to the door to the room, which was what prompted the Greek to cross over to Kambyses as silently as he could move. The Parthian was gazing down at the floor in disgust, but the appearance of Anaxagoras' sandaled feet caused his head to raise, and he saw the Greek press a single finger to his lips.

Then, in a normal tone of voice, Anaxagoras said, "Excellency, forgive me for confusing you. I didn't come to ask your permission, but I'm worried about my family." He hesitated, then said a bit more loudly, "And I wanted to ask you to prevail on Caesar to allow you to send a decree under your name that my family is not to be harmed because of my work."

Even as he was speaking, Anaxagoras, noticing that a chest next to the couch had accumulated a fine coat of dust, was using his finger to write something on the surface. Fortunately for both of them, Kambyses immediately divined the game Anaxagoras was playing, except his initial thought was that it was a trap. What had puzzled him almost from the moment of his capture was the question; why was he still alive? And, not just alive, but being so well treated? Both sides involved in this war, from the very moment Caesar's army had crossed into Parthian territory, had based their competing strategies on an incomplete understanding of how the other side operated. Instead, the leadership of both Parthians and Romans had formulated their respective plans using the fragmentary information about the other side, gleaned in a variety of ways, and both sides had suffered nasty surprises as a result. Before the first real clash in the battle on the ridge, Parthians had accepted as an article of faith that the combination of cataphract and horse archer was unbeatable by Roman Legions; they learned that this wasn't the case in the form of jagged lead missiles and carefully chosen terrain. However, as Kambyses well knew, since Caesar had admitted it to him, the Romans had been equally sure that the Parthians didn't use artillery when defending a city, nor did they know about the Parthians' use of naphtha. Now, as he watched Anaxagoras tracing out a series of words, but using the Parthian characters instead of Greek, Kambyses was still suspicious that this was a trap, but the real question was, at whose behest? Never far from the Parthian's consciousness was the recognition of the presence of spies who reported to Orodes; that he was trusted by the former King of Kings and knew the identities of these spies meant that he knew Anaxagoras wasn't one of them. Regardless of this knowledge, Kambyses was equally sure that Phraates had his own stable of men who fulfilled the same function as those belonging to the dead Orodes, which meant that it was possible that Anaxagoras had been recruited to work for the new king. At the same time, Kambyses couldn't be sure that this Greek hadn't changed allegiance now that the Romans had conquered his city, and simply wanted to be on what Anaxagoras thought would be the winning side, meaning this was a trap set by Caesar, not Phraates. His strong suspicion that the former was more likely was based in another fragment of knowledge about the Romans, and that was their reverence for the law. Kambyses had been acting in his capacity as commander of the city, and Caesar himself had said he bore no malice towards the Parthian for his use of the naphtha; Caesar had also pointed out that his men didn't feel the same way, which had been borne out by the murderous looks and muttered threats of the guards who had been outside his door since his capture. But, Kambyses reasoned, as he studied Anaxagoras' face as the Greek continued drawing figures in the dust, if he could be caught acting in concert with a spy, then the Romans would have the pretext for executing him. In the span of time it took for Anaxagoras to scribble his hasty message, Kambyses had decided that, whatever this Greek was up to, he wanted no part of it. Then, when Anaxagoras was finished, he glanced down disinterestedly, his mind already made up, yet he went ahead and read it anyway. Stiffening suddenly, he glanced up to stare hard at Anaxagoras, in whose face he read even more potently the truth of what Kambyses had just learned.

"Well," he said at last, his voice slightly raised to match the level that Anaxagoras had used what in real time was just a few heartbeats before, "I'm not sure whether or not Caesar will allow it, or if it will do any good. But, yes, Anaxagoras, I will do what I can to protect your family."

"Thank you, Excellency," Anaxagoras' voice throbbed with the emotion that one would expect at Kambyses' agreement to help his family. "I will be forever in your debt."

With that, the Greek left, leaving Kambyses to carefully wipe the dust from the chest, erasing the words that told him that the Greek's family had been slaughtered in the sack of Seleucia, and that he was now irrevocably bound to the Parthian cause. How he planned to help, Kambyses didn't know; what he did was that having the Greek working in his capacity would only aid in the fight against the invaders. From Kambyses' viewpoint, his own captivity was a temporary condition; when the moment was right, he was determined to escape and return to Phraates and offer his sword once more to the service of the House of Arsacid. Whether or not the young king would accept him, or part Kambyses' head from his shoulders, was in the hands of Ahura-Mazda, although he felt fairly confident that bringing his king Caesar's head instead would smooth over any possible resentment on the part of Phraates and enable Kambyses to keep his where it belonged. First, however, he had to be patient, and it was in this one characteristic where the Parthians were superior to Romans. He would wait and watch; then, he would act.

It was when Caesar was in Alexandria almost four years before that he had gotten the idea, which was prompted by Cleopatra taking him to see the mausoleum of Alexander, the Macedonian king who had earned the title of Great. His initial thought when he viewed the remarkably well-preserved corpse wasn't about Alexander, oddly enough, but of Pompeius Magnus. Do you see the difference, now, old friend? he thought with amusement, sadness, and a tinge of scorn. You gave yourself the title of "Great," but this man *earned* it. Standing there with Cleopatra, even Caesar wasn't immediately aware that a seed had been planted; for this delay, he blamed the chain of events that first caused, then were caused by his presence in Alexandria in the first place. Nevertheless, over the course of time, the idea began blossoming, and now, as he stood on the ramparts of Ctesiphon, looking down on the sweating, cursing men who were using a combination of gestures and swipes of their *viti* in their attempts to turn raw *tiros* into Gregarii, albeit through the man standing next to each Centurion who was relaying the given commands, his mind was elsewhere. Although he was facing east, his mind's eye had swept past Susa, visualizing the vast expanses of barren desert, and the harsh, jagged mountains, beyond which lay Bactria. And, beyond that? When Caesar turned away from the rampart to return to the palace that had become the *praetorium* of a city that was being transformed into another example of Roman efficiency, the Dictator for Life had a smile on his lips, already working on the details of his plan to surpass a man known as "Great." By the time Caesar is done, they'll have to invent a new word to describe his deeds, he thought with a real pleasure and sense of anticipation. Caesar was ascending to a level of greatness that would change the world.

Epilogue

While Caesar was busy across Our Sea, in Rome, Marcus Antonius was thoroughly enjoying himself, in the manner that had already made him famous. Whether it was trying to harness four Numidian Lions to a chariot, which turned out to be a miserable failure, or insisting on being one of the "boys" in the Festival of Lupercalia who ran naked around the Forum, Caesar's Master of Horse couldn't remember a time when he had had as much fun. Nevertheless, he was reminded on a daily basis by the likes of Marcus Tullius Cicero that there was the business of running Rome, a much drearier occupation than he had believed possible. Perhaps the only satisfaction he took from the office was when, as he had been instructed, the moment the courier had galloped from Brundisium to Rome, carrying the dispatch Caesar had sent on the fastest Liburnian that he had arrived safely with his army intact, Antonius carried out the orders Caesar had given him by executing those conspirators Caesar had deemed must die. This was the first of what would be many moments when Antonius, tasting from the cup of absolute power, found it quite to his liking and considered exceeding Caesar's instructions by having the head of the man he considered the worst of the traitors, Marcus Junius Brutus, added to those Caesar had listed and whose heads now adorned the Rostra. Somehow, he had managed to restrain himself, but it had taken quite a bit of willpower on his part, particularly since Brutus insisted on strutting about Rome, relying on the power of Caesar's forbearance and mercy alone to save his miserable skin. Oh, Antonius was well aware that the meetings had resumed in secret, along with the whispering plots, yet somewhat to his disappointment, Brutus had managed to stay away from these small gatherings. Cicero, on the other hand, was another matter altogether, but even the aging orator and self-styled "champion of the Old Republic" could detect no falsity in Antonius' booming greeting when he answered the politely worded "invitation" to meet Antonius at, of all places, Pompey's former residence, which had been appropriated by Antonius after the great man's defeat.

"*Salve*, friend Cicero!" Antonius' voice under the best of circumstances had a booming quality to it, which he liked to remind anyone and everyone was due to his massive chest. "Thank you so much for coming to see me on such short notice!" Pausing only long enough for the pair to embrace and exchange the obligatory peck on each cheek, Antonius joked, "Trying to manage all the chickens wearing Senator's purple is very trying, I know!"

Knowing such unsubtle jibes were an integral part of every visit with Antonius, Cicero managed a polite smile, and played along as much as he could stomach. "Yes, *Magister Equitum*, it is quite the ordeal trying to, as you say, *manage* these chickens so that we can conduct the business of the Republic. Now," he took the seat Antonius proffered, folding his hands in his lap as he asked with a sour smile, "what business is it that our esteemed Dictator wants us to address?"

Antonius' smile froze on his face, as did his body just before reaching his own chair, his mind racing with what he was sure, and was correct in thinking so, was a veiled message. While he kept the smile, he allowed himself to drop heavily into his seat; of course, he chided himself, I should have known Cicero has spies of his own.

"I have to say I'm greatly relieved," Antonius said, summoning as much false sincerity as he dared. "It's good to know we don't have to waste both of our valuable time on me informing you that a message has arrived from Caesar, since you already know."

"No," Cicero lied, supremely unconvincingly, "that was just a surmise on my part." Now the older man offered Antonius his own version of a fabricated smile as he said lightly, "Since that's the only time we see each other these days, when you have instructions from Caesar."

"You know," Antonius slapped a hand on his desk, taking a petty pleasure in seeing the way Cicero jumped in his seat at the sharp sound, "you are absolutely right, friend Cicero! It seems we only get to be in each other's company when we have something dreadfully boring to discuss. So," Antonius' smile grew so broad that Cicero had the sudden thought that the ends of his mouth might meet each other in the back of his head, "I'm inviting you to dinner as my guest, tonight! I'll make sure my cooks are informed, and I'll spare no expense!"

"That is *very* kind, *Magister*," Cicero answered, trying to make sure his face didn't betray the furiously working mind behind it as he tried to unravel what game Antonius could be playing; the idea that Antonius had any desire to spend time in his company never crossed his mind, nor did he have any relish for the idea of listening to this muscle-bound oaf blathering on about whores and debauchery. "I'm afraid I have already made plans for this evening. Perhaps, some...."

"Cancel them," Antonius' words were quiet, but it was the instantly vanished sense of good humor that informed Cicero he wasn't being issued an invitation.

Despite the contempt with which Marcus Tullius Cicero held Marcus Antonius, he never lost sight of the reality that Antonius was a very, very dangerous man, especially when he was clothed in the power that came from being Master of the Horse. That he was *Caesar's* Master of the Horse made him doubly dangerous, and while Cicero had been called a lion in the Senate, he had long since understood that when it came to physical courage, the gods had seen fit to deny him much of that quality.

"Then," the words he heard coming out of his mouth were certainly in his voice, but Cicero's face and tongue seemed so numb that it was if someone else was speaking through him, "by all means, I would love to come."

"Good!" Once more, Antonius slapped a hand on his desk, the icy menace vanishing as rapidly as it had come, and he was all conviviality once more. "I know Fulvia will love to see your...." Antonius paused as if trying to think of Cicero's new wife's name.

"Publilla," Cicero supplied, and felt a prickling of anger, "but she is no longer my wife."

"Ah, that's right," Antonius tried to look embarrassed. "I'd forgotten."

No, you didn't, Cicero thought savagely, allowing his mind to rage at what he knew was a calculated slight designed for the sole purpose of embarrassing him, *him,* Cicero! Cicero, the *Optimate,* who's been reduced to this, eating with a man who's little better than a Gaul!

Outwardly, Cicero's tone was equally pleasant as he assured Antonius, "There's no reason that you should remember, *Magister.* It was an inconsequential event, and you have so much on your mind. Which," he reminded Antonius gently, in a silent signal to the other man that now he had had his fun, it was time for the real purpose of this summons, "is why you wanted to see me, I believe?"

"Ah, yes." Antonius slapped his forehead, exaggerating the gesture in the same way he did all things: bigger, grander, and more vulgar than they had any reason to be. "You're right, of course.

Forgive me." Picking up a document, Cicero instantly recognized two things about it; the seal on it, which was broken, was unmistakably Caesar's, and it was written on vellum and not a wax tablet, meaning that this was a message Caesar expected to be treated as if it was a law. This realization caused Cicero's stomach to twist, in a combination of anger at yet another reminder of the absolute power Caesar wielded over every man who was a Roman citizen, and fear of what it might contain. When Caesar had announced that Cassius was going to be taken with the Dictator, Cicero had lived in an almost constant state of terror. Despite Cassius' assurances that he had destroyed all of the correspondence between not only the other conspirators in the failed attempt on Caesar's life, but with Cicero himself, the old Senator's imagination was so vivid that he would wake himself at night, sweat soaking his nightclothes, sure that he had heard a pounding on his door by men who had been tasked with dragging him away to an ignominious death. Only after hearing of Cassius' escape did Cicero breathe easier, although this turned out to be short-lived; indeed, there *was* a knock on his door in the dark watches of the night, but it hadn't been because of men sent by Antonius, at the order of Caesar. Instead, there had been a message, cryptic in nature but clearly understood by Cicero, from Cassius himself, who had informed him of his escape. For days that stretched into weeks, Cicero had waited to be questioned about his knowledge of Cassius' whereabouts, yet despite being in Antonius' presence at least a dozen times since then, the brawny *Magister* had never even mentioned Cassius' name, and from everything he could tell, neither the Dictator nor *Magister* seemed the least bit concerned that one of the principal, and most vehement, members of the conspiracy was now roaming the vast world out there. Rather than set his mind at ease, the subject of Cassius' whereabouts ate away at Cicero, making every summons by Antonius not only unpleasant, but in some ways terrifying. And, knowing Antonius, Cicero was sure that he was being tormented up to this moment, as Antonius seemed to take an inordinately long time unrolling the scroll.

"So," Antonius' voice made Cicero jump in his chair, but if the other man noticed, he didn't give any indication, "our Dictator has conquered both Ctesiphon and Seleucia, and has invested both."

"Already?" Cicero gasped, momentarily forgetting his fear for his own safety.

The twisted smile Antonius offered him was the first genuine moment the two of them shared, as the *Magister* tried, unsuccessfully, to keep from sounding bitter as he replied, "Have you forgotten what Caesar's capable of? Whatever he sets out to do, he does."

Cicero was sure there was more meaning to Antonius' words than appeared on the surface, and when it came to the subject of Caesar's competence, if they had known each other's minds, the pair would have seen how they were running along the same path. Both of them, in different ways certainly, had been eclipsed by the blazing brilliance of Caesar, and neither of them were built in such a way that they didn't view this reality with a great deal of resentment.

"But," Antonius continued, "he's given instructions about his plans for this new territory that is, or *was*," he corrected himself, "controlled by Parthia and is now ours to govern."

"Cleopatra," Cicero practically spat the Egyptian queen's name, certain that Caesar was going to cede control of this strategically important area to her.

Consequently, his shock was profound when, in response, Antonius shook his head, "No, although I admit I thought the same as you. But no, the old boy has other ideas for this part of Parthia." Taking a breath, Antonius continued, "He's turning it into a Senatorial province. And," suddenly, Antonius seemed to have trouble getting out this next bit, which Cicero understood the moment the words were out. "He's appointed the boy as *Praetor*."

"The 'boy'?" Cicero's first response was bewilderment, followed quickly by horror. "Not *Caesarion*, surely!"

"No," Antonius laughed without any humor, "not that boy. The other one."

"Octavian?" Cicero found he was tightly gripping the arms of the chair he was in, as if he was afraid he would suddenly fall out. "But...but the boy's not even old enough to be a Senator!"

"Oh?" Antonius thrust the vellum document out towards Cicero, saying flatly. "He is now. By decree of our Dictator for Life."

Only then, as Cicero's mind tried to absorb this cataclysmic shift in their world, did the idea come to him, striking him with the power that ignorant people claimed was contained in the lightning bolts thrown by Jupiter. Antonius doesn't want me to come to dinner to kill me, he thought; he's as unhappy about this as I am, probably more so. Suddenly, Cicero regarded the man who, just moments before, had been a sworn enemy, seeing him in a completely new light.

"You know, Marcus Antonius," Cicero spoke thoughtfully, but was careful to look the other man in the eye, "I think we have a great deal to discuss tonight."

Cicero got his answer, in the form of a grim nod, and Marcus Antonius placing a finger alongside his nose in a sign that was used by Romans of all classes and needed no interpretation by Cicero. Standing to leave, when the two men embraced again, the atmosphere in the room was different, and the old Senator took the long way back to his own residence; there was much to think about.

Historical Note

One of the nice things about writing historical fiction is that the author can sometimes stretch what we do know from the historical record to cover parts of what we don't know. That is the case here, specifically with the route Caesar chooses in his invasion of Parthia, and in the spirit of full disclosure, I didn't arrive at this on my own.

While I can't remember the exact specifics as far as the name, or "handle" of the person who posted this, during my far-flung attempts to find any snippet of research material that I could about the Parthians and their military during the First Century BCE, I came across someone who offered what I think is an interesting hypothesis. Specifically, the idea that the route planned by Caesar for his invasion was actually used instead by Marcus Antonius, at least the very first part of it.

The more I thought about it, the more this seemed to resonate with me as being not just possible, but likely. Marcus Antonius was a charismatic character, and certainly had some capabilities in different areas, but nothing I have ever seen suggests that planning was one of his strengths. Consequently, it seems likely to me that he would simply dust off the scrolls containing the detailed plans created by his former leader and mentor, Caesar. It makes sense, on a number of levels, that Antonius simply followed the blueprint laid out by Caesar a few years earlier. And it seems very Caesar-like to me that he would specifically avoid retracing the steps of Marcus Licinius Crassus, taking the most direct, but least-watered route into the Parthian heartland.

However, I diverge in a major way, because I have Caesar crossing over to follow the Tigris River, and the point where he does so, just north of Mount Masias, or modern day Karaca Dag, Turkey is the point where the two rivers are in closest proximity, being a bit more than fifty modern miles. Thanks to the miracle of Google Earth, I "walked" the ground, just to make sure that the route was navigable to an ancient army on foot. The tradeoff is in the ruggedness of the upper Tigris; the river has cut through the rock in several places so that it is at the bottom of a gorge. This would have made for slower going, but once past that barrier, the river led directly to Ctesiphon, albeit in a very meandering way. One advantage of making a crossing where I describe is that Caesar and his army would have been able to

485

follow the Tigris as it moved east, before turning on its north/south axis, so there would have been a steady supply of water. By my calculations, this would have added at least three to four hundred miles to cover, but at the same time, the security provided by the river would counter the difficulty posed by the extra miles.

As I always try to do, the terrain described in the first Parthian ambush is as accurate as it's possible to get without actually being there, as is the site for the battle on the ridge. For those interested in such things, the precise location is Latitude 37.449919°N and Longitude 41.898159°E. The river descends through a gorge, while making a large loop, and while I'm certainly no Caesar, if I was the commander, I would shorten the distance by cutting across, particularly since the ground has finally begun to flatten out. Conversely, if I was the Parthian commander, I would have my ambushing force use the cover of the dry watercourse a half-mile to the east of the location above.

The battle on the ridge is located at Latitude 37.101133°N and Longitude 42.369326°E, which is essentially the borderline of Turkey, Syria and Iraq. Hopefully readers will forgive and understand that I chose to scout the terrain virtually, and not actually visit the site, given its location. I love my work, but I love my head more, and want it to stay firmly attached to my neck for as long as possible!

On my description of the siege of Ctesiphon/Seleucia, I suspect that the purists and experts in Parthian history might take some exception to my description of the two cities as being essentially conjoined. I want to make it clear this is my own invention; I couldn't find any evidence that suggested the presence of the three bridges joining the two cities that I describe.

Having said that, what we *do* know is that Ctesiphon started as an armed, military encampment across the river from Seleucia. Once it became a city, while I suppose it's possible that the two cities co-existed side by side and operated as completely separate entities, once both came under the control of Parthia, it seems likely that they would essentially link the two. In a modern context, I would point to Dallas-Fort Worth in my home state of Texas as an example of what happens when two cities are not only close in proximity, but share the same ownership.

Finding information about the Parthian army, and more importantly, its organization proved to be quite a challenge. Ultimately, I leaned on the resource I found online in the Iran Chamber Society, and an article by Professor A. Sh. Shahbazi for my description of the *washt, drafsh,* and *spad,* and the numbers of men each of these units contained.

Finally, on the use of naphtha, I got my information about the location of deposits from Strabo's Geography; whether it was used in the manner I described at this point in history is hard to tell. Again, I tried to put myself in the sandals of the Parthians, and if I had this as a resource, I would use it. Hopefully, the method in which it's employed, and how the Parthians come to possess the kind of artillery that we do know wasn't a normal feature of their armaments, won't ring false to readers.

CPSIA information can be obtained
at www.ICGtesting.com
Printed in the USA
FSHW02n1048241018
53252FS

9 781941 226148